THEIR DEEDS COME IN MANY FORMS:
DECEPTION AND PASSION,
BETRAYAL AND TRUE LOVE . . .

RALPH BEHR. His father and his grandfather were self-made real-estate men who struggled with a dream. Now it's his turn. He intends to build three 150-story towers in the middle of Manhattan—but everyone, from the mayor to the man on the street, is dead set against it. . . .

GAIL BENEDICT. Fiercely moral and independent, she's a convict's daughter whose life has been a crusade against all that Ralph represents. To please her aging father, she marries Ralph in name only—and keeps her contempt a closely guarded secret. . . .

SIMON KRAMER. He's tough, he's rich, and he's unscrupulous. Ralph's chief competitor, he's consumed by his determination to steal or halt Ralph's new project—at any cost.

LORNA GARRISON. Slim, dark, successful, and terribly chic, she was once Ralph's mistress—until Gail came along. Now the only desire in her heart is revenge. . . .

MILO BENEDICT. An artiste with grandiose airs, he divorces Gail so she can marry Ralph. But he's an invisible force behind the scenes, his hatred for Ralph ready to explode at any provocation. . . .

AMANDA BROOKHOUSE. She's everything that Ralph ever wanted: beautiful, blond, poised, and wealthy. And she actually loves him and wants to marry him—but there's a hitch. . . .

These are only a few of the characters who plot and plan in DEEDS—a riveting story of the very rich, the very powerful, the very exclusive who call Manhattan home. . . .

Also by Joseph Amiel
Published by Fawcett Gold Medal Books:

BIRTHRIGHT

DEEDS

Joseph Amiel

FAWCETT GOLD MEDAL • NEW YORK

To Nancy for her love and endurance

A Fawcett Gold Medal Book
Published by Ballantine Books
Copyright © 1988 by Joseph Amiel

Library of Congress Catalog Card Number: 87-30847

ISBN 0-449-14522-0

This edition published by arrangement with Atheneum Publishers, a division of The Scribner Book Companies, Inc.

Manufactured in the United States of America

First Ballantine Books Edition: January 1989

Prologue

From his penthouse office in Behr House, Ralph Behr had been watching the night, hot and sweaty, slowly pin the day to earth. Only far to the west, well beyond the Hudson, was the day's bloody shoulder still struggling against inevitable defeat.

He shifted his gaze downward, to the insect-sized men and women far below who shuffled slowly through coagulating amber light in shirtsleeves, shorts, halter tops, as little clothing as possible to alleviate the intense heat that had gripped the city for days. He imagined them looking up with awe and longing at the illumination deposited atop the city's towers like snow capping great mountain peaks.

He could see much of Manhattan from here and several of the skyscrapers he had erected. Proud of them, he was prouder still of having accomplished so much so young, and in New York City, which he considered the locus of the world's most talented people—the best of the best, the winners. Usually he was in motion; he hated inaction, the waste of precious time and the boredom of it. But now he could only wait impatiently for the telephone call from his lawyer at the negotiating session. He was too well known to attend himself—the seller of the property would surely recognize him and raise the price exorbitantly, realizing that the parcel had to be part of a larger site Ralph was assembling for development. In this case, the seller could ask almost anything and Ralph would be forced to pay.

For two years his agents, pretending that they themselves were the actual buyers, not even knowing that Ralph Behr was their ultimate employer, had been quietly using chains of front corporations on his behalf to buy up individual properties in that area. Tonight, Ralph's lawyer was attempting to close on the purchase of the last piece in the jigsaw puzzle that made up the full assemblage, the key piece. Without it the others were useless. The old man had stubbornly refused to sell, insisting that he wanted to pass on to his son the family's auto-body repair business, located in several of the buildings on the site. He had finally agreed to sell only after another garage was found to which he could relocate.

No one, ever, had built anything higher than the project Ralph envisioned erecting on the site. He had constructed it a hundred times in dozens of configurations in his imagination, perhaps thousands of times if one counted the first vague, shining edifices that had risen in his boyhood imagination. He could almost see it gleaming in the distant darkness, its three skyscrapers piercing the night like slivers of glass. "Topless towers," Marlowe had called them. The image from a play Ralph had read in college had stuck in his mind like his first fireworks display.

The private-phone line rang, and Ralph leaped at the receiver. That would be Phil Rountree.

"There's a snag," were the lawyer's initial words. "The old man wants to break the deal."

"How much more does he want?" Ralph asked grimly.

"It's not money. We were going over the contract of sale and got to the part about having to transfer good and marketable title to the property—the standard requirement. His lawyer explained that it gave us the right to cancel the contract if the title-insurance company finds some defect with the ownership rights. He jumped up and called me an 'oily crook trying to cheat him.' "

"But he owns the property, doesn't he?"

"Sure, but until we hear back from the title-insurance company that's checking it out, we can't really be sure there isn't some sort of technical problem with his title."

"How long have he and his famly owned the property?"

"Fifty, sixty years maybe. Before that someone else owned it another fifty or sixty."

"And he's serious about breaking the deal? It's not just a negotiating tactic?"

"I think he means it."

Ralph considered only briefly. "I agree to what he wants. Sign the contract his way."

"As your attorney, I have the obligation to warn you that—"

"Phil, stop thinking like a lawyer. Be realistic. If he walks out now, we'll never get him back to the table. I've already spent millions to buy the surrounding parcels that don't make sense without this last piece."

"Don't just jump into this—"

"When the plane's going down, Phil, you jump . . . and hope

your parachute will open." Ralph's soft voice was wrapped about a steel core. "I expect a call back from you in twenty minutes with the news that I own that parcel."

Ralph hung up and buzzed his secretary on the intercom—Myra never left before he did. She was to telephone Lorna, his date for the evening, that he would be late. He had already changed into one of the tuxedos hanging in his office dressing room.

He now went to the bar installed behind the teakwood wall paneling. He removed a bottle of champagne from the refrigerator, uncorked it, and poured some into a glass, which he set beside the telephone. He would drink from it only when Rountree called with the good news. Then he returned to the window, reorienting his gaze by means of the succession of familiar lighted promontories situated to the south of Behr House: RCA, the Helmsley Building, Pan Am, the Empire State, Chrysler, Con Ed, the World Trade Center. He finally located the coveted patch of darkness at the lower end of Manhattan and locked his gaze on it, superstitiously willing the last parcel to become his. There, in that dim quadrangle, his hope for immortality awaited him.

When Ralph Behr walked into the ballroom, heads turned and hands stretched, as if toward a young sovereign. Nodding, smiling, stopping for a word or two, he moved with an athlete's litheness around groups in evening dress who twisted deferentially or enviously toward him as he passed. A slim, dark-haired woman in black accompanied him, shaking hands and chatting as she followed just behind him.

On the other side of the room, Dan Ahern, who covered real estate for *The New York Times*, was pointing out prominent guests to his companion: developer Simon Kramer, the charity's guest of honor, who was rumored to be donating a million dollars when he accepted their Man of the Year award later in the evening; Morris Weitzman, who had three buildings going up in Midtown and was in a fight with the community and local officials over every one; Bob and Joan Eigen, up from Palm Beach, where he was developing real estate; Arnold Dale and his wife, she beaming as proudly as in the ads that showed her tyrannizing over their frightened apartment-sales staff.

"If you could bottle the ambition in this room," Ahern concluded, "you could light New York City for a year. They're all

3

here because they want something. The little ones from the bigger ones, the bigger ones from the biggest ones."

Marilyn Watkins was used to the cynicism Dan Ahern imagined protected him from being fouled by the men he wrote about. She herself pursued gossipy stories for a local tabloid newspaper. This wealthy real-estate crowd was new and a bit intimidating to her.

"Who do the biggest ones want something from?" she asked.

"God, probably . . . if he'd joint venture."

The commotion near the door drew their attention.

"That's Ralph Behr, isn't it?" she exclaimed, unprofessional excitement in her voice.

"The American hero himself."

"He looks younger than I thought."

"He's thirty-six," Ahern replied grumpily, envy edging into the habit of disdain. "You'd be a successful real-estate developer too if you started out with a father who owns fifteen thousand apartments. Every few years another one of these comets flashes across the skyline: Bill Zeckendorf, Donald Trump, now Ralph Behr. Most burn out and plummet like a piece of coal."

"Do you think I could meet him?"

"He's like all the rest," Ahern grumbled, his lower lip disappearing for a moment into the thickness of his blond mustache. "Someone should offer a reward to the first team to scale his ego."

Ahern knew he should go over there too; Behr was news, and several other reporters had cornered the guy in an impromptu press conference. Marilyn following closely on his heels; he began to snake toward the front of the ballroom.

Those encountering Ralph Behr for the first time were invariably surprised by several things about him. A couple of inches over six feet, he was taller than he appeared to be from a distance or on television and better looking, with a boyish expression that also tended to reduce his size in the mind's eye. The vibrant brown-green of his hazel eyes and the intensity of his gaze were further small astonishments; his eyes held the other person as ferociously as if he had grabbed a fistful of shirt. But as soon as his interest waned, he would instantly move on to something new that might devour his curiosity. His voice was also surprising: despite a circus-barker reputation for dynamism and self-promotion, he spoke with disarming softness.

The woman beside him, Lorna Garrison, was in her early thirties. She carried herself stiffly erect, a study in self-discipline.

Her nose was well shaped, if a bit long, and her skin was drawn tightly against high cheekbones and the hollows below. Frosted brown hair was slashed at a fashionable angle just above her eyes, which were dark and deeply set. Her black gown, with its sharply tailored, sequined jacket and straight floor-length skirt, enhanced the handsome severity of her appearance. She was a partner in a politically influential public-relations firm that represented many of these real-estate developers, but not Ralph Behr, who was a master at getting himself publicity. Her brief glances seemed to cover the entire room, even as her attention was warily focused on Ralph's bantering with one of the reporters.

"Mr. Behr," a trade-magazine reporter asked deferentially, "what do you see ahead for New York City real estate?"

"Everyone is always saying New York's overbuilt. But New York's the mecca, where it's at. Everyone who's anyone in the world wants to live here. There's always room for one more good building."

Another reporter spoke up as the first hurried to scribble down the unremarkable quote. "How does Patagonia look?"

"Sure you're not just looking for a betting tip, Eddie?" The others chuckled, knowing the man to be an avid racetrack fan. "His ankle's coming along well. He should be ready for Saratoga."

Ralph Behr was staring at Marilyn. Nervous, she felt compelled to ask a question. "Any new projects on the horizon?"

His gaze did not waver. "I wasn't going to announce it yet, but since you put the question directly . . ." He lowered his voice, as if confiding to the circle about him. "I'm celebrating tonight. Just a few minutes ago I sewed up a big assemblage in Lower Manhattan. I'm planning to develop an office building, a hotel, and an apartment building there. Each one will be a hundred and fifty stories high."

"A hundred and fifty stories!" Even Ahern was impressed.

Ralph's broad smile swept the circle. He had been hoarding that news, like a man waiting to yell, surprise party!

"Taller than the World Trade Center and the Empire State Building. Nearly forty stories taller than the Sears Tower. New York City is the greatest city in the world and should have the tallest building in the world. I'm going to give it—" he paused to increase the drama "—the three tallest, most spectacular structures ever built by man."

"You're serious," Ahern observed.

"Preliminary plans are almost finished, and the model will be ready next week. The towers are only the beginning. They'll be

5

at the edge of a huge, circular atrium, along with three department stores and the world's finest, chicest shops, four-star restaurants, the works. This is more than a project, it's *the* real-estate project of our time."

"Where is it?" a reporter wanted to know.

"I can't reveal that just yet . . . one or two loose ends. But I bought the last parcel only half an hour ago."

Ralph cast a glance at Lorna, his grin indicating his triumph at having surprised even her along with everyone else while planning this massive undertaking. She seemed hungry for the information; she fed on such fare. The reporters seemed to be groping futilely for questions that would afford them a grip on the immensity of what he was proposing: to build the three tallest structures the world had ever seen.

Lorna was concerned. This was big news—the reporters would be on the phones within minutes filing stories that could well make page one. She pulled Ralph away.

"Damn it, Ralph, Simon Kramer is going to be furious. This is a big night for him. He invited these reporters here to cover his award, and you stole the spotlight from him again."

Ralph feigned innocence, but the smile was impish. "I can't help it if they print what I say."

Lorna, too, was now grinning. "Naturally, you also can't help it that all their stories will be filed by the time Simon delivers his speech." She paused. "You really *are* planning this project, not just fishing for newsprint?"

He crossed his heart, the boyish expression conscious now. "Want to see the site?"

"Oh, God, could I?"

He laughed. "I could get anything out of you in return for a secret."

"Ralph, if you're telling the truth about this thing, it really is the greatest real-estate project ever built."

"You bet it is." His face grew serious. "If I take you there, you have to give me your word not to reveal the location to a soul until I'm ready."

She nodded.

"Swear it."

"My God, you're a suspicious man. Ralph, you know if I say I won't tell anyone where it is, I won't."

"Let's get out of here." He started to walk toward the door. She reached forward to halt him.

"We'd better wait until the dinner is over. Kramer's going to be angry enough when he reads about you in the morning papers without your leaving an empty space on the dais."

"Hey, I wouldn't want to spoil Simon Kramer's party."

The heat seemed to have sucked all the oxygen out of the night and left a vacuum that propelled pedestrians by the power of inertia. Even the short walk beneath the canopy's lights, from the hotel's revolving doors to the silver-gray limousine, was oppressive.

Lorna fell back against the cold leather seat. Ralph gave his driver the address, and the car door closed to seal them in.

"Kramer gave the most pompous, boring speech New York has heard in years," Ralph grumbled.

"It wasn't that bad. Besides, I like Simon."

"All that phony cultured suaveness? You just want his business."

The project site was in a deteriorated section of Lower Manhattan. The limousine parked beside an empty lot that formed an outer corner of the four-block expanse. As Ralph and Lorna walked onto it, the heat fell upon them like walls collapsed by a fire. The streetlamps, tall pickets guarding the periphery of the sidewalk, seemed to aim their small yellow suns at the improbably dressed couple who disputed the hegemony of the rubble and the tenacious claim of the crabgrass tufts.

Ralph pointed out the spots he had chosen for the three towers, the department stores, and, in the land's very center, the atrium. Someone had planted a garden there, on an empty lot at one of the inner street corners. He told Lorna he planned to bury the intersecting thoroughfares beneath the atrium and construct turn-offs into subterranean parking garages.

Then he fell silent and stared upward at the stars searing the night.

"Nobody's ever done it before," he finally declared with passion. "A hundred fifty stories. Nobody. Do you know what that means?"

"You'll be a billionaire."

"Nearly two thousand feet high. Nobody's ever built a project like this one."

He picked a stone from the debris at their feet and threw it upward as hard as he could. He continued to stare into the blackness into which it had disappeared.

"Three towers reaching toward heaven." He grinned at her. "If I never build another thing, I'll be remembered forever."

"Are you going to name it after yourself?"

"After my father. The Henry Behr Center. I want to honor him with something that will knock the eyes out of the sons of bitches who turned their backs on him and my grandfather."

"He's got to be thrilled," Lorna said.

"I'm going to surprise him."

Ralph's gaze drifted upward again. "The towers will be made of steel," he said. The last word hung in the air as if he had hammered the sound from an anvil to demonstrate the metal's strength. "Only steel can go up that high."

Lorna failed to notice the intensity in his voice. She pointed to a couple of tenement buildings on a part of the site that abutted the lot. "Who lives over there?"

"Squatters. The guy who owned that parcel said they just started moving into the empty buildings one day. They don't have any right to occupy the apartments—they don't have a lease or pay rent—but he never threw them out because it kept the buildings safer to have people living in them."

Ralph's arm swept a wide arc. "You have no idea how incredible this site is. Forget the seediness of the neighborhood, the debris, the disreputable characters slinking around out there. Instead, look at the transit lines and the wide avenues that go right by it. Look at how close it is to the financial district. Shopping and residential areas around here are starting to come back. Most important, look at the zoning code. Zoning makes this a miracle just waiting to happen. That piece over there with the tenements is zoned residential, and I'll put the condo tower on it. The rest of the site is zoned commercial. I have the right to build anything I want and go as high as the moon."

"And you don't have to get the city's permission for any of it?"

"Not for a damned thing. Well, maybe some tax abatements we're entitled to and for putting those streets that cross in the middle underground, but if they try to block me, I'll do it another way. But why the hell shouldn't they give those to me? I'm going to turn this whole slum area into a jewel."

"If you've already bought the last piece, why didn't you want to tell the reporters where it's located?"

"My title-insurance company is taking a little longer than usual to check the chain of title on this one." He pointed. "That big garage over there."

Lorna was surprised. "You mean you bought it before you knew whether the title was good?"

"If I had waited, and this last parcel had gotten away from me, the whole project would have gone down the drain and left me

8

sitting with three and a half worthless blocks. Besides, when I do make the announcement, it will be with bands marching and flags waving. I want to have the model ready. Everything."

"You can't handle the press alone on something this big."

"We'll see." He flung an arm around her. "What do you think?"

"It's awesome," she answered huskily. "Those three towers will dominate New York's skyline. You weren't exaggerating. The greatest real-estate project ever built."

She pulled his head down to hers and kissed him hungrily. "Jesus, I'm turned on."

"If that's all it takes, I'll build one of these suckers every week."

Ralph undid his bow tie and the top shirt button and slipped down into the mauve club chair. He crossed and extended his feet before him. Lorna had lowered the living-room lights and put on soft music. Through the wide windows at the end of the room, he could see, across Central Park, the shapes of buildings formed out of tiny lighted squares. Usually, as soon as they got back to her place or his, the two of them were so aroused they could barely wait to undress, but tonight she said she wanted everything to be just right. She had gone to the kitchen for champagne.

Ralph reflected that he had dated her for a couple of years now and still enjoyed her company. That was something to a man who had a reputation for running through relationships like an express train past local stations; he attracted women easily and became bored with them even more easily. Certainly she had good taste and a sense of style: the way she dressed, this apartment. But it was something about the intensity of her interest in him that kept him going out with her, as if she was trying to wrench an equivalent interest from him. That was flattering and intriguing in occasional doses.

Ralph sensed movement and looked up. Now absolutely naked, Lorna was carrying into the room a Lucite tray that supported a champagne bottle and glasses. Her body was lean and sharply angled at the joints, a testament to her self-discipline. She set the tray down on the end table and then glanced up wickedly.

"This is your night. Whatever you want. Here's a preview."

She poured one of the glasses full, then stood and dipped her index finger into it. She slipped between his legs, bent over him, and ran her wet finger across his lips.

Ralph licked at the wetness. "Miss, do you have any of those little goldfish crackers to go with it?"

Smiling, she dropped to her knees. "No goldfish."

Her hand undid his pants and drew out his penis, already lengthening.

"How about those nacho things?" he asked.

Her head began to lower to his lap. "Say another word, and you're an inch shorter."

Later, they made love together in her bedroom. When they finally lay spent, her head in the crook of his elbow, her eyes remained on his face, lit only by the reflection from the thin stripe of light that extended from the crack in the doorway and across their bodies like a sash.

"The first time I met you," she reminisced, "was at the East River Tennis Club. Do you remember that?"

"No."

"A long time ago. I had been the youngest deputy mayor in history. My new husband and I were just starting our PR firm and I was learning that he was a lousy businessman and worse in bed. You were a brash kid from Brooklyn with a rich father and a great backhand who hadn't built so much as an outhouse on your own yet, but you had more confidence than developers who'd built a dozen buildings. I fell for you like a ton of bricks. I was twenty pounds heavier, and you wouldn't look twice at me. That day I went on a diet and promised myself several things: to divorce Chet, to find a new business partner, to do a million a year in billings—and last, but I assure you far from least, I vowed that someday I would fuck you. All the other things came easy. But it took me until almost three years ago to date you and a few weeks after that until I could get you into bed."

"Why are you telling me all this now?"

"Because now I want more." She hesitated only an instant. "I want to marry you, Ralph."

"That's what this performance was leading up to?"

"It wasn't a performance. It was a way of showing how good I could be for you. Nobody will ever make you a better wife. I'm as ambitious as you, and I know everyone worth knowing. And God, but I want you so much."

She kissed him again, grinding her mouth on his. "No, don't say anything now, tonight. We have plenty of time. Think about it. You'll never find a woman who understands you better or is a better lover. I would kill for you."

She rolled on top of him and stared down into his eyes, a verdancy as dark and obscure in the dim light as the secret at the heart of a forest.

"You're like me, Ralph. There are no rules for people like us. That's why we get what we want in life. And why we're dangerous."

Ralph lived on the top two floors of a Fifth Avenue apartment house which had been the first project he had ever built on his own. He had kept the penthouse. The rental apartments were eventually sold to their occupants at a handsome profit. It was after two A.M. when he let himself in, bow tie dangling untied on either side of an open collar, hair a little messy. Usually the butler left only the foyer light on when Ralph was out, but tonight the rooms beyond were lit as well. Ralph smelled familiar cigar smoke and went into the living room. His father sat in a tall wing chair facing the entrance.

"If I'd known you were here, I'd have been home earlier," Ralph said and strode across the Turkish carpet to kiss his father on the cheek, a ritual of affection Ralph's maturation had not ended.

Henry was seventy-seven years old and, although he had given up trying to lose the extra weight that had accumulated over the years, he was fit for his age. Only occasional shreds of gray at his temples wove through a fairly full head of black hair. His eyebrows too were a bit gray, and bushier now than when he was younger. The jowls drawing down the corners of his mouth only partially divulged his age, while making him appear more contemplative than he was. All in all, the passage of years had been kind to him.

Ralph's success had been on a scale so remarkable that envy or meddling by Henry was out of the question. He concentrated on managing the apartment buildings he had built or bought in the outer boroughs and rarely visited Manhattan. Ralph occupied himself with new projects here, which was where the vast increase in their net worth had occurred. Ralph still took the trouble to consult with his father before embarking on a new venture, and Henry appreciated the courtesy, but both men knew that it was just that.

"Been waiting long?" Ralph asked.

"Since about ten."

"How could you be sure I'd come home tonight?"

"You hate to sleep in someone else's bed. Since you were a boy."

Ralph ran a tired hand through his hair and fell back onto the sofa. "A problem? Everybody well?"

"Fine, fine," his father said, brushing away that area of conversation with a wave of his cigar as he paused to recall his approach. "As of the end of last month, I calculate you and I together, our firm, we're worth in round numbers two hundred million dollars."

"Give or take a few million either way that's probably accurate. And?"

"Half of that doesn't belong to us."

Ralph was too startled to react. Then he thought it might be one of his father's infrequent jokes. "If you're going to tell me the IRS is our silent partner, I'd be inclined to agree with you."

Henry shook his head. "Abe Weintraub."

Ralph was bewildered. "Who the hell is Abe Weintraub?"

"He and I were in business together in the early fifties."

Ralph searched his memory. "That accountant you once owned some buildings with maybe, what, twenty, twenty-five years ago."

"Twenty, exactly twenty. We were partners, down the line. We had a few small apartment buildings, a couple of commercial taxpayers, but we were partners."

"So you were partners on some buildings then. But you said that he owns half of our assets. Not our *present* assets."

"There was no other way. I never told you before probably because I was hoping he'd die or something else might happen to him. Or . . ."

Ralph was growing angry. "Or what—that it wasn't important enough to bother me with?"

"I was ashamed," Henry retorted, his voice rising to meet his son's, then dropping into a timbre of humiliation as he began to speak again. "Not that I did anything wrong, but it was a . . . stain, I guess would be the best way to describe it."

"Maybe you'd better start from the very beginning and take it very slowly."

Henry relit his cigar to give himself time to choose the right phrases that would best begin to reveal to his son the ugly secret he had harbored for twenty years, the secret on which all their prosperity had been built. He blew the smoke toward the ceiling and watched it for a few seconds before lowering his gaze to his son's.

12

"We had built up a nice little real-estate business, nothing major, but enough to give us a solid income. That was when I heard that Hampshire Gardens was for sale."

Ralph nodded. Hampshire Gardens had been his father's first large real-estate purchase: twenty-one apartment buildings, four to ten stories high.

"I was working on the owner to bring down the price and trying at the same time to stop him from turning the deal over to brokers, who could get him maybe thirty, forty percent more than we were offering. Abe's job was to find the financing. That was always his job. Finding the properties and negotiating for them was mine. A few days later he told me he had a bank willing to give us a big mortgage and that I should close the purchase with the owner. I did, while Abe worked with our lawyer to draw up the contracts. But I never imagined that he had done something illegal."

The butler, a middle-aged Englishman named Deighton, appeared in the archway leading to the foyer. He wore his robe over pajamas and carried a pot of coffee, which he substituted for one left for the elder Mr. Behr on the marble coffee table earlier in the evening. After Deighton had poured coffee for both men and left, Ralph instantly swung back to his father.

"What was it this partner of yours did illegally?"

"He inflated the figures we'd be paying for Hampshire Gardens in the documents he gave the bank. You know, to get a bigger bank loan, so we wouldn't have to put up any money of our own as equity. Hell, we didn't *have* any money."

"Didn't the bank talk to the seller or hire an appraiser to check out the value?"

"Any price can be justified—you know that. Look, the bank didn't *want* to know the real value. The whole thing went through because the bank president was Abe's buddy." Henry punched the air with his cigar. "What Abe did was understandable—what with our having only a few thousand dollars between us. But he never told me about it—only that everything was taken care of. He had gotten a great mortgage, he said, and I didn't have to worry about a thing. The closing went through. Abe signed on behalf of our partnership."

Henry took a long drag on the cigar, trying to put off the moment when he must go on. Finally, he looked back at his son.

"A few days later one of the bank auditors happened to do some checking and found out what the real puchase price was."

13

"You're saying that this partner of yours used fraud to obtain the mortgage. Well, he got caught at it, so that's his bad—"

"Let me finish," Henry interrupted forcefully. "When Abe was about to be questioned by the grand jury, to see whether they would indict him—and it was certain they would—he threatened to testify that I was in on the whole thing from the beginning. That wasn't true, but he was desperate, and he knew there was no way I could defend myself against that kind of a lie—after all, I was an equal partner with him. The point was he wanted to make a deal with me."

Ralph leaned forward. "What kind of a deal?"

"His proposal was that he would take all the blame if he secretly remained a partner in my business while he was in prison. I would provide for his family with cash in the meantime and then give him half of what I was worth when he got out."

"And you took that deal?" Ralph asked in disbelief.

Henry nodded. "I signed a contract that he hid in a vault somewhere and a false confession he could release if I double-crossed him. I had to go along. Either both of us went to jail or he did. There was no way I could prove I was innocent if he refused to testify for me. We were both sure he'd be out in a couple of years at the most, and then the partnership would end. Look, he was already a partner in whatever we had. And we still owned Hampshire Gardens; the bank directors were so afraid of bad publicity because their president had been in on it with Abe that they agreed to let me keep the property if Abe pleaded guilty and everything was hushed up."

"But that was twenty years ago."

Sadness flickered on Henry's pursed lips. "It didn't work out like our lawyer thought it would. The judge suspected there was more to this guilty plea than met the eye. He decided to make an example of Abe. He sentenced him to consecutive prison terms on the various counts, which meant Abe would have to serve a minimum of twenty years. The judge figured with that heavy sentence hanging over him, Abe would then bargain for a shorter one by offering to spill the beans about everyone else who was involved."

"But he didn't?"

"He's been in prison all this time. And Hampshire Gardens was the beginning of our fortune."

"And, now that he's getting out, you want to turn over half of it to him."

"It's his."

Ralph jumped to his feet. "What the hell does that mean—
his? He blackmailed you into signing something. All right, there's
a contract. You have to give him something. What were you two
worth twenty years ago? A couple of hundred thousand? Half a
million with Hampshire Gardens? Double it. Give him a million. Two. Hell, give him five! He'll be happy as a pig in shit.
He can live like a king for the rest of his life." Ralph's voice
dropped. "But half? Half of what I built up was worth
maybe twenty million free and clear when I started. Half of
another hundred and eighty million dollars he had nothing to do
with? That I left in both our names only because we always
agreed that what I was building up was mine and that you would
pass your part on to me and Jeff? Now you tell me that all along
I've had a partner who gets the giant share! Well, there's no way
I'm going to give that money—*my money*—to some crook! Even
if he spent a *thousand* years in prison!"

"Half!" Henry repeated in a voice that admitted of no argument. "That could have been me in there. I never blamed Abe
for pressuring me. Maybe if I had been the one in charge of
trying to find the financing, I'd have done the same thing he did.
Maybe I would be the one getting out of jail after twenty years."

"Then give him half of what you built up *before* I joined you."

"How long would it have taken you to get where you are
without that capital behind you?" The older man shook his head
firmly. "He has a contract, and it's very clear. Besides, if I don't
give him what's coming to him, he can turn over my confession
to the D.A. There's no statute of limitations on fraud. When
Abe gets his money, I get back the confession."

Ralph tossed up his hands in anger and frustration and spun
away, striding to a window. He stared at the park without seeing
it and then, in control of himself, went back to the sofa.

"What will people think when we just hand over half of
everything we own to a convict? They'll know damned well why
he's getting the money and what you did to stay out of jail."

"Abe and I were worried about that, but I think we came up
with a solution that allows you and me to transfer half of our
assets to him without arousing suspicion and without having to
pay heavy taxes. Actually I came up with it, and it works."

Henry sat back and took a sip of his coffee. He spoke more
quietly, hoping to reduce the tension in the air. "Abe isn't very
healthy and doesn't really want the money for himself. He has a
daughter named Gail. I guess she's thirty now." Henry wanted to

look at his son when he said the next words, but could not. "The way around all of these problems is for you and Gail to marry."

"What?" Ralph was flabbergasted.

"Just hear me out. It wouldn't be a real marriage. You'd go out together, be seen together in public so that there could be no doubt in anyone's mind that it was a real marriage—the servants here and everyone else would consider you just like any other married couple. But in private, even though you both lived in this apartment, you would lead separate lives. More married couples than you can imagine really live like that anyway."

Henry hunched forward to the front of the chair as he spelled out the rest of the plan. Except for a couple of million dollars accumulated in his own name over the years, he would immediately turn over to Ralph all of his interest in the firm. Canceling some large liabilities in his own name would allow that to be accomplished without a big tax bite. Then he would retire. When his other son, Jeff, was a little more mature, Ralph would take on the obligation of financing him, as he himself had done for Ralph. Ralph and Gail would sign a prenuptial agreement that would grant her half Ralph's property in the event of divorce or death. In two years, when no court could doubt the marriage had lasted long enough for the wife to be entitled to a substantial settlement, Gail and Ralph would be divorced.

"You're finished?" asked Ralph, who had been barely able to contain himself throughout his father's explanation.

Henry nodded.

"Good! Then let me tell you: you're crazy if you think I'm going to get married!"

"You have a better way?"

Ralph fell silent and worked through every scenario that appeared to make the slightest bit of sense. Each one had a fatal defect. He had already rejected a simple transfer of cash or property; its purpose was transparent and it would trigger a huge gift tax. A sale of half their buildings with no down payment and a low-interest mortgage would impose a capital gains tax on the Behrs and debt on the Weintraubs. Contriving some sort of lawsuit that the two sides might appear to be settling would also alert the authorities, who might wonder why the Behrs did not defend it in court, which would doubtless cost them far less. Only a marriage and subsequent divorce accomplished everything the two old men wanted.

Ralph reached for his coffee. It had grown cold, but he did

not notice. "I'll grant you that it works. And I agree that you don't seem to have any other choice."

"I'm doing this at your expense, I know, Ralph. It creates certain inconveniences for you for a few years."

"Inconveniences!"

"Call it . . . I don't know . . . a favor to repay me for whatever help I've been to your success . . . or one of those things you sometimes have to do for family. They're the only ones in the world who care about you and, when it gets down to it, who really mean anything to you, right?" He himself would have sacrificed everything he owned for his own father—if only he could have.

"But keep in mind," Henry continued, "none of us can dare risk telling a soul that the marriage is a sham. If word got out, the government would invalidate the marriage, and this whole transfer would come tumbling down. The government would start to dig up the past. Look, even a rumor about why you're marrying Abe's daughter could destroy a reputation I spent my whole life building up."

Throughout the conversation Ralph had been focusing on the loss of half his fortune, but at that moment the realization sank in that he would actually be marrying this unknown woman, living here in this apartment with her, having meals with her, going out with her. And only they and their fathers could be allowed to know the truth, and probably his brother as well. But no one else. "This girl Gail?" he finally asked. "What's she like?"

"Pretty."

"That's something, at least."

"One little complication, though . . ." his father added after a moment of hesitation. "She's married. To an artist."

"Just a little complication."

"She's already agreed to fly to the Caribbean for one of those quickie divorces just as soon as you say yes."

"What does her husband think about it?"

"He's all for it, I understand."

"I'll bet he is."

"They'll remarry after the two years are up."

"And then he gets to share all that money."

Two years! Ralph thought despondently. Two years of living with some woman he didn't know, who would end up a hundred million dollars richer for doing nothing but hanging around. This could not have come at a worse time, just when he needed the firm's full resources behind Behr Center's development and his total concentration focused on the effort. Now that he had announced the project, all the jackals would go on the attack to gain some personal advantage: the politicians and the misguided community do-gooders would be snapping at his heels, and every powerful real-estate developer in the city would be employing political influence to cut himself in on the deal. Of all the times in his life to have this woman dumped on his back, now had to be the worst. But he couldn't turn his father down. He loved him so deeply and admired him even more. His father had gone through so much to get where he was, had struggled so long and hard to build a good life for his family. Ralph knew that if his father had asked him to give back everything, not just half, he would have. He felt a pang of sadness that he would have to wait for a better time to tell his father that he intended to name the new project after him.

"All right," Ralph finally conceded with resignation. "All right, I'll do it."

He instantly felt wounded, impaired, earthbound. He had always been a superb natural athlete—twisting, dipping, faking, then breaking for the basket and leaping high above the others to score: unstoppable. That sense of the inevitability of his triumph in whatever he did had remained with him. Until this moment he had glided through life, over life, as if those between him and his goals were schoolchildren flailing vainly at his irresistible moves. But now, blindsided, crippled by a circumstance he could not have anticipated, he felt as if that perfect grace was suddenly gone and his luck fled, as if he would forever be hobbling down the court on one good leg, like a bird trying to fly with a shattered wing.

Ralph took a deep breath, trying to clear his face and voice of the gloom he felt.

"When's the happy day?" he asked.

BOOK ONE

Raphael's Story

Chapter 1

Although he did not know it, Ralph Behr was following in a family tradition: The men in his family had usually married under strange circumstances. Once they truly fell in love, their devotion to that woman never wavered. But that woman was not always the same one they had married.

Ralph's great-grandfather, Haim Behar, had lived in Salonika, a cosmopolitan Greek city on the Aegean that was part of the Turkish Ottoman Empire. He had been forbidden to marry his childhood sweetheart by the young woman's father, a rabbi who had arranged "a great match" with the son of an important rabbi from Constantinople. Hoping to force her father into permitting the marriage to Haim, she became pregnant by him, not knowing that she was already dying of leukemia. She was finally allowed to marry him on the day that she went into labor, so that the child, who was born prematurely, would be legitimate. Weakened by the exertion, she died late that same day. The child was Raphael, Ralph's grandfather.

Izzy Weintraub, Gail's grandfather, was also born that year, but in America, on the Lower East Side, where his parents had settled after leaving Russia. He and Raphael first met when both were young men. Not only were they not yet married, but Raphael was not yet Behr and Izzy was not yet Weintraub. The families they later formed had known each other since, in the way that lives bump into each other and somehow are then propelled along routes which bring them together again and again, although that seems the most unlikely eventuality at the time. In fact, had it not been for Raphael, Gail would doubtless never have existed.

For his part Ralph owed more than the accident of descent to his grandfather. Whether passed down genetically or by means of the history and myth that surrounded his forebear, much of what Ralph Behr had become was a legacy from Raphael. Pride, for one, combined with a confidence that, in some of the family's

21

males, appeared at times to verge on arrogance. His name, for another, Ralph having been chosen as an Americanized version of Raphael. In many ways, he had inherited more from his grandfather than had his own father, Henry. Certainly, he had inherited the compulsion to build higher than anyone else ever had.

Raphael Behar first saw the Eiffel Tower on a cold spring day in 1905. The structure seemed alive to him, a swaggering black colossus produced by an act of creation that was more God's than man's. At that instant—nearly dizzy as he stared straight upward from its strong steel legs planted wide apart on either side of him to the very crown, proudly pushing back the gray sky like an African giant's head—he knew that he had to be an architect, to spend his life creating such magnificence. Tall buildings, broad squat ones, sprawling ones that beckoned generations of families, stately ones to which men could come to worship or make laws. And someday, someday, a building taller than this, the highest, finest giant of a building any man had ever built.

At twenty, Raphael was a good-looking, gregarious young man with black hair carefully in place and eyes that were a surprising hazel beneath the black eyebrows. Those characteristics too would be passed on to his grandson. He was of medium height and slight build. Despite his father's attentive concern, being an only child had forced Raphael to care for himself to a great extent and, as a consequence, he had developed at an early age a self-assurance evident to all who met him.

Young women were partial to his looks, he knew. Even in the restrictive Middle Eastern society in which he had grown up, his natural confidence and conversational facility had allowed him to develop a sense of ease around them, which served to enhance his attractiveness.

Raphael had welcomed the opportunity to take time off from the university and, as his father's business-trip companion, make his first visit to Paris. He had been helping out in the family trading business since childhood and had a good head for it. The assumption had always been that he would eventually join his father in business. Money was a necessity he relished, but he could muster little eagerness for a lifetime dedicated to trying to sell higher than he had bought. His greatest pleasures came from intellectual endeavors, from drawing, and from socializing with his friends. He was doing well enough at his studies, but not so well as he could have if he had believed they were leading somewhere else than to a lifetime's dissatisfaction as a merchant. But, in that dazzled moment in front of the Eiffel Tower, for the first time, he apprehended the possibility of another career, one that would provide intellectual and artistic fulfillment.

Haim Behar had made a good profit on the shipment of lemons he had brought and found he could buy French cookware at an advantageous price for sale back home. He told his son that the order would not be filled for two weeks and let the young man enjoy that time free of care. Raphael spent his days wandering about the city sketching buildings and monuments. Haim spent those days with doctors, grimly confirming that his own physicians had been correct in their diagnosis. He had tuberculosis, and it was terminal.

Each night, at dinners together that were very precious to Haim, Raphael gaily told of his day's wanderings through the city, of his evening's plans. Raphael was an entertaining conversationalist, and Haim would laugh at his son's stories until tears ran from his eyes or the coughing began. Haim said it was a lingering cold. Raphael was concerned, but had no inkling of the true nature of his father's illness. The young man's bond to his father was strong and deeply loving. That heritage too would be passed down through the generations to Ralph.

Haim had never remarried, had never even been with another woman, Raphael was quite sure. After dinner, when Haim retired to his hotel room, Raphael would frequent the left-bank cafés favored by other young people from all over Europe: painters and sculptors breaking free of what they considered the tyranny of Academy realism, poets proclaiming a titillating decadence, performing artists of every type, and all those who sought their company. He soon made the acquaintance of an art student who introduced Raphael to his wide circle of unconventional, exhilarating friends. French was the international language, and Raphael's school French was good. As could most Europeans, he could converse in several languages. In his case they also included the Greek and Turkish of his homeland and excellent, if formal, university English learned to help his father correspond with London importers. Raphael told the other young people that he intended to return the following year to study architecture, which was now true, and they accepted him as one of them.

All the way back on the train to Salonika, Raphael's head was filled with the gaiety of Parisian life, of its vivacious women, and of dozens of buildings he had seen and sketched. Raphael's

23

reveries were interrupted only by his father's worsening cough. Haim appeared weaker. When Raphael expressed his concern, Haim at last confessed that he was dying.

Raphael cried and hugged his father. He begged him to see another doctor—perhaps in Switzerland or Berlin or London was someone who could cure him. Gazing into the hazel eyes that had bewitched him the first time he had glimpsed Raphael's mother, Haim gently made his son understand that nothing could be done, that there was no hope.

Haim adored his son, but he was a realistic man and tried to evaluate his son objectively: Raphael was likable and possessed of the very important knack Haim had tried to nurture in him of being able to ingratiate himself with people. At times Raphael seemed poised beyond his years and quite shrewd in achieving his ends. At other times, overly naive and trusting, he could get carried away by a faddish idea or a person who was clever in returning his amiability. The boy's good heart, which had always been a source of joy, now troubled Haim. Would Raphael be hard-minded enough to protect himself against the temptations and threats that would assault him? The boy's instinct for self-preservation had never been tested. What would happen when Haim was no longer there to protect him?

Rocking through the European countryside that night, father and son talked about Raphael's future. The young man admitted that he wanted to return to Paris to become an architect.

Haim slept little that night, pondering. His plans for Raphael to enter his business, he realized, had been somewhat selfish, based in part on his own desires to perpetuate what he had built and to retain his son's company in his later years. Architecture was probably a good profession: The world was full of buildings, and someone had to design them, so the boy would be able to make a living. Haim was far more worried about the location than the profession his son had chosen.

The Salonika region had always been a precarious homeland for Jews, even those who had achieved some prosperity. Haim's opinion was that his people had been able to survive since the Inquisition forced them from fifteenth-century Spain only because the tension between the Christian Greeks and the Moslem Turks often caused both to forget their antagonism toward the Jews. After he himself was dead, his son would have no reason to remain.

But France? Fresh in Haim's mind, in the mind of every European Jew, was the recent Dreyfus case. By framing a Jewish

24

captain for treason with forged documents, French army officers had succeeded in unleashing a waiting, snarling anti-Semitism from behind France's false facade of tolerant gentility. Only recently had the truth of the anti-Jewish plot been forced into the open by Dreyfus's supporters. Haim did not want his son to put down new roots where hatred would always lie in wait behind the next door, where the centuries had also hardened the class lines that might otherwise impede his clever, ambitious young son's progress to prominence and wealth. Paris had exposed Raphael to luxuries he had never before imagined—and to a desire for them that his father recognized. Better for him to settle in a place where everyone was free and a stranger, Haim thought, a country of minorities where none was dominant, where Jews—everyone—had legal rights and opportunities.

"Not France," Haim announced the next morning in Ladino, the ancient Spanish still spoken among themselves by Mediterranean Jews forced out of Spain four hundred years earlier. "America."

"France is the center of the world."

Haim chuckled gently. "And the women there are very beautiful and very liberal with their favors." His expression grew serious again. "In France the anti-Semitism is as entrenched as the sewer system."

"America is where foolish dreamers go or those with nothing, not even an education, the laborers."

"Raphael," his father remonstrated gently, "I hope you do not think me one of the fools who believes the streets there are paved with gold. A man must work hard to succeed everywhere. But at least in America everyone starts out with a fair chance."

To make his father happy, Raphael weighed the value of emigrating to America. Despite enticement by the lively urbanity of Paris, he conceded that America made some sense. It was young and growing. There, he had heard, new buildings went up every week, every day, and the language would present little problem.

A cough suddenly exploded in Haim's chest which, catching his son's eye, Haim turned to dramatic advantage. "I'll never see your children, but I'll die knowing that in America they are safe."

That night Haim wrote a letter to his wife's brother, Nissim, who had gone to "New York, America" years before to seek his fortune. He asked his brother-in-law to watch over Raphael, who intended to emigrate there and study architecture.

Father and son quietly began to liquidate their inventory and to collect all the money owed. Haim's strength began to fail faster and earlier than expected. The doctors insisted he go into the hospital. Only a few days after that, Haim's largest customer, who owed him an enormous sum, confessed insolvency. Raphael kept the news from his father, allowing him to die believing he had bequeathed his son a solid inheritance with which to begin life in America. After expenses were paid, Raphael would be left with only a small amount.

The letter from Nissim in New York arrived a few days later, expansively inviting the young man to America. This was a marvelous country, his uncle wrote, full of opportunity for those with the ambition and means to set themselves up. New York was a city of wonders, of miracles, with fine architectural schools. He would personally introduce his nephew to the professors. Raphael could stay with him until he had found a place of his own—there was plenty of room in his fine, spacious apartment.

There was no doubt now that Raphael's destination would be America. Even if he had been inclined to go back on his vow to his father, he was far too poor. Without money with which to begin in Paris, one had little future. Without money in America, one was in the same boat as every other future millionaire, or so it was commonly believed. He wrote back to inform Nissim of Haim's death and that he would be leaving at the end of the month for America.

In the next few weeks, Raphael liquidated what little else he could. Finally, on the day he was set to leave, he hired a horse and carriage and was driven to the cemetery to say good-bye to the mother he had never known and the father who had never loved another woman. Not because he believed in God—Raphael considered himself far too modern for that—but out of obligation to his parents' beliefs and to make some parting gesture, as tears ran down his cheeks, Raphael recited the prayer for the dead over the twin graves.

Then, summoning the strength to turn away, he climbed back into the carriage for the trip to the railroad station. The train would take him to Genoa, where he would board a ship for America. Only memory was left to hold him here, and he would carry that with him wherever he went.

In 1905 Harlem and the Upper East Side were a curving swath of small nations squeezed up against one another north of Central Park and east of Fifth Avenue. The nearly homogeneous enclaves expanded and contracted in response to the pressure of immigration: Germans, Irish, Italians, and over fifty thousand Jews from many countries.

The Irish teamster amiably discoursing on every sight they passed that warm fall morning did not notice the despair into which his passenger had fallen. Many of the West Side neighborhoods through which the open, horse-drawn wagon rumbled north from the piers were shocking slums, with wooden shacks crowded up against each other. Perhaps for that reason, Raphael conjectured, the people all seemed to be out on the sidewalks; the streets bustled with activity: pushcarts, peddlers, women chatting, children playing tag around their legs, dangerous-looking men lounging in doorways.

The driver stood to pull the mismatched team to a halt as the wagon, now headed east on 116th Street, approached a rundown tenement building. Women on the sidewalk were chatting with a man leaning casually from a first-floor window. Handsome, with an abundance of straight black hair combed into a pompadour, he was joking and chucking one of them under the chin. Uncle Nissim.

"Raphael!" Nissim flung wide his arms to greet his young nephew with an embrace and to express his sympathy concerning Haim's death.

Raphael was surprised to find his uncle home from work so early in the day.

"Things have been slow for tinsmiths," Nissim explained as he supervised the teamster's placement of the steamer trunk beside a patch of linoleum in the tiny parlor. "But my wife has a good job with a hatmaker."

Raphael was shocked. "Your wife works!"

"In America everyone can work," Nissim declared ebulliently. "Having your wife work is what it means to live in a free country."

"I saw pushcarts," Raphael observed. "You could rent a pushcart and make money that way until you find a regular job."

Nissim shrugged. "What could I sell that someone isn't already selling?" A benevolent smile appeared on his face. "And I wouldn't have been here to welcome my nephew from the old country."

"How long have you been home like this waiting for me?" Raphael asked as he paid the driver the fare and let him out of the apartment.

"Two, maybe three weeks."

Raphael was appalled that his uncle would let a single day go by without earning money. Nissim agreed and, delighted by his nephew's concern, grandly pointed out the ancient sofa. The stuffing mushroomed through gaping tears in the upholstery.

"Boarding in a fine room like this would cost you three or four dollars a week anywhere. Because you are my nephew, the last relative I have left in the world, I will charge you only two dollars."

"No wonder you stayed home three weeks to wait for me."

Nissim bent his head apologetically. "In advance."

Raphael handed his uncle two dollars.

"It's nearly lunchtime," Nissim remembered. "I'll start making some good, strong Turkish coffee and set the table. Why don't you go to the grocery on the corner and buy some cheese and bread? Also fruit and some more coffee to welcome you with."

Raphael had hoped that living at Nissim's would reduce his expenses and stretch his meager capital. Whatever was left by the time he found a job would provide some of the tuition at an architectural school. But a different sort of education had begun—his education in survival.

"It's fortunate you have no children," Raphael remarked to his uncle. "They couldn't afford to live with you."

Nissim opened his arms wide again to embrace his nephew. "Welcome to America!"

Over lunch Nissim expounded on several elaborate plans he had concocted to make untold millions for them both. All he needed was investment by his nephew. Raphael explained that his means were small and intended for an architectural education. Peeved to learn that his nephew was not rich, Nissim accused him of having arrived under false pretenses, but grew more ingratiating when he realized that an argument might cause Raphael to demand the return of the two dollars. He knew the ways of America, the "ins and outs, the ropes," he said buoyantly. Raphael's father had entrusted the young man to his care, and he would not shirk that responsibility. He would take possession of Raphael's nest egg, no matter how small and unworthy it might be, and turn it into a fortune for them both.

Raphael graciously and firmly declined the offer. Taking his sketchbook and pencils from his trunk, he excused himself. He intended to spend the afternoon strolling downtown along Fifth Avenue, which his uncle had assured him was the chicest boulevard in the city.

In later years, when Nissim was an old man working for Ralph's father as a building superintendent, he would recount stories to young Ralph about his grandfather and the early days in New York. Even then, Nissim was still filled with outlandish schemes to become a millionaire, and even then women would still be buttoning blouses and quickly redoing makeup when Raphael arrived at the little ground-floor apartment. In several ways Nissim became a tutor by example for young Ralph, who learned to treat every encounter as a potential negotiation for advantage.

Raphael found a job that very first day in New York, totally by accident, but not one that he had foreseen in his lavish dreams of success in America. And that very same day, it became the cause of his happening to meet the man who would eventually be Gail's grandfather.

The mansions that lined Fifth Avenue were as grandly impos ing as any he had seen in Europe. He was pleased to note that care had gone into their design, as well as into the design of the electric streetlamps, which were tall and stately. Trees shaded the pavement. The people were tastefully, if a bit less smartly, dressed than in Paris, he thought—the men mostly in top hats, the women in chastely low-hemmed, high-necked dresses. Motor cars and hansom cabs shared the avenue.

As he neared the business area, he gradually became aware of another difference. The people seemed to move more briskly, more purposefully, their heads jutted forward a bit more. Given the barest of gaps in the traffic, the younger ones, and even some of the older, raced across the street, disregarding the bleating horns and the insults. This was clearly a country in a hurry.

At Thirty-seventh Street, Raphael stopped to look in the windows of the Tiffany Store Building. Just east of it, a residence was being constructed, and he ambled over. A young, well-dressed man, with blondish hair in what was probably permanent disarray, stood before the entrance to the building taking shape. He was talking animatedly and pointing to the plans unrolled before him on planks supported by sawhorses. The listener was the foreman and, Raphael excitedly surmised, the speaker was the architect. Raphael approached the blond young man just as the foreman was leaving.

"It is a handsome building," Raphael began, careful to enunciate each word clearly. "Are you its creator?"

"The architect? Oh, no," the other young man said in some embarrassment. "I'm only apprenticing in his office."

"I hope I will someday too be an architect, but I am only now in this country today."

"Your first day? Why, your English is quite good."

Raphael and the young man, Trevor Everett, began to chat, at first about Raphael's observations during his first few hours in America and then, enjoying each other's unexpected company, about their backgrounds. Raphael became enraptured by the dream of joining the other young man as an apprentice. How right was the decision to come to America. This was indeed the land of opportunity. Even walking down the street the first day, he had run into someone who could help get his architectural career underway.

"Perhaps there is room for another apprentice where you work?" he asked.

"Do you know mechanical drawing?"

"I can draw."

"No, mechanical drawing. To make up plans."

Raphael hung his head. He would have to study mechanical drawing before he could hope for a job with an architect. Sensing Raphael's dismay, Everett offered to introduce him to the man whose house was going up in front of them. George C. Boldt was the owner of the Waldorf-Astoria Hotel. Not only was he building this new town house, the young man confided, but he was erecting a magnificent castle on one of the Thousand Islands. The work would be in the hotel and not architectural work, but at least Raphael could earn a living while he studied.

Grateful, Raphael agreed. As the two young men walked the three blocks south on Fifth Avenue to the hotel, the American pointed out the white marble facade and the tall Corinthian columns of Stanford White's Knickerbocker Trust Co. building. Delighted by its derivation from the ancient temples of his homeland, Raphael showed his new acquaintance the drawing in his sketchbook that he had made of a similar, classical Parisian structure, the Madeleine. Everett admitted his envy: his dearest wish was to visit Europe and see with his own eyes the great buildings there.

"You will do it, Everett," Raphael exclaimed exuberantly. "Just as I have come here, you will go there someday and see with your own eyes."

The Waldorf-Astoria was a conjunction of two imposing hotel buildings constructed on the sites of what had been the homes of

30

two branches of the Astor family. In 1890 William Waldorf Astor had decided that he would live permanently in England and that a hotel would be a valuable rental property on the site of his Thirty-third Street home. The man selected to build, own, and operate the hotel was George C. Boldt, who had come to America as a teenager and worked his way up to the proprietorship of a small but superbly run hotel in Philadelphia. A few years after the Waldorf Hotel's opening, William Waldorf Astor's cousin John Jacob Astor chose to raze his own home on the northern half of the block front and enter into an arrangement for Boldt to build a larger hotel on it that would be integrally joined with the Waldorf, but could be severed in case the arrangement failed. The names of the two twin hotels were forever joined. New York had never seen anything like the opulent furnishings and attentive service of Boldt's Waldorf-Astoria Hotel.

Everett led Raphael into the hotel for a brief view of the ornate lobby before whisking him to a separate entrance on Thirty-fourth Street, beside a florist's shop. The stairs led half a flight up to the mezzanine and George C. Boldt's office.

As they were being admitted, Everett glanced at his companion, "You will have to shave your mustache. Mr. Boldt does not permit facial hair of any kind on his staff. Clean-shaven faces, he feels, appear more hygienic to his guests."

Raphael had only an instant to shoot his new friend a surprised look before the door opened; he had fancied that the mustache made him look like a mature man instead of a boy. Boldt, who appeared to be in his fifties, was at his desk reading some papers. The first thing Raphael noticed was the man's close-cropped beard and mustache.

Boldt removed his pince-nez glasses as he stood up to greet the young men. In a middle-European accent, he asked about progress on his residence, and Everett raised a small problem his employer wanted resolved. Boldt then asked if Raphael was also employed in the architect's office.

"He aspires to be an architect some day, Mr. Boldt," Everett replied. "But it is his first day in New York, and he is seeking employment."

Boldt smiled, and Raphael was taken with the kindliness of the man's expression as he inquired where Raphael was from. Observing that immigrants from that part of the Old World were uncommon in New York, Boldt then asked what languages

Raphael spoke. The long list did not seem to satisfy the hotel owner.

"We have a great need for waiters, but without a knowledge of German . . ." Boldt shrugged. "It is essential that a guest from Berlin or Paris be able to come fresh from the steamer and know that here he will be instantly understood."

"I do not intend to be a waiter," Raphael replied. He was appalled by the idea. He was a gentleman, a young man with an excellent education, an artist. Such an offer was an insult. He was about to depart when Boldt spoke again.

"I myself began as a waiter and could not have begun at a better place. A good waiter has an excellent opportunity to learn by observation and rise in the world. A waiter learns human nature and the value of never-failing courtesy and that the customer, who provides the income in any business, is always right."

Everett interposed himself. "He is very quick, Mr. Boldt. I'm sure he could quickly learn German and be very useful to the hotel."

"Look up at the ceiling," Boldt directed.

Raphael did so.

"Without looking down," the hotel owner continued, "tell me exactly what items are on my desk."

Raphael did not know whether to laugh at the childish game the man had proposed or simply to leave and not stoop to his demeaning level. Irritation won out, and he decided not to depart before demonstrating his talents to this dictatorial Mr. Boldt who thought so little of him. As well as he could with his limited vocabulary, Raphael named the items: a desk pad and blotter; a brass pen set containing a bottle of ink; a photograph of a woman in a silver frame; several papers—letters, Raphael assumed, because stamped and canceled envelopes lay nearby. "That is all, I think."

Raphael stood up to leave.

Boldt appraised Raphael with more interest. "Observant. That is important. Every employee here is responsible for the well-being and enjoyment of our guests, even if a particular job is not his. Your manners are good, your appearance." He nodded. "All right. See Oscar. Tell him I have hired you and you are to work with a waiter who can teach you German while you are learning to wait on tables." Boldt told him what the wages were and what tips he could anticipate.

Raphael hesitated. The income was excellent for someone

with no other prospects. His uncle Nissim was often out of work and earned less when he did have employment. Raphael was proud, but he was not foolish.

"Thank you, Mr. Boldt."

"I expect you to be able to converse with me in German in one month. One additional matter," Boldt began.

"I had intended to shave my mustache this very night," Raphael responded.

Boldt smiled. Despite a touch of arrogance about the eyes, the young man was indeed quick to anticipate another's desires. He was a young man to keep an eye on. He would do well in America.

Oscar told Raphael that he would start the next day. He was expected to serve in tails, which the hotel supplied, but he would need to buy his own dress shirts. Heinz, the waiter Oscar named as his mentor during his training period, suggested that he try a shirt store on Delancey Street on the Lower East Side; prices were far more reasonable than in the stores along Fifth Avenue.

"Usually with Jews you have to bargain," Heinz remarked, "but that one starts with his lowest price and then takes less."

Raphael caught sight of the impossibly tall tower long before he reached Twenty-third Street and was stunned by it. He hurried toward it. Stopping impatiently at a street corner to let a carriage move past, he counted the floors. Twenty! A slim and elegant wedge twenty stories high! Paris had ornate facades, but no building so modern, so striking as this. This was what he had come to America for.

He stood in front of its entrance, staring upward in awe, blocking pedestrians who hurried by; women whose skirts swirled upward in the drafts caused by the tall building and the men trying to glimpse their ankles.

Pointing to the street sign on the Twenty-third Street corner, a large policeman with a walrus mustache jerked his thumb to indicate Raphael must move on. No ogling the ladies' ankles in his purview.

"Twenty-three skidoo!" he ordered, his accent as Irish as that of the teamster who had driven Raphael from the pier.

"What is it called, the building?" Raphael asked, bursting with curiosity.

"The Fuller Company Building, but everyone calls it the Flatiron Building."

"Of what is the building made?"

"Steel." The policeman was used to the question. "A steel frame."

Again steel, Raphael observed. Like the Eiffel Tower. The Greeks and Romans, the Gothic-cathedral builders, had all erected exquisite structures, but all were earthbound because they lacked the knowledge of building with steel.

When a woman opened the door to leave the building. Raphael noticed the elevator inside the lobby. Steel to gain the height, he reflected, and an elevator because people cannot easily walk up more than maybe four or five floors at most; the lessons are all around me if I keep my eyes open.

The signs and clothing changed abruptly when Raphael crossed the Bowery, leaving the Italian and entering the Jewish section, where many women wore ill-fitting wigs and, even in the heat, the men wore skull caps or black derby hats and their dark suits covered layers of shabby clothing. Pushcarts formed a line along the gutter that slowed pedestrian traffic on the sidewalk to a trickle. Store signs were written both in English and Hebrew letters. But Raphael did not recognize the Hebrew words, until he sounded out the names "Goldstein and Weintraub," which he recognized as Jewish names from Northern Europe, where Yiddish, not Ladino, was spoken; the Hebrew letters were being employed to write Yiddish. In English the sign declared that Goldstein and Weintraub were tailors.

Such signs covered every storefront, hung from every shop. As Raphael made his way deeper into the Jewish section, the profusion of people and smells became stifling. He had to push his way through.

At Allen Street a train rattled along the elevated right-of-way. Amplified along the dark tunnel formed by the track structure above and grimy buildings with saloons on both sides, the sound crushed down on him. A woman accosted him. He turned the corner and found someone who was able to direct him to the shirt store on Delancey Street.

He entered. Boxes were crammed onto shelves that reached to the ceiling and were heaped in piles everywhere. Shirts tumbled out of many. Noticing Raphael, a young man of about his own age hurried to the front to wait on him.

"May I help you?" he asked in unaccented English.

Raphael explained what he was looking for. The other young man went scurrying through boxes in what seemed to be a futile effort to locate the correct merchandise. Each time he pulled out a box, others would topple off that pile. Several times the right boxes turned out to have the wrong shirts in them.

To make conversation as the young man hunted for the shirts, Raphael recounted his recent run-in beneath the elevated subway and then asked, "Where does one meet respectable young women?" The man's face reddened. "You are asking the wrong person. I don't know many girls. Day and night my mother is after me to find a nice girl and settle down."

Raphael sensed the other man's shyness. "I think you would like to meet a nice girl too, I am right?"

"It isn't as if business is so good that I have money to support a wife," the young man rejoined, his eyes averted.

"This is a busy street."

The young man finally found the right box and the right shirts.

"Didn't you see the sign over the door?" he said as he handed Raphael the box. "Vishnetsky."

"And?" Raphael asked, holding one of the stiff shirts up for examination. It was a fine shirt, as fine as any he could have bought in Paris.

"If you were Russian, you would understand. My father was a Russian Jew who died last year and left me the store. This whole neighborhood is full of Russian Jews. They see a name like Vishnetsky on the sign, and they don't believe we're Jewish. They left Russia to get away from people with names like Vishnetsky. Names are important in America."

"That is easy. Change your name."

"Vishnetsky has always been our name, for generations." He extended his hand. "Izzy Vishnetsky."

Raphael lowered the shirt and shook his hand. "Raphael Behar. I wish to ask you a question, Izzy. Is it better to starve as Vishnetsky or to prosper as Goldstein?"

Izzy reflected a moment, then shook his head. "The fellow next door is Goldstein."

"Then Lipschitz or Weintraub." Raphael tried to remember other names he had read as he walked the narrow streets.

"In English Lipschitz is not such a good name."

Raphael extended his hand again. "Happy to meet you, Mr. Weintraub."

Izzy sounded it out. "Weintraub. I like it. It's a good name." He tried it again. "Weintraub. Izzy Weintraub."

"How much for the shirts?" Raphael asked.

"Keep your money," the other said, as he refolded the shirts and searched around for a bag in which to place them. "You deserve it for the advice and my new name."

"Vishnetsky or Weintraub, I think the way you do business you'll always be in trouble."

"Already I feel different," Izzy said in a gush of feeling. "This is the first important step I have ever taken with my life. Do you understand that? Generations from now my family will celebrate this day that I took on this new name. Perhaps your family will be there too, as honored guests."

"You have a problem," Raphael observed skeptically. "You are a romantic. That is a good thing for a poet or a painter. It is not a good thing for a man who wishes to sell shirts. I sometimes have such feelings that come rushing like a big wave, but I . . ." Raphael searched for the English word. "I *control* them. I must control my life to gain my success."

Izzy stared into Raphael's eyes for a long moment. It was his own turn for skepticism. "Maybe the wave has not been big enough yet."

When the big wave did come, her name turned out to be Sally, although Raphael did not know that for a while. And, as Izzy had predicted, she swept away all of his new friend's pretensions of self-mastery.

Chapter 2

Raphael first caught sight of her one afternoon, after his drawing class at the Cooper Union, as he was hurrying out of the building toward the subway. He thought she was the most remarkable-looking creature he had ever seen—not simply beautiful, but remarkable looking. She wore a long, dawn gray dress and seemed to glide with serene self-possession, like a tall clipper ship with pristine sails and perfect grace past grim and smoke-blackened freighters. He turned to get a better look, and his natural self-assurance then propelled him toward her as he calculated how to manage an introduction. But the crowd of other

36

students surging between them was too great, and he lost sight of her before he could fight his way through them.

Raphael's instinctive determination to go after what he wanted was another legacy to his son, Henry, and then to his grandson Ralph. They all understood as well its corollary on this most commercial of islands: success brought acceptance. That knowledge, from which was to be formed both Henry's apartment empire in Brooklyn and Ralph's psychological passport to cross the river into Manhattan, was the very promise that first sustained Raphael as he hauled plates to and from the kitchen for the benefit of oblivious diners; even in moments of deepest depression, Raphael knew that his father had been right about his coming to America. What each of the men in turn would someday be forced to learn was the corollary's bitter converse: that a reversal of fortune brought rejection, and how they faced it determined their destinies.

As unsuitable as he considered a waiter's job, Raphael worked hard to do it well; his experience as a diner with his father in fine European establishments and his cultivated manners made for swift progress once Boldt and Oscar had assured themselves of his competency in German. The latter was pleased to find unnecessary in Raphael's case such usual admonitions to newly recruited dining-room staff as Do not reach across the table to pour water; Do not serve toothpicks with the check; Do not stop to watch how much another waiter is tipped.

Raphael had been working for several months when a call came that a waiter was needed upstairs. The rainy night had been slow for Raphael. The few groups of diners who *had* turned up had insisted on sitting in more favored parts of the dining room, which were the coveted stations of waiters with more seniority. He was delighted when the captain righted matters by choosing him to help out in Charles G. Gates's suite. If rumors were true, hundreds of thousands of dollars were crossing the gambling table there each night and winners were often generous to attendants.

From the newspapers which Raphael read every day as part of his self-education and from back-of-the-house gossip, Raphael had learned quite a bit about Charles G. Gates. He was the fast-living son of John W. Gates, better known to the public as "Bet-A-Million Gates," who had turned his thirty-dollar-a-month barbed-wire salesman's job into control of the barbed-wire trust. Since then, the older Gates had made and lost fortunes at the gaming tables and on Wall Street. His gamble on the Spindletop well had put him back on top again and set off oil fever in Texas. Charlie did not have his father's business acumen, but he had the same taste for gambling, drinking, and high life and, thanks to his father, access to vast wealth. He had recently ridden at great speed to New York in his private railroad train, checked into his father's old rooms at the Waldorf, and declared the party on.

As Raphael wheeled in serving carts of food, the men were gathered around a large table playing poker, their heads nearly obscured by clouds of cigar smoke. A few female escorts sat on sofas at the other end of the large, ornately decorated room. The players had decided to sup later and take snacks while they played. Occasionally, as Raphael offered a drink or a selection from a tray, the players would hand him a tip or stuff one in his pocket, barely taking their eyes from the game.

Several were crude, uncultured men, Raphael noted, men who must have risen from poverty to great wealth. They were overweight, as if their appetites for money, for excitement, and for food were all bound up in the same hunger that had motivated their success. Two of the other men were in their twenties: one was a shrewd player who seemed to weigh both the cards and the psychological makeup of his opponents before he committed money to the pot; the other, whose name was Bobby Houghton, was handsome and elegantly dressed and played carelessly, impulsively, seemingly to stimulate himself with the hope of relieving a deep ennui. Gathering from the conversation that he was a rich man's son, bored by the position he filled in his father's company, Raphael surmised that he was someone who had everything and was able to take pleasure in nothing. Charlie Gates seemed like that as well. A heavy drinker, he would often overvalue his hand and plunge heavily, hoping to bluff the others. When he lost, he would laughingly exclaim that it was only money, "the cheapest commodity in the world," and insist that his guests have another drink. With a trace of envy, Raphael estimated that any one of the poker pots some of these men took so lightly would allow him to quit working and study architecture at his ease.

"Where's Lonsdale?" Bobby Houghton asked. "You said he'd be here."

"After the opera," Charlie Gates assured him. "He won't disappoint me. I'm in the Amalgamated Lead deal with him."

"No wonder you're in a celebrating mood," another commented.

Half an hour later there was a knock at the door. Raphael

answered it. Lonsdale turned out to be a tall, striking man in his late fifties with graying hair and an aristocratic manner. He wore a black silk top hat, tails, a white waistcoat, and a white tie. Raphael's gaze shifted to the woman beside Lonsdale, and he felt a spasm in his throat that rolled to the pit of his stomach—the same young woman he had glimpsed at the Cooper Union. Tall and swathed in a pale blue cloak, her face appeared tiny and childlike in the hood, fragilely beautiful, with an alabaster-pale complexion and large blue eyes.

Raphael smiled indiscreetly at her as he took her wrap. Up close she was even more beautiful than he had thought her at first glance. She was young, perhaps his age or so, and her skin was fresh and flawless. As she threw back the hood and turned to let the cloak slip from her shoulders to his hands, her dark hair was very near him. She wore it up, in the current fashion, but had allowed a few wisps to hang down along her neck. He had never seen anything so erotic as those few soft hairs caressing her neck. Inhaling her perfume at that same moment, he felt weak.

Again, Raphael noted that she seemed to glide as she proceeded across the room beside her escort, her blue silk gown whispering about her. Bobby Houghton seemed to know both Lonsdale and her, exhibiting vitality for the first time that evening as he rushed over to say hello. All his attention was fixed on her. Her face remained expressionless, as if she floated within a bubble that shielded her from the sounds and sights and thoughts of a sordid world.

Lonsdale took a seat at the poker table. She did not join the women, but took a position directly behind him, her hand resting on his shoulder. Raphael guessed she was his daughter. He revealed his cards only to her. Occasionally, he would turn to her, awaiting a nod or a shake of her head. Her solemn expression did not change, whether he won or lost.

After a while, Raphael noticed that she was staring across the table at the shrewd young man who had been a steady winner throughout the evening. As unreasonable as he knew it to be, Raphael felt a surge of jealousy. But then he noted that her eyes were fixed on the young man's hands, and he too began to watch them. Once in a while, as he dealt, the young man's lower fingers flicked at the bottom of the deck, and the young woman invariably advised Lonsdale to fold his hand. Once Lonsdale grew irritated, again showing her his cards, which obviously were promising, but he reluctantly threw them in when she insisted. Invariably, the heavy-browed young man would win his deals.

After several hours, only he and Lonsdale were winners. The biggest and loudest loser was Charlie Gates.

Lonsdale stood up and turned to his companion. "I've bored you long enough, my dear."

He rolled some bills into a tight little tube and slipped them into the young woman's glove. She did not seem aware that he had done so.

"She's my good-luck piece," Lonsdale announced to one and all.

As the group made its way to the supper table, the talk was of the hands that had been won and lost and, occasionally, of business. The women entered eagerly into the conversation, glad at last to be included. Bobby Houghton jumped to take the seat on the other side of the dark-haired young woman with Lonsdale. Charlie Gates, at the head of the table, was now sloppily drunk. Disregarding his own escort, he kept trying to woo her as well, while also trying ineptly to court her important banker companion. Raphael tried to catch the dark-haired young woman's conversation. However, except for an occasional reply to a direct question, spoken too softly for Raphael to hear, she was silent and her gaze distant, as if her thoughts might now be walking along the uncharted coast of an undiscovered civilization.

Most of the hotel's menu was in French, and Raphael was in the habit of translating for those Americans he sensed would not understand that language. Only when he began to do so here did her attention fasten on him, her gaze become rapt.

She ate lightly and, turning down dessert, indicated to Lonsdale that she wished to leave. When Raphael held up her cloak for her to slip into, she unexpectedly turned to stare at him or, rather, through him with eyes so translucent, so composed, and yet so unexpectedly cynical, they appeared to have seen the beginning of time.

That look, into which Raphael could read nothing, neither interest nor even awareness of him, sealed his fate. He was wildly in love, seized by the same sort of total, improbable, unreasonable infatuation that had overwhelmed his father to the exclusion of all other women and, for good or ill, would strike each of the men descended from him.

For a while Raphael had avoided seeking a room of his own; it would cost him far more than the sofa he used only long enough for a few hours of sleep and homework before catching the subway downtown for work or school or the pleasures he had begun to discover in the city. Although Nissim's wife was amiable and Nissim was infectiously good-humored company, Raphael considered him a moocher or *shnorrer*, as it was termed in the Yiddish he was picking up. When Nissim realized that the Cooper Union provided free education and, thus, Raphael's small nest egg was still untouched, he started to concoct grandly chimerical schemes for businesses they could found together, based on his nephew's capital and his own genius. No matter what time Raphael returned to the apartment, Nissim was waiting up, eager to discuss his newest scheme.

Because of its lower rents and proximity to the Cooper Union, Raphael began to search for a room on the Lower East Side. The failed Russian revolution of 1905 had sent a new wave of Jewish immigrants to seek refuge in America, a large number of them in that densely overpopulated district encompassing Rivington, Orchard, Stanton, Ludlow, Broome, Eldridge, Essex, and Hester streets. The great majority had grown up in Jewish ghettos or rural villages in which their meager education and social behavior revolved around ancient religious texts and long-acknowledged custom; to Raphael they appeared to have emigrated, not from Europe, but from another age. What he pitied most about their situation was that they were lost here, struggling to stay afloat in a system where the threat was, not to them politically as a religious group, but to them economically as individuals. Nothing in their previously sheltered lives had prepared them, he decided, to confront the great truth of American democracy: that economics here treated one and all callously, but more or less alike. Here no one forbade their traditional way of life, but it was irrelevant, even self-destructive. They could choose not to work on *shabbos*, the Saturday sabbath, but their sweatshop employers could instantly find someone who would.

Each time Raphael entered the congested streets lined with colorful, overflowing pushcarts, he might have been gladdened by their similarity to the Middle Eastern bazaars he had left behind, but he was instantly repelled by the feeling that he had become trapped in a human anthill where hundreds of thousands slaved joylessly in stacked, tiny chambers until their barely noticed deaths. Fearful of sharing their fate, he was simultaneously ashamed of his own dread that gentiles were lumping him together with them. I am somebody! he would cry out silently as if to remind himself.

In the fall Raphael found a room he could afford in a building that faced away from the heart of the district. Although he

41

became friendly with several of the other young people who lived there, Raphael considered that this new dwelling, like his present station in life, was only a way station. He shifted to day work at the Waldorf-Astoria, so as to take the evening courses necessary for an architectural degree and so as, occasionally, to be able to enjoy the city's pleasurable nightlife.

Although he devoted less time to study than before, he was conscientious about attending his classes at the Cooper Union. He scanned the halls for the dark-haired young woman, but did not see her there again, nor at the Waldorf. When he finally did see her, it was in the most improbable place of all.

Raphael had not been to synagogue since coming to America; moreover, he had felt relieved to be rid of that obligation since his father's death. But the approach of Yom Kippur had provoked a deep melancholy. Only a year before, he and his father had sat side by side in the third row of their synagogue in Salonika, as they had done since he could remember, and so, out of respect for his father on that day set aside for soul-searching, he had accepted his friend Izzy Weintraub's invitation to his *shul* and then home for dinner to break the fast.

Although the Hebrew accent was different from the one he had been brought up with, he tried to follow along and maintain some interest. After the ram's horn had been blown at the end of the service and he had stepped outside the synagogue, Raphael was suddenly jolted by the sight of that perfect and perfectly remembered face. She stood beside a small older woman.

"Who is she?" Raphael asked Izzy excitedly, gesturing. "Do you know her name? Who is she?"

Izzy turned to the friend beside him and pointed her out. The other man leaned over to Raphael. "We all call her Shaineh Sally. You know what *shaineh* means? Pretty. She calls herself Sally, but her real name is Sima. She's a Russian Jew. She started as one of the girls at Rosie Hertz's. She sure worked her way up in the world."

"She's a whore?" Raphael was shocked and disheartened by the knowledge.

"She's a whore like Rockefeller is an oil salesman."

"What is that supposed to mean?"

"Men spend on handkerchiefs for her what you and I would be grateful to make in a year."

Raphael felt his heart breaking. At that moment, she noticed him, and recognition seemed to flicker across her face. She walked over to him.

"You work at the Waldorf-Astoria," she said. Her voice bore almost no accent, but she enunciated her words very slowly and carefully, as if laboring not to make an error.

"And I have seen you also at the Cooper Union. I'm studying there at night to be an architect," Raphael added, to make her understand that she might have met him as a waiter, but that the defect would soon be corrected.

"You are from France."

"I *speak* French," he replied, conscious of his accent in English. "I'm not from France."

She thought for a moment. "People in society speak French in restaurants. I wish to learn French. I will pay you."

Raphael was deeply offended. He had finally gotten a chance to converse with her, and she had tried to hire him like a servant. This . . . this *prostitute* had tried to buy his services!

"I will not waste my time teaching a useless woman to order in French from waiters who understand English," he said, proud of the derision he had managed to instill in his response.

He swept past her, head high. Even as he did so, he found it impossible to erase from his heart the false image of a pure and ethereal angel that radiated from her face. He had been captivated, and now was torn by two irreconcilable emotions: by abhorrence that she was a Jewess who sold her body and by desire to possess her. He slept poorly that night.

The next evening, when Raphael arrived at the Cooper Union, Shaineh Sally stood beside the entrance. She had obviously been waiting for him. Raphael had made up his mind to have nothing to do with her, but the sight of her face made him tremble despite his intentions. The very coolness of her stare ignited desire.

"You said you also attend the Cooper Union," she enunciated in the soft, careful speech he remembered. "I have studied art here to improve myself."

He did not respond, but he could not break away either.

"I still want you to teach me French," she said. "Why are you not interested? As I said, I will pay you well."

Raphael was contemptuous. "I am sure you can. Lonsdale gave you a roll of money."

"Hundred-dollar bills," she added, pride now infusing her voice. "But I won five times that for him."

"You don't come cheap."

"Girls who do deserve what they get."

Teeth clenched in rage and infatuation, he replied, "We'll make a deal. You're a businesswoman. One French lesson by me for an hour in bed with you. If we're both satisfied, we can go on to lesson two."

For the first time Raphael saw emotion flood her face. She was furious. "I am not some street girl you can buy. Graham Lonsdale is my friend and my . . . *only* escort."

Raphael stared deep into the bottomless blue of her eyes. "*That* is my offer. Take it or leave it."

Her thoughts were an uncharacteristic jumble. He tipped his new gray derby and strode into the building.

"Wait!" she called after him, her tone reflecting her amazement. "I will take it."

On his day off from work, Raphael walked the short distance from his tenement building to the address near Washington Square that Sally had given him. He was surprised to find that her home was a handsome federalist town house. A young Irish maid admitted him and led him into a large, well-furnished drawing room. The furniture was very modern and obviously chosen with care: straighter, simpler lines and lighter woods than the ponderous Victorian look still popular with many. Sally stood up when he entered. She wore a gray chiffon dress. Her mother, a frail woman, was just leaving to shop for food. Raphael could not tell whether she knew what her daughter did for a living, but she appeared to receive the respect due a parent.

Raphael complimented Sally on one or two pieces of furniture that were particularly well designed. He noted the pride she took in the house as they walked through it to her sitting room overlooking a rear garden. The focus of the room was a superb antique French desk. What intrigued Raphael most were the books on it and on the shelves behind it. He picked one of them up, an English dictionary that had clearly seen much use. Another was an English grammar book, again much used. Open on the desk was a French beginner's reader Sally had only recently purchased and evidently had begun to study in preparation for his visit.

He drew up a seat next to hers at the desk to begin the French lesson. Her scent, which had floated through his waking and sleeping dreams, made him dizzy. He fought to concentrate on his first words. But his arm brushed against hers, and his voice caught. When she tried to repeat his French phrase, hers seemed to catch as well.

44

By the end of the hour, the lesson had become as erotic as if they were already lovers. When she tried to repeat *ma chere*, he corrected her with a finger placed gently on her lips.

"No," he whispered, *"you* must say *mon cher."*

"Mon cher. How do I say that I want to make love to you?"

"For that you kiss me."

She leaned toward him very slowly. Just before their lips touched, she whispered, "And naturally it must be a French kiss."

Sally was as passionate in bed as she was cool in her demeanor outside of it. Naked, she was even more beautiful and, without the clothes that provided true or false clues, even more of an indecipherable, compelling mystery. After making love to her, Raphael felt exhilarated and gripped by fascination. He was obsessed with knowing everything about her. He pressed her to tell him about herself.

She sat up and drew on her peignoir.

"It has grown quite late," she said, her speech careful once more.

At the front door, he told her he would continue the French lessons for free if she wanted them, whether she slept with him or not.

She laughed, the first time he had ever seen the seriousness break. "I was going to say that in the future you need not feel obligated to give me French lessons when we make love. But I do not want you coming here. From now on I will come to you."

Most mornings, Raphael paced his little room impatiently until Sally arrived. He gave her a French lesson, and then they made love.

He tried asking her questions, but she evaded giving answers. The mystery she maintained both irritated and intrigued him. She seemed almost a spirit who materialized into the shape of a passionate woman once each day and then disappeared. Several times he became petulant, refusing to continue the lovemaking until she told him about herself. When she reached for her clothing, he relented and coaxed her back into bed.

Once, he insisted that the next time they meet at her house. Was she ashamed of him? No, she said, shaking her head. But her soft tones were adamant. "It is an unnecessary danger."

Rather than risk losing her, he bit off his vexation. Why was he so enamored of her? he agonized. Although his first year in

America had hardened him and filed off much of his innocence, his basic nature was still effusive, open, subject to being swept up in his enthusiasms. In contrast to his confident declaration to Izzy, it was actually *she* who was always in control, carefully shielding herself and her ambitious intent behind her impassive beauty. His own mind could be playful, but she had no interest in or talent for flirtation, which he found strange in a woman who drew men to her. Her conversation could be penetrating, but she kept the topics impersonal. She seemed to attach values to everything, usually material values, swiftly losing interest in matters to which she could not. In no way was she sly or underhanded, but her manner unsettled him: direct when addressing him, focusing on him fully; distant at other times, as coldly indifferent as the first time he had seen her. Even when he thought them closest, when they were joined by their mutual passion, he sensed in her a selfishness, a self-involvement that excluded him.

He realized that he hardly knew her at all. What were her feelings toward him? he demanded she reveal. She left without answering, but she ruminated on his dissatisfaction with the little of herself that she gave him each day.

She arrived the next afternoon without the French book.

"I will trust you," she said tensely, as if she had wrestled all night with that issue.

She was born in a village near Odessa and was twelve when the Cossacks descended. They massacred all the men, including her father, and burned all the houses. She hid in a cupboard. Afterward, only survival was important to her. All illusions were at an end, the foremost being God. To be killed because of the way one worships God, she explained to Rapnael, would mean God cannot or does not wish to protect his worshippers or else that he does not exist. One would have to be a fool to believe in such a God.

With help from relatives in Odessa, who probably feared their asking to move in, Sally and her mother bought passage to America.

Her mother was lost in the New World, but Sally, despite her youth, quickly realized that the streets here were paved with gold only for those who used their skills and opportunities wisely. She found a job sewing garments in a sweatshop and brought home piecework for her mother. Her work was dreary and endless. Seeing her value in men's eyes, she decided that they would be her means out of poverty. Her price would be very high, and she would despise them for paying it.

Raphael asked whether it was true that she had once worked for Rosie Hertz.

"No, it was not like that," she replied adamantly. Sally had been only fifteen at the time, but she had gone to Rosie herself and struck a deal. If Rosie taught her what she needed to know to please men and loaned her the money to be seen at the right places uptown, Sally would pay her half of what she earned the first year from the wealthy man whose mistress she would become.

"After expenses," Sally carefully added. "To you I may be a prostitute," she told Raphael with no self-pity, recalling one of their earliest conversations, "but to a man I wish to attract, a man like Graham Lonsdale, I have learned to be a dream he must pay dearly for. I left Sima Rabinowitz at immigration in Castle Garden. I've worked hard to make myself into Sally Robbins, who speaks without an accent and creates a stir at the finest places and among the finest people. I have money now, and I will have much, much more."

Raphael had so many questions, but she halted him. Maybe another time. Would he please hold her for a while? she asked so quietly he almost failed to hear her. They sat on the edge of his bed, and he held her. For the first time they did not make love before she left.

Now that she trusted him, Raphael could ask other questions. He learned that Graham Lonsdale was her only other lover now and had been for more than a year. To keep the interest of a woman so much younger than he, Lonsdale understood that he must be generous with his gifts, for one thing paying the rent on her town house. But the town house lease was in her name, she pointed out. As to why she continued to live near the Lower East Side if Lonsdale and the social circle she aspired to join had long since moved uptown, she explained that although she felt no pull toward other Jews—and her visit to the synagogue on Yom Kippur was no exception—she remained for the sake of her mother, who would have no one to talk to away from the Jewish section. Here her mother had only a short walk to the grocer who could understand her, the butcher, other women she knew. Sally's men friends might suspect she was Jewish, but probably did not. When she finally did move uptown, it would be because Lonsdale or, if that relationship failed to last, one of his successors had offered her more than the expensive gifts they knew she required; it would be because one of them had offered her marriage and entree into the upper class.

Raphael jumped angrily to his feet. "Then why do you continue to see me if you have Lonsdale?"

She owed him an answer. Although she engaged his eyes directly, her voice was almost inaudible. "I do not mean to climax with him, but my body often betrays me. With you the choice to make love is mine. I don't hate myself for my pleasure."

Her answer infuriated Raphael. "What about love? What about me? You never want me to talk about myself. You want me to hide myself and my feelings like you do."

"I know you want to be an architect," she countered. "You study for that at the Cooper Union."

"But why? Why do I want to be an architect? What do I feel? Why do I go crazy waiting each day for you to arrive, afraid that this time you will not and I will never see you again?"

She chose the question she wished to answer. "You want to be an architect to become rich. What we all want to do. Also, for respect. Several are in society."

"I want to build beautiful things," he shouted with passion. "Long after I am dead, my name will be on the cornerstones of the most beautiful buildings of our time—the greatest, tallest buildings in the world."

"Perhaps," she replied after a long pause for thought, her eyes never leaving his. "But you want more to be rich, Raphael Behar."

A knock sounded at Raphael's door on a morning Sally had told him she would not be able to see him. Overjoyed by the change in her plans, he rushed to open it and was confronted by a young woman he had never seen before. In her early twenties, he guessed, she carried two inexpensive suitcases and wore the sort of old-fashioned clothing he associated with immigrants just off the boat from Eastern Europe. Her features were too irregular for her to be pretty, her eyes too deeply set and close together, but she was pleasant-looking, with a trim figure of less than medium height. A kerchief was knotted tightly beneath her chin to control curly chestnut-colored hair that refused on all sides to be contained. Her most compelling feature was a very determined expression.

"I am Hannah Moskowitz," she announced in Yiddish.

He waited for her to tell him the purpose of her visit.

"Hannah Moskowitz," she repeated, as if to a slow child. "I am here to marry you."

She thrust a letter at him. From what he could gather, a matchmaker in her town had arranged her marriage to a young man who had emigrated to America several years before. His mother had negotiated on his side. This letter to her was his concurrence. Raphael recognized the young man's name. He had resided in the room before Raphael and had long since skipped out of town to avoid paying back rent and other debts. He was believed to be living somewhere in the South, but no one was sure. Raphael tried to explain as well as he could to the young woman.

"That is impossible," she firmly maintained. "I do not have a photograph, but your description is the same as the one your mother gave me."

"Do I sound and look like I grew up speaking Yiddish?"

She thought about that for a moment and nodded. "You are not Shmulke Lubovkin. Tell me when he will be back."

Again, Raphael explained that he had left New York and no one knew his whereabouts. Only then did the young woman's shoulders slump. She looked around her, suddenly understanding that she was marooned thousands of miles from anyone she knew. After several seconds in which, head buried in her chest, she appeared to weigh her alternatives, she straightened up and strode into Raphael's room.

"I will stay with you for now. In exchange, I will cook and clean. But understand," she added, her chin now lifted, "you will not touch me."

No amount of argument could persuade the young woman to leave. Raphael summoned the building's superintendent to reinforce his argument that she must go and, if she still refused, to force her to do so. But her frontal attack swiftly routed the other man, who slipped away murmuring disjointedly that a pipe needed fixing. Raphael's sympathy for her fled a few minutes later when she shoved aside his clothing, fastidiously folded in the chest of drawers, to make space for her own. He sprang forward and began to stuff her clothing back into one of her open suitcases, but she, just as quickly, replaced it with clothing from the other. This might have continued indefinitely had Raphael not stopped to look at his clock. If he did not leave immediately, he would be late for work. With little choice but to put off her eviction until later, he rushed from the room.

He returned at the end of the day to find her still there.

"I have had time to think," she announced. "You have no wife. But I must learn more about you before I marry you."

"Oh, no," he countered, "I do not intend to marry you simply because you happened to knock on my door."

She paid no attention to his demands that she leave. She had prepared his supper and began to lay it on the table. "You are acting difficult because your stomach is empty."

"I do not want to eat. I want you to leave my home."

"Eat," she ordered.

There seemed to be no way to make her listen to reason. For lack of an alternative, he sat down to the meal, some sort of stew.

After a single mouthful, he lay down his fork. "You are a terrible cook."

"I will improve."

"I do not *want* you to cook for me."

"That is the arrangement. I cook for you. In return I live here."

"That is *not* the arrangement," he shouted. "There is no arrangement!"

She was now evaluating him. "I think I am right. You need a wife. You are lucky that I need a husband. The Lord had a plan when he put you into Shmulke Lubovkin's room."

"If God is a matchmaker, He is a very poor one. Why not go back home. The immigration people will arrange for your passage."

She shook her head adamantly. "I chose to marry Shmulke Lubovkin because he was in America, where Jews can live without being afraid, where women can get an education."

Raphael had seen a similar vehement indignation in the young women leading street-corner rallies to gain the vote or a clothing workers' union. This country seemed to attract such angry women, Raphael decided.

"What kind of work can you do? Maybe if you had a job I could get rid of you."

"I cook."

Raphael's eyes rolled up. "Can you sew? There are jobs for women who can sew."

"I cook better," she admitted.

"Then you'll starve," he informed her, shaking his head, scooping up his schoolbooks and fleeing.

This Hannah Moskowitz was like tar in his hair. How could he get rid of her before tomorrow morning, when Sally arrived? How could he even explain her? Of one thing he was sure, this was a determined young woman. She would not just go away. Perhaps if he found work for her, he could convince someone in the building to take her in as a boarder. Hungry, he headed toward a delicatessen on Delancey Street.

The sign for Weintraub's Haberdashery caught his eye. The store was closed, but Raphael could see Izzy inside trying, amid the chaos of his merchandise, to take inventory. An idea seized Raphael that would have momentous implications for his descendants then impossible to foresee.

Raphael knocked on the door and was admitted. He immediately gripped Izzy's hands in his.

"Tonight, Izzy. This very night you have a date with a wonderful girl. I've told her all about you, and you are just the sort of man she likes."

"I must do inventory."

Raphael shook his head, accepting no refusal. "Inventory tomorrow night, Izzy. Tonight, you finally have a date."

"I'm no good at small talk, Raphael. What will I say to her, that I want to find a girl to marry? I will scare her off."

"She is a serious girl, Izzy. Your kind of girl. Believe me, talk about marriage will not scare off Hannah Moskowitz."

The wedding took place two weeks later. Raphael gave Hannah away because he was the closest approximation of a relative she had here. He was happy for his friend Izzy, who wanted a wife, but would never have had the nerve to find a bride on his own, particularly one with so much character. Even before the wedding, she had begun to organize the store and make it more attractive to customers. But Raphael pitied him as well. Izzy would never get his way in anything again. Raphael's fondest wish for his friend was that the marriage produce no female offspring—Hannah's genes would create a line of she-tigers.

Less than a year later their son Abraham would be born. Raphael would be both delighted and relieved, unaware that his concern should then have shifted to his own future grandson.

Trevor Everett finally made up his mind to spend a year in Europe and had been trying to convince his employer to take on Raphael as an apprentice in his place, pointing out that Raphael's drawings of proposed buildings rendered from the blueprints were especially noteworthy and that he was well on his way to obtaining his architect's degree.

Raphael was interviewed by Everett's firm and then for several weeks received only inconclusive reports of his candidacy's progress. Sally warned him that the firm would never hire a Jew, that he would have done better to hide his background when applying. Raphael continued to wait, with hope diminishing little by little each day.

The night before Trevor was to embark for Europe, Raphael and several of Trevor's male friends gave him a dinner. The drinking lasted long into the night. It was a wonderful place this America, this New York, Raphael crowed. Trevor should cancel his trip immediately: Paris was decadent, effete. New York City, vital, exuberant, was the city of the future.

The other young men lived uptown. At Twenty-third Street they all parted company, and Raphael weaved happily home alone. He never saw the men who began to follow him along an avenue claimed by both Irish and Italian street gangs until a patch of darkness finally provided cover to jump him.

When he woke up, he was in a hospital ward. Bandages covered his head, and it hurt horribly. A doctor was bending over him. The man seemed pleased that Raphael was awake and explained that he had been found on the street with a fractured skull and no money, probably the victim of a robbery. He prodded and pricked Raphael at various points and declared himself satisfied that the patient would make a full recovery. Raphael should consider himself very lucky, the doctor told him. The streets of this city were a no-man's land.

When the doctor left, Raphael noticed Sally, in a prim black dress and hat, sitting on a chair near his bed.

"How do you feel?" she asked.

"All right," he mumbled and tried to sit up. He groaned with the pain. "I have to let them know at work that I can't make it in today."

"I telephoned them. Does it hurt badly?"

He nodded and closed his eyes. When they opened again, she extracted a piece of paper from her handbag. "As soon as you are well, you have an interview as a draftsman with Harrison Courtney's architectural firm."

She placed the piece of paper on his night table.

He pushed himself up and struggled against the pain to express his contempt. "Another one of your close friends?"

"Yes, but not in the way you are suggesting. I thought you would be pleased."

"I won't take charity from you."

"Then you're a bigger fool than I was when I slept with you for a French lesson."

What choice did he have? "Thank you," he said. After all his brave talk about his ambitious dreams, he resented her being the one to set his feet onto a path toward them. His voice was bitter. "Why must even your favors sound like payments?"

"I wanted to help you."

"You owe me nothing."

Her brow knitted, as if analyzing her motives for the first time. "We . . . we . . . rely on each other."

"And now you have dropped by to find out when I will be available again for you."

She was silent for a moment, then spoke grudgingly. "I have been here since yesterday morning, as soon as they told me at your building what had happened."

Raphael just stared at her, as if that was the most extraordinary statement he had ever heard.

When Raphael had recovered, he went to see Harrison Courtney and was hired. The head of the eminent architectural firm had often dined with Sally when she was accompanying his old prep-school friend Graham Lonsdale and seemed unaware either of her roots or those of his new employee. Raphael was pleased that he and the others in the office had accepted his story that he was French. Raphael did not need to deny he was Jewish; the matter never came up. He continued to take evening courses at the Cooper Union and to see Sally whenever he and she could.

For a while the new job focused Raphael's ambition, which had become dissipated over the long time he had had to wait to realize it. That he had obtained the job through Sally continued to bother him—and that he could see her now only on Saturday and Sunday afternoons. Once, in his bed after they had made love, he fumed that he despised Lonsdale for being able to buy her body, for keeping her.

She replied that Raphael misunderstood. They kept each other, in a manner of speaking: Lonsdale kept her with his money and social position; she kept him, not really with her body, but with her mind.

Raphael grabbed her roughly. "I want to see you all the time and be the only man in your life."

"That is a luxury I cannot afford."

"You disgust me!" he shouted. "I will not see you again!"

53

His resolve lasted two days. He left flowers on her doorstep and a note that asked her to forgive him.

The next Saturday at noon she knocked on his door, and their affair resumed, more intimate in what they revealed to each other, more poignant in their silent acknowledgment that no matter how long it might last, the relationship was temporary.

A year went by and then a second. Like the other young men in his office, he hoped for advancement in the firm. As he gained experience and knowledge, he was given more responsible work—plumbing and electrical layouts—but he noted that qualified men who had been with the firm for many years had not yet been named partners. How long would he have to wait with only the mere hope of advancement? Perhaps the partners, he worried, were aware that he was Jewish and tolerated him only because he was a useful drone? He vacillated between periods of intense concentration on his job and periods of frantic, unfulfilling nightlife.

Growing increasingly depressed about his chances for advancement, he began to pay more attention to Nissim's get-rich-quick schemes and actually invested some months working with his tinsmith uncle to develop a steam engine for airplanes. On the night they determined that the weight-to-power ratio made it infeasible, he got very drunk and showed up at Sally's doorstep in the early hours of the morning. She refused to admit him. He recognized Lonsdale's carriage parked at the corner.

For a week Raphael waited in anguish, uncertain whether Sally would appear at his door the next Saturday.

The knock came precisely at the customary hour. He rushed to open the door. Sally stood there, glaring at him. She did not enter.

"If you had stayed on my stoop one minute longer, I would have summoned the police. I told Graham that I had never seen you before in my life."

"It eats me up to know you are with him."

"Graham is a good man. He is also a considerate lover, or tries to be. Many men in his position do not. He treats me with respect."

Raphael clapped his hands to his ears and spun away. "I do not want to hear anymore. If I were rich, you would not have to—"

"You are poor, Raphael," she countered sharply. "He is rich."

Raphael inhaled deeply and turned back to the dooway. "It will not happen again."

His need to grow rich became an obsession, not merely to be successful or happily fulfilling his desire to design buildings, but rich.

When the new semester began, Raphael spent the nights after school scouring the city for real-estate opportunities.

One Saturday afternoon in early 1909, he took Sally to a narrow, rundown building in the east Seventies. He had been bargaining with the owner and could acquire it for three thousand dollars in cash if the owner took back a second mortgage. The bank that held the first mortgage had indicated it might be willing to increase the mortgage's amount so as to allow him to demolish the present structure and put up a residential brownstone he was sure could be profitably sold! He had fifteen hundred dollars and then some. He wanted to know whether she was willing to be his partner and invest the other fifteen hundred he needed.

"I'll do better than put up cash," she replied. "I'll find you someone who'll agree to buy the brownstone from you on the basis of your plans, before you have to take title from the seller and pay the cash he's asking, maybe even before you have put down the ten percent on contract."

Rather than being elated, Raphael was furious. No doubt she would be going through her file of past or potential lovers to find one who would do a favor for her.

"My plan is strictly business," she replied scornfully. "I know several people who are looking for a new house. We would use their cash deposit to buy the property as partners. A bank would finance construction because we are sure of a profit up front."

He wrapped her in a hug. "Partners? Better than partners! Marry me, Sally! Marry me now, and we'll struggle through this together."

Sally smiled indulgently. "It makes no sense."

"What makes sense? To wait around for Lonsdale to ask you to marry him. He never will."

"Then someone else who can afford me."

"Goddamn it! Are you really the sort of woman I try not to believe you are!"

"What advantage are you offering me? To support you when you fail?"

"I won't fail. You have to risk something for happiness."

"I know what I want in life." She averted her eyes, and her

voice was very low. "What if I told you that Bobby Houghton has asked me to marry him?"

"Houghton?" Raphael was stunned. "You love me. You know you do. You've told me."

"When we were making love. I can't be responsible for what I said then."

"But you can't marry Houghton. What do you know about him? Do you even like him?"

Sally pulled away. "Marriage to someone like Bobby is what I've always wanted. Do you know that he is worth twenty million dollars? As his wife I will be accepted into society."

"And what about the men who know about your past?"

"Time will erase that."

"Marry me, Sally. Right now. While I have nothing, only dreams. Someday I'll give you wealth. And something Houghton never could—joy every minute we're together and despair every minute we're apart."

"It's too big a gamble."

"After you marry Houghton will you still hide your mother from his family? Will you still be worried that you might be using the wrong fork? Or that he might find out about Sima Rabinowitz?"

"You should marry a fresh young thing, Raphael," she said carefully, but now haltingly, as if fighting to maintain her self-control. Within her doubt he glimpsed his hope.

Embracing her, he laughed. "This is America. Here we newcomers, we can become anything we want to be. Marry me, Sally. You and I will become rich and important. But we'll also be happy." He kissed her. "You love me. You know you love me."

She stared silently at him for a long moment, thinking, weighing one value against another, the known future against the unknown.

"Promise me, Raphael!" she erupted fiercely. "Promise me that all those things will come true!"

"I promise."

Years later, on their anniversary, after he had made good on all his promises, he asked Sally why she had changed her mind that day and married him, instead of Bobby Houghton. Was it simply love? he asked. Or, he added jokingly, did his good looks have something to do with it?

She remained silent, but there appeared on her face the

enigmatic, self-engrossed smile that could still entrance and infuriate him.

"Well," he asked again, "why me instead of Houghton?"

The smile slowly widened while she gazed at him.

He grew irritated. "Well?"

"What makes you think Bobby asked me to marry him?"

"You told me he did."

"What I said was, 'What if I told you that he asked me to marry him?' "

"You . . . you mean he didn't?" Raphael sputtered.

Hardly ever had he seen her laugh without restraint, but she was doing so now.

He grew angry. "All these years you had me believing that I won out over him, and he never asked you?"

She nodded and then laughed harder. She put her hands around his neck.

"Why did you let me believe it?" he stormed.

She refused to allow him to pull away. "You were so . . . so changeable, always finding something new to become excited about. What you needed for success was to focus all your energy on it, to be really committed." She put her forehead against his. "I needed your promise."

BOOK TWO

Henry's Story

Chapter 3

Raphael's son, Henry, would never need such encouragement. He had inherited his father's ambition in full measure, undiluted by any inclinations that might divert him. What he lacked was the artist's bent that underlay his father's manner and provided much of his motivation.

Henry Behr adored his father, but his stomach tied into knots whenever his parents visited him at prep school. There was no mistaking his mother's upper-class breeding; her son believed her to be the last descendant of an old Boston family. But Raphael Behr spoke with a foreign accent and sometimes was embarrassingly effusive. His father's disturbing habit, for example, of touching people to emphasize a significant point made even Henry's mother cringe. Later, she would quietly try to correct the mannerism, even as she simultaneously explained to Henry that it simply emanated from his father's compassionate nature, which wanted to express the warmth he felt for people. To Henry, however, it seemed to scream aloud for all to discover and ridicule his father's secret conversion from Judaism. His parents had been members of Grace Church for as long as he could remember, were on good terms with many rich and prominent people, and had subtly fostered the rumor that Raphael's roots were in the European nobility; yet Henry was terrified one of the other boys—so formally correct toward their own parents—would guess that his father was originally an immigrant Jew who had shortened his name from Behar to Behr.

Henry was far more comfortable with his father back in the city. There, away from the condemning eyes of the other boys, he took pleasure in his father's ebullience and happily reciprocated his demonstrative affection. They rode their horses together in Central Park, and Henry accompanied his father to the office or, even more wonderful, to construction sites. During these visits Raphael would always take the time to instruct his son in some construction detail and would convey his excitement at the sight of an idea growing out of a hole in the ground in the form of concrete and steel, pipes and wires, granite, brick, and glass. Henry treasured the intimacy of those moments—it was like discovering a secret part of his father—but he was not similarly stimulated; apart from the money at stake, he considered one building much like the next. Once in a while Henry was allowed to sit in on negotiations. That rough-and-tumble warfare was the part of his father's business he liked best.

Although the newspapers claimed that Raphael Behr was one of the richest builders in New York, Henry did not know whether that was true—his father refused to comment upon such speculation. Rather, what was important, his father said, was that one had the means to live well and go on doing what one loved. Raphael both designed his buildings and owned them. Henry knew that he did not have his father's artistic sense and could never be an architect, but such people could be hired, like other tradesmen. The critical, the daring, function was to be the owner, who took the risks and reaped the rewards of building. Working the system better than the next man, outsmarting him in a deal—these required the shrewdness he knew he possessed. His father did not talk much about the past, except to tell his son that an essential lesson he had learned from observing his own father in business was that who you know can often be more important than what you know. Henry understood his father's purpose for contributing heavily to political campaigns and spending so much time cultivating relationships with important judges and politicians—Mayor Jimmy Walker himself had dined several times at their home. Zoning problems and aggravating lawsuits always seemed to be resolved in his father's favor. That's the way things work in New York, his father taught him, with a regret in his voice Henry could not explain.

Assured of eventually taking over his father's empire, Henry knew that he was a privileged young man. He could picture himself someday in the important clubs, smoking after-dinner cigars with Phippses and Whitneys and Morgans and Vanderbilts. He knew several young men from such Olympian families and several more by sight, and he was determined to join their ranks.

Henry's feelings toward his mother were far more complicated. Sally Behr was a stern and exacting figure, a disciplinarian who demanded his best behavior at all times. Whereas praise came from his father unstintingly and undiscriminatingly, it was rare from his mother, given only when truly deserved; going off to prep school felt almost like a reprieve. But Henry also grew up entranced by her beauty and her energy in undertaking social activities and working for elite charities which could create access to figures who were important for her husband's business and their rising position. Inevitably, hers became Henry's image of a truly desirable woman, and Henry became determined someday to marry someone whose beauty everyone would envy him for possessing, and whose status would ensure his own.

The crash that began at the end of 1929 happened only a few months after Sally's sudden death from a cancer no one suspected had been consuming her liver. Raphael was devastated, but later he was grateful she had not lived to see his destruction, the end of the life he had promised her. Both of them had believed in the American Dream, in the idea that with hard work and vision one could climb inexorably upward. Raphael had gradually forgotten the dangers always waiting to spring out of the darkness. He never realized he was putting his weight on a thin crust of snow that hid a bottomless crevasse.

Initially, he had thought the crash would not affect him. All his money was in real property, almost none in stocks and bonds, but he had borrowed heavily. Now that the succession of buildings he had constructed over the past twenty years had brought him wealth and position, he had begun to design and erect the kinds of buildings he had imagined as a young man, the kinds of buildings that would be admired long after he was gone.

Raphael had several new buildings under construction, including one that would be the tallest ever, the Behr Building. After years of dreaming about it and sketching it at home late at night, the foundation was in place and the steelwork was already several floors up. Raphael was caught in the middle. The depression had so destroyed the real-estate market that no tenant would pay the rents required to make the new buildings profitable, particularly the very high rents he needed at the Behr Building. When one bank went under, he had to abandon construction on the building it was financing, while subcontractors threatened to stop working on his others. Expenses were crushing him on all sides because many of the tenants in his older buildings, commercial and residential, could no longer afford the rent and were moving out or just closing down. The bad times dragged on. As new buildings neared completion, they could attract few tenants at rent levels sufficient to pay interest and principal on the financing. That was when Raphael went to his friends at the banks and learned that he had no friends there. They had their own problems, they told him; they would defer nothing, stretch out nothing, renegotiate nothing. As his empire began to crumble, Raphael turned to personal friends, for many of whom he had done favors over the years. They turned a cold shoulder.

One still-wealthy financier dismissed him with the advice that he go to his own people, the Jews. Everyone knew the Jews had lots of money squirreled away. Weren't they positively gloating about this depression? Hadn't they caused it in order to buy up assets cheaply. "Go to other Jews."

As he left, stunned by both the financial rejection and being considered a Jew, it occurred to Raphael that he barely knew any others.

In some ways the city had returned to the condition in which Raphael had first encountered it: the people out on the streets, peddlers soliciting their business. But the buildings were emptying now, and the same people who had once put in interminable hours to make a living and gain a foothold in this new utopia could find no work.

At first Raphael fought to overcome his difficulties, but as they dragged on and he saw himself encircled with no way out, Raphael seemed to lose heart, overwhelmed by the humiliation of failure and ostracism and by the effort it would take to begin again with nothing, this time without the incentive of doing it for Sally. By the time the Raphael Behr Real Estate Co. finally went under, he seemed to be sleepwalking—eating food or signing papers that others put in front of him. Within days his personal bankruptcy swept away whatever he had left, including the building in which he lived.

Raphael roused himself enough to realize that he had to find a place to live, if not for himself, then for his children. Henry, nineteen, was completing his first year at Princeton and knew nothing about the catastrophe that had befallen them. His daughter, Melinda, three years younger, was still in high school. Unable to afford an apartment in Manhattan's decent neighborhoods, Raphael decided to look elsewhere, subconsciously relieved that relocation would also prevent him from having to face each day the shame of running into people he knew.

Although Raphael had barely kept in touch with the Weintraubs as his own social position increasingly diverged from theirs, he phoned the shirt store. Admitting his misfortune, he asked if Izzy knew of an apartment in his Bronx neighborhood. Raphael waited through the mortification of answering the questions Izzy insisted on asking: How could that be? He had been so rich, so successful. What had happened? Finally, Izzy understood the seriousness of Raphael's predicament and handed the phone to Hannah, who took control of the situation as usual. She knew that the ground-floor apartment of the building where they lived was vacant. The rent was low, and she thought she could talk the landlord into foregoing a security deposit.

"Whatever it is, I'll take it," Raphael mumbled.

When Hannah arrived at the landlord's office, Raphael and Melinda were already there, their belongings in several suitcases. They all took the subway to the new apartment. Raphael had not ridden in a subway in nearly twenty years.

Raphael had wanted to spare Henry the pain of their predicament as long as possible. His son was so dear to him. How he had looked forward to Henry, after college, joining him in business. All that he had hoped to give his children, all that he owed them, would now never be. Henry was scheduled to return from college in a few weeks and that was soon enough to break the terrible news. Then it would be unavoidable.

When that spring morning arrived, Raphael woke early, dressed with great care in a favorite blue suit, the last his tailor had made for him, wrote a short letter, and then left the apartment. He had only a single nickel in his pocket, which he used to enter the IND subway station. He walked to the front end of the platform and then off the edge of it just as a D train rushed into the station. His letter was found propped on his dresser beside a small life-insurance policy, which would benefit his children. Excluded from the bankruptcy foreclosure, it had been purchased many years earlier to help out his uncle during Nissim's short and unsuccessful stint as an insurance agent. The policy contained a clause prohibiting cancelation if the insured committed suicide.

Izzy and Hannah arranged for a modest funeral at the Sephardic synagogue upstairs on Jerome Avenue. By then Melinda had been able to locate her brother by waiting outside their old apartment building. At first Henry refused to accept that his father was dead, that everything they owned was gone, that others now lived in their apartment. When Melinda sank cross-legged to the pavement and broke down in tears, Henry finally realized that his stubbornness was aggravating her very real grief, and he went along with her up to the Bronx.

Shaken, bereft, he alternately asked questions and brooded, but none of it quite pierced the inner shell that surrounded his assuring reliance on circumstances he refused to believe had changed. He tried to insist that the funeral service be held at Grace Church. He relented only when Melinda told him the choice had been his father's, but that seemed as preposterous as everything else he had heard.

The funeral service was Henry's first participation in a Jewish ceremony, except for the time he was made to attend Abe Weintraub's bar mitzvah, which had set him fuming for days. He had met Abe Weintraub only once before in his life, when his father had invited the Weintraubs to their apartment, so their son could see parades from the Behrs' window. Henry was disgusted by the oriental trappings of his father's funeral service—the people here, he was told, had come from the same part of the world as his father. The synagogue was not even a proper building. Rather, it was a large, second-floor room above a candy store that was reached by means of steep stairs. Wooden chairs formed rows on three sides of a large Turkish carpet. Henry was most appalled that on the fourth side, at the head of the room, the clergyman was wearing a barbaric shawl and hat and chanting mumbo jumbo. Thank God his friends had not been invited to this place. The only people here that he knew were the Weintraubs, and he barely knew them.

After Henry and Melinda had been driven back from the cemetery and were finally alone in their apartment, Melinda handed her brother the letter. He went to the window to read it:

Dear Children,

It hurts me more than I can ever say to know that I have failed you. Only by dying can I leave you anything to go on with. The insurance policy provides each of you with $6,000. That should be enough to live on while you finish school if you are both careful.

Henry, I know that you and Melinda have always fought, but you have only each other now. Please try to take care of her until she graduates from high school and can take care of herself.

If it can be done without too much bother to anyone, I would be grateful for the traditional Jewish funeral I grew up with. I was the only one who did not understand that I was always a Jew.

Please believe that I do this because I love you,
    Your Father

Only then did the full desolation of his father's death descend on Henry, and he began to cry.

He walked to a corner of the room and leaned his forehead into it. Melinda waited long minutes while her brother sobbed. Finally, when he had regained some control of himself, he turned back to her and was surprised by the hard look in her eyes, but then she had known longer about their father's death, time enough for the sorrow to become tainted by anger.

"Don't count on the six thousand dollars."

"What do you mean?"

"Mr. Weintraub checked. There isn't any. *Tio* stole the money."

"Uncle Nissim?"

"Dad bought the insurance from him years ago, but Nissim borrowed all the cash in the policy for himself. He figured Dad was so rich he didn't need it."

"He took it? All of it?"

"And he lost it too. He's a tinsmith, and he figured Prohibition was his golden opportunity to go into business building stills. The police got wind of it and closed him down."

Henry was disoriented by the profusion of catastrophes. "Christ, how could this happen? We were so rich."

"This is the depression, Henry. Wake up! It's happening all over."

Henry began to cry again. "Why didn't Dad tell me he was in trouble?"

"*I* wanted to"—her voice turned sarcastic—"but Dad didn't want to disturb the prince's studies."

Henry wiped his eyes and took deep breaths; there were problems he must think about.

"Oh, God, how do I afford school next year?"

"Ask for a scholarship."

"Are you kidding? With *my* marks?"

"Dad kept telling me how well you were doing."

"I didn't want him to get annoyed. Only proles study."

Melinda cut him off. "You didn't want to disappoint Dad, so you lied to him instead."

Henry brightened. "Maybe Nina's folks can help out. They're really top drawer. She and I were going to announce our engagement this summer. At her parents' country club."

"It would have been nice to tell your family." Melinda was still angry, but her voice was tired. "If you go back to college, how do I pay the rent here? Mrs. Weintraub says I can work in their store, but that won't be enough."

Henry's voice rose. "Maybe we won't be able to afford to send you away to school or even private school, but you're going to finish high school. Dad was clear on that."

"At the end Dad didn't know which end was up."

Henry dropped to the sofa beside his sister. "This is all insane. If we just take our time and don't act as if the world has come to an end, things will work out."

She looked at him as if the insanity were his.

Henry Behr was well over six feet tall, which his mother had attributed to her own father, and had inherited a pleasing combination of his parents' facial features: Sally's clean profile and strong chin and Raphael's open expression and hazel eyes. He would pass on these physical traits to his own son Ralph.

Although he had neglected his studies and his youthfully unrefined competitiveness had so far found an outlet only in sports, Henry was not lazy. Rather, he was a young man trained to become an upperclass businessman and gentleman and, in better times, would have slipped effortlessly into that life of responsible ease. Highly ambitious, he would have increased both his wealth and his social position in due course. He had some talents: good at math, the sort of personality others were drawn to, clever at getting his way. Unfortunately, the pragmatic side of his character, inherited from his mother, had lain undeveloped because his barely troubled life had floated above the exigencies which might have molded it.

Melinda had been blessed with both her mother's practicality and enough of her looks to be considered a pretty girl. She also possessed, as did so many young people growing up in the pleasure-obsessed times just past, a wild streak.

Because it had already been paid for, Melinda finished up her sophomore year at the private school she attended, but worked after school and on weekends at the Weintraubs' shirt store. She did not know whether they really needed her or were taking pity on her situation, but jobs were too scarce to refuse out of pride.

Henry glided through the last weeks of Princeton's year in a daze. He had been expecting to spend the summer with Nina. She had promised to send him a letter, after she had checked with her parents, inviting him to their country house when her classes at Smith College were over. Her parents liked him, she said, and would be delighted to have him. But the mail from her had mysteriously stopped coming. That was not like Nina, who had diligently written to him twice each week.

On a Saturday afternoon, he telephoned her parents' Fifth Avenue apartment and asked for her. Perhaps she was ill and had returned from school early. No, the butler told him, Miss Pollard was still away at school.

Henry telephoned her dormitory at Smith. An older woman—probably the housemother—stated that she was under orders not to allow Miss Pollard to speak to Mr. Behr. Henry exploded into brutal language, demanding that Nina be put on the phone and threatening the woman. To no avail.

Furious, uncomprehending, Henry set out for Northampton. Having only a few dollars—he had counted on his father replenishing his bank account—he hitchhiked.

He slept in a field and early the next morning, a Sunday, tried to meet with Nina at her dorm, but the housemother refused to summon her. His first impulse was to storm past the woman and force his way to Nina, but if Nina was not there, the police might seize him before he could find her. He retreated, as if leaving for good, and took up a post behind some trees well down the path leading from the dorm. After a while he saw her leave the dorm with the housemother and some friends. They were dressed up. He followed at a distance. When they entered a church, he slipped into a rear pew to observe her.

He never tired of looking at her, and he could do it now without her becoming self-conscious. Nina was the most beautiful girl he had ever seen: finely fashioned nose and mouth, delicate facial bone structure, crown of blonde hair turned gold in places by the sun while she was playing outdoor sports. She had an innocence that thrilled him. Not the kind that would cause her to refuse to kiss him—in fact, she had kissed him goodnight on their very first date—but, rather, she was so refined and yet so fresh. After he met her every girl seemed plain and dull. They had met at a coming-out party the year before. Soon she had trusted him enough to let him bring her not only to the usual outings and night spots frequented by her social set, but also secretly to the daring places she had only heard rumors about: jazz speakeasies and private parties attended by show people. She was drawn to his masculinity, a reckless strength absent in the other young men she knew, and was excited by his disregard for the conventional behavior of her upbringing. She thought him dashing and his looks divine. It really meant something to both of them when she invited him to be her escort to her own coming-out party. When she admitted that she loved him, he did a back flip, an actual back flip, outside her front door.

Just before the benediction, Henry went back outside the church and waited on the steps so that Nina could not avoid speaking to him. The housemother saw him first and tried to block him off from Nina, but he sidestepped her easily.

"It's all right, Mrs. Gregory," Nina said. "I'll have to speak to him sooner or later."

Henry led her down the steps and away from the others. Under a linden tree that shaded them, he turned to look at her again. She was only half a head shorter than he.

"Did your parents really order you not to see me?" he asked.

Nina dropped her eyes. "Yes."

"Why?"

She was silent.

"For God's sake, tell me why."

"Please don't make me have to say it."

She glanced shyly up at him, but his mouth was determined. Her eyes dropped again before she dared to answer. "Because you're poor now."

"You said you loved me. More than anything, you said."

She lifted her face and then her gaze. "I meant it, Henry, I really meant it. I've cried myself to sleep every night."

"Then to hell with what your parents want."

"It isn't that easy."

Her eyes began to fill. Henry reached out to hold and comfort her. She raised her hands to fend him off.

"What do you expect me to do—" Henry blurted out, "just give you up and walk away?"

"If you love me, yes."

She took a step back, inhaling deeply to gain her composure.

"Things are a bit shaky for my own family right now. A good marriage would help things all around."

"You make it sound like you're on the auction block. Is this something *you*—not your parents—*you* want? Give me an honest answer. You know how much I love you."

"Enough to give me up?"

"Yes," he said softly, "if that's what you *really* want."

Tears were falling slowly down her face now. She was silent for a long while, then spoke in a whisper.

"That's just it. I've always had everything I wanted. I don't know how to be poor, Henry, and I'm not very strong, like some of the other girls. No matter how much I love you now, I would become desperate without money and end up hating you."

"That's it, then," he finally responded. "I'll always love you, Nina. Nothing changes that."

For a long while he stared at her face, trying to memorize the exact shade of blue of her eyes and the soft dip of her eyelashes. He strained to remember the perfect sculpture of her nose and the soft feel of lips that curved like rose petals.

Suddenly, he spun around and began to run across the lawn as fast as he could. He leaped a hedge and continued to race down the middle of the road until he was miles away and could barely breathe.

The next weeks were harrowing for Henry, as he tried to come to grips with so many things at once: with the loss of his father; with the loss of Nina—if not dead in fact, she was as good as dead so far as his own life was concerned; and with the realizations that money was now very precious and that he could not return to college. He discovered that jobs were scarce as well, no matter how long and conscientiously he looked. His father's tragedy, Nina's rejection, his sudden poverty all drove home to him a single lesson: to win at any cost. It was a lesson he would instill in his son.

He knew a little bit about real-estate development, but no one was doing any building. He had always been attracted to finance, but telephone calls to his parents' old friends or his own proved fruitless. Word of his changed circumstances had obviously circulated quickly, and several people even refused to take his calls. Was the rejection due only to his destitution or to his Jewish forebears as well? He knew only that in either case, he had contracted a repulsive disease. He found himself hardening and growing up quickly.

Izzy Weintraub had paid the first month's rent on their apartment, and it looked as if Henry and Melinda were going to have to impose on him for an additional loan to tide them over a bit longer, when Nissim rang their door bell one night. Henry could barely control his fury.

"You don't want to see me," Nissim declared brightly.

"Not unless you brought the twelve thousand dollars."

"Do I look like a man who has twelve thousand dollars?"

"No, you look like a man who's already spent it." His great-uncle sported a tan set off by a wide Panama straw hat and a white suit. His Mediterranean accent added to Henry's impression that his father's uncle resembled a gigolo awaiting the arrival of the tour ships.

Nissim appeared hurt at not being believed. Then he smiled broadly, sure that Henry would be eager to hear of his good fortune. "Everyone wants me to make them a still."

"Then you can pay us something on account," Henry replied as he admitted Nissim to the apartment.

"That money was your father's investment in my liquor-distilling company. Everything was lost when the police put it out of business. Those are the risks you take in business."

"Did my father *know* he was investing in your distillery?"

A wave of Nissim's hand displayed his scorn for such narrow thinking. "Raphael Behr was too busy and important a man to be bothered with small details."

Henry had run out of what little patience he possessed. "What are you here for?"

"To do you a favor. I loved your father like a son. More than a son." He stepped up and embraced Henry. "I want to help you and Melinda. Where is my beautiful niece?"

"Working late."

"And you also will have a job. Then you will think good of your uncle." He took a seat on the sofa and placed his hat on the end table, the lone table in the living room. "I have a job for you."

"You're serious."

Pride gleamed in his eyes. "Not one of my stills ever blew up. People like that. But landlords are not so easy. I found a basement in Brooklyn to build the stills. The landlord knew your father."

"What's his name?"

"Johnny Manzanatto."

"I don't remember Dad having any dealings with a Johnny Manzanatto."

"Years ago. Johnny worked as a laborer on some of your father's construction sites when he first came to America." Nissim's voice became mournful. "Johnny was very sad to hear that Raphael died. He said your father was always a stand-up guy and wanted to help out. He needs someone to collect rents—someone big and strong—so I thought of you."

"He has a job for me?"

Nissim leaned forward confidentially. "Because he trusted your father, and I told him you were the same kind of guy."

72

"And you want to be sure whoever he hires doesn't alert the police that you're building stills again."

Nissim's beneficent smile blazed forth again. "For my nephew, anything!"

Henry went to work collecting rents for John Manzanatto, a darkly olive-skinned Italian, known behind his back as Johnny Mulatto. He was a boastful little man, who hinted that the cash with which he was buying up so much distressed real estate emanated from his activities as a bootlegger, one of the few activities producing cash for investment. Most of the buildings were in the Jewish areas of Brooklyn, and a smart young man like Henry was very useful. He quickly learned the ways of his new environment: how to work around things and to keep his mouth shut. He could act Jewish or Christian as the situation required, and he made a good impression on the local politicians and the do-gooders when he went down to discuss building violations and the like. Johnny also liked that he was tough. When a huge stevedore tenant who owed back rent threatened to throw Henry down the stairs if he didn't beat it fast, the stevedore found *himself* flying down the stairs a second later.

Deprivation hardened Henry, paring away the prep-school polish he could no longer afford, to expose a cold-eyed wiliness. Each month Henry made the rounds to collect the rents, ignoring the dispiriting hard-luck stories, yielding to which would cost him his job—he knew he was always just one sharp word from Johnny away from their predicament. The rest of the time he was concerned with evicting tenants unable to pay, renewing leases, getting leaks repaired and then haggling with the insurance people for reimbursement, seeking out better prices for coal in the winter—the general minutia of managing buildings. Henry learned fast and was particularly adept at arranging terms and financing, but he felt he was simply slogging through his days with no hope for better and no end of the drudgery.

Henry and Melinda continued to live together until she was graduated from high school, an obligation both felt they owed their father. The arguments between them had started up again only weeks after his death, Melinda insisting she could handle her own life very well without his interference. Henry had felt an inchoate impulse to hold together the family's remains, but was unable to instill a similar impulse in Melinda, who seemed to become more waywardly headstrong the harder he tried to keep her in line. Soon after high-school graduation, she left the

Weintraubs' shirt store for a better-paying job waiting on tables at a Bickford's and, a month after that, moved in with a musician also waiting on tables there.

Henry found that the change in his own circumstances, combined with the dreariness, the hopelessness, of the times, had made New York a bleak and oppressive place. Where once he had thought of the buildings as jewels of great and quantifiable value glittering in the vault that was the city, they seemed now like massive teeth that ground down the people scurrying fearfully among them. One place seemed as depressing as another; Brooklyn was where he worked, so he gave up the Bronx apartment and rented a smaller one on Ocean Parkway.

Henry submerged his daytime cares in a hectic nightlife. He was particularly drawn to the Broadway–Times Square district of Manhattan, where the play of lights, neon loops and shifting incandescent patterns created make-believe images in the night that hid the heavy substance of real life. When he slept with a woman, he invariably did so at her apartment, from which he could leave when he wanted, regaining his privacy and concealing from her the skimpiness of his means. The women were simply a way to pass the time and to release sexual tension. None of them could ever touch his heart.

As years passed Henry continued to earn a small, secure salary during a time when many in the population were starving, but what he wanted most—to buy a building of his own—was denied him. Once or twice he pursued other opportunities, which invariably failed to pan out, often simply because he had no capital to pursue them. He was forced to learn patience. Finally, he talked Johnny into selling him, over time, one of the buildings he owned, with title going to Henry when he finished paying for it.

Henry used nearly all the cash he had in the bank to make the down payment and gave up his few luxuries from then on to accumulate the money to pay the monthly installments. By early 1942 he had almost paid off the price and anticipated the property soon being transferred to him. Then one night the bottom dropped out. Passing a newsstand after sharing a sandwich and cheese cake at the Turf Restaurant with a Copa girl he was seeing, he heard the news dealer call out, "Brooklyn mobster found dead in car trunk. Get your paper."

Automatically, Henry threw down a coin and picked up the *Daily Mirror*. He glanced at the lurid photo of a corpse stuffed into a car trunk, the bloody bullet-holes sprouting like flowers on the sport shirt. The name Johnny Manzanatto leaped at him from the caption.

The police had sealed off the real-estate office by the time Henry arrived. They questioned him and then released him when they were convinced that he knew nothing. He went to Johnny's house to offer the widow his sympathies, promising to look after her property. He made sure she understood that he was only a payment away from owning the building on Avenue U.

Two days later Henry attended the funeral. A friend surreptitiously pointed out a pallbearer whom rumor indicated was the hit man for a powerful mob boss who had ordered the murder. Later, Henry observed him consoling the widow.

The next day two men with bulges in their jackets knocked on Henry's door and announced that he had been summoned to a meeting. When they took off his blindfold, he found himself in a large wooden warehouse, on the waterfront he reasoned, because he could hear ships' whistles and could smell salt water. He was facing the mob boss, a surprisingly young man in a brown suit and turned-up gray fedora. The man had small eyes that Henry could barely make out in the gloom and, for some reason, that scared him more than the men who surrounded him.

"Johnny's wife says you told her you own one of my buildings," the man growled. He had a hoarse Italian accent that seemed ominous.

"One of *Johnny's* buildings. Almost. I've been paying for it over time. I've got one more payment."

"Johnny was killed because he tried to take what didn't belong to him. Don't make the same mistake."

"I've been paying him for two years for the building on Avenue U. I have all the receipts."

A toss of the boss's hand indicated his dismissal. "It wasn't his to sell."

"What about my money?"

"So, he was stealing from both of us. That's your problem. I took care of mine."

"I put every penny I had into buying that building. I own it." Henry said, his voice rising in anger.

A hand cuffed him hard on the neck.

"Talk polite!" a voice behind him ordered.

"You got a choice," the boss declared quietly. "You forget we ever had this conversation and beat it."

"Or?"

"There is no 'or.' "

Power, Henry brooded. The only thing that matters is power. That's what gets you what you want and protects you. The mob had muscle. The bankers exerted less brutal forms of coercion, but the result was the same. You could lose whatever you had if you didn't have power to guard it.

Discouraged, with no prospects, Henry decided to do the patriotic thing and use his local political connections to gain an officer's commission in the army before he was drafted.

Preparing to leave for training, Henry went to his sister Melinda's apartment to say good-bye. She was still living with her musician boyfriend, who for months had been out of any kind of work, even waiting tables. He had been offered a job in a California band, and she had convinced him to take it.

"A lot of people are picking up and moving to California," she told Henry. "It's like the last frontier out there, a place to start over."

A postcard forwarded to Henry two years later would inform him she was working in a ship-building plant in San Diego, a later postcard that she had married the plant's owner, deemed essential to the home-front effort. Every few years after that a Christmas card or a christening announcement would arrive. Later she would divorce him and marry a man whose family for generations had owned several square miles of Los Angeles.

In June of 1942, by means of a useful connection, Lieutenant Henry Behr was assigned to London. His real-estate experience had won him a job on the military staff building facilities for the American troops expected in the coming months.

For a dozen years Henry had known little joy, not understanding how there could be joy when he was neither rich nor on his way toward becoming rich. In London, the war colored every thought, every action, every conversation. Death was so close; the German blitz was flinging bombs about London like a grotesque dart game. There, life itself seemed very precious, and hope was reduced to a place in the soul where peace waited like a bulb in frozen ground. There, Henry began to enjoy life again.

A gaiety born of desperation gripped many in London; restraint, sobriety, and chastity were niceties relegated to a time when people could be sure they would live to see tomorrow. When Henry left work at the end of the day, some sort of party invariably awaited him.

One night the air-raid sirens went off, and Henry and some

others, whiskey glasses and bottles still in their hands, descended to a shelter in one of the Underground railway stations.

Convivially, he offered drinks to people seated nearby on the concrete platform. One was a young woman several feet away. He could not make out her features very well in the darkness, but had noticed her staring upward at the ceiling ceaselessly, as if the enemy planes were visible through it.

"How can you drink," she asked sternly, but also with some curiosity, "when the Nazis do showers of death upon us everywhere?"

The young woman herself had a German accent, and Henry was intrigued by her slightly ungrammatical, almost literary speech. "Sounds to me like a damned good reason to drink," he answered.

"You do not know them," she answered, her gaze still fixed on the ceiling, "what they can do."

She told him her name was Rosalie Mayer. She and her family had been fortunate enough to escape from Berlin just before the war started. Her father was a jeweler. They were able to smuggle his inventory out of Germany and to England, sewn into their clothing. After the Germans began the bombings, they had tried to leave England as well, but were unable to do so. Henry found the young woman's frankness refreshing after a steady diet of English reserve.

When the all-clear signal sounded, Henry invited her to join the party about to recommence. Afterward, he escorted her home. They began to date, and he drifted into her circle, which included refugees from all over Europe who had sought sanctuary in London. Many had earlier stashed money in English banks or had escaped with enough to live well. Often, they displayed a cultured savoir-faire. Henry found exhilarating after a dozen years among Brooklyn shopkeepers and politicians and Broadway sharpies and show girls.

Rosalie was also the first Jew he had ever dated, and the differences piqued his interest. She was pretty enough, he thought, in a soulful Semitic way. She had dark hair and dark, haunted eyes; a slender body with an abundant bust that appeared more surprising than alluring; and the very earnest manner that had initially intrigued him. At first Henry had speculated that her seriousness resulted from not being comfortable in English, that greater vivacity must be evident in German, but a friend who spoke German informed him she was humorless in that language as well.

One night, after a dinner party given by two of her friends, he asked her if she wanted to go back to his apartment for a drink.

"Yes," she replied after a moment of reflection, "it is time we do sex."

They embarked on an affair. She was very taken by him; he, as usual, stayed uninvolved. In fact her novelty quickly wore off, and Henry was ready to end the relationship when she telephoned him. It was urgent that she see him, she said.

They met at a small pub he frequented near the Admiralty. He intended to tell her he no longer wished to date her.

She was nervous when she entered and surprised Henry by ordering a whiskey from the nearby waitress before sitting down. He decided to hold off with his own announcement until she told him what was on her mind, which she would do at once, he knew; she had little ability to make idle conversation.

"Henry, a bomb exploded last night on our block. The next building to our hotel is fallen down. The one on the corner is a hole in the ground."

"That's horrible." He had come to accept that whether one lived or died in London was a matter of luck, not of virtue. "My parents and I escape here to be safe from the Nazis. But soon they will be here too. Or they will kill us all from the sky. England is not our home; it was a place to be safe. But only America is safe, far enough and strong enough to keep us well. My parents have business friends who arrange passage for us on a Red Cross ship returning to America. In a convoy. We can obtain a visa to enter, my family and I, if you will marry me."

Henry had no doubt about his lack of feeling for her. He tried to be gentle. "I'm not interested in marrying anyone. I don't think you and I—"

Perhaps sensing what he was about to say, she interrupted before he could form words that might become barriers. "Please, allow my completion. It is important what I want to say."

He nodded.

"Henry, I love you. I do not know if you feel likewise to me, but I love you the same even so. I wish our marriage to be a real marriage, but if that cannot be, I wish you to marry me anyway."

"But, if I don't want to be married to you—"

"Then my father will pay you five thousand American dollars to marry me. So we can go to America before the next bombs come. My parents, they will not go to America without me."

Henry stared at her without believing the words. He had struggled and scraped along for a dozen years and had nothing to show for all that work. Now, simply because he happened to be an American citizen to whom this refugee woman was attracted, he could snap up five thousand dollars. Maybe more.

"Make it ten, and you have yourselves a deal. American soldiers need permission to marry, so I have to pay off certain people."

Her mouth shook momentarily. "All right, ten. Do I understand right that you do not wish to be married to me but for the money?"

"Now isn't the time for me to consider marriage, Rosalie."

"I hope when you know me more after the war, in America, you will think about it again."

"We'll talk about it then," he replied to make her feel better.

He slept with her that night, to make her feel some hope of holding on to him and because he knew she would soon be out of his life. Hell, for ten thousand dollars, she deserved it.

Chapter 4

When the war was over, Henry returned to Brooklyn. Some of the ten thousand dollars went for living expenses until he found a small building he could afford to buy with the rest of it. He realized when the deed was signed that this was the first time since his father's death that he was actually free, not dependent on anyone's goodwill for a livelihood.

Rosalie continued to live with her family in an apartment on Central Park West. In London she had helped her father try to reestablish his jewelry business. After settling in New York, however, he joined with a partner he had known in Germany, which allowed Rosalie to recommence the German literature studies broken off when she and her family escaped from Berlin. After a few years she mustered the courage to begin work on the research for a biography of Goethe.

That she was still in love with Henry, he could tell during the few occasions he saw her: when papers needed signing for immigration or the IRS or when accompanying her to occasional social affairs at which his presence was required as her husband. She had quietly consented to obtain a Reno divorce after she and her parents obtained their citizenship papers, but Henry did not press the matter once the papers had come through; the marriage was no bother to him and, in fact, provided a convenient excuse in severing attachments to other women.

Henry's primary concern was his real-estate business. So much time had been lost during the depression and the war, almost as if his ambition had slumbered through them in hibernation. Now it had woken, when the season for it had come around again, and he was bursting with eagerness.

After buying that first building, he retained Abe Weintraub for accounting services. They had not been close during the years Henry lived in the Bronx—Abe was older than he, and the two were separated by the even wider chasm of their social standing while growing up—but Henry knew Abe was smart and reliable and would not charge as much as other accountants.

Abe was of medium height and prematurely balding. His facial features were well-formed, but rarely appreciated because shyness caused him to avert his gaze and his posture to stoop. By dint of hard work and low fees, Abe had built up a modestly profitable accounting practice during the depression and was trying to reestablish it. He had spent the war years stateside, after being pulled out of basic training to untangle the base's snarled paperwork. Hannah and Izzy had been overjoyed that their son would not be sent to the front. Abe guiltily felt he was somehow letting down his country. Afterward, he returned to his old room at his parents' apartment in the Bronx, both to save money and because they were getting on in years. The only difficulty was having to put up with his mother's nagging that it was time he found a girl and got married. His life in peacetime was as boring as before.

When Henry, who had no cash left, approached him to become his partner on a second building he had located, Abe did something uncharacteristic. He decided to risk his capital, give up his accounting practice, and join Henry in business. With all the returning servicemen, he foresaw a need for housing. Real estate could become a good business again. There came a time when he reproached himself for that decision, the only impulsive act of his entire life, although for a long time the partnership was successful and compatible.

Whether the partners were building or buying or financing, Abe made careful and astute analyses before they took any major action, working out on paper all the variables and risks with an exactness that was alien to Henry's more spontaneous nature. Like his father, Henry had a talent for making friends, which allowed him to uncover opportunities that would never have been presented to his reserved partner. Both men were willing to work long hours and sacrifice present income in order to build up capital for future expansion. The trust that gradually arose between the partners began to make them close friends. Abe's caution induced greater prudence in Henry, and his shyness was eased by increased prosperity and exposure to Henry's affability. He began to date more, usually the daughters of his mother's acquaintances, whom she arranged for him to meet. "Thank God," Hannah said, "you have a mama who knows you don't find a wife by sitting in your office doing figures and hoping."

By 1950 the partners' business situation had eased considerably. They owned and managed a number of small apartment buildings that were producing a solid income, and they were building two more. They had hired a bookkeeper-secretary and someone to manage their property. Most of their time was devoted to finding new buildings. They began to ease back on the hours they had to work. It was decided that Abe would try to cultivate more of the people at the financial institutions and Henry a more important group of brokers, lawyers, general contractors, and investors than those with whom they presently dealt.

One night Henry attended a formal charity ball in Manhattan as the guest of a socially prominent lawyer he had known in prep school and recently begun to retain as a means of access to the man's contacts. Henry had worked his way around their table and was beginning to survey the ballroom. Perhaps he might even spend the rest of the evening hunting for a wealthy single woman here. At forty years old, he knew he was good-looking in a rugged, masculine way when compared to the effete types in this crowd; good prep school; a year at Princeton; good war record; and a business of his own, which differentiated him from the leeches sucking at upper-class ankles.

He strolled to the edge of the dance floor to watch the women gliding by. Suddenly he gasped. Over her dance partner's shoulder, he glimpsed a woman's face too well-remembered. No one could be that impossibly beautiful. Still. Thinking and breathing both ceased. At that moment the woman's own gaze shifted into Henry's. She halted for an instant, like a deer hypnotized by

81

oncoming headlights, then nodded to her boyish partner in dismissal. Henry stepped into her arms in his place.

"Never once, in all this time," he said, "did I ever believe I'd see you again."

Without another word they danced for several minutes still staring at each other. When the music ended and people began to move off the floor, Henry asked the question that had formed out of chaotic emotion.

"Are you happy?"

Slowly, as if tearing the admission out of her flesh, Nina shook her head.

Henry spoke again. "I'll meet you tomorrow at noon under the clock at the Biltmore."

Without walking her back to her table or even waiting for her reply, he strode away.

He was at the Biltmore an hour early. Exactly at the stroke of noon, she arrived, her eyes wide and frightened and compelled to stare silently into his.

He led her to the elevator and then down the corridor to the room he had reserved. He closed the door behind them and embraced her. They kissed, and Henry felt all the lost years melt away. He undressed her, his fingers shaking, marveling that she was here, with him, and then stunned by how beautiful her body was, how fresh still her skin.

They made love. Nina screamed when she came, her eyes wide open, as if blinded by light after a lifetime in the dark.

The love affair that began again that afternoon was the only truly passionate one of Henry's life. It was also so for Nina, who had never made love to any man except her husband.

Within six months after ending her romance with Henry, Nina had married a man a dozen years older than she. The alliance had been a brilliant one for her and a fortunate one for her family. Her husband was an eminent banker from one of America's wealthiest and most esteemed families. A widower whose first wife had nearly died as a result of the birth of their second child, he had undergone a vasectomy, quite common in his circle by then, fearing what might happen if she gave birth again. Shortly afterward, she had been killed in an automobile accident. After two years of grief and loneliness and concern that his children were growing up without a mother, he asked his sister to help him find a suitable bride.

Nina's name was on the list his sister carefully drew up,

82

although he expressed some doubt because Nina was young and might be accustomed to more outgoing companionship. He invited her to dinner, was instantly taken both by her beauty and by her youth, which he decided had produced an innocence and natural compliance that were in her favor. Her family background and demeanor were excellent, and her graciousness would make her a valuable escort and hostess for his extensive business entertaining. After several weeks in which they spent a good deal of time alone together and with his two children, for whom she seemed to have genuine affection, he explained that the woman he married could never have children of her own, but must be content to be the mother of his.

Nina pondered the decision deeply. She was not in love with her future husband and doubted if she ever could be. He was an authoritarian who had been reared to assume power. His life organized down to the minute, he would dictate precisely how their lives were to be lived, she knew. But her most important priority in marriage had become financial security, particularly after seeing what its absence had done to Henry and his family. The vast wealth of this well-respected, if formal and undemonstrative man, could ensure the luxury she required.

When they married, he propped up her father's factories long enough to arrange for their sale, as he had promised to do, and she gracefully slipped into her role of wife, mother, and hostess. Amid almost unimaginable opulence, her life slowly began to petrify. Inwardly, Nina was strangling to death. That is, until the chance meeting with Henry Behr at the charity ball. Dynamic, impulsive, masculine, he had fanned the last ember in a heart turned nearly to ash.

A dead part of Henry's being also seemed to come alive. He had forgotten he could be this happy with a woman. He was desperately in love, even more desperately than in his and Nina's youth, because he had lived so long amid the bleakness of being without her.

The day after their first rendezvous, Henry arrived at his office at eleven. His first question to Abe was whether he had received any phone calls. Abe's response was a wide smile.

"What's so funny?" Henry asked.

"You. My guess is you're in love."

"What makes you say that?"

"Well, you didn't come in, or even phone in, all yesterday. That's never happened before. Today, you show up three or four hours later than usual. Instead of shuffling through the mail to see if we received any checks—your invariable habit, by the way—you asked if anyone telephoned. That's got to be love."

Henry could no longer restrain the grin. "And you're an expert, I suppose."

"You don't have to have the disease to recognize the symptoms. Who's this extraordinary woman?"

Henry's face turned grim. "Let's just say that I can't talk about it and leave it at that."

Chastened, Abe dropped his gaze to the spreadsheet on which he had been working and, when a decent interval had passed, suggested they look at the figures on the deal he had been examining.

In the months that followed, Henry and Nina met clandestinely several times each week. She was the dream of perfection made flesh to a man who had forgotten how to dream, a summit of everything he had almost attained as a young man before fate cast him down. Layers of restraint peeled off each of them like disguises. She admitted that when they were apart, she counted the hours until their next meeting. She loved him.

"Then leave your husband," Henry finally said after they had made love in the Manhattan apartment he had rented solely for the times they could be together. "Marry me."

Nina began to shake. "Don't say that! You can't imagine what he would do. He would destroy you financially if he even suspected our affair, much less that I intended to leave him."

"I'll sell whatever I own right now, and we'll go somewhere and start again."

Nina's face collapsed into sorrow. "Nothing has changed, Henry. I still have very little of my own. And so do you, for all your brave talk."

"I've been happier these last months than ever in my life. You too. You know that's true."

"And terrified all the time of being found out." Nina's hands had moved instinctively to cover her nakedness.

Henry reached for her. "We've wasted too much of our lives. If you won't tell your husband you're leaving, I will."

She grabbed his hands. "Oh, God, Henry, don't! Please don't! Promise me you won't say anything! And you won't bring up marriage again!"

Nina had become so agitated that Henry feared he might lose her forever if he continued the discussion.

That night, alone in the Manhattan apartment, obsessed by thoughts of her, Henry decided the only way to induce Nina to leave her husband was if she became pregnant with his own child. He unrolled the condoms he kept in his night-table drawer, put a large pinhole at the end of each, and then rolled them neatly back up again.

Henry said nothing more about marriage and waited out the months. Three months went by before Nina exhibited the tension upon meeting him that indicated she might know she was pregnant. She kissed him perfunctorily when their apartment door was closed and began to pace the room.

"I'm pregnant," she suddenly cried out without looking at him. "I went to a doctor in New Jersey and used another name. He confirmed it."

Henry moved to embrace her. "That's wonderful."

Her nails cut into his arms. "You know my husband is physically incapable of having more children. We hardly even sleep together anymore. What shall I do?"

"Marry me."

"You weren't going to bring that up again."

"What did you expect me to say?"

She turned on him, displaying a fury born of ultimate fear. "I'm not going to marry you! Can't you understand that. I will *not* leave my husband! My home! My position!"

"When he finds out about the child, you'll have to."

"If he found out, I'd kill myself."

Henry's illusion that motherhood might force her to seek a divorce ended with those words.

"Then I presume you're thinking about an abortion."

Nina shook her head indecisively, as if she had not faced up to any choice.

Henry was unsparing. "If you kill my child, I'll go to your husband myself and tell him about us."

She sank to a seat at the edge of the bed and began to cry, her head swinging from side to side. "I don't want to kill the only baby I'll ever have."

Her utterance was the silver flash of hope for which Henry had been angling. They talked for several hours, working out possibilities. When she left, a plan had been decided upon.

Her husband was scheduled to leave for a long business trip through Europe and the Middle East. She was a tall woman, and loose clothing could probably conceal her growing abdomen until he left. Then, claiming that her mother—now a widow living with her sister in Charleston, South Carolina—was ill,

Nina would move in with her until the birth. Her husband preferred to have very little to do with her family and would not bother her there.

Once she gave birth, Henry would take their baby. He would arrange matters so that no one, not even the child, would ever know she was the mother. Henry intended asking Rosalie, to whom he was still married, to care for the child as her own—as their own. Rosalie was a serious, levelheaded woman who would make a good mother.

Also decided, without either of them having said a word about it, was that Henry and Nina's affair was at an end.

Although she was eager for children, the price Rosalie exacted was that she and Henry begin to live together at last as a true husband and wife. After deliberation, Henry agreed. Like his father and grandfather, he had married under strange circumstances. And although his wife was a woman of character, he was in love with another woman and always would be.

Rosalie put aside her literature studies and the Goethe biography to dedicate herself totally to her new family. She made an attentive, even a somewhat overprotective mother, in part because she felt that Henry, when home with them from the office, tended to excessive strictness in trying to curb the boy's naturally strong will. She sometimes wondered how much of Henry's fondness for the child derived from paternal pride and how much from his love for the child's mother, whoever she was. Ralph was a clever, endearing little boy, and Rosalie's unstinting approval allowed him to develop a confidence in his own worth.

When his younger brother was born, Ralph was hurt by his mother's shift of attention. He was old enough to understand that the new baby necessarily took up a good deal of the time that used to be his, but he felt resentful nonetheless. She loved the baby more, he thought. After a few ineffectual stabs at recapturing all of her attention, he focused more on his father, whose attitude had not changed, but had merely broadened to include a second son. Ralph adored his father and wanted to emulate him despite the sense that gradually grew in him that they were always competing. As time passed Ralph became increasingly determined that his father's success was the marker he would aim for and surpass.

For several years it had been Henry's custom on the Saturday before Christmas to take Ralph into Manhattan. Father and son would look at the animated displays in the department-store windows, then go to F.A.O. Schwarz to pick out a special present and then to Rumpelmayer's for ice cream.

Each time the same tall blond woman in a long fur coat, sometimes dark brown, sometimes white, would be sitting at a nearby table. She would begin to talk to them, mostly to Ralph. The first year she purchased a gift from the front counter for him. From then on, she always had a gift waiting when he arrived. He had become her young friend, she said, and she had no other young friends to whom she could give a Christmas gift.

On their way home to their house in Brooklyn Heights after that first Christmas trip together to Manhattan, his father told him that meeting the tall blond woman was a secret between father and son, a kind of bond they could share. They would never tell anyone, not even Mom, about it. They would tell her that they had bought him the second gift when they went for ice cream.

On the Saturday before Christmas Day of 1961, when Ralph was ten years old, the blond woman arrived late at Rumpelmayer's, very anxious that he might have left already. Relieved to see him, she scooped Ralph up in her arms and kissed him.

That night and for a long time afterward, Ralph brooded about that meeting and a question he wanted answered. Mom would get furious at him for asking it, as she often did, although she rarely became angry at Jeffrey, his younger brother. His father, he decided, would not answer him and might even end the Christmas ritual altogether, costing him his only chance to gain the answer. So, with a patience few would have believed possible for a boy so impatient about other matters, he waited out the year until the Saturday before the next Christmas.

Ralph tossed and turned in his bed that Friday night. They were late getting started the next day because Mr. Weintraub, his father's business partner, and Mr. Weintraub's mousey wife and five-year-old daughter, Gail, had been invited for a holiday breakfast. Gail kept coming into his room to play with his trains, even though he warned her not to and kept herding her out. Ralph tried to be polite, but was delighted when they left. He hurriedly put on the new tan cashmere overcoat his mother had bought him at DePinna's to match his father's and rushed out with his father to the Cadillac.

His father drove more quickly than usual over the bridge into Manhattan and waited with the motor running while he trotted past the display windows at some of the department stores. They parked in a garage near F.A.O. Schwarz. Without having to be told they were in a hurry, Ralph swiftly picked out his own gift and one for Jeff and then matched his father's brisk pace up Central Park South to Rumpelmayer's.

The tall blond lady was waiting at the same table where they had all sat the year before. She smiled at Ralph's approach and opened her arms, embracing him. Then she released him enough to have a good look. Henry took a seat across the table from her. This was the moment Ralph had chosen.

"You're my real mother, aren't you?"

The woman's face turned white, and her lips separated without her making a sound. She glanced in terror at Henry, her eyes accusing him of having broken their pact.

"No, Ralph," Henry essayed weakly, "she's a friend we met here. Your mother is home. How could you say that?"

Ralph's eyes shifted from one adult to the other, resting at last on the woman. She did not have to tell him. The guilt in her eyes, her inability to deny his assertion, were his answer.

She sprang from her chair to flee.

"No, wait—" Henry exclaimed, jumping up to stop her. He banged against the table, knocking her water glass to the floor with the sound of a cymbal crash. She slashed his hand out of her way and rushed on, out of the restaurant.

Henry stood watching her for a long while. When he turned back to his son, his face was composed.

"Crazy lady. That's what happens when you try to be nice to strangers."

Ralph said nothing.

That incident ended their pre-Christmas visits to Manhattan. Ralph was sorry. Manhattan dazzled him: the huge buildings thrusting into the sky, the people handsome and handsomely dressed, scurrying by because they must have important things to do. He was sorrier not to see again the beautiful woman who was his real mother, but he had learned what he had to know. And knowing it was both another bond to his father and, although he never consciously acknowledged it, another barricade behind which he could defend and rally his growing independence from him.

BOOK THREE

Ralph's Story

Chapter 5

"I haven't slept much trying to figure out how to say this. I guess I'd just better get it out."

Ralph Behr ceased speaking as Lorna Garrison poured coffee into his cup. He had left here only hours before, after they had made love and she had pressed him to marry her. Now, Ralph was back in Lorna's apartment after telephoning to say it was urgent he see her. In the few hours between, he had agreed to marry a woman he did not know as a means of transferring to her the staggering sum of one hundred million dollars and thus of keeping his father out of jail.

Lorna had proposed marriage the night before, perhaps mistaking her own strong emotions for their reciprocation or his engrossment in business as a sign that he would consider marrying a woman who shared that interest and enhanced his efforts there. Ralph had had good times with Lorna and terrific sex and they had a lot in common. She had often been useful to him, he would admit that. And there was that intriguing, flattering intensity about her passion for him; he had the feeling she would claw through stone to gain him. Within that intensity he could also sometimes glimpse an equally intriguing nucleus of vulnerability— the denied, unpopular child willing herself to become the sleekly alluring woman and the nexus of political and business intrigue.

But being diverted by her and kept interested by her interest in him was as deep as his feelings for her went. Her appeal was to his appetites and not his yearnings. She offered only more of what he already had.

Ralph did not articulate that vague perception to himself; he had concluded simply that he had no desire to marry Lorna Garrison. Moreover, he had not intended to tie himself to a wife for a long time and probably, unless he could see some advantage in it, forever; he had grown up witness to his dissatisfied father's outbursts of irritation, his mother's alternating nagging and stoicism, and the periods between of their ragged toleration.

Ralph was a relatively courteous man, not because he was particularly sensitive to other people's feelings, but rather because he was usually too preoccupied for such awareness. Thus, he took care to employ the forms of social courtesy that allayed the negative reaction his self-involvement could cause. However, even if he did not break the news of his marriage personally to Lorna out of fairness, he would have done so as a precaution. Crossed, she could be vicious. When he had left her apartment last night, he had intended to avoid a reply to her proposal and, in fact, to avoid her for a few weeks so as to let things cool off and impress upon her that good times together were as far as their relationship was going to go. But he could not take that route now. He knew he must inform her right away, before she read about it or heard it from someone else; delay would not change anything—the arrangements had all been made.

Despite Ralph's objections, Lorna had insisted on making breakfast for him. Smiling, bubbling, she kissed Ralph and then took the chair across from him. Fork aloft over her scrambled eggs, she sat erect, alert, her brown tip-frosted hair precisely in place. She loved even the worry pinching his brow, she thought, and the few strands of his dark hair that fell across it. He was so handsome—intense, nearly green eyes in a slim, engrossed face; perfectly tailored dark suit draped on a tall body; unseen muscles coiled to propel him instantly at a project or a woman with total self-assurance that he would get his way, even with she herself, who was so used to getting hers. She thrilled to that strength in him, to never quite being able to anticipate what he would do, to never quite being able to control him. He is the supreme prize, she thought.

"Have you considered my proposal?" she said lightheartedly, nearly laughing at the grimness of his expression. His phone call this morning, his urgency, had precipitated her expectation, her certainty, that he was returning to propose.

"I'm going to marry another woman," he said. "A couple of days from now, in fact."

Lorna stared at him in shock.

"It was kind of sudden," Ralph confessed.

What more could he add? he wondered. That he had no choice? Damn! He was being dragged into that marriage kicking and screaming. For God's sake, he was losing a hundred million dollars! He considered admitting that this had nothing to do with her, maybe flattering her about how pretty and sexy she looked in that filmy night thing she was wearing and making clear that he wanted to continue seeing her, that this was just another little deal he was involved in. But he instantly rejected the thought. She would either despise his character or insist on knowing more, and then she would dig and dig until she pieced together the whole incriminating story. No matter which course he took, he feared she would be vindictive. Better not to chance her discovering anything, he decided. Better a clean break with no openings she could probe for information to smear him and his father in print and on TV stations everywhere.

"Who's the woman? Do I know her?" she asked, her cheeks swiftly reddening.

"Her name is Gail."

"Does this goddess have a last name?"

"Yes. Weintraub, I guess," he mumbled.

"You guess."

"Look—"

She interrupted him forcefully. "What does she look like?"

"Well . . . I don't . . . you know," he mumbled.

"I'll make it easier," she said sarcastically. "Is she taller than I am? Shorter? Blond, brunette, or redhead? Is she better looking than I am?"

"She looks like, you know, very nice."

"That beautiful!"

"Lorna, I don't really want to go into all this."

"You don't what?" she hissed. "You cold-hearted son of a bitch! You don't want to talk about it? Last night you let me go on about loving you and wanting to marry you. And all the time you were engaged to another woman. You just wanted one last fuck."

"It isn't really like that," he offered lamely. "It all happened after I left here."

"*After you left here!* Where did you find her? On a street corner?"

"She was someone I thought was out of my life forever," he replied with some honesty. "And now she's suddenly back. It all happened in the last few hours. Believe me, I hate to do this to you. I have no choice."

"It's bigger than both of you!" She plunged her fork into the small mound of scrambled eggs on her plate. "You've made me a laughingstock in front of the entire world. The gossip in this city will be about nothing else for weeks. I'll never live it down."

Ralph stood up. "I'd better be going."

"One more question," she demanded. "And at least have the

decency now to be honest with me, Ralph—you owe me that."
Lorna waited for his nod before continuing. "Is sex with her as good as it is with me?"

"The truth is I don't know what sex is like with her."

"You asshole!"

After he let himself out, Lorna remained seated, staring at his empty chair. She loved Ralph Behr so much, more than she had ever loved any man, and he had thrown her over for a woman he claimed had suddenly appeared out of his past. Losing him was as painful as if he had died, but worse—death did not also bring humiliation. Not the kind of woman who cried, she brooded for a long time without moving from her chair. Her instinct was to hurt Ralph as badly as she had been hurt. And then she remembered something he had mentioned about his new real-estate project.

Lorna went to the telephone and dialed David Hodge. One of the state's most influential real-estate lawyers, he was an old friend who had fought alongside her through many campaigns on behalf of many clients. She had learned to ask only important favors of him because he asked only important favors in return. Needing Hodge's government influence to smooth the way, Ralph had retained him for several early projects, until a change of administration in Albany had brought in a new governor with different allegiances.

The conversation was brief and to the point, the salutations cursory. Hodge promised Lorna that in strictest confidence he would phone a good friend at the title company Ralph used and ask what was holding up the title insurance on Ralph's new project. Lorna indicated her willingness, if necessary, to demonstrate "in green" her gratitude to the title-company man for divulging that little bit of confidential information. She would owe David Hodge a very large and probably ultimately more costly favor.

Just after eleven o'clock, Hodge phoned her at her office with the information. She ruminated on her possible moves for a long while afterward. Then she telephoned Simon Kramer.

As she suspected, Simon Kramer was enraged that all the publicity generated at last night's charity affair had gone, not to him, who had been named its Man of the Year at a cost of a million-dollar donation, but to Ralph Behr, who had announced a huge new project. She assured Simon she had tried to prevent Ralph from stealing his thunder, but Ralph had insisted. That was why she was telephoning—to invite Simon and his wife to a dinner party this very night as a way of demonstrating her dismay over the incident. No, of course, Ralph wouldn't be there. She couldn't stand his egoism, the way he treated people. Last night was so typical of his despicable behavior. As a matter of fact, she was so angry at him she might just share some damaging secret information about his newest project with another developer.

Simon Kramer said he would change his plans for the evening. He and his wife would be glad to attend.

When they hung up, Lorna pulled out her A list and went to the very top. A senator maybe or an ex-cabinet official. A TV-news personality would look good. And, certainly, big money. In spite of the late date, she would need real luminaries to impress Simon Kramer. That was the whole purpose of tonight. At the end she would suggest they have a private lunch tomorrow, at which, if all had gone well to that point, she would lay her cards on the table.

Simon Kramer was in his early fifties and coolly poised. He had hawkish features that were not unattractive, a short beard and mustache that gave him an intellectual air unusual in real-estate men, and thinning black hair turning gray, which he wore combed back. Over years spent in the construction business, he had built up political ties which proved invaluable to him after he expanded into development. Lorna had chosen him for her scheme because of his grudges against the man who had scorned her, but also because he possessed qualities she had admired and been attracted to in Ralph: both men were dynamic and successful, and lurking within their ambitiousness was a killer instinct—Ralph's clothed in boyish, high-spirited competitiveness, Simon's in cultured gentility.

At the dinner party at least, events went along as Lorna had planned them. She looked dazzling in black chiffon that partially veiled a low neckline, and Simon focused all his attention on her. Certainly, she concluded, she put Simon Kramer's vapid wife into the shadows. Lorna had met many couples like them: powerful men who married too young the arid women the financial cost now prevented them from divorcing. Simon was suitably impressed by the other guests—none in real estate to dim his own luster. Out of earshot of his wife, he mentioned to Lorna that he would like an opportunity to talk further with her and, in fact, was the one to suggest lunch the next day.

Lunch, however, proved more of a sparring match than Lorna had anticipated. She arrived at La Grenouille a careful five minutes late, only to find that Simon was not yet there. She chafed for another five minutes until he arrived without an apology. After the way he had reacted to her last night, she expected him to throw himself at her, maybe even come right out and proposition her—she had been counting on something like that to gain control of the conversation. Instead, he paid scant attention to her, as if his mind and interest were elsewhere, doubtless aware that he was annoying her. He knows how to play the game, she thought, and found with surprise that that in itself aroused her, as did the authority he exuded when he finally stopped making notes on other matters and turned fully toward her. She groped for an opening that would allow her to assert control over the direction of the dialogue. Without meaning to, he provided it.

"What's your thinking on how to sell Ariel Tower?"

She feigned ignorance.

"The apartment house I'm building on Second Avenue." He was peeved.

"I haven't seen it," she replied after a moment of seeming to be attempting to recall the project. "I've heard, though, that it hasn't got the cachet of the one Ralph Behr built nearby."

Simon smiled thinly. "I hadn't heard that. I'll admit that sales—for both of us—have been slower than we projected."

"Simon, you're attracting Miami Beach north, not the glamorous names that will draw buyers who can pay the prices you're asking. Celebrities have to believe your building is the only place in New York to be. That's the same reason my guests all canceled other plans to be at my apartment last night."

"I was impressed," he admitted.

"You were supposed to be. You need to hire a firm that can enlist names like those and then get them into print."

He parried. "You said something on the phone yesterday about Ralph Behr's new project being in trouble."

"I think I know something that might give another developer a shot at it. Why don't we look at the model apartments in Ariel Tower?" Lorna tipped her head forward to gaze at him through her eyelashes. "I think you and I have interests in common."

Having the right product to sell was essential in obtaining the publicity he'd need, Lorna asserted as she moved through the model apartments that had been rapidly furnished on the second floor while the rest of the building climbed upward. She suggested layout changes Simon should consider making in order to enhance the sense of luxury on which she believed sales here depended. Two of her ideas required partition walls to be moved in two of the apartment lines. Simon nodded several times, but said very little.

"I'd also want you to throw out all this junk furniture and hire a different top interior designer to do each apartment," Lorna tossed off as they inspected the final apartment. "When they're done, I'll stage a charity dinner in them with fabulous guests. I can put this building in headlines around the world." Lorna stepped closer to Simon. "My fee is ten thousand dollars a month, a minimum of three months, you pay all the expenses, and I'm cheap at twice that."

He gazed at her a long time before replying. "There are too many sales people around for us to talk here. I want you to see the penthouse. We can talk there. I want to talk about Ralph Behr."

Neither spoke in the elevator that took them to the top floor. They stepped out onto an open concrete floor with exposed concrete columns and beams, the rawest sort of space. Outer walls and windows had enclosed it only a day or two before. Lumber and pipes and electrical wiring were stacked in piles.

"I have no love for Ralph Behr," Lorna began. "Neither do you. We'd both like to pay him back in kind. Would you be interested in stopping the new project he just announced?"

"I might be."

"You *would* be," she corrected. "You'd have him by the balls. And I'm the only one who knows how. I want a twenty-five percent interest in anything you get out of it—which might even be a piece of Behr Center."

"And you want me to hire you to publicize this building?"

"You need me," she said.

"I *want* you. It amounts to the same thing."

A slow smile lifted her mouth. "Down the line?"

"Right here."

Never taking her eyes from his, she swiftly removed her clothes and lay back naked on the cold concrete.

Several minutes later two workmen on a scaffold lowering themselves down the outside of the building happened to look through the window. Lorna caught sight of them over Simon's shoulder and blew them a kiss. Simon yelled at them to get the hell away and mind their own fucking business.

A few days later three City Hall reporters covering a long Board of Estimate hearing just recessed for a lunch break were

97

walking swiftly along the street. The heat wave had not let up, and they were eager to reach the air-conditioned coffee shop. They would not usually have paid attention to the silver-gray limousine that stopped in front of the Municipal Building, but Dan Ahern noticed the Behr license plate and the antennae sprouting as if the vehicle were Air Force One. They stopped to watch Ralph Behr and his father emerge with an elderly woman and a young man.

"What would those two be doing at the Municipal Building?" Ahern asked.

"A meeting?" reasoned a reporter with the *Daily News*. "Then why isn't he at City Hall?"

The third man, Lowery, with *New York Newsday*, had once covered real estate. "The other guy is his brother. I think the woman is his mother. Why would they *all* be here?"

"I may be crazy," Ahern remarked, "but wasn't that a bridal bouquet Ralph Behr was holding?"

The three men gaped at each other for an instant and then took off in a run for the Municipal Building. They dodged the vehicular traffic scooting through the archway at the large building's base and then into the south doorway, through which the Behrs had entered. They missed the elevator, but watched the indicator stop one flight up. They ran for the stairs and charged up to the second floor, where they caught sight of the Behrs entering the chapel waiting room at the Marriage License Bureau.

Lowery expressed what the other reporters were thinking: that if the marriage was Ralph Behr's, they had a great story.

"Lorna Garrison maybe," Ahern figured. "They were at the real-estate dinner together a few nights ago."

The reporters briefly discussed sending in one of their number to find out what was happening, but none was willing to wait outside. They rushed at the door together and then struggled through it like a ball of grappling tag-team wrestlers falling between the ropes. They came close to knocking down a very pregnant young woman clutching a marriage license in one hand and her grim-looking boyfriend's wrist in the other.

The Behrs were gathered at the side of the blue room. Other people sat in rows facing each other across a center aisle leading to the closed chapel door. Ralph held a small bouquet of purple violets, tied with long, pale purple ribbons. He recognized Dan Ahern and nodded resignedly. His plan had been to fade into the barely differentiable public moving through the marriage process and then issue an announcement later on. Moreover, having the wedding performed here by a city clerk simplified matters. Ralph's wife-to-be was Jewish, and he had been raised as a Protestant, although he had little interest in religious matters.

"You're getting married?" Ahern hazarded.

Ralph's nod lacked its usual enthusiasm.

Ahern pressed on. "What's her name?"

"She's very shy, not used to crowds and publicity."

"Come on, Ralph, I'm only asking her name."

"Gail Benedict," Ralph admitted. In the car his father had told him that she went by her husband's last name.

"Gail Benedict! *The* Gail Benedict!" Ahern could not restrain the whistle. "Not used to crowds? If we're talking about the same Gail Benedict, she *manufactures* crowds."

At that moment a young woman and an older man entered the room. Henry Behr moved toward them. Ralph scarcely recognized Abe Weintraub from his childhood: the older man's face was gaunt and his complexion a pale gray, whether from prison or illness Ralph could not tell. Weintraub walked haltingly and looked far older than his father. Only the man's eyes appeared vital; they stared at Henry Behr with hatred. For that and for the blackmail he had concocted to rob the Behrs of what was rightfully theirs, Ralph hated the man with an equal intensity.

Ralph's gaze shifted to the young woman.

Gail was shorter than average height with long chestnut-brown hair plaited into a single braid. Her eyes were large and gray under eyebrows drawn together in anger. Her nose was straight and pert, though oddly out of character with the stormy expression in her eyes. Her mouth was wider than he would have liked. She was nice-enough looking and might even have been passably attractive, Ralph decided, if the entire impression she seemed at pains to make was not so jarring and so annoying. She had returned from the Caribbean with her divorce decree yesterday afternoon in plenty of time to dress presentably for the wedding, if only for appearance's sake. Instead, she had chosen to wear faded jeans and a cheap cotton blouse.

All in all, he decided, little about her would have attracted him if they had met socially. And then his heart sank, and he finally understood Dan Ahern's remark. He recognized her from a TV news report he had seen a few months back. Caustic and belligerent, she had been leading some kind of demonstration and haranguing public officials. They had appeared to detest her. Yet, he was *marrying her*. Shit!

"Dan, could my bride and I have a moment alone?" he asked in what he hoped passed for groomlike passion.

The reporters commandeered telephones to summon photographers. Ralph turned his back to block them from the conversation. His father was quietly introducing Gail to the others and reacquainting them with Abe.

"I'm Ralph Behr," Ralph said directly to the young woman. His tone was pleasant. He was hoping to establish an amicable relationship in order to make the next two years as painless as possible.

She nodded. "I saw your ad glittering on your limousine's license plates."

"Look, this marriage is costing me a hundred million dollars. I like it even less than you do."

She fixed him with a cold stare. "Let's just get it over with."

"One thing, this room is loaded with reporters."

"Trust you to make your wedding a media event."

"While they're watching, try not to show your animosity."

"You really want the impossible."

"Force yourself. You have a hundred million reasons." He shoved the bouquet at her and slipped his arm through hers. The smile he flashed at onlookers felt like it was dripping from his face like wax.

A friendly judge had waived the waiting period, and the City Clerk's office had expedited the arrangements. A waiting clerk took the papers and Ralph's ten dollars and handed him the license.

As the wedding party moved into the adjacent room, where the ceremony would take place, Lowery called out to his journalist colleagues, "They're getting married *here!*"

The other reporters slammed down their phones and hurried to join him.

Ralph concentrated on Gail as they moved past Lowery. "My angel!"

Her answering smile looked lethal. "My pet!"

Ralph took his place beside Gail in front of the clerk.

"The ring?" the man asked.

Ralph stared at him, uncomprehending.

The man recognized Ralph and grew nervous. "The ring for the . . . umm . . . bride."

"Is that really necessary?"

"Well, it's traditional."

"We're very modern."

100

Henry leaned forward and handed his son a spectacular diamond wedding band he had bought that morning. Two circles of pear-shaped diamonds, their larger ends abutting, formed a herring-bone pattern. It was a lavish peace offering.

Instead, appalled by the ring's extravagance, Gail glared at Ralph as he placed it on her finger.

The disconcerted clerk asked Ralph, "Are . . . are you going to wear a ring?"

"You've got to be kidding."

The clerk swallowed hard, looked over at the bride, who was also glowering at him, and then back at the groom. Ralph gestured impatiently. The clerk performed the service hundreds of times a week, but he was now so nervous that he forgot the opening phrase and, once he got going, rushed through the ceremony, stammering and stumbling over words he had spoken innumerable times, turning to Gail when speaking to the groom and Ralph when speaking to the bride.

"I now pronounce you man and wife," he concluded with a great sigh of relief. "You may kiss the bride."

"Thanks," Ralph said and shook the man's hand.

"The bride," the man repeated, "you may kiss her."

"Right," Ralph said. He took a deep breath and turned to her at an angle that would shield her hostility from the reporters at the doorway craning for a better view.

"Darling," he pronounced.

"Dearest," she responded in a voice that rang out like an alarm.

At that moment Ralph knew exactly what it must be like to kiss dry ice. Two years! he moaned silently.

As he lifted his head, he found his mother's arms around them both.

"Congratulations," Rosalie sobbed. "I'm so happy for both of you."

Ralph looked over at his father, whose expression indicated he had taken his usual course, which was to keep his wife in the dark.

A lot of hand-shaking and well-wishing followed, mostly from the reporters.

"Where's the honeymoon going to be?" Ahern asked.

"Paradise!" Gail uttered in a loud sigh and rolled her eyes dreamily toward Ralph.

The reporters seemed pleased with that answer and wrote it

down. They started to ask other questions, but Ralph begged off and shepherded the two families toward the exit.

At the elevator Rosalie pinched Jeff's cheek. "If only I could live to see my baby married." She turned with some heat to Henry. "Or to see him finally a partner."

"Rosalie, now's not the time for that," Henry replied.

"How are the condo sales going at Second Avenue?" Ralph asked his younger brother, partly to change the subject.

Jeff was slow in replying and relieved when the elevator doors opened. "A lot of possibles," he said heartily as he stepped quickly into the elevator. "We're getting a lot of recognition in the marketplace."

"What are the numbers, Jeff?" Ralph asked with some impatience as he stepped into a space beside his slightly shorter brother. Jeff invariably resorted to reassurance whenever Ralph, as frequently happened, criticized his managing. Ralph knew the technique to be a transparent ploy to evade unpleasantness.

"Twenty-eight sold. Seven down payments. I think. Three in contract. Look, there are twenty thousand new apartments on the market in this city. It's not my fault that people aren't rushing to buy right now."

The elevator doors opened on the lobby, and the wedding party moved toward the street.

"I didn't say it was," Ralph retorted. "But I expect you to have some recommendations on how to correct the situation."

"I'm working on that, Ralph," he said too quickly. "I need a couple more days."

"What about the brownstone? You've had three months to find a tenant."

The brownstone was an East Side property Ralph had surreptitiously acquired as part of an assemblage he was putting together in order to build a luxury apartment house on the land. Until all the parcels were purchased and he was ready to demolish, a management company fronting for the Behr Group was renting out the acquired buildings on short-term leases. Jeff was in charge of that entire operation.

"It's the short duration of the leases," Jeff said. "We can't risk taking on residential tenants—they're too hard to evict in this city. And it's tough to find commercial tenants willing to go in when they know we can cancel at any time."

Ralph stepped aside at the front entrance to let the others through and to complete his conversation with his brother. He felt sentimental about the little brownstone. His father had pointed it out to him when he was a teenager, the first building his grandfather, Raphael, had ever put up. Family legend had it that his grandparents had married a few days after his grandmother had found a buyer for the building. But sentiment did not obscure business needs or his brother's sluggish performance.

"Jeff, we have this same conversation every time I bring up the brownstone. Somewhere in New York there has to be an office tenant willing to rent short-term at our price."

Abashed, Jeff nodded. Ralph placed a hand on his shoulder. "Let's go over this whole thing next week."

The wedding party was standing in awkward silence on the pavement near the limousine when Ralph and Jeff reached them. The reporters were only a few paces behind. Two photographers summoned by phone were running toward them from City Hall. Ralph guided the wedding party into the limousine, at the same time trying to smile happily at the clicking cameras.

"One of the bride and groom!" a photographer called out.

Ralph and Gail beamed out the open window until the limousine pulled away and rounded the corner. Riding backward beside Henry, Ralph shifted position to face Gail and her father, who sat beside his mother Rosalie in the rear seat. The ex-convict's dark eyes were squared on Henry's and bore the glint of jubilation.

What a shameless, evil bastard! Ralph declared to himself. Willing to hurt anyone and do anything for money, even go to prison. Someday he would repay this outrageous robbery by Abe Weintraub, but for the foreseeable future he would have to live with the situation, with this Gail. He had determined that he would make her presence in his life as pleasant for himself and as unintrusive as possible.

"I've asked my cook to make lunch for all of us. I know this isn't the happiest of occasions, but at least we can try to get off on the right foot."

The limousine made a second turn. Gail bent toward the driver.

"Stop here, please." She turned to Ralph. "Look, let me lay it out right at the beginning. I don't like you or anything I've ever read about you. You represent everything I oppose: greed, bullying, the vanity of seeing your name in newspapers or on buildings. Understand that I only agreed to this marriage charade because it was important to my father. All he has to show for twenty years of hell is the money he's entitled to. It's part of our deal that you and I have to live in the same apartment, go out socially, and appear to be a real married couple. But I'll be damned if I'll spend a single second more with you than necessary. I have a lot more important and less distasteful things to do."

She dropped the bouquet onto the seat behind her and stepped out of the car, extending a hand to help her father out as well. She leaned back in to ask something. "What's the address of your apartment?"

Ralph told her, then added, "The cook will have dinner ready early tonight. Remember, we're supposed to look married to the servants too. No matter how much we dislike the idea, this is our wedding night."

She grimaced. "Don't wait up."

No one spoke for several blocks. The violets lay on the seat, the ribbons trailing onto the carpet. Everyone avoided looking at them. Finally, Ralph addressed his father.

"Why didn't you tell me she hated me?"

"It doesn't make any difference."

"I have to live with that bitch."

"It had to be done. We've agreed it's the only way out. Now that she knows her father pleaded guilty to keep me out of jail, she hates us for it—me *and* you. If it was up to her, I'd take her father's place in jail, and she'd burn every dollar coming to the two of them."

"And she's only going through with it because her father wants her to."

"And her husband."

"Great!"

They rode much of the way uptown in silence. Rosalie turned her face toward the window.

Ralph invited the others to his apartment for lunch, but no one was hungry. Usually his schedule away from his office was packed with a succession of closely timed meetings, but he had cleared his schedule completely today because of the wedding and because he intended to take his father to see the land that was to become Behr Center. Abe Weintraub had been delighted to exclude both that immense and costly complex and Ralph's Upper East Side assemblage site from the marital assets to be divided under the prenuptial agreement his daughter was signing— neither project was certain yet of profitability nor had even commenced construction. That agreement would later serve as the couple's divorce property settlement. Behr Center would be totally Ralph's, and he considered it his means for recouping everything this woman and her father had stolen from him and for making many hundreds of millions more. And yet, the project meant far more to him than money: it was his masterpiece, his immortality.

"I'm naming it after you," Ralph said to Henry as they stood on the sidewalk across from the low-slung garage buildings that had completed the assemblage just a few days ago. Beyond were the three additional blocks that comprised the sprawling site, covered mostly by empty lots, a few small stores, and some dilapidated tenements. "The Henry Behr Center."

His father did not reply.

"You want me to, don't you?"

Henry was overwhelmed by the vastness of the site. "It's a great tribute, Ralph, a hell of a tribute."

"I thought every time they drove past it would be a slap in the faces of all those Establishment bastards who shafted you and your father when times got rough. One thing you taught me: you better look out for yourself. Everybody else is only looking out for themselves."

Henry nodded and threw his arm around his son's shoulders. "If I taught you that, then I did a good job."

The Behrs drove uptown to a building under construction on Second Avenue and conferred with the supervisors. Henry had learned not to interfere. Ralph's sharp eyes caught and corrected every potential problem Henry had noted and more: a misaligned beam; cheap bathroom fixtures a subcontractor had slipped in; slow delivery of some material to the site.

Very early, his son's business ability had shown itself so overwhelming that Henry's competitive urge had slunk away, leaving only pride and a feeling of being almost an outsider to all of this, almost unnecessary. Manhattan, always wracked by intermittent convulsions of growth, had changed dramatically since he was a young man. These glass-skinned buildings were bigger and sleeker; there were also so many more laws and rules, more approvals to be obtained, and more adversaries to be overcome than in bygone days. The magnitude of the numbers, the very style of doing business was alien to Henry. And despite Ralph's appearance of deference, Henry was glad when the tour was over, and he and Rosalie could repair to their summer home on the Jersey shore.

Ralph and Jeff returned to their office on Madison Avenue at four o'clock. Behr House was a skyscraper with a lobby atrium containing three floors of shops. Access could be had from

Madison, Park, and both side streets, which increased the foot traffic and enhanced retail sales, justifying the high rents he was charging. The office floors were fully rented less than a year after opening, with his own firm taking one floor. He was pleased with the architecture and by the building's success, but other developers had built similar projects. No one had ever built anything on a scale to equal the three sky-high towers planned for Behr Center. That would be the greatest project ever built. It would astound the world.

"You're here!" the receptionist exclaimed as Ralph, a step ahead of his brother, pushed through the glass doors into the modern pale yellow and umber decor. A broad smile broke across her face. "Congratulations!"

"What for?"

Her smile faltered. She lifted her copy of the afternoon paper to show him the front page. It read: BEHR MARRIES WOMEN'S LIBBER. Beneath that was a larger photo of Gail and him framed by the limousine window. His grin, he decided, looked almost idiotic enough to be the real thing.

"Thanks."

He marched grimly down the tan-carpeted corridor to his office.

"Congratulations, Ralph!" Ben Rogovin, his executive vice president, called out and rushed from his own office with a hand extended.

Ralph mumbled his thanks and fielded questions about the blushing bride, trying to duplicate the newspaper photo's idiotic smile.

"What a surprise!" Rogovin went on. "None of us even knew you were dating her."

"We didn't want it to slip out to the press," Ralph said as he moved past him into his office.

Myra, his secretary, jumped up to kiss his cheek. "When we read the paper, we were sure you'd be off on your honeymoon."

"Big disappointment. Too much to do right now."

Ralph reached for his list of phone messages and scanned them. He broke into a smile and slapped the list against his palm.

"Charles Brookhouse telephoned," he called out to Ben Rogovin.

"Just tell him to send over the money," the other joked.

Ralph told Myra to return the call and entered his office. The Brookhouses had always run Metrobank like a private fiefdom. Charles's father had been the sole heir to his own father's huge fortune and had built Metrobank into a global giant that rivaled Citibank, Chemical, and Chase for hegemony in New York. Charles had inherited his father's reins when the latter retired. He himself had become a world-renowned financial elder statesman and played a large part in refinancing the heavy debt run up by several South American nations.

Metrobank had been seeking to expand its commercial real-estate lending. Ralph, who had been trying to determine the right source for Behr Center's financing, had asked a mutual friend to arrange for him to have lunch with Metrobank's chairman. Ralph had never had a failure, each building having been more successful than the last. He was currently the industry's "hot" developer, and financial institutions were fighting to do business with him. Some, though, would offer terms that would be too restrictive, some were too small, and all would attempt to obtain a different "kicker" on top of the usual interest. But Metrobank might just be hungry enough for his business to settle for straight nonrecourse mortgaging.

Ralph and Charles Brookhouse had hit it off well at their initial meeting. Ralph had mentioned Behr Center only in passing, knowing that men of Brookhouse's background and era rarely talked business on a first visit, more rarely still over lunch. Now he would find out if Metrobank was interested.

"Yes, I enjoyed our meeting too, Charles," he said into the receiver after the exchange of greetings. For all his self-confidence and despite being a Yale graduate, Ralph was at heart a Brooklyn kid who spent his summers playing ball at the Parade Grounds and going to Coney Island to pick up girls. He had not yet overcome the awe of being on a first-name basis with Charles Brookhouse.

"That project you're planning downtown," Brookhouse said in quiet upper-class tones. "It piqued our interest. Perhaps you'd be interested in discussing our potential involvement in the financing."

Ordinarily, Ralph would have sold the hell out of the project, but one did not take that approach with a man as understated as Charles Brookhouse. "I hadn't really considered it, but I'd certainly be pleased to tell you about the project. The architectural model will be arriving next week. If it isn't too much of an inconvenience, I'd like to invite you and any of your people to meet next week in my offices. The model can show you better than plans or renderings what the project will look like."

"My appointments secretary will call yours to arrange a suitable time. By the way, I'm having a small luncheon for a few friends who have expressed interest in a pet charity of mine. I'd like very much for you to be included."

Ralph knew a quid pro quo when he heard one. "I'm honored that you asked, Charles."

"My appointments secretary will convey that information as well."

"Excellent. Until the luncheon then."

They said good-bye and hung up. "Excellent," Ralph repeated aloud in amusement. He had never used *excellent* that way before. The Brookhouses of the world had that effect. Ralph went to the door.

"Myra, his 'appointments secretary,' will be calling my 'appointments secretary.'"

"Does a raise go with my new title?" she teased.

Ralph chuckled, but was already looking again at the message list. "Rountree said it was important?"

"Yes."

"Get him for me."

For two years Phil Rountree's firm had been doing the legal work on the secret land acquisitions for Behr Center. Rountree was close to the governor, who had once been a partner in his firm, and had solidified that relationship for Ralph. Ralph had learned from his father that the right lawyer was usually the one who could open doors to the right politicians.

Ralph immediately heard the concern in Rountree's greeting.

"What's up?" Ralph asked.

"A problem with the deed on that last parcel. You know that I've been after the company for the title insurance report. They claimed it was taking longer than usual because they had a complication to check out. They just called."

"And?" Ralph asked impatiently. He was shuffling through his mail as they spoke.

"And there's one hell of a complication with the title all right. You'll recall that I warned you about buying that last parcel outright instead of waiting until you were sure you had good title to the property."

"And *you'll* recall that the buyer was an old man whose family had owned that garage property since God knows when and doesn't understand contracts and title insurance and all the legal rigamarole. He would have backed out if we had insisted on doing things the legalistic way."

"Maybe. Or just maybe he's smart as hell."

"The problem, Phil."

"At first I thought one of our young lawyers had made a mistake, but there was really no way for him to know."

"I've got the part about it not being your firm's fault, Phil. What I want to hear now is the problem." Ralph had put down his mail.

"Well, originally the land was part of a farm owned by the Van Leeuwans, Dutch settlers in Nieuw Amsterdam. In the eighteen hundreds, the Van Leeuwan family sold off what was left of the land in two halves. Your half was conveyed after they sold the other parcel to a man named Cartright. Cartright seemed to have insisted on this crazy easement which is creating all the difficulty. He got a perpetual easement that allowed him, his family, his heirs—you name it—to cross the half of the land he didn't own. Your half. And, oh, yes, any of his 'cattle, sheep, goats, or wheeled vehicles.' He probably wanted to get to a road or a stream on the other side. However, when Van Leeuwan sold that other half of the land to someone else, he didn't give a full covenant and warranty deed and made no reference to the easement he had already given Cartright."

"You mean the buyer of that other half—*my* half—never knew he didn't have clear title?"

"Right. Both deeds of sale by Van Leeuwan were recorded. The difficulty occurred because someone way in the past tampered with Cartright's deed in the city records."

"What kind of tampering?"

"The title company brought in a handwriting expert to look at it. X-rays show the original ink was eradicated and a meaningless sentence forged in its place. When tracing a title in the records, you always investigate all conveyances from a seller, not just his sale of that particular property, so as to avoid just this sort of problem. But, from then on, anyone who was checking the chain of title when buying your property would be unable to find Cartright's easement and couldn't know that this deed was burdened by an easement that gives the adjacent owner the right to cross any part of your land forever."

"Even a hundred fifty years later?"

"That makes no difference. There were a lot of paths and alleyways to go through, so Cartright and his descendants probably never questioned their right to walk across the other parcel. I gather the property may still be in the Cartright family."

Ralph rarely raised his voice when angry or anxious, but now his speech quickened and the inflection became more emphatic. "You're telling me that any structure I build has to allow for people from across the street strolling through with cows and goats?"

"And their wheeled vehicles."

"That could be bulldozers."

Rountree hesitated a moment. "Yes. Or ten-story cranes."

"How did the title company notice the forgery?"

"They've been in business a very long time and have documents that are called 'title plants' that were created from the original records. They found the easement in their old title plant for the conveyance from Van Leeuwan to Cartright."

"And they won't insure the chain of title without excluding the easement that destroys any chance I have to build," Ralph replied heatedly.

"Sorry," the lawyer sympathized.

"How do we fix it?"

"Either buy the other owner's right to cross your land or buy the land itself to extinguish the easement. It's the parking lot across the street."

"Find out who owns it. Use a dummy corporation and buy the entire parcel. If we try to buy only the easement, he'll get suspicious and know that he's got me over a barrel."

"Right."

"Immediately, Phil! And if you can't do it, I'll find someone who will."

Gail spent a long time talking with her father on a bench in Riverside Park. He held her hand all the while, as if to assure himself no barrier remained between them, and he kept staring at the boughs shading them.

As they had been forced to do for Gail and her late mother during Gail's childhood, the Behrs were now providing Abe Weintraub with an ample income until the two years passed and she received half the Behrs' net worth. She had come to feel that the prospect of that wealth for her had kept Abe alive during his prison years. In accordance with his wishes, Henry Behr had also located for him an apartment overlooking the Hudson River and the New Jersey Palisades; Abe claimed to have yearned for such a view in prison, but Gail suspected part of the reason was that he felt he might be a burden if he lived closer to her—her apartment with Milo had been way downtown and with Ralph Behr would be on the East Side. Her father assured her he would be fine as soon as he adapted to freedom and the way life had changed on the outside. A synagogue was only blocks away, and good doctors; and the very first day out he had become entranced by the food stores along Broadway: pillow-plump peaches and sweet melons, half a dozen varieties of apples and pears, nuts and cheeses and the smoked fish he could recall from his childhood. Along with his wife's passing and so many years of isolation had gone the desire for female companionship. He had been the prison librarian and was content to spend his days among books. A branch library was only a short walk, and the number 5 or 104 bus would take him directly to the main library at Forty-second Street. Like a starving man at a banquet, his visit there had made him dizzy with its richness.

The afternoon was nearly over when Gail finally left her father listening to a Mozart quartet in his new apartment and took the subway back downtown. She was hours overdue at the Women's Action Coalition. Many artists had migrated eastward from Soho and other areas where prosperity had pushed rents beyond their income. Some had moved into ancient buildings in the East Village and the Lower East Side and began to fix them up. Gail and her husband, Milo, and many of their artist friends now lived there side by side with Hispanics and elderly Irish and Eastern Europeans and working-class and welfare families. A few blocks south was the Delancey Street location her father had once pointed out where, long ago, his parents had owned a shirt store.

The subway car's graffiti screamed dissonant, disjunctive colors at her. She retreated into her own thoughts. With nothing to do but think on the subway and then during the walk from the station to the Coalition's office, so close to her home, she was overcome once more with a dislocated feeling.

Events and emotions had rushed upon her so swiftly these last few days. Joy at her father's coming release was overwhelmed by shock at his assertion that he had saved Henry Behr from prison in order to preserve for her his own half of the Behr's growing wealth, which now totaled two hundred million dollars. Then had followed her sadness that so many years had been, as her father had always maintained, unjustly stripped from him; and finally there was dismay at the marriage plan her father proposed, which entailed divorce and separation from Milo. She had tried to weigh the arguments for and against entering into this sham marriage with Behr—or Boor, as she had begun calling him—but there hadn't really been enough time to think it through properly, she thought. Finally, she had agreed to her father's entreaties, raced to his old lawyer to review and sign the papers which the Behrs had already signed and which then went into a bank vault, and flew off to the Caribbean. One minute she was married, the next divorced, and the next meeting her new husband and marrying him.

Milo had been positive that getting so much money, the things they could do with it, was worth what they would have to go through. But two years was itself a kind of prison term. Although they would be able to spend occasional nights together—my God, they would go crazy otherwise—they would have to be very discreet. Her greatest fear was that the time apart would change the way they felt about each other. Not on her side, she was certain—she would always love Milo. But how could she be sure he would still feel the same way about her when the two years were up and she divorced Ralph Behr and got her settlement? How could she be sure that Milo would not have fallen in love with someone else or come to value his freedom too much to remarry her, as they had planned?

The wretched displaced feeling had returned the moment she agreed to marry Ralph Behr and relinquish the security that marriage to Milo had brought her. That same anxiety had assaulted her after the father she loved so much had gone to prison, taking with him her feeling of safety and instilling within her a raging anger at the arbitrary authority that had the power to seize him on charges he denied and at her father's business partner, who showed up each month with money he claimed was offered out of kindness toward the family of his fallen partner; her own father insinuated it was the man's ransom to remain free.

She had been only ten years old when her father had been imprisoned. Unable to express her anger or unhappiness to her mother, a pretty, quiet woman, Gail's discontent churned and expanded within her. Everyone in the neighborhood knew that her father was in prison. Some taunted her. Others merely shunned her. A few, like the grocer, were too effusive in their solicitousness. Soon, she learned to reject her schoolmates before they could reject her, parading her differences, deliberately dressing in counterculture sandals and African blouses, a single braid down her back, emphasizing what she deplored and then flaunted as the plainness of her looks. Unlike them, she was high-minded and devoted to humanistic principles.

She was not quite fifteen when she began to travel into Manhattan for rallies and volunteer efforts: the women's movement, the antiwar movement, the environmental movement, the disarmament movement. She marched on Washington, on City Hall, on everyone and every institution she perceived as threatening the helpless and downtrodden, unleashing almost indiscriminately at whatever authority she sensed was doing evil the fury she felt at the forces that had ravaged her own life. She had an inner vision of herself as a Joan of Arc or, because she had bound herself so tightly to Judaism during that period in her life—the single tie she could manage to her orthodox father—as a Judith, setting out alone with only her faith to cut down the powerful, the rich, the corrupt. Even as she kept aloof from her classmates and told herself she was morally superior to them, she knew that they did not need to prove their virtue because their fathers were not in prison.

When the time came for Gail, who was highly intelligent, to attend college, she chose New York University rather than the Ivy League college that had offered her a scholarship. In the city she could remain engaged in all her causes and study the subjects that interested her. While she flung herself into sociology and psychology and history and gradually came to focus on the condition of women, she began to study painting and found not only that it aroused her, but that to her amazement her professors considered her talented. She thrived in the cosmopolitan atmosphere of college and Manhattan. There too she had met Milo, who was a real artist and had encouraged her timid aspirations. Even after she was graduated and pursued her activism professionally, she continued to paint, stopping only when she feared that two serious painters in one family might endanger her marriage.

Although her youthful religious zeal had lessened a good deal, she continued to eschew pork and shellfish, eventually simplifying matters by becoming a vegetarian. Friday nights she lit candles at home and was surprised and delighted that Milo was enthusiastic about the candle lighting too. His own commitment to Judaism was casual, but he considered the ritual a way to honor his dead parents' memories. He had placed their photos reverently in the living room.

As time passed and she grew more certain of the miracle of being loved by Milo, Gail's life took on a serenity it had never experienced. Her anger diminished, or perhaps became funneled into those causes for which she could be most effective. Her youthful fears and insecurity faded into dim memory. Only now, like a threatening face suddenly turned on her, had she suddenly become aware that growing up with a silent, passive mother and no father, an orphan in all but name, had simply caused her fears to burrow like locusts beyond the borders of her consciousness. Now, great fortune awaiting her or no, divorce had caused the ground beneath her to shiver ominously; deep in their hidden nests, her fears rustled their wings.

In their five years together, Milo had become her refuge and buttress, allowing her, because she was no longer alone, to feel as strong as she had always tried to appear.

Last night had been awful for her: making love to Milo, she had felt like a stranger in her own bed, her own home, knowing it would be the last time she could be there for the next two years because of fear that a nosy neighbor in the building might start asking questions. All this morning she had stared at artwork they had collected and furniture she had stripped and stained. Finally, she had wandered into Milo's studio and curled against a wall to watch him paint. When he finally noticed her, the tears were streaming down her face, and he spent the rest of the time before she had to be at the Marriage License Bureau comforting her.

Now, as Gail walked down familiar streets, past little stores run by familiar tradesmen and unlikely storefront art galleries, and stopped to chat a moment with mothers she knew pushing strollers home from the park, she began to feel a lessening of the despondency and disorientation whirling within her. She glanced at her ring finger. The diamond wedding band seemed to her to glitter like a Broadway marquee denouncing her to all she passed. She dropped it into the side pocket of her shoulder bag and extracted the wedding ring Milo had given her. Wearing that again, as she had done for so many years, suddenly seemed great comfort, visible proof of their marriage's strength and continuity despite this nominal interruption.

In sight at last of the Coalition's premises, she skipped onto the curb with a smile and quickened her pace.

Soon after moving to this neighborhood, Gail had been horrified when a woman neighbor she knew had staggered into her apartment bleeding and bruised, clutching her two-year-old child to her bosom. The woman's husband had returned home drunk and had beaten her. She had escaped with her baby when he went to the bathroom. She had sensed that Gail would not be afraid to take her in.

Gail did more than shelter her. She gathered together a group of activist women, many of them artist friends, rented an empty store and began the Women's Action Coalition to help battered women. Gail obtained government funds and private grants to open a hot line and was able to hire some full-time professionals, albeit at miniscule salaries. First one and then a second "safe apartment" was rented. Battered women and their children could stay there for a month while recovering physically and emotionally, with psychological counseling, and seek residences of their own apart from their abusive male companions. Gradually, the Coalition branched out into redressing other women's problems, into rape counseling and abortion referrals, and then into neighborhood problems, such as housing and arranging for more police patrols and better street lighting to make the streets safer at night. A neighborhood newsletter was started and annual gatherings planned to instill community cohesiveness and to raise money. Gail's reputation spread. She found herself being called upon as a leader in a wider spectrum of women's issues. But her headquarters and heart were at the Coalition.

Because of the heat, the door to the Coalition's storefront office was propped open when Gail entered. A volunteer manning the hot line was seated with another woman behind the folding table along one wall. Both were stuffing envelopes with a fund-raising plea and a note changing the date of an upcoming lecture on the rights of rent-controlled tenants. Gail smiled hello as she strode to the metal desk that barred the way into the partitioned-off back rooms. A woman in her thirties sat behind it typing.

"Hi, Carla," Gail said.

"The Ford Foundation grant application," Carla explained. "If the foundations sent us just five bucks for every grant application we submitted, our money worries would be over."

Carla was Gail's best friend and lived in the same building as Gail had with Milo. She was a large, earthy woman with electrically frizzy black hair parted in the center. She wore a red halter top and patched jeans. She was a sculptor, and her small salary at the Coalition comprised nearly all her income.

"Sorry I'm late," Gail apologized.

Carla pulled the application from the typewriter and looked up. "A problem?"

Gail shook her head, not ready to discuss it yet. She had not told Carla or anyone else she was divorcing Milo, nor even confronted the problem of how she would do so. "What's been happening?"

"Lee Greenspan called. Can you be part of a panel for Women Fight Back?"

"What are they fighting back against?"

"She said it was none of my business."

"About a year ago I sat on one of her panels. She kept trying to get me to say that men's genes make them all violent. Turn her down for me, please, Carla."

A pretty black woman came out of the rear area. On her way to an evening job, she carried books in a shoulder bag. Her name was Brenda Clay, and she would be entering her senior year at NYU in the fall. She idolized Gail and had put in untold hours as a volunteer at the women's shelters.

"Catherine Rodriguez was back this morning," Brenda reported. "She was beaten up again by her husband."

Gail's brow wrinkled. "I thought family court had granted her an order of protection."

"When she tried to serve it on him at his job last night, he beat her up."

"The cops were supposed to accompany her."

"They told her they couldn't be bothered."

"Damn it!" Gail welcomed the rush of anger that assured her she was still her old self. "Did you talk to the precinct captain?"

Carla spoke up. "I did. He says no one was available."

"I want a policeman to go with Mrs. Rodriguez this afternoon," Gail ordered. "Stop off first at the station house and get someone. If you get any flak, call our lawyer right away and tell her to have the court expand the order immediately. We have to be tough about this. The cops have to know we'll go after them unless they give us the protection we're entitled to."

Gail went to her office at the very back of the premises. A few minutes later, when she was on the phone, she heard voices far louder than usual up front. As soon as she could, she extricated herself from the phone call and hurried to the front to help Carla.

A stubborn-looking young woman in a navy blue suit stood before the metal desk.

"There you are!" the young woman cried out as Gail emerged from the rear. "I'm Marilyn Watkins." She explained she was a reporter and named her newspaper. Gail grimaced: it was one of the more lurid news publications in the city.

Word had gotten out that Ralph Behr had returned to his office. Reporters had jammed the elevator and waiting areas there, but he was refusing to see them. Deciding to go after Gail, Marilyn had rushed down by cab on the chance that she would be at the Coalition, at worst hoping to track her down through co-workers.

"How long before the marriage did you know Ralph Behr?"

Carla stood up protectively in front of Gail. "This crazy woman insists you got married today to Ralph Behr, of all the guys to pick out. I told her you were already married and to get lost."

Marilyn held up an afternoon paper and prodded, "Look, you're going to have to talk to the press sooner or later. Wouldn't you rather it was someone sympathetic to your views?"

Uncharacteristically, Gail was at a loss. She glanced over at her friend, then back at the reporter. The commotion had drawn the other women as well.

"I . . . I was hoping we could keep the marriage private."

Carla was stunned. "You really *are* married to Ralph Behr! I'm your closest friend. At least you could have let me know, after all the things I've confided to *you*."

"It isn't like that. . . ." Gail began in the combative tone into which the nature of her job and her fierce sense of commitment often caused her to slip. Then, the words turned halting. "I . . . promised not to say anything. To anybody."

Marilyn moved closer to her. "Why did you divorce your husband for Ralph Behr? How did the love affair start? Did your husband know about it?"

"I . . ." Gail tried to begin once more and then could find no words. She stared first at her hurt friend and then at the reporter, whose pencil was poised implacably above a steno pad.

For the first time she understood how very public would be what she had naively assumed was simply a private arrangement that entailed periodic social appearances. She had unwittingly allowed her life to become gossip fodder.

Gail broke for the door and out onto the street. An empty cab was going by. She flagged it down and jumped in.

"Where to, ma'am?" the driver asked.

"Just drive."

They headed uptown. Gail's distress made it difficult for her to regain control of her thoughts. After a while, when she could think of nowhere else she could go, she gave the driver the address of Ralph Behr's apartment house.

Chapter 6

Ralph was on the phone in the living room when Gail was ushered in, still feeling a little numb. On the marble coffee table was the bouquet she had left in the limousine. She withdrew the diamond wedding band from her shoulder bag and, leaning over the coffee table, shoved through it the long, narrow cone formed by the violets' ribbon-wrapped stems.

Noticing her presence, Ralph stood up and gestured to a chair. He held his hand over the mouthpiece and muttered to her that he was usually not home this early, but so many reporters were trying to get into his office that work became impossible. He had slipped down the emergency stairs and caught an elevator to the basement.

Noting that he too had been dismayed by the furor their marriage had aroused, Gail conjectured that maybe they might have enough in common after all to stumble through the next two years in a kind of cooperative detachment. She looked at the bookshelves to gain a sense of his taste in books. Ralph concluded his phone call and hung up.

"These books have never been opened!" Gail exclaimed. "Even the old ones!"

She held up one volume of a leather-bound set of Dickens's works.

Ralph shrugged. "Probably. The decorator purchased them."

Surprise slid into a disdain that justified her earlier contempt for him. "One decorator just passes them on to the next, from generation unto generation, and nobody ever opens them."

Ralph smiled, purposely ignoring the sarcasm in her tone. He was still hoping to put their relationship on a more amiable and thus less troublesome basis. "Most people who can afford to buy books that look like that are too busy to read. Let me show you around."

He stopped, noticing what she had done with the diamond wedding band. "Look, if you don't like it, don't wear it. When

118

we're divorced, you can sell it. But at least be discreet enough until then not to let the servants know how you feel."

She nodded and dropped both the flowers and the wedding band into her shoulder bag before following him out.

A library, billiard room, dining room, kitchen and servant's quarters made up the rest of the floor. Ralph confided that the dining and billiard rooms were the only two he visited very much, the former infrequently because he ate out so often. He had made good pocket money hustling pool in college. The strategy and subtle skill could still engross him completely when he wanted to clear his mind. Gail was aghast at the kitchen, huge and ultramodern in design: black and dark red, stainless-steel appliances. A staff of three were waiting there to serve dinner: cook, maid, and the butler, Deighton, whom she had already met.

"Well, that's it," Ralph declared as he led her out of the softly lit dining room. "At least the first floor." He gallantly corrected himself. "Your home now too."

"And what's upstairs?"

"A bunch of bedrooms and bathrooms. Pool. Gym."

Gail's expression darkened. Her body tilted forward as she steamed toward the stairs and up to the top floor like a destroyer into high, rough seas.

"You really do have a pool!" Gail stared in disbelief at the white tile and marble room with Ionic columns that opened, through sliding glass doors, onto a fully equipped gym on one side and a wide terrace on the other. Tables and chairs were grouped at one side of the pool.

"I wouldn't get to exercise enough otherwise," he explained.

"So you just snapped your fingers on the eighth day and created a pool up here."

He looked askance at her. "Do you have any idea how much it costs to build support for the weight of that much water this high up?"

"Do you get the feeling we're not on the same wavelength?"

Ralph led her along the corridor past the pool and exercise room to the other side of the floor. The second bedroom was hers.

"If you don't like the way it looks, you can have it redone."

Gail gazed around the large room: wide bed with a modern cream-colored headboard; a very wide chest of drawers; TV, stereo, and other electronic devices built into the matching cream-colored wall unit beside it; thick powder blue carpet;

pastel shades of velvet on modern armchairs grouped around a parson's desk at the far end of the room; dressing room adjacent to a marble bathroom; indirect lighting. Handsome but impersonal, she thought. This could be anybody's bedroom. Maybe if I put some interesting prints on the walls. Maybe curtains instead of those thin metallic blinds.

She walked to the window, overwhelmed by the luxury of so much space to herself, space that continued outward beyond, widening into a park now edged in red-gold. "It's fine," she said turning back. "There might be a couple of things I'll want to change once I move in."

"Your clothes are already put away. I sent the chauffeur for your luggage this afternoon."

She opened the nearest top drawer of the chest. Her panties were carefully folded by color in several piles. Next to them her bras had been placed in a large clear-plastic envelope, beside one for her stockings. Scarves in the next drawer. Sweaters in two others. Then nightgowns. She had never been that neat in her own home.

"Look, all this was very nice of you," she said without animosity in her tone for the first time. "To take care of it for me, I mean."

"If you need anything, just ring for Edie, the maid. She'll get it for you."

Gail nodded.

"Or tap on the door." He opened the door on the opposite wall from the bathroom. "My bedroom is in here. I figured because of the servants we ought to have adjoining bedrooms, so I had a door put in."

He had explained to the servants that he and his new bride kept such unpredictable hours that adjoining bedrooms made more sense than one bedroom for both.

Gail examined the door. "There's no lock on it."

"I figured a lock would look pretty suspicious to the servants."

He strode to the electronic wall-unit beside her bureau, not noticing the fury building up behind her eyes. "All the best equipment," he pointed out. "If there's any record you want, any videotape, just call that phone number there, and they'll deliver any hour of the day or night."

He sat down on the edge of the bed. "Look, Gail, now that we're finally alone it gives me the chance to say something I've been wanting to tell you all day. If we're going to live together for two years, at least we should try to get along—you know, get to know each other a little bit, so we can relate like a husband and wife."

Gail exploded. "You really are a contemptible creep! Get out of here!" Gail grabbed Ralph's arm and pulled him up. She pushed him roughly through the doorway between the bedrooms. "You can get to know whomever you want and do whatever slimy relating you want in your *own* bedroom, but don't you dare ever open this door or set foot again in mine!"

"Are you crazy? If you were the last woman on earth—"

He never finished the sentence. The door slammed in his face.

Imagine that plain-looking bitch even thinking that he wanted her! he fumed. He had a good mind to charge back in there and tell her off. But she'd probably get too much satisfaction out of his bursting in. Then she could say it proves again how low he is, coming back to rape her or something like that.

He spun around and stalked to the center of his bedroom. What a miserable woman! He had acted with utter politeness and cordiality toward her, under the most vexing circumstances. For her part she had jumped to misconstrue his every word. Well, his goodwill was at an end. From now on she was just a necessary piece of furniture around here, like a chair or a table. In two years, he would be able to redecorate and clear her out.

Then he noticed that someone, the maid probably, he reasoned, had thoughtfully turned back the blanket and top sheet on both sides of his bed. After all, this was their wedding night, and the servants logically assumed they would be sleeping together. He made a mental note to mess up the other side of the bed before he left in the morning.

Gail's anger had not abated when she joined him in the dining room for supper. "Half a dozen families could live like kings here."

Ralph circled the table to his place opposite Gail. "If they can afford it, they can have it. That's the incentive to be rich."

"Ralph Behr, the embodiment of the American dream: rich boy makes good. A lot of people have trouble just paying the rent and groceries."

"We can get into that some other time. I gave at the office."

The maid entered with a tray. She placed cups of soup in front of Gail and Ralph.

"I gather the apartment meets with your approval?" Ralph asked in a tone that was far more amiable toward Gail than he was feeling.

"Did you pick the painting?" She gestured toward a modern French street scene on the wall above the buffet. She considered the style mannered and unfelt, cranked out to ensnare the untutored eye.

"I found it in a store in Paris. The owner said the guy was going to be big."

"Big? He could wallpaper the world."

"I liked the colors. Bright. The decorator picked out the other paintings, mostly put up things that went with the color scheme. To tell you the truth, if you had asked me what was on the walls in any of the rooms I couldn't tell you."

"That's what they look like."

Ralph smiled joylessly. "I can see tact is going to be your strong point."

Gail was seething. "You may find this difficult to believe, but thousands of artists live on the hope that someone like you will come along with empty walls and buy the work they've created out of the fibers of their soul."

"I buy what I like."

"Someone with your money has an obligation to educate your taste in art and *then* buy work you like because it's good and expresses something significant. Did you ever take an art-history course or spend any time in museums?"

"Bores me to death."

"What excites you?"

"Business. Building things. Negotiating. Winning. And sports—watching them, but more often playing them. My race horses winning. Movies once in a while—a good comedy."

The maid magically appeared to whisk everything into the kitchen as soon as the spoons were laid beside the soup cups.

"What excites *you?*" Ralph asked.

"Helping people in trouble. That excites me a lot. Art. Dance. Books. Time with my friends. Cooking for them. Good conversation. Movies too, but I'm sure not the same ones as you."

Deighton entered carrying broiled steaks on a silver tray. Right behind him was the maid with a tray of assorted vegetables.

He offered the tray to Gail, who inquired, "Would anyone be offended if I didn't have steak?"

"Is something wrong with the steak, ma'am? Perhaps you'd like it well done."

"No, I'm sure it's fine. I just don't eat meat."

"Would you like Cook to make you something else?"

"No, the vegetables will be fine."

She took full helpings of the vegetables. Ralph put a steak on his plate and a few peas he would probably not eat.

"Red meat will kill you—" she commented as the door closed behind the last servant out of the room.

"Hell, I live on the thin edge."

"—and in less than two years if I'm lucky."

Ralph had asked Jeff to come by with some legal papers that would be delivered after Ralph left the office. Gail and Ralph were just leaving the dining room when he arrived. Waiting in the lobby were friends with whom he was going off for the evening.

"I didn't want to bother you. I figured you two would want to spend some time getting acquainted."

"I'd be safer spending time with Jack the Ripper," Gail snapped and turned for the stairs.

Ralph stared after her in fury. "Jeff, bring up your friends. I'm in the mood to party."

The glass doors between the pool and the terrace had been opened. Deighton was serving drinks and Edie hors d'oeuvres to the three people with Jeff. Rock music pounded out of the sound system at full volume. Ralph leaned against the open door to the outer corridor and smiled happily at Jeff, who stood uncomfortably beside a well-dressed young woman.

"Gail said she was tired and wanted to sleep," Jeff reminded his older brother. "Maybe this isn't the best time for a party."

Ralph ignored him. "Introduce me to your friend."

"Maggie Stanhope. My brother, Ralph Behr."

Maggie Stanhope was a tall crisp-looking blonde, a type Jeff knew his brother favored. He had not intended for them to meet. He was crazy about Maggie and for months had been trying without success to attract her interest. He didn't need her attention diverted to his brother. Ralph wouldn't try to steal her, he knew, but she was promiscuous as a cat and might well want him.

"Ralph just got married, you know," Jeff interjected, his gaze fixed on Maggie, hoping to note a flagging of her interest in Ralph.

"That's right!" Ralph called out to others. "Tonight's my wedding night." He lifted his champagne glass. "A toast to my wedding!"

A figure in a dressing gown appeared in the doorway.

"What timing!" Ralph declared. "The little woman herself."

123

Gail glared at him. "I've been trying to get to sleep, but this noise makes it very difficult."

"Did our wedding night wear you out?" he replied with mock solicitude. He winked exaggeratedly to his audience.

Jeff spoke up. "Maybe we better go."

"The party is just getting started. Champagne for my queen." He began walking around the pool toward Deighton. "Just the pick-me-up she needs. And oysters, Deighton. Plenty of oysters. But I don't know how much more my poor body can take."

Embarrassed, Jeff nodded for Maggie to move off.

"Look, I'm sorry about this," he said to Gail in a low voice when they were alone. "Ralph insisted I bring everybody up."

Perhaps her inclination toward the underdog was influencing her, Gail thought, but this morning she had felt sympathy and liking for Jeff, who had tried so hard to please Ralph. "I imagine it isn't easy having him for a brother."

"He's a great guy, he really is. But he's used to getting his way."

"Particularly where you're concerned?"

Jeff glanced sharply at her and then off toward Ralph. "I know this . . . this arrangement isn't your idea. Ralph does too."

"Funny how I believe the sincerity from you and not from him."

"Let me do my best to clear everyone out so you can get some sleep. Give me about fifteen minutes."

She smiled. "Thanks."

Gail disappeared back down the corridor, and Jeff went over to cajole Ralph into letting the party end.

Ralph had joined Jeff's friends. A man in jeans and silk shirt was showing a fantastically thin wristwatch, a recent purchase at Cartier, to a young woman dressed in purple who was puzzling over which of seven parties and events listed in her appointment book they should drop in on first this evening.

Maggie Stanhope, christened Margaret Garrett Stanhope, had moved to the side of the room and was pondering her own problems. Her allowance had been cut off by her social-register family months earlier, after they read one too many stories about the dissolute disco crowd in New York in which her name had been prominently mentioned. It was a life she was reluctant to give up, but clearly could not afford to continue under present circumstances. She owed her landlord three months' rent, and he was threatening to evict her. Bloomingdale's and a slew of other retailers had long since cut off her credit and were now threatening to sue for what she owed them. The telephone company—God, what would she do without a phone?—had given her only three more days to pay up or lose her service. She had danced all the way to the end of her lifeline and now needed a way to make a lot of money fast and steadily. She had studied business at college, but had no marketable skills or employment record to adduce her qualifications for a high-paying job. With her extensive contacts, the answer was obviously to go into business for herself, and she had been trying to think of a business that could yield high profits quickly, but her lack of capital was an obstacle.

For personal and financial reasons, she would like to have aroused Ralph Behr's interest, but she had not and probably no amount of trying on her part would change that. His brother Jeff, however, was a different matter. Jeff was obviously infatuated with her, always hanging around her, always confiding in her, particularly his trials with his demanding brother, but she had not paid much attention. She liked strong, rich men. Jeff wasn't particularly strong and, although he doubtless earned a very high salary, didn't seem to have much capital of his own. Yet, observing the two brothers now in conversation together and remembering some of the things Jeff had told her triggered an idea, a way to repair what at present was her very precarious future.

As they left Ralph's building, Maggie took Jeff's arm and suggested they leave the others. Perhaps they could have a look at that brownstone he had recently told her his brother had criticized him for failing to rent.

"But, my God, Maggie, a whorehouse!"

Jeff had shown her through the building. Only now, as they stood once more in the dimly lit entrance hall, did she reveal her scheme.

"It would be the perfect tenant for you. High rent, higher than anyone else would ever pay you, and there'd be no other tenants in the building, so no one would complain. The place is perfect. All those bedrooms. I could be in operation in a few days."

"Hey, you're talking gangsters and pimps and long jail-sentences."

"I'd hire only beautiful young women, not professionals, aspiring actresses and dancers who'd work here two or three nights a week to make enough to keep them well-fixed and able to pursue their careers. I can think of half a dozen right now who'd jump at the chance if they were sure the men were the right sort. Do you know what we could charge for girls like those? I'd run it like IBM: strict business rules for the girls' behavior, marketing, security, financial controls." Maggie's enthusiasm grew as she visualized what she would create here. "The brass plaque outside would say this was a design firm, and that's exactly what it would say on the lease, so you'd be protected. The reception area would be here and have a desk with someone to greet people and answer the phone and make certain we knew the men before we allowed them into the salon."

"The salon?"

Maggie took Jeff's hand and drew him into the center of the first-floor space. "Here. I could furnish it well enough from department stores in a few days to get started. The look would be simple: large modern furniture, grays and whites and blacks. I could finish the decorating after we were in operation and had the cash flow." Her eyes glittered in the dim light. "Only the finest clients. They'd know the girls here would be beautiful and elegantly dressed and always act like ladies. They could count on our being discreet. Diplomats who needed escorts, corporate executives in town for the evening. Sometimes the girls would go to them or the men could come here. They could always drop in and find a girl who appealed to them and take her upstairs to our suites or out for the evening first. They'd know that our girls were clean and would never embarrass them at dinner or a club."

"I don't like the sound of that 'our.' "

Maggie stood very close to Jeff, her breasts just brushing against his shirt. "No one would ever know you're my partner. Every month we'd share the profits. I'd take credit cards and checks from the steady clients, made out to the design firm, but you'd always get your own share in cash, so there'd be no record of paying you. Think of the kind of money a place like this would bring in." She moved closer, her lips nearly brushing his. "Think of all those gorgeous women working for you. And you could have any of them. You'd be a king with your own harem."

"Jesus!" He hesitated. "There are too many risks."

"The only risk I see is that your brother, Ralph, will continue to belittle you for not finding a tenant for this building. Say yes to me, put up a bit of capital—I could get most of the stuff on credit—and you'd knock him over with the kind of rent you'd be getting for this white elephant. If he had thought of it first, believe me this place would already be a fuck palace. But he didn't, you did. The guys who make it are the guys who can ride the risk and make it carry them where they want to go. I get weak in the knees for them every time."

Her hands wandered purposefully to his crotch.

He tried to think. Everything drew him to her reasoning. "We intend to build here," he declared. "As soon as I give you notice the lease is canceled, you're out, understood?"

"Whatever you say, Jeff."

She slid down his zipper and slipped her hand into the fly. "Just as long as it's yes."

Chapter 7

Heshy Rubin had been standing on the sidewalk outside Behr House since six in the morning waiting for Ralph Behr to arrive for work. Oblivious to him, pedestrians pushed past and around him as if he were a buoy in one of the swift waterways that separated this island from mainland. Heshy was a short, rotund man just past fifty with a habit when he was nervous of running a hand through his thinning hair, as if checking for loss. He had dressed with particular care this morning: black and white hound's-tooth-checked jacket with sharply angled lapels, white tie and shirt, black mohair pants, and pointed patent-leather shoes with tassels. He was a habitual smoker but, so as not to antagonize Ralph Behr with a mound of cigarette butts on the sidewalk, took care to extinguish each stub by walking to the corner and flipping it through the sewer grating.

Heshy was a commercial real-estate broker whose luck had been running bad. All his life he had scrambled in the small-time end of the business—finding tenants for small stores and offices—but he had not closed a deal in almost two years. His old firm had dropped him, and six months later he had had to run out on the rent for the hole-in-the-wall office he had sublet. Even his poker skill, which had always seen him over the rough periods, had deserted him. He owed everyone. At one time he had felt he was only a deal or two away from holding this whole town in the palm of his hand, but now he felt like a cockroach scurrying along the streets without hope of finding cover from these buildings that were stomping him to death.

You had to be born rich, with every opportunity, to get the best of this place, he had thought despondently as he lay on the sofa at his girlfriend's apartment, reading a gushing newspaper article about Behr's whirlwind courtship and marriage: you had to be a Ralph Behr. At that instant Heshy was struck by the greatest idea he ever had, an idea that could turn everything around for him. But in order not to be cut out of the deal, it was essential that he see Ralph Behr personally. The problem was that Behr would not recognize his name and thus would not take his telephone call. So he had to stake out the building where Behr's offices were located. Sooner or later, he would get a chance to speak to him.

This morning, however, a water-main break several blocks north had caused traffic to detour and Ralph's driver to let him off at a side entrance. Even when Heshy knew that Ralph must already have arrived by another entrance, he continued to wait. Perhaps Behr might come out for lunch or an appointment. He had to speak to Ralph Behr directly. This single idea was his only prospect, all he had left to sell.

Ralph's first phone call that morning was from Earl Peters, the head of Peters and Patterson, a large ad agency. Ralph had served with him on a fund-raising committee and had had dinner with him once to discuss the potential for selling condos by means of TV. This was tourist season, and the hotels were full. Peters had an important client coming into town for an ad presentation and needed a hotel room for him. Ralph had Myra check their hotels and five minutes later called back to confirm a room. "Only for you, Earl."

The same thing happened twice more with other acquaintances before nine o'clock. He had set a policy of holding out three rooms until noon at each hotel. It racked up a lot of favors.

Next, Ralph phoned several key people in the city administration, offering to undertake major renovation on a dilapidated subway station near the office building he was rehabilitating in the financial district. Ralph was prepared to donate funds and his construction skill for the renovation in return for the city agreeing that he could move the station's entrance from across the street to what he could frankly maintain was a much safer location: within the retail concourse of his building. That would guarantee a lot of subway riders walking past the shops and allow Ralph to charge the retail tenants higher rent.

Ralph's first meeting of the morning was with his executive vice president, Ben Rogovin, to go over a deal to buy the building next door to their rehab. Ralph did not think anything would come of it. The sellers were not yet desperate enough to take the price he was offering, but anything higher made little sense, considering the glut of office space hitting the financial area now. However, if he could arrange the subway-station relocation, he could extend the retail concourse into that adjacent building and thus increase the building's value. A higher price would then be justified.

Ralph enjoyed chewing over the deals with Ben, who took the same pleasure he did in analyzing pitfalls and devising strategies, in the twists and turns of the negotiations, in besting the other guy with brains and bluff and timing. He paid Ben a lot, but you had to pay for a guy of his caliber who wasn't ever going to own a piece of the business.

Some developers negotiated like guerrilla fighters, always trying to slip behind the enemy's lines to grab more contractual territory, battling to the death over every point, setting traps in the contracts that would provide grounds for later attacks in court. Ralph was far more pleasant to deal with, but for all his charm and good humor, no less fierce than those more obvious marauders. Maybe every man for himself wasn't the way it should be, but that was the way he knew it was.

Ralph had a compulsion to make deals. He saw opportunities everywhere and was addicted to the action and to feeding his hunger for increase, but he was disciplined in calculating the risks. He entered only into deals that provided him with some edge. Often that edge was simply his confidence in being able to create the favorable factors necessary for success, to evaluate the risks differently, and to envision possibilities lesser developers could not. Huge numbers did not intimidate him if they totaled correctly on the bottom line; they made the game fun.

Jeff knocked on the open doorway. "You got a minute?"

Rogovin gathered his papers. "We were just finishing up."

Jeff took the chair that Rogovin vacated.

"You look excited." Ralph remarked. "How were all those parties last night?"

"Terrific." The unexpected reference to the previous night momentarily disconcerted Jeff, and he had to concentrate to remember the phraseology he had rehearsed. "Ralph, remember yesterday you and I were talking about the brownstone. Well, I think I have a tenant for it. A European design firm. I've been working on it for a while, but didn't want to tell you until it looked probable."

"How much?"

"Ten thousand a month. It comes to over forty dollars a square foot."

"That's great. How good is the tenant's credit?"

"I'm checking into that. One thing I made clear. This lease is strictly short term. We can cancel at any time."

"Great going."

Ralph was genuinely pleased with him, Jeff could tell, and began to breathe easier. He stood up. He didn't want to give Ralph time to think up other questions. "I've got the broker on the phone in my office."

"Triple-net lease?" Ralph asked as Jeff walked toward the doorway.

"What? Oh, definitely. They pay all the operating expenses, taxes, and insurance."

Jeff stopped in the doorway. Ralph's eyes were fixed on some papers before him, his mind already elsewhere and Myra buzzing his intercom to brief him on his schedule for the day. "Don't forget," she reminded Ralph, "you've got to be at the reception for the mayor tonight."

Jeff slipped away.

"Damn!" Ralph remembered. "I agreed to raise funds for something or other for the city." He couldn't miss this. The mayor was antagonistic enough toward him and his family as it was. "You'd better get, uh . . . Gail for me."

"Would you happen to have her phone number?"

"Why would I have her number?" he answered without thinking.

Myra began to track down Mrs. Ralph Behr a/k/a Gail Benedict. A few minutes later she buzzed Ralph again to let him know his wife was on the phone.

Ralph closed his door, manufacturing a shy smile for Myra as he did so, and picked up the phone.

"What is it?" Gail demanded to know after his hello.

"Lovely to speak to you again too," Ralph replied with an equivalent amount of belligerence. "The servants told me the blushing bride took breakfast in her room this morning. Might have looked a little more appropriate if the happy couple had eaten their first breakfast together."

"Coffee and juice was all I could stomach."

"I hope your health improves during the day. I've got some bad news for you. The bride's presence is also required tonight. An important function. Six thirty. The mayor and a lot of top people will be there. And everyone will want to meet you."

"I've got a previous appointment. Tell them I had a headache."

"And be driven out of town by the snickering."

"Bad choice of illness," she admitted.

"I've got to be there, so you've got to be there. It would look funny if I showed up alone so soon after the wedding. I'll make a deal with you. We should be finished fairly early. Then you can go on to your other appointment."

He told her the time he would pick her up at the apartment and that he expected her to be dressed well. "And that doesn't mean the jeans are freshly laundered."

"How I dress is my own business."

She hung up. He expected the worst.

Ralph rushed home from a late meeting to pick up Gail only a few minutes before the mayor's reception was to begin.

Edie, the maid, was at the door, bubbling over about something in the living room! He followed her in and was confronted by mounds of open gift boxes displaying silver and crystal bowls, trays, candlesticks, goblets, and much more.

"What is this stuff?" he demanded to know.

"Why, your wedding presents. They've been coming all day."

"Oh, shit!" he moaned and went upstairs. He knocked at Gail's door.

"Come in," she called out.

He opened the door to find her standing in front of the mirror that extended above the width of the double chest of drawers, brushing out her long chestnut-brown hair. She was wearing an embroidered peasant blouse with short, puffy sleeves and a wide skirt.

"Why aren't you dressed? We've got to leave in a couple of minutes."

She turned on him in a fury. "This is the best outfit I own. Boy, I knew I could count on you for an insult."

"That's it? That's what you intend to wear?"

"Do you know what this blouse cost me in Yugoslavia?"

"You overpaid. Look, we're not going to visit Marshal Tito's tomb. This is for grown-up American people wearing normal dress-up clothes. I would have let you know if they were going to have square dancing."

She glared at him. "This is how I dress. This is what I wear."

He turned away and began to close the door. "I'll make up some excuse for you."

"Oh, no." She charged to the door and swung it back open. "It occurred to me after we spoke on the phone that this is my chance to corner the mayor. I've been trying to get some action from City Hall for four months."

"You get to the mayor on your own. Don't use my connections for your nonsense. I've got a business to run."

"You're not cutting me out of this."

She strode by him down the corridor.

"Maybe I can find you a hoe and a wheelbarrow," he remarked as he followed her, "and you can recruit him into the 4-H Club."

Gail halted and turned. "I happen to be pretty well known on my own. And I'll be damned if I'm going to change who I am for you."

He tried to control his own anger and appear reasonable. "You're going to stick out there. Our incompatibility will stick out. That's not something either of us wants." He took a deep breath. "Can we call a cease-fire to this war, Gail? We have to be together for another two years. I don't care what you wear, only whether it reflects badly on me or makes people wonder about our marriage. Believe me, if you want bloody warfare for two years, I'm a master at that."

"No, I don't," she conceded. "I've got more important things to do, and I suppose you must also. All right, a cease-fire."

It seemed appropriate to shake hands, so they did, and that seemed childish, so they both chuckled self-consciously and headed toward the stairs.

The reception for donors to the City Betterment Fund was held at Gracie Mansion, now handsomely restored to its historical beauty. Staying out of the spotlight was not something to which Ralph had ever devoted much practice, and he found it especially difficult with so many people wanting to meet his new wife. Women in elegant dresses were gliding into the room, and here he was with a woman who looked like something out of National Geographic. He intended to beat a hasty retreat just as soon as the mayor appeared and he had paid his respects.

Morris Weitzman took the cigar from his mouth with one hand and stuck out the other for Gail to shake. A rough-and-tumble real-estate developer in his sixties, he had built his empire on the foundation of a family flooring and drywall business that supplied many of the city's general contractors.

"He's arrogant and too big for his breeches," Morris began with an affectionate glance over at Ralph, "but you've got to know all that by now. He's also a hell of a kid. Congratulations."

Ralph made the introduction. He liked Morris and disregarded the griping he occasionally heard that Morris was never satisfied, no matter how much he had amassed. Ralph had always found Morris a straight shooter. Making money was the point of doing business. Hell, he himself was no different. No businessman worth a damn was.

Weitzman pinched Ralph's cheek and turned back to Gail. "I first met this guy when his father was building an apartment project in Fort Lee, and he walks in to tell me I've got to cut the price on a drywall subcontracting job I'm halfway finished on. Right?" Ralph laughed and nodded. "I mean he wasn't more than twenty-two, twenty-three, and he walks right in and practically demands I cut the price. Remember what the mid-seventies were like in this business? Rents are going to drop, he tells me, and all the subcontractors are going to have to cut their prices fifteen percent or he's closing down the job. What a kid!"

"You still made a good profit," Ralph remarked.

Morris winked at Gail. "I always make a good profit."

Gail spoke up. "A friend was on the committee when you were converting the Crofton Hotel to an office building. You were supposed to submit plans to restore the old lobby for their approval. Instead your people came in on a Sunday and just ripped it out."

Weitzman raised a finger. "We were only in discussions. Nothing had been finalized."

"You were the only one at that table who thought there wasn't an agreement," Gail rejoined with some heat. "You already knew you were going to make millions from that office building. You had a duty to spend a few thousand dollars extra to keep that beautiful old lobby as it was."

Weitzman closed his eyes and slapped his cheek in mock dismay. "A do-gooder!" He glanced shrewdly at the other man. "Ralph, my boy, you're going to have a hell of an interesting marriage."

Others were now crowding around Ralph and Gail to offer their congratulations, and Gail soon felt herself tossed about by the tumult. Developers, industrialists, architects, broadcasting executives, financiers, lawyers—lots of lawyers. So many people that she could not keep track of, much less converse with. She recognized some of the faces and many of the names and found it appalling that they were all eager to ingratiate themselves with Ralph Behr. She was right about these money-grasping, mover-shaker types: They were all "You scratch my back and I'll scratch yours"—no integrity, no character, no values. Her own friends seemed doubly precious to her.

The mayor was tall and easy to spot when he entered the room. Plagued by corruption scandals like many others before him, the mayor was working hard to build goodwill.

Ralph had shifted from a brief conversation with a black state assemblyman to one with a labor leader who was head of the construction trades council. Ralph had made it a policy to separate himself from direct dealings with the unions by always subcontracting all of his construction work. But, again, keeping open the lines of communication never hurt. Ralph failed to notice that the mayor had greeted his way through the people between them. Just as he turned away to seek him, Ralph heard a memorable New York City accent at his side.

"I understand congratulations are in order, Ralph," the mayor said, beaming at Gail with practiced avuncularity.

"Thanks, yes, Mr. Mayor. Perhaps you know Gail."

"I'm delighted, Gail," the mayor said. "May I kiss the bride?" He leaned down and pecked at her cheek.

"This is a momentous time in your life, Ralph—marriage, huge project. I hope the project is in the city's best interests."

"No doubt of that. Blighted area. But the zoning, everything, is already favorable. Nothing about it should trouble you."

"I'm the mayor. Let me be the judge of what troubles me." A broad hem of dislike seemed sewn around the mayor's words. "The deputy mayor tells me you talked to his people today about fixing up the subway station near a building you're doing."

"Do you know that station? It's dark, full of crime, falling apart. I wanted to clean it up—not just for my project, but for the neighborhood."

The mayor eyed Ralph skeptically. "Just a good Samaritan?"

"My gesture makes good business sense," Ralph rejoined frankly. He judged that the time was right to force into the open an issue that had increased the animosity between them. The Behrs had been heavy contributors to the mayor's unsuccessful opponent. "I hope you can understand that despite the great respect I have for you, loyalty to an old friend meant we had to back him in the mayoral race."

"Certainly. And I hope you can respect my own loyalty, which goes back a great deal further."

Months would pass before Ralph would come to comprehend what he meant.

The mayor turned to Gail, good humor back in his expression. "Speaking of what troubles me, I can testify as a result of personal experience that this little lady is going to give you quite a bit of trouble from now on. She does me. I understand you're hounding my people regarding something new."

"More foot patrolmen," Gail replied.

"Everyone always wants more police."

"We've worked up comparative figures that demonstrate the need. Violent street crime has jumped in a couple of areas in our district more quickly than most places in the city—assault, robbery, rape—but it's been dropping where there's a higher percentage of street cops."

"Tell you what, I'm a fair man—any honest person in this city will tell you that. I'll have someone meet with you to look at your figures. If they prove your case, we'll allocate more of the new rookies to your area. What could be fairer than that?"

"Thanks. We really need it." Used to prolonged hand-to-hand combat against the city bureaucracy for every inch of ground, Gail was honestly astounded by the mayor's receptivity. She knew that being here, with Ralph Behr, had a lot to do with it—a by-product of the token favors, like trinkets or small hostess gifts, that powerful people accorded each other for what to them were minor matters. But she had also glimpsed the mayor's enmity toward her new husband.

"He doesn't like you very much, does he?" Gail asked Ralph with undisguised glee when the mayor had moved on to chat with other guests.

"Let's go."

"Not yet. We just arrived. I'm beginning to enjoy myself. What does the mayor have against you?"

Ralph had no objection to telling her what was commonly rumored anyway. "It goes back to the old days in Brooklyn, when the mayor was just starting out in politics. I don't know exactly. My father says it happened because he backed his opponent in some local race. All I know is there's an old grudge."

"And now that he's mayor you and your family are on the outside."

"Working my way back in. Sooner or later we'll need each other." In explanation he waved his hand at the group around

135

them. "But he doesn't want to make it easy. The deputy mayor he mentioned doesn't make it any easier either. A young guy with a big ego. Wants to show that he can put it to Ralph Behr."

"And can he?"

Ralph's voice registered disdain. "It's like going one on one with a dwarf. I've beaten him hands down without half trying every time. Once I had to take him to court to get what was coming to me from the city, and the city lost on every point. You probably read about it. But the mayor still backs him, so I try not to antagonize him."

"Sounds like he must be doing all right if he's getting under your skin like that." She was enjoying what she supposed was Ralph's discomfiture. "Is he here?"

Ralph scanned the room and then nodded toward the far corner. As Gail spun around to follow his gaze, he noticed the two people who were talking to the deputy mayor. One was Lorna Garrison. The other was Simon Kramer.

"You said you had another appointment," Ralph muttered and began to steer her toward the entrance past a new group of well-wishers. His peripheral vision caught sight of Lorna as she separated from her companions and cut across the room to block his progress. Ralph could not avoid her. The innocent expression pasted around her fixed smile presaged unpleasantness.

"Lorna Garrison, I'd like you to meet Gail Benedict or . . . Gail Behr, rather."

"I'm surprised you two haven't decided what name she'll take," Lorna said with exaggerated concern. Her smile widened.

"Either one will do fine," Gail replied warily.

"She's cute, Ralph," Lorna said to him after a moment's appraisal. "But I was hoping you had outgrown 'cute.' I suppose it's still the Brooklyn in you."

Gail smiled—this Lorna had picked the wrong woman to try that stuff on. She raised her own voice so that those nearby would be sure to hear. "You must still be carrying a torch for Ralph. How sad! Perhaps you should seek professional help. They say a psychiatrist can do wonders for depression from unrequited love. So nice meeting you."

Gail yanked Ralph's arm along with her and out of the room.

"You were dynamite!" he exclaimed as they strode out of Gracie Mansion and toward their car.

"Going out with her sure doesn't say much for your taste!"

"What do you mean? She's a very attractive woman."

"If you like sleeping with a black widow spider. You must be blind, Ralph. That woman is a killer."

"View the situation from her standpoint. With no warning I suddenly announced I was marrying you."

Gail stopped to face him. "You mean you were actually serious about her? Ha! A hundred million dollars doesn't even come close to what you owe me!"

By the time they reached the parked limousine, they were recounting the incident and laughing. Ralph helped her in.

"You know, all the time we were there," she observed, "no one ever once mentioned the good of the city."

"What's that?"

"Are you really that callous and selfish?"

"What I meant was who the hell knows what's good for the city? Give away too much to the poor, the city sinks back into insolvency, like in the seventies. Put limits on rents or raise taxes too high, no new buildings go up and business and people leave the city. For all your liberal sympathies, I'll bet if the city tried to take too much from you and give it to the poor, you'd holler bloody murder."

"Some of us have a sense of social responsibility. We're a single human race on a single planet."

"That kind of sentimental thinking will get you nowhere." Ralph did not wish to pursue a discussion that would lead inevitably to argument. "You said you had another appointment. Where?"

"A little gallery is exhibiting some friends' work. They're having an opening-night party."

"That's a public kind of event. The press may be there. It seems to me something you and I should attend together."

"They're mostly all friends."

Ralph had grown enthusiastic. "It might be a fun evening. Besides, you knocked my taste in pictures. Educate me."

"All right," she grudgingly agreed. "Just one thing. Can we park his thing around the corner from the gallery? I've been putting off explaining our marriage to my friends. This . . . this locomotive won't help. I don't think they'll understand."

Ralph had punched a number into the car telephone. As he waited for the other party to answer, he turned to her with some thorniness in his tone.

"If you want your friends to get the impression that you think you're slumming, that you don't consider them good enough to visit in the kind of car they have to assume we travel in . . . Get

137

used to it, babe. This is the life other people would sell their souls for."

Ralph turned abruptly to the phone with an apology. Something had just come up, he said, that prevented him from meeting the other man for dinner.

Gail watched him as he spoke—dark blue suit, rich as sin, a yahoo when it came to art—and was overcome with dread about the evening ahead.

The gallery was a basement Ralph would have missed if Gail had not been with him—she rushed from the limousine before it came to a stop, to separate herself from it. When he reached the bottom of the old iron stairs and entered the gallery, Ralph could not find Gail among the many people who filled the simple room, brick walls painted white and the ceiling a web of plumbing and track lighting painted black. Not knowing anyone and this being an art gallery, Ralph figured the appropriate thing for him to do was look at the art. A large painting beside the door accosted him with clashing colors and maimed body parts. He stepped forward to read the card beside it. *Odalisque 1*, it read. The next painting, much like it, was titled *Odalisque 2*. In fact, he noticed, all the paintings along this wall appeared very similar and seemed to bear that Odalisque title.

"This guy has an S and M problem," Ralph commented to a man standing beside him observing *Odalisque 2*.

"Cosmara is a genius!" the man spat back, taking his eyes off the painting only long enough to fling a look of contempt at Ralph.

Ralph moved along. A woman stood with a notebook and pencil at the end of the row, in front of *Odalisque 7*.

"They say he's a genius," Ralph remarked.

She laughed deprecatingly. "He confused actual space, virtual space, and historical context so badly it's a joke. He should be painting houses."

The adjacent wall bore even more jarring paintings by several other artists, and Ralph scanned them quickly. He grew more bewildered and angrier at the affront to his sensibilities as he noticed metal debris welded together and placed on stands. Just like they were sculpture, he remarked to himself. Little in Ralph's life had prepared him to assess this avant-garde art. He had occasionally visited homes where the paintings were just colors, but never were they as outrageous as here.

When he caught sight of Gail, she was talking to three women,

138

dressed more or less like she, all of whom were staring at him. Deciding he was expected to meet them, he started forward. Two immediately moved off as if he had thrown a switch. The other, a black woman, her brow furrowed, continued to speak to Gail.

Ralph stopped and turned his attention once more to all those body parts along the first wall. During this closer inspection he noticed that a couple of the paintings seemed to feature what appeared to be vaginas. He stepped nearer, not quite believing that a serious artist would paint such smut. No mistaking that shape. Sharper realism than a pornography magazine photo, he thought. Disgusted, he went to get himself a doughnut.

"Without a word to anyone!" the black woman was remonstrating with Gail. "How long have Sam and I known you and Milo? We had to read it in the paper."

"Those things are very personal," Gail responded.

"If you feel that way, why are you bothering to justify it to us now?"

"I'm not justifying it. I just want you to hear it from me. You're my friends."

The woman crossed her arms. "You used to tell me how in love you were with Milo, remember? What happened to that? If you really care what I think, Gail, I'll tell you what I think. When Ralph Behr got the hots for you, you saw your big chance and went for the money. Milo was in the way—too bad. I'm not condemning it. I might do the same thing. But don't try to tell me it has to do with anything other than pure self-interest."

Gail shrugged off her failed attempt to create an explanation that would satisfy her friend and turned away. She ought to find Ralph. It didn't look good that she was leaving him all alone in a room full of strangers. Damn! She had always steered her life unerringly toward values that mattered. Everything in her life had now become appearances.

She glanced once more at the door and then scanned the room for Ralph. It's just like at the mayor's reception, she observed as she moved to his side: here too people were eager to meet him, a few because he was famous, more because he was rich. The gallery owner understandably was one of the latter. He launched into a supercilious pitch intended to induce Ralph to buy one of the Cosmaras, preferably with the highest price tag. Feeling a responsibility for having brought Ralph here and fearful he might actually swallow the man's gobbledygook, Gail was about to step in. But Ralph was too self-confident; he simply said that he didn't know much about art, that Gail was introducing him to it, and that he wasn't ready yet to buy anything. He even remained courteous when Al and Mimi Benton came over to berate the design quality of his buildings. Gail assumed it was the closest these Marxists had ever come to a real-live capitalist.

Carla, her closest friend, joined her then. Carla stared at Ralph for a moment.

"All right, he isn't just rich, he's good-looking too. I guess that's reason enough. You're forgiven." She offered her hand to Ralph as he parted from the Bentons. "Hi, I'm Carla."

Gail listened to Ralph and Carla for several minutes. He could be ingratiating as hell, she observed, relieved that Carla had warmed to him; the two years would be a lot more bearable if her best friend could at least accept the idea of her remarriage. Perhaps her trepidation about the evening had been groundless. Carla was volunteering to explain the artwork to Ralph. Gail looked at her watch and then at the door. Still early. Having not yet congratulated Cosmara on his show, she moved off in his direction.

She recognized the commotion at the door as heralding Milo's entrance. He stirred excitement in those around him like one of those grand old touring cars pulling dust swirls into the vacuum behind it. Gail craned to catch a glimpse, her first sight of him after nearly two emotionally trying days apart.

Milo Benedict was tall and slim with dark hair that rose majestically from a high forehead and then swept outward and floated downward to his shoulders. His nose was long, but thin and well-carved and his cheekbones high and prominent, as if to accentuate the artistic nature of the man who bore them. His eyes were bright and dark, although much of his facial expression was produced by his eyebrows, which arched and dipped and knitted continually and independently of each other. His mouth—Gail adored his mouth—was as elegantly curved as a violin. He would be dressed to catch the eye, she knew, to stand out, to contrast with the sartorial inattention of many of their artist friends. She grinned when she finally drew close enough to the entrance to see him. His clothing did not disappoint her prediction: sheer salmon-colored shirt, its sleeves pushed up; black linen trousers; and the sandals he always wore in the summer.

She watched him with an indulgent smile: everything about Milo compelled attention. One hand held a glass of white wine. The other gesticulated grandly as he spoke. He was either telling a joke or making a generalization about art that dared those in his entourage to debate to him. None of them would. Instinctively, she wished she could fling a challenge at him and have one of their laughing, intellectual clashes, with each driving the other farther out on a limb until she yielded because he never would. But that would not be seemly now. She must appear genteelly disengaged and yet barely able to tolerate his presence.

Then she heard his voice deepen with contempt, "Is that great devotee of the arts, Ralph Boor himself, really here? A man has a right to meet his wife's husband."

Gail realized that he must have been drinking for some time. She rushed to head him off. "That's enough, Milo."

"Ah, my sweet heiress," he said gently. He looked about them, a playful expression gradually forming. "And there's Br'er Bear himself," he announced in a comic Southern accent.

Ralph Behr had made his way to Milo. Gail introduced them.

Milo used his own slightly greater height to stare condescendingly downward at Ralph, his accent now his own. "I have truly been looking forward to meeting you. The newspapers report that you say you like the real-estate business because it's so creative. What a wonderful choice of words! 'Creative.' Tell me—may I call you Ralph?—are you an architect?" He glanced about at those in his party, as if they were all in on a joke.

"No."

"Then on what does this creativity center?"

"I create the total conception and then implement it."

"And make all the money."

A small smile flickered at the corners of Ralph's mouth. "Which proves how creative I am." Perhaps the man was merely trying to reinforce the scenario the three of them were playing out, but Ralph saw no point in continuing this argument in front of all these people. "Sorry about what happened."

Milo seemed determined to pursue it. "Isn't the spurned husband expected to be wracked by poisonous jealousy?"

"I hope there're no hard feelings," Ralph said, maintaining the fictional posture.

Milo stared at him for several seconds and then burst into laughter. "How could there be?"

Ralph too now realized that Milo had been drinking. "I think we ought to go," he murmured to Gail.

Gail spoke softly to Milo. "There isn't any need for this. You know that."

Milo suddenly grabbed the back of her neck and pulled her face toward him. She glanced nervously about and resisted for a

141

moment, but he pulled harder, insisting, until she kissed him deeply. After a possessory stare at Gail, Milo turned back to Ralph with a nod of his head and a reassumption of the Southern drawl.

"Good night, Br'er Bear. *Au revoir*, Momma Bear."

Then, once more breaking into a throaty laugh, Milo strode past, his entourage following.

When he and Gail were in the limousine, Ralph finally spoke to her again. "We're going to keep running into both of them at these functions. Lorna has a lot of real-estate and political connections. Milo and you, I gather, have a lot of friends in common."

He nodded to his chauffeur, and the car began to move forward. "Where do you want to go for dinner? It will give us a chance to talk and get to know each other a little better. How about Le Cygne? I can give them a call, so the table will be ready when we arrive."

"Sorry. I'm meeting Milo in a few minutes. A friend's away on sabbatical this year, and Milo has the keys to his apartment."

"You mean you're going to walk out on me after I broke my dinner appointment."

"I didn't tell you to break it." She was on the edge of the seat, peering out to catch sight of the street signs.

"You're really looking forward to going to bed with that character!" Ralph observed with disbelief. "I know he was your husband, but the guy's a windbag, all show and talk."

"How could you possibly expect to understand a man like Milo?" Gail retorted hotly. "An artist, a free spirit?"

"He's a parasite."

"Parasite? He worked his way through school with a job every summer on construction and demolition crews. *You're* the parasite! Making *deals*!" She spat the word as if it were an obscenity. "Getting rich off the sweat of others who do the real work."

"Those deals put a lot of people to work. Speaking of which, from what Carla tells me, he hasn't sold a painting or had a job since you married him."

"That's none of your business!"

"A guy with talent could work in advertising as an art director and paint his own stuff at night and on weekends. At least he'd have some self-respect."

"He sure had you pegged. Money really *is* all you think about, isn't it?"

"Hey, I wasn't the one who divorced my wife for the big

142

bucks. Don't kid yourself about what money means. It makes you a hero to a lot of people. Your buddies in there, who go all weak in the knees about Michelangelo and Picasso, they sure seemed eager to meet me."

"Stop here," Gail called to the chauffeur.

The car came to a halt, and she stepped out.

"Milo shouldn't have said what he did in front of all those people," she offered Ralph with only a slight intonation of apology. "He had a little bit to drink, and his ego might have been bruised because he didn't expect you to be there . . . and didn't want his friends to get the impression—you know, because of the fast divorce and marriage—that I left him for you."

"That's the point. They're supposed to think that," Ralph grumbled, shaking his head in disbelief. "You two deserve each other."

He told the chauffeur to get going.

Despite the early-morning drizzle, Heshy Rubin had once more taken up his post at the Madison Avenue entrance of Behr House. And once more he failed to confront Ralph Behr, who again entered by a side access. He would have liked to have waited inside the lobby, but that was a sure means to get thrown out by the building's security force and then kept far away. Heshy turned up his collar and continued to stand beneath the awning, as if waiting for someone he was scheduled to meet there.

When a street peddler took up wary residence on the nearby corner, Heshy bargained the price of an umbrella from three down to two of his scarce dollars. Protected now from the rain, he ventured a dash across the street to a cigarette machine and back. Lately, his girlfriend had been on his back to stop smoking for reasons of health, but having bought the cigarettes out of the saved dollar, he felt guiltfree about smoking them.

Soon after, the rain stopped, and the sun came out. Heshy threw away the umbrella disgustedly. Two bucks down the drain.

Nothing to do but keep waiting.

"Myra," Ralph called out without looking up from a set of plans for Behr Center he had been studying. "Get Phil Rountree for me."

Phil would be in his office by now. The title problem had been in the back of Ralph's mind all night. He wanted to make sure his lawyer was solving it by buying up the adjacent parcel.

Rountree greeted him with, "I was about to call you."

"What about the parking lot?"

"The guy hasn't returned my calls. His secretary says he's out of town, but she put me on hold first before coming back on to tell me that. I've done some checking on him. He inherited a few pieces of property, bought another, and manages them. Just small buildings and that parking lot. His mother's sister was married to a Cartright and left it to him when she died."

"Phil, I've got to be downtown in a little while for a meeting with the MTA and some city-agency heads about that subway station. Give me the guy's name, address, and phone number."

"I promised I'd take care of it."

"The name and address, Phil. I'll handle it myself."

Ralph rushed out of the building so quickly that Heshy Rubin was taken by surprise. Heshy hurried after him, but the building attendant stepped into his path to block him, and the limousine pulled away from the curb before he could catch Ralph's attention. The attendant threatened to have him arrested for loitering. In better times Heshy would have slipped him twenty and been done with the annoyance, but that twenty meant too much to him right now.

"There's twenty in it for you *after* I get a chance to speak to him."

"Beat it."

Heshy moved off and lit a cigarette. He knew he would have to be careful now, perhaps stand most of the time here at the corner away from the entrance. In one way that was better. He could watch two entrances at the same time. Somehow he had to get Ralph Behr to hear what he had to say.

God, he promised, just get Ralph Behr to make this deal with me, and I'll give up smoking—forever. I swear it. All you have to do is just get him to listen to me.

He glanced up to seal the bargain and then went back to smoking, trying to memorize every sensation. Forever was a hell of a long time to go without smoking, no matter how rich he would be.

Ralph hammered out some rough terms with the agency heads. The details would be left to lawyers and subordinates. One of the men tried privately to pump Ralph for the location of the huge new project he had announced, claiming he might be helpful in identifying potential government subsidies or tax abate-

144

ments. Ralph tactfully resisted. Announcing early had been useful in generating interest in the project, Ralph told himself. A little mystery kept it on the front gossip burner. The longer he could keep it a secret, the farther along he would be before the vultures descended.

Ralph grimaced at the shabby exterior of the small office-building that occupied the address Phil had given him. A little fixing up and the landlord, who also owned the parking lot he was there to buy, could get five bucks a foot more for space here. A man that lazy should not be too tough to deal with.

The company name Ralph was seeking was painted on a frosted-glass door at the end of the corridor. Beneath it were several more names of real-estate corporations the man doubtless used for different purposes. No bell. He knocked. A young woman's voice called out from within. He tried the door, but it was locked. Then he heard footsteps, and the door opened a crack, a chain pulled taut at chest level. The young woman's eye gazed at him with suspicion.

Ralph gave her his name. She continued to eye him.

"You look like him," she said, but was dubious.

In these surroundings he understood why. He held up his American Express card. "I'd like to see Mr. Drogin."

She laughed with nervous apology and swung back the door. "I guess that's why they say you shouldn't leave home without it."

Lined with old filing cabinets, the office was as drab and in need of paint as the rest of the building. She went to the open doorway of the inner office.

"Mr. Drogin," she announced, still incredulous. "Ralph Behr is here to see you."

Drogin was in his fifties. He had the high paunch of a once muscular man. A mustache dropped into parentheses around an incidental mouth.

"Jesus, this is really an honor, having you here, Mr. Behr. It's a little dirty now. We're going to paint the place, but haven't had the time. This is really an honor."

Ralph had decided to be more or less straightforward. He declared that he was interested in buying Drogin's parking lot as an inexpensive place to park construction vehicles he would need further uptown. He named a generous price, but warned that he was going that high because he did not intend to bargain.

"I can't understand it," Drogin responded. "All the years our

145

family had that property no one ever approached us. Suddenly, all this activity."

"Someone else approached you?"

"Yeah," Drogin said apologetically. "If I had known you were interested, Mr. Behr, I wouldn't have listened to them. And not just because you're offering more money. Believe me, it would have made me proud to sell the property to a man like you. You know, something to tell my grandchildren about."

"You've already sold it?"

"Same thing. Signed a contract of sale. We close at the end of the month, but it's ironclad, that contract of sale. They pay the last ninety percent, I deliver a standard deed. No loopholes."

"Who's the buyer?"

"A dummy corporation represented by a broker. Wouldn't tell me the name of the principal."

"Maybe I can check it out," Ralph said, not bothering to hide his disappointment.

Drogin hesitated a moment. "As a matter of fact, I have a pretty good idea who the principal is. My secretary happened to overhear when the broker made a phone call to the buyer."

"You mean you had her listen in."

Drogin shrugged with a little smile. "The broker asked to speak to a Mr. Kramer. When this Mr. Kramer got on the line, the broker called him Simon."

Ralph brooded on the turn of events all the way back uptown. Why Simon Kramer of all people? All his buildings were in prestige areas. Why suddenly a property in a deteriorated downtown area right across the street from where no one knew Ralph was building?

The limousine coasted to a stop in front of Behr House. As Ralph stepped onto the curb, a short, round man he did not recognize, wearing a loud black-and-white checked jacket, rushed up to him.

"Mr. Behr, I've got to see you," Heshy Rubin said.

"Call my office." Ralph strode past him without stopping.

"But it's really important. Something you'll want to know about."

Ralph was nearly through the glass doors being held open by the lobby attendant when Heshy shouted out, "I have a major tenant for that hundred-and-fifty-story office building!"

Ralph stopped and turned back to get a good look at Heshy Rubin. "How major?"

146

"Twenty, maybe thirty floors, maybe forty."

That was a massive amount of space; a tenant that big could ensure the success of the entire building. Despite the unorthodoxy of this meeting and the flamboyance of his garb, Ralph decided a man who was trying to hand him a line of bull would be hiding his nervousness better.

"Tomorrow morning in my office. Nine thirty."

"You bet!" Heshy replied enthusiastically. "I'll be there. On the dot."

Ralph disappeared into the building. Heshy stared after him for several seconds, then popped a cigarette into his mouth. He was about to light it when he remembered his vow. He crushed the matches and shoved them into his jacket pocket, but kept the cigarette jauntily between his teeth. No good to jump to extremes, he admonished himself. One step at a time. He turned toward the attendant.

"You cost yourself twenty," Heshy taunted him.

A half a block later Heshy remembered his girlfriend's reluctance to slip him in to see her boss, Hanssen, the head of that insurance company. Behr would be thrilled to get a triple-A tenant like that, but what if her boss had already found new space or was going to stay put in the old building or he didn't like Behr's location or wouldn't pay what Behr was asking in rent . . . or a million other what ifs that had soured deals in the past? He would go up to her office right now and stay there until she gave in and asked Hanssen to see him. Heshy was determined to talk the man into agreeing to see Ralph Behr about leasing space. Then he would have something concrete for tomorrow's meeting with Ralph Behr.

Heshy lit the cigarette without thinking, and then cursed himself for inadvertantly jeopardizing his rare moment of good luck.

Only if I make the deal, he declared to the sky. The agreement was always only if I make the deal.

Peter Brower, the architect on the Wall Street rehab, was exiting the elevator as Ralph was entering. He had just met with Ben Rogovin. Ralph held open the elevator doors long enough to rush order a rendering that showed the proposed subway renovation.

"I've got to lock the city into the deal with a press conference as fast as I can."

"What subway renovation?"

"Find a good place inside the building to put a new subway entrance, so that we can walk the pedestrians past a concourse of shops. But don't show the shops in the rendering. This is strictly to close the deal with the city."

Ralph allowed the elevator doors to close, brooding once more over what he had learned from Drogin.

By the time the doors opened on his floor, he had figured out the culprit. As he passed Myra and entered his office, he said, "Hold nine thirty tomorrow, and get Lorna Garrison for me on the phone."

When Lorna's secretary reported that she was not coming in to her office today, he picked up the phone receiver himself and punched in the number of her apartment.

After several rings Lorna answered, a bit out of breath. "Hello."

"I guess I have you to thank for Simon Kramer buying that parking lot across from my property."

"Why, Ralph, how nice of you to call."

"I'd like you to give Simon a message for me: how much does he want for the property?"

She was silent for a short while, and Ralph thought he heard some odd sounds.

"What's happening there? Are you all right," he asked.

"Oh, I'm just fine," she responded. "Why don't you give Simon the message yourself, Ralph? He's right here."

The sounds through the receiver grew louder. Then he heard her voice again. "You see, dear Ralph, at this very moment he's fucking me. And both of us, at the very same time, you son of a bitch, are fucking you!"

Her laugh became a rising moan, and then she slammed down the phone.

Chapter 8

The negotiations for a neutral place to hold the summit conference between Ralph Behr and Simon Kramer entailed all of the delicacy and behind-the-scenes maneuvering of that between the leaders of superpower nations. The envoys were Ralph's secretary, Myra, and her counterpart in Kramer's office. Seeking every small edge, one side would suggest a time and place that provided it with some psychological advantage—a shade of dominance or of implied concession by the other side. The latter would inevitably turn it down with due apology and a claim of unbreakable prior commitment. Finally, Kramer's secretary insisted that her employer would be leaving the city after attending the Metropolitan Museum's party to accord important donors an opportunity to view new Impressionist acquisitions before they became part of the permanent collection. Mr. Behr could attend as her employer's guest—they could have their discussion there.

Ralph greeted the proposal with some consternation. "Talk about the home-court advantage!" He whistled. By meeting at the museum, he would be ceding the high ground to Simon Kramer, who prided himself on his cultured image and would doubtless take the opportunity to demean him. But if he turned down the site, Kramer would make him wait days, maybe weeks, for another date. At the very least, Ralph decided, he ought to be prepared.

He immediately telephoned the Met's director for an invitation, correctly reasoning that the latter would not lightly dismiss a potential donor of his magnitude, and then, at the offices of the Coalition, Gail's artist friend Carla. She agreed to administer a crash course on the Met's new acquisitions and told him to meet her at the Witkin Gallery, a bookstore specializing in art books. They had a lot of buying to do. "Not looking dumb," she reasoned, "takes a lot more knowledge than just saying a few things that are smart."

Myra then telephoned Simon Kramer's secretary with the reply that Mr. and Mrs. Behr were already planning to attend the Met party and would be delighted to see Mr. Kramer there.

When Gail returned home that night after dinner with her father, she found Carla lecturing her husband on Monet in the library, a room which contained even fewer books than the living room. Carla and Ralph sat across the ponderously ormolu-encrusted eighteenth-century desk from each other, art books piled between them. Earlier, Gail had expressed her doubt to Carla that Ralph's recent exposure to art had motivated this hunger for more knowledge. Of one thing she was sure, he was not going to the Met because of any sudden awakening to art.

"How's the pupil?" She asked.

"He remembers everything. Pins me down with sharp questions." She smiled at Ralph. "He's got an A going so far."

Gail was not swayed. "Do you feel any different about art?" she asked him.

"Not much," he answered honestly. "I understand a lot better what they're trying to do, and I'm beginning to recognize the different styles now, but an old picture just isn't important enough to get all that excited about. There are thousands of them."

"Like buildings," she retorted.

"People *use* buildings. They're part of people's lives, they form their cities. Art's just a good excuse for a few people to think they're smarter and have better taste than everyone else."

Gail shrugged pointedly to Carla, but a question was preoccupying her friend. "He says there's an upstairs. He's kidding, isn't he?"

Gail frowned. "That's what *I* thought. Want to borrow a swimsuit?"

Carla fell into a stunned silence.

"Welcome to ABC's Wide World of Excess," Gail quipped.

"This is heaven," Carla sighed.

"That's the problem. You find yourself getting used to it."

"He says Bergdorf Goodman's sending over a gown for you. I guess they really do those things. I have trouble getting some schlocky shop to hold a blouse for me till payday."

"Send it back, Ralph," Gail declared with immediate irritation. "Or, if it's so important to you, wear it yourself."

Carla was appalled. "Send it back?"

Gail turned on her. "If anyone understood, I was sure it would be you."

"We're not talking high treason here."

"Send it back!"

The dress was still on Gail's mind when she and Ralph were proceeding up the broad flight of steps in front of the Metropolitan Museum of Art.

"What the Coalition could do with that money!"

"It wasn't a choice. This isn't 'Let's Make a Deal.' You get a large allowance each week now, a lot more than the price of that dress. And two years from now, you'll have a fortune. You can do whatever you want with your money."

Gail halted for a moment and stared at Ralph in some confusion. Despite the deliberation that had gone into her decision to enter into this marriage, the certain attainment of vast wealth still remained abstract numbers, a resolution agreed to, but not

150

assimilated. She had trouble equating even the amount now deposited each week into her bank account with anything as concrete as an actual dress. She shook her head slightly, as if to clear it, and proceeded up the stone steps to the entrance.

The reception was being held in the André Meyer Gallery, where the new paintings would be hung. Gail noticed Ralph eyeing the gold letters spelling out the donor's name above the gallery's entrance.

"Jealous?"

"Not if you have to walk down all these corridors to find the place."

Captivated by the collection, Gail began to dawdle over every painting. Ralph left her and quickly strode through the gallery, looking over the new acquisitions and glancing occasionally at a few other paintings that caught his eye because the colors were bright or because they too had appeared in Carla's art lesson. He paid more attention to the other guests. He was used to knowing the important people at public events, but everyone looked important here, and he recognized very few. When he did, he introduced himself and was relieved at the nod of awareness that his name provoked. Their own names were a roll call of distinguished families. What he begrudged them was how comfortably they chatted to each other, that they had known each other since childhood.

He caught sight of Simon Kramer standing among several men, gesturing toward a painting. Ralph was determined not to go to him. He planted himself before the new Cézanne and waited for Kramer to work his way down the wall to him.

"An unexpected surprise, Ralph, to find you in a museum," was Kramer's greeting.

You son of a bitch! Ralph thought. You had to try for the cheap shot. Here goes.

"I wouldn't have missed this Cézanne for the world."

"What is it that you like so much?" Kramer asked, ready to pounce.

"For one thing the painterly massing of form. For another, that effect of the sun's heat he achieves by using a limited palette: ochres and browns and yellows. That gives the picture a harmony based on color. Don't you think so, Simon?"

"Yes, yes, indeed."

"Gentlemen"—he turned to the others with his hand outstretched—"I'm Ralph Behr."

A few minutes later Ralph and Kramer had moved away from other people.

"What do you want for the land, Simon?"

"Half your project, and you put up all the cash investment."

Perhaps Kramer had misunderstood. "I'm talking about a price for that parking lot."

A look of intense rancor replaced Kramer's suave gentility. "You ruined the most important night of my life, Behr, but now I've got you! You can't build a doghouse on your land without me!"

"You're really serious."

"You're lucky I'm letting you have half!"

"We're wasting each other's time." Seething, Ralph turned away to leave.

"Mark my words!" Kramer called after him. "Without me you'll never build on that land!"

Behr Center sprawled across the far end of the conference room and rose nearly to the ceiling. Created in secret and costing a quarter of a million dollars, the scale model contained details as small as benches, trees, and pedestrians along outdoor walks. A smaller model would soon arrive that could be more easily carried to the innumerable meetings of governmental and community groups with a real or imagined interest in the project.

Employing a small telescoping pointer, S. N. Watanabe—small, bespectacled, austere—barely indicated one of the miniature towers. Its curtain walls, made of mirrored celluloid, were lambent with the sunlight that had itself come slanting through the glass curtain wall which formed one side of the conference room. His voice was very soft, and the bankers had to strain to hear his presentation.

"The widely separated vertical strips of black marble that extend the length of each tower accentuate its height, while the use of moderately reflective glass—even in the upwardly angled panels which create the setbacks—is, of course, intended to minimize the building's bulk and accommodate the project to the far lower scale of the surrounding neighborhood. To avoid the visual predictability of the traditional rectangular skyscraper, each tower's geometry was varied. The hotel, for example, has five *unequal* sides. Because the project covers so much land in an otherwise blighted and desolate neighborhood, we felt justified in creating our own urban environment, convinced that future development will follow its lead."

152

Born in Japan and raised in America, S. N. Watanabe was one of the world's preeminent architects. Ralph and he had jointly developed the design. Ralph had almost fired Watanabe after the latter's first rough sketches, when Watanabe had presented plans for "glass palaces, lost in the sky." Ralph had heatedly declared that the project's whole point was to be visible and *not* to get lost; the towers must look every bit as tall as their hundred and fifty stories, "like they're punching a hole right through the sky." He was determined to build something that would represent the aspirations of this century as Notre Dame and the Eiffel Tower did theirs. The two men's association had been saved when Ralph hit upon the idea of black granite strips running up Watanabe's glass towers and when Watanabe realized that Ralph could not be cowed by an imperious, artistic manner and possessed himself an instinctive, if sometimes overstated, sense of good design.

Reflecting now on his choice of Watanabe, Ralph was pleased: no one else combined that knack of monumentality and elegance. But he had also chosen Watanabe for another reason: the renowned Japanese architect had the cachet to impress the arty sycophants who molded opinion in New York. No one was better too at speaking the jargon that awed the architectural critics; in their rave reviews whole paragraphs out of Watanabe's mouth would appear unchanged, as if constituting their own opinions. Naysayers, who sprouted in New York like dandelions, might attack a lot of things about Behr Center, but once they learned the name of the architect, they would fall all over each other to laud the design.

At that moment Charles Brookhouse spoke up. "I understand a primary obstacle to building skyscrapers at this height is the wind."

"I was just about to mention that point," Watanabe replied. He nodded toward a gray-haired man in his fifties wearing a rumpled suit. "Eli Steinman, the structural engineer, is in the forefront of scientific investigation of methods of lateral stability by means of active controls. Normally, a strong wind would cause the top of a building this tall to oscillate back and forth so far out of line that people in the upper stories would become sick. We propose to counter that oscillation with a new technology: 'flexing tendons,' cables that run up within the building and, directed by a computer, stiffen the building on the windward side to prevent its bending."

Brookhouse appeared to Ralph to be engrossed, although it

was tough to read any emotion on the man's face. Beside him, James Fowler, dressed in a nearly identical dark three-piece suit, watch chain looped across the vest he wore, despite it being summer, glanced at his superior surreptitiously, as if seeking a clue for his own reaction.

Ralph found his mind wandering. Two newspaper reporters and three from TV had telephoned to interview him for a reaction to his wife's demonstration that morning. Taking their cue from Martin Luther, she and a dozen other protestors had attached their own Ninety-five Theses to the door of Saint Patrick's Cathedral in a protest against Roman Catholic stands on a variety of issues, among them women's and homosexuals' rights. No doubt lingered in Ralph's mind that he was the only spouse who had been contacted by the press—and probably the only spouse who would be named in their pieces. He envisioned headlines like BEHR'S JEWISH WIFE ATTACKS CHURCH TO BACK QUEERS AND BABY-KILLING. Ralph refused to take the calls. Unsuspectingly, though, he did take a call from a syndicated talk-show host, thinking the latter might be asking some favor, such as a hotel reservation. It turned out he was calling to induce Ralph to appear with Gail on his TV show. The topic—Ralph grimaced visibly at the recollection—was why opposites attract.

Ben Rogovin was staring at him. Ralph composed his expression and nodded that he was all right. All right? Damn it! The woman was a constant source of embarrassment to him. How could he keep his mind on business knowing that she was out there somewhere, like the plague, inflicting grief on him as if he were some biblical victim? Giving her and her crooked father the hundred million was almost easier to endure than living with her for two years was going to be.

An instant before the listeners realized Watanabe had ended his presentation, Ralph shot forward in his seat, thanking the architect and, in the same breath, asking the bankers to flip open the materials they had been handed. Now it was his turn. No more fancy window dressing and, particularly important with a guy like Charles Brookhouse, no self-praise about his own accomplishments clothed in false modesty. They knew what he had done and what he could do—that's why they were here. After skimming over the highlights of the market analyses, which justified the high projected rents and sales figures he anticipated, Ralph cut straight through to the heart of the economics: expected revenues and the bottom-line operating profit.

"Metrobank needs a flagship project to attract major developers and put you into Manhattan real-estate lending in a big way. This is it. Behr Center will be the most important and conspicuous real-estate complex ever built. I want to borrow one and a half billion dollars. You can see that profits will cover the debt service twice over. As a result of the apartment sales, we'll have a positive cash flow by the third year. I think those are impressive economics. What do you think?"

Ralph observed a barely perceptible look pass between the bankers. In his late fifties, slim, Charles Brookhouse had pleasant looks: eyes a faded blue color, deeply etched nasolabial folds descending toward a future meeting place beneath his chin, and thin, graying hair.

"We are suitably impressed as well," Brookhouse began in flatly delivered, measured phrases. "The project is important to the future of New York and deserves all the superlatives. We appreciate your bringing it to us first. If the figures stand up to scrutiny, then we will be pleased to offer you the loan commitment on terms I'm certain you'll find acceptable—with certain provisos."

Fowler leaned forward and raised an admonishing finger. "Certain provisos."

"A billion five hundred million," Rogovin confirmed. He wanted no mistaking the loan figure.

"A major proviso would deal with the office building," Brookhouse cautioned. "As I understand it, you intend first to begin construction on that tower, while delaying other construction until the office building is partly occupied and can provide a more extensive base for attracting hotel guests and residential and retail tenants. However, our own calculations make us somewhat wary about the office market in Lower Manhattan. The total amount of unrented new space downtown comes to nearly the equivalent of all the office space in Philadelphia. Thus, we wish to see substantial rent-up in your proposed office building before you begin construction."

Ralph had been anticipating such a demand. "A broker has already set up a meeting for me with the head of a large insurance company that might be taking over a million square feet."

Ralph had found that power made all men who wielded it alike in many ways, but that what was important to know was what made each of them different. As Brookhouse spoke at length about the social benefits he foresaw deriving from Behr

Center, Ralph realized what it was that differentiated Charles Brookhouse: unemotionality so great that all the blood seemed to have been drained from him, courtliness so deeply ingrained as to seem the necessary twin of the privilege of his birth, and the absolute conviction that he would be obeyed without question.

Recalling the banker's earlier allusion to a pet charity in which he hoped to seek Behr's involvement, Ralph had been waiting for the curve. It broke a lot farther than he had expected.

"How much do you know about Cal Coolidge, Ralph?"

"Excuse me?"

"Our thirtieth president, Calvin Coolidge, how much do you know about him?"

"Actually, I don't get as much time to read as I'd like, Charles." Then he added hurriedly, "But I always wanted to know a lot more about Calvin Coolidge."

"I'm pleased you don't know much. It proves my point."

Ralph relaxed. "Well, great."

"One of our nation's tragedies is that so few Americans are acquainted with the contribution made by Calvin Coolidge."

"It must have been immense, Charles."

"I've given a great deal of thought about how best to make Americans aware of the great man's achievements." The merest resonance of evangelism invaded Brookhouse's flat tones. "We have to add Calvin Coolidge's likeness to the faces on Mount Rushmore."

A satisfied smile flitted over the older man's lips as he sat back to await Ralph's reaction.

"That's . . . umm . . . Mount Rushmore! And Calvin Coolidge! Well! That's really . . . something!"

Regarding Ralph's incredulousness as approval, Brookhouse continued. "When I was seven years old, my father took me to his home. You know what Cal Coolidge said to me that day?"

"Something extraordinarily important, I'll bet."

"Nothing!"

"Nothing?"

"Not a word. The wisdom of what he was trying to impart to me, the very essence of the man, was restraint."

"Restraint," Fowler murmured, as if he were saying amen.

"Restraint," Ralph repeated, and his face took on the look of a man glimpsing far horizons. "How very important that philosophy has been in my own personal life, Charles."

"Would that Silent Cal's successors had followed his course, instead of attempting to extend the government into every corner

156

of our lives." Brookhouse lifted a finger. "Restraint in all things. Economy, in word and deed. Our family has contributed a good deal to the effort to add his noble image to Mount Rushmore, but we need financial and spiritual help from others to convince the administration to shoulder part of the cost of the carving."

Ralph shook his head in sorrow. "All those wasteful programs, while something like this is ignored."

"Then I can count on you, I'm sure, to be at the luncheon for prospective donors."

"Right now my cash is heavily committed because of Behr Center." Ralph paused for emphasis. "But I'm sure that as soon as your bank loan reimburses me and begins to fund development, I'll be in a position to contribute generously."

"That seems fair," Brookhouse conceded and stood up. "My hand."

When the bankers and the architect had been escorted to the elevators and had departed, Ralph continued to stare at the elevator doors, musing about Brookhouse.

"Kings must have been like that before there were constitutions," he observed to Rogovin, then added almost to himself, his voice trailing off, "How rich do you have to be?"

A moment later, he jumped high into the air and exultantly slapped the ceiling. "One point five billion dollars! Can you believe it? It sounds like something out of the federal budget. We've got the money. We're on our way."

Rogovin remained somber. "We've been beating our brains out for days, and still haven't figured a way to prevent Simon Kramer from stopping the whole thing."

"I have."

Rogovin's face brightened. "He'll sell to you?"

Ralph made a derisive sound.

"What then?" Rogovin asked.

"I'm going to have his property, easements and all, condemned by the state of New York and then turned over to me."

The entire Behr family frequently gathered for dinner together on Friday night. Rosalie had been making plans for an elaborate meal to welcome Ralph's new wife, partly because she thought it was expected of her and partly because she had spent much of her life as an outsider and felt impelled to make the young woman welcome. Ralph begged off and instead invited his father to a quiet restaurant in Brooklyn, where his father's home and office had long been located and where he hoped they would not be disturbed and could talk. Far more cautious about important matters than he allowed himself to appear, Ralph was used to soliciting other opinions, making certain before he acted. Because of the restrictive effects of the arrangement with Gail that forced the pretense of a normal married life, he could discuss the true state of affairs with only two people: one was his brother, Jeff, who had to be told the truth because the family's fortune had suddenly been cut in half—but Ralph usually felt more like a parent than a brother to Jeff. His father was the other.

At first Ralph and Henry chatted about how the business was going since the latter's retirement: the co-oping of the old apartment buildings, a short wildcat strike at a construction site over work rules imposed by one of the subs, a delay in the delivery of special ceiling fixtures for the office rehab, and the problem posed by Simon Kramer. Ralph explained that he had arranged to meet with the governor in an attempt to induce the state to condemn Kramer's property and sell it to him.

As they ate their appetizers, father and son touched desultorily on a few other business matters. Finally, out of courtesy and a residuary of guilt, Henry was forced to inquire about Gail. Some time had passed since the wedding.

"How are things working out between you two?"

Ralph shot his father as much of a reproach as he would permit himself.

"A standoff. She hates me just about as much as I can't stand her."

"I heard you two looked like a happy couple at the mayor's function."

"That was a few weeks ago. You must have read about the little spectacle she staged outside of Saint Patrick's since then? The cardinal himself called me after that one."

"What did you tell him?"

"He tried to threaten me. I got so pissed off that I wanted to say, 'I'll keep my wife in line if you do the same with yours.' "

"Oh, God, you didn't say that? We'd never be able to put together another construction crew in the city of New York."

"No, I just told him her views upset me too, but she has a mind of her own."

Ralph was fuming. "You know who's been in my apartment the last two nights? Half the radical organizers in New York. People you couldn't believe. I came home and found them sprawled all over my living room. I couldn't just throw them out, right? She's supposed to be my darling little wife. So I

158

smiled and went upstairs . . . like I was a guest there. We had it out afterward, and she told me she always had them to her other home and didn't intend to stop now." Ralph shook his head in disbelief. "*Her* home! Do you believe her nerve? She expects me to be the one to make all the adjustments. Tonight I posted Deighton in there to make sure they didn't steal anything. With my luck, they'll have him throwing firebombs at me when I come home."

"No matter how it appears, this can't be easy for Gail either," Henry suggested by way of appeasement.

"Don't you believe it. She's got it all. The money is only for starters. I have a public reputation to protect, but she can do any kind of a damned-fool thing she wants. What can I threaten her with? One word from her, and you're in prison."

Henry tried to assert some sort of equivalency of annoyance. "She's separated from her husband. That can't be easy."

"She sees that ass all the time. Everybody is getting laid but me. Jeff drags his butt into the office in the morning like he spent a night with the Rockettes. 'Poor jilted Lorna' spends lunch hours in the sack with Simon Kramer. And me, the old playboy, I haven't been with a woman in weeks. I'm climbing the walls. What am I supposed to do, prowl the singles' bars? I'm married. And if I did happen to find someone, she'd better live alone because I sure can't bring her home."

Henry shrugged contritely.

Ralph went on. "The worst thing about it is that she's so damned brazen about taking everything. She acts like all this is coming to her, and *I* owe *her*. Her father's a thief, but she acts like *we're* the criminals."

"Her father was the same way. He never had any sense of shame about what he did to me."

The entrees arrived, and Ralph changed the subject.

"Did you see Dan Ahern's piece on me and the new project in the *Times* today?" Henry shook his head, and Ralph pulled out the clipping. "Not bad. I thought he might use the new subway station to take a cheap shot at me and make himself look good, but he was very fair."

"Did he mention me anywhere?"

Ralph pointed halfway down the clipping. Henry read that part first and then went back to the beginning to scan the rest of it.

Dan Ahern's treatment of Ralph Behr was also a subject of discussion at a restaurant in Greenwich Village. He and Marilyn

159

Watkins were having dinner near her newspaper's offices when Max Borah walked by and stopped to speak to Marilyn. Small and sour-faced, at thirty-nine Max was an investigative reporter who was the fearsome star of her paper's staff. Marilyn introduced the two men.

"That was some lovey-dovey article on Ralph Behr," Max observed acidly. "If it wasn't *The New York Times*"—he heaped sarcasm on the title—"one would think you were doing PR for the boy-o."

Ahern was unflustered. "If there's nothing there, Max, I don't manufacture it."

Marilyn wanted to interrupt and calm the waters, but Max was too quickly incensed. "Meaning that I do?"

"That series you wrote on him a while back. Columns of insinuation, but no smoking gun."

"Right from the start he was making those cozy tax-abatement deals with the same politicians he and his father had contributed heavily to. The son of a bitch won't take my calls. But where there's smoke, someday I'm going to find the fire."

"That's just it, Max," Ahern observed philosophically, "he doesn't have to take our calls. The real problem we have with guys like Ralph Behr is that he's rich and powerful, and we envy the hell out of him for it. We're jealous. We make up our minds that he—anyone—can't get that rich honestly; otherwise, we'd be rich too, right?"

"Ralph Behr represents the worst of America, a corruption of the American dream into greed and manipulation and egotism. Where are our values when a guy can become a hero just because he's successful? The rock star as real-estate mogul. You can't honestly like a guy like that."

"I don't know—I've never thought about it," Ahern replied. "But I will tell you one thing I admire about him. Behr is one of the few people I've ever followed who truly enjoys walking on a high wire. It's dangerous, and I like to watch him do it."

"There's got to be another side to this Behr Center deal. All this talk, and no one even knows where the site is," Borah added pointedly. "I don't know what he's hiding—tax deals, city approvals he shouldn't have gotten, zoning violations he has to get fixed—shit, who knows? But I'm going to dig, and I'm going to find it."

"Whether it's there or not?"

"Oh, something's there, all right."

*   *   *

When his dinner with his father was over and they had parted, Ralph headed back to Manhattan in his limousine. Having fired five drivers this year, the last one for ferrying drugs for pushers in his off hours, he had not bothered to learn the new man's name. Ralph promised himself to do so if the man lasted into September. "Take the Brooklyn Bridge," he instructed.

A few minutes later, the Gothic stone towers loomed up against the night and the skyline beyond, welcoming him, exhilarating him. The Williamsburg and Manhattan bridges, with towers of trusses and bolts, had always seemed to him like erector-set afterthoughts flung across the East River. But the Brooklyn Bridge had dignity and grace and strength. And it was the first—that was important, not to be a copier.

The guys who built those other bridges—nobody remembers them, Ralph had noted when his grade-school teacher was telling the class the history of the Brooklyn Bridge, but every kid in school learns about the Roeblings. Ralph assumed that every boy wished someday to build something so terrific that he too would be remembered forever. After school that night he revealed his desire to his father.

Henry brought his son's fantasies back to earth. He explained that the bridge was built to increase land values in Brooklyn, which then consisted mostly of farms. The cynicism in his tone deepened into reproach as he recounted how his own father had harbored a desire like Ralph's that became an obsession—in his case to build the tallest building in the world—and how the banking clique had destroyed him.

That Saturday Ralph had ridden his bike to the bridge and gazed at it. Beyond was Manhattan. He would be the one, like Galahad, to pursue the family's destiny back over the bridge and make the dream come true at last for all the Behrs before him. And everyone would know his name forever.

Chapter 9

Unable to think of anything more exciting to do, Ralph had returned home and spent the evening, bored, mostly watching TV shows he was not interested in and shooting pool. Only when, just before he was about to change for bed and Deighton knocked on his bedroom door to ask whether Mr. Behr wished him to wait up for Mrs. Behr, did Ralph realize that she was not yet home.

Ralph simulated unconcern and, claiming that Gail was at a meeting scheduled to run late, told Deighton to go to bed. Actually, Ralph was very concerned. Not about Gail's safety— the more morbid her fate the better—but about the appearance to the building's employees and his servants of her bounding in at an ungodly hour after another of her trysts with her ex-husband. Just the night before, admitting that she had been with him, she had returned back here at eleven. But it was already past midnight. Irritated, Ralph made up his mind to give her a strong lecture on her responsibilities to their arrangement just as soon as she came in.

Four hours later, with still no sight of Gail, Ralph was raging, pacing up and back in his bedroom as he conjectured on her infamies. By now he could only deduce that she was an unbridled nymphomaniac, oblivious to her shame and to the danger into which she had placed everyone, her own father included. Of all the women to have been thrown together with!

Ralph heard Gail's steps just a moment before her outer door clicked shut. He exploded into her bedroom through the connecting door.

"Do you have any idea what time it is?" he erupted.

Gail glanced at her clock radio. "Two minutes after four."

"Well, what do you have to say for yourself?"

"It's late, and I want to get to bed, so please get out of here."

"That's all? You traipse in here at four in the morning, just

162

about announcing to the doorman, the elevator man, and all the servants what you've been out doing, and that's your apology."

Gail stared, frowning, at him.

Ralph thrust his finger at her. "We had a deal. You could see lover-boy Milo once in a while and very secretly. But you're practically moving back in with him. This insatiable sex drive of yours isn't just your own problem, you are jeopardizing me and my family by your reckless—"

"Is that where you think I was—with Milo?" she asked, her own anger now aroused.

"Where else could you have been? I don't see any broken bones, so you weren't in the hospital."

"As a matter of fact," Gail railed back at him, "that was exactly where I was most of the night, getting a woman's arm put into a cast because her husband had broken it . . . and the cut in her scalp sewn up . . . and the cigarette burns he had put on her face treated. The rest of the night I was helping her and her children settle into a safe hotel room, until we can move people around in our shelters and find a place for them there."

Ralph did not speak for a moment but then, a broad smile affixed to his face, he said, "Just worried about you out this late, that's all. Good night."

He strode back toward the connecting door.

"Oh, no you don't!" she shouted and caught up to him.

"This is off limits," he reminded her.

She ignored the warning and followed on his heels into his bedroom. She was just getting warmed up. She had had enough of his disapproving glares after few very short and very occasional hours with Milo and enough of his misplaced resentment for being thrown into this situation.

"You sanctimonious hypocrite!" she exclaimed. "You're feeling so self-righteous. You waited up all night just because you thought you had the evidence to make me apologize so that you could feel morally superior."

Ralph entered his dressing room and began unbuttoning his shirt. Gail scurried around in front of him to make sure she had his attention. She was going to let him have it once and for all. Suddenly, a thought occurred to her, and she burst into laughter.

"You're jealous. You've got no one yourself, not even that spider woman. So you condemn me for being normal."

"Unlike you," he rejoined, tossing his shirt across the top of the wooden valet, "I take very seriously my obligation not to risk

163

exposing the real nature of our relationship and jeopardizing us all."

"I'm right, aren't I? You haven't been with a woman since our wedding."

"By choice, I assure you," Ralph responded airily. "Celibacy is good for the soul. You ought to try it. As a matter of fact we could do it together, a kind of family activity to prove the purity of our love." Ralph kicked off his shoes in the direction of the shoe rack.

"Very funny. I'll bet you think I enjoy living here with you? Let me tell you that I hate it. It's like being trapped in an enemy camp. I don't have a moment's peace of mind here."

Ralph nodded and began to unbuckle his pants. "Mental cruelty. You can use that for our divorce." He shifted to a falsetto. "He abused me, your honor. He gave me a beautiful apartment and maids and a large allowance, but he didn't approve of my having sex with my ex-husband. Deep down I'm sure he secretly wanted to have his way with me. In fact he even undressed while I was in his room."

"What?" Gail suddenly realized that Ralph was standing in his jockey shorts and was about to slip those off.

"You pig!" she yelled.

"You weren't invited in here, ma'am. Your rules, remember?" He dropped his undershorts. "I'm about to take a shower. If you'd like to continue this chat in there . . ."

Gail rushed out of the dressing room and toward her own bedroom.

He called out to her, "They say you have to expect these little squabbles early in a marriage."

For nearly thirty years, Watchman Fidelity Property and Casualty Insurance Company had stolidly resided on the eastern flank of the financial district. Heshy Rubin was waiting outside the entrance to the old granite-sheathed high-rise when Ralph arrived, carrying a long cardboard tube. The morning was hot, and the short, chubby real-estate broker was anxiously mopping his sweating face with a white handkerchief. As they proceeded into the lobby, Heshy hopped around Ralph to open the door and then trotted past him to push the elevator button.

"Mr. Behr, this guy is really . . . I guess you could say eccentric, Mr. Behr. He's used to having his own way, if you understand what I mean. The building has been sold, and the insurance company has to get out in two years, when their lease expires. But he's crazy; he refuses to believe he has to move. He hasn't lifted a finger to find new space. He tells his board of directors he's waiting for the right opportunity to present itself, like it's going to come down the chimney at Christmas, if you understand what I mean."

"I understand what you mean. I've done a little research of my own."

George Hanssen had been the chief executive officer of Watchman Fidelity for twenty-two years. He was in his late sixties and, still vigorous and in firm control of the board of directors, exhibited no inclination to retire. He was a spare man in every way: small, thin, and impatient with those who wasted his time by wasting words.

"You have ten minutes," he announced before greeting Ralph. "If you can't make your point by then, you're a damned fool and not worth the trouble."

Heshy shrugged his shoulders worriedly at his girlfriend, Hanssen's secretary, as she closed the door behind the three of them.

Not bothering to shake Hanssen's hand, Ralph advanced to a window in his office that overlooked the East River and placed over it a large artist's sketch of New York City as if seen from the top of his own proposed office building. Held in place by cellophane tape, the sketch showed sailboats skimming along the brightly sparkling river and, in the distance, larger ships plying the lanes into and out of the harbor. Ralph explained that the view was the same as Hanssen's present view, although a bit farther uptown.

Hanssen stood in front of the covered window, hands skeptically on his hips. Finally, he turned.

"I don't like what I read about you, Behr. You're a big talker, a big spender."

"Just publicity, Mr. Hanssen," Heshy interjected. "Helps him sell his real estate."

Hanssen ignored him, focusing his attention on Ralph. "They also say you're a playboy, a womanizer."

"He's married now, Mr. Hanssen," Heshy again interjected.

"Sit down, Heshy," Ralph told him without taking his gaze from the insurance executive.

Hanssen tipped his head at Ralph. "But I'll give you that you're a smart one. You made the effort to find out I like sailing, and I like to watch the water out this window."

"And you'd be able to, all the way out to sea and up the

Hudson on the other side. You'd be higher than in any other building in the world."

Hanssen stared for several minutes at the sketch filling the window. Time was ticking by, but Ralph said nothing. Heshy had retreated to the far end of the room and taken a seat on one of the forest green leather sofas. He kept glancing at his watch, and despite the air-conditioning, continued to sweat. Hanssen finally turned and went to his desk. He pulled a single sheet of paper from his center drawer and handed it to Ralph.

"This is what we need. How much?"

Ralph read carefully. Nothing out of the ordinary and a lease duration and space requirements close to those on which he had already predicated his calculations.

"Forty-eight dollars a square foot."

"That's higher than I've been quoted for other buildings."

"So's my building. The highest in the world. And the finest."

"We've been offered land in New Jersey and Connecticut with great tax breaks and subsidies."

"Most of your employees live here, and so do you. Moving out of the city would disrupt the entire company. With our own cogeneration plant, you'll have competitive electrical rates." Ralph gestured at the piece of paper. "Take this much space, and I'll name the building after your company. What's that worth in advertising?"

From the cardboard tube Ralph withdrew site maps, floor plans, and colored renderings of the office building and all of Behr Center. He explained where the project would be built and the advantages of the site. He stressed the fact that it would be part of a spectacular complex and described what was pictured— the atrium, the retail stores, two other towers.

"What's the schedule for building all of this?" Hanssen asked.

Ralph told him. Hanssen's gaze shifted back and forth from plans and renderings to the sketch in the window.

"If all those other buildings and gazebos don't get built," Hanssen finally remarked, "we'll be sitting sky-high in the middle of a slum looking like the biggest damned fools since the jackasses who insured the *Titanic*. What I want is a right to cancel at any time before we move in if you don't meet those other dates."

Ralph was confident about his construction schedule, but if something unforeseen caused a delay in starting any of the other buildings, he would already have built the tallest office building ever and no longer have a major tenant for the bulk of the space.

Interest on Metrobank's mortgage would be running night and day like a clock, with no rental income coming in to repay it. He tried to dissuade Hanssen, but the insurance-company executive was adamant.

"All right," Ralph conceded, "we have a deal."

They shook hands. Ralph was overjoyed: things were falling into place very quickly. Measured against the huge benefit of that lease, he was glad to take the risk.

Hanssen tilted his head, his expression bordering on contempt. "I still don't hold with a man who thinks he has to put his name on everything that drifts by. . . ." His eyes wandered over to the rendering of the office tower. ". . . but you sure have one handsome building here."

"And your time is running out," Ralph commented.

Descending in the elevator, Ralph broached the brokerage fee. Heshy had been prepared to haggle over it, expecting a skimpy figure, now that Ralph had sewn up the tenant. But the figure was a fair one: three million dollars with payments over three years commencing when and if Watchman Fidelity took occupancy. Ralph would send him a confirming letter by the end of the day.

Heshy was wrapped in stunned ecstasy as he watched Ralph's car pull away from the curb, waving at it like a boy at a parade. He had hit the jackpot, the lottery! He was rich! Rich! Whatever he had ever wanted was his. An apartment on the park, a Florida condo, a limousine twice as long as Behr's! Whatever he wanted.

And then he remembered the conditions. He wouldn't see a penny until the insurance company moved in two years from now. And if they didn't move in, nothing! If Ralph Behr fucked up with a single delay in starting construction on any piece of the project in the next two years, he, Heshy Rubin, would be out the whole three million bucks!

"Oh, shit!" he moaned aloud. "Oh, shit!"

He could not make up his mind whether to laugh or to cry. He placed a cigarette in his mouth. He was reaching for matches when he suddenly recalled his vow and stopped stone dead.

No money for two years—maybe ever—and yet, he still had to give up cigarettes from this very moment until the day he died because, sure as hell, he had a deal for the space. He couldn't risk trying to weasel out of it now. He glared at the sky.

"You tricky son of a bitch!"

*　　*　　*

167

Ralph had always resented the World Trade Center. He considered the twin towers a couple of oversized aluminum fence posts displaying little grace and less beauty. Imposed on New York City by an overbearing state government, they had glutted the city's office market in the bargain. But the World Trade Center was where the governor's office was located, so that was where one went to see him.

As he walked through the retail concourse, Ralph took note of one of the few elements he had always liked about the project: stores were located between the elevators and the subways, so as to assure constant foot-traffic past the retail areas—and a reason for it. That kind of thinking had gone into his subway-entrance relocation and into Behr Center's commercial corridors as well.

Getting close to the governor had been difficult at first: Ralph had been born wealthy and reared, albeit by a Jewish mother, as a Protestant inclined to mask his feelings; while the governor came from working-class Catholic parents who had emigrated from Europe. A man who displayed his emotions freely, the governor was also leery of those outside his circle until they had proved their loyalty. Hiring Phil Rountree, the governor's ex–law partner, had helped bridge the gap somewhat, but the two men had finally found a personal common ground in their love of sports.

The governor was standing at the door to his office. He had on his jacket and was reading a letter. He shook hands and spoke while he read.

"My wife put your wife on the board of the disabled kids luncheon, didn't she? We thought she'd enjoy the fashion show and meeting the other women. She should be over there now with the others."

The bag lady meets Calvin Klein! Ralph muttered to himself. Talk about culture shock!

"Yes, I suppose she is," Ralph said aloud.

"Good, you can surprise her. We're going over there." He looked up and stuck out his hand again, a wide smile on his face. "Hey, my congratulations. Our wedding gift arrived, didn't it?"

Ralph nodded. "Beautiful. We really loved it." He thought it was a crystal bowl, but was not sure. "You got my thank-you note?"

The governor nodded. "Appreciated it."

He quickly signed the letter and led Ralph back toward the elevators.

"The secretary of health and human services was supposed to stop off in New York to speak on his way back from a conference in Brussels, but his plane was delayed over Newfoundland. I'm filling in." He chuckled. "It was the best my wife could do on short notice. We can talk in my car. Your car can follow."

"We look like a funeral," Ralph commented as the two limousines moved up the avenue adjacent to the Hudson River. Because of deterioration, this lower stretch of the West Side Highway had long since been torn down for safety reasons. Years of citizen court action had finally killed a plan to replace it with Westway, a predominantly federally funded highway built as a tunnel half-submerged in the river and running parallel to the shore. The area between would have been filled in to create more property for land-scarce Manhattan.

"If you'd have been in charge of Westway," the governor remarked, "it would have been finished by now with no headaches."

"Thanks, but I've got my own headache right now, and I could use some help from you."

"I'm listening."

Ralph explained that an oddball easement tied to the parking lot across the street from where he was planning to build his new development was holding things up. The governor began firing questions to dig out the facts. Finally, he asked who the owner was.

"Simon Kramer."

"And you say he bought the parcel just to tie you up."

"He has it in for me. I guess I tweaked his nose once too often. Because of that he's holding up a project which would revitalize a large part of lower Manhattan."

"Kramer snubbed me when it looked like I didn't have a chance for governor, and then he tried to jump on the bandwagon when I won the primary. I accepted his contributions, and I'm pleasant to the man, but I owe him nothing."

Ralph had known all that. He awaited the governor's next sentence.

"What do you need?"

Ralph outlined his plan. The Urban Development Corporation, a powerful state agency known as UDC, was charged with the responsibility of using its extensive real-estate development powers and its funds to build projects in conjunction with private builders that would eliminate urban blight and increase employment. One of those powers was condemnation, the right of a governmental entity to seize a private owner's property by paying its fair market price as determined by a court.

"Not an hour ago the head of a large insurance company threatened to move out of the state," Ralph concluded. "I talked him into taking space in my new office building. If my project can't go forward, the city and the state lose six thousand jobs."

"You're not exaggerating. Six thousand?"

Ralph raised his hand as if taking an oath. "But I need UDC to condemn that parking lot and sell it to me. For its fair market value, of course. But things have to move right away. That area is a slum, and until I came along no one was interested in revitalizing it."

"I agree with you. That area needs development desperately."

"Except for you and a few others, no one knows exactly where my project is. But somehow Kramer found out and bought the parcel to make trouble. The more I can accomplish until word leaks out and the kooks and community SWAT teams start arming themselves, the fewer problems there'll be. If I'm not up and building on schedule, that insurance company is out of New York."

"What's my downside?"

"The mayor might get annoyed. Cities usually don't take kindly to the state coming in and condemning their land without their approval."

The governor's mouth tightened, and his face turned red. "Did you hear what he said about me on the radio last week? I could have said a lot worse about him, but I've never dealt with people that way. He's close to Kramer, isn't he?"

Ralph nodded.

The governer jabbed a finger at Ralph. "This project is important for the state. You've got it."

He buzzed a bodyguard in the front seat and told him he wanted to speak to the head of UDC right away. He turned back to Ralph.

"You don't happen to have anything in mind for Buffalo, do you?"

Gail was speaking to an elderly woman when Ralph arrived at the luncheon. The woman wore an elegant silk dress and discreetly dazzling diamond earrings and a diamond brooch. He noted that Gail was dressed like someone who had wandered in from a picnic. She slipped her arm through Ralph's and kissed him adoringly on the cheek.

"Darling, I've missed you so much," she said.

Ralph peered warily at her, but she was already introducing him to the elderly woman. Ralph recognized Annabelle Grinstead's name instantly. She was a grand dame of New York City philanthropy, a contributor to and on the board of several venerable cultural institutions. She broke into laughter at the mention of Ralph's name.

"Yes, of course, the Fifth Avenue Flasher. I don't know why your wife calls you that, but I find it frightfully amusing. From what I had read about her in the papers, I didn't know what to think, but I must say she is such a delight. You're a lucky man. You'd better watch her every minute though. She can charm and cajole anything out of anyone. In fact I've just promised to help her raise money for that wonderful work she's been doing at those women's shelters of hers. They're so much more"—she searched for the right word—"more *specific* than the sorts of charities with which I'm usually associated."

At that moment the governor's wife rushed up to them. "Oh, God, Ralph!" she exclaimed, tears of laughter began rolling down her cheeks. "The Fifth Avenue Flasher! This poor child has got to be protected from a menace like you."

Ralph glanced lovingly at Gail. He certainly *had* better watch her every minute, he thought. The woman was a loose cannon. All he could hope to do was limit the damage by not leaving her side whenever they were out together socially.

He kept her arm locked against his side until the luncheon was over and he had instructed the chauffeur to transport her downtown to the Women's Action Coalition. He would gladly walk to his office to be certain that she had been safely removed.

At the first street corner he telephoned Phil Rountree in order to fire off a list of items for the lawyer to handle. As he waited for Rountree to pick up, he scanned the food carts selling ices, ice cream, souvlaki, falafel, Chinese specialties, salads—one even selling hot dogs. One man was hawking earrings to passersby, another sets of kitchen knives and portable radios. Pedestrians forced their way through small gaps between those loitering to eat or shop. The secret of this city, Ralph thought, is that in some way or other everybody here is always selling something.

Ralph heard Rountree's greeting in the receiver.

"Phil, a couple of things: I've just lined up our first major office tenant at Behr Center. It's Watchman Fidelity. I'll dictate a memo setting out the major lease terms, and you and Ben can negotiate the rest of them. Prepare a letter informing Metrobank that their condition has been met, and we want a firm loan-commitment letter from them. I may have to do some fast explaining when they figure out that Watchman Fidelity has an out, but we'll worry about that then. Next, everything is on track regarding wiping out Kramer's easement. The governor will direct UDC to condemn Kramer's parcel and turn it over to me. I meet with the UDC head tomorrow. He'll have his people rush things through so we can show good title to our construction site. Let's hold off a bit on evicting the squatters until UDC commits itself definitely with a directors' vote. But be ready to go at a moment's notice. I want to demolish and have foundations dug for the office building before winter."

"We're researching whether you have to go to the community board to review the plans with them."

"And waste another six months. I'm counting on the fact that we won't have to with this one. You assured me that because I don't need a zoning change, I can build there as of right."

"The law is one thing. Public opinion about skyscrapers that high may be another."

"Let me tell you, Phil, if the law is on my side, I build."

Ralph and Gail had few public social obligations during the next weeks and saw very little of each other. The few times they dined at home together they ate quickly and silently and had coffee sent upstairs, where they took their cups to their respective rooms. The exception was the night Ralph invited Jeff to dinner. Gail engaged Jeff in a long, attentive conversation and joined the brothers afterward in the living room.

"She's trying to lull us into letting down our guard," Ralph later remarked to his brother, "so she can nuke us."

The rest of the time husband and wife kept out of each other's way. Ralph spent nearly every waking hour getting Behr Center off the ground. Heartened by her shelter program's positive reception among the wealthy women with whom her marriage to Ralph put her in contact, Gail began to devote much of her time to planning a major fund-raising operation, so that, at last, the program could be enlarged and the staff cease its helter-skelter scrambles for funds to keep the doors open.

Gail and Annabelle Grinstead and the three women she had invited to join the committee were late beginning lunch at Le Cirque because heavy traffic had caused one of them, Eloise

McCauley, to be late returning from her Connecticut country house. They were all very excited about this new cause because it promised to be so relevant and, "Well, it's so contemporary, isn't it?" Eloise commented after her lengthy apology. Her friend, Carolyn, assured her that it was—she had seen discussions of it on "Donahue" and "Oprah Winfrey."

Gail considered the latter two to be "ladies who lunch," rich women who had little but lunch and shopping to occupy their days. Well, if she could induce them to make donations and raise money from their crowd, it was well worth her time. Far more intelligent were Annabelle, the no-nonsense grande dame of philanthropy, and Diane Northwood, a handsome, superbly groomed woman in her thirties, who was the wife of the heir to a tobacco-company fortune.

As they ate, Gail spoke first about the larger issue of violence against women, its causes and implications. She hoped that her descriptions would challenge them, provoke them to ask questions, unsettle their complacency so that they would want to become involved. Annabelle patiently prodded Eloise and Carolyn along. So well, in fact, that by the end of lunch and during the trip downtown in Annabelle's limousine, they were deeply engaged in the discussion.

"I'd like you all to meet Catherine Rodriguez," Gail said as the women entered the anonymous three-bedroom apartment in an East Village residential building. A Hispanic woman in her late twenties sat at a typewriter table in the foyer, practicing what she had learned that day in typing class. Gail explained that the Coalition had arranged for Mrs. Rodriguez to take courses that would give her the job skills to earn her own living and not be financially dependent on a man.

"He beat me pretty bad a lot of times. I didn't know where to turn. A friend told me about this place. I wasn't alone after that. That gave me courage to leave him, you understand?"

"We obtained a court order of protection for Mrs. Rodriguez and had him barred from their apartment," Gail informed the others, "but her husband consistently refuses to obey it and, on several occasions, lay in wait to attack her outside their apartment house. The safest thing was for her to leave the apartment and take refuge here."

"Will you divorce him?" Eloise asked.

Mrs. Rodriguez bit her lip. Gail was forced to answer for her. "She's Catholic. She won't divorce him."

Gail led the visitors through the living room, encouraging

173

them to speak to the sheltered women and the latter to tell their stories. Finally, they ended up in the small kitchen, where they were introduced to Maureen Stroud. Serenely pretty, very young, with wiry red hair, she was bathing her infant son in the shallower of the kitchen-sink basins, while laughing and cooing to him. Carolyn could not take her eyes off the baby and begged to hold him. Maureen wrapped him in the towel and lifted him into the woman's arms. They all took seats in the small living room.

"Maureen," Gail began gently, "these women want to learn more about our programs, so that they can help us raise money. May I tell them why you've come here?"

Embarrassment seized the young woman. She struggled with the decision before nodding her acquiescence. She kept her eyes down as Gail spoke.

"Maureen may look older, but she's only fifteen. She came to us when she was eight months pregnant—after her father demanded that she put the child up for adoption as soon as it was born. He has a history of violent action toward her and her mother. Maureen feared he might kill it."

Carolyn, who had been smiling at the infant and brushing his cheek with her finger, looked up with a stricken expression.

"Couldn't you go to her father," Diane asked Gail, "and try to educate him? Other girls have gotten carried away, and the world didn't end. After all this is his grandchild."

Gail hesitated and placed her hand protectively on Maureen's before she answered, "He's also the child's father. He has forced her to have sex with him since she was ten years old."

"Oh, God!" Diane exclaimed, giving voice to the revulsion they all felt. Carolyn stared numbly at the baby, suddenly not sure what her attitude toward him should be.

Only now did Annabelle, who had already spent time here, speak up. "Now, you understand why I felt what Gail and her people are doing is so important."

"What about therapy for some of these men?" Diane wanted to know.

"Few of the men are willing to go for help—some of the better-educated ones maybe. We don't have the funds for separate groups for the men, and we feel it frightens and inhibits the women to have men in their sessions. Anyway, we don't know how much good it does for the effort we would have to put in. We can't do everything."

Annabelle had already requested that Gail limit the fund-raising to the battered women's shelters and programs, excluding the community activities that emanated from the Coalition's storefront headquarters. The women's sympathies, she knew, would clearly lie with the plight of the abused women and children, which touched them each as women regardless of socioeconomic differences.

As they all gathered at the front door, Gail felt the afternoon had gone well and was optimistic about gaining their help.

Eloise's voice caught before she could make the words audible. "This is just awful. This is happening to women who love their men and their children just as much as we do and who suffer for it. My husband's office will send a check in the morning, and I will serve on the permanent committee to help raise whatever you need."

Carolyn agreed as well. Gail realized that these women were not what she had thought. Their energy might not be harnessed to all her causes, but they were compassionate and willing to educate themselves and then to contribute in whatever way was appropriate for them.

Diane, who had appeared to be the most shaken by what she had seen and heard, held back to speak privately to Gail. "Just raising money isn't enough. It's too easy. Seeing these women makes me realize how very lucky I am. They have nowhere else to turn. I want to help financially too, but if I can be of some help by working here, I would very much appreciate your letting me."

Gail kissed the other woman's cheek with impulsive gratitude. During the course of the afternoon she had come to like Diane, and now the thought crossed her mind that perhaps they might even become friends. But when she was bidding the women good-bye until they met again to begin planning for fund-raising, she was struck by how unlikely that could ever be with as lofty a creature as Diane.

Because of her feminist prominence and her involvement in art, Gail had been asked to join a committee to stage a major exhibition of the work of contemporary women artists, to be supported by notable women's groups. The previous meeting had foundered over objections to isolating women from other artists, which some claimed automatically demeaned their work as incapable of competing on an equal basis with males, and to limiting the endeavor to female visual artists to the exclusion of female composers and writers. Some of the feminist leaders stumped for

175

a major festival to feature the work of a wide variety of contemporary creative women in commemoration of a major feminist anniversary. Research into an appropriate anniversary was to be undertaken before this present meeting.

The gathering was at the loft home and studio of Kary Kelly, a well-respected painter with whom Gail had become friendly when both had taken a life-drawing course years before. They had gone different ways professionally, but had remained good friends.

Kary was a tall, dark-haired woman with a reputation for unsparing candor. Her eyes were dark as well and seemed to possess only two expressions, shifting from fierce to kind and back again with little gradation between. Gail's announcement of her name into the intercom at the front-door vestibule was followed by an inordinate delay before she heard the buzzed release of the vestibule's inner door. After climbing the flight of steps, Gail had to ring Kary's doorbell—her hostess was not at the door waiting as she usually was for her guests. When it opened, Kary stood beside it like a guard, her lips pursed and her eyes vindictive.

"I didn't think you'd come."

Gail had encountered too much suspicion and resentment since her marriage to mistake their cause in Kary. "You too, Brutus," she said lightly, hoping that the jibing reference to the hostility she had been facing would end the matter, but the woman's countenance did not change as she replied.

"Milo is a friend of mine."

"I thought I was too."

Kary nodded. "Come in."

Most of the women had already arrived—a few well-known feminist leaders, the rest artists. Gail knew all of them. Even among those who did not register resentment when she greeted them, Gail could sense reserve and even withdrawal. Rich now, different from them, she had become a remote object of envy, scorn, or perhaps both. A couple of the women sensed her discomfort and tried to converse with her, but the awkwardness was clearly palpable. Whatever happened to sisterhood? Gail wondered. All were relieved when the meeting started and they could pay attention to the agenda.

Gail left as soon as the meeting ended. Despite her self-righteous scowl, she was deeply despondent. She used the time traveling to the borrowed studio apartment where she was to meet Milo consciously trying to regain her equanimity.

176

She arrived a quarter of an hour late, but Milo, always so punctual, had not yet arrived. Her initial reaction was relief at not having been the tardy one. She took a seat and began to go through some papers she had brought with her from the Coalition.

An hour later, Milo still had not shown up. Very concerned by then, Gail wanted to try locating him, but had to discard each method that came to her to track him down; she could not risk questions about why she was so determined to locate the man she had been in such a hurry to divorce.

Gail had met Milo almost immediately after she entered NYU. They had literally bumped into each other outside one of her classroom buildings, she carrying books, he one of his canvases. Several years older than she, already out of college and not taking courses at NYU, Milo was at the center of a large circle of its art students and teachers and of artists in the area. He was clever and strong-minded with a magnetic manner and the lean good looks of an esthete. He invited her to join him for coffee. They talked until after midnight. She found his charm; his certainty and integrity about what was right and wrong; his active, almost dominating intellect; and his burning desire to be a great artist irresistible. He walked her home, concerned about the dangers lurking at such a late hour. He did not even try to kiss her, saying that he did not want her to get the wrong idea about his intentions.

Clever, sarcastic, unyielding in her moral values, at eighteen Gail was a pretty, easily angered young woman who burned with a sense of righteousness. Below her chestnut hair was a forehead often knotted by the intensity of her emotions. Milo was the first person she had ever met, girl or boy, woman or man, wise enough to see through her defenses and strong enough to overcome them. Soon she found herself very much in love with him. Only then did he confess that he himself had fallen in love with her that very first day. They began to live together in a loft they renovated. They married a few years after she was graduated from college, although Milo had pressed her to marry him from the earliest days of their living together. She treasured that sense of propriety in him, of older and more enduring values, despite the Bohemian nature of their lifestyle.

She found her anger, which had come to seem an almost permanent part of her makeup, like her eye color or her height, melting to a warm and loving nature, sometimes abundantly so in reaction to her having suppressed it for so long. She felt grateful for having been rescued from the grimly unrelenting self-sufficiency into which she had been forced so early in life. Milo became her lover, husband, friend, her sanctuary, and if he was sometimes arrogant or insensitive, she usually let it pass, remembering that he was an artist—high-strung, creative—and that he loved her. She was terrified to lose the love on which she so depended.

She needed that sanctuary because she was still a whirlwind of energy for every cause that called upon her or that provoked on behalf of people oppressed in some way that rage always so near her surface. "Your causes," Milo would jokingly call them, as if they were pets or a porcelain-thimble collection instead of people crying out to her. Oddly, that made the crushing load seem somehow a bit more bearable. But once, during an argument, he asserted that her compulsion for causes was no more than a blatant compensation for the injustice done to her father. She exploded, telling him that she had no illusions about the probable roots of her indignation, but simply to ascribe her motives to a childhood trauma demeaned the wrongs done to her father and to the people she tried to help and the sincerity of her efforts. He broke off the argument instantly then, understanding that he had probed too thoughtlessly to her essence.

Suddenly, the door of the borrowed apartment burst open, and Milo strode in. Usually immaculate in public, he still wore his painting clothes and had forgotten the dinner he was supposed to bring, but his expression was ebullient.

"The painting is flowing, Gail, like a river pouring out of the end of my arm."

"Why didn't you call? I've been worried sick that something might have happened to you."

He took her in his arms. "I wish you could see it. Reds that spin and dance. A yellow that sears your eyeballs off. And all balanced like a high-wire act."

She was distressed to realize that he had been drinking again, which he seemed to be doing much more lately, but the genuineness of his joy mollified her. "It's been so long since I've seen you this excited about your work."

He turned rigid. "You're right, what good does it do?"

"Milo, they can't all be closed-minded. I know you'll find a gallery that believes in you."

"Like that mangy woman who kept marketing the junk art while my work languished in the back room."

"There have to be others. Sooner or later—"

"I'm a pioneer, you know that. They're intimidated by work so

178

far out on the frontier of contemporary art. They want the easy sell, the commercially accessible."

"You always said financial success didn't matter, that history was art's true judge."

Milo lifted his head and looked away. The lamplight behind illuminated his profile like an aureole. "It hurts when a pandering hack like Cosmara is the darling of the art crowd or a facile, superficial dauber like what's-his-name who used to live in a room at the back of the Harrises' place—"

"Matson?"

"Matson. When a Matson is selling that painted debris he glues onto canvas for ten thousand dollars apiece. It's not the money, it's going so long without the recognition."

Her heart ached for him. "If only there was a way to get your work noticed."

"There is." He seized her arms. "I've thought of a way. We could open our own gallery. You and I. And not just my work, but Cleo's and Ted's, Smitty's and John's. All our friends who have talent and haven't been discovered yet."

For a moment she had been caught up in his enthusiasm. Now she halted, to make him see the problems. It would take a hundred thousand dollars, maybe more. *Probably* more.

"But, you have it," he rejoined. "You have millions, or will in a couple of years."

"If I had the money now, you know I would do it for you, but I don't."

"But Behr could give it to you. On account, I mean, and deduct it from what you get after the divorce."

"I suppose so, if that had been our agreement, but it wasn't. I get my share in two years. You know that."

"It's pocket money to him. If you ask him the right way, there's no reason for him not to do it."

"Milo, I can't talk to him. He's an animal!" she fumed. "Why, the last time I had anything like a conversation alone with him he ripped off his clothes and tried to pull me into the shower with him."

Abhorrence contorted Milo's features. "We knew it wouldn't be easy. I despise him too, but the art gallery could be a breakthrough for me."

"Just knowing he's in the next bedroom disgusts me, and you want me to beg him for—"

Milo kissed her. "Just present the proposal to him. You aren't

179

asking that much of him, when you consider how long he's keeping us apart and forcing us to wait for the money."

"He has no honor, no integrity—"

Milo kissed her again, bundling her in his arms, knowing it made her feel safe. "And how little the amount is compared to the sum you'll ultimately receive."

"I guess I could present it to him," she said, relenting.

His chin rested on top of her head, which lay against his chest. "Our home is very lonely without you."

"I miss you so much."

She thought about what she had promised Milo. "Ralph is going to Saratoga in a few days and is adamant about my appearing there with him. That's the last thing in the world I want to do, but he has some dumb horse running there, and it's supposed to be a very social scene, so I guess I do have to go with him." She paused for a moment to consider what the social commitments would entail. "If I agree to go and play the loving wife in public for a day or two, I'll have a chance to talk to him on the way up."

Milo smiled with relief. "I knew you wouldn't fail me."

Before she left in the morning, she slipped five hundred dollars into the pocket of his trousers draped over the back of a chair. He relied on her money, but she did not want to shame him when he took it.

Chapter 10

Ralph usually awoke earlier than Gail, drank a glass of milk and ate a doughnut, and then descended to the limousine for the trip to the office. The car was available for Gail if she wanted it after her own breakfast, but she shunned it, preferring to take a subway to her destination, which was usually the Coalition's offices.

The next morning, however, Deighton knocked on Ralph's door, not with the customary tray and newspaper, but with a message that Mrs. Behr was awaiting him in the breakfast room. Ralph finished dressing and joined her.

"You want me to go to Saratoga," she began almost angrily. "How can I?"

"I don't follow you."

"I haven't . . . you know . . ." Her expression alternated between irritation and anxiety. Finally, she blurted out, "They dress differently. Don't tell me that it comes as a surprise. You've pointed it out often enough."

"You're worried about what you'll wear in Saratoga," Ralph replied with a small grin.

"Laugh. Go ahead. I know it's very funny to you."

"No, it's not, you are. As if you were going to the dentist for an extraction."

"It's all so phony."

"Yes. But people think clothes are important, so they're important."

Gail took a deep breath, but her voice was very small. "I don't have the vaguest idea of what's fashionable and what's not."

"Just look at some magazines." Even as he said it, Ralph noticed the stack of fashion magazines open in front of her. She must have stayed up late or woken early to pore over them. "You can hire a fashion coordinator."

"Oh, no! Not like some mining heiress who just snowshoed out of the Klondike."

"Maybe a friend who's well dressed."

"And admit it? As if I was an infant? I'm supposed to know how to dress."

"You want me to go with you, is that it? You want me to go with you, but you can't bring yourself to ask me after I've been telling you for months that—"

She exploded, "If you dare say you told me so, the whole thing is off."

Ralph tried hard to look serious. "I have one early appointment I can't break—at Watanabe's office. Why don't you come with me and then we'll go shopping."

She murmured a very low thanks and, now more relaxed, started to take another sip of her black coffee, all she could bear this early in the day, when she noticed Ralph's chocolate doughnut and milk. "Do you eat that for breakfast every morning?"

"Not always. If I'm in a hurry, I grab a Milky Way."

"That's the way children eat."

"It's a lot healthier," he countered, "than all that caffeine and no food."

181

"Look, I shouldn't have mentioned it. I appreciate your going with me."

A spasm clamped Gail's unreliable stomach as Ralph bit into the chocolate doughnut.

The meeting was held around a small conference table in Watanabe's private office. Watanabe presented and Ralph eventually approved a daring architectural scheme for the atrium, which was the focal point of pedestrian activity in Behr Center: an immense circular concrete plaza open to the sky, but protected from the elements by a clear plastic dome. Ralph had decided that elevating the plaza would provide a distinctive feature for the project and leave cavernous space beneath it, if the potential audience was there, perhaps for movie theaters, which would draw people to the project at night.

Watanabe's scheme to elaborate those ideas placed the slab twenty feet high on three legs at its outer circumference. The legs were the bases of arches that grew increasingly slim as they soared and crossed high above the plaza and also bore the weight of the plastic dome. The three towers and, between them, department stores and other retail structures, would be placed around the plaza's periphery, so that their main entrances would be on that level and face inward onto the plaza. Escalators in the towers and in the center of the atrium would descend to the ground and subterranean levels, where mass transportation and parking were located.

The streets crossed the center of the project at grade level. Watanabe's scheme avoided the potential controversy and delay that would ensue if Ralph sought the city's permission to bury the streets below ground.

Eli Steinman, the structural engineer, assured the others at the meeting that for all of its appearance of floating insubstantiality, the concrete arches on which the slab rested and which rose high above it could be designed with sufficient strength to bear safely the weight of the plaza's enormous width and high dome.

Ralph had confidence in Steinman's opinion, as well as in Steinman's associate, Larry Carlacci, a young structural and construction engineer who had recently supervised his building of an apartment project. Both men had already proven to Ralph that despite the daring design, their structural specifications would create a strong, solid structure.

Gail had been prepared to be bored by the architectural talk, but found herself enthralled. She had no idea that such care went into the planning. Here Ralph was in his element, and his insistent manner and assumption of authority no longer seemed out of place. From what little she had read about the project and her preconceptions about Ralph Behr's flamboyance, she had expected a gaudy carnival look, but the project was handsome in appearance and imaginative in concept, although she could not discern its location. Even Steinman, she gathered, had been given only subsurface information, not the address.

When the meeting ended, Ralph and Gail stayed behind so Ralph could discuss several additional matters with Watanabe. They had just begun to talk when a telephone rang. A grimace flickered briefly on Watanabe's normally impassive face. After several rings Ralph suggested that the architect answer the phone, but he refused. When the ringing continued, Watanabe felt called upon to explain.

"That's my private line," he declared with clipped pique. "That can only be my wife."

Realizing that he must now explain further, the Japanese-born architect confessed quietly, "How I envy native-born Americans, who are not subjected to the incompatible matching that often occurs in arranged marriages."

Watanabe mistook as sympathy the look that passed between his guests.

The first stop was Bendel's. A tidy, pleasant-faced saleslady, her hands clasped before her, greeted them as they stepped off the elevator. The store's head had alerted her to expect them. Gail's first reaction was defensive; she started to say that they were just looking and would call her if they found something they wished to purchase. Eyeing Gail's peasant blouse and jeans, Ralph interrupted to inform the sales lady that he was the one requiring help—he was making his wife the gift of a new wardrobe; she had just donated hers to the fund for Yugoslav Widows and Orphans. He did not even bother to glance back at the laser-beam stare that he knew must now be melting twin holes through his back.

Ralph sat in the open area at the rear of the floor and watched as Gail timidly appeared before him in a succession of outfits. He was surprised that in the right clothes—a tailored suit, for example—she revealed a trimly attractive figure. She noted that his taste in accepting or rejecting a garment was exercised with swift sureness, as if he were evaluating proposed designs for a building. In his mind, she realized, she had been categorized as another project.

At one point Gail flounced out of the dressing room wearing what looked almost like a jumper, for the first time that day a large smile lighting her face.

"No," Ralph told the saleslady.

"But I love it," Gail insisted. "It's the only one I picked out myself. The colors are wonderful: bright blues and yellows."

"Maybe in a painting, but they're so bright they detract from your own hair color. Mainly, though, it's too young for you; it makes you look like a child, not a woman."

Gail glanced plaintively at the saleslady, whose nod indicated that Ralph was confirming what she herself had told Gail in the dressing room.

An hour later Gail and Ralph deposited their many packages in the limousine. Gail, exhausted, collapsed against the seat.

"I hadn't realized what condition those luncheon ladies have to be in for this. If I never do it again for the rest of my life, it will be too soon."

"We're just getting started. I had my secretary make appointments for us at Bill Blass, Geoffrey Beene, Oscar de la Renta, Mary McFadden, and Carolyn Roehm."

Gail's eyes appeared to be drowning. She had planned to be reasonable about the prices of the items she chose, but to her surprise, Ralph never asked the cost of anything. Sumptuous garments followed each other in such profusion that she soon lost track of every showroom they visited and everything they bought: evening gowns, suits, cocktail dresses, day wear, light flowered dresses for Saratoga, sportswear, slacks, shoes, coats, blouses, hats, gloves, lingerie. To all her other reasons for hating him, she added his wastrel spending on her.

Milo had located a large space in Soho, the now trendy area South of Houston Street, that was about to be vacated. Although she immediately went to view it, Gail was so busy at the Coalition that only as the limousine was picking her up at the Fifth Avenue apartment before the trip to Saratoga did she begin to think through how she would ask Ralph to transfer funds to her for the art gallery. Her five suitcases filled the trunk. Ralph's two sat beside the chauffeur. Ralph was deep in conversation with Ben Rogovin outside Behr House when the limousine pulled up. Ralph waved the other man into the car, made a perfunctory introduction, and continued their conversation. Gail assumed they were giving the associate a lift to a nearby appointment before she and Ralph continued the drive up the Thruway to Saratoga.

The car swung into the heliport at the edge of the river and up to a green-and-white helicopter with the Behr Group's name printed boldly on the sides. For a moment Gail conjectured that they were dropping the other man off here, until the chauffeur opened the door for her.

"Oh, no," she exclaimed to Ralph. "Not on your life."

"We're attending a cocktail party in two hours and a ball later on."

"Ralph, I suggest we put off the cocktail party and take a leisurely ride up the Hudson, perhaps have a nice conversation, and then, when we get up there—"

"This is the chauffeur's weekend off," he told her, wishing he had taken the trouble to learn this one's name. He placed his hand firmly in the small of her back and, pushing her out in front of him, continued his speech. "I know how concerned you are about the rights of working people. He put in such long hours this week. I'm sure you wouldn't want to deprive him of these few days of free time."

"Are you really off?" she asked as she emerged onto the asphalt.

"Yes, ma'am, until Mr. Behr returns."

Knowing she had been manipulated, but unwilling to betray her values, Gail glumly continued on toward the giant grasshopper that waited to swallow her. Discussing the art-gallery proposal when she was in the cabin with Ralph would take her mind off the terror of being borne aloft by a craft without wings. But Ralph had not finished his business agenda and directed Rogovin to join them in the cabin. The pilot could deposit Rogovin back in Manhattan after dropping off Ralph and Gail in Saratoga.

While the two men continued their talk, incomprehensible to her in its real-estate jargon, the helicopter gently lifted up and away to the north, nonetheless leaving a very tense Gail sure she was about to throw up all over her new Geoffrey Beene outfit.

As Gail's equilibrium returned, she tried not to watch the unrolling of the geography below for fear of provoking her nausea again. Instead, she stared across the cabin at Ralph. The day before, her friend Carla had asked what he was like as a person, and Gail was franker than she had intended because the question had been on her mind—she was having a hard time

185

figuring him out. Measuring her words carefully, she had said, "I suppose more than anything else, I'm the kind of person who is galvanized into action by my fears. I undertake causes I want to believe will be worthwhile enough to crowd them out. You see, I have to trick myself into believing that there's a point to life, that taking action can overcome despair. But Ralph never seems to be troubled by anything. All those layers of complications are totally absent in him. He seems to have no irony, no fear."

Now Gail watched him more than listened as he laid out strategies to his aide. She imagined that in an earlier day, with a different scale of achievement, he might have aspired to be an Alexander or Attila or Napoleon, insensitive to the anguish and tragedy that keened behind his progress toward glory.

"He's like some animal perfectly formed by a hundred million years of natural selection and survival of the fittest to be exactly what he is," she remembered telling Carla. "He's galvanized only by his own ego, his own massive, rapacious ego."

"If you really think he's like that," Carla had asked in shock, "why did you marry him?"

Only then did Gail remember that she must cover up. She smiled. "I envy him really, for not agonizing over everything like so many of us do." Then, with something close to admiration in her voice, she added, "I don't think he fears even death."

And as she watched him, she realized that that too was probably the truth.

In August every year the New York City racetracks suspend operation for a month, and thoroughbred racing moves upstate, north of Albany, to the town of Saratoga Springs. The area's natural mineral waters were the original attraction for summer visitors, and later its racetrack and illegal gambling houses. Rocking chairs lined the wide verandas of grand Victorian hotels along Broadway then. When the gambling casinos were closed down, the track, with its month-long race meet, remained, as did the thoroughbred yearling sales and a polo field, all of which continued to draw the upper-class horsey set back to their opulent summer homes. A performing arts center was built for summer cultural events. And, of course, there were still the parties, the profusion of parties.

Nearly a year before Ralph had rented a mansion and, in the weeks preceding this trip, had used his contacts to be certain that he was invited to the major social events during his stay. He knew some of the people who would be at the ball, of course, primarily those who owned racehorses, but he was very conscious of not being part of that crowd, and he did not want to risk the humiliation of being snubbed. His horse would be running. Everyone would know he was in Saratoga, and everyone would know if he was not at the best parties.

The ball was held at the Canfield Casino, now restored as the home of the Museum of the Historical Society of Saratoga Springs. They traveled to the ball in an open, horse-drawn carriage Ralph had rented.

"This transportation is ludicrous," Gail had warned him.

But, arriving at the casino, Gail found a line of carriages ahead of them waiting to discharge passengers.

Filled with misgivings as they entered and greeted their hostess, Gail wore a white McFadden with a floor-length pleated skirt, halter top and low back, which she had been assured would be considered summery, yet elegant and restrained. Gail felt that she had sneaked her lumpish, graceless body into someone else's clothes and that everyone could tell. Because she was here with Ralph, she could not hide; people stared at them and came up to greet them, even people who did not know him, but wanted to.

A woman she recognized approached. "Diane!" she greeted her with delight. "Thank heaven there's someone I know here."

"You look lovely, Gail. You have such fresh, healthy looks."

Gail determined to take her mind off herself and have a good time. Diane Northwood introduced Gail to her husband, and then the husbands were introduced around. The men began to talk business, and Diane guided Gail to a nearby group of women whom she wanted to hear about the women's shelter program.

Ralph was relieved when Gail left. Subdued, perhaps because of the new clothing and the surroundings, accompanied by someone she knew, Gail was not apt to foment trouble for him, and he could be more relaxed. Diane's husband introduced him to some other men, and then Ralph began to wander about alone, weaving his way around the guests and the waiters and around the unlikely assortment of street entertainers sprinkled about the premises: jugglers, sword swallowers, magicians, clowns, singers, tap dancers.

The band struck up a Dixieland number, and several young couples jostled him on their way to the dance floor. The room had grown warm and noisy. Ralph walked toward the garden for some air.

A tall young woman was standing in the doorway, her back toward him, her blond hair in the moonlight a cascade of silver that fell onto her bare shoulders like a bridal veil. At that instant she turned around, and he saw her face, so exquisite, so perfect, so innocent, that the face of every other woman he had ever seen seemed coarse by comparison. The moonlight danced along her cheek and the lines of her nose and brows and lips, making her appear as ethereal as the light which revealed her. She looked straight at him. Her eyes were blue, an inky blue in the dimness, and she too seemed transfixed.

Later, when he thought about it, he was amazed that for all those long seconds, not a single person in that crowded room crossed the open floor between them to break the enchantment.

"What's your name?" he asked when he had moved to her.

She took a long time to answer, as if alighting from a realm where words are unnecessary for communication.

"Amanda," she finally said.

"Mine is Ralph."

Her laugh sounded like crystal bells to him. "Everybody knows who you are."

Ralph suddenly felt very stupid, unable to think of anything to say, fearful that she would walk off unless he did. Groping for words, he asked, "Have we ever met?"

"Do you think we have?"

She spoke slowly, allowing long silences to elapse, unconcerned about filling them. Her eyes, like matched sapphires set wide apart, never wavered in their gaze; unself-conscious, they revealed nothing of her beyond their appearance. She reminded him of a young Grace Kelly patiently awaiting coronation. Her perfect beauty combined with her self-assurance to maintain effortlessly a spell that had always before evaporated for Ralph as first impression dissipated on acquaintance.

Ralph was about to ask her last name when he noticed her gaze shift to the side. He turned.

"What a pleasant surprise, Ralph, to find you here. You've already met my daughter, I see. Is your wife here with you? I'd like to meet her."

The speaker was Charles Brookhouse, his new banker. Saddled by a married state he could not easily explain away, Ralph felt gripped by anxiety. He scanned the room.

"Right over there, as a matter of fact."

Had Brookhouse mentioned Gail, Ralph wondered, as a precaution against an unwanted attachment between his daughter and a married man or was it simply courtesy on his part?

A few minutes later, when the five of them were together chatting, Ralph decided that the purpose had been courtesy, and possibly an opportunity to learn a bit more about his new borrower. Ralph harbored a twinge of concern that Gail might fling barbs at this pillar of banking and society, whose wealth was founded on a robber-baron forefather's aggressiveness. But Gail had obviously been having a good time this evening. She was vivacious and, incredibly to Ralph, began to elicit an amused nature from Charles Brookhouse, a man whom he had always found to be unrelievedly grave.

Brookhouse insisted that the Behrs fill the empty places at his table for the dinner. Gail's wit was in good form, and bearing none of the malice she often displayed toward Ralph, she kept the group entertained. Ralph too laughed and joked and held up his end of the conversation, but his mind was occupied by the blond young woman sitting very coolly several chairs away from him, on her father's other side. Between them was her mother, a pretty woman in her forties who resembled her daughter. Several times he tried to engage Amanda's eyes, but could not. She possessed in ultimate form everything that he craved in a woman, and he was in agony, fearing that he had lost her.

When dinner was over, as Brookhouse and his wife were saying good-bye to Gail and another couple who had been at their table, Amanda turned away from them and toward Ralph.

"I understand you're a horseman, Mr. Behr. I know you have a horse running tomorrow. Do you ride?"

"Yes."

"Would you join me tomorrow morning? I have a big brown stallion you might like."

He could phone the caretaker at his country home and have his riding clothes driven up overnight. "I'd love to. But there's a yearling filly I have to look at first thing. She comes up for sale tomorrow night."

Amanda's eyes lit. "Could I go with you to see her? We could ride afterward."

"Eight o'clock at the yearling barns."

She nodded and smiled, as if to an old family acquaintance, and shifted her attention back to her father.

That night, for the first time he could remember, Ralph was unable to sleep.

* * *

His riding clothes arrived at dawn. Ralph dressed immediately. He drove the blue Mercedes 500 SEC he had had customized into a convertible through the countryside until it was time for him to be at the yearling barns.

Ralph had no inherent love of rustic scenery, of nature proliferated into grass and flowers and trees. He could recognize its beauty, but viewing was a passive act, and it bored him very quickly. At such moments he yearned to click swiftly from that vista to the next, as if viewing a slide show. For him land existed mainly as the stage for what man, or rather *he*, could build upon it. Today, though, his senses were alive to his natural surroundings: he heard brooks skipping over rocks near the roadside, saw flowers punctuating with color the landscapes he traversed, and savored the warm breeze rustling the trees that crowded each other and leaned out over the road, waving at him as if he drove along a parade route.

Finally, Ralph headed the car toward the yearling barns. His love of horses had started young. His father had first put him on a horse at two and a half, much like Henry's own father had done with him. Ralph could still remember continuously slipping off, his legs too short to grip the pony's flanks, and his father always being there to hoist him back up by the seat of his jodhpurs. He could remember too the thrill he felt at controlling the huge animal.

Bobby Bakst, the trainer of his racehorses, and Eddie Gorman, the manager of his Kentucky horse farm, were waiting for Ralph as he drove up. Amanda was not. Bakst was an ex-jockey who, in preparation for the day he would retire, had become an assistant trainer while waiting for a broken collarbone to heal. He had ridden for Ralph several times and his insightful comments afterward convinced Ralph to offer him the trainer's job, replacing an evasive trainer in whom he had lost confidence. In his forties and fighting to get down to riding weight, Bakst happily took the job and yielded to the last five pounds. He still acted as exercise boy on the better horses in the stable and had galloped the best of them, Patagonia, that morning, to loosen up the horse's muscles.

"It was all I could do to hold him. He's as fit as he could be without a race under his belt. He needs the race today to be ready to go a mile and a quarter in the Travers."

"Tell me about this Secretariat filly," Ralph said.

Gorman, a lanky Kentuckian, spoke up. "She's the best year-

190

ling in the sale. The Nijinsky colt looks better on paper than he does in the flesh. Ankles look suspicious."

"OK, let's see the filly," Ralph ordered.

A few minutes later a groom emerged from the horse barn with a chestnut filly on a halter. She walked with her head up, prancing lightly.

A black BMW drove up. Amanda was at the wheel. She strode quickly toward them, as beautiful as he remembered her, but fresher and more vibrant-looking in the daylight.

"Sorry," she said to Ralph. "I really tried to be on time. I was closer this morning than I usually am. I hope that counts."

"Your being here counts."

"What do you think?" Ralph said, motioning toward the filly.

"She's the Secretariat filly, isn't she?" Amanda exclaimed. There was a spark in that enthusiasm that Ralph found immensely appealing. "Oh, Ralph, she's gorgeous." She dropped her voice to keep the groom from hearing. "I guess I shouldn't have said that out loud if there's a chance you might bid on her."

"It doesn't matter. With her breeding she's no secret."

"*Will* you bid on her?"

"I'm going to buy her. If you'll let me, I want to name her Amanda."

Ralph could not decipher the young woman's expression and feared he had overstepped propriety—they hardly knew each other, and she believed him to be married. Damn it! He was.

As they walked to the Mercedes, she spoke up. Her voice was clear and untroubled. "I was afraid you were going to name her after your wife."

"I want to explain about my wife." Ralph's own voice was somber; he had been rehearsing all night what he would say.

"You don't have to."

Ralph stared at Amanda in astonishment.

"It doesn't matter to me about her, not yet anyway. You barely looked at her or spoke to her all night."

"But I *want* to explain."

Amanda considered that for a moment. "After we've become lovers."

Ralph halted and stared at Amanda.

She spoke again. "I want you to be sure first that I'm in love with you."

Amanda knew the riding trails around Saratoga and led the way up into heavily wooded hills. She was a superb rider, back straight, toes up in the stirrups, hands quiet above the pommel. Along a wide, fairly level stretch, she suddenly broke into a fast gallop, catching Ralph off guard, laughing back over her shoulder. He raced after her, but then she slowed her mare to a walk and, beaming at him, guided her onto a path he did not see until his own horse was already in the woods, climbing the hill behind her.

They emerged onto a clearing at the top of the hill and pulled up their horses. Amanda leaned over to Ralph and kissed him. She tasted like pine and flowers, and the simultaneous assault on his senses made his flesh feel about to burst through his skin. He jumped from the saddle and reached up for her waist, lowering her gently into his arms. This time they kissed more deeply, pressing hard against each other. Although he held her in his arms, she seemed paradoxically insubstantial, a creature almost as much of his fantasies as of flesh and bone.

Reluctantly, he separated from her and tied the horses' reins to tree trunks.

"When I found this place," she said, "years ago, I knew that when I made love for the first time here I wanted to be in love."

"And you're sure you are?"

She smiled and kissed him lightly, her arms around his neck.

He led her to a knoll, beneath an ancient tree. He spread his jacket on the far side, away from anyone who might approach on the hidden path they had taken, although Amanda assured him she had never seen another soul here.

She lay back on the jacket. He sat beside her, staring down at the flawless being who had told him she loved him. The light through the shifting leaves caused her hair to shimmer like gold dust spilled about her and her eyes to sparkle as if luminous sea creatures swam deep within them. The mystery of the enchantment that suffused her and held him captive seemed to be buried at the bottom of the blueness.

"Tell me again," he said.

"That I love you?"

He nodded.

"I love you," she said. "I have waited all my life to love a man like you."

She put her finger to his lips before he could offer his own pledge. "Please don't. It's enough to me, it's everything, that I love *you*."

He stretched out beside her and drew her against him, seeking her lips once more. Then, rising onto an elbow, he began, very deliberately, to open the light cotton blouse she wore and then the sheer bra, which fell to either side of her breasts. Her breasts were full, but her nipples delicate and pink. Like a child's, he thought, exactly as they should be. He bent to kiss one of the nipples, feeling it with the tip of his tongue and the shudder that followed, like an earth tremor.

He unbuckled her belt and then opened her jodhpurs, pulling down the zipper. Suddenly, she began to laugh. He understood why only when he saw her pointing to her boots.

"All the times I imagined making love here," she said, finally managing to speak through her laughter, "I always forgot about the boots."

They helped each other to undress and, when both were naked, lay down again together.

"Everything," he whispered, "every single part of you, is beautiful."

"And we are in our own little Eden."

She was already wet when his hand finally slid from her breast to the hollow between her legs. Her eyes closed, and she bit her lower lip in response to surges of sensation.

When he lowered himself over her, her legs drawn up and wide, she let out a little cry and then slowly, almost involuntarily, began moving in rhythm with him. He tried to hold off, to give her time, but he desired her too much and could not. He pulled out of her only an instant before he came and fell through the greenness until he opened his eyes, and she still was there.

Chapter 11

Ralph had already left to view the filly and meet Amanda by the time Gail awoke. When Diane telephoned soon afterward, Gail accepted an invitation to breakfast with her and her husband at their house nearby. She returned only a few minutes before Ralph did.

"Oh, there you are," she called out when he entered. "Deighton wants to know if we're taking lunch on the rear patio."

He was smiling. "Sure, sounds fine. Beautiful day. We don't have to be at the track until three or so. My horse is in the feature. Just give me a couple of minutes to take off the boots, shower, and change."

She was already seated at the glass table on the patio when he returned.

"You seem in a good mood today," she greeted him. She hoped to keep the conversation pleasant between them.

"Couldn't be better. You?"

"Very uncomfortable. I couldn't wait to get back here."

He sat down at the place setting opposite her.

"Where were you?"

"Diane and Avery Northwood's. She telephoned and invited us over for breakfast. You were already gone, so she asked me over alone."

Gail recalled something. "They kept calling their house, which was immense and really magnificent, a cottage. At first I thought it was a joke. But he doesn't joke—ever."

"I forgot to tell you, they call these places cottages. Kind of reverse snobbism."

"Like Marie Antoinette and her friends dressing up as shepherdesses. Oh, for the simple wonders of poverty!"

"That Northwood woman seemed down to earth."

"Ralph, I really think she's terrific. She was one of the women Annabelle Grinstead invited to the Coalition."

He nodded. "You mentioned that last night, when you introduced them."

"But she's so different around him, as if she's got to be on good behavior. He's so stiff and formal. When they speak to each other, it's like diplomats at a conference. I felt so uncomfortable. With you, even with all our disagreements, I never feel that I can't say and do what I want. It's as if she's on permanent probation. She had told me that she wanted to work a few hours a week as a volunteer at the women's shelter. Her husband must have refused to let her. It was so sad and embarrassing when she told me she had changed her mind."

"She *might* be on permanent probation."

Gail's puzzled expression caused Ralph to elucidate.

"A prenuptial agreement that leaves her very little if they're divorced."

"Do you think that might be it? Oh, God, to live one's life like that!"

"She lives well. Obviously, it was worth it to her. One of the reasons you might feel like an equal is because financially you are. The way I look at it, in the end everything, especially relationships, comes down to power—financial, psychological, what have you."

Gail was about to object that she would not compromise her self-respect, regardless of her finances, when a thought stopped her. "A lot of the women who come to us for help just can't leave their men because they need the financial support, so they continue to take the abuse."

Deighton appeared with crabmeat appetizers and iced tea.

Amanda was on Ralph's mind. "I guess it's important for a woman to have enough money to feel secure. But I'd feel like some kind of sponger if she paid for anything, like I wasn't much of a man."

Thinking that he was referring to Milo, Gail was about to take umbrage when, guiltily, she recalled that she hadn't thought about her pledge to seek funds from Ralph since their trip to Saratoga began. "Ralph, I've been waiting for a chance to talk to you about something financial. About an advance against the money I'll be getting."

Gail explained that she and Milo wanted to start an art gallery. He had found space in an area of Soho known for galleries. They needed the initial rental payments by the first of next week or they would lose it. When Ralph questioned her about the exact amount required for construction, for operating costs, for a reserve and how all of those figures tallied against expected revenues, Gail's answer each time was that she did not yet know.

"You don't have the slightest approximation of a business plan, but you're ready to put money down on the space?"

"Milo is sure we'll lose it otherwise."

"And Milo has a lot of experience in these things."

"Look," Gail began, her anger rising out of her chagrin, "the money will be mine in two years. This is a very small sum in comparison."

"Right now, we are partners in everything but Behr Center and some East Side property. If you build an art gallery, whether I like it or not, I'm your partner, not good old Milo."

Now Gail had greater cause for anger. "Your objection is to Milo, right? You don't like Milo, so you don't want me to have the money."

"What I think of Milo has nothing to do with it. What does is that you have no conception of how to run a business, any business. I've picked you up at that Coalition and gotten a look

195

at the way you handle finances—receipts in shoe boxes, when there *are* receipts, almost nonexistent bookkeeping, no long-term planning. Which means that, second of all, I'm the one who'll look bad. And I've worked too hard at succeeding to have my reputation ruined by the two of you playing at being patrons of the arts."

"You already assume we'll fail, as if you're the only one who knows how to run anything."

"Tell you what, you want an art gallery? Fine, we'll go into the art gallery business. You and I as partners, not Milo. Whatever role you want to assign Milo is fine—tell people it's part of your divorce settlement—but you and I own it. I approve all major decisions—and all major expenses. And I expect a logical business plan."

"Talk about power hungry! Why do you always feel you have to control everything. You're just a better-disguised version of Avery Northwood."

"And we start with my sitting down with this landlord of yours."

"You're saying I have no other choice."

"Partners, all the way."

Gail stabbed her last piece of crabmeat. "Partners."

"Horse racing is a vicious and cruel sport. You rich people force these poor creatures to run by putting a man on their backs to whip them and yank at their mouths and kick sharp points into their ribs." Gail had been cross since lunch had deteriorated into snide insults and a few fast bites of food. "But the greatest cruelty is perpetrated on the poor bettors. They lose their rent money and starve their families—I've seen them. The rich people who run the sport work hard to keep them addicted because their betting provides the money that supports racing. The sport of kings. Hah!"

Earlier in their marriage Ralph would have defended his position, pointing out that no one was forced to bet, that people did so in the hope of winning, not of losing, and that all sports attracted gambling, the profits of which were better funneled into government programs than into the pockets of organized crime. Today, though, as he drove the Mercedes into the horsemen's parking area, he only half heard Gail's criticism; he was far too inured to her disapproval to pay much mind, and he was far too happy. His thoughts were on the expectation of seeing Amanda very soon: she too would be at the track.

196

Ralph was sure he was in love. Despite his disparagement of men who fell fast into that state of foolish euphoria, he was feeling wonderful. He enumerated Amanda's attractions. She was beautiful—incredibly desirable. She was intelligent, gracious—certainly she was accomplished: a linguist, a horsewoman. She came from the cream of society, a name as renowned, as coveted, as Vanderbilt or Whitney or Rockefeller.

"God, I wish I had brought a book," Gail groused as Ralph handed her a pair of binoculars. He turned the car over to the attendant, handing him a five-dollar tip.

"Thanks, Mr. Behr," the attendant exclaimed. "Good luck today. Should I put it on Patagonia?"

"That's a question you'd be better off asking the horse," Ralph replied. He did not bet himself—winning or losing a few thousand dollars seemed meaningless—and he never gave betting advice to others, so as not to be blamed if they lost.

As Ralph and Gail rode up the escalator to the box seats, it occurred to him that he had gone longer today without telephoning the office than he could ever remember on a weekday. He had felt no need to do so, and only now thought about telephoning because the sight of the track made him remember that New York State racetracks contain no public phones, a holdover from the pre-electronic betting age when conspirators, right after a race, telephoned the results to colleagues outside the grounds, who then rushed to place bets with bookmakers unaware that the race had already been run.

Saratoga is a very old track that still retains its country-fair look. The open brown wooden stands run nearly the length of the stretch and are protected from rain and sun by a shingled roof supported by tall wooden posts and topped by pyramid-shaped spires. Gail was charmed by the stands and by the grass and hedges and by the lake with waterfowl in the infield area that was at the center of three concentric tracks: dirt on the outermost and turf covering the inner two.

The attendant led them to their box. Gail pointed out that two rows down and several boxes to the right the Brookhouses were sitting with some other people. Ralph had himself noticed the Brookhouse box the instant he entered the area. Amanda turned, as if she had been checking for his appearance all afternoon. For the merest instant she caught his eye before she smiled noncommittally at both of them. She wore a light blue flowered dress that set off her eyes and made her skin look dusted by sunbeams. Why hadn't he noticed her tan this morning? he wondered, experiencing a tinge of self-accusation. Because he could not remember lighter patches on her body, he decided that she must sunbathe nude. The image of a nymph flitting among trees flashed through his mind. The thought aroused him. She looked so beautiful that he ached at the separation that kept him from touching her.

"The biggest surprise of this trip was eating dinner with the Brookhouses," Gail remarked. "People in real life don't do that. Did you know them before last night?"

"Only Charles. He's the lender on Behr Center."

"I like him, Ralph. What a shock that is! You can't know how many times I've imagined him as the image of corporate evil incarnate. He isn't at all what I thought he was like. He's very reserved and formal, of course, but he has this strong sense of responsibility that motivates him entirely. He reminded me a lot of my father."

If Ralph had not been preoccupied with thoughts of Amanda and people had not been seated near them on both sides, he might have glared at Gail or even told her off once and for all.

Several races were still to be run before Patagonia's stake race. Between races Gail went strolling on the grounds with Diane and several women she had met the previous evening. Much to her surprise, she found she enjoyed the entire experience: the socializing; the colorful, country atmosphere; being so close to the horses she could feel their breath as they pranced by; and the culminating thrill of the races themselves. People from every station in life were mingling here for a festive day. She had never understood the extent to which these swift, beautiful animals mounted by tiny athletes were engaged in a sport, and that betting was not necessarily a disease, but a means of participating in the victory.

When it was time to walk to the paddock to watch Patagonia being saddled, Ralph's hope that Gail might remain disinterested had become fruitless. She wanted to join him. Amanda was waiting beneath the tall oaks as they approached. Gail greeted her warmly. Flanked by both women, he entered the grass enclosure. Onlookers leaned over the white rail fence.

Ralph regarded his program. Patagonia was number three. Gang Tackle, number four, was the only serious contender. Like Patagonia a class runner out of training for several months, he too was now being pointed for the fall classics. Unlike Patagonia, he already had a race under his belt, which he had won easily. Ralph caught sight of him just as he was entering the paddock, a heavily muscled bay. Patagonia was lighter and thinner and skipped nervously at the end of his groom's bridle. He had finished his two-year-old campaign with victories in a couple of major stakes that made him runner-up for an Eclipse Award. A training injury had forced him to miss the Triple Crown, but a lackluster group of three-year-old colts had left the rest of the year wide open for him.

While the jockey's attendant looked on, Bobby Bakst and his groom placed the pad and cloth beneath the narrow leather saddle and fixed it atop the colt by means of elastic girths they buckled tightly beneath the horse. The grooms then walked their charges around the dirt path worn out of the grass oval until the jockeys sauntered into the enclosure. Although twenty years older, Bakst was no bigger than Montez, the jockey engaged to ride Patagonia. Gail was fascinated by the sight of the two little men discussing strategy beside an animal which towered over both of them. Bakst inquired whether Ralph wished to add any comments. Ralph reminded Montez that the colt tended to shy away from the whip if it was shaken at him. Then they all wished each other luck, and the groom gave Montez a leg up onto Patagonia. One more loop around the paddock, and the horses filed out and toward the track.

"What do you think?" Ralph asked Amanda as they walked back to the boxes with Gail.

"How has he looked in training?"

"Bakst says 'great,' but that he isn't quite racing fit yet."

"Gang Tackle is a speed horse. If no one runs with him and pushes him, he might have too much left at the finish."

"Patagonia's not going to let him get a big lead, and he's not going to lose," Ralph declared, as if willing the horse to absorb some of his own determination.

Amanda laughed and brushed his hand for a moment. "If only you could run for him."

"With the right filly waiting at the finish line," he replied with an easy smile. "Will you come to the winner's circle?"

"Stop by our box afterward."

Amanda moved apart from them, appearing absorbed by an ice-cream stand to one side of the escalator rising to the building's spectator level.

"Amanda Brookhouse and you?" Gail murmured in utter surprise. "Beauty and the beast. Jesus, you work fast."

"Don't tell me you're jealous."

Gail eyed him with scorn.

Bakst joined them in the box just before post time. Patagonia and Gang Tackle closed as co-favorites at three to two. The starting gate was at the head of the stretch. Patagonia was slow to break from it, hung back all the way down that straightaway, and continued to lope with the pack along the back stretch while Gang Tackle opened five lengths on the second horse. Gail grabbed Ralph's arm.

"What's your jockey doing?" she yelled over the noise. "You said he couldn't let that other horse in red get a big lead."

"My horse broke slowly."

"The pace is very fast," Bakst commented defensively. "Montez probably thinks Gang Tackle will wear himself out."

"I hope he's right," Ralph declared.

Around the clubhouse turn, Patagonia began to move around horses. At the head of the stretch, he was second, with the five lengths still to make up. Gail was screaming now.

"Come on, Patagonia! You can catch him! You can catch him!"

Gradually, the gap between the horses narrowed, but also the distance left to the finish line.

Gail beat on Ralph's arm. "Oh, God, he's not going to catch him!"

Ralph was silent. Inside his voice was low and intense: You're going to make it. You're going to make it.

"Come on, you lovely horse!" Gail yelled and then, again and again as she jumped up and down, "Come on! Come on!"

With less than two hundred yards to go, Patagonia started to move faster, his head and neck thrust forward and lower and his legs reaching farther. Gang Tackle was game, not slowing at all. As he saw Patagonia move up alongside him, he tried to reach down within himself for that extra burst, as Patagonia had done, but could not. They flashed past the finish line with Patagonia a neck ahead.

"He did it!" Gail was yelling, hugging Ralph and jumping up and down. "He did it! What a lovely, wonderful horse!"

They and Bakst dashed downstairs, taking congratulations all the way. Ralph hugged Patagonia's head, sweat and all.

"What an athlete you are! Incredible."

They all reached up and shook hands with the jockey and quickly posed for pictures before he jumped down to go to the scale. Sportswriters were waiting outside the winner's circle to interview Ralph. Then the group hurried back to the box seats.

"He was breathing hard," Bakst pointed out as they walked,

"but Montez says he could have gone farther. We may just have ourselves a top three-year-old, Mr. Behr."

"He's the best horse in America!" Ralph declared jubilantly. "The best!"

Ralph purposely chose a route that brought him past the Brookhouses. His gaze was on Amanda and the elation and pride on her face.

"Congratulations, Ralph, Gail," Charles Brookhouse murmured. "Your horse ran a courageous race."

Charles and his wife offered their hands to shake.

"He's terrific!" Amanda added enthusiastically, and her smile conveyed that she was not speaking only about the horse.

"The others with us would like an opportunity to congratulate you, I'm sure." Charles turned to the three people in the row behind them. "Baron and Baroness von Dunkheim."

Ralph reached up, shook hands with the German couple, and turned to the older woman beside them.

"My stepmother, Mrs. Brookhouse," Charles announced.

Ralph looked at her for the first time. In her eyes was a terror she seemed to be trying with all her strength to hide. Ralph immediately understood why. The woman was the tall blond lady, his natural mother.

Ralph left the racetrack within minutes. Driving back to their house, Gail's excitement was such that she failed to notice Ralph's had fled and that he was nearly silent. What little attention he paid to her consisted of muttered annoyance at her proprietary pleasure over the success of "their" horse. She insisted on reminding him that they were partners, as Ralph himself had insisted on pointing out to her about the proposed art gallery only this morning.

Ralph fled to his dressing room as soon as they reached the house. They would have to change for the evening. He had been deeply shaken by the encounter with the blond woman—he still thought of her as that, although he had not thought of her at all for many years. Momentary questions about who he was, something of which he was so solidly sure, flitted in and out of the fear that preoccupied him, the fear that the romance with Amanda that had engulfed him so swiftly less than twenty-four hours ago might be doomed.

Stepmother, Ralph repeated to himself. I'm positive Charles had said stepmother. Ralph could even remember having once heard that Charles's father, Otis Brookhouse, had been widowed

201

with two small children, Charles and his sister, before marrying for a second time. Ralph himself was thus unrelated to Amanda, whose biological grandmother had died half a century earlier.

He knew so little about her, bits and snatches, but was in love with what he was certain were the important things. He felt desire for her whirling within him as he brought to mind her beauty and delicate gentility and the social grace that could be engendered only by birth into so elite a family. Subconsciously Ralph, who was so logical and practical, had been waiting all his adult life to be swept away by a romance that appealed to neither of those qualities. If he was to fall in love, he wanted it to be with a goddess.

His sham marriage was obstacle enough to his winning Amanda, but now there was her grandmother. His thoughts halted at the word, and he realized he must face and assimilate the more telling fact: that Nina Brookhouse was his biological mother, half of her genes were his. And he must face too that he hated her for spurning him.

Physically, except for the aging of her skin and the grayness undulating dark to light in her hair, she looked much as he remembered her: she was tall and slim; she carried herself with an elegant straightness of spine and civility of manner; she was still beautiful. He stared at himself in the bathroom mirror, seeking the resemblance to his mother. The shape of their faces and of their noses and eyes were similar, though not their eye color. His were almost green, hers blue, a color close to Amanda's, despite the fact that the two women had no blood relationship. Ralph calculated that Nina's love affair with his father, which had produced him, must have occurred well after her marriage to Otis Brookhouse.

With Henry retired Ralph had not bothered to consult him when he approached Metrobank for Behr Center's financing. Several times in the past, whenever Ralph had mentioned feeling out Metrobank for financing, Henry had dissuaded him for reasons that seemed superficial. Now Ralph understood why.

Ralph was not given to sustained introspection. He quickly decided that he and Nina had no more relationship than a foal would have with the mare from whom it was taken at birth when she refused to nurse it. Chromosomes could have been contributed by anyone. Thank God they had not also been contributed to Amanda. He refused to consider whether some unacknowledged part of him was eager or even mildly curious to know more about Nina. He knew who he was and what he wanted. He wanted Amanda.

The men and women in evening dress about to enter the Fasig-Tipton sales pavillion glowed pale pink in the early evening light, making them appear to be the charmed and fantastical deities that careworn, envious mortals believed them to be.

Ralph had invited the Brookhouses to the final night's yearling sale and was chatting with Patricia Brookhouse, Charles's wife, whom everyone called Patty. Gail and the others stood several yards away, where Charles had fallen into a conversation with a French art dealer with whom he was acquainted.

"I must tell you," Patty Brookhouse confided to Ralph, "Charles is absolutely enchanted by your wife. He thinks you two are a splendid couple. Stability is very important to him, you know. I imagine it's partly the banker in him. He wants to be certain that those to whom he lends are solid and reliable. He takes it badly when he finds that his trust has been misplaced."

Ralph could discover no sign in her face that she intended her words as a warning. Born a wealthy patrician with roots firmly planted in Puritan soil, Patty Brookhouse was reserved and undemonstrative, much like many others in her social class. But Ralph was also beginning to appreciate that this traditional upperclass wife and mother, tactful and yielding, also possessed the poise he had observed in her husband and daughter. His own self-confidence stemmed from a certainty about what he could do, *theirs* from what they were entitled to be.

As they spoke he glanced frequently over at Nina. She wore a gray and red gown with a narrow skirt that accentuated her height and slimness. A small ruby necklace and matching earrings completed the ensemble.

"Amanda and her grandmother seem very close," Ralph commented, observing the smiles that often passed between the two in recognition of a shared reaction.

"Yes, they are. In some ways, I'm a bit embarrassed to say, she's closer to my daughter than I am."

The sale was beginning and the Secretariat filly would be coming up early, so Ralph motioned for the others to begin heading inside.

Although the astronomical prices for thoroughbreds had descended somewhat in recent years, a top yearling could still cost a fortune at auction and a stallion with a fine racing record command many millions when syndicated for breeding to those eager for its progeny.

Only the auctioneer's inducing singsong interrupted the tense silence as the bidding on the Secretariat filly reached two million dollars. Ralph's first and only bid—two million two hundred thousand dollars—won her. In the ensuing hubbub, as Charles offered his congratulations, Ralph gallantly indicated he would name her for Amanda, his banker's daughter, and Nina instantly suggested that naming the filly for Ralph's wife would be more appropriate. Gail politely declined with the quip that her blood pressure could not stand having items that cost more than a dollar fifty named for her.

As the group left the sales pavillion and headed back to the horse-drawn carriage that would take them on to a party for the evening, Gail pulled Ralph roughly aside.

"A goddamn horse! You just threw away two million two hundred thousand dollars on a goddamn horse! Half of that money was mine. I'm warning you, don't you ever spend that kind of money again without consulting me!"

Rage instantly seized Ralph. "You're warning me?" he hissed with equivalent heat. "With what, some more blackmail, you little thief. How I choose to spend *my* money is *my* business. *My* money! *My* business! You get me angrier than any woman I've ever known. You might not stay alive long enough to enjoy your share."

Gail glared at his balled fists and shot him a look of utter contempt before she turned away.

At the party Nina chose the moment to speak privately to Ralph when Amanda and her mother were being introduced to one of Charles's international banking customers. She led Ralph away from the protective light of the huge yellow-and-white-striped tent and into the dimness at the rear lawn's edge, near a long flower bed.

"I do not want you and Amanda to see each other," Nina said.

"You think that we do?"

"I know my granddaughter. I can see she's in love with you. What I do not want for her is to become involved with a married man."

Ralph took no care to rein in his sarcasm. "Just any married man or *me?*"

"Both."

"Because it brings your own sins a little too close to discovery?"

"I'd rather leave past . . . occurrences out of this discussion."

"That's really what I was for you, right? An unfortunate occurrence."

She stared at Ralph for a long while, but he could not discern what she might be feeling. Finally, she spoke, "Mr. Behr—"

"Don't you think our relationship is close enough for you to call me Ralph?"

She hesitated and then began again. "Ralph . . . I am having this very painful conversation purely out of concern for my granddaughter. She is young and still inclined to inappropriate enthusiasms. You are a married man, which is sufficient reason for me to demand that you break off anything with her that has already begun or that you may be contemplating."

"*You* were married when you had an affair with my father. Maybe it's a family trait."

Her face grew whiter in the light slanting from the tent's open sides. "I know the pain she'll endure as a result of her impetuosity."

Ralph's voice was passionate with anger. "I don't like people who walk away from their responsibilities. I don't walk away from mine. I won't walk away from Amanda. Judging from your own history, I assume you understand all too well how people must sometimes marry for reasons having nothing to do with love or emotional commitment. That's all I'll say about it."

His voice lowered, but not the intense anger that drove it. "So, we both have secrets. The only difference is that I *know* yours. I *am* yours. If you try to interfere again in anything concerning Amanda and me, I will take great pleasure in disclosing it to the world. Mother!"

Ralph left her there and returned to the locus of light and music and people. Amanda approached him.

"Will you dance with me? It seems strange that we've made love and never danced."

He led her to the crowded dance floor and guided her into the middle, where they would not be seen from the tables.

"Amanda, I want you to know that I'm not the sort of man who gets married to a woman and then has affairs, although that's the way it might look."

"Is that what you were talking to my grandmother about?"

"She was concerned for your sake. Did you tell her about us?"

"She sensed it at the racetrack today. She worries about me, but I can take care of myself very well."

"Don't feel you're on your own here. I want you to know what

205

I told her. I don't take this relationship lightly. I won't walk away from my responsibility to you."

Her feelings while he spoke to her had been hidden behind her impassive expression. But now a warm smile blossomed from it.

"I haven't asked you to make any commitments—I want you always to remember that."

Ralph engaged her eyes. "Will you promise not to reveal something. To anyone?"

"I told you it doesn't matter about your wife," she said.

"It does matter, and it should."

"Then I promise."

Ralph led her off the dance floor. His emotions had never been stirred by a woman before. He needed a moment to think things through. He turned back to her when they were at the far end of the hors d'oeuvres table, where they would be alone and appear to have stopped for a bite to eat.

"Gail and I did not know one another on our wedding day," he began. "We had to marry for reasons having nothing to do with any feelings for each other. I've never slept with her. The arrangement will end in two years. That gives you and me time to get to know each other, to . . ."

She smiled indulgently. "I know you. I know I love you. Two years won't change that."

"And I love you. But it's very important until I *am* free that you never tell anyone what I've just told you. Your father and mother must always think I'm just a friend of the family and a client of the bank."

"But we'll still see each other."

"Yes, but only when no one knows."

"That isn't important."

"Tomorrow morning. We'll go riding again."

He took her by the elbow to guide her toward her parents; he and Amanda had been off alone too long.

Charles and Patty were standing with Gail and some friends. Gail appeared to say something which caused Charles to break into the tight-mouthed smile that Ralph now knew denoted convulsions of absolute hilarity. Ralph would have to tread the next two years very carefully.

"Does it bother Amanda that you're married?" Gail wanted to know when they were driving back to their house.

"She said it didn't matter about you."

"I'm sure she did."

Ralph's hostility, raw from their repeated squabbles, was instantly inflamed. "What does that mean?"

"It means that Amanda Brookhouse is very used to getting her way—in everything."

"Meaning me."

"If that's what she wants right now, yes."

"I don't take orders from anyone!"

Gail laughed. "If she wanted you to crawl across a desert on your belly, you'd crawl."

"Bullshit!"

"Not because you're weak," Gail explained, "but because she's a Brookhouse, and she knows how desirable that makes her, especially to someone like you. Winning her puts the stamp of approval on your climb up, Ralph. She legitimizes you."

Ralph flashed a startled look at Gail and said nothing more.

Chapter 12

On Sunday evening the helicopter flew Ralph and Gail back to New York City. Twilight was settling like dust after a storm, causing the streetlamps and the buildings flecked with lighted windows to sparkle in the early darkness like jewels clutched in the island's fist. Ralph's limousine was waiting for him, a radio-summoned taxi for Gail. It took her right from the helipad to the apartment where she would meet Milo.

She had had a wonderful time in Saratoga Springs among the rich against whom she had so often inveighed. As a result, she was feeling somewhat guilty. She missed Milo very much, doubly so because Ralph's disappearances, doubtless to sneak off with Amanda, reminded her of her own sexual cravings. By telephone she had already informed Milo that she had procured the money for the art gallery, but with some conditions.

She arrived at the little borrowed apartment to find Milo struggling over the financial statements Ralph had insisted be prepared. Convinced that Ralph had demanded control solely to humiliate him, he was fuming over what he termed "the Boor's tyrannical interference."

"Should I turn down the money?" Gail asked.

Milo reached out his arms and drew Gail onto his lap. "You did a marvelous job inducing him to fund our gallery. If you're able to put up with him day in, day out, I guess I can live with him too." His voice was filled with melancholy. "Why do people like Behr, whose every waking moment is devoted to greed, get such power over the rest of us?"

Milo's spirits rose when that thought led him to recount an incident that had occurred the previous evening while he and a group of their artist friends were gathered for drinks and talk at a local bar. Cosmara had maintained that the Renaissance produced great art because wealthy patrons had made the artists economically secure, which allowed them to concentrate on exploring in their art the revolutionary trends coursing through the culture.

"You could be sure that a panderer like Cosmara would embrace the materialistic view," Milo commented, "given the way success has perverted what little talent he may once have possessed. I was loathe to bother, but everyone urged me to refute him." Milo shrugged, slyly smiling. "What could I do?"

Gail listened attentively as Milo recounted the debate. Although she guessed he had been drunk again and more bitter than witty, she laughed at the right places and smiled the rest of the time. And all the while she was praying to herself that the exposure the gallery would afford his work would drain from Milo the terrible jealousy corroding him.

Although she was reluctant to admit it to herself—so important to her was her belief in her self-sufficiency—she relied on his strength to shield her from all the terrors outside the castle the two of them comprised. Her angry, forbidding, love-denied childhood, which had forced her to muster nearly insupportable fortitude, had generated in her an extravagant gratitude toward Milo; astonishingly, as plain as she knew herself to be, he had chosen her from among all women to share his life and to sustain her through hers till death them do part. However, she had sadly observed how, little by little, the last few years had parched him, leaching out the zest for life that had long made her dizzy with lovesickness for him and leaving behind in him only a raging, understandable thirst for recognition. More and more, he had been trying to slake that thirst, to overcome the apprehension of failure, with alcohol. One reason she had capitulated to the marriage with Ralph Behr was out of the hope that if Milo felt financially secure, his despondency would end.

As she had anticipated, Milo was exhilarated when he finished telling her the story. He kissed her exuberantly, and they soon made love. To Gail it seemed like the early days of their marriage, when Milo's spirits sang and his body became lusty simply out of the pure joy he felt at his own virility, the potency of his irrepressible creative energy.

On Tuesday at noon, Ralph joined them at a booth in the coffee shop near the office of the landlord. He scanned the budgets and projections Milo gave him. Several incisive questions skewered the assumptions on which the calculations were based. Milo raged and disputed until he and Ralph made some phone calls to gallery owners they knew. Eventually, more accurate cost, operating, and revenue figures were plugged in and new estimates agreed upon. Only then would Ralph allow their group to proceed to the landlord's office.

Initially, Milo tried to make some negotiating points, but he soon lapsed into silence and let Ralph do their bargaining. The meeting ended with the landlord imploring them to take the space for nine hundred dollars less rent a month after an initial three-month grace period, during which he would contribute twenty thousand dollars as his share of renovation costs.

"You did a very good job," Gail had to admit.

"It's how I make my living," Ralph told her.

Milo was tight-lipped and said only that he was going home to design the interior and wanted no interference from Ralph with that part of the process.

Ralph replied, with equal firmness, "No construction starts until I approve the plans."

Gail was feeling kindly enough toward Ralph that she suggested they have dinner together at home that evening. As it turned out, Gail left a message at his office that she would not be able to make it. Arriving back at the Coalition, she had found waiting for her a group of tenants with a major problem. She immediately scheduled an emergency meeting for that night.

Gail stood at the head of the Coalition's large front room, conferring with John Rosenthal, president of the tenants' group, and Fletcher Crane, a lawyer she had called in. Crane was on the tall side and prematurely gray. He wore a yellow bow tie, a blue seersucker suit, and a yellow-and-blue-striped shirt that tightened over a small paunch. She guessed that his choice of half-glasses worn at the end of his nose was an effort to appear thoughtful and folksy and disguise his toughness. Rosenthal, on the other hand, in washed-out jeans and rolled-up shirt sleeves, eschewed affectations of dress. He was less complicated and both more interesting and more engaging. Shorter than the lawyer, with a red beard and mustache and lively blue eyes, he was a painter who was beginning to gain a reputation for his large-scale energetic art and was personally respected by others for his instinctive knack of being able to induce others to work together.

Nearly all of the hundred or so folding chairs were filled, and other people milled in the back of the room. Through the wide storefront windows, a few stragglers could be seen approaching.

Gail went to the center of the room. Carla, who was acting as secretary, rapped sharply on the table at which she sat to take notes. Another woman was moving down the center aisle getting the names along both sides. Gail was filled with pride that people in her neighborhood now almost instinctively turned to her organization for help, a mark of how far the Coalition had come since its first struggling days and how much wider its concerns ranged than the abuse of women. By some it was known as the Neighborhood Coalition or, simply, to all, the Coalition. Slowly, the worried babble hushed, and she began to speak.

"My name is Gail Benedict. Most of us know each other. I've been asked to help organize resistance on the matter facing all of you tonight. The Coalition has been through similar battles against landlords, and we believe many forms of defense can be mounted. I've asked Fletcher Crane to join us tonight. Fletcher is a lawyer with a lot of experience representing tenants. He's had a few hours to investigate the circumstances surrounding the eviction, but before he fills us in, I'd like to—"

"Mrs. Behr!" A small man with a pinched face had jumped to his feet. He was waving a steno pad. "I have a question."

"We'll take questions later," Gail replied and was about to continue her remarks.

"My name is Max Borah," the man said, ignoring her. The room became silent. His exposés of the underside of New York politics had made his name famous. "Why are you hiding from these people the fact that your husband is the landlord who is trying to evict them?"

Gail was shocked. Her voice barely audible above the eruption of sound in the room, she asked, "Do you have any proof?"

"My story in tomorrow's paper will report that Ralph Behr owns those buildings and intends to build the huge project he's planning partly on the land where Artists' Haven is located. I repeat, Why are you hiding all that?"

The room exploded into a battleground of cries and comments and shouted questions. Gail was stunned. Her life was so separate from Ralph's it had never occurred to her that they might collide.

A taller man beside Borah began to hand out early copies of the newspaper. Gail recognized him as a neighborhood resident whose wife was a secretary at the paper.

Gail took a copy and quickly scanned the article. Borah had not guarded his words; he seemed very sure of his facts: he and an associate had spent weeks tracing corporations and chains of titles in Albany and New York City and also appeared to have an informant at Ralph's law firm. He declared unequivocally that Ralph intended to build his massive Behr Center among the small buildings and empty lots at the edge of their community. To do that, he would first have to demolish the two tenements that had been restored by the residents to become Artists' Haven.

A young woman named Dorothy Graham stood up. Gail had known her since the woman and her husband, both young architects, had moved into the neighborhood. Gail and Milo had even attended a party in her home.

"Why did you keep all that from us, Gail?" Dorothy Graham cried out reproachfully. "Did you think we were too stupid to find out? Jimmy and I have broken our backs to repair the plumbing and wiring and make the building a decent place to live. Now that property values are starting to go up a little, sleazy developers like your husband come around and want to steal it back. How could you do this to us?"

Gail was at a loss. "I honestly didn't know that—"

"Just give us a straight answer," said a man she knew from community-board meetings. "No bullshit. Does your husband own our buildings or not?"

"I . . . I don't know," she admitted.

"Bullshit!" the man shouted.

"Bullshit!" another agreed.

Several people were shouting at Gail now. Alice, a heavy woman who was a frequent volunteer at the Coalition, got the crowd's attention next. "We had a deal with the landlord that he wouldn't sell without offering us a chance to buy the buildings from him first. What the hell happened to that?"

211

"It wasn't in writing," another reminded her hotly. "We shouldn't have trusted that slimy bastard."

"Him?" a man at the side of the room yelled. He pointed at Gail. "We even got double-crossed by *her*."

Everyone was talking, many shouting accusations at her. Gail wanted them to know she had been totally unaware of Ralph's machinations, that she was on their side. But the more she tried to quiet the crowd, the louder it grew. Finally, John Rosenthal, the head of the residents' group, stepped to her side.

"They're not in a mood to believe anything you tell them."

"But I really didn't know about this thing. I'm as angry about it as they are."

"I know you are," he said kindly, "but they're focusing on you and not on the problem. Maybe it would be better if you left the meeting."

Gail sadly regarded the irate mob that until a few minutes ago was comprised of her friends, and then she returned to John's sincere gaze.

"You're right. I'm in the way here."

She grabbed her jacket off the back of Carla's chair. Carla tried to catch her hand to speak to her, but Gail pulled it back too swiftly and broke away, pushing a path through the standees blocking the center aisle, not looking at any of them.

Once outside, her pace could quicken. Digging angry, wretched tears out of her eyes, she rushed down the amber-tinted sidewalk past darkened stores. The distrust they had expressed hurt her deeply. Wrongly accused and yet rightly judged by their circumstantial standards, how could she hope to be believed? They were desperate, too worried to be reasonable. She was now an enemy to her friends about to lose their homes, and a stranger to the organization she had single-handedly built. All thanks to Ralph Behr!

Gail found him at home taking supper upstairs on a table in his bedroom. He was in his shirtsleeves, tie open. A Mets game was on television, but the sound was low and his attention was focused on the pile of papers before him. As usual he had the telephone pressed to an ear.

"How much do you think it will take to buy it?" he was saying into the receiver when she charged into the room.

She took up a position directly in front of him, beside the table. Her tone was menacing. "You have exactly one minute to get off that phone before I rip it out of the wall!"

Ralph seemed to pay her little mind. "It's not worth anywhere near the forty-three million, even if you throw in the out parcels." He paused, then spoke again. "I'm interested at twenty-eight million. That's not an offer to buy at that price, understand, just interest. When you're ready to come back down to earth, get back to me."

He hung up and turned to Gail. "I'll get it for thirty. If I want it. Change your mind about dinner?"

"Over a hundred people who live at Artists' Haven are faced with eviction," she fumed, "with not having roofs over their heads. They don't have thirty million dollars to throw around."

"Oh, the Borah story. I'd have liked another week or two before announcing the location, but it was bound to leak sooner or later."

She was disgusted. "I can't get over how calmly you're sitting there. I take it the story is true."

"As far as it went. What it glossed over was that those people just broke into the buildings one day and started living there. Those buildings are slums."

"Maybe by the standards of this palace, but those buildings are their homes."

"They have no leases."

"They *saved* those buildings, with their sweat and their money. The landlord was overjoyed to have them there."

"He's no longer the landlord. I am, and I want them out."

"And just where do you expect them to live?"

He shrugged. "That's not my problem. Their moving in illegally doesn't put an obligation on the rest of the world to care for them."

Gail's eyes were blazing. "No matter how often you demonstrate it to me, I still can't believe how coldhearted you are."

"I pick my own charities. And your buddies are not going to bully me into putting them on my list. I have big plans for that property."

"Big plans, big man! And not a single qualm about the little people you're crushing along the way."

Ralph stretched out, his feet crossed, his thumbs hooked into his belt. "Wake up, Gail! This isn't the nineteenth century. Tenants are voters and have a lot of clout. The problem here is that your friends, which is what I assume from your concern they are, don't have any *rights*. None! And I do. You're always telling me how determined you are to protect people's constitutional rights. What about mine? Those people want to take my

213

property and haven't any legal right to do it. Why aren't you defending me?"

He smiled boyishly, as if he had just been struck by the most tremendous idea. "Tell you what—I'll pay your Coalition, that you say needs money so badly . . . I'll pay you guys to defend my rights. Call it public relations. Ten thousand dollars a month to clear my good name and move the project along in the community."

"You're a lowlife!" she hissed.

He chuckled. "And you're a hypocrite. . . . Maybe even a bigot."

Gail spun around and stalked toward the door.

"That's it?" Ralph called out. "You're going to quit just like that, when the fight's just getting started?"

"Bastard!" she snapped and then fled, but only as far as her own bedroom. Alien territory, but the single bit of space in all the world that remained in any way still her own.

Even before ten o'clock the next morning, when Ralph's hurriedly called press conference would begin and he could announce the project officially, many people were already at work trying to stop its progress.

Dorothy and Jimmy Graham had spent the night surveying every building within what Max Borah's article claimed were the boundaries of the new project. As soon as the sun came up, they began to photograph structures that might conceivably be considered worthy of protection from demolition by the city's Landmarks Preservation Commission. Husband and wife functioned like two parts of the same machine, as if they had a single brain.

Employed by architectural firms engaged in restoration work, both knew the procedures to gain landmark status. Despite their outrage at eviction, the Grahams had to admit that little on the site was architecturally noteworthy: around them, like unsightly outcroppings among the empty lots, were arrayed the most decrepit and undistinguished of tenements, warehouses, and garages. Only when Jimmy muttered that these were just typical run-of-the-mill nineteenth-century commercial buildings did a possible course of action occur to Dorothy.

"Maybe that's what we argue: that these are prime examples of nineteenth-century commercial stock, nearly all of which have been demolished. The whole area is one big museum. And that's what makes it unique."

"But it's just ugly and nondescript," Jimmy replied.

214

Dorothy was the more practical. "We haven't got anything else to push."

Jimmy shrugged and pulled out a mechanical pencil and the small, spiral notepad he used for jotting down ideas. "Okay, how about, 'a superb, highly endangered example of the commercial architecture that characterized New York City's bustling mid-nineteenth-century business life.' "

"Good enough, I guess. We can always add phrases like 'rare historic zone' and do some research on people and businesses that might have been located here."

While Jimmy set up long shots, Dorothy concentrated her own camera on architectural details that might enhance their argument: cornices, lintels, archways. They had to hurry if the prints were to be ready in time for their meeting later that day with a preservationist who had an antipathy to contemporary high-rise architecture and close friends on the Landmarks Preservation Commission.

The first that Harold Gaber heard about the evictions was when he bumped into Steve Bailey on the takeout line at the corner luncheonette. He had dropped in to pick up a cheese Danish and a coffee to take upstairs to his law office. Harold was just past thirty with a struggling neighborhood practice. To gain visibility he had joined the local Democratic Club and had won a seat on the local community board, gradually rising to the chairmanship. As a result more legal work had come his way: some immigration stuff, a couple of store leases, a few criminal trials, a succession of cut-rate divorces he could do with forms (he charged more if the spouses' haggling required him to go beyond filling in the blanks), but nothing significant. His hope was that, in a few years, his widening circle of connections would provide an in to run for some office or for a judgeship, but that was only the scantest of hopes right now.

Steve Bailey had been at the tenants' meeting the night before and, after filling Harold in, asked with some vehemence, "How do you stop a guy like Ralph Behr?"

Harold instantly recognized that he had the sort of issue he could ride to prominence.

Son of a bitch! he kept repeating happily to himself all the way to the newsstand, where he picked up the paper in which the story had broken. He read the article as he walked upstairs to his office. Son of a bitch! Ralph Behr is trying to ram this megaproject through, and I'm in a perfect position to stop him. The worst that can happen is that he has to hire me to do legal work for him, to get me on his side, and the best is that I look like a hero for trying to stop him and maybe get a shot at running for the state assembly.

He spent an hour at his metal desk skimming law books and then began making phone calls to arrange an emergency meeting of the community board that night. He would personally have flyers distributed in time to alert the public to tonight's discussion of the "potentially devastating impact" that Behr Center would have on the area. Although he possessed too little specific information about the project to know precisely what his objections were, Harold pulled a yellow pad from under a pile of books and papers and began to draft his speech.

The deputy mayor had come up with a very similar scheme, although somewhat grander in its choice of personal goals. There was a chance that the presidency of the city council would soon become open—the incumbent was rumored to be considering a try for a statewide office. The deputy mayor was convinced that the publicity he could gain from denouncing a gargantuan development, sure to overwhelm its neighborhood, would earn him a lot of public support and get his name known more widely. After all, the little guy doesn't side with rich people like Ralph Behr. As soon as he read the morning papers, the mayor would probably send him a memo ordering him to block the project simply because the Behrs were involved. The last time that had happened, the mayor had stayed in the background and forced his aide to be the public point man in the battle. Behr had won easily in court and, the deputy mayor was convinced, had taken pleasure in making him look like a bumbler.

The deputy mayor thought for a while. Rumors were widespread that Lorna Garrison was still angry as hell over the way Behr had dropped her and married someone else, her transparent disinterest in his fate fooling no one. She could help publicize the city's fight against Behr's project while making sure that his own name received prominent and favorable mention among the electorate. She could also be a potent force in raising money from her clients for the run for the city-council presidency, or even the mayor's office when and if the current mayor stepped down. He could almost see himself in one of those TV ads, tie open, shirtsleeves rolled up, shaking hands and talking to ordinary people; he wet his lips as he imagined them nodding their heads. Furthermore, a lot of developers would like to build a project like this one, he reasoned. Why the hell should Ralph Behr be the only one with a shot to build it just because he sneaked around buying up land? Maybe there was a way to throw the whole thing open for bidding—in the interest of good government—and let other big developers go for it as well. Those guys would probably be grateful to contribute if he showed that sort of evenhandedness.

The deputy mayor immediately set several city departments and a team of city lawyers to work investigating the legalities of Behr Center. He made clear that he was interested in blocking it. Then he telephoned Lorna Garrison.

Since the abortive meeting at the Metropolitan Museum, Lorna had been chafing for Simon Kramer, her partner and lover, to take action, but he had insisted that logic required they wait until Ralph actually announced he was building across the street from the parking lot Simon had purchased out from under him. Only then would the easement that allowed Simon to cross Behr's property at any point become valuable. She rose late because a social engagement the night before had run longer than anticipated, made herself coffee, and began to read the *Times*, the first of half a dozen newspapers she customarily skimmed in the course of a business day, a necessity in public-relations.

In the Metro section she came upon the article that repeated Max Borah's report, while adding that Ralph Behr had called a news conference in his office for ten o'clock, at which he was expected to announce the location of Behr Center. She was about to telephone Simon Kramer when the phone rang with a call from the deputy mayor.

She considered him a shrewd but drab man and felt no particular affinity for him. But the mayor had put a lot of power over real-estate development in his hands, and with so many of her clients in real estate, he was a useful ally. As she suspected, he was phoning about Behr Center, but had not taken the trouble to choose a tactful approach.

"I know how much you dislike Ralph Behr," he began.

"If you mean that I believe he fails to take the good of the city into account in his projects, that's probably a fair assessment of my views."

"That's what I meant. I'm really furious about this new project he intends to build downtown. Three gigantic towers overwhelming everything around it, tying up traffic, polluting the air probably. How do you feel?"

"A very insensitive plan, as far as I can see."

"Well, I thought you might feel that way. Perhaps you and I could have lunch today to discuss it."

"You know," she added, as if it was a sudden thought, "I might ask Simon Kramer to join us. He feels much the same as I do about Ralph Behr's tactics. And he just happens to own the property right across the street from Behr's."

The deputy mayor was pleased: Simon Kramer was a heavy political contributor who could be very useful to him. The date was made—at Lorna's office at one, where they would be able to converse privately.

Then she phoned Simon. He told her that he had already arranged for one of his lawyers to attend Ralph's press conference in the guise of a reporter. The announcement itself might well be cause enough to obtain a court order halting construction of the project on the ground that any building would be a barrier to his free exercise of his easement.

John Rosenthal and several others who lived in the Artists' Haven buildings tried to gain admittance to the conference room at the Behr Group's offices, but having no press credentials, they were turned away. The young lawyer at the firm retained by Simon Kramer wrote an occasional consumer-advice column for a weekly newspaper published in the Long Island community where he resided. His press ID card passed muster.

The room was jammed with the press and with several local TV-news camera crews. The lawyer had to squeeze into the back row. He switched on his tape recorder, held up the microphone, and what he heard hit him like a falling safe.

After trumpeting the project's virtues and having the architect, Watanabe, do the same from his perspective, Ralph Behr ushered to the podium the head of the State's Urban Development Corporation, who announced that its board was delighted with the salutary effect Behr Center would have on the blighted area. UDC, he continued, intended to aid in the revitalization by using its powers of eminent domain to condemn the parking lot across the street as a land-use improvement project. UDC would then sell that land to Ralph Behr for him to construct "at his own expense as a goodwill gesture a public park for all of the community to enjoy."

Ralph then spent the next ten minutes modestly describing the glories of the park and the community's incredible good fortune in benefiting from his largesse.

Lunch at Lorna's office took on a far more fevered tone than had been foreseen when the date was made that morning.

All day, tenants in the targeted tenements organized, met, and picketed. They assaulted the Manhattan borough president's office and the city council president's office, as well as those of several councilmen, assemblymen, and state senators. A barrage of press releases fell on the media. More importantly, other tenants sought out key people in city and state agencies with jurisdiction over matters that had the potential to halt development: the City Planning Commission, the Landmarks Preservation Commission, the Public Development Corporation, the Buildings Department of the General Services Administration, the Department of Transportation, and the Office of Environmental Impact of the state's Department of Environmental Protection.

"My head is spinning from all the names and initials you're flinging at me," John Rosenthal finally exclaimed in his apartment late that afternoon, during a briefing he and several other tenant-committee members were receiving. "EPA, DOT, GSA, PDC. I can't keep straight who's who and what's what. Let me try to go through this in my own words. The main point is that even though Behr claims it doesn't, the project might still violate zoning."

"That would be determined by the City Planning Commission," Dorothy Graham pointed out.

"And might require action by the Board of Estimate," her husband, Jimmy, added. "That's made up of the mayor and the top city officials, who have the final voice."

"Okay," John recapitulated, "the law requires that if the building differs from what's permitted under the zoning code, then Behr will have to file an environmental-impact statement, which could take months."

"And months. Even to get the EIS's paperwork right," said Sandy Beamer, an urban planner temporarily out of work and thus delighted to have some use for his expertise.

"Which would mean," John reasoned, "that Behr might be forced to redesign the project or it might even be stopped altogether if he fails to satisfy city planning and the state environmental people that the project won't have a negative impact on the environment."

219

Dorothy jumped back in. "Even though, except for the buildings we're in, there isn't much other residential development around there, we could still tie things up by claiming Behr needs an environmental-impact statement to prove he's not changing the general character of the neighborhood from low-income housing."

"Or we could prove that he'll cause a lot of air pollution because of all the cars coming in to the project," Sandy Beamer interjected—he had been waiting a long time to make the point.

"They call that one SIP," Jimmy pointed out.

"So what you're telling us," said John, "is that we might even be able to hold up Behr long enough for the authorities to change the zoning to a new classification under which his building no longer qualifies."

All three advisers smiled proudly at that.

John was impressed. So was Allison Jenks, also a tenant-committee member. "But how can you change the zoning rules after Behr has already fulfilled all the requirements under the old rules? I know Ralph Behr is an ogre and we're fighting for our homes, but does that sound very fair?" she asked.

"This is our city!" Jimmy growled, astonishing John with his vehemence.

"Well, sure," agreed John.

"Those are our homes. Whatever it takes to win!" Sandy added.

"This is war!" Dorothy chimed.

John scratched his red beard and thought a bit. "It's a wonder anything ever gets built in this city. Maybe this is heresy, but I almost feel sorry now for Ralph Behr. If you guys weren't on our side, I'd think you were dangerous."

"Thank you," said all three.

Ralph arranged for his brother, Jeff, to join him for dinner at the Upper, his private club on the East Side. Only fifteen minutes late, Amanda Brookhouse was still properly apologetic. Jeff sat beside Amanda during drinks and dinner, as if she were his date, but anyone paying attention could not have mistaken the looks exchanged by her and his brother.

"What do you think of her?" Ralph asked when Amanda left the table for the ladies' room.

"She's beautiful."

"What else?" Ralph pressed him.

"She's everything a man could want in a woman."

Ralph would have been delighted with his brother's response if he had not sensed some annoyance being held back.

"All right, what's bothering you about her?"

"Nothing about *her*."

"Then what?"

"It's too silly to talk about."

"Come on. My feelings won't be hurt."

They never are, Jeff thought, but what he said was what had been on his mind earlier. "I know it's crazy, but your going out with her doesn't seem right." He cast about for the correct words and then settled on those that had come to mind. "It's as if you were somehow cheating on Gail." His gaze dropped. "I told you it was silly."

"Silly?" Ralph sputtered. "It's absolutely crazy."

Amanda was soon back at the table. Ralph implored her to order the bombe for dessert, an elaborate ice-cream confection that was a specialty of the club. She tried to beg off, but he ordered it for her, and she yielded. He declined to order something for himself, however, saying that he was full. Amanda then refused the bombe, which she had ordered only because she thought him reluctant to take dessert alone.

"You know why he insisted like that?" Jeff suddenly exclaimed with an undertone of reproach that caught Amanda and Ralph off guard. "Because he doesn't know how else to impress a girl who's as rich as he is."

Amanda broke into a smile and turned to Ralph, putting her hand gently on his. "Is he right?"

"The dumbest thing I ever heard. I just wanted you to try their specialty."

Ralph glared at Jeff, and the latter turned sullenly silent. Dinner was quickly concluded.

The limousine dropped Jeff off a few blocks from the club. Watching his brother and Amanda pull away, he allowed the feelings of envy and frustration to flood over him. She was charming and very desirable, and this golden dream of a golden girl was obviously in love with Ralph, to whom everything perfect seemed to come so effortlessly. Fuck! Guilt instantly and inevitably followed upon that thought because Jeff looked up so to his brother.

Jeff turned and walked uptown and then east to the brownstone on the side street. God, he was horny and needed a woman. He rang and could sense an eye peering at him through the peephole in the door. Then the door opened, and the brawny doorman bowed as Jeff entered.

"Good evening, Mr. Jones."

The small redhead at the reception desk smiled as he approached. "Good evening, Mr. Jones."

He hadn't had her yet. Maggie said she wasn't one of the girls, that it was more businesslike to put someone at the front desk who wasn't available to the customers. But he thought she was always particularly nice to him, nicer than she would have to be, even if she did suspect he was an owner. One of these days he was going to take a crack at her. Jesus, she was making five hundred a week just to smile at customers and take phone calls. For that kind of money she ought to come across with more than a smile's show of appreciation.

He was about to stop and chat with her when he noticed Maggie in the salon, as she called it. He glanced into the room. Not recognizing either of the men who sat on the gray office-style sofas there, he proceeded past the receptionist and into the room. Maggie and several well-dressed young women were conversing with three men. Maggie excused herself and led Jeff to her office, the men's laughter trailing after them.

"I was hoping you'd drop in tonight," she said. "I've just been looking at the books. We're already breaking even, but cash is short. When everyone's back in September, business will be booming."

"How much are you looking for now?" he wanted to know.

Maggie bolted the door behind them and unlocked the safe. She opened the books and pointed to the totals. No doubt about it, business was climbing. Taking a seat across from him at the sleekly modern beige desk, she outlined her marketing plans for the fall then handed him a page of figures.

He looked up. "This says you need thirty thousand dollars more capital by September."

"And you'll also notice that the thirty will be paid back by November, and part of the original sixty as well. A cash-flow shortfall has to be expected in a start-up operation."

Maggie spun around and flipped on the personal computer behind her. A few moments later the printer burped out a graph and then a spread sheet.

She spun back, showing him the graph. "If business continues to increase at only the present rate, so that the slope of the curve remains constant, you'll have all of your original investment back by the end of December, and we'll be in profits as well. But the summer is traditionally slow. The big spenders, the business-men, the diplomats, they're all out of town." She turned to the spread sheet. "Given what I believe is a justifiable assumption of increased revenues after Labor Day, just look at how high the figures climb in the coming months."

"And you can't do with less than thirty?"

She pointed to a column of numbers. "There are expenses."

"I'll give you ten tomorrow and ten next week. Then we'll see where we stand." He remarked sourly, "Is my twenty thousand high enough to buy you for the night?"

"I don't mix business with pleasure." Then she smiled, relax-ing her sternness. "You don't want me, Jeff. I'm old stuff to you. Cass is here tonight. She was asking about you earlier. She mentioned she hadn't seen you in a while. She really likes you."

Jeff laughed. "All the guys who come through here—are you ever tempted to give one of them a whirl?"

Maggie was already opening the door. "Cass," she called out. "A friend of yours is here." She glanced at Jeff. "You drive her wild."

Ralph turned the key and swung back the door. "I've given orders to the hotel staff. This suite is never to be rented. It's only for us."

He handed her a key of her own and stepped back, allowing her to pass into the suite. They had entered the elevator sepa-rately, as if strangers. All the way up to the penthouse floor he had fretted that the hotel's decoration might not be to her taste. She was used to the most sumptuous decor, but always re-strained, dignified. Perhaps she might find hotel furnishings and colors too garish.

"I can always have these rooms redone if you're not happy," he said.

"The suite is lovely. The deep blue carpet, the soft lighting. It's very romantic."

"I chose it for us because of the view." The living room was spacious, with floor-to-ceiling windows extending around two sides. He pointed south. "See that dark patch past the Con Ed building."

"Yes."

"That's where I'm putting up the three tallest buildings in the world, the ones your father's bank is financing. The most monu-mental real-estate project ever. You've got to go back to huge public works like the Great Wall of China and the Egyptian pyramids to find anything even close. But those weren't just one man alone. Whole nations were mobilized for those."

She squeezed his hand. "There's no one like you."

Pleased, he turned back to the room. "You're sure you like the furnishings here?"

She put her arms about his neck. "They're perfect for the sort of person who would come to a place like this." Seeing his doubt, she repeated, "It makes me feel very romantic."

"Jeff was right about one thing."

"What's that?"

"You're very beautiful."

The low light created a sheen where it touched her brow, nose, lips, and chin, and deep shadows where the planes of her face curved away. Her eyes, light blue in the daylight, were cobalt now, with bright dots swimming in the corners. He kissed her, his desire to possess her as great as their first time. If there were problems that posed barriers to their future—his marriage, her grandmother—they were at that moment too pleased with each other to care.

Nearly everyone interested in the community board's hearing regarding the Behr Center eviction controversy had a TV set on from ten to eleven-thirty that night, flipping from channel to channel. Three network-owned TV stations and two independents had sent camera crews to cover it despite the lateness of the hour.

Gail had spent the evening at Carla's, after an awful day at the Coalition's storefront offices, in which she felt herself excluded from all the activity generated to obtain publicity for the eviction-threatened tenants: the press releases argued over and then run off on the mimeograph machine, envelopes typed with addresses culled from the Coalition's press lists, the intense conclaves among the resistance leaders and her colleagues with experience in landlord-tenant battles. She had kept to herself in the back office for as long as she could take it, and then at four went off to meet Milo at the new gallery, to learn what he was planning. As she crossed the Coalition's front room and headed for the door, the others' relief spread out behind her like skywriting.

Gail played distractedly with the pasta primavera Carla had prepared. She wanted so to give vent to her distress by talking about what was bothering her: about the hurt she felt at being distrusted and avoided by her friends; about the difficulties of living with someone as annoying, as thoughtless and self-interested as Ralph Behr; about Milo's corrosive depression; about how sad it was that Carla was the last of her friends who did not avoid her now that she was married to a rich celebrity, except for the few who seemed eager to latch on to her for their own financial reasons. Gail wanted most of all to convince her best friend that she had known nothing of Ralph's plans to evict the Artists' Haven residents because she and Ralph lived totally separate lives, and even hinted gingerly to that effect. But, of course, Gail could not actually discuss any of those matters outright. She could disclose nothing.

By ten o'clock, the conversation began to trail off, and they turned on the TV set, eager to learn what had happened at the community-board hearing.

Channel 5 was first with a report and then channel 11. Both had reported the essence of community-board president Harold Gaber's speech, in which he denounced Ralph Behr's callousness for trying to throw brilliant artists and widows and children out in the cold. That statement left both of the women somewhat puzzled—neither could recall a widow in the project, and for days the outside temperature had hovered around ninety. Gaber stoutly asserted that he, as head of the community board, would stand against Ralph Behr and the evictions and prevent him from building his "gigantic monstrosity" in their backyard. Then refuting Ralph's declaration the previous day that the project already conformed to all the zoning requirements and needed neither citizen review nor official approval, Gaber aimed his forefinger at the lens and asserted that it was impossible for any honest man to conform to all the zoning requirements and that he did not trust a man or project that did.

Artists and others fervently portrayed the battle as one between the forces of light and art against those of darkness and greed. This was housing for the heartless rich to force destitute genius artists into the ranks of the homeless and inflict too much development and too many people on the area. An architect proclaimed that the plaza's wide expanse made the structure inherently dangerous. And just about everyone criticized the height of the towers.

Several elected officials were then shown denouncing the project. They stood behind the community, they said. In his speech, John Rosenthal tried to pin them down to specifics in obtaining a number of favorable actions: first, a determination from city planning that an environmental-impact statement was required; second, landmark status for "this rare district of historic importance"; and third, a change to make the zoning conform to the lower height and bulk of the surrounding locale.

The clips of speeches were intercut with shots of cheering listeners the two women recognized: Milo, who had somehow gotten a place on the podium (looking wonderful in his yellow cotton jacket, Gail thought); Fletcher Crane gesturing professorially to one of the legislators, the community board, several Coalition volunteers; and various people from the area.

Only during the channel 11 piece, after Gail lustily cheered the TV remarks of an architect disparaging the project, did Carla finally believe that Gail had been sincere in asserting ignorance of her husband's intention to build on the site of Artists' Haven. The speaker blasted it as an oversized amusement park and Ralph Behr for scarring New York's skyline for untold years to come. As soon as the reporter concluded the piece, Gail hurriedly thanked Carla for the dinner and rushed off. She did not wish to allow her friend time to raise the question of why, if Gail felt such antipathy to Ralph Behr, she had married him.

"Exceptional and unique character?" Ralph shouted, nearly jumping out of bed and overturning the pastry plate brought up for them by room service. "Rare area of historic importance? It's a slum, a miserable, decaying slum!"

He quieted down when the channel 4 reporter ticked off the tenants' upcoming defense tactics. Ralph was neither surprised nor worried by them. The buildings department had already approved the office building plans, and the eviction process had already started. The latter was a judicial matter, thank God, and far less subject to the political opportunism now crawling out of the woodwork. Most significantly, none of the people gearing up to fight him on the evictions knew that the battle could drag on for quite a while without causing him too much distress because the residential tower, which was slated for that parcel, was not scheduled to begin construction for a very long time.

"Do you see the guy in back?" He pointed. "That's my wife's husband—ex-husband, I mean. The one in the yellow jacket."

"He's handsome. Artistic-looking."

Ralph appeared too intent on his own thoughts to have heard her comment. "Can you beat that? I'm financing an art gallery for the guy, and he's out there trying to kick my teeth in. I'm surprised my wife isn't there too, packing box lunches for the lynching party."

Chapter 13

By noon the following day a secretary at the Rountree law firm had admitted under interrogation to an affair with Max Borah "and maybe saying more than I should have" and was summarily fired.

With the leak now closed, the real-estate and litigation departments of the Rountree law firm could begin to prepare papers for lawsuits Ralph was about to start and those he was expected soon to be defending. They found themselves joined by Gary Frost and his firm, whom Ralph had also retained. Frost was a notoriously tough litigator who, like Ralph, hated to lose.

In addition, Ralph had sought Jeff's, Ben Rogovin's, and then, as he often did, his father's opinion by phone from the latter's Jersey Shore summer home regarding the tactics he should pursue against the mounting opposition to Behr Center. Jeff counseled a prudent watch-and-wait posture. Ever the strategist, Rogovin supported a more aggressive attitude, so as to put the other side on the defensive. His father's characteristic advice confirmed Ralph's own prospective game plan: attack—everywhere and everyone!

The next day, as a *Daily News* photographer caught his shocked expression, Harold Gaber was served with a summons and complaint for impliedly defaming Ralph Behr by his statement on television that only a dishonest man could claim no zoning changes were required. Ralph Behr was asking a hundred million dollars in damages. At that moment the community leader's personal bank account contained a hundred and twenty-seven dollars and thirty-four cents. A reporter with some legal training realized that the case was more than simply a clever ploy to silence a critic and sway the public: a favorable court decision for Ralph would establish that no zoning changes were required for the project, a judicial precedent which might then be used to halt lawsuits by opponents who maintained otherwise.

The activity in the weeks that followed was frenzied. Ralph, his staff, those he had engaged for the project, like Watanabe, and those willing to take up the cudgel for him as a favor vied with Artists' Haven residents, spokespersons for citizens groups, and community-board members in lobbying city and state officials. Lawsuits and applications were announced and filed in profusion. The ranks of Ralph's opponents were swelled by local activists and environmentalists fearful, first, that gentrification would sweep over outlying neighborhoods once Behr Center was built—with richer home-seekers moving in, and rents rising to the point that present residents would be forced out; and second, that the quality of their lives would be irreparably harmed by sky-high towers blocking the sky and casting long shadows throughout the day, by the masses of people the project would house and attract, and by the unavoidable increase in traffic.

Architectural historians and urban planners—arcane and anonymous professionals who had been ignored for years—were suddenly courted on all sides for favorable opinions: the former about the importance or unimportance of the Behr property to the history of New York, and the latter about the project's effect or lack of it on the area.

A city-council member, known for espousing radical views on behalf of populist causes and for an extreme inability to comprehend or appreciate economic realities, introduced a bill to force Ralph Behr to abandon his plans and, instead, to build luxury four-story housing for the poor. She immediately found herself at odds with many local residents who were quick to declare that the area had quite enough poor people, thank you, without building spectacular housing to attract more. She decided to change her bill to require Ralph Behr instead to turn over the projects profits to the poor—and to build it in the South Bronx.

The landmarks commission began the process of determining whether any of the present buildings should be protected from demolition, but the citizens groups were annoyed to learn that Ralph had already hired as his own counsel for the landmarks controversy the law firm they themselves usually retained.

City planning's experts also worked late into that first night and the second and the third. They examined the tiniest details, made and remade all the square-footage calculations, and tried to reinterpret the zoning language. All to no avail. Ralph had been absolutely correct in his assertion that the project had somehow been made to fit perfectly into the existing zoning regulations; he had an absolute right to build the project as set forth in the plans submitted to the buildings department. Knowing which way the wind blew from city hall, the head of city planning immediately began the process of rewriting the area's zoning.

Because of Ralph's celebrity and the spectacular nature of the project, the media treated the controversy as something between a presidential campaign and the Super Bowl. Statements outlining the city administration's viewpoint were all issued by the deputy mayor, who both reporters and Ralph pointed out to the public was Ralph's old adversary. And although the deputy mayor took great care to maintain that the administration was objectively studying the Behr Center issue, as did everyone else, Ralph knew precisely what side the administration was on.

Ralph was enjoying himself and the battle enormously. His senses sharper, his intuition keener, he came alive at such times, like a warrior king in the midst of a new military campaign, as if the rest of his life were merely preparation and resting up for it. Ralph devised a profusion of tactics to keep his opponents on the defensive. Now was the time to call in all the chits—to ask repayment for favors he had done influential friends over the years—and to barrage the press with announcements, interviews, and contrived events to draw coverage, all intended to keep the public and as many public officials as he could favorable to him. A pinnacle of that effort, which merged his public efforts with his personal self-image, was the *New York Post* political cartoon which depicted him as a lone knight, his lance forming the three towers, charging at an array of evil-looking black knights who were termed the Four Horsemen of the City's Apocalypse and were defending themselves with weapons labeled squatters, slums, self-interest, and deterioration. He obtained the original drawing and had it framed and placed on his office wall.

Gail's heart was with her friends and their fight to retain their homes and the present texture of the neighborhood. Didn't they know that marriage could never cause her to betray a lifetime's principles, a lifetime's selflessness? Occasionally, her help was solicited in order to pump her for clues about Ralph's future moves, she felt; rarely was information freely offered about her friends' own plans. She found it easier on all concerned to spend as little time as possible at the Coalition's headquarters. However, late one afternoon, she stopped in to sign checks and found a discouraged group sprawled in folding chairs and perched on the edges of tables. John Rosenthal greeted her.

"Any great ideas for us?" He shot a silencing glance at a woman who appeared about to object.

"I do have one thought." Gail chose her words carefully. "To stop the developer from tearing down your apartment buildings, you're placing a lot of hope on obtaining landmark status. My experience tells me you're going to fail, and those buildings will come down unless you can make them too valuable in another way."

"So, how do we do that?" the woman challenged her.

"Our greatest resource down here is artists, right?"

"Okay, so?"

"At the far ends of both buildings are side walls with no windows. Why not ask two really important artists among us to paint murals on them?"

Rosenthal understood instantly. "The buildings would then be art treasures, too precious to demolish. Good thought. Thanks."

Gail smiled and then retreated to her office, anxious not to endanger the small bit of trust she saw emerging onto several faces.

"You really stabbed me in the back!" Milo was enraged, angrier than Gail had ever seen him. "The most prominent public art project in years, and you didn't use your influence to have me chosen as one of the artists."

They stood in the center of the art gallery. Workmen were erecting walls in the rear and demolishing them in the front. Ralph had devised a fast-track construction schedule which required coordination from all the trades, but which would have the gallery finished nearly two months earlier than originally anticipated. Gail moved to an unoccupied corner of the gallery after she noticed that a man installing ventilation ductwork nearby had stopped working, perhaps in order to overhear the altercation.

"I couldn't," she whispered, when Milo was standing close enough again. "People are barely talking to me as it is because I'm married to Ralph."

"The murals were your idea, I heard. They were ready enough to listen to you then."

"They need really well-known artists," Gail pointed out with some hesitation, wary of wounding him.

He glared at her. "A commission to do just one of those murals, just one, and the publicity would have made me a major painter."

"Milo, don't you think I would have suggested you if I had thought I could have influenced them?"

"I don't know," he said sullenly, his gaze on Ralph Behr, who was across the room speaking to the general contractor and another man.

"Even if my suggestion would have made a difference, how would it look for me to nominate the ex-husband I'm supposedly feuding with? You, me, Ralph—we're all trapped by this damned arrangement."

"Don't give me that," Milo fumed. "You love the attention you're getting now, the luxury. Someone said they saw you being driven somehere in his limousine yesterday."

Milo stomped off to speak to a workman, leaving Gail to fight back tears. She spun away. She did not want anyone to see her crying or to say anything that might widen the unexpected breach. Without Milo she had little worthwhile in her personal life. She took a deep breath and straightened up. Walking toward him, she was about to utter a conciliatory phrase when she noticed Ralph approaching.

"Oh, Jesus!" she muttered.

Ralph began speaking to Milo while he was still several steps away. "We're going to have to leave in that first wall. Vito says it's a bearing wall."

"That wall isn't in my plans—you'll remember that you insisted on approving my plans. You even said you liked them," Milo replied forcefully. "It has to come out. I want a large open space."

Ralph stared at Milo for a moment, as if trying to contain himself. "When you and I went over the plans, you assured me that that was not a bearing wall."

"Does that make a difference?" Gail inquired of Ralph.

"Only that if we take it out, we will all be knee-deep in old building."

"Your sarcasm isn't helping," said Gail, bristling herself.

Ralph shifted back to Milo. "The wall stays in. That's a given. So we now have a shorter front area and a second gallery room behind it."

"We can certainly support the building some other way than that ridiculous wall," Milo declared.

"With a steel transfer beam and supporting columns on the sides," Ralph contended with some derision. "Vito and I agree: all that will probably cost a hundred thousand dollars to put in. That's major construction."

"I understand the implications of installing a transfer beam," Milo retorted. "The gallery's outstanding design feature, however, is the long, wide expanse that greets visitors. The gallery will look skimpy otherwise."

"Our finances will look even skimpier. Paying off the annual interest expense for an additional hundred thousand dollars of construction costs would require ten or twelve thousand dollars more income a year. That cripples the bottom line."

Milo swung around, facing Ralph directly. "That wall comes out."

Ralph locked gazes with him. "You paying personally for it? Because if you're not—and I sure don't see how you can—that wall stays."

"You're beginning to bother me a great deal, Mr. Boor. You're here only because you insisted on being Gail's partner in this business. Or do you have a more personal interest on her behalf?"

"In Gail?" Ralph was as shocked by the insinuation as Gail had been, the difference being that he could scarcely restrain his laughter as he responded. "I guarantee you she's safe from me, Milo."

Now Gail was the one irritated. "And just what is that supposed to mean?"

"Let's just say that you're not my type and I'm not yours."

Milo interjected, "Are you both finished with your denials?"

Ralph grimaced impatiently. He turned to the contractor. "Vito, ask the engineer if the wall will support an archway on either side. That might open up the room a little."

Gail glanced hopefully at Milo.

"Archways would be acceptable" Milo yielded. But Gail could hear resentment in his voice, for not getting his way and for not being the one to come up with the possible solution.

When they were alone again, she asked Milo, "Can we see each other tonight? He'll just have to go up to Saratoga without me."

"I've made other plans."

"Couldn't you change them?" she asked softly.

He paused, and then he smiled sheepishly. "That guy just gets under my skin. I start to worry about all sorts of things because you're living with him."

"Oh, Milo, if there's one man in the world you don't have to worry about, it's Ralph Behr. You're the only man I could ever love."

"I love you so much," he replied softly. He put his arms

232

around her waist. "How about if I make my special Greek salad?"

Gail exhaled in relief and smiled brightly at him. "You know the way to a girl's heart."

A few minutes later, when Milo went to the makeshift office in the rear to interview a prospective gallery employee, Ralph pulled Gail aside to inform her that she had better make clear to Milo that he was to make no major business decisions, not only in construction, but in operation as well, without Ralph's approval.

"You keep trying your best to put him down," Gail rejoined heatedly, "as if this were some macho contest between you two."

"I don't trust his business sense. That's the long and short of it," Ralph replied. "Or much else about him. But he's your problem. Just don't make him mine."

Gail held her temper and changed the subject to her decision not to arrive in Saratoga until the next morning.

Ralph had no objection. "As long as you're there tomorrow in time for the Travers. At the party I'll tell Diane and some of the others on your fund-raising committee for that women's thing you're involved with that you're too busy working on their opening-night benefit at the art gallery."

Usually, Gail was infuriated by Ralph's refusal to consider, or even distinguish among, matters he simply lumped together as "women's things." Like his unwillingness to bother remembering the names of his succession of chauffeurs, she thought. But she was struck now by the realization that he could easily have refused to finance the art gallery after the residents of Artists' Haven—some of whom would show at the gallery—rose up against his efforts to clear them from the tenements. She had made no pretense of her sympathies.

"Why did you keep going with this gallery when it was clear I was on the other side in the eviction matter and ready to help the tenants any way I could?"

He seemed surprised by the question. "We had a deal."

"That's all?" she replied, surprised that having given his word had been reason enough for him.

Ralph grew wary. "If you're thinking that Milo was right, that maybe I've got a thing for you, let's be clear about that. Not even a quiver."

Gail's expression revealed her distaste for his grossness. "Don't try to flatter me."

*　　*　　*

233

Saturday morning Gail flew to Saratoga to join Ralph—the Travers would be televised nationwide, and her absence might appear suspect. She too had become a fan of Patagonia and was looking forward to the race. She was also eager to escape the tug-of-war pulling at her on all sides.

Ralph had given many interviews this past week to sportswriters and broadcasters seeking a story about the upcoming horse race. She herself had asked why the race seemed so important to him. "It's the prestige race for those people," he had confessed. Although contemptuous of the social climbing inherent in his answer, she understood whom he meant: the socialites who ran thoroughbred racing, the ruling circle whose inherited riches had sustained family stables and breeding farms for three and four generations. Several of them, she gathered, had entered quality colts.

For an instant after arriving at the east-side helipad, Gail had found herself taking pleasure in the opulent convenience of having a helicopter awaiting only her. Recalling Milo's admonition that she might be getting used to the potentially self-indulgent life that marriage to Ralph Behr could provide, she made up her mind to detest the entire decadent experience. Only a few minutes after vaulting the Tappan Zee Bridge, she became entranced by the tiny farms and forests and towns scrolling past between the borders of the Hudson on the right and the Thruway on the left. Ralph was waiting with the Mercedes in the driveway of the Saratoga house when she landed on the front lawn.

"Not bad for a Brooklyn girl, huh?" he quipped, his half-mocking smile indicating a prescience about the inner conflict in which she was engaged. She glared at him and, while Deighton held the car door, slipped into the seat beside him.

When Patagonia won, pulling away from a colt owned by Wellington ("Pudge") Terwilliger III, stymieing once again the latter's quest to join two previous generations of Terwilligers as a winner of the Travers, Ralph was aglow with the pride of victory. Television sportscasters interviewed Ralph, first alone, then with the trainer and jockey, and finally with Gail. He seemed to draw energy from the admiration of onlookers: the jockey who admitted his greatest worry had been "letting a great guy like Mr. Behr down," the sportscasters who nearly exceeded their allotted broadcast time, and especially the bettors and well-wishers thrilled to be able to wave their winning tickets at him or call out their congratulations.

"Proud of me?" he asked a beaming Amanda as he returned

234

by way of her box. She was there without her parents, who were committed elsewhere that weekend. His manner turned slightly caustic a moment later when he turned to her grandmother. "How about you, bursting with pride as well?"

When she and Ralph were on their way to their own box, Gail observed to him, "You seem to know the elder Mrs. Brookhouse pretty well."

"We share a birthday," Ralph replied.

He twisted abruptly to accept congratulations from people seated along the aisle and, noticing Pudge Terwilliger, complimented him on his fine horse, who "just had an off day."

Back in their seats, Ralph commented privately to Gail that Patagonia could beat Terwilliger's mule running backward any day of the week.

"You couldn't bear to be self-effacing," she remarked. "Patagonia just won by a mile, but you had to make sure I knew how good *your* horse was."

"You really do your best to ruin it for me. Would it hurt you to swallow the criticism and just try to get along with me for as long as we're forced to be together?"

After a moment of reflection, Gail confessed, "As a matter of fact, it would."

But she did try to make the rest of the afternoon at least amicable, so that her own weekend might be peaceful, and was relieved to learn that Ralph intended to spend much of his free time away somewhere with Amanda.

At the end of the day, Gail and Ralph drove to the stable area. The red, white, and blue pattern Ralph had chosen for his silks—the jockey's identifying shirt and cap—was visible everywhere: on the grooms' shirts, the feed and water buckets, the horse blankets. For a full year, he pointed out to her, his colors would also adorn the canoe that floated on the lake at the track.

A hot walker was still cooling out Patagonia, leading him along the shedrow, the dirt path located between the building containing the stalls and the barn's outer posts. Under a sheer blue blanket, the horse came into view around the corner of the barn and ambled toward them. Ralph went up to the colt and nuzzled its dark bay nose, speaking too softly for Gail to hear. Words of praise, she imagined. The horse dropped its head to Ralph's side jacket pocket, nudging him gently. Ralph laughed and reached in, pulling out lumps of sugar he always brought as a treat and feeding them to Patagonia from an open palm. He hugged the horse and stepped back to allow the groom to recommence the shambling walk around the covered path. Ralph remained watching until the two had disappeared around the far corner.

"There goes a great one," he remarked as much to himself as to Gail.

"He made a lot of money for you today."

Ralph eyed her with irritation. "Planning to start a labor union for racehorses?"

He strode by her toward the Mercedes.

"What's the matter now?" she asked, catching up to him. "Don't tell me you haven't thought about how much you won."

"Frankly, until you brought it up, I hadn't. You're really the one who's obsessed with money."

"Me?"

That night, Gail kept her tongue as Ralph reveled in the partying and the adulation he received as owner of the Travers winner. He made his way from table to table, from group to group, determined to meet everyone worth knowing but surprising Gail with his modesty and graciousness: foreign statesmen, film stars, European nobility, and a generous assortment of Phippses, Whitneys, and Vanderbilts, whose families had inhabited the summit of the American social system for generations. Gail found herself awed by these people, despite her strong political bias against privilege, and disgusted that many displayed awe at being introduced to Ralph.

At night, when the parties ended, Ralph met Amanda in the guest house at the edge of the property he had rented. They made love a bit more swiftly than in the past, some sense of routine having entered the process. They were lying on the bedcovers when Amanda raised a matter that had been on her mind for a while. She had been reticent to do so earlier because it dealt with a subject she considered far more personal than sex. It dealt with money.

"You really enjoy your money, don't you?"

"Not you too."

Amanda was taken aback. "If it bothers you to talk about it . . ."

He propped himself up an elbow. "No, it's just that the subject seems to be coming up a lot today. I enjoy money, yes. Don't you?"

Amanda smiled. "Very much. But people always act as if one should be guilty about having money and enjoying the spending of it. That seems idiotic to me. I have nothing to be ashamed of.

236

I didn't exploit anyone to get it. I just inherited it, so it's mine to spend and enjoy."

"Did you always know you had it?"

She shook her head. "I had a vague idea that we were better off than most, but I was very sheltered. At eighteen, my father explained about my trust funds, because the first portion of principal was about to come to me outright." She dropped her eyes. "The only way I can comprehend all that money is to think of it as a huge mountain. It was there before me and will be there when I'm gone. I blow by it, scraping a little off, but the mountain hardly notices."

"Is there anything you want to do with your life?"

"I respect people who work, but they do it for the money." A small grin escaped her. "I certainly don't need more money."

"I don't have to work for a living anymore either, but I really love what I do."

"That's why it's different for you . . . and people like your wife who have a burning desire to save the world." She paused. "Ralph, all my life I've wanted to be only a good wife and a good mother, especially a good mother; to be there for my children when they need me, no matter when. That's what really matters in life."

Mesmerized by her beauty, enchanted by her fresh candor, Ralph kissed the tip of her nose and tried to convey the delight she afforded him and the admiration he had for her elemental aspiration.

Later, Amanda invited Ralph to spend Labor Day weekend with her at her family's Newport cottage. There would be lots of parties. She grew petulant when he explained that the place and the circumstances were far too visible.

"But you told me you didn't have a real marriage, so what harm could there be?"

Ralph grew concerned, his voice firm. "I said no one but you could know that, especially your father. You mustn't tell anyone or act in any way when you and I are in public that would lead people to think there's anything between us."

"Of course, if you don't want me to, but it all seems so unnecessary and really isn't fair to us."

"Not one word," he warned her. "Some things just have to remain secret."

"How very odd!" she observed before she kissed him. "You sounded just like Granny when you said that."

* * *

237

The mayor's administration was still reeling from a major scandal that had exploded in a chain reaction across several city agencies and involved graft and self-dealing by public officials and by political leaders close to the mayor. The mayor himself had not been implicated and still retained some popularity. With the mayoral election only a little more than a year away, he was carefully choosing issues and forums that would sustain his popularity and thus his chances for the reelection he so keenly desired. But every ambitious politician, every business-person whose economic well-being depended on ties to city hall, was weighing the mayor's chances of survival.

For days the deputy mayor had been laying plans and gingerly broaching with prominent developers the question of what might be buildable on the four blocks which comprised Ralph Behr's site "if for some reason," as he coyly put it, "Ralph was unable to go forward." After Labor Day he began meeting with prominent builders in earnest and in confidence. He was helping the mayor to court these men with hopes of potential profit from entrance into the project, but he was also cautiously feeling them out about their interest in supporting him if he himself ran for public office. He was talking about the city council presidency, but there was little doubt he was also eyeing the mayor's job, if the latter's reelection efforts faltered.

One of those to whom the deputy mayor spoke was Simon Kramer, suggesting that he might be wise to commission an architect to begin planning a project on the Behr Center site. Feeling confident about their deepening relationship since meeting at Lorna Garrison's office, the deputy mayor revealed to him a bit more of his personal political plan than to the others. He knew that Simon was close to the mayor and expected no commitment, but left feeling encouraged by the developer's supportive attitude.

Early the next morning, a Tuesday, Simon joined the mayor for a private breakfast meeting at Gracie Mansion for which he had pressed on an emergency basis. Like many astute politicians, the mayor was a suspicious man who valued and repaid tested loyalty. Simon reasoned that confidential disclosure of the deputy mayor's tentative feelers—with a little exaggeration—could be the means to demonstrate yet again his own loyalty to a mayor who had helped him in the past and could be far more helpful now.

"The guy is trying to do an end run around you, locking up

your supporters and their backing. He's taking their money away from you—and you're letting him."

Simon paused to let the mayor consider what he had just been told. The deputy was his key aide, dear friend, and protégé. When the mayor finally looked back up at Simon, his expression was determined.

"I've had inklings something was odd. He's been evasive the past few days. This finally pins down why. You've always been straight with me, Simon—a real friend. I'll be straight with you. I want to run again, but the big contributors are scared that if they back me, they'll either get tainted by those damned corruption prosecutions or else that I'll lose, and their money will go down the drain."

"Because you're acting timid; you're on the defensive. You've got to take the bull by the horns again, show what you're made of. The big donors have to know that unless they back you, they could lose their access to city hall. If they want to be with a winner, they'd better be with you."

The mayor eyed Simon shrewdly. "Are *you* behind me?"

This was the moment Simon knew could cement his relationship with the mayor for good and give him leverage in the Behr Center matter. "I believe in you, Mr. Mayor. I believe that you're the finest public official this city has ever known and that you can win reelection if you're prepared to fight for it with bare knuckles, no holds barred. If you are, I'm prepared to back you to the hilt. I'll be your finance chairman, if you'll have me, and loan you up to five million dollars and raise the money to make good on that loan. In short, I'm giving you virtually a blank check to go out and win again."

The mayor deliberated for several seconds. "You know, I've been thinking about the way Ralph Behr has been trying to ram through that project of his. You've got rights there. The people of New York City have rights there. And he's running roughshod over them. A project of that magnitude needs a developer who has the city's welfare at heart. Someone I can trust."

The mayor's antagonism to Ralph Behr's plans was aggravated when, that same day, the brash developer announced he was commencing construction on the office tower, as if the city had no voice in what was built within its borders, as if the mayor had no say.

The next day, the mayor called a press conference. He roundly denounced the office-tower's construction start as an arrogant affront to the city and to the democratic process, "coming as it does on the heels of our recent reasonable request for time to study the project's impact on the community. In light of the crisis created by Mr. Behr's threat to the well-being of the people of New York City, I am ordering the buildings department to revoke their approval of his building plans while we reassess matters. One approach we are considering would be to initiate condemnation proceedings and seize the property, in order to institute the far more democratic process of opening the bidding to all responsible developers in accordance with guidelines drawn up by city planning. We would then be able to make sure that anything built on that site, which everyone agrees is one of rare historic importance, enhances and doesn't exploit the community."

The mayor gave way to the head of the city planning commission, who distributed the agency's development guidelines. He then introduced several prominent developers, who praised the fairness of the plan and declared that they were looking forward to making bids. With four full blocks involved, there was room enough for everyone. Simon Kramer pointed out that he already owned a sizable parcel and had long been planning development in the area. A representative from Lorna Garrison's public-relations firm distributed press kits of his proposed development containing ambitious sketches and majestic verbiage.

The following morning Ralph and the governor presided at a press conference, along with the head of the state's Urban Development Corporation. The governor defended constitutional property rights and the value of Ralph's project to the people of the locale, to the city, and to the state. He warned that if the city instituted condemnation of the property, the state would use its own powers, if necessary, which superceded the city's, to condemn the property on Ralph's behalf. Ralph announced that his lawyers were filing court papers at that very moment to enjoin the city from proceeding with its "unconscionable plan."

For the next several weeks, charges were traded back and forth on television and in the newspapers, the most conspicuous being the mayor's that the state was trying to force its will on the people of New York City and the governor's that the mayor was disregarding the good of the people on behalf of his campaign-contributing cronies in real estate. And when the state supreme court soon thereafter ruled for Ralph and against the city, Ralph issued a statement that he would break ground for the office building immediately.

Ralph's greatest vexation, however, was not with the progress of events, but with the unfavorable light which the opposition was increasingly able to induce the media to cast on him. When he and Gail attended a university-president's dinner party, he aired his dissatisfaction with a powerful figure at *The New York Times*. He mentioned an article they had run about the tenants' fight to keep their hard-won homes, another about the murals noted artists were painting on the buildings and the preliminary injunction they had obtained to stop him from blocking their effort, and a third that maligned him and misrepresented factual matters in his past. His announcement of the ground-breaking had been slipped in at the end of a human-interest article on the artists. The *Times* official found him very thin-skinned about his image, but agreed that fairness dictated a major article about him and offered to have a profile on Ralph written for the magazine section.

The next afternoon Dan Ahern came to Ralph's office for the first of what turned out to be many long hours of interviews and several days of tagging along after Ralph. Integrity, particularly his own, was very important to Ralph, who viewed the world as being divided into one hemisphere for those with integrity—a very small group, mostly limited to family members and a few close friends—and the far hemisphere for those without. As soon as someone betrayed a trust or acted in a manner Ralph took to be dishonest, that person was immediately and irrevocably deported to the dark half, where a large and growing colony of reporters now resided. Ralph determined to allow the truth to do his selling for him. And until he found his trust betrayed, he was prepared to believe that Dan Ahern would report the facts honestly and fairly, and that was really all he wanted.

Ahern arrived a few minutes early and was astounded to find Ralph Behr just finishing autographing a stack of eight-by-ten glossy photo portraits of himself that had been requested in the mail by total strangers. Ralph admitted he never failed to be surprised—and slightly embarrassed—by it, but did it, he said, because it seemed to matter to those who had asked. Although the requests had increased since the Travers (particularly from young girls who wanted photos of Patagonia), Ralph took pains to include a little note with each autograph.

The initial interview lasted two hours, and Ahern had obtained some interesting, if not earthshaking, background material: Ralph idolized his father and the memory of his grandfather and, while growing up, wanted to emulate and surpass their achievements. With his father working long days away from the house so much of the time, his early years had been spent principally with his mother, who had instilled in him her strong moral values. Ralph had not been an outstanding student, taking more pride in his athletic feats at Yale. Confirming the impregnable self-image at which Ahern had always marveled, Ralph claimed never to have given a thought to the critics in the early years who considered him simply a rich boy playing at real estate. The most interesting reaction had been to the question, "If you build Behr Center, what will you do then?" Ralph had appeared puzzled for the moment, eventually wondering aloud whether "anything after that could be worth doing."

The interview was drawing to a close when the intercom buzzed. A Miss Watkins was outside, waiting for Mr. Ahern. Dan apologized for the interruption; he had asked Marilyn to meet him here for their evening's date, but had not reckoned on the receptionist interrupting the interview to announce her arrival. Having remembered the pretty woman at the dinner for Simon Kamer, Ralph invited her to join them. But he remembered also which newspaper she worked for and, after greeting her, had some sharp comments about the bias he thought Max Borah had shown. Ralph sensed that her apologetic discomfiture derived from her own embarrassment over the sleaziness of some of her paper's reporting and of the gossip-mongering slot into which she had been shoved there.

After the reporters left Jeff entered to discuss a matter and found a somewhat saddened older brother, who confessed, "Those two work on rival papers and can date. I'm in love with a wonderful girl—you said yourself that Amanda's wonderful—but I have to sneak around back alleys just to see her. Why couldn't *you* have been the poor sucker who had to marry Gail?"

"Because you were the one with the assets." Smiling, Jeff shook his head. "I'm very happy being a bachelor."

"I was too."

On the day of the ground-breaking for Behr Center's office tower, several thousand demonstrators surrounded the site, blocking construction crews and dignitaries from getting through. The TV cameras showed it all. The governor termed it a tragedy.

In private, however, he told Ralph Behr that the continuing confrontation between the state and the city was appalling and had to end. The spectacle of the state threatening the city with unrequested condemnation, forcing this development down people's throats, would arouse massive enmity against both of them personally. Ralph was not running for public office and could afford to antagonize voters. He himself was not about to. Moreover, admonished the governor, Ralph could not possibly get his project built if the city continued actively to fight it; what if, to take only one example, the mayor blocked street access and routed all traffic away from the site. Ralph needed the city's cooperation whether he admitted it or not. The governor had just spoken on the telephone with the mayor, who had agreed to meet alone with Ralph an hour from now in an attempt to resolve the matter.

Ralph tried to object that right was on his side, but the governor was adamant. He would support Ralph only up to a point. And that point had been reached.

The sky had darkened, but Ralph still chose to walk from the World Trade Center to City Hall, using the time to review his arguments against city interference and what he might be prepared to yield to gain the mayor's support. The conversation never got that far.

When Ralph arrived, the door to the mayor's office was open, and he could see the city's chief executive in his shirtsleeves. Noticing Ralph, he frowned, but nodded for him to enter, and the room began to empty. The deputy mayor hung back.

Ralph addressed the mayor forcefully. "I understood we were meeting alone."

The mayor's gesture dismissed the deputy, who closed the door behind him.

"Maybe if we had talked earlier," Ralph began, taking a chair across the desk from the mayor, "before your deputy's personal animosity toward me could get in the way, you and I could have hammered out solutions to the problems without all this mess."

"He isn't the one blocking you. I am. He's been following my orders for the most part."

Ralph threw up his hands in exasperation. "So that's it. What *is* it you have against my family?"

"You really don't know, do you?"

"Know what?"

"You ask what I have against your family. All right, if you're really sincere that you don't know, I'll tell you."

The mayor sat back, his fingertips touching each other and, for an instant, his bottom lip. Then he began to speak. "Twenty years ago or so, I was living in Brooklyn, working as a lawyer. I had grown up there, and my best friend was an Irish boy named John Moran. We had grown up on the same block and had gone through school together and had been close friends all the time. Both of us went to the same college in the city. I went on to law school, and he took a job with a bank and got a business degree at night. John rose quickly. He was very smart. He was still in his thirties when he became president of the bank."

Ralph settled back in his chair. He did not know where this story was leading, but the mayor clearly intended to take his time.

"John was a fine man with a fine family. Three children and one more on the way. Catholic families are like that, you know. John was well acquainted with your father. Everyone of any substance in Brooklyn was well acquainted with your father, who had friends everywhere. One day your father submitted a proposal to John to finance a real-estate property he wanted to buy. Well, the numbers looked very good—there seemed to be a lot of collateral there. An appraisal backed the valuation. John granted the loan at a solid rate of interest. But a few days later, a bank examiner who happened to be doing the annual audit grew suspicious because the appraiser's signature looked different from the way it looked on the appraisal for a different property in the bank's portfolio. He phoned the appraiser, who said he knew nothing about the property your father owned. He had never even seen it. The property turned out to have been bought by your father for a lot less than he claimed to have paid—the bank put in all the money to buy it, your father none."

Ralph could sit still no longer for what appeared to be a baldfaced attempt to concoct a false justification for the mayor's spite. "My father was able to finance out on a lot of his properties— that's normal in the real-estate business—but if you're saying—"

The mayor cut him off. "A check of John Moran's desk revealed an envelope with five thousand dollars he couldn't account for. It looked to everyone that John had fraudulently granted the mortgage in return for the payment. He was stunned; he felt disgraced, he had known nothing about the fraud. From all appearances, though, he was guilty. Another man might have defended himself, but John was crushed to think others believed he had acted illegally. He felt he had failed the bank by not investigating closely enough when he granted the loan, that he had betrayed the trust placed in him, that he was dishonored beyond repair. He could no longer face people. He committed suicide."

"Look," Ralph countered. "I'm sorry about your friend, but if my father did anything wrong, the banking authorities would have locked him up."

"Your father is a very clever man. He never signed any of the papers, although he negotiated that loan. He was the one who worked it out with John, the one John trusted. Your father didn't pull a trigger or anything, but he knew how important John's good name was to him. As sure as if he *had* pulled a trigger, by framing him Henry Behr killed my friend."

Ralph jumped up from the chair in a fury, and only the desk between them prevented his getting to the mayor. "I don't want to hear another lie from you about my father! Your lousy crook friend probably killed himself because they had the son of a bitch dead to rights!"

The mayor never flinched. "I'm firmly against the state high-handedly condemning land without the city's approval so you can erect your skyscrapers without our having a say in the matter. And I don't like having a political enemy in the position of building the city's most important project, someone who can embarrass me if the slightest thing goes wrong. Make no mistake, with everyone trying to get me to stop your project, I'm not about to let you walk off with the biggest plum we have."

Ralph finished what he felt the mayor had left self-protectively unspoken. ". . . when you can make a whole bunch of campaign contributors happy by letting each one develop a piece of it and promising them all sorts of zoning and tax-abatement sweeteners and granting them bonus space in their buildings!"

The two men were at an impasse. The mayor had agreed to this meeting out of concern that his apparent impotency against the state might induce voters to consider him irresolute or, worse, a captive of the real-estate developers now clawing to bite off a piece of the project. But it galled him to think that if he yielded, Henry Behr would win once more. The mayor eyed Ralph, deliberating.

"Even though I don't trust your father, I'm not the kind to blame you for his transgressions. Ask anyone—they'll agree I'm a fair man." He paused, his fingertips once more reflectively against his lips. "Tell you what," he finally decided, "I'll give you the name of someone to look up and talk to who was there. Are you willing to be equally fair by checking into what really happened?"

"If there were witnesses against him," Ralph scoffed, "he would have been charged with something."

"Your father had too many friends. They were all willing to be

245

satisfied with the way the evidence looked on the surface. They were glad to take scapegoats instead. Here's my offer: you be fair about piecing together the truth about what happened, then I'll be fair about evaluating your proposal to build Behr Center."

"What's the name of this property you claim my father acted fraudulently on?" Ralph demanded.

"Hampshire Gardens."

Chapter 14

The taxi carrying Ralph out of the blackening morning plunged into the Brooklyn-Battery Tunnel he had always regarded simply as a road to negotiate the obstacle of the East River. Now, it seemed a blind passage toward a black and dreadful possibility, where his soul would be sorely tried. Everything about the tunnel appeared direful, from the soft hum, quieter than silence, to the fluorescent lighting that cast a garish pall on the vehicles sealed like coffins and moving in an endless funeral procession.

He shivered. This was not like him, Ralph reasoned, this anxiety, this what? overdramatizing things. He had no doubt that the mayor's charge was baseless, a politician's fabrication to justify a grudge against a man who refused to support him. Ralph tried to turn his thoughts elsewhere, but he could not. An accusation had been made against his father, against what he considered the honor of the family name, and until innocence was affirmed he himself would be on trial. As impossible as it seemed, if guilt could be proved—there, the dread again—then his name would make him responsible.

He had dismissed the limousine and taken a taxi to be less conspicuous. But a smell of urine and gas was nauseating him. The driver claimed not to smell anything. Either he was lying or too used to it to notice or be affected. As the cab emerged from the tunnel, a heavy summer rain began to fall, obscuring the view from the windshield except for the brief instant after each wiper's pass.

"You smoke?" the man inquired in a deep voice that sounded like an indictment.

"No."

"Christ, all day long, just driving people from one place to another, you need something. It's a hell of a rotten way to make a living." The cabbie's eyes were dark slits in the rearview mirror. "I know you, right? You're somebody."

Ralph shook his head. The man was silent except for the condemning gaze in the rearview mirror. When they arrived at the destination, and Ralph had paid him, the dark slits were still staring.

"I know you."

The bank entrance, at the corner of a busy commercial block, was just across the pavement. He ran from the taxi, swerved to avoid a woman hurrying by with her umbrella held low and forward against the rain, and ducked into the bank. Plastic-laminate countertops and other modern furnishings could not disguise the grand solidity of the space: inlaid marble floors, marble walls rising to a vaulted ceiling.

Ralph immediately spotted, seated behind the railing, a thin man with white hair. Through round glasses the man's light blue eyes fixed on Ralph as he approached, assessing him. The taxi driver's stare had been like an inquisitor's. The white-haired man's was like a prophet's who has grown weary over the years from the burden of too much knowledge.

"Mr. Gleason?"

The man nodded and slowly rose. "You wanted to talk about John Moran, you said on the phone."

"The mayor thought you might be able to tell me about him."

The elderly man stared a while longer into Ralph's eyes. "Too much time has passed for it to matter."

"It still seems to matter to the mayor."

"Bless him for that." Gleason paused. "Why don't you just ask your father, accept what he tells you and leave it at that?"

"The mayor has a different version."

"Mr. Behr, trust me on this. Sometimes it's better not to know things that are dead and buried."

"If it's the truth, I do. If it's the truth, it matters."

Gleason considered that statement with a gravity Ralph had thought reserved for Judgment Day. "We'll see, Mr. Behr."

Leading the way to the conference room, he closed the door behind them and chose a seat across from Ralph.

"All right," he began softly. Then his voice strengthened. "I trust you know the background."

Ralph repeated what the mayor had told him. "John Moran committed suicide after an envelope was found in his desk that contained five thousand dollars. A bank examination had raised questions about a mortgage given to my father and his partner to buy a group of buildings. Moran appeared to have taken a bribe to make the loan."

Gleason nodded. He spoke slowly, as if laboring to bridge the years wih memory. "I had just become the loan officer then. The mortgage on Hampshire Gardens was the biggest loan the bank had made up to that time. John was concerned about my inexperience, so he more or less took this one over himself. The first and last time either of us met your father's partner, Weinstein—"

"Weintraub?"

"That was it, Weintraub. The first and only time we ever met him was at the closing. Right here in this room. Different furniture, but the same room. We dealt with your father on everything—the terms, the appraisal—but Weintraub was the partner who came to the closing and signed the papers. They were partners. Either one could have signed. But Weintraub seemed to think that we had insisted he be the one to sign, that we wanted to make sure the other partner was in agreement on everything Henry Behr had worked out."

"I still don't see why so much emphasis is placed on the fact that my father didn't sign."

"Well, it only became important when we learned about the fraud. The papers contained a clause that said the bank would obtain the appraisal—the mortgagee would pay for it, but the bank would obtain it. Your father volunteered to call the appraiser and set him to work. He named a reputable appraiser, and we agreed. The appraisal came in on the man's stationery, so we never even thought to doubt it."

"The point you're making here, I gather, is that it looked from the papers like the bank had arranged for the appraisal. Did Moran suspect my father had acted fraudulently?"

"He refused to jump to any conclusions about your father's guilt before calling him in to get his side of the story." Gleason halted, disconcerted by a memory. "John was too good-hearted. Suspicion was bound to fall on him too, because of the appraisal, but he refused to accuse your father or call the police before giving him a chance to clear himself. When your father arrived the next morning, they spoke alone in John's office. I don't know what was said. I remember watching the door and wondering what was happening. Suddenly, it opened, and John stood there. Your father, who was behind him, left the bank without saying another word."

Gleason bit his lip, then regarded Ralph again. "The police showed up an hour later with a search warrant and found the envelope in John's desk. Weeks afterward, after John was dead and Weintraub had pleaded guilty, the mayor and I had a long talk. He wasn't the mayor then, of course, just a friend of John's who was shocked and saddened by what had happened and, knowing John, just couldn't believe he would do something like that. Well, I told him exactly what I'm telling you, and it occurred to me then that with his back turned to go to the door to let your father out of his office, John would not have been able to see your father slip the envelope into the desk."

"Then how did Weintraub get implicated?" Ralph was disturbed, not only by the elderly man's story, but by the plodding, sincere solemnity with which he told it.

"The envelope was Weintraub's, with his home address printed on it and had his fingerprints all over it—and John's. John told the police that your father had handed him the envelope, which he opened. He said that it contained the cash and that your father told him he could either apply it to the project as equity—it wasn't nearly enough—or keep it for himself and get the bank examiners to look the other way. John said he became angry and shoved it back at your father. But your father denied knowing about the money or the appraisal."

"So, it was Moran's word against my father's. The police, who were right there, believed my father."

"That's true, and they didn't seem to put much importance on something I found so strange: all the time he was in the bank for that meeting with John, your father wore gloves. It was spring, a little on the chilly side, but I remember thinking it didn't seem cold enough to wear gloves. I mean, this is Brooklyn. No one's that fancy here."

"This is all just a lot of suspicions."

"Except for the envelope and the money. They had Weintraub's and John's fingerprints on them, and they were found in John's desk. And, of course, the loan papers were all signed by Weintraub, so any fraud looked like it had been his doing. But Mrs. Robbins swears she looked into John's desk drawer a short time before the meeting with your father, to get the bank's seal for signing some papers, and there was no envelope in there. So one way or another, the money had to come from your father."

The evidence against his father was starting to accumulate. "Is she still with the bank?"

"Yes."

"One thing I don't buy," Ralph said sharply. "If my dad was guilty, the police would have arrested him. The D.A. would have put him on trial."

"It was easy not to. John looked so guilty: he had been accused of acting to defraud the bank, and he had killed himself that same day, right after being asked by the directors to resign. The evidence was strong against him, and his suicide seemed to confirm it. Weintraub looked like the party who had bribed him and was willing to take the blame." Gleason fixed on Ralph's gaze with his own. "The talk was that the D.A. was an old friend of your father's."

Mrs. Robbins confirmed what Gleason had reported, that she had seen no envelope in Moran's desk a few minutes before his father's visit. And one other thing: that night, right after John Moran's death, she had spoken to her friend Olga Beranich, who worked for Henry Behr and Abe Weintraub. As a matter of fact, several months earlier she had recommended Olga to Henry Behr, who had mentioned that he was seeking to hire a secretary-bookkeeper. Olga told her that she was very worried. After coming into work that morning, she had gone to the office safe for the checkbook. She immediately noticed that the five thousand dollars in cash recently put there was missing. She had seen it in the safe the night before, when she locked up the checkbook. Police detectives had been there to question her, and she explained about the missing money. They told her it had turned up in John Moran's desk.

Ralph tried to recall why Olga Beranich's name seemed familiar. And then he remembered she had been the notary who witnessed the signatures on the secret document he had been shown that shackled his father with blackmail while Weintraub waited out the years in prison.

Logically, he should question those law-enforcement authorities who could still recall what had transpired, but that might arouse their suspicion. Instead, he looked in a phone book and telephoned the Olga Beranich who, as Mrs. Robbins correctly guessed, probably still lived in a Slavic neighborhood in Greenpoint. The voice of the woman who answered the phone was frail and full of trepidation, but she yielded before Ralph's insistence. A phone-dispatched taxi drove him out to see her.

Ralph rang her doorbell on the fifth floor of the ancient building. It was answered by a sliver of an old woman's face behind the chain that secured the door. He spoke softly, but received no response for many seconds. Then the door swung back. A small woman dressed in black and a drably patterned shawl was revealed. She was trembling.

He followed her into the living room. Ralph's depression was deepened by the barrenness of the room: everything carefully dusted, but there were no photos, only a single cheap reproduction of a crucifixion painting on one of the faded yellow walls. The landlord had doubtless bullied her into not fighting for the paint job to which the law entitled her. The fringed, stuffed furniture was worn but serviceable. Linoleum covered the floor. A television screen stared at them.

"Mrs. Beranich, I understand you used to work for my father."

The faint motion of her head indicated assent.

"What did you do?"

She finally spoke. "Everything. Bookkeeping. Typing. Whatever had to be done. I was the only one in the office."

"Besides my father and Abe Weintraub, you mean."

She nodded again. Her lips were quivering. Ralph leaned forward to comfort her. "I just have a few questions to ask, and then I'll go. No need to be nervous. Do you have any children?" he asked, simply to put her at ease.

Her eyes widened. "My son died," she said stiffly. "In a car accident."

"I'm sorry," Ralph said, now feeling doubly awkward. "It's difficult to be alone."

He asked about family and what she did during the day, but the woman was not inclined to be talkative.

"I'm sorry to have to bring up unpleasant matters," he finally said, "but I have to know certain things. Mrs. Robbins—you remember she was the one who suggested I speak to you—she says you mentioned at the time of all the trouble that you were worried about an envelope with five thousand dollars that was missing from the safe the day it turned up in the bank president's office."

The old woman nodded.

"Did you tell that to the police?"

Reluctantly, she began to speak. "They only wanted to make sure that the envelope was the kind Mr. Weintraub used for his personal letters. It had his name on it. I would have told them the rest, but they didn't seem interested."

"The rest?"

"Your father telephoned Mr. Weintraub at home the afternoon before and said he was out of town. He asked Mr. Weintraub to take the five thousand dollars out of Mr. Weintraub's personal checking account right away, before our bank closed—it was late in the month, before the rents came in, so there wasn't enough cash in the company account. Your father told Mr. Weintraub he needed it to make some payment to a contractor who was insisting on a cash down payment before he would take on some repair work on one of their buildings. That's why the money came from Mr. Weintraub's personal account and it and the envelope had his fingerprints on it. Mr. Weintraub put the money into the safe that night, and it was gone the next morning."

Ralph felt numb. But he refused to consider the implications of what she had said until all the questions were asked and he was absolutely sure. "Anything else?"

"I came in early the next morning, like always, and the janitor mentioned to me he had seen your father going into the office late the night before."

Ralph sat motionless and unspeaking for a long while. Finally, he said, "You're sure about the janitor. He said my father was there after you left the night before."

"Yes."

That was the most damning fact of all. His father had had access to the money between the time it was locked in the safe at night and the time Olga Beranich found it missing the next morning. Although surface evidence incriminated Abe Weintraub and John Moran, at every point, behind each fact, lurked the shadow of his father.

"You notarized the agrement my father and Weintraub signed when Weintraub was just about to go to trial."

The woman began to shake harder now, her eyes pleading for him to go away.

"Just this last question, Mrs. Beranich, I promise."

"I don't know anything about their agreement," she blurted out, her eyes wide with terror. "Just leave me alone."

Ralph suspected she could be so shaken by the question only because his father had threatened retaliation so strongly if she even spoke about the document that she still feared him, even after some twenty years.

Ralph decided he would not gain any more from her and stood up. "Thank you. I'm sorry to have had to trouble you."

He left her there, staring at him in alarm, and made his own way to the front door. He stood outside it, rooted to the old hexagonal tile floor. He could not remember ever feeling so desolate. Everything pointed to his father being a crook and his father's success having been built, not on the inexorability of the Behr talent in which Ralph had grown up having faith, but on fraud. The immense admiration he had for his father and his father's principles might well have been the result of a loving son's gullibility in the face of a lifetime of deceptions. Even his father's assertion to him of innocence in the Hampshire Gardens affair might have been a cynical ruse to gain Ralph's agreement to the scheme that saved his skin. The beliefs Ralph had always held dear were shattering.

Gleason had been right when he warned him not to inquire too deeply. Ralph had been too thick or loving or sure of himself and his father to heed him. Even if his father proved to be innocent, it *would* have been better not to be put through this, not to be filled with this anguish, not to have all his loyalties battling each other in this way. However, Ralph was not the sort to turn back once he had started down a path, however dark it might be and whatever might lurk there waiting to assail him. He had to know the truth about what had happened in that banker's office twenty years earlier, regardless of the personal ordeal that ensued.

Ralph raced through the blinding rain to the waiting taxi, the day nearly dark as night. Spotting a candy store, Ralph halted the driver and ran inside to use the telephone to make further transportation arrangements.

Reminiscences descended on him of innumerable candy stores, almost interchangeable with this one, oases of delight that had drawn him when he was growing up as a boy in Brooklyn. One wall was lined with rows of magazines and comic books, like psychedelic clapboard siding. Soda-fountain spigots arched high and majestically like a trio of swans above the counter that ran much of the length of the store, and black vinyl mushroom stools on stainless-steel stems sprouted deferentially before it. At the counter's near end was a hill of sweets, bins of penny candy and rows of packaged candy and gum, that ascended to a graying, heavyset shopkeeper who was talking to a customer. Ralph walked past them and began to dial the pay phone nearby.

"It isn't easy, this country," he overheard the customer saying.

"In Russia everybody had job. Guaranteed. I was engineer, important. What I am now? Night watchman. I make nut peas."

"Peanuts," the other man corrected him.

"And I'm lucky to have that. Everything here is struggle."

"Are you sorry you came?"

Ralph halted his own conversation to listen.

"No, for my kids, I'm glad. Because we're Jews, my kids would never be allowed to have college. They have no future there. Here, yes. And here," he admitted, "they love it. Is country for my children."

For a while in the taxi, Ralph thought about his grandparents: Raphael and Sally Behar, who had died well before he was born, and Otto and Bertha Mayer, who were the parents of his mother, Rosalie. Immigrants, they had come here under varying degrees of duress, to find the better life he could now take for granted. Not one to delve without purpose into the past—the pursuit of present satisfactions motivated him—he knew very little about them and sensed that what little he knew was constructed out of scattered half-phrases broken off of legends about themselves they had created after arriving to build new lives. Even his mother, with her sweetly comic accent and occasional odd choice of words, refused to make the past a real place for him. "What difference does it do? We're all Americans now. That's the point, isn't it?" she told him once when he was young. Another time, she declined with the admission, "I would cry."

The only certain sense he had about them all, particularly about his mother, was that they had all adhered to ethical principles, despite conditions that may have forced them, in order to survive, to cross the line into what one or another country's authorities might have deemed illegal—like his own necessary marriage to Abe Weintraub's daughter. However, if the witnesses to whom he had spoken today were to be taken at face value, Ralph would have to believe something about his father that was inconceivable to him: that right from the very start of the Hampshire Gardens deal, he had crossed over, not only the technically legal boundary, but also the moral boundary between right and wrong.

The rain had let up, and the helicopter swept across the stretch of water between New York and the Jersey Shore as if atop the wide wave of night rolling in behind it. A rented limousine met the helicopter when it landed and conveyed Ralph the few miles to his parents' beach house in Deal.

He had told his secretary to phone ahead, but his mother was arriving only as he pulled up. For a perfunctory moment, she expressed regret over not being available to prepare dinner or to join him and his father, but she was much too excited about what she had begun to do to sustain the posture. She had returned to college for some summer courses and was attending a seminar tonight at a professor's home, but her ultimate aim was far more demanding. She took Ralph's hands and sat him down on the sofa across from her.

"I am going to make a biography of Goethe. What do you think?"

She sat back to judge his reaction. Ralph had to scratch around in his memory to recall who Goethe was. He remembered her once telling him she had put the work aside when she married.

"That's a big job for someone your age," he said.

"I should have started twenty years ago, when you and Jeff were both in school all day. Where did the years go?"

Ralph found her effort incongruous. "You're a . . . a mother . . . a wife and a mother."

"You and Jeff are adults now."

"What will Dad do for company? He doesn't go to the office anymore."

She shrugged her shoulders. "That is his problem. I invite you all summer and you suddenly show up. Before you lie to me and say nothing, tell me what's wrong."

Ralph deliberated a moment. "I'm afraid I'm going to have to lie and say, nothing's wrong."

"Is this 'nothing wrong' something with you?"

"No. Something I want to find out about from Dad that happened in the business a long time ago."

"As long as it isn't with you. I read some of the things they say about you in the paper and worry. Your wife," she asked with more emphasis than the question deserved, "how is she?"

"Fine."

"It's a shame all this. You need a wife, Ralph. Maybe not this one, but a genuine wife to you. You aren't as much like your father as you like to think."

Ralph wanted to ask what she meant by that, but sensed the question might open wounds she had long ago determined to suffer silently. He hugged her instead and watched her face break into a delighted smile.

"I know Jeff was always your favorite," he admitted, "but I still love you, Mom."

Her expression grew serious. "That is not true. I did not love him more. I had to protect him more. You're a tough act to follow."

"Ralph!"

His father entered the living room jovially. Ralph stood, and Henry threw an arm around his son.

"She was telling you about the courses she's taking?" Henry shook his head with a chuckle. "Normal women crochet or play bridge."

Henry drew Ralph toward the room's entrance, ignoring Rosalie. "We're eating at a wonderful restaurant, the Old Mill Inn in Spring Lake, just a few miles from here."

Ralph turned back to kiss Rosalie good-bye. "I'd like to hear more about this Goethe thing some time."

She kissed him and smiled up at him. "You really wouldn't, but then, to me, after all these years a building is still only a place. Be good."

Ralph walked out of the room, musing on her customary, offhanded farewell. That he be good had always been her main concern, and it had always somehow seemed appropriate even when she was wishing him luck on the outcome of a game. He knew that many of his values had come from her—he had admitted as much to Dan Ahern in that interview—but he had always assumed those were also the values of a father too busy to spend the time inculcating them. Now, he would find out.

Totally razed by fire in 1985, the Old Mill Inn had been rebuilt to incorporate a sense of its original nineteenth-century profile in a handsome, modern structure that was nearly all glass in the rear and overlooked a scenic lake. Led to a table in the Green Room, father and son ordered a Scotch and a tomato juice respectively and, while waiting, watched the waterfowl paddle across the lighted water. When the drinks came, Henry joked a bit with the waitress and then told her they would put off ordering dinner for a while.

"The food's very good here," Henry remarked as she departed. He took a sip of his drink and sat back to listen to whatever his son had come to discuss.

Ralph started chronologically, at the point, early in the day, when the entire matter had suddenly been presented to him by the mayor. He related that conversation and then, leaving nothing out, showing how each person's testimony had corroborated the others', carefully traced his path of inquiry among the people to whom he had spoken at the bank and then to Olga Beranich.

"She's still alive," was Henry's sole, noncommittal comment. Ralph could discern nothing from his father's expression.

Finally, with no facts remaining to be recounted, Ralph had to pose the question forming itself all the while he had been speaking, all that day. He took a deep breath and peered into his father's eyes.

"I have to know. Did you fake all the figures for that mortgage and then frame John Moran and Abe Weintraub when it looked like the truth was about to be discovered?"

Henry's expression remained unchanged, although his eyes narrowed slightly, as if he was assessing the facts laid out before him. Then, leaning forward, he set his elbows on the table and faced his son. Suddenly, he winked and grinned broadly.

"Do you really think I was going to let myself get sent to jail when there was a way to blame it on someone else?"

At that terrible instant Ralph wished more than anything that his father had lied, had denied all the evidence, no matter how damning, that he was not smiling smugly, as if the matter concerned merely a clever tactic he had used to buy some property.

"Then it's true."

"Hampshire Gardens was the big chance I had been looking for. But there was no way we could come up with the capital to buy it—or that Abe would have had the guts to do what I did. So I made up a cock-and-bull story for him. I told him the bank was willing to give us a hundred percent mortgage because it had some shaky loans outstanding to the project's owners that a sale to us and this new mortgage would clear up. He believed me. And the bank believed the phony figures and appraisal I put together." Henry shrugged modestly. He saw a lesson in this for his son. "The trick in having people believe you is believing everything yourself while you're selling it."

"Why did you think you had to do it?" Ralph asked in a strained whisper.

"If it was up to Abe, we would have remained small-timers the rest of our lives, as long as he had enough to live comfortably on. There was no way a drudge like Weintraub was going to risk even what little we had for a shot at real wealth, although I'm sure he would have been delighted to share half the gain if I had pulled it off." Henry chuckled. "As a matter of fact, I did, didn't

257

I? The bank's directors were so worried about the bad publicity and their own responsibility for having voted to give me the mortgage in the first place that, when Abe pleaded guilty, they were glad to wash their hands of it."

"So Abe took all the blame in return for your signing that secret contract, and you got off scot-free."

Henry's smile, drawn back from his teeth, had become an expression of intensity. "I was broke when my father died. From being brought up with millions, I was suddenly so broke I didn't even have the money to bury him. Nothing. I couldn't even finish college. From then on all I did was struggle to get rich again."

Henry gestured at his son. "You've had money all your life. When you needed equity to start out with, I put it up for you. I was rich by then. What do you think you would have done if you had been in my shoes, desperate to make it really big"—his speech turned sarcastic—"without a rich father willing to back you, and you saw a Hampshire Gardens, your big break, just sitting there smiling at you?"

Ralph stood up abruptly.

"I hope not that," he said.

He strode toward the Green Room's entrance and heard his father's words calling after him.

"Of course, you would. You have my ambition. You know it's worth it in the end."

Despite the evidence mounting all day, Ralph had refused until that terrible moment to accept his father's guilt. Henry's admission had shocked and distressed him utterly. Ralph was the least naive of men; his career depended upon a shrewdness that grasped the motives of others and then determined how best they might be used to obtain his own goal. But the cynical opportunism suddenly, proudly exposed, the callous disregard for what to his father were irrelevancies of right and wrong, the total lack of remorse for causing the death of one man and wasting the life of another had stunned Ralph and increased his anguish a hundredfold. Perhaps because his father was so lacking in contrition and had built on the tainted bounty of Hampshire Gardens the foundations of what eventually became Ralph's own empire, Ralph was overcome with all the guilt he felt should have been his father's. Rarely had that emotion ever pierced Ralph's self-confidence. Its newness to him exacerbated its effect and added to his torment. And entwined about guilt was his grief at realizing that, like a scrim that conceals the real action taking place behind it, the hereditary superiority on which his certainty of success had always rested had been a delusion; the Behr family's heritage of greatness to which he presumed he had been born heir was only a crook's manipulations and, before that, a colossal bankruptcy. He no longer felt entitled to anything he had achieved. None of his success seemed earned; all had been stolen. Its legitimacy was as contrived as his own, as wrongfully gained as his father's wealth and respect and as spurious as his grandfather's upper-class position. Nothing in Ralph's life, even his hardest-won victories, seemed free of shame or capable of restoring the pride that had always filled him.

Loving or not loving his father did not enter Ralph's mind—he would love him always, if only for being his father, and would do nothing to harm him—but the irrevocable relationship added to the guilt Ralph now bore and to the compulsion to exculpate the family name somehow for the terrible crimes his father had committed. There had to be rules. Right had to be right and wrong had to be wrong or else no one was safe, or else there was no up or down, east or west, yes or no, no winner whose gains would be safe from a loser entitled to swipe it all back, nothing that would last. The possibility that the purpose of life might not be clear, as he had always conceived it to be, and might in fact be obscure or, God forbid, absent entirely, threw his values into conflict. To Ralph, fulfillment depended on the game's being fair—succeeding was not the same as winning. But to Henry success appeared to be measured solely by money and actually depended upon those he bested gullibly playing fair. Ralph was appalled that his father had considered the code of honor for which John Moran had killed himself simply a weakness to exploit and had triumphed, not as a result of shrewdness others would applaud, but of dishonesty he would have to lie about the rest of his life. And what was owed to Abe Weintraub, Ralph thought at last, who had been robbed of twenty years of life, of others' respect, of a wife who died before he could return, of a daughter's growing up? And what to that daughter for all her heartache? Ralph had despised them both for what he had been led to believe was their vile blackmail.

Now, moving high above Manhattan, trying to pick out below his penthouse where she might have returned for the night, he felt a desperate urgency to apologize for what had been done to Gail and to her father. Now, a hundred million dollars no longer seemed a heavy price.

Gail felt increasingly abandoned by her co-workers at the community headquarters and ostracized by her friends, who considered that her marriage made her a traitor either to their interests or their class. Milo was resentful when she exhibited involvement in the art gallery. She dreaded the tension and the inevitable arguments during Ralph's visits to the site and having to act as intermediary between them. She had become almost grateful for emergencies at the shelters because they afforded her the increasingly rare feeling of being needed.

She returned home late that evening after a long and difficult day at the shelters. She let herself into the lower floor of the apartment she shared with Ralph and was about to ascend the stairway when a sudden movement across the hall, in the library, caused her to stop short. The quietness of her step had obviously caught Ralph by surprise. He had half-risen from the small sofa and awkwardly jerked his hand upward to halt her from moving on.

"I've been waiting to speak to you," he called out.

Oh, God, he was the last person with whom she wanted to speak. She moved into the open doorway. "Can we make it quick? I've had a very trying day."

He sank back into the sofa. Perhaps it was the single, dim lamp in the corner, but he looked haggard, Gail thought. The clothing was as neat as always, the black hair precisely in place. But his eyes were sunken, his manner uncharacteristically slow and anxious, like a man who has suffered a stroke.

"I . . ." He fell silent and just stared at her.

"Is something wrong?"

He bit his lip and slowly nodded. "I want to apologize."

"For what?" She was impatient now.

"For what my father did to your father. I didn't know until tonight that he had."

"You just found out?" she asked dubiously.

"I'm sorry. I wish there was something else I could say."

Gail sat down beside Ralph on the sofa. "You're serious."

He nodded. "My father admitted it tonight."

She shrugged. "It doesn't change anything."

"Not for you," he said, shaking his head with a sad, slow resignation too overwhelming to be feigned. "I was always so proud that in our family we operated on the up and up. It still seems inconceivable that my father would steal and then frame other people. Or that he would lie to me."

Thinking she might be about to reply, Ralph placed his hand on her arm. He had more to tell her. "Whatever I might have said bad about you or your father I want you to know I regret it."

Gail stared at Ralph incredulously as he inquired, "Do you think if you invited your father here for dinner, he would come?"

"I could ask."

"I'd like to meet him, you know, and ask his forgiveness." Ralph slowly shook his head again. "Twenty years of misery . . . and all the time he was innocent."

"I'll ask him here," she repeated and stood up, at a loss as to what else to say and, surprisingly, embarrassed by Ralph Behr's candor.

More surprising still to her was finding out that he had a conscience.

Chapter 15

At the tense meeting with the mayor the next morning, Ralph offered a curt, almost noncommittal acknowledgment that what he had learned in Brooklyn the day before might possibly be viewed as implicating his father. The mayor nodded, accepting the vague statement as an admission. He admitted, for his own part, that he had once looked into constructing a case against Henry Behr, but found it impossible without the testimony of his ex-partner, a highly unlikely offering from a man who had chosen to spend twenty years in prison rather than implicate Henry Behr. The mayor would have to be satisfied with the lesser punishment he hoped he had just inflicted: Henry Behr's loss of his son's respect.

Ralph did not trust the mayor to keep his word to be fair about examining the implications of Behr Center; too often in the past the man had proven to be only as dependable as his momentary self-interest. But, in this case, the mayor's promise coincided with his need to resolve the controversy—already there were fears that his inability to stop construction at Behr Center was being taken as ineffectualness by the electorate. He had analyzed Ralph's project extensively, and his major objection had not changed: this was too important, too conspicuous a project for the city to rely on a single developer. The mayor wanted others involved.

Barely hiding his contempt for what he viewed as the mayor's attempt to reward major backers, Ralph adamantly refused. Finally, the mayor narrowed his demand to a single developer who would be a joint venturer with Ralph and "protect the city's interests." The developer he named was Simon Kramer.

Ralph's tone remained calm, while inwardly he raged at the mayor's demand. The project was his. The vision had been his. He had taken the financial risk during assemblage, had borne the front-end architectural and legal costs, had obtained the financing and the major office tenant. If the mayor wanted other reasons why it was a poor idea, Ralph had a lot of them: He and Kramer detested each other. They were both strong personalities who would clash on every point. And, most of all, he didn't need Kramer or anyone to do the project—he was ready to go.

The mayor stuck to his guns, contending that bringing in Simon Kramer circumvented another of his objections: as a matter of principle, the course of the city's development was its own business, and he would fight vigorously to prevent the state, like an occupying army, from appropriating land in the city, whether Kramer's parking lot land or anybody else's. Ralph was going to have to deal with Simon Kramer.

Ralph suspected some deal between the two men or some favor being repaid, but he knew he was trapped. The governor was ready to withdraw his offer of UDC condemnation in the face of possible voter resentment. Better to act now, Ralph realized, before the mayor suspected that the governor's support might be weakening. Ralph agreed to attend a meeting with Simon Kramer at which the two developers would explore a possible settlement. The mayor said he would have the deputy mayor sit in as a disinterested third party.

The initial meeting was to take place at the offices of Garrison McLaughlin, Lorna Garrison's public-relations firm. Ralph arrived with Ben Rogovin and Phil Rountree on his flanks. Lorna appeared in the reception area shortly after he was announced. She had obviously dressed with care: a scarlet-and-white print silk dress, gathered on one hip, that showed her figure to advantage.

A triumphant smile flickered on her lips. "You should never have crossed me, Ralph."

Instead of answering, Ralph turned to Rogovin and extended his hand, palm up.

"Damn!" Rogovin complained and reached into his pocket for a ten-dollar bill, which he placed on Ralph's open palm, while explaining to Lorna, "I told him you had too much class to gloat. He said you didn't."

Enraged at the insult, Lorna turned on Ralph. "You prick!"

Once more Ralph put out his hand toward an exasperated Rogovin, who slapped another ten-dollar bill on it. Lorna raised her hand to strike Ralph. He held up a warning finger.

"Don't you think you've cost him enough for one morning?"

Lorna spun on her heel and stalked back out, the men following behind and winking to one another.

The deputy mayor and David Hodge, hired to represent Kramer's legal position on the matter, were both waiting in the conference room, but not Simon.

"I think I've heard this song before," Ralph declared. "If Simon isn't here in five minutes, this meeting and this attempt to join us together is over."

Knowing Simon's tactic of arriving ten minutes late, Lorna tried to argue that traffic was heavy and that it wouldn't be fair to the people of New York for Ralph to leave. Ralph merely glanced sardonically at her and then down at his watch. At five minutes past, he stood up and led his companions from the room.

Simon Kramer arrived exactly ten minutes late to a meeting which had already ended.

Delegated to begin the rapprochement process, Hodge telephoned Ralph with the called-for pacifying speeches ("Simon said he had never seen the traffic so horrendous. He was *mortified*, believe me, Ralph, *mortified* that you got the idea he had purposely done such a thing."). Ralph agreed to accept Kramer's phone call. Five minutes later Simon telephoned to invite Ralph to dinner at his home that night.

"Just us and our wives. No lawyers. No officials. They only make trouble. The mutual respect we have for each other—I'm sure we can work things out. I must confess, Ralph, with your interest in art, I'm eager to show you my own collection."

Myra immediately began going down the list of Gail's phone numbers and reached her at a shelter apartment. Gail said she could make it the next night, but had an appointment to see Milo tonight.

"I'm sorry," Ralph apologized. "If it's any comfort, I had to break a date with Amanda. By the way, I told Kramer you don't eat meat."

Gail was disarmed. "That was really thoughtful, Ralph. If tonight is that important . . ."

Immediately after hanging up, Ralph told Myra to inform Kramer's secretary that his wife was a vegetarian.

Ralph and Gail arrived punctually at seven-thirty at the apartment overlooking the East River. Simon was waiting at the front door beside his wife and maid to welcome them with a great show of jocular hospitality. Wearing a nearly identical navy suit and red tie as Simon, Ralph worked at returning the small talk. Each man was making an effort not to allow the larger matter that was the purpose for the visit to become obscured by small irritations.

Gail was struck by an amusing comparison she kept to herself: heads of state must exhibit a like kind of artificially amiable behavior when visiting each other to seal peace treaties. Her own relations with Ralph, which had been similarly disagreeable, if less stilted, had undergone a subtle change since she had come upon him the night before, distraught, waiting for her in the library. His genuine remorse had moved her. Without being conscious of the difference, she no longer felt the instinctive need to distrust him or to keep her guard up quite so high. To help out she stepped forward and put her arm through Simon's.

"Ralph tells me you're an art collector."

The entourage proceeded into the long gallery.

"Isn't that a Jacques Lipshitz?" Gail inquired about an abstracted bust of a man's head. Noting how proudly her host preened his short, pointed beard, she added, "A very important name."

Her conclusion was that the collection was a good and extremely costly, if safe, one: highly eclectic, but unassailable. Among the pieces were a seventeenth-century Dutch still life, a Renoir, a Picasso, two Miros, a Giacometti, a Beckman, a Shahn, a Motherwell, and a Rauschenberg. Although many of the works were not of the artists' first quality, Gail was delighted to see a number that were and complimented Simon appropriately. Occasionally, she would turn to Ralph with a remark like, "A good Dubuffet, don't you think, Ralph?" He would halt, stare at the work, and then nod his concurrence. By the time dinner was served, Simon's congeniality had become genuine.

Preoccupied by the apartment's dramatically modern layout, decoration, and lighting, Ralph was able to focus his attention on the matter which had brought them together only when they sat down at the black glass dinner table. For the rest of the evening, the two men gingerly explored potential approaches to a joint venture, both waiting to give the other man time to get used to the small ownership share they themselves were willing to relinquish, knowing that too direct an approach could cause a breach. At the door Ralph suggested lunch at his office the next day. He was dour in the limousine on the way home.

"Did it go well?" Gail asked.

"Did you see his home? The right thing would have been for me to reciprocate and invite them to dinner at my apartment, but it's decorated like a bad joke compared to his."

Gail kept silent.

"All right," he remembered reluctantly, "you tried to tell me the first time you came there. It looked all right to me," he grumbled. "Kramer worked in his father's construction company and went to school at night, did you know that? All that cultured facade is something he just picked up, but look at that apartment." Ralph brooded a while longer before speaking again. "I'm tearing my whole place out and doing it over. How good was his art collection?"

"What did you think?"

"Me? What do I know?"

"Not much, but what did you think?"

"The Picasso didn't look all that terrific to me. I liked a few of the others." He told her which ones.

"Your instincts are good."

"How much would it cost me for a collection like that?"

"I have no idea. And you don't just do it overnight. It takes time to put a collection together. But why would you want one like that?"

"The prestige of it," he admitted openly. "It opens doors."

"Sure, but why artists who've already made it? You'd be just like most other rich collectors."

"And there's something wrong with that?"

"The way to stand out and make a real name for yourself is to go after the new artists before they're discovered. You have an edge other collectors don't have: You're a partner in an art gallery. You'll be seeing the new artists first. You can pick the best of them. In a few years they'll be the important artists. You'll own their works for a fraction of what they'll bring then and have done something valuable for art."

"Sometimes it looks crazy to me."

"As crazy as the first time you were exposed to it?"

"No," he realized. "I'm getting used to it. Would you help me pick what to buy?"

Gail grew excited. "I'd love to. Would half of it be mine?"

Ralph frowned. Their prenuptial agreement dictated upon their divorce a split of all his assets except for Behr Center and the East Side assemblage. "You're learning too. Yes, half would be yours. We'll decide who each piece will go to when we buy it. One thing, though, I don't care if he's going to be the next Rembrandt, absolutely no Milos." He remembered something else. "Look, when you invite your father over, be sure to tell him I'm redoing the place."

"Ralph," she laughed, "he's been in prison for twenty years. It's really not going to matter."

"Well, maybe, but just remember to tell him."

Ralph and Simon's polite jabbing and feinting continued through the next day's lunch and progressed to serious punching at the following day's session with all attendants present. Twice Ralph threatened to walk out and once Simon. During a break Hodge and Rogovin worked out a proposal each presented to his principal. Both balked and demanded changes. Simon wanted to be a half owner. Ralph wanted to hold him to twenty-five percent with a minimum investment of fifty million dollars, regardless of how great a share the banks lent. They settled by agreeing that Simon's share would be thirty percent, with a fifty-million-dollar minimum cash investment, but five million dollars would be deducted for his signing over the parking lot. Kramer Construction would act as general contractor on all the work not yet under construction and receive the normal fee for doing so. That meant Simon would be responsible for building everything but the office tower, for which contracts had already been signed with another contractor. An apparatus was set up to ensure that Simon's construction company would be kept to a low bid and penalized if it failed to build in accordance with a rigorous schedule. Ralph insisted that Simon deliver a completion bond to guarantee that the insurance company would complete Simon's portion of the project if he failed, for any reason, to do so. However, if it came in on time and on budget, Kramer could make a hefty profit.

The deputy mayor returned from the telephone to assure the others that the mayor had approved those parts of the arrangement which affected the city, as a result of the newly joined partners' agreement to shift one tower slightly in order to keep its shadow from falling so prominently on adjacent avenues and their promise to try their best to work out a fair settlement with the squatters. For his part the mayor would guarantee to meet the city's obligations, which included approving any tax abatements to which they were entitled, mitigating the site's traffic problems, pushing through any reasonable street changes, and targeting more low-income apartments for other parts of the community district, so as to defuse activists pressing for them at Behr Center.

Lorna arrived at the meeting with champagne and a list of actions to be taken to gain the most media attention when making the announcement to the press. Simon took her aside and apologized for not being able to obtain a contract for her firm to publicize the project.

"I tried as hard as I could for you, but Ralph wouldn't budge," he told her. "This meeting will break in five or ten minutes. I've got to meet my wife at eight, but that should still give us time to celebrate privately back at your place. On the way we can talk about what I can do to convince him."

In fact, Simon had not raised the issue of a public-relations contract for Garrison/McLaughlin, nor did he intend to. Lorna was pestering him for a quarter of his ownership share—seven and a half percent of the deal—and putting up nothing. That was a very fat tip just for providing him with some information and spreading her legs from time to time. She was in his hair enough as it was. Any time he needed her services for PR, he could always buy those too.

The next day the mayor called a press conference. With newspaper, TV, and radio reporters, and their tape crews elbow to elbow in the city-hall hearing room, he proudly expressed his pleasure that Ralph Behr had revised the plans to develop Behr Center and had agreed to "my request that a concerned citizen like Simon Kramer be involved." Both men beamed when the lights swung around to them. Then the mayor upstaged the settlement by announcing, in order to end all the speculation, his intention to run for reelection the following year.

"Behr Center will be the catalyst for the rebirth of the East Side of Lower Manhattan and a vivid demonstration of my administration's vigorous leadership in building the new New York. Make no mistake about it, Behr Center will be a showplace for all the world to marvel at. But it will also be a symbol of this administration's progress toward the year two thousand."

Gail had invited her father to dinner that evening, and Ralph went home early feeling very strange: both guilty and beholden toward a man to whom he had never done an unkindness, a man whom he hardly knew. He had declined his own father's dinner invitation for that same night with a lie about the nature of the conflicting engagement, instinctively recognizing that dinner with Abraham Weintraub would be considered disloyal. He had always been so self-assured and close to his father that he could not remember having lied to him before, or even having felt the need to lie. But then, never before had he known that his father had lied to *him*.

"Thank you for coming, Mr. Weintraub."

Abe Weintraub had been out of prison for months now but still appeared spindly and frail, if somewhat ruddier. He kissed his daughter on the cheek, stared at Ralph without seeming to notice the outstretched hand, and then silently surveyed his surroundings.

"There was a time I could look at a building in any part of the city," he said matter-of-factly, "and tell you within one percent what it was worth. One percent. Like a trick monkey. Values are all different now."

"Did Gail let you know how badly I felt about what my father did to you?"

"What did your father tell you?"

"He admitted framing you."

Abe gazed at Ralph, his dark eyes large and piercing within the caves of their sockets. He seemed to be listening to some silent recording replay precisely the dialogue between Ralph and his father. Abe shook his head. "I think he *enjoyed* admitting it."

Discomfited, Ralph turned and gestured toward the living room, trying to think of words that would restart the conversation. The old man walked the few steps and stood at the portal to the living room, his eyes slowly taking it all in. He shuffled to the room-length window and gazed at Central Park for a long while before turning his back on it. "You live well, Ralph Behr." His tone seemed both free of personal bias and tinged with bitterness.

Deighton had entered and approached him with hors d'oeuvres. Abe seemed unable for a moment to understand who the liveried butler might be. Then he nodded to himself and, declining the food or a drink, walked to a deep armchair and slowly seated himself. When Deighton withdrew, Abe spoke again.

"So, tell me, Ralph Behr, why is your conscience bothering you so much that you feel it necessary to ask his forgiveness?"

"Because it wasn't fair to take your freedom from you."

"It wasn't fair," Abe repeated sardonically. "No, I suppose not. So, it wasn't fair."

"I'd hate to think I gained as a result of your grief."

Abe said nothing more; he seemed content to sit quietly and stare at Ralph. Gail had taken a seat, but used to her father's silences, also seemed in no hurry to make conversation.

"Was prison difficult?" Ralph asked.

"A foolish question. I did not have my freedom, my family. I could do nothing for them. And I was innocent."

"How did you spend your days?"

"A better question. They let me care for the library. I was able to read, to study."

"College? What?"

"In the morning the Talmud. The rest of the day philosophy, ethics. A little of this, a little of that. I enjoyed the solitude. At night, for pleasure, I read science fiction and played chess."

"You played chess by yourself?"

He nodded. "I was allowed to live alone in a cell too small for two; the other prisoners called me the rabbi; they left me alone. I don't expect chess is a game that interests you." When Ralph shook his head, Abe observed, "Your father could never see the point of it either. It bored him. Like you, he loved business, where the attack and strategy, the rough and tumble, were for real."

Ralph interrupted. "Was Hampshire Gardens the only time my father . . ." He faltered as he had trouble choosing a word that would not derogate his father.

"Acted criminally?" Abe finished acidly. "Hardly. I tried to restrain him in the beginning, but he simply stopped telling me."

Ralph reacted to a timbre that sounded like self-righteousness in the old man's tone. "Did you threaten to break up the partnership if he continued . . . or did you just stop asking him?"

"We were talking about chess. When your father framed me was the first time I understood that I had to react to the traps in life as if I was in a chess match." Abe smiled thinly. "He was shocked when I demanded the secret agreement and threatened

269

to testify against him in court unless he signed. He never expected that from me. He thought he could grab it all and put me into prison as well."

"I'm surprised you didn't want revenge, to force him to go to prison too. Wouldn't you have been able to negotiate a shorter sentence that way?"

Abe regarded Ralph with disdain. "The desire for revenge is like a worm that eats away the soul; it may eventually destroy the object for that revenge, but it will certainly destroy the soul of the seeker. The Talmud considers hatred a grave misdemeanor under Jewish law. So, I do not seek revenge nor hate your father, but I did seek to retain what should have been mine. I knew to the penny how much Hampshire Gardens was worth. With an asset like that in his hands, Henry Behr could begin to build a fortune. I wasn't about to let him cut me or my family out of it. In a sense I became *his* jailer; he was working to build up my fortune because half of everything he made continued to be mine."

Abe glanced at his daughter, his expression softening, then back at Ralph. "In most men's lives, if they're lucky, a single moment arises when they face a choice that can bring them wealth, success, security for their families. If they don't act then and there, they are consigned to failure forever. Most men stumble, become frightened, maybe don't even recognize the moment for what it is until it's too late. I gradually recognized how devious your father was, but even from the beginning I knew that he could make my fortune. I grabbed the moment with both hands. Gail, her children, her children's children, will be rich forever."

Gail moved from her place on the sofa to kneel beside her father. "You know that isn't important to me."

Abe stroked his daughter's chestnut hair. "It *is* important. I grew up poor. Don't believe the nonsense made up to deceive poor people into accepting their powerless condition. In our society money is the tool to control the things that can impede your life, to change it whenever you wish. I wanted that for you. Don't throw away what I sacrificed my own life to give you."

She nodded her head obediently. "I won't."

When it seemed appropriate, Ralph stood up and suggested dinner.

Two candles sat on the sideboard in the dining room. While Gail lit them, Abe covered his head with his hand. Ralph knew the ritual: his mother recited that Hebrew prayer over candles every Friday night, her principal assertion of her own religion in a family she had agreed could follow their father's Protestantism. Once when he was a boy, Ralph had accompanied her to synagogue for the last hours of the services on Yom Kippur, the Jewish day of atonement, on which she told him God judges whether you are worthy of continuing to live for the next twelve months. They were not like the genteel church services to which his father occasionally took him. Sounding primitively all around him were unintelligible chants which the prayer book translated into self-accusations that provoked disturbing thoughts.

Gail had prepared her father a kosher meal, which was served on a new set of dishes. As they began the meal, Ralph asked Abe about the Talmud. He could not understand why anyone would study something for twenty years. Once you learned something, that was it—you went and did it.

Abe's eyes lit up. He explained that the Talmud was a compilation of scholars' learned commentaries made over many centuries on the Mishnah, the Jewish law derived from the Old Testament. The joy of studying it was in the dialectical process, the give and take of brilliant rabbinic minds in disputation about correct Jewish behavior.

"Even if my body was imprisoned," he said, "my mind could be curled on a bench at an ancient rabbinic counsel. All my reading, my studies, liberated me. I could be hovering above a supernova or debating free will versus determinism with the great philosophers. I could flash to the beginning of time or the heart of man or the universe's outermost boundaries. And always, because I had no other concerns, I knew I was close to God. Perhaps that was God's plan for me. Like Job I was innocent and my family taken from me, but God rewarded me."

"Would you mind telling me about the Hampshire Gardens business?" Ralph asked.

"If you don't mind knowing how your father lied and cheated to destroy my life," the elderly man replied.

As he listened to Abe recount the events leading up to his imprisonment, Ralph was struck by a notion that seemed too astonishing for him to accept: that Abe Weintraub had actually enjoyed prison. Ralph reproached himself. The man had suffered unbearably, irreparably. He pushed the odious thought from his mind as he heard Abe saying something to him.

"I've been thinking about why you felt it was important to apologize to me."

"Do you have an answer?"

Abe nodded. "You're a lot like your grandfather Raphael. Even your looks. Even when you were a little boy."

"In what way?"

Abe had barely touched his food, but pushed his plate back and, elbows on the table, intertwined the fingers of both hands meditatively. "Your character sometimes gets in the way of your best interests. Your father would never make such a mistake."

Gail's eyes rolled up in disbelief. "Dad!" He had promised her to essay courtesy tonight, given Ralph's sincere remorse.

"I thought you—" Ralph caught himself and, despite the elderly man's aspect of bitter enmity when he mentioned Henry Behr, chose a different word from *hated*. "I thought you disliked my father."

"I do. But judged from his own perspective, life is simple and probably very satisfying, in the way a child is satisfied once he stuffs himself on his favorite candies. Life for your father does not have the complications it has for other men. He simply goes after what he wants, no qualms either way."

Ralph found himself fidgeting at this recitation of his father's rapacity. "What was my grandfather like?"

"My parents idolized him. Not only when he was rich, which would have been understandable, but when he was poor too. He introduced them to each other, you know."

"Grandma and Grandpa?" Gail was surprised, her own curiosity stirred.

"A day or two after my mother arrived in this country."

"Anything more you remember about my grandfather?"

"He was only average height, but the look of him was impressive. He *looked* like a man of character. He was always forthright when he spoke, with a European accent I always thought was elegant, especially compared to my mother's. And he dressed elegantly too. My father used to say he had the best eye for shirts of anyone he knew. Henry, his son, was my age, but he came from another world, the world of Manhattan, of rich people. I always assumed he was like his father, that he had character, that I could trust him. Instead, he ruined me."

"He didn't, though, did he?"

"What is that supposed to mean?"

"What my father did was inexcusable, but in an odd way, I'm getting the idea he gave you exactly what you wanted in life."

Abe leaned forward expectantly, prepared to enjoy debating the proposition about to be posed.

Ralph ticked off the points of his reasoning. "You weren't

comfortable in business, maybe not even in the outside world, with its demands and responsibilities, where you were always forced to wrestle with your conscience and make uneasy compromises, maybe even to live with a woman who bored you or didn't you give you any peace of mind, I don't know. You're a man who's much happier retreating into the world of books and ideas, who can spend twenty years examining arguments made by rabbis a thousand years ago. And my father gave you the perfect excuse to retreat: you'd done nothing wrong and had even provided for your family with that secret agreement, so your conscience was free of guilt. You could blame my father for having stolen your freedom from you and enjoy it at the same time. Most people would go crazy there, but for you it was perfect. Everything was so simple. And all the while, the richer my father grew, the more justified you could feel in having sacrificed yourself for Gail. In a way you were as selfish as my father. You enjoyed prison."

"That's the most detestable thing I've ever heard!" Gail exclaimed.

"If I'm wrong," Ralph said quietly, "I'll apologize. Your father prides himself on being an honest man." His eyes shifted. "Mr. Weintraub, am I wrong?"

Confronted by an indictment of the rationale with which he had justified his life for the past two decades, Abe's mouth curved downward and drew tightly together. He thought a long while. "Why do you ask?"

Ralph too was deeply pondering his answer. "Not because I wish to exonerate my father," Ralph said slowly, thinking as he spoke, "but to understand it all. For days I've been thinking my father was totally evil, and everything we owned and built up was stolen, poisoned somehow. I felt guilty for having benefited from your suffering. But I'm beginning to think it's more tangled than that: even someone like you, who was blameless, wanted it to happen. I think you're a hypocrite. You might not have admitted it to yourself, but once my father committed the crime, which you would've never had the nerve to do yourself, and had you trapped, you became his self-righteous but very eager partner."

Abe seemed tired, his reply evasive. "Which brings us back to a question I asked you very early in the evening. Do you still feel it necessary to ask my forgiveness?"

"Yes. But now I wonder about something that I never even had doubts about before: who I am."

"Earlier, I said you reminded me of your grandfather, who

273

had talent and initiative, but floundered when faced with a crisis. Now, I'm not so sure. Maybe it's better to be like your father, who had immense ambition and no talent, but succeeded when the chips were down because he had no morals either. Or are you someone else, Ralph Behr, whom we'll know only when the time comes for you to face your crisis?"

"You haven't told me if you enjoyed prison," Ralph reminded him.

Abe sat silently for a long while. Then he shifted in his chair to face Gail. "Forgive me, baby. I was happier in prison than ever before in my life."

The next few weeks witnessed a sputtering and then a cessation of attempts to reconcile what the squatters were demanding ("The world and my head on a platter," Ralph groused) with what Ralph was willing to give them ("He won't be happy until we're begging in the streets," they proclaimed to the press and officials still sympathetic to their cause). During that time, site and foundation work proceeded on the office tower, while the artists chosen by the residents completed their murals on the side walls of the two disputed tenement buildings. Simon Kramer stewed as he waited to get onto the site to begin his own construction efforts. He claimed that his access to the site was blocked by the tenements, which prevented him from beginning to construct the expansive elevated plaza that would form an atrium at the center of the three towers, the department stores, and the smaller shops.

"Time's running out on the date the contract requires me to start," he fumed. His tone became accusatory. "You knew how difficult those bastards would be about relocating."

"No more than you when you agreed to the terms," Ralph replied. He then explained that the eviction action was moving forward briskly, putting pressure on the squatters to settle soon.

"Someone should just chase those bastards out, so we can level those shacks and get to work."

"Those walls are too precious to tear down," Ralph teased.

"That penalty clause means a lot more."

"I thought you were an art lover."

"Shakedown artists is what they are," Kramer muttered angrily, "figuring I'll just sit back and take this shit."

For a time the art gallery threatened to become a target for the angers and frustrations of the artists in the community, some of whom resided in the disputed tenements, and the rest of whom were antagonistic to Ralph's project. Gail's persistent refusal to be abashed soon overcame her artist friends' reluctance to deal with her. Most were not yet well known and needed the exposure at what promised to be a major gallery and the sales it might generate for them. Milo was a whirlwind of energy, exhorting the workmen about the last details, hiring staff, cajoling promising artists to show, and working till the early morning hours on two large paintings that would complete his own contributions to the gallery. As he put it to those expressing distaste at representation by a gallery owned in part by the enemy Ralph Behr, "This is an entirely different matter. You, me, Gail, even Ralph Behr—we're all in it for the same thing, to sell the paintings and raise the artists' market value. Behr knows how to make money and he knows how to get publicity, right? Isn't that what we're all looking for?"

A precarious truce built on mutual self-interest was established.

The vernissage was held for the artists and their friends and family the night before the formal opening. This was a far different crowd from what could be expected at tomorrow night's black-tie affair to benefit the Coalition's shelter program. Not the least of the differences was the far less expensive and often haphazardly chosen wardrobe. Both Ralph and the Artists' Haven residents viewed the evening as an opportunity to recommence negotiations on an informal, less hostile basis.

Ralph arrived early to view the show and confront the problems and last-minute confusion he was sure he would find. Happily, everything was in readiness for the evening, and he congratulated Milo on the fine job: construction finished on time and without lagging problems, the design having produced a grand and inviting space, the art was well displayed, and preparations for the party were completed. Milo accepted the praise warily, anticipating the concluding criticism that invariably set off their altercations. When the barb did not strike, Milo's smile relaxed, and he grew buoyant.

Even someone as contentious as Ralph Behr had been forced to admit that everything had been carefully attended to, Milo thought with a pride he considered justifiable under the circumstances. This gallery embodied all his aspirations for the future. How could a coarse plutocrat like Ralph Behr, on whom life's privileges had been showered at birth, comprehend the anguish of watching one's talents go disregarded for lack of the leverage to compel others to take notice? Tonight marked the beginning of his ascension; he had refused to be ground down by adverse forces but, grasping the reins, had directed those forces where he, not they, willed. The gallery would make him a prominent figure in the art world. And, most importantly, it would at last provide the means to raise his own paintings to their rightful eminence among the spires of contemporary art.

"I intend this gallery to be a beacon, not for what's stylish in contemporary art," Milo confided, "but for what's best, what truly captures the spirit of the times."

To toast the launching of their new venture, he offered Ralph a drink from the open bar set up at the end of the main exhibition room. Ralph accepted a white wine so as not to give offense and clinked glasses with Milo.

Gail arrived at that moment and caught sight of the two men. Fearing trouble, she hurried to them, but Milo's affable expression eased her worry. She took the glass of wine he handed her.

"Pleased?" he asked.

"Yes, it's beautiful. You've done a wonderful job. Hasn't he, Ralph?"

"I've been telling him that."

"Except for the damned arches," Milo commented. "But I guess that couldn't be helped."

Gail raised her glass to Milo. "Even the arches look good."

She sipped her drink. Milo joined her with a large swallow before turning to Ralph.

"Gail tells me you've become a collector."

"Yes," Ralph replied. Gail had been escorting him to other galleries, and they had already begun to purchase artwork to be installed in his apartment when the new renovation and decoration were completed.

Expansive now, Milo declared, "You've never seen my work, have you?"

When Ralph shook his head, Milo gestured with his glass at one of the walls. Ralph smiled, as if appreciatively, and walked toward it. Milo followed at his side.

"What do you think?" Milo wanted to know. They stood in front of a large painting composed of clashing colors.

"Interesting." Ralph hated it.

"Milo," Gail interjected, "Ralph thinks it would be less . . . umh . . . suspicious if he doesn't buy your work."

Milo paid no attention. "I wanted to submerge context into the purity of color."

"You've certainly succeeded." Ralph did not understand what

he meant, but finding little he liked in the painting, thought it easy to believe something had been submerged.

"I've priced it at thirty-five hundred dollars," Milo pointed out.

Gail was shocked. Chagrined, she looked over at Ralph, but he merely nodded and kept his silence.

"Of course," Milo continued, "as one of the owners, you would get a discount. People from the *Times* and *Art News* may be coming tonight to review the show. Once they like something, it skyrockets. You won't be able to touch one like this for under ten thousand."

"Lots of luck," Ralph offered and moved on to look at other paintings.

Milo stared after him, not certain whether to take umbrage at the curt dismissal or to write it off to Ralph Behr's customary impatience.

"God!" he commented to Gail. "The man is really insufferable! Not an ounce of graciousness or tact in him."

"Actually, he can sometimes be very human. I don't think he meant anything by it."

Milo shot a glance at her, vexed by her unexpected leniency. "What precisely do *you* mean by it?"

Gail smiled reassuringly at Milo. "Only that he's not really quite the monster we always pictured."

"If your point is that the man has been useful—yes, I'll give him that," Milo said with a shrug, his indignation abating. A small smile crept onto his own face. "Even if he did it with your money."

Gail laughed. She loved him so; she wanted to throw her arms around his neck right there, but they were being watched by too many shocked old friends, who appeared to be burning with curiosity at the sight of the recently divorced couple in conversation. Before she could think of anything to say, Milo downed the rest of his wine, flashed her a loving smile, and excused himself to greet incoming guests. She noted the bounce in his step, his arms opened wide in welcome, and grew less troubled, despite observing on the faces of several women the attraction he exerted.

It had taken years for Milo to still the jealousy in her that she came to understand resulted from being insecure about her own looks. Often she would be wrenched awake, shaking from the terror of dreams in which she found him making love to other women. Milo's gentle assurances gradually stilled her fears and made her realize that his gregariousness and good looks would always draw women to him, but that he loved *her* and had no desire to reciprocate their feelings. She was glad to have been the means for providing him with this gallery and the role he had always coveted: host, high priest, and creator of a temple of his art.

As Ralph slowly made his way around the gallery, he found himself excited by the work of several artists. He was gaining confidence in his ability to respond to art with a more open and knowledgeable sensitivity. Pleased by his choices, Gail informed Theresa, the gallery's manager, of the works they wished to purchase. In order to dispel any notion that they may have set prices low for personal advantage, she and Ralph had already established a policy that none of their purchases would be final until approved by the artist.

Once or twice, Gail tried to introduce Ralph to the artists, but the conversation proved so labored that she was glad to flee as soon as Dan Ahern and Marilyn Watkins came up to thank Ralph for inviting them. When the two reporters excused themselves to go, Ralph was left alone. He recognized several people from public hearings and TV interviews eyeing him, but they chose to keep their distance. No way, he decided, would he belittle himself by making the first move to meet people who had insulted him in every public forum in the city.

As soon as Carla entered the gallery and pushed her unruly electric hair from her eyes, she caught sight of Ralph standing alone, quarantined by a no-man's-land. She liked him, and her down-to-earth sociability was offended to find him so isolated. She strode up to him, grabbed his hand, and, like a tackler breaking up the wedge of blockers for a kickoff return, successively forced her way into each cluster of people. Carla knew nearly everyone, and she introduced Ralph in ways that would prompt further conversation. She interrupted John Rosenthal, who was chatting with several other Artists' Haven residents, with the surprising news that Ralph had purchased one of his paintings.

"Subject to your approval, of course," Ralph quickly added.

"Why would you buy my painting?" Rosenthal wanted to know. He had debated with himself for weeks over the ethics of showing here and now regretted the decision.

"I liked the action in it," Ralph explained. "It kept pulling me in and swirling all around me. Yet it all seemed to be balanced. Does that make sense?"

"That's what I was trying for. That's it exactly."

"I've got a lot to learn. Carla helped a lot," Ralph remembered.

Several in the group ventured to tell him how impressed they were by the gallery. Ralph spelled out the plans for promoting the artists. The initial tension began to dissipate as views were exchanged. Finally, Ralph returned to Rosenthal's painting.

"I admire anyone who can create something that's never been there before."

"But not enough to leave all of us alone," Rosenthal tweaked him.

Ralph smiled. "I think it's in both our interests to work something out. I'm willing to discuss relocating you, even converting loft buildings for home and studio space for you, but those buildings come down."

"Even with the murals on them?" Carla asked. She and many others had come to believe that putting prominent artwork on the buildings had checkmated Ralph.

"I didn't put the art there. They're not my responsibility. I intend to demolish those buildings. And the sooner the better."

The reaction was acrimonious, but Ralph's refusal to lose his good humor or even to raise his voice—he considered this similar to any other negotiation—had a calming effect on the dialogue. The others began to respond to him, not as a powerful foe, but as a rather ingratiating, even charming, human being, with aims they could comprehend, while still opposing them. Many were overwhelmed in the presence of a luminary like Ralph Behr. The evening became quite convivial.

The room was crowded when a critic from one of the art magazines slipped into the gallery. He had almost finished touring the room when Milo recognized him and hurried up to engage him in conversation, informing the man not quite accurately that he was one of the gallery's owners. Pressed for an opinion about the show, the critic remarked that several of the artists were first-rate discoveries, several more were promising, and only one did he actively revile, finding the work immitative, pretentious, superficial, and totally undistinguished. He gestured at Milo's paintings and offered to be magnanimous about not mentioning that artist because of the high level of all the other work.

Milo's expression contorted, and he shouted. "Out! Get out of here!"

The embarrassed man moved through the crowd in the direction of the entrance. Milo ignored the shocked glances about him and had the bartender pour him a drink to get his mind off the incredible insult.

He spun around, and his eye fell on Ralph Behr speaking to a fairly large group of people, who were laughing amiably. His gaze might have moved on if Gail, who had been acting as a hostess, had not chosen that moment to direct one of the waitresses toward the group and then lingered a moment to join the conversation. The sight, as he conceived it, of his wife and his friends dazzled by a lout whose only attribute was exorbitant, undeserved wealth filled Milo with jealous rage. He strode toward them, calling out in a voice too loud as he approached, "Did the famous collector utter words of infinite cleverness? It's amazing what money can buy, even the adoration of the art world."

Gail anxiously eyed Milo and the glass he carried. "Ralph was just telling us about the time he and I were at a gallery and the man asked if Ralph might be interested in a Man Ray. Ralph became irate because he had never heard of that artist and thought the gallery owner was offering him a male prostitute."

"No one could accuse our Ralph of being gay, isn't that right, my sweet? We have your testimony to the contrary."

"That wasn't the point of the story, Milo."

"Ah, no, but it's my point—or, rather, *his* point that's in question." He glanced at her with disgust and then allowed his gaze to circle the group. "Are there any others here that my lovely ex-wife may have slept with?"

Ralph stepped in front of Milo. "I think Gail is owed an apology."

"What an interesting puzzle that presents! Do I apologize for sleeping with her or because I implied that *you* sleep with her?"

"Because you're out of line on all counts."

Milo's mouth curled with repugnance. "I think I've had just about enough of you! Enough of your money! Enough of your power to squeeze the people around here out of their homes! Enough of your boasting in that modestly boyish manner! And more than enough of your sniffing around my wife's crotch!"

Milo drew back the glass, as if about to fling it dramatically in Ralph's face. Ralph's left hand snapped forward and clamped onto Milo's wrist. His right grabbed the shirt material at Milo's throat and pushed him backward hard against the wall. His face very close to Milo's, he spoke in a whispered hiss the others could not hear. But they could see the terror on Milo's face.

"If you ever speak disrespectfully to Gail or to me again," Ralph warned, "I'll rip your throat right out of your body. And no more drinking on the job. This is a business, not your personal playground."

Ralph stepped away and, turning his back on Milo, reentered the group, continuing the conversation as if the intrusion had never occurred, disdaining even to accord Milo the dignity of keeping him in sight to guard against his possible retaliation. Milo simply stood where he was for a moment, the glass held oddly in the air against the wall, his eyes darting from one to another of the shocked bystanders. Gail reached out toward her humiliated mate, uncertain what to do. That served only to augment his humiliation. He threw his glass to the ground and stomped away. When Gail was finally able to disengage herself discreetly from the group to find Milo, he was gone.

In the early hours of the morning, residents at Artists' Haven were rousted from their beds by several loud crashes and the collapse of one end of a building. When the dust had cleared, what appeared to have happened was that someone had driven a ten-story construction crane the block and a half from the office-building site to the tenements. Two swings of the cement bucket smashed through opposite ends of the two low-rise tenements. Fortunately, stairways and not apartments were behind those mural-painted walls. The tenants escaped without injury.

Awakened by a phone call just before dawn, Ralph rushed down to the site, now illuminated by police spotlights. With all the other buildings razed for blocks around them, the two old tenements stuck up like the last, decaying teeth in an empty mouth. Police personnel were questioning the residents and examining the crane, the land, and the damaged structures for clues. A man had been seen running away from the crane in the dark, but no one could provide a description. Residents and onlookers milled at the edge of the commotion with reporters buzzing about them like flies.

Noticing John Rosenthal and his wife, Marti, trying to move belongings from their apartment in the collapsed building, Ralph shook off a reporter and approached them to express his sympathy for their loss and his relief that no one had been injured. Rosenthal stared at him incredulously, as if at a contrite executioner. Ralph offered to dispatch staff down here to find temporary housing for now-homeless residents and stood by his offer to develop permanent housing.

He returned to his car and telephoned his brother, Jeff, and Ben Rogovin, assigning them the task of setting up an office to locate temporary lodging for those forced out of the buildings. Reporters began arriving, and Ralph repeated his statement of distress and sympathy. Eyes more darkly underlined than usual by lack of sleep, Max Borah was standing with pad and pencil out when Ralph hung up.

"It's a little early for you, isn't it?" Ralph commented.

"Did you have anything to do—directly or indirectly—with demolishing those buildings?"

"No. Did you?"

"What's that supposed to mean?"

"They say a great reporter will do anything for a good story."

Borah eyed Ralph with a look that conveyed both the malice he harbored for people of Ralph's ilk and for anyone who would impugn his journalistic integrity. "You're the prime suspect, Behr. You had the best motive for doing it—instantly rids you of your tenant problem."

Ralph's expression conveyed his own angry contempt. "If you're accusing me of attempted murder, be very sure you can prove it, because I have a nasty habit of suing people who lie about me."

"If you didn't do it, who did?"

"You really expect me to guess at something even the police don't know?"

"Any hunches then?"

Ralph stared at Borah without replying.

Borah pressed on. "A little birdy told me you got into a fight last night with your wife's ex-husband. True?"

"Sorry to disappoint you. Not a punch thrown. Call it a discussion of artistic differences."

"Seems strange that you'd be in business with him in the first place."

"A very civilized divorce. It sounded like a good business opportunity. Incidentally, you might want to tell your readers about the great young artists whose work we're showing there at our art gallery."

Ralph ducked into the car, waved good-bye to Borah in the same motion, and directed the driver to head uptown. Borah brooded as he watched the long silver-gray limousine glide swiftly away, like a fish too infuriatingly clever to be hooked. Christ, he hated that bastard's smug show of aid to the residents almost as much as he hated his evasiveness. There had to be something more here, something Behr was hiding. But what? According to Marilyn Watkins, who had dropped into the paper's offices late the night before to file a story on the evening's parties around town, the impression at the gallery had been that husbands one and two had had some kind of dispute, which would be natural, she thought, considering how abruptly Gail Benedict left number one to latch onto the wealthy number two. Regardless of Behr's explanation, it still didn't make sense for both men to go into business together. Maybe more was there than met the eye, he thought, but not enough was showing above the water for him to spend the time to dive below. He had more than enough on his plate with the trials and investigations that stemmed from the municipal corruption scandals still going on. But he sure intended to keep an eye on Ralph Behr. Sooner or later something might just jump up at him out of the box.

Ralph's thoughts as he rode uptown were not on Max Borah, but on Simon Kramer, who was his own prime candidate for culprit. His strongest inclination was to storm Simon's office and accuse him of having ordered the demolition, but Simon beat him to it with a furious phone call that arrived at Ralph's office just as Ralph did. Simon did not seem to be disturbed by the incident, but rather at Ralph's having attempted it in such a way that he, Simon, could be implicated. Ralph did not know whether to believe the other man's innocence, but as he sat in his office and thought, Ralph remembered Milo's abrupt disappearance from the art gallery and Gail's once remarking that he had worked summers in construction jobs while in college, maybe it was even demolition.

When Ralph phoned her to refresh his recollection, Gail became incensed at what she characterized as his attempt to smear Milo.

"You're the lowest! Everyone's sure you did it, so you try to shift the blame to Milo. He was one of the first to volunteer his services at the Coalition when we took in families after the building collapsed."

"If he *is* the culprit, thank him for me. He did me a favor—whether he intended to or not."

"Every time I tell myself you might have a speck of principle in you, you do something to remind me what an opportunistic rat you are."

Ralph hung up on her to take the phone calls from the press that were lighting up his telephone console.

The D.A.'s office took immediate control of the investigation. By innuendo, the first newspaper and broadcast reports directed the blame toward Ralph and, to a lesser extent, to Simon

Kramer, based on their well-publicized fight to evict the tenants and pull down the buildings. Guests at the vernissage the night before quoted Ralph's remark that the buildings were coming down, "the sooner the better." Art critics mourned the damage done to the murals, and Ralph was again quoted as having said the night before that he wanted to get rid of the murals.

Ralph issued a statement to the press expressing shock and dismay at the incident and relating his efforts to house the residents. Then he conferred with Mickey Kohler, a top criminal lawyer, about how best to clear himself of the imputation of guilt. At the end of their meeting, the lawyer telephoned the D.A. to assert that Ralph was willing to appear before a grand jury to answer all charges. Ralph then added that to his press release. Lorna grudgingly admitted to her client Simon Kramer that Ralph's innate instinct for public relations had prompted him to undertake precisely the actions she would have advised. She issued an almost identical statement to the press in Simon's name.

By the time Ralph returned to his office, angry pickets were marching up and down in front of his office building. He waited for the clamor to quiet a bit, wanting to assert his innocence and that he was as upset about the incident as they, but went up to his office when their angry shouting continued unabated.

The black-tie charity party at the gallery that night had little of the congeniality for which Gail had hoped. Noted collectors and critics had been invited, in addition to socialite and celebrity guests, but the artists made little effort to hide their suspicion that Ralph had ordered the demolition. Some of the guests liked the art. Some even bought pieces. But for the most part they confined themselves to conversation with friends.

Milo was a lively host, doing his best to charm potential patrons, as if the previous night's fracas had never occurred. Two differences were his occasional wary glances at Ralph and the fact that he did not drink. As usual unattached women gravitated toward him, and Gail was forced to exercise a good deal of self-control not to rush to his side and protect her territorial rights. She finally relaxed when he caught her eye and winked conspiratorially, communicating to her how funny he found it that all these women considered him a bachelor.

One of the buyers was Charles Brookhouse, who was a noted art collector. He mentioned in passing that he was also sending a substantial contribution to "Gail's cause," although Ralph was convinced he had no idea what it was. Ralph knew the Brookhouses had received invitations, but believed Amanda had convinced them not to come. He had been nonplussed when she and her parents arrived.

"They like you and Gail a lot," she whispered. "Father didn't want to disappoint Gail." She smiled. "I didn't argue very hard. You and I haven't been able to see each other too much lately. I missed you."

She squeezed his hand. Ralph was certain everyone in the room had taken notice.

Later on, as the Brookhouses were leaving, Charles reminded Ralph about his commitment to the Cal Coolidge fund.

"How much do you think is appropriate, Charles?"

"We'll discuss it on the plane."

"The plane?"

"Next Tuesday morning. The entire committee is flying to—"

"Mount Rushmore?"

"Washington, for a meeting at the White House."

"About time they took notice, Charles."

"Oh, by the way, Ralph, my sympathies over the unpleasantness last night."

Fearing its collapse, the city ordered evacuation of one of the damaged buildings. The second would require extensive work. Such questions as who was going to do the work and when were instantly shoved into the background on Friday when a New York court ruled that the occupants of both buildings were residing in them illegally and could be evicted. The residents declared their intention to appeal.

Ralph telephoned John Rosenthal and proposed a generous settlement. Although he appeared to hold all the cards, he recognized that the residents' ability to delay eviction until all their legal remedies were exhausted could prove costly and might throw off the tight construction schedule. It was in everybody's interests to settle.

One week later, the residents were housed elsewhere temporarily while seeking permanent housing with the large settlements they had received, and workmen had carefully removed what was left of the mural walls, as called for by the agreement Ralph had made, turning them over to the artists, who had nowhere to display or store them. Within minutes cranes and bulldozers had leveled the empty tenement buildings.

At nearly the same time, a spokesperson for the police department announced that a lack of fingerprints, eyewitnesses, or other leads dictated dropping the investigation into the crane attack on Artists' Haven. As with most crimes in the city, no one would ever know the culprit.

Fall was well underway when the city withdrew the last of its legal challenges to the building of Behr Center, leaving assorted community groups to fight on alone. One group was able to induce a federal judge to issue a temporary order restraining further construction until he could hear testimony on the question of whether Ralph was required to obtain an environmental-impact statement that assessed Behr Center's effect on the area's low-income tenants and the massive increase the project would cause in population, traffic, potential noise, potential air pollutants, and just plain building bulk. The battle continued.

Chapter 16

Over the next few weeks Ralph was forced to spend much of his time either giving, preparing to give, or listening to legal testimony. Evenings were devoted to running his business. Although they spoke at least once a day and, even with Ralph's pressed schedule, were able to steal a few odd hours together at their hotel suite, Ralph had very little time to be with Amanda.

One Friday afternoon, with the weather having returned to summerlike warmth, he finally slipped away for the short helicopter ride to his Westchester house. The servants had been given the night off, and he let himself into the house.

One reason for his being there that weekend was an invitation to visit the Brookhouses' nearby estate the next day—Gail would be joining him in the morning. Another was being alone with Amanda for an entire night.

He had begun to learn more about Amanda. As she gained confidence, she exhibited more of her personality and less of her impassive facade. She was conservative in her tastes and very organized. Permissible behavior was defined by a mysterious catechism which separated those initiated into her class from the excluded, and she transmitted some of its subtler points to Ralph by graciously suggesting he modify some bit of behavior she thought might be construed as socially ill-mannered or, what was almost as bad, conspicuous. She took meticulous care to display flawless manners and dress, which left her unassailable; was reticent about undertaking new ventures and lowering her defenses unless she felt absolutely safe; and although her poise belied it, she was inclined to become anxious in the face of any controversy, which she tried to conciliate.

Once having made plans, she tended to become agitated and preoccupied when changes arose for which she was unprepared, as if an internal clock were trying to lift events back onto the rails laid out in her appointment book. Yet when she and Ralph were engaged in activities that she had anticipated, or the shift in her schedule was to become available for the odd moment Ralph could manage, she radiated joy. And, always, always, she was beautiful.

Her days were crammed with activities—Ralph was amazed at how busy she appeared to be yet few that bore personal consequence. Although she had completed two years at the acceptable junior college attended by many in her crowd, she decided against matriculating for another two years at a senior college to gain a full degree. What was the point, she asked, if she had no interest in a career? She read a good deal and was, thus, constantly expanding and educating her mind. She was, she felt, "finished" in the fullest and most traditional sense of the word: that is, prepared to assume her place as an exemplar of her social class, as the future wife of a prominent man, and as the mother of children who would be trained in their responsibilities as she had been.

Amanda and Ralph had already ridden and were in the large eat-in kitchen. An expert cook, she had placed her endive salad on the table. He broiled steaks, for which she had prepared a chanterelle mushroom sauce. Miniature vegetables were waiting to be lightly sautéed. She deftly cracked and separated eggs, then stirred into the yolks ingredients for the sauce of her dessert, *oeufs à la neige.*

"Are you sorry that spending the evening with me is keeping you from that party you were supposed to be at?" he asked.

"Granny was upset when I told her I was seeing you tonight. She had arranged for her friend's grandson to escort me."

She held up the spoon for him to taste the sauce and happily reciprocated his smile after he did. "I love being with you."

"What if he had been good-looking?"

"Then I would have slept with him, of course."

Only after the stunned look had seized Ralph's face did she laugh and kiss him, and he realized she had been joking. But it bothered him that he could not tell beforehand that she had been.

After dinner, while they were walking in the garden, she said she felt very romantic and hinted that he make love to her on the grass, like the very first time. Ralph kissed her and suggested that with the evening growing chillier, they go upstairs to the bedroom overlooking the garden. Sensing her disappointment, he gently embraced her and they lay down.

Ralph did not enjoy the act very much. Although he was happily surprised by what he took to be a sexual assertiveness on her part, the grass was cold and wet and he had to work very hard to perform. Amanda did not seem to notice. She lay open to him in a kind of dreamy oblivion. Ralph found it odd that she could be both so unemotional and so daringly fanciful about sex at different times. She later confessed that her adventurous moods were often prompted by a desire to flout the conventionality that stifled her while growing up. She was as intriguingly independent as he had perceived her to be when he first set eyes on her, but in ways he had not anticipated.

The disjunctive nature of Gail's life—the sudden shifts she had undergone among husbands and economic means and social classes—grew wearisome during the course of that fall. She became short-tempered and slept poorly. She felt like her brain contained a dozen Gails who lived on different planets, where alien inhabitants forced each to speak a different language in which they imposed conflicting demands. As executive director of the Coalition, she had diverse programs to oversee and influence to regain among many people who still opposed, or even pursued lawsuits against, development of Behr Center. Much of her time was spent fund-raising, widening a network of wealthy contributors and the means to reach them. The art gallery was prospering, and her efforts helped to cultivate collectors and promising new artists to whom she had access. And, once in a while, the outside world still called upon her as a prominent feminist figure and organizer and as an expert lecturer in matters of male abuse.

Her personal life transformed that hectic schedule into a source of anguish. Milo was by turns sullen, overly expansive, and depressed. Gail's relationship with him was increasingly troubled due to his hostility toward Ralph, on whom he seemed to have fixed, she surmised, as a symbol of his discontent. Although she never discovered Milo drunk at the gallery, he usually turned up drunk for their nights together, which had been growing less frequent. Her hope lay in the pleasure he seemed to derive when she praised his effectiveness in establishing the gallery so quickly in the art world; she thought he might be pondering making a future as an art dealer.

The fall social calendar called upon Gail and Ralph to spend a lot of time together. Her attitude toward him, once so uncompromising in its resentment of the privileged life he had built upon her suffering, had become uncertain, confused by aspects of his character revealed during the dinner with her father, particularly by Ralph's stubborn and unexpected integrity. Her surprising discovery that for all his shrewdness, Ralph Behr was a well-meaning man had done much to lessen her antagonism toward him. As a result their relationship had slid into an amicable camaraderie occasionally punctuated by teasing banter.

"This bedroom is a mess," Gail observed upon arriving at the Westchester house the next morning. Amanda had long since returned home, but Ralph's clothing was strewn about the floor.

"The servants won't be back till later."

"My God, Ralph, I suddenly got it. You drop your clothes on the floor out of a higher social responsibility! If you hung them up, you'd throw two dozen people out of work. Ralph, I've been so wrong about you."

Laughing, Ralph finished knotting his tie and slipped into a blue blazer. A few minutes later he was at the wheel of the Mercedes and driving them along country roads to the four-thousand-acre Brookhouse estate in nearby Connecticut. There various family members had erected homes offering obeisance to the mansion built by the founder of the family fortune, Amanda's great-grandfather.

Revered by his descendants and considerd an object of robber-baron loathing by historians of nineteenth-century American industrialization, the latter, who had backed Ford, Frick, Rockefeller, and Guggenheim growth, had left a twin legacy to his only son Otis: a tradition of iron-fisted domination of relatives and employees and a fortune of seven hundred million dollars, which had increased considerably since. His descendants, Amanda among them, had received substantial trust funds, but the great bulk of the family's assets and the control of Metrobank still resided in Otis's vigorous, if ancient, hands.

The guards checked their list against Ralph's and Gail's driver's licenses, then allowed them to proceed through the tall iron gates. The road to the main house beneath the tall shade-trees touching branch tips above them took nearly ten minutes to travel. As they emerged into the clear, they caught sight of a tennis court. Amanda was playing tennis with a handsome young man. Nina and an elderly man in tennis whites were seated on a veranda beside the court.

The road looped around a huge front lawn. The Mercedes drew to a halt at shallow steps ascending to the entrance of a mansion built on the scale and style of a British palace. The butler informed them that "young Mr. Brookhouse and Mrs. Brookhouse," whom they guessed were Charles and Patty, would join everyone at lunch. He led them to their suite, where Ralph changed into tennis garb and Gail into a skirt over a bathing suit.

A servant chauffeured them to the tennis court in a four-seater golf cart. Curt and wary, Nina greeted them and introduced the handsome young man as Cobleigh Barnwell, known as Cob. Ralph surmised he was the young man with whom Nina had been trying to match her granddaughter. The elderly man was now on the court, and Ralph recognized him as J. Otis Brookhouse, Nina's husband and a legendary figure in American banking. He was now rallying with Amanda. Tall, slightly hunched at the shoulders, and still lean, he moved surprisingly well for a man who had to be in his mid-eighties. Longevity ran in the Brookhouse family. Otis's father had died, still hearty at ninety-four, in a car accident.

Ralph observed Amanda with pride and pleasure. Long legs lightly tanned, beautiful face intent on the game, blond hair whipping out behind her as she ran, strokes clean and strong, he thought her the image of flawless grace. Sure of herself, always maintaining a small vault of reserve he could never quite penetrate, she was very much a Brookhouse, envied by one and all for her social position, so rich on her own he could be sure she was attracted to him and not to his money. He had finally found the perfect woman.

Amanda waved and, beckoning Ralph to replace her on the court, trotted over. She introduced him to her grandfather at the net. Up close the elder Brookhouse looked a good deal like his son, Charles, but his brow was heavily wrinkled and the nasolabial creases were deep crevasses matched by parallel canyons from cheekbones to jaw; his hair was white; and his gaze was hard. He looked far younger than his years.

Although Ralph had concentrated on basketball during his formative years, he was nonetheless a strong enough tennis player to have made the higher ranks of his high school team each spring. As he took his place the court, he was reluctant to hit the ball with any force at the elderly man across from him. His easy lob came whistling back at him.

"Basketball was your game, wasn't it, Behr?" Otis called loudly across to him.

Nina instantly grew nervous for her husband's health. "It's a hot morning, Otis. Perhaps Mr. Behr isn't in shape."

Otis glared at his wife and drove the ball just above the net right at Ralph, who returned it hard into the corner. The old man's age-shortened strides transported him faster than Ralph had expected; Otis reached and returned it. The rallying continued for several minutes. The old man had probably never possessed sleek form, but he seemed capable of returning every shot.

Any inclination Ralph may have had to ease up against his elderly opponent was overcome by a very strong hunch that losing, even in these rallies, would have cost him the latter's respect. A no-win situation: he would be hated for winning and scorned for losing. He decided to win graciously. As they walked off the court a few minutes later, Otis wore an angry sneer.

"It doesn't say much for you if a man my age could look that good against you."

Ralph chose to be tactful. "It says a lot more about you. You play a fine game."

Nina was on her feet as her husband approached. "You were wonderful, Otis. He made a few lucky shots."

"Good game, sir!" Cob Barnwell exclaimed to Otis.

Otis's eyes, however, were on his granddaughter. "What did you think, pumpkin?"

Amanda kissed his cheek. "You played beautifully. But Ralph was too much of a gentleman to lob you or go down the line when you were at the net."

Instead of exploding as Ralph had anticipated, Otis chuckled, his face only slightly more expressive than at rest, and threw an arm about his granddaughter. "One of the psychological advantages old people can count on."

Amanda was his favorite, Ralph sensed, who could get away with saying things to her grandfather that others could not.

As they drank iced tea served by an attendant, Otis interrogated Ralph about Behr Center. Although ostensibly retired, Otis appeared to be continuing to run the bank through his son. He was fully informed about the terms of Metrobank's loan and declared that he had acceded to the loan only after Charles convinced him that the bank had been lagging in real-estate financing. Judging by what he had read about Ralph, however, his own assessment was that Ralph's cockiness made him a credit risk.

"Think a lot of yourself, don't you, Behr?"

Ralph stared into the other man's eyes. "I'll tell you what I think about myself. I'm a great real-estate developer who can deliver what I promised your bank."

The old man returned the stare without giving any indication of his thoughts and then stood up to head back to the main house. Nina followed a step behind him. Ralph concluded, on consideration, that Otis's animosity toward him did not derive from knowing that Nina was his mother. A proud, vindictive man, Otis would never have allowed the bank to finance him, perhaps would even have tried to destroy him, had he known.

After Ralph and Gail had changed their clothes, they were shown to the study, where Charles and Patty had been reading the morning newspapers. The two couples exchanged greetings and moved into the wood-paneled English Gothic dining room. Staring upward in admiration at the elaborately fan-vaulted ceiling, Gail asked if the room had been taken from an actual English house of the period. Charles explained that it had been, as had several other rooms, and that the interior of the house had been designed around them.

Amanda entered the dining room at that moment, followed by Cob, now dressed in white slacks and tennis sweater. Later, Gail laughingly confided to Ralph that she could imagine Cob as the vacuous male ingenue who continuously bounces onstage in drawing-room comedies to voice the cry, "Tennis, anyone!" The last to arrive were Otis and Nina, and that seemed expected by the family members. Otis did not wait for others, but rather was waited upon.

"My son tells me you've agreed to join his Cal Coolidge committee," the elder Brookhouse began.

"Yes," Ralph replied, unsure of what the other man's attitude might be on the subject.

"I gather you're trying to flatter him. You can't be as foolish as he about honoring one of the most negligible presidents in our history."

Although Ralph was growing peeved, he did not want to alienate the old man, who was both his banker and the grandfather of the woman he loved. "It's the solid Yankee values that I feel are valuable. They're getting lost today."

The family members smiled, so Ralph decided that had probably been the correct answer. He could not tell from Otis's contemptuous expression or from his words because, doubtless aware of Gail's background, the old man had shifted to a new topic, the women's movement, which sparked a debate that lasted all through the meal. Several things became obvious. Otis Brookhouse was clearly the power in his family, for all of his son's appearance of authority to the outside world. His antipathy toward Ralph seemed to stem from a need to prove that he could still best a younger man who had earned an arresting reputation, that he was still the dominant male of the pride. His contempt was not limited to Ralph, but extended toward his deferential son and the opinions of the elder Brookhouse women, however timidly expressed.

As coffee was being served in the drawing room, Gail let drop that she would be in Washington, D.C., for a convention of a national women's organization the first week next month.

Charles asked if that meant she was proabortion. Gail replied that abortion was a woman's personal choice. When he asked Ralph, the latter's quick, emphatic response that it was a form of legalized murder provoked a shocked reaction from Gail.

"That's easy for someone who can't get pregnant to say. I'm absolutely stunned you would take that position."

"Strange you two have never discussed something so basic," Otis was quick to note.

"Whirlwind love-affair," Ralph swiftly rejoined. "We didn't have much time for talk." He thought a moment and then pointedly caught Nina's eye as he said, "I think my own reason for being against abortion is a very personal one."

Amanda had sat quietly through lunch, but her grandfather now wanted her opinion. "Oh, I'm for it, but not as a matter of principle, as Gail is. It's a simple issue of what's practical at the time. If I didn't want to have a baby, there should be no reason why I should have to have it."

Cob nodded vigorously, but Otis was displeased by his granddaughter's liberality. "The younger generation seems to have principles which rise and fall purely on self-interest."

"It's not a question of generations. Most women feel like I do. What do you think, Granny?"

"Yes," Ralph repeated, "what do you think, Mrs. Brookhouse?"

Otis turned to his wife. The color had risen to her cheeks, but she smiled at her husband and said softly that she agreed with his stand against abortion.

Hoping art would prove a less divisive topic, Patty moved to defuse the controversy by telling her father-in-law about the handsome exhibit she and her family had attended at the art gallery owned by the Behrs. She then invited the others outside for croquet.

"Grand!" Cob exclaimed.

But Gail was nettled by the dominance of the men and the passivity of the women. Defying the solemn stodginess of the atmosphere, she suggested that she and Charles instead go rowing across the lake to the village while the others played. As she later remarked to Ralph, for all his stern dignity and, doubtless, his aplomb among international bankers, Charles seemed naive in many ways; exposed almost entirely to the insulated women of his own class, he in turn was captivated by Gail's candor, what he took to be the outrageous daring of some of her ideas.

While chatting with Ralph beside the croquet turning-stake, separated from the others, Amanda expressed delight at learning that Gail would be away in Washington the beginning of the month. That was the week of an important charity dinner Amanda was scheduled to attend, and Ralph could now be her escort. He claimed that her parents would object or people might suspect what was happening between them, but Amanda had often been escorted by male family friends and was sure her mother would not object. Such arrangements were common at public events.

"I want to spend the night with you at your apartment in New York," she said with a directness that caught Ralph off guard. "You can give the servants the night off, like you do at your country house. I always feel so tawdry at the hotel." She smiled slyly at him. "Let's sneak off to my bedroom now and make love."

Generally, Ralph enjoyed venturing into potentially dangerous situations for the pure thrill of surviving them, not only whole, but triumphant. For a while he had spent his weekends racing cars. If he alone had been at peril, he would have slipped away with Amanda then and there, the chance of discovery enhancing the sexual thrill. But caution was now called for because of all the other people who would be exposed to danger if the true basis of his marriage were detected. Wed too recently for their marriage to appear to be curdling or for a court to judge the agreed-upon split of assets equitable, he and Gail had to continue to appear to all the world like an ordinary married couple.

"Give up a hot croquet match just for sex?" he scoffed. "Never." He then grew serious. "Going to that dance and my apartment afterward are just too risky."

Amanda remained firm. "A man, if he loved a woman, would want to take her back to his home."

She looked so pretty at that moment, so much in love with him, that he finally said he thought he could arrange it. His unvoiced concern after viewing the subdued period furniture and fabrics in the Brookhouse home was that she would hate the new modern look that had just been installed in his apartment, which now struck him as unalterably tacky. As soon as he returned to New York, he would throw out all the new furniture, bring in a new decorator, and insist the job be finished by the beginning of the month.

On Monday morning Ralph, Jeff, and Ben Rogovin flew to Boston on a chartered jet to examine a downtown office-building site being offered them. Standing across the street from the parcel, Jeff expressed enthusiasm and grew irked that Ralph slighted him by giving more weight to Rogovin's negative assessment. Ralph finally shrugged his shoulders.

"Everybody wants to build in New York. What the hell are we doing *here*? We could build Buckingham Palace here, and no one would ever know about it. Let's get cracking on that East Side assemblage."

Less than two hours later, they were back in Manhattan, stopping off on their way to the office for a quick look at how things were proceeding at Behr Center. In the air they had phoned Watanabe's and Steinman's offices, so that the architect's and structural engineer's associates assigned to the project would be there when the group arrived. Ralph did not know Watanabe's project architect, but he put a lot of stock in the opinion of Steinman's man, Larry Carlacci. Ralph was still seeking a construction representative and, because of the complexity of the plaza's concrete structure, had induced Carlacci to take over some of those duties in the interim. Ralph liked the young engineer's scrappiness, and he had been able to bring a Behr Group apartment project in on schedule. Although the courts were still preventing Simon Kramer from commencing his segment of the construction work, Carlacci's biggest complaint was about the difficulty of obtaining cooperation from Simon Kramer on the preconstruction aspects. Ralph assured him that Simon had not been his choice either, but that they would both have to learn to live with him.

Ralph had just reentered the limousine when the phone rang. The caller was Gail, and she was distraught, hardly able to speak. She told him as much as she could over the phone, and he assured her he would be right there. When he hung up, he asked his companions to switch to a taxi back to the office and directed the chauffeur to take him to the art gallery.

Ralph found Gail in the office with the manager, Theresa. Gail was ashen, her eyes fixed on the floor. He closed the door and asked her to tell him everything she had learned. Gail tried to speak, but her voice caught. Ralph turned to the other woman.

"Milo left here Friday about noon and hasn't been seen since," Theresa began. "I went to the bank this morning to deposit several checks that came in over the weekend. They told me Milo had withdrawn everything on Friday from both accounts, seventy-three thousand dollars. I couldn't understand it, so I phoned Mrs. Behr here to see whether she knew anything."

"That's all the information you have?"

Theresa nodded.

"Did anything unusual happen Friday morning?"

"Not that I can recall." Theresa pondered a moment. "An art magazine arrived with a review he had been waiting for. It was pretty hard on Milo's work, but he didn't seem that upset to me."

Gail looked up. "Something terrible has happened to him, I'm sure of it. Someone must have forced him to withdraw the money and then to drive off with them because he could identify them. I'm terrified, Ralph. I was going to call the police, but maybe that will endanger him. I didn't know who to turn to for help but you."

"Have you tried to phone his apartment?"

"There wasn't any answer. Should we call the police?"

"Let's go over to the apartment first. Maybe somebody saw him."

There was no answer when they rang the doorbell. Gail still had the key and let them in. The living room was undisturbed. Gail rushed into the back of the apartment. Ralph had just noticed a photograph on the mantel when he heard Gail's cry from a far room—not a call for help, but a wail as forlorn as a lost child's. Ralph ran to find her. Dresser drawers and clothing had been strewn about the bedroom. Gail was huddled on the edge of the bed, staring about her, her wide mouth bent down at the ends like a sad clown's.

"His clothes, the suitcases, his paintings—all gone." Tears were running down Gail's cheeks. "He ran away."

Ralph sat down beside her and put his arm around her. She buried her head in his shoulder. He tried to say comforting words, but could not say the ones she wanted to hear, that Milo had just gone away for a few days and would be coming back. He now had good reason to think differently.

"It's that damned money," she finally was able to say. "He couldn't live with the burden of my having all that money."

"No, I think that's what he was after all the time. I think he couldn't live with the rejection of his art."

Gail's mouth firmed angrily. "Milo and I were married for years before he knew about the money. You always hated him, and now you're taking the opportunity to pile it on."

"Gail," he said gently, "that photo in the living room. The woman in black. Who is she?"

"Milo's mother. She died before Milo and I met. Her name was Gail, like mine. He derived a lot of comfort from the coincidence."

Ralph took a deep breath. "You don't know how sorry I am to tell you this. She isn't dead. I met her only a couple of months ago."

Gail stared at Ralph incredulously. "No, she's dead."

"And her name is Olga . . . Olga Beranich."

"It's Gail. He told me so many times how wonderful it was I had the same name."

"She knew about the contract between our fathers. She worked for them. She typed and notarized it."

"No!" Gail insisted, wanting desperately to disbelieve the implications of what Ralph was saying. "No, that couldn't be. She's dead."

"I can take you to where she lives, but I don't think she'll be there any longer . . . now that I know her address."

Gail nodded, but when she started to stand up, she began to sob and collapsed against the unmade sheets, her cheek pressed to them, her hand stroking them.

"Oh, Milo. Oh, Milo," she kept whispering.

Ralph had guessed correctly. Olga Beranich's next-door neighbor verified that Olga had left with suitcases Friday night, shortly after her son arrived. When Gail showed the woman a photo of

Milo she still carried in her wallet, the woman confirmed that indeed the man was Olga's son, Milo Beranich. She had met him visiting his mother several times over the years.

All the way out in the limousine to the Slavic enclave in Greenpoint, Gail had been silent, pressed into a corner, staring sightlessly out the window. Now the fear of what she might learn had been replaced by knowledge. Her face, often pugnacious with its nose turned up at the very tip like the peak of a cap and her eyes large and angry, seemed lifeless, as if the vital force within her had died with her illusions about Milo.

Gently, Ralph explained his reasoning: Olga knew from typing the contract that Gail's father stood to inherit half the fortune the Behrs were amassing. Through mutual acquaintances she must have kept tabs on Gail and her mother over the years. Gail's entrance into NYU provided her artist son with the opportunity to contrive a meeting. Milo was charming, attractive. Gail fell for him.

"How can you be so sure?" Gail wanted to know, a small part of her still unwilling to relinquish the last morsel of hope that Milo had married her for love and not money.

"He lied about his mother and changed his name. He lied when he told you she was dead and that, like you, she was Jewish. Why else would he have done all that?" Ralph took her hand. "It's true I didn't like him, but I feel really sorry about this. My family has hurt you more than we can ever repay. No amount of money can repay it. And now this too."

When they were emerging from the Brooklyn-Battery Tunnel, she looked over at Ralph and said, "The money really separates us from other people."

"The money and what began it all," he agreed.

She did not understand.

"The contract," he explained, "Hampshire Gardens, your father going to prison."

"Oh, I thought you meant what my father told you about his parents, that your grandfather introduced them."

The next weeks were very trying ones for Gail. No mention of Milo's larceny was made to the police, in part for self-protection— Milo might disclose the purpose of her recent marriage—and in part because Milo had meant too much to Gail for her to press charges. She even admitted to Ralph feeling better knowing that Milo had the money. Discussing her anguish with her father would be difficult after a lifetime of separation from him, particularly now that she could no longer evade the truth that he was an inherently self-centered man consumed by his own interests. Also, she did not want him to feel that either her initial entrapment or later abandonment by Milo were somehow his fault. She simply told her father that she was pleased to be free of Milo and left it at that. If he noticed that she had exchanged her old gold wedding band for the diamond one she wore when marrying Ralph, he never mentioned it.

Just as Ralph was the only person to whom she could turn upon learning that Milo was missing, he was the only person with whom she could express the devastation she felt at being duped and abandoned by a husband everyone believed she had already left for another man. With the antagonism dissipated between them, she was free to confide in Ralph about her tortured emotions and was grateful for his willingness to listen. At first she feared he might be listening out of politeness or the remnants of guilt, but her need was so great to talk out every sentiment, to examine every detail of her shattered, manipulated union that she pressed on and found that Ralph's concern did not lessen.

For his part Ralph no longer felt comfortable discussing his business problems with his father, and Jeff still seemed like a kid to him. Ralph found that Gail was an intelligent and sympathetic listener. Although not required to do so for appearance's sake, several times he asked her out to dinner.

Despite his proclivity for self-promotion, she observed that Ralph seemed uncomfortable talking about himself, rather than his actions and projects. She began to appreciate both the hazards and the choices he faced in business—most financial, an occasional few moral. He weighed the latter as carefully as the former. She sensed that he still experienced distress regarding his father's deceit. In that, she and he, who had initially appeared to have nothing in common, were strangely joined.

When Gail left for the convention in Washington, she reticently asked Ralph if she could call him from time to time just to talk. The coldness she had early sensed from feminist colleagues had not abated in the months since marrying Ralph, adding to her feelings of displacement. She viewed the convention as an opportunity to reestablish relationships and to regain her place among them.

The next day, the federal court handed down its decision, ruling that both Ralph and the governmental agencies involved had acted in conformity with the law in all respects. He was free to proceed immediately with construction on Behr Center, without the need for an environmental impact statement. Within an hour Simon Kramer's crew was on the site, and Ralph was there presiding at an impromptu press conference to record the first piece of earth-moving equipment, a clamdigger, ripping its first large bite out of the empty lot.

Entering the main entrance of his hotel with Amanda on his arm was a strange experience for Ralph. They had often been there together, but had always entered separately and met only in their suite. Tonight they were attending a charity ball and would be observed by hundreds of people.

"I guess it's okay because we have our clothes on," he joked.

At the entrance to the ballroom, a woman Amanda knew came up to say hello. Ralph thought he saw a question about his presence in her eyes.

"Her family and I are old friends," he rushed to assure the woman.

A perversely mischievous smile on her face, Amanda made a proprietary show of adjusting his black bow tie.

"Known her since God knows when," Ralph added. "Client of the bank. Play tennis with her grandfather."

The event was being staged for an eminent scientific and medical research facility. Ralph's chair was beside a Nobel Prize-winning biologist, who described his work to the others at the table in simple terms, but seemed much more interested in Ralph's work.

The others at the table, old friends of the Brookhouses, were all from rich, old-line families, but they too fawned over him. Pudge Terwilliger made it a point to come over, and Mitten Cornell, and a good many others. None thought it scandalous that he was accompanied by Amanda Brookhouse. On the contrary, because they all knew he was married, they assumed that his presence with Amanda meant that he was a very trusted friend of one of the most powerful families in America. Ralph quickly relaxed and, stimulated by their admiration, allowed his natural buoyancy to show.

Amanda was usually reserved in public. Tonight, however, she felt no reluctance to display her pride in being with him.

Elated when he took her back to his apartment afterward, she pronounced it very handsome and the decor wonderfully homey. He discovered one reason for her determination to view his apartment when he led her upstairs: she immediately went to see for herself that Gail had a separate bedroom.

Turning back to Ralph's bedroom, she told him, "For the first time I really feel you belong to me."

Ralph took her in his arms and kissed her, aroused by the satisfaction and excitement being with her always instilled. With surprise he realized as well that he had not made love to a woman in his own apartment, in this bedroom, since marrying Gail. Amanda had been absolutely correct about the importance of coming here to be with him.

Compliant and affectionate in her lovemaking, Amanda enjoyed knowing she could summon such passion from him. Eventually she too was transported into an orgasm that shook her with pleasure.

Dan Ahern joined Ralph at the apartment for dinner when Gail returned from Washington. He had dined with them before in the course of gathering material for his *Times* article, and they felt at ease in his company. Gail did not restrain her criticism of the convention for ignoring the problems of minority women and women suffering wage discrimination and physical abuse, all of whom were not well-represented among delegates.

"The only issue there that wasn't abstract was the barrier that marrying Ralph has put up. Deep down, nobody really trusts me anymore." She glanced at Ahern. "I don't mind bringing it up because I feel so angry about it. They clam up around me and slight me, and then they probably tell each other that money has changed me and I put on airs now."

"She thinks money separates us from other people," Ralph recalled.

"It sure does," Gail affirmed.

"Money is just a way for people to know how much you've accomplished," Ralph argued, and he described the deference shown to him a few nights earlier at the dance given for the Institute—he did not mention that Amanda had been his companion. "I sat beside a famous scientist, a guy who won a Nobel Prize. That's something, but he idolized me and what I'd done, like a kid asking for Phil Simms's autograph. A lot of other people there did too. Really rich people."

Gail laughed. "I'll bet you loved it."

"What do you think is the significance of that incident?" asked Dan Ahern, who had been taking notes.

"I could have raised a billion dollars from investors that night."

Lorna Garrison's anger at having been discarded by Ralph might have lessened by now if her love life had been happier. She was not used to a relationship with a married man and was irked that commitments to his wife invariably took precedence over those to her. Moreover, although Simon Kramer was a strong man, which she liked in him, he could also be demanding and manipulative. She might have broken it off if she had another man in her life who attracted her or if she had already wrested from him a document attesting to her one-quarter ownership of his Behr Center share or if she were not billing quite so much from his other projects. But none of those had yet occurred, and so every mention of Ralph Behr or his wife in the newspapers or by friends restoked the humiliation which she felt he had visited on her and the desire to repay that humiliation in greater measure.

Yet she might never have stumbled upon the means if she had not committed in the spring, well before she and Ralph broke up, to stage a lavish cocktail party at Ralph's hotel for the introduction of a new product in a line of cosmetics her firm represented. Still steaming at the injustice of providing catering business to her fickle, ungrateful ex-lover, she arrived early to make certain her account executive had everything in order. The banquet manager was an old friend, whom she knew from his previous job and whom she always tipped lavishly because his surveillance was so essential to a successful event. He also provided her with wonderful gossip.

"What's up, Paolo?" she asked, once she was sure the details were in order. "How's Mr. Behr?"

She mentioned Ralph offhandedly, mostly because being at the hotel made her recall him so strongly, but the odd expression that came over the banquet manager's face caused her to press the question more strongly.

"You know something, right? About Mr. Behr? You can tell me. I can be very generous."

Paolo deliberated briefly. Self-interest won out. "He can't know where you heard it. You must promise me."

"Of course. What is it?"

"Well," he began, his eyes gleaming, "one of my waiters was sent up with food and champagne one night to a suite Mr. Behr keeps only for himself and doesn't allow the hotel to rent out. He

302

happened to catch a glimpse of a young blond woman through the open bedroom door. He didn't think anything of it. He knew Mr. Behr was married. But a few weeks ago he was working a charity dance, and he noticed Mr. Behr with the same blond girl. He asked me who she was. I knew her, of course. She was Amanda Brookhouse, not Mrs. Behr."

"Amanda Brookhouse! He's sure it was the same woman?"

"Absolutely. He became positive a week or so later when Mr. Behr attended a real-estate dinner here with his wife, whose hair is a kind of reddish brown and who is shorter, he says. No, he is sure the woman upstairs was Amanda Brookhouse."

Jealousy and delight mixed into the single emotion of having stumbled upon an oasis of revenge at which she could finally slake her thirst. The fact that Amanda Brookhouse was such a stunning catch, a social climber's dream, exacerbated Lorna's anger and confirmed her belief that Ralph was a user who hopped from one woman to the next for the advantages he could obtain. Even so, she reasoned, although Ralph may have had a playboy's reputation, he was not mindlessly casual about relationships with women. She was convinced his commitment to her, for example, up until the very last moment, had been genuine. If that was so, then it seemed strange, she reasoned, that Ralph would undertake an affair with Amanda Brookhouse such a short time after his sudden and presumably passionate marriage to Gail Benedict. Unless there was another, less apparent reason for him to marry Gail Benedict.

For a moment she considered telephoning Max Borah immediately—he had once phoned her to ask questions for a story he was writing about Ralph. But passing on gossip would not be enough to prod a tough reporter like Borah; she needed to figure out some way for Borah himself to prove that Ralph was having an affair with Amanda Brookhouse. That might then lead him to seek proof that Ralph's marriage was a fraud undertaken for some sinister purpose. She had a feeling that the means would come to her in the same way that this information had—by keeping her ears open and being patient.

Chapter 17

The fall should have been a happy time for Ralph. Behr Center was finally under full construction, and space in the office building was renting well to smaller tenants. He was deeply captivated by and on good terms with Gail, who was no longer the major source of irritation to his peace of mind she had been for a while after the marriage. But with greater frequency than this man who had known only good luck in his life was used to, the concluding months of the year also brought their share of difficulties that caused him to brood anew over thoughts and doubts that originally began to trouble him when he learned of his father's duplicity. Even small tribulations seemed fraught with deeper significance.

The first occurrence was Jeff's admission that he had taken an apartment for himself with river and park views in Symphony House, a handsome luxury building Burt Resnick and his family had just built. Jeff kept to himself that he had hired a top interior decorator to furnish it at a cost of over half a million dollars—he intended to borrow much of the money, which he would repay out of his secret brownstone profits. Ralph was furious that his own brother, who could choose for free any vacant apartment in a Behr building, would shell out good money to another developer and thus deliberately proclaim to apartment-seekers that a Resnick building was better than one built by Ralph.

"That's just it," Jeff told him. "I would still have been living in one of *your* buildings."

Ralph considered Jeff's action the most adolescent form of rebellion, an excellent indication that Jeff wasn't yet responsible enough to be provided with the funds to begin developing on his own. Jeff was deeply hurt that his older brother could not see his side of it and still did not seem to appreciate his work or his feelings. He discussed the dispute with his mother and with Gail, with whom he had become close. Both women tried to make Ralph see Jeff's point of view, his need to be on his own.

Ralph agreed not to hold the incident against Jeff, but for a long time he felt very let down by him.

Once a week during most of the year Ralph gathered with some of his old college friends for early-morning basketball games at the Y. These pick-up games attracted many ex-college athletes and even some pros in the off-season. Once a top player who had been named all-Ivy in his senior year at Yale, Ralph considered himself at thirty-six to be still in his prime and took pride in proving it.

One morning a new player was added to the opposing side, a classy guard who had played a few years before on a championship Georgetown team and who was now introduced as a rising star at a big Wall Street investment bank. The young man and Ralph guarded each other, and Ralph felt as if he were playing in slow motion: moves he should have made effortlessly felt awkward, holes closed up an instant before he arrived, the kid was past him on fakes he should have laughed at. Growing angrier and angrier at himself, he put a fake on the kid to get to an opening to the right of his center on the high post, where he could put down a short jumper. But the kid was with him all the way and blocked the shot, leaving him twisted off balance in the air. He came down on the side of his foot and hit the floor in pain.

His orthopedist assured Ralph it was only a bad sprain and taped the ankle tightly. He limped into his office two hours late, feeling very old. He was a bit shaken too by the recollection that he had envisioned himself as hobbling back and forth on a basketball court the very night his father revealed that he would have to relinquish half his wealth by marrying Gail Benedict.

Easily the most distressing of Ralph's trials had involved Patagonia, who had had a superb year, sweeping the fall three-year-old stakes, defeating older horses in the Marlboro Cup, and was training brilliantly for the Breeders Cup Classic. Ralph had announced the colt would be retired to stud afterward. For days before the race, the press had run stories about Patagonia and his celebrated owner.

Patagonia had been skimming easily along the backstretch in second place, seemingly able to take the lead at any time. Suddenly, he stumbled. The jockey later reported having heard a snap and knowing instantly that the colt had broken a leg. The outcome of the finish became secondary to most onlookers. The jockey pulled the colt to a halt and jumped off; Patagonia stood on three legs, the fourth dangling. The crowd and the TV commentators were stunned. The horse ambulance rushed Patagonia to the stable area. The broadcast ran late to interview the jockey, still overcome, who reported that his horse had stepped into an unseen depression, covered over by a light cake of soil that gave way. As the young man spoke, slow-motion replays circled the foreleg that suddenly broke in two.

Within hours top veterinarians arrived, and Patagonia was operated on. Ralph could not remember feeling such grief. He had loved this horse as he had never loved any other. Patagonia had been the fiercest of competitors, who would fight his way through any opening to get to the finish line first. He was the purest champion Ralph had ever encountered.

Ralph was with Patagonia throughout the operation, wracked by the agony of watching knives cut skin, stainless-steel screws bite into bone halves they locked together again, and needles sew soft tissue back into place.

Newspapers ran the story on the front page, and news shows that night led off with a report that the operation had been a success, but saving the life and breeding bloodlines of this horse America had taken to its heart rested on how well the horse would behave afterward. When he woke and felt the pain in the leg and saw the bandages, would he remain tranquil and allow the months of healing to occur or would he try to rip the bandages off and slam himself against the harness that held him, making it impossible for him to survive? TV crews kept showing up outside the mobile operating room, hoping to relay some word back to a horrified nation. Over and over, on the verge of tears as he spoke, Ralph could only repeat that they were praying Patagonia would pull through, but no one could be sure until he woke how he would react.

Gail had been at the track with Ralph, as she had for all of Patagonia's races this year. Amanda had come as their guest. Both women had remained throughout the night, nearly as distraught as Ralph. Both had grown to love the colt. Once in a while Ralph wanted to talk, but most of the time he stood alone, staring at the sleeping horse who had come to mean so much to him or standing in the doorway of the next stall, stroking the stable pony, Patches, Patagonia's inseparable companion since he first arrived at the track. The piebald was restive, his head high, listening worriedly because he could not hear his friend moving around in the next stall.

The women spent much of the time talking. Amanda was particularly eager to do so. She had been unable to confide her feelings about Ralph to anyone else because of his warning about the danger.

"I know I'm not to mention it to outsiders," Amanda finally was able to bring herself to say, "but something's been on my mind, and I just want to be sure about it." She hesitated. "This sounds so strange . . . but I have to ask whether you mind my relationship with Ralph. You two really do intend to divorce, right?"

Gail nodded. "But that's got be kept confidential."

Amanda appeared relieved. "I knew Ralph wouldn't lie to me. He is really very honorable, but I couldn't understand why you would willingly give him up, so I had to be sure."

"We married for business reasons. We have no romantic interest in each other."

Despite the gloominess of the occasion, Amanda, who had always been quiet in Gail's company, became exhilarated and talkative, allowing Gail finally to see in the young woman the disarming graciousness that had attracted Ralph. They spoke about Ralph and how hard he would be hit if Patagonia did not pull through.

The conversation turned to other topics and, as the hours of the night ambled by, the two women developed a friendship. Gail had missed the companionship that the necessity of concealment from friends like Carla had stolen from her and was as pleased as Amanda to be able to speak a bit less guardedly about her relationship with Ralph, although she still kept potentially damaging details to herself.

Occasionally, Ralph would wander over to the women to report the horse's condition or simply to express his worry. Dan Ahern arrived at dawn, during one of the latter moments. Ralph shook his head when Ahern asked whether he had any objection to his being there. Ralph's mind was consumed by his concern for Patagonia.

"He's going to pull through this. The doctors say the break set perfectly. All he has to do now is let it mend, and he can live the life of a raja on the farm." He bit his lip and peered at the stall into which the tranquilized colt had been placed to recover. "Just let it mend," Ralph urged in a whisper. "Don't fight it."

Later, they all watched as the colt, hanging in a harness that kept weight off the injured leg, began to wake from the drugs. Tethers on either side of his bridle held Patagonia's head immobile. His groom stroked his nose comfortingly. But as soon as the colt was aware of the cast on his leg and the harness, he became frantic, rearing and kicking to free himself from them. He fought to get his teeth near the cast and rip it off. He was in an angry frenzy. Ralph jumped into the stall with one of the vets and the groom. Long minutes passed while they tried everything to pacify him. They put the stable pony in with him, hoping that would calm him as it did when he was going to the track to train or the starting gate to run. Patagonia remained wildly fractious.

"He's too much of a competitor," Ralph called out to the others. "He doesn't understand it's for his own good."

After hours of trying to calm down Patagonia, when all the doctors agreed that the colt would continue to fight savagely to get at the cast regardless of the measures they took, Ralph had to make the decision.

"Don't let him suffer."

He turned away when the injection was administered and leaned against the wooden stall door. Tears poured down his face. The women, nearly as emotional as he, led him away.

"How could he die? He was running so easily," Ralph kept repeating.

Ralph dropped to the grass. "He could beat any horse on earth. He was all fight. The best. He never gave in." Ralph glanced back at the stall. "That's what ended up killing him."

He stared quietly at the sky for a long time, the suffering in his face giving expression to his thoughts. "Those races, the Breeder's Cup today, beating older horses, they seemed so important. I wanted the world to know he was the best. Why couldn't I have been satisfied and just retired him? What did another race more or less mean?" He paused for a while, then dropped his eyes. "What does any of it mean?"

Gail spoke up. "He fulfilled himself, Ralph. He was a racehorse, a great racehorse. He died trying to do what he was born to do."

"Maybe. Or maybe just what I wanted him to do."

Dan Ahern took notes.

A few days later Ralph invited Ahern on a tour of Behr Center. For a long time, when Ralph was starting his day near her office at the Coalition, Gail had refused rides downtown. Lately she had begun to accept, exiting the limousine one avenue away. But Ralph wanted her to see his project too, and today they all drove straight to the site.

A huge hole that would eventually cover the greater part of four city blocks was growing. Into it would be placed the foundations for the arches that supported the plaza, for the other two towers, the three department stores, and the other retail space.

"You can't really tell anything yet," Ralph said a bit nervously, wanting them to like it. He led them to the corner of the site where the office tower was already under construction. Trucks and cranes were parked beside it, and men in oddly fitting helmets clambered along the exposed girders.

He explained that the footings beneath the concrete foundation had to be placed on the island's granite bedrock in order to support the tower's weight. No matter how good the engineer's test borings were, you could never be quite sure just how far down you would have to go to hit solid bedrock, so the cost of foundations was always unpredictable. Then he described the steel structure already rising several stories into the air above the foundation columns.

"Poured concrete would be too heavy for a building this tall," he said, "all that weight at the top pressing down on the columns below. They would have to be so massive on the bottom that the building would be as wide as the pyramids. That's why we're building with steel girders. They're bigger and maybe closer together at the bottom than at the top, of course, but they're a lot stronger for the weight than reinforced concrete and allow a much lighter skeleton for the building. We'll also have some lateral supports, and a lot of those are built into those angled facades you saw on the model."

He stared at the structure for a moment. "There's something about steel. Something in the gut. Something strong and tall that gives me the feeling that I'm building a ladder to the sky."

He remained silent for a long time, continuing to stare at the steel lattice growing upward. When he spoke again, Dan Ahern took more notes.

Ralph had been well known before, particularly in New York, although many people had considered him a smart-aleck pleasure-seeker who used his father's wealth to steamroll over poor tenants and erect flashy buildings that he bragged about. Patagonia's tragedy now made Ralph not only nationally famous, but a sympathetic figure, with whose suffering everyone who had lost a pet or even a human loved one could identify. When Ralph donated Patches, the still-forlorn stable pony, to a camp for underprivileged children, two networks filmed stories that focused on Ralph's hope that the presence of adoring children would rouse the pony from his melancholy.

Lorna Garrison paid Ralph the respect of a grudging smile while watching the evening news over supper. This was John D. Rockefeller handing out dimes to tykes or Babe Ruth visiting children's hospitals. Her view that Ralph had cynically concocted the pony donation to gain popularity made it easier to reinforce her hatred of him.

Her temper had simmered just below the boiling point for weeks as she glimpsed Ralph's face peering at her from a succession of magazine covers at newsstands, at her dentist's office, and, worst of all, on her own reception-room coffee table. But she finally erupted one Sunday morning in January when she took the *Times* off her doormat and brought it in. Flipping through the sections, she came upon a smiling portrait of Ralph on the cover of the magazine section. She flung the paper across the room, terrifying the cat, who knocked over a lamp that sparked and sizzled after it broke.

Too angry now to reflect on the evidentiary strength of the tidbit she had been harboring, she searched for Max Borah's home number in her address book.

Borah was just finishing Dan Ahern's *Times* article while sprawled on his bed beside a dull young woman picked up the night before at a party, whom he was conspicuously ignoring so as to induce her to leave.

"It's a puff piece, another goddamn puff piece!" he roared, startling the young woman, who had just about given up hope of regaining the attention he had shown her the night before. "Makes him sound like fucking Hamlet, not like the greedy, conceited bastard he really is!"

"Who?" the young woman asked.

Borah looked oddly at her, not understanding why she was speaking to him. He had not spoken to her. Just then the phone rang. The caller was Lorna Garrison.

After they both agreed that the article whitewashed Ralph Behr unconscionably, Lorna revealed that a waiter had seen Ralph in a hotel suite with Amanda Brookhouse. "He's only been married a few months. There's something fishy—sinister, perhaps—about his marriage."

Borah was overloaded with stories he was pursuing about the municipal corruption trials, but his reportorial enthusiasm was aroused by the combination of his annoyance at the *Times* article, this rumor of adulterous scandal, and a recollection that Marilyn Watkins had earlier also speculated on the odd suddenness of Ralph's marriage to a feminist. Borah averred that he was interested, but only in the context of responsible investigative journalism, to demonstrate that Behr's sexual misbehavior was part of a pattern of immorality that extended to some criminal act—in business, maybe, or in his relations with public officials. He intended to do some digging, but a waiter's belief that he had glimpsed a blonde through an open doorway wasn't enough. For all anyone knew, Behr and his wife got it on by wearing wigs and kinky costumes in hotel rooms.

Lorna stomped about for nearly half an hour after hanging up with Borah. Then she used the magazine section to line the cat's litter box before beginning to read the rest of the paper.

Ralph waved the magazine section at Gail with great vexation when she entered the breakfast room to join him for breakfast. "It's Ahern's article," he fumed. "The first paragraph is about Patagonia's death, then he writes, 'Behr's eyes, normally a compelling hazel, looked like shards of shattered green-and-orange glass as he stared with bewilderment into the sunrise, trying to comprehend the death of the horse he loved so. "I wanted the world to know he was the best," Behr told us with grim quietude. "Why couldn't I have been satisfied and just retired him? What did another race more or less mean? What does any of it mean?" Ralph Behr is a man struggling to comprehend exactly that.' "

Ralph looked up. "The guy sandbagged me. I was too emotional to be careful about what I was saying. I'll bet that idea runs through the whole article. Here, listen to the garbage in the next paragraph: 'Behr evidently continued to deliberate about the significance of his accomplishments. A few days later, while inspecting the skeleton of the massive office building just beginning to rise from its foundation, he suddenly conjectured aloud, as if continuing to express his earlier thoughts, "Maybe a person's life just *is*, and that's it, that's all. I used to think being famous was important. But more and more, it's just a sales tool." ' "

Ralph glanced at Gail again. "I never thought he would lie like that—just make up quotes and write that I said them."

"You did say that," she reminded him.

"All right," he seethed, "but he should have kept my personal thoughts off the record. Any honorable guy would have. Did he ever give you the idea that he intended to ambush me like that?"

She knew he was not seeking her opinion. Indeed, he immediately read on, stopping every few minutes to read a line or two or make a comment that allowed him to let off steam. Although

Dan Ahern had recounted his subject's history, he had used his access to delve deeper into Ralph's psyche, making evaluations that Ralph himself might not have yet been ready or willing to make.

As he neared the ending, Ralph began to read aloud more slowly, more reflectively. " 'Is the image we have of Ralph Behr a true one or does he conjure it up with the same dexterity as the publicity that keeps him constantly in the news? The impression one gets is that for a long time he moved comfortably in the role which we ascribe to him. His fans write to him for signed photos or stop him in public to ask for an autograph, elevating him to the high plateau inhabited by such other high-income idols as rock singers, athletes, and movie actors. And he experiences no sense of self-consciousness as he signs. The celebrated Yale basketball star who built an awesome business empire, the man of action who seized success but can still care about the grief of a stable pony, has become an avatar of our national values, an authentic, if superficial, hero.

" 'When I first met Ralph Behr, I sensed that he thought of himself as a hero too. But lately he has begun to have his doubts. The accidental death of a racehorse and a twisted ankle in a choose-up game might not seem ominous to most people, but they have roused Ralph Behr to confront his mortality. He has always submerged himself in life and identified with its accepted forms, unthinkingly oblivious to their transience. He is becoming painfully aware that his sporting triumphs and the edifices he builds to increase his wealth and enshrine his fame merely deny death; they do not overcome it. Now, at the age of thirty-six, building the tallest and, according to him, the most spectacular real-estate project ever, Ralph Behr wonders what, if anything, will.' "

Ralph flung the newspaper to the floor. "Shit! The guy's a sleazeball."

"I was there when you said a lot of those things."

"But he twisted them, made them into things I never intended."

"What bothers you about the article? I think it's pretty complimentary in many ways."

Ralph's mouth twisted uncomfortably. He spoke reluctantly. "He makes me look like a weakling . . . an idiot wimp who isn't bright enough, on the one hand, to understand what's happening and, on the other, can barely make a decision because he's agonizing over life and death and that crap."

"First of all, Dan was just doing his job—" she began.

"Look," he challenged her, "I've accomplished in ten, twelve years what few men accomplish in a lifetime, right?" She nodded. "I've got an image as someone who's unbeatable. People want to make deals with me because I come through, and that guarantees they'll come through too. An article like this . . ." He trailed off.

"Makes you look human and not godlike," she finished for him. "You *are* human. There's nothing wrong with people knowing that—they'll like you a lot more for it. It's the side that made *me* like you."

"The world is full of enough ordinary people who pass through the world and don't leave a trace."

Early the next morning Max Borah stormed the managing editor's desk and demanded Marilyn Watkins's services to do the legwork on a story about Ralph Behr. Stories about big real-estate political contributors were a special favorite of Borah's and a natural for the populist audience to which he appealed, but the managing editor remembered having once let him spend several weeks futilely trying to get something on Behr. Borah seemed to harbor animosity toward the developer for some reason, and Marilyn was already hard at work on several other stories, but the managing editor yielded immediately, having no desire to test his own power against Borah's. Not only was Borah very close to the publisher, he was now the paper's major drawing card.

"Max," Marilyn moaned, "can't you find someone else? One of the new kids." The way she viewed it, Borah was sending her on a hunting expedition from which he hoped she might return with a carcass big enough to interest him.

"I need someone with experience. You had some ideas about how hurried his marriage was, remember?"

"I've got too much on my plate as it is."

"You want to share the Pulitzer with me for the piece, don't you?"

"It's all yours."

She knew Borah never shared credit with anyone and doubted that anything shocking would turn up on Ralph Behr. Deep down, she did not want it to. She liked Ralph Behr. He was neither boring nor neurotic, she reflected, as was the case with so many successful men. Rather, he projected an open charm and, perhaps because of his aura of wealth and achievement, seemed effortlessly masterful. As Dan Ahern had once observed, his only sin was refusing to apologize to Borah for his success.

But she could only smile at Max Borah and agree to try to fit the assignment into the rest of her schedule. Borah could have her out the door and on her way to the unemployment office before she had poured her second cup of coffee. He had a habit of losing interest in stories which did not promise huge rewards. She hoped that would occur here.

Several weeks later Ralph fulfilled a commitment to attend a fund-raiser cocktail party for a congressman to whom he had already contributed heavily. He avoided Lorna, for whom such affairs were the lifeblood of her business, but chatted a while with the deputy mayor, who seemed eager to rebuild bridges he had burned between them, now that the mayor had become willing to deal with Ralph.

The deputy mayor spied Marilyn Watkins making her way toward them before Ralph did. Preening, he invited her to join their conversation, but eventually took his leave when he realized to his disappointment that her attention was primarily directed at Ralph. She had put off looking into Ralph Behr's affairs for a long while, but Max Borah had become insistent. Ralph had recently heard from friends that she had been making inquiries about him. Bored, with no company for the evening, intrigued at the prospect of playing cat and mouse with a pretty woman seeking to dig up dirt on him, Ralph remarked that his wife had a commitment this evening and invited Marilyn to join him for dinner.

She became so disconcerted when the restaurant turned out to be Lutèce, where she had dreamed about eating, but had never been before, that several minutes passed before she had relaxed enough to start asking questions. Ralph soon gathered that the target of her inquiry was his marriage to Gail.

"You have to admit," she pointed out, "that her divorce and marriage to you were quite sudden. Then you went into business with her ex-husband. I tried to check out that episode with him, but he hasn't been seen in weeks."

"What are you getting at?"

"I'm not sure. But I always come back to the glaring incongruity of you two as a couple. It's as inconceivable to me as if you had married Madonna . . . or a member of the Red Brigade."

"Ain't love grand!" Ralph replied with an ingenuous smile.

"Seriously, how long have you known each other?"

"Can't you just accept that two people can meet, fall in love, and decide to spend the rest of their lives together?"

314

"Nowadays people shack up together first. Marriage is a last resort."

"You really are an idealist. Marilyn, I'll tell you anything you want to know about my projects, my business, but I don't talk about my personal life. That's nobody's concern but mine."

The waiter was placing the appetizers before them. After their first bites and comments, Ralph deftly changed the subject to Marilyn: her career, where she grew up, her life since moving to New York, her feelings for Dan Ahern, what Max Borah was like to work with. And all through the meal, Ralph saw to it that the wine kept pouring freely.

As coffee was served, Marilyn returned to the subject. "You two together, it just doesn't figure. For a couple of newlyweds," she scoffed, "you two display less affection in public than the main event at Madison Square Garden."

"Who does figure? What's normal?" Ralph had become irritated by the probing. "This conversation ends right now. My private life remains strictly that—private."

"I'm sorry," she apologized. "My only justification is that people want to know."

"They don't have a *right* to know gossip. Is that why you became a reporter, to shovel that manure at them?"

She shook her head and turned back to her coffee. "I remember now, it was to save the world, while having a house in suburbia, an ambitious yet sensitive husband, and two point three kids." She paused. "People rarely get what they want in life. They just get what they get." She paused to look at Ralph. "That's what makes you so damned enviable. You go out and take the whole pie while the rest of us fight over the crumbs."

In January an old girlhood friend of Lorna suddenly called her for lunch. The woman and her husband were stopping in town briefly on their way to Saint Croix for a month.

As they sipped their drinks at Côte Basque, the woman explained that her husband had wrenched his back and could not ski and had talked her into putting their Sun Valley ski house up for rental for the month. Reluctant to let others use her house, she had relented when the broker finally divulged that the tenant would be Ralph Behr, imploring her not to tell anyone because Behr had insisted on anonymity. If he thought the owner knew, he might not take the place. The price was very high, and Behr needed it for only the first ten days of February, but he would be willing to pay for the entire month if the house had everything

315

he wanted: handsome and spacious, right on the mountain, marvelous views, but totally secluded from the view of others. The broker had orders to dismiss any servants, stock the house with food and wine, and place four bottles of champagne in the refrigerator. Lorna's friend had decided to rent in part because she was sure Ralph was planning a romantic tryst with Lorna, whom she trusted to take good care of her house.

Lorna snapped off a bread stick and curtly rejoined that she had given Ralph Behr his walking papers many months earlier.

"Oh, dear," the woman explained, "have I done something wrong?"

"Not at all," Lorna assured her.

Ralph normally basked in publicity and enjoyed being the center of public attention. He had never sought anonymity or seclusion in the past. Lorna's instincts screamed out to her that he had to be taking a girlfriend with him, undoubtedly Amanda Brookhouse. If Max Borah wanted unmistakable proof of Ralph's adultery, she was now in position to give it to him—photos and all.

Marilyn's assessment that Max Borah would probably lose interest in Ralph Behr seemed to be proving accurate. He had not raised the matter since her dinner interview with Ralph several weeks earlier. She had undertaken a bit more research, but troubled by Ralph's assertion that she was trafficking in trash, and with Borah's interest having waned, had turned to her own stories. However, she found herself dissatisfied. Ralph's prodding had also served to awaken her to the insignificance of the sort of journalism into which she had become slotted. She had spent many days worrying about the problem before the afternoon that Max Borah rushed to her desk with a gleeful expression on his face. He insisted she join him in a vacant hallway so no one would overhear. He lit a cigarette and demanded first to know if she had learned anything new about Ralph Behr.

"Only that his wife's father was released from prison just before her wedding," she replied warily. "He served twenty years for some kind of fraud."

"Jesus, really? Maybe that fits in somewhere with what I'm working on. Lorna Garrison is convinced she can prove he's got an affair going hot and heavy with Amanda Brookhouse."

Marilyn's eyes widened. "How can she do that?" Marilyn found herself feeling surprisingly jealous of Amanda Brookhouse.

"Behr has rented a house in Sun Valley where they can fuck

with no one the wiser. We're all flying out there the same night they arrive, this Friday. I've arranged for a local photographer to take pictures when we break in."

"I'm supposed to go with you?"

"Won't be necessary." His lips formed a circle in front of his nicotine-stained teeth to emit a smoke ring. "I wouldn't be caught dead on skis and, shit, I hate the cold, but I've waited a long time to catch Ralph Behr with his pants down. And now I'm going to do it. Literally."

"Are you sure you really know the way?" Borah growled at the local photographer. The latter was driving them in a rented four-wheel-drive vehicle. It bounced and slithered through the darkness along the narrow, snow-covered road that wound up the mountain.

Snow had been falling since Borah and Lorna arrived at the ski resort, and he had never been so cold. The heater had conked out after the auto-rental agency had shut down for the night, and he was freezing despite the warm clothing he had purchased: two pairs of long thermal underwear, a bright red ski outfit, and huge foam-rubber-lined boots that made him feel ridiculous. He had removed his gloves and was vainly rubbing his hands together to revive his numb fingers.

"We've been driving for hours. If they aren't here, so help me God, Lorna, I'll kill you."

"It's been only twenty minutes. For the third time, I checked with the company he always hires his jet from," she replied. "They flew him and a woman here this afternoon."

"What if they're out to dinner?"

"They won't be. Too many people would recognize them. Besides, this is their first night alone. Ralph isn't the kind to waste it going out to dinner."

"You better be right," Borah warned.

The driver finally pulled to a halt at a point in the road that looked to Borah exactly like the rest of the bramble through which he had been driven. The three of them began to trudge through the snow, slipping and sliding. Twice the photographer admitted to having taken the wrong path in the dark, and they returned to the car to seek it again. They were cold and miserable.

"Through there," the photographer suddenly pointed at the darkness. His flashlight picked out a wooden sign with the chalet owner's name carved on it.

"Jesus," Borah grumbled and shoved his hands back into the

frigid gloves. "I can't believe people would put themselves through this just for the chance to break a leg on long planks."

Lorna directed the photographer to lead the way once more into the woods. She followed and, a moment later, Borah hurried to bring up the rear, crashing fearfully among the branches.

The house was placed on a knoll that gave onto the entire valley. Glass sliding doors that led to the wooden deck and wide picture windows were lit from within, but covered by blinds that blocked off the interior from view. The three trespassers could hear lush violin music emanating from what appeared to be the living room. They tried quietly to open the front door and windows, in hopes of catching the adultery in progress, but all were locked. Then in a whisper they discussed breaking through a glass door, but decided that might constitute a criminal act.

"Maybe if we climb to the second story," Lorna suggested, "we'll find an unlocked window."

Borah glared malevolently at her and stepped up to the door. He had a plan.

"Avalanche!" he shouted, as he pounded on the door. "Avalanche!"

He stepped out of the way to give the photographer a clear shot when the two came running out naked or, at best, clutching clothes they had scooped up in their flight to escape death.

The door swung open and the flash went off, revealing Ralph and Gail, their arms complacently around each other, fully clothed.

"What a surprise!" Ralph cried out. He turned to Gail. "You know Lorna Garrison and Max Borah, don't you dear?"

"Yes, of course," she replied, "you're the woman who was so devastated when Ralph married me."

Ralph flashed a pleasant smile. "How did all of you find out we were here?"

Lorna was the first to recover her composure. "My friends own this house. We . . . we were coming to surprise them. I didn't realize they must have rented it."

She glanced at Max Borah, who was glaring at her like a hanging judge.

"If you ever cross my path again," he hissed, "I'll cut you up so bad in print you won't have a client who would dare to hire you."

Ralph stepped forward to brush off the snow that had dusted Borah's face and red ski suit during the walk through the woods. "You look exactly like Santa Claus, Max. Ho! Ho! Ho!"

Borah knocked away Ralph's hand and stomped off down the path from which he had just come.

"Max," Ralph called out to him, "I can't let you leave on a cold night like this without a warm drink."

"Fuck off, Behr!" Borah shouted back over his shoulder.

Chapter 18

"You were great!" Ralph shouted, grabbing Gail in a bear hug and swinging her off the ground in a wide circle as soon as the door was closed.

She was laughing as hard as he. "They looked so foolish. Did you see their faces when they realized I was the woman with you?" Another peal of laughter rang from her throat.

"I loved it," he shouted again, lowering her, but continuing to hug her. He planted an enthusiastic kiss on her lips. Ralph suddenly realized what he had done and pulled his arms away self-consciously. Equally self-conscious, Gail pulled down the bottom of her sweater, which had ridden up.

"Thanks for agreeing to come here," he said. "You probably had a hundred other things you'd rather have been doing."

"I'm as much at risk as you if someone discovers why we got married. This should silence them once and for all."

"Lorna looked as if she never wanted to hear my name again."

They laughed again, but not with the same lack of restraint. They could not remember ever touching each other before, much less kissing, without its having been staged for onlookers.

"How about some champagne to celebrate?" Ralph remembered. "There should be some in the bar refrigerator."

"Great."

They walked back from the vestibule where his skis stood against the wall and up the few steps to the open kitchen and dining area. Beyond was the wide, handsomely furnished living room. The main bedroom was reached from the living room through a door on the right. Between the two was a fireplace that opened onto both rooms. The bar was near the fireplace. Additional bedrooms were located downstairs.

He had asked Gail to replace Amanda on the trip in the hope that that would end the snooping. Marilyn Watkins had come to his office the day before, claiming it was urgent she see him immediately. Very upset, she explained that Max and Lorna were planning to trap him in Sun Valley with Amanda Brookhouse. Maybe reporters had a right to stake out presidential candidates that way, she maintained, but not private citizens; whatever his personal life might be, she did not believe it was the public's business. Ralph thanked her for revealing the scheme to discredit him and, praising her integrity, asked how she could continue to work with the sort of colleagues who stooped to that level. Marilyn admitted that she had indeed quit her job and was seeking to leave New York; Ralph's comments at Lutèce had alerted her to how hardened New York had made her and the subconscious toll the pace and callousness were taking on her. Ralph made calls to friends in smaller cities to which Marilyn expressed an interest in moving.

As Ralph wrestled with the champagne cork, he commented to Gail, "I think it would help for us to be seen openly together around Sun Valley, just like any other married couple on vacation. But if you'd rather not, if you'd rather go home, I understand."

"Oh, no. I think it's a good idea . . . you know, to make sure no one doubts we're really married."

The cork flew high into the triangular space defining the cathedral ceiling. Foam spewed from the end of the bottle. Gail laughed and thrust her glass forward to catch the champagne. When Ralph had poured his own glass, he lifted it to make a toast, but all he could think to say was that Gail was a very good sport and admitted he hadn't expected that, considering the way their relationship began.

"There are a lot of good things about *you* I wasn't prepared for either," she replied. "Amanda is a lucky girl."

"Thanks."

Ralph had not thought much about Amanda most of the day and evening. The flight out had been enjoyable. He and Gail had played an intense, teasing game of backgammon to see who would get to sleep in the master bedroom. Gail surprised him by turning out to be a killer at the game and admitting she had played it to make money in the downtown coffeehouses when she and Milo were running short. It had occurred to him then that despite having lived with her for months, he was acquainted with only her most visible facets and that, astonishingly, she was great fun to be with, companionable.

"I feel really bad about Amanda," he confided. "She was looking forward to our spending this week together."

"I know," Gail replied in a tone that she hoped emphasized her sincerity about the matter. "I tried to reach her by phone to tell her how much I wish I didn't have to be here in her place."

"We'd be foolish, though, not to have a good time as long we're here."

"That would be really foolish," Gail agreed.

They touched glasses and drank.

"Look, that kiss I gave you before," he began somewhat diffidently, "I hope you didn't think I was trying to come on to you or anything. I didn't mean anything . . . you know, anything intimate by it."

"Oh, I didn't think that at all. It was a very friendly kiss, just friends."

Ralph laughed. "Who would have thought the day we got married that we would end up friends?"

Sun Valley was the first great American ski resort and truly popularized the sport. W. Averell Harriman, chairman of the Union Pacific Railroad, decided that a luxurious ski resort, like those at which he had learned to ski in Europe, would increase passenger traffic in the West. His emissary scouted western mountain areas until he came upon the little town of Ketchum, Idaho, described by one person as little more than a wide spot in a road that led to nowhere. Harriman agreed that it was perfect, bought up a forty-three-hundred-acre ranch, began construction of a first-class hotel, and hired Steve Hannigan, the publicity man who had put Miami Beach on the map, to do the same for Ketchum. Ironically, Hannigan hated the cold and winter sports, but he understood that if like-minded Americans were to be lured to travel all the way to Idaho to take up skiing, they would have to envision the sport as fun, easy, elegant, safe, and, of course, not cold. He convinced Harriman to rename the area Sun Valley, to put in a glass-enclosed heated swimming pool, an outdoor skating rink, fine dining, and an orchestra for dancing, and to set the railroad's engineers to work on investing some means to carry people up the mountain. The latter effort produced the first chair lift, adapted from a device in South America that transported mountain bananas to a railroad siding.

321

Sun Valley Lodge opened at the end of 1936 to the music of Eddy Duchin and his orchestra. Hannigan lured Hollywood stars and the wealthy sports-minded and publicized their visits. Ketchum was gradually transformed into a town that combined colorful ski-resort design with low-slung Old West architecture. Over the years notables continued to be drawn to its quiet elegance. Harriman convinced Ernest Hemingway to make his home near Ketchum, where he could fish and hunt. The Kennedys learned to ski there, and the Shah of Iran. Sun Valley retained its well-deserved cachet.

Gail had never skied before, but by ten o'clock the next morning, Ralph had overseen her purchase of ski boots and clothing and the rental of short skis on which to begin learning. Several of the salesgirls recognized Ralph, and one asked for his autograph just as Gail emerged from the dressing room in a turquoise outfit she was trying on. She caught Ralph's eye behind the young woman's back and mimed throwing up at the thought that anyone might want his autograph. Ralph broke up laughing and had to turn his own back on Gail to sign his name.

He had decided to be the one to give her her first lesson, and they drove the short distance to Dollar Mountain, a gentle hill excellent for beginners.

"How good an athlete are you?" he asked when they were well up the slope.

"I can walk without falling down."

"What sports did you play in school?"

"Sports were organized, gung-ho, cooperative, and acceptable. I was against everything they stood for."

Ralph took a deep breath and launched into an explanation of the snowplow, so she could stop. Once she had gotten the hang of it and felt safe, he pointed out that one did not ski straight down, but descended the slope by skiing back and forth across it. Weight on the inside of her uphill foot would shift that ski onto its inside edge and turn it back across the hill, slowing down her speed at the same time. She could then turn back the other way by applying weight to the inside of the other foot, which was now atop the uphill ski. To his amazement, she did the basic maneuver perfectly on the first try, with none of the bent-over trepidation he expected.

"It's a lot like turning on your inside edge in ice skating," she had discovered. "My mom used to take me to do that when I was a kid."

Slowly, they zigzagged their way down to the lift. She found getting on and off the chair lift harder than skiing.

"That thing is a menace!" she announced after he picked her up from the snow at the top.

"You're doing fine. Let's try some more turns."

By afternoon, they had shifted to Mount Baldy, the main ski area, and Gail was moving down the novice slopes with some confidence and a wide smile. She was exhilarated by the sense of freedom and motion. Ralph was impressed. He had expected to leave her with an instructor for the week, meeting her at each day's end. Now he could anticipate exploring more difficult trails over the next few mornings while she took lessons, and then to having fun skiing together the rest of the day.

It was four o'clock when they stepped out of their bindings and hefted their skis at the bottom of the Lower Warm Springs run. Ralph winked at Gail as they passed the previous night's photographer pressed against a building, trying vainly to appear inconspicuous. He snapped their picture.

The Creekside was packed with skiers getting acquainted over after-ski drinks and lining up dates for the evening.

"Looks a little crowded," Gail remarked, as she faced the wall of bright sweaters and ruddy faces that seemed to admit no passage.

"That's the fun of it."

Ralph plunged into the mob, pulling her far smaller body along behind him.

"You look just like Ralph Behr," one young woman observed as he slid by.

"People tell me that," he replied, "but I don't see it myself."

They found a tube of space near enough to the bar for Ralph to order drinks. Gail finally had a chance to look around. Her first thought was that the men and women were intimidatingly gorgeous. The merely attractive need not apply.

"Fast track," she mumbled.

"You can hold your own."

Gail blinked and then smiled. "You don't really mean that, but thanks anyway."

"I do." He smiled at her. "And if they ever decide to hold a revolution in this place, you're indispensable."

"You'll be the first to go, Capitalist."

"I figure knowing you gives me connections with the guerrillas. Come the revolution, I'm planning to be out there selling you other guys Uzis and discount guillotines."

323

Ralph ordered Bloody Marys and turned back to find Gail gazing again at the people about her.

"I'm sorry I'm ruining your fun," she said.

"Funny. I was about to apologize for ruining yours. Here you are on vacation, finally over, I think, your depression about Milo, and you have to have me tagging along wherever you go."

"I'd run right home if you weren't here. I'm not sure I'm the swinging-single type. I feel like defective goods. This sort of thing repels me. I've never really lived alone. I wasn't at college very long before I met Milo, and I haven't been on my own since. Like I said, this is a very fast track for someone like me."

"You have this image of yourself as an unattractive little mouse. I can't understand it. You're a terror to politicians, enormous fun to be with, and you're very pretty."

"Be careful," she said, with little conviction in her voice, "I may start believing it."

Ralph had spoken honestly. Her looks had grown on him. The wide mouth and slightly turned-up nose that did not appeal to him on first meeting now seemed all-American-girl fresh. The brownish hair now seemed bright with glints of red that set off her gray eyes; he could barely recall how instantly angry they could become, but only that they were always lively. He raised his glass.

"Here's to us."

Grinning, she raised hers. "The really good-looking girl and the really lucky guy she's dragging along."

"The realest," he agreed and touched his glass to hers. That superlative became a joking slang phrase they used with each other.

After a plate of cheese nachos, Ralph suggested going back to the house for a sauna and Jacuzzi. They could then nap until dinnertime.

"I'll pass on the water sports," she told him. "I didn't bring a bathing suit."

"A towel will do. The heat will take a lot of the soreness out of your muscles."

She started to protest. Ralph cut her off.

"Hey, we're just pals—roommates, if you look at it that way. I'm the one person you can walk around in front of in a towel who's not going to get any ideas."

He led her out of the bar area.

Gail first poked her head into the sauna and with the greatest reticence allowed the rest of her body to enter the small wooden room. A huge blue towel enveloped her. Only her toes below and her head above were exposed. Ralph, already sweating from the heat, stared in amazement that so vast a towel even existed. He himself had wrapped a normal-sized yellow towel around his waist.

"Afraid you'll catch a chill, Pocahontas?"

"I'll do it my own way, thanks," she said a bit curtly.

Ralph leaned back and closed his eyes. "My father took me to the Luxor Baths in Manhattan when I was small. He said his own father used to take him to a Turkish bath, and going reminded him of his father. Funny, when I think of it now. My father is the most unsentimental man. Hardly mentions his father, except when I ask, but he somehow felt he had a duty to take me because his father took him."

"I don't understand."

"He said it was the least he could do for his dad, who was a good man."

"What was your father like when you were growing up?"

Ralph started to say he was great and then stopped to muse on the matter. He found it difficult to speak against him, as if his father's crime and cover-up had been slips in an otherwise blameless life. He assessed Gail for a long moment. He had fallen into the habit of candor with her and decided he could trust her with his true feelings.

"He was gone a lot. Building the business. And when he did have the time, he could be tough on me. Once I really worked hard on a paper in high school—up all night to do it. When I told him I got an A minus, he just asked me, wasn't an A better than an A minus? I mean he was proud of me, but it was rough to win his approval."

"I think pride is different from approval. Pride is about oneself, not the other person."

"Breaking away became a necessity for me—going into business for myself. There couldn't be two stars. I just knew it had to be me."

"How did you get him to fund you?"

"He hoped I'd be in business with him, but he knew I was too independent for that. Instead, he provided the capital for me to go out on my own. I'm sure he also got tired of me telling him how to run his business. He was really very generous. He put several million dollars into my hands, and I was only a couple of years out of college. That's when I finally knew how much he loved me."

"Maybe he just thought he could make more money by using you a different way."

Ralph glanced sharply at her. "What does that mean?"

"A couple of weeks ago Dad told me that after about seven or eight years in prison, he became unhappy at how slowly your father's wealth was growing and warned your father it didn't justify his staying in jail and putting his family through the rest of his sentence without him. Your father came back to him with a plan. You were eager to build in Manhattan in a major way, and he would fund you. Dad said he didn't want to rely on someone so young, but your father convinced him to wait a bit and see how you did."

Ralph's eyes blazed. "I don't believe a word. My dad gave me that money out of pure generosity and love. We kept our assets and profits pooled together in the beginning because he could use the tax benefits from what I was building better than I could. That's the truth, whether you believe it or not. Look, I know it's hard for you to be objective on the subject of my father."

"I won't deny I hated him," Gail admitted. "He was the man in the camel-hair coat who brought money to us every month and was free while Dad was in prison. How could I not have hated him?"

"And by association, me."

"You were easy to hate, and I was very unhappy. I pictured you and your family living a luxurious life."

"Don't tell me that we turned you into a radical."

"A lot of men in authority seemed to be causing everything bad in my life. They called my father a criminal, locked him up, guarded him day and night. They said Americans were free, but I saw blacks and women who were sure getting a raw deal. Typical child of my time."

"Then why pick Milo? He always seemed like a dominating bastard to me."

"That was only during our last few years together, I think because he felt so powerless. When I first met Milo, he was sure of himself and so sure of his talent. I loved him, and he seemed to love me back. That meant a lot to a girl who grew up without a father, never dated in high school, and probably scared off any boy who might have wanted to ask." Her eyes lit in recollection. "I had a crush on Walter Gordon. He was a couple of years older than I was and the only person in my school I used to see regularly at rallies and demonstrations. I was sure that he would

326

notice me and realize we were soul mates, but he never even knew I was alive."

"With me it was Jane Carter. She lived down the street in Deal, where we spent the summers. I was fourteen, and she was three years older and a knockout."

"Never gave you a tumble, huh?"

"Well, to be truthful, when her parents were away at a wedding one weekend—"

Gail punched Ralph in mock anger. "You're supposed to make me feel good by telling me your own teen years were awful."

"Would you feel better if I confessed there was no Jane Carter?"

"You made her up?"

"No, but if it would make you feel better . . ."

Gail laughed. "I was right to hate your happy adolescence."

Ralph stood up. "Ready for a quick shower and then the hot tub?"

Two showers and a large Jacuzzi were located in the same softly lit, tiled room. Through the glass doors at one end they could view the valley and the far hills. Gail emerged from her shower just as Ralph was walking down the steps into the tub, and she followed. Once seated across from her, shoulder-high in water, he removed his towel and laid it on the tile floor behind him. Gail was first shocked and then, realizing he would not see her nudity beneath the churning surface, felt chagrined in her oversized towel. Very carefully, she unwrapped it, tried her best to wring it out, and placed it behind her on the floor.

"You can get herpes like this," Ralph said offhandedly.

"What?"

"I'm joking. It's all fresh water and constantly filtered."

She relaxed. The warm water felt wonderful.

"I must seem terribly unsophisticated," she said.

"No," he replied. "Is that how you feel?"

"In the beginning, certainly. First, the limousine, then that massive apartment with servants tiptoeing around like shadows. I couldn't put down a napkin at dinner without a fresh one instantly taking its place. One reason I never tried to use the sauna there or anything in the pool area was because the whole setup seemed so decadent. I told myself you were the incarnation of a depraved Roman emperor."

"Remember the fights we had over your clothing?"

"That seems a long time ago." She grew reflective. "I really had no idea how much taking the money—marrying you—would change my life."

"You sound like you regret it."

"A lot of it. I think if you had been just an ordinary guy—" She corrected herself. "—just a *rich* ordinary guy, Milo wouldn't have run off when he decided he had kidded himself all those years about his talent as a painter. But he felt he had to match your—what, your style, I guess."

"The seventy thousand dollars had nothing to do with it?"

"That was just running-away money—the means to escape a situation he couldn't endure. He won't blackmail us if that's your concern. He's not a bad man, Ralph, just one who kept trying to cover up the fear deep down that he couldn't cut it on his own." She shrugged her shoulders and eyed Ralph pointedly. "That he was ordinary."

Ralph lay back, his arms spread atop the lip of the tub. "What would he think if he saw us now?"

"He'd think the worst. I always used to think the worst of your intent too. Seems silly now, doesn't it?"

She realized that Ralph was staring earnestly at her, more serious about his answer than she had intended with her question.

"No," he said slowly, "he had reason to be jealous. It just took me a long time to wake up to it."

"Oh," Gail said. She was having trouble breathing. "I told you I'm not very sophisticated, Ralph, but I *am* direct," she finally was able to say. "And if I'm getting these signals wrong, please tell me right away before I make a total fool of myself." She halted, gathering courage to say more. "I hope they mean that you want to make love to me because right now that's what I want."

Ralph did not answer, but moved beside her and very slowly lowered his lips to hers. They kissed for a long time. Disoriented, all she could think to say when they drew apart was, "I guess I got the signals right, after all."

His hands moved over her body, slippery in the water, while he and she wound about each other—spiraling, cavorting water-beings. Then he reached down and lifted her from the water in his arms. All she could think was that if he stumbled and fell, they would break legs or hips, which seemed somehow farcical after coming safely through her first day of skiing.

His bedroom was next door, and he lay her on the bed. The covering quilt darkened wetly beneath her. He stretched out beside her, looking in amazement at her body and into her eyes.

This happening between them would have seemed so improbable during the belligerence of those first weeks, so abhorrent.

Gail breathed him in, and his smell was arousing: virile and clean. Her eyes closed to concentrate on his touch moving gently along her curves and finally to her breast. Spasms spread from her nipple through her body. She moaned softly. And then moaned anew as each commenced. Finally, she reached her arms up toward his neck, drawing him to her, kissing him deeply, opening her mouth to his tongue, replying with hers. She could feel his hardness pressing up between her legs and spread to take him into her. She groaned uncontrollably at the incredible, fondly remembered sensation that rose from deep within her.

A moment later, arched upward, she was atop him, then leaning over to kiss his neck, his ears, to stroke his body. His hands were on her breasts, his palms gently rubbing her nipples in circles.

"Come," she urged him softly, like an incantation. "Come. I don't want to come without you. You're too wonderful. Come. Come."

She exploded only a moment before he did.

That night, when they returned from dinner, Gail joked he was really sneaky enough to try anything to win back the master bedroom.

"The realest," he confessed.

They made love again and again that night. He had never considered that she might be so erotic. Her passion entranced him. His unexpected sensuality delighted and surprised her, in part because she had unconsciously accepted Milo's claim that his own artistic nature elevated him above other men as a lover. Ralph behaved puritanically in public, she discovered, simply because he believed sex belonged in the bedroom, and there he felt no limits. They finally fell into an exhausted sleep in each other's arms.

Next morning, Gail's moans derived from a different cause.

"Oh, God, I can't walk," she whispered hoarsely as she tried to stand up and get to the shower before making Ralph breakfast.

"You've never skied before."

Ralph went downstairs and turned on the Jacuzzi. By ten o'clock, they were back on the slopes. But at the end of the day, they did not waste time by stopping first at the Creekside.

*   *   *

Ralph had always grown anxious away from the office on vacation, or else bored. Either way he invariably spent a good part of his vacation on the telephone doing precisely what he did the rest of the year. This time, however, he did not reveal his phone number and called his office only twice during the ten days he and Gail were away, just in case a crisis had arisen in his absence. When Ben Rogovin tried to gain his opinion on a less-than-urgent matter, Ralph cut him off, saying it could hold.

Amanda telephoned him once, and he asserted that he missed her. At that moment, feeling very guilty, he did. He remained taciturn for several hours. Gail was so high-spirited talking with the waiter at dinner, however, that Ralph began to laugh and soon put the issue of whether he was being disloyal to Amanda out of his mind. After all, he reasoned, he hadn't yet made a commitment to Amanda that would warrant fidelity. They were wiser to take their relationship a slow step at a time. And, besides, he reasoned, even a man having an affair is allowed to make love to his own wife. But the latter line of thought was so patently ludicrous that he found himself smiling and Gail asking him the reason. He answered that he was having a wonderful time. The world beyond Sun Valley began to seem very far away again.

They skied every afternoon together, particularly enjoying the glades. By the end of the week, she was confident enough to ski the easier runs on the bowls. One day they took off to try cross-country. At night they went to restaurants and bars and discos and, once, a horsedrawn hayride. They could not get enough of each other's bodies. They made love in the sauna, the tub, the shower, on the carpet before the fireplace, and, until the early morning hours, in bed. And they talked with an openness and trust that surprised them both. Sun Valley became an endless idyll.

They were very quiet on the plane ride to Ralph's Lexington, Kentucky, horse farm to view the yearlings and the two-year-olds being broken for racing. They would go on to New York the next morning. After dining with Eddie Gorman, the farm's manager, and his wife, they slept together in the main bedroom of the main house, but they did not make love. Each acted uncertainly, stiffly, toward the other, as if waking from a dream. Neither was sure how the other felt away from the isolation in which their romance had flourished. Neither knew what the passion they had just shared meant in real life.

* * *

On the plane ride home, when contemplating the state of the responsibilities facing her, Gail made up her mind that her marriage to Ralph had made it impossible for her to allow the Coalition to continue directing the raft of neighborhood activities that often opposed Behr Center. The many demands made on her time by the neighborhood center had stalled important initiatives that could help the abused women who had always been her primary interest and the Coalition's original purpose. She decided to concentrate on that cause and turn the neighborhood center over to those running it, perhaps with Carla as its head. Many of its volunteers would be relieved by her departure.

At the storefront office, she told Carla and several others what she intended and phoned their lawyer to have him draw up whatever papers were necessary for the Coalition to disassociate formally from the neighborhood center. With a sense of an unwanted burden having been lifted from her back, she happily departed with her files to the larger of the shelter apartments and set up a temporary office.

Immediately, she found herself engrossed by the sorts of problems she cared deeply about. The week away had given her a fresh perspective on areas that ought to be addressed: more job-training programs and day-care volunteers to allow the women to work during the day. The psychological counseling could be improved, so the women could face their traumas more effectively. She feared that the psychological problems affecting the children were being largely ignored, and she wanted better programs for them too. Two apartments were not big enough to handle the women needing help in the community. They could use a large building, she decided. And, once she had that operating well, perhaps a second in a different part of the area. She would have to increase the staff and the fund-raising. Higher pay was essential if she was to hire more people and keep them; she had lost too many because of the abysmal wages she could barely afford. Despite having to work at a paying job and completing college, Brenda Clay, for example, was doing unpaid the work of two full-time people.

Gail had finally become used to the idea of having money in the bank and had begun to provide a large segment of the budget, but so much more was needed. She would ask Ralph to advance a substantial donation from her share of the assets to get started on the new initiatives.

As the day wore on, she wondered about Ralph's dinner plans, if she ought to call the cook to prepare something for them. She phoned Ralph at home and at his office, but could not reach him. For ten days they had not been apart, but perhaps, she thought, she was assuming too much when she assumed that they would have dinner together tonight as well. She did not know precisely what sort of relationship he intended now that they were back. The circumstances here were very different. One large factor was Amanda, whom they had carefully avoided discussing all the time they were away. Amanda would not go away, nor would Ralph's feeling for her.

At that moment Ralph was at a fund-raiser for the Museum of Modern Art to which Amanda had invited him weeks earlier. She claimed at the time to those sending out invitations that she did not want to lose Ralph Behr's growing contemporary collection to the director of the Metropolitan, who had been actively wooing Ralph since he had attended their donors' party.

Separation from Ralph during the vacation she had intended to take with him had left Amanda anxious and missing him. During their first minutes together, he felt strangely removed, as if standing back out of the scene and watching it and himself from a distance. Soon, though, her conversation provoked a response from him, and he began to enjoy himself. As he had done in Sun Valley, he temporarily put out of his mind the conflict his emotions were loathe to face between his enchantment with Amanda and the unexpected attraction for Gail that had gripped him. One thing he did not want to do right now, he decided, was add to his inner confusion by sleeping with Amanda tonight. If he remained with her after the party, he reasoned, she would expect that. In fact she would probably be hurt and suspicious if he did not seem as eager for it as she seemed to be.

Standing alone before a painting, she whispered as much to him. "All I could think of when you were gone was how much I missed you. You too?"

Ralph's mumbled affirmation seemed to satisfy Amanda.

"I figured you must have met women out there. I know you," she laughed. "You'd get terribly bored just spending time with Gail." When Ralph did not answer, she added. "Did you?"

"Did I what?"

"Did you date anyone in Sun Valley?" She laughed again. "You didn't have to spend every night with Gail, did you?"

"As a matter of fact I did. Good company." Ralph felt proud of having kept within the letter, if not the spirit, of the truth. He was relieved that Amanda did not yet expect their relationship to be exclusive. He found that odd and a bit deflating: he expected that she would have wanted to tie him down. He wasn't sure that he really understood her.

Amanda squeezed his hand. "Grandma insisted I go out with Cob. After a week without you, I must admit he looked very tempting," she said with a shrewd smile that seemed to calculate precisely how much she could faze him.

"What do you mean Cob looked tempting?" He found himself feeling jealous, and angry at that failing in himself.

"He's very good-looking, that's all."

"He's an airhead."

"He's already a partner at Morgan Stanley."

"Figures."

"He's very nice."

"And you were horny. So . . ."

"Ralph, nothing happened. We went to a party, and he dropped me off at my apartment house without even getting out of the cab." She turned to Ralph directly, apology in her eyes for having upset him unnecessarily. "I'm sorry I made you jealous. Nothing happened."

"I'm not jealous," he pouted.

"It isn't fair for me to tease you about sex, after you were forced to spend ten days with Gail. Let's get out of here as fast as we can. I'll meet you at the hotel suite."

Gail had not expected Ralph to be pacing up and down impatiently when she arrived home, but she had thought he might have left a message for her. There was none on the foyer table. She ordered a light supper sent to her room and went upstairs. After opening the door between the bedrooms, she could not decide whether to put on her nightgown or stay in street clothes. She sat stiffly at her desk, going over the week's mail. After a few hours the silliness of remaining fully dressed in her bedroom well after ten o'clock—when she had recently spent so many hours naked with him—eventually forced her into a white nightgown and peignoir.

A few minutes before midnight, Ralph arrived home. Although he was successful at displaying an impassive demeanor which prevented his business opponents from guessing at his aims and motives, living with him had taught Gail to read subtle signs of his emotions. Right now, she decided, he looked very guilty indeed.

"Did you see Amanda tonight?"

He nodded. "A fund-raiser at the Modern."

"You've become quite the art connoisseur. 'The Modern.' "

"She sends her regards."

Gail realized that she had been interrogating him and had no right to do so. "Thanks. How is she?"

"Fine. Really well."

Gail practically had to bite her tongue to keep from asking whether he had made love to her. "Did you go anywhere afterward?"

He nodded.

"You look beat," she observed, again with more sarcasm in her tone than she intended.

He looked at her abruptly and turned away.

Now I've gone too far! she exclaimed to herself. She started to enter his bedroom to ask about his day when she realized he was going into his bathroom to shower. How many nights had they showered together and made love in the Jacuzzi? She wondered what he would think if she joined him in the shower now. Did he want her to or would she just be pushing herself on him? Why would he want her to if he had just bounced all over a bed with Amanda? She was in agony over undertaking an action she had done instantly, unself-consciously, only two nights before.

Oh, my God, she suddenly realized, I'm in love with him! The knowledge had struck her without warning, before she could raise a defense against thinking about it, as she had been so careful to do all the time they were together in Sun Valley. Her thoughts were all confusion. She needed to think.

She closed the door between the bedrooms part of the way and turned off all but the dimmest illumination in her night-table lamp. Slipping under the covers, she propped a book on her knees. In case he did come in, she did not want him to think she had been waiting for him.

She was sure of it now: just the hope of seeing him made her giddy with anticipation. She was in love with Ralph and felt like a fool. She reasoned that after suffering rejection from Milo and the loneliness of long weeks alone, she had been so eager to feel wanted in Sun Valley that she had allowed herself to make the age-old mistake of falling for a man who had simply considered her a handy lay. Well, why wouldn't he? She *had* been. Eager and willing and grateful. And she had given as good as she got, so no recriminations there. They were pals, they had told each other. The best of friends. And what are friends for? she added, unable to strain the bitterness from her thinking.

334

She heard the water cease to run in his shower and simply sat there and waited.

Ralph emerged from the bathroom in a white terry-cloth bathrobe, still drying his hair and still in confusion. He had taken Amanda to a small restaurant in Little Italy, correctly assuming he would not be seen there by anyone who knew him. He told Amanda that he had twisted his back while skiing, and it would be a while before he could undertake anything as athletic as sex. She was so understanding that he felt like a heel. But at least that was better than trying to make love to her before he had sorted out his feelings. She had looked compellingly beautiful too: every facial feature chiseled flawlessly, large blue eyes intent only on him, a deep cleft in the neckline of a black dress she had doubtless bought to emphasize her sexuality. Several times during the evening he told himself his scruples were idiotic—he had made no commitment to anyone. Hadn't Amanda even admitted that she expected him to sleep with other women?

Gail too had looked wonderful tonight, he remembered, waiting for him when he came home, smiling, the door open between their bedrooms. What could I say to her, he wondered: I haven't slept with Amanda, so let's fuck? Or maybe, Let's not fuck? Seeing Gail had aggravated his perplexity. He had gone to the shower to clear his head. He certainly could not raise the problem with Amanda—she would think he had lied all along to her about his marital relationship. Perhaps he could discuss it with Gail. What could he say to her, though? Either she expected some sort of promise from him or else she had simply been glad to have him around for recreational sex and would burst his delusionary balloon if he divulged his conscience qualms, making him feel like a fool. When he was younger, with other women, he had expended little thought on the consequences of his lust, floating through the years in a state of mindless, self satisfied vigor. What had weakened him like this?

He stood at the crack in the doorway between the bedrooms, trying to remember how easily he had spoken to her in Sun Valley about his family and his business, his plans and his concerns about the future. They had nourished each other. They had also amused each other. There had been no awkwardness. If she had wanted their relationship to continue the same way, however, he thought, she would have left the door open, not practically closed like this. She was too polite to close it all the way, but her clear intention must have been to let him know she did not want him in there. Jesus, she had been sarcastic about his having been with Amanda! He grew angry at what he perceived her attitude to have been, and then he grew self-righteous. He had been so utterly, so conscientiously principled tonight, and yet Gail had assumed the worst. She must think him some kind of exploitative libertine who would jump on any woman who gave him half a chance. "You look beat!" she had said before he went into the shower and before that had made some crack about him trying to impress Amanda as an art connoisseur. She seemed to be making it very clear to him that the fun and games she had permitted in Sun Valley weren't going to continue, that the fencing match was about to start again.

He marched to his bed, not sure about his conclusions, but sure that he wasn't going to let himself be hurt by leaving himself open to rejection by her.

Gail thought she heard him at the door. She declined to call out to him, afraid if he was not there that he would interpret her action as an attempt to lure him in and that she would not know what to say when he entered. She quickly went to the door. If he *was* there, then she would be sure that his uneasiness too derived from not knowing what to do about the new situation in the face of the old circumstances to which they had returned. But just as she reached the door the lights in the room beyond went off, and she slowly returned to her bed.

Chapter 19

The next morning, when she arrived at the breakfast room, having made up her mind not to get off on the wrong foot and to try to recover the lost ground in their relationship, she learned that he had risen very early and left the apartment over an hour before.

Ralph had wanted to review the work at Behr Center very carefully before his meeting with Simon Kramer. He picked up Jeff on the way downtown. The construction rep they had recently hired was waiting at their trailer when they arrived. He handed each brother a long list containing design changes Simon was demanding. The two developers had displayed extreme tact in avoiding confrontations since becoming partners, recognizing that they would have to work together for several years. The changes, however, raised a conflict in attitude between the men which Ralph knew could no longer be sidestepped.

When the group went out on the site, he observed the progress that had been made over the past week, how much wider the excavation had grown, and noticed that in one corner the first footings, which would bear the foundation, had been laid. Refusing to let slip by the slightest detail that was not quite right, he made comments, and the rep took notes. In the future, Ralph told him, he expected more careful work out of Kramer's people and the rep himself to catch more problems earlier.

Simon appeared amiable when the meeting began at his own construction trailer. He commented on Ralph's tan and asked whether Ralph and his wife had had a good time in Sun Valley. Ralph reasoned that Lorna had informed him of their whereabouts, although probably not her discomfiture upon confronting them. Each partner brought the other up-to-date on his particular area of responsibility, and then they moved onto future planning. When Ralph stated his impression that Simon seemed to be aiming to cut corners on the construction, Simon blew up.

"Damned right, I'm cutting corners," he declared unapologetically. "Everywhere I can. Do you know how far behind those fucking squatters put us, and then the holdup on the licenses until everybody and his mother finished investigating why the tenements were knocked down? We couldn't get on this land for months. Then the ground was frozen over, and we hit boulders and outcroppings bigger than that fucking Mount Rushmore carving you squeezed five thousand out of me for. You could have carved a dozen goddamned Calvin Coolidges on the rock under those old garages."

Ralph held up Simon's list. "These changes you want—I'm not going to approve them. They'll make the buildings and the plaza look like every other high-rise project going up in the city."

"I never saw so much wasted money. Those finishes your plans call for are exorbitant. You could substitute for every one of them, and no one would ever notice. It adds up to millions you're wasting."

Ralph heatedly declared that he wanted to put up a complex so distinctive, so overwhelming it could charge the highest rents in the world and get them. Angrily, Simon retorted that he wasn't going to go broke just so Ralph could build a monument to his monumental ego. The battle was joined.

Anticipating years of squabbling, Ralph was still out-of-sorts when Gail telephoned him late in the afternoon. They had long-standing plans to attend the opening of the new exhibition at their art gallery that night. Now she asked him to meet her earlier than they had arranged because, having decided to expand the Coalition's shelter facilities, she had located a building for sale and would be meeting with the landlord. She and Ralph could go right from that meeting to the gallery.

At the door of the shelter apartment to which Gail had moved her office, Ralph found a large, beefy man in a dirty blue parka exchanging furious words with her. She stood behind the front door and spoke to him through the small crack permitted by the chain. Her single eye fixed the man with an implacable stare. Inside was his girlfriend, Ralph quickly gathered, whom the man wanted back. Gail was relaying the woman's statement that she would not return to him, she did not want to see him again. Uneducated and a halting speaker, the man appeared deeply frustrated in the face of Gail's articulate refusal to admit him. He kept repeating that he needed Mary Anne, and Gail had better let him pass.

"I just want to see her and talk to her," the man cried. "I know she'll come back if I can just talk to her."

Gail pulled the door closed.

Greatly pained by the recollection when Ralph asked him what had caused her to seek shelter here, the man mumbled that it was nothing. He had just had a little too much to drink the other night. His woman friend wouldn't stop nagging him about his drinking and that he should be trying harder to find a better job. He just pushed her around a little to silence her. He wouldn't be much of a man if he let her go on saying those things, right? But these women *here*, they were the problem. They were putting ideas into her head. They were keeping him and Mary Anne apart.

Ralph recognized in the man masculine feelings, frustrations, and apprehensions with which he and any normal man could identify. Not that he himself would ever do so, but he understood how a woman could wear a man down with criticism to the point where he exploded into physical retaliation to gain her capitulation. Gail, for example, could irritate him instantly without half trying. Ralph talked the man into going home and giving Mary Anne some time to cool off. The man agreed she might be willing to meet with him if he tried to stop drinking and let her friends know he intended to change his ways toward her.

As they walked the two blocks to the building Gail was seeking to buy, she and Ralph fell into an emphatic argument about what had just occurred. To Gail the man was a dangerous bully who compensated for his lack of self-worth by beating up a woman. To Ralph he was just a guy having a run of bad luck he couldn't handle, who couldn't express his feelings and resorted to asserting himself with a little shoving. He added that the man's girlfriend probably provoked the whole thing to feel wanted and she enjoyed it until, maybe, he exerted a little too much force. The words were about the couple involved in the recent incident, but fretful and uncertain about the other's feelings since returning to New York, they were giving vent to the strain of their own muddled relationship. Even as she argued with him, Gail berated herself for her vehemence; she wanted his love and had once again succeeded only in irking him.

After viewing the building and the landlord, they debated about whether she really needed to buy a building, the overhead it would impose on her organization, and the value of interceding in domestic controversies.

The opening-night reception at the art gallery was well underway when they arrived. The gallery had proven profitable, and Ralph appreciated the observation point it afforded him inside the contemporary art world. He found he enjoyed mingling with the offbeat, spontaneous artist crowd and picking artists and works that could prove valuable later on. Most of all, he liked the stamp of cultivation that gallery ownership and his art collection placed on his image, which had been dented a bit by the artist-squatter dispute; he could no longer be written off simply as a greedy and insensitive businessman.

He had just moved on from chatting with a now-established painter whom the gallery had discovered and a critic who had been a frequent writer about the gallery's newer artists when he noticed Gail in an intense discussion with their manager, Theresa. He could always tell the extent of Gail's interest in a conversation by whether she had her hands on her hips. Chest out meant that she was arguing ferociously. Head tipped off center meant she was greatly intrigued by what was being said. Her hands were now on her hips, her head was tipped, and her eyes were very wide.

"Listen to this, Ralph," Gail said hurriedly as soon as he was beside them, glancing away from the other woman for only an instant. "Theresa's friend was out in California and ran into Milo. He has his *own* gallery in Venice, California."

"Does that mean you're ready to go after him for what he owes us?"

Gail appeared hurt that he had raised the issue. "I'm just glad to know he's well and getting his life together."

He was incredulous. "You're glad? He robbed us."

Drawing Ralph with her, Gail stepped away from Theresa, whispering so the latter could not overhear. "We've been through this before. He took the money to get away when he could have tried to blackmail us instead. The poor reception his paintings received and trying to compete with you put a lot of pressure on him."

"You make it sound like his larceny was my fault."

She turned back to Theresa. "Did she tell you anything else?"

The young woman hesitated. "He's living with Carrie Donaldson."

The remark struck Gail like a blow in the face. "She's a . . . a . . . she's window dressing. No personality and no brains."

Ralph intervened. "Is she rich?"

Theresa nodded. Ralph's glance at Gail conveyed self-satisfaction at his assessment. Embarrassed, Theresa excused herself.

"Carrie Donaldson is all wrong for him," Gail continued. "He'll be bored in no time."

"I don't believe I'm hearing this. Maybe women really do want to be pushed around."

"That's a deplorable thing to say."

"Don't tell me it's normal to worry about the happiness of the man who conned you and stole from you."

"I can't just turn my emotions on and off depending on who I happen to be with. Perhaps you can."

"You did a pretty good imitation of it last week."

"Do you think last week could have been something that just happened and now it's over?" She waited, hoping, for him to deny it.

"I guess maybe we both feel that way," he replied defensively. He waited for her to say that she didn't.

But both were unwilling to risk the rejection that might ensue if they lowered their guard.

"We're still really good friends, though?" she asked.

"The realest. Pals."

They separated then, as they had just separated from emotions they could not clarify or justify. They both felt alone and sad, as if watching a train that carried a loved one away forever pull out of the station. Their pride was hurt too, but they had saved face by not admitting that the brief affair had touched them more deeply.

Stoic, but quiet, Gail gave no hint of her grief as she later rode uptown in the limousine with Ralph. She was a strong woman, she told herself. Maybe the affair with Ralph or even her feelings for him now were a pardonable stage she had to traverse on the path from the loss of Milo to independence. Every woman going through what she had was fair game for an attractive man's flattering word and warm bed. The trick was in not allowing yourself to make more of it. She began to consider herself very sensible in having seen it for the interlude it was.

Ralph too had been wrapped in his own thoughts. He had concluded that she was still in love with Milo, even if she refused to recognize it; although working all day with women drawn subconsciously to dominating men, she was blind to her own affliction. Or maybe he and Gail just weren't right for each other, he conjectured. God knows, they had fought like caged animals since the moment they met. Maybe the temporary cease-fire of the last months was the most they could expect; he and Gail had simply gotten carried away by the atmosphere at Sun Valley. He was fortunate to be so levelheaded about it, he concluded, before things with Gail really got sticky and endangered his relationship with Amanda, the woman who was really right for him.

Ralph was relieved that events had, at least, dictated a direction out of the confusion that had assailed him since returning and that he no longer had to hide from Amanda an intimacy he was maintaining with Gail. He phoned Amanda as soon as he got home. He announced that his back was now feeling great, and he couldn't wait to be alone with her.

Gail sensed no ambivalence in the firm way he closed the door between their rooms.

When Rosalie was accepted at NYU, one of her first acts was to visit Gail's office nearby. Since then they had lunched together half a dozen times and spoken twice that number on the phone. Her return to education had given her a new confidence and a touchstone with her academic, as well as her Jewish, past, a Jewish past she had submerged since living with Henry. Gail was the first member of her family she invited to the Passover seder she decided to have.

Henry was jovial in welcoming her to their home and wryly mocking during the abbreviated readings and ceremony that accompanied dinner. Gail tried to conceal her enmity to him. Jeff and Ralph struggled to understand the arcane rituals which harked back to the Jews' exodus from Egypt, but they felt almost as awkward as during their first meal with chopsticks. What gave Ralph pleasure, however, was the shining look in his mother's eyes.

After a while Ralph noticed also that a change had occurred in he relationship between his parents since his mother's decision to return to school. She no longer accepted her husband's authority without question; she now seemed good-naturedly to do exactly what she wished. Henry appeared powerless to curb her surprising independence and resigned to treating that as well with a wry irony. His own days were tedious; he was bored by retirement and itching to find an activity that would occupy him.

Afterward, Gail pointed out something else she had observed about Henry. He seemed to talk a good deal now about his past accomplishments. During the course of the evening he had mentioned how much he used to enjoy visiting the bookkeeping department the first days of the month to watch the rent checks being opened and to observe the mounting totals. They imparted a sense of well-being. Henry asked Ralph whether he felt the same way. The younger man admitted that he had not even stopped by the old Brooklyn office, where the rents were collected. Besides, he added, the totals were invariably just about the same as the month before. Gail later told Ralph that at that moment, she thought she glimpsed in Henry a deeply bitter resentment toward the son who had supplanted him so completely. Ralph attributed her impression to her long-standing dislike of his father.

She was far kinder in her attitude toward Jeff, with whom she had become good friends over the three-quarters of a year since the wedding. Although he had earlier confided to her his desire to start his own firm because of his conviction that he would never be treated by Ralph as an equal, she had also sensed beneath his cockiness anxiety about taking such a fearful step. This night, perhaps because of the influence of the wine, he raised the issue directly with Ralph.

Ralph answered with equal candor. "Things are a little precarious now. Half our assets will go to Gail and her father, and I've had to sink a lot of my own money into the two projects they're not involved in, the property you're assembling for us on the East Side and Behr Center. Metrobank will let me mortgage out on the office tower at Behr Center only after we have an eighty percent rent-up. Kramer is buying into the rest of the project, but he pays in stages, over time—when he can offset the payments with his construction fees." Ralph glanced at his father as he mentioned Metrobank. To his recollection he had never told his father that the Brookhouses' bank was his financing source. "The point is: everything is on the line right now, and I need your help. As soon as I've got a little more breathing space, I'll be glad to talk about it. By then you'll have more experience. Frankly, you could use it."

Jeff did not want to argue that last issue in front of his parents, with Ralph no doubt eager to demonstrate total recall of all his mistakes. He contented himself with grumbling to Gail about Ralph's unfairness. It was a way too of gaining her attention. He thought her the most warmly sympathetic woman he had ever met. Unfortunately, he had begun to notice a sharp lessening of her hostility toward Ralph. Tonight, the conviction had taken hold of him that she might even be slipping into active attraction to his brother. He could not tell whether Ralph reciprocated that feeling, but Jeff assumed his brother would be a fool not to take advantage of the convenience of a sexual relationship. He decided that patience was his best strategy in winning Gail. When the couple's divorce ended Ralph's claim on her attention, he himself would be in a perfect position to build upon his friendship with Gail and press his own suit.

Since surfacing several months earlier, the discord between Ralph as developer and Simon Kramer as general contractor had increased. The gentlemanly polish Simon had occasionally projected was now rarely in evidence, replaced by belligerence. He had risen from scant means to his present wealth in the construction business by being tougher than the next guy. Equally stubborn, Ralph was determined not to yield on points he believed were essential to the quality and, ultimately, the success of the project. Both men were used to getting their way. All that kept them from coming to blows at times was their mutual interest in getting Behr Center built on its very tight schedule.

During a heated meeting at his office to resolve many matters in dispute between them, Ralph found his own construction representative often siding with Kramer. When the latter tried to convince Ralph that a cheaper, untested window should be substituted for the make specified on the plans, Ralph had had enough.

"Who are you working for here?" he demanded to know.

"You, of course."

"Not anymore, you're not. Is he still working for *you*, Simon?" Upon receiving no answer, Ralph added. "Then I guess you've lost both jobs."

Emitting protests of hurt outrage, Simon loudly denied the charge. Ralph ignored him, pointed a finger at the rep, and ordered him from the room.

After the meeting Ralph drew into his office Jeff and Larry Carlacci, the young structural engineer supervising Behr Center for his employer. Ralph asked Jeff to take a more active role in overseeing construction and Larry to wear two hats for his engineering firm: becoming Ralph's construction rep for an added fee to his firm while continuing to oversee the structural work. The young man knew construction inside and out and he could not be bought. Carlacci was eager to take on the job; Behr Center was the most important project he had ever worked on, maybe that any structural engineer had ever worked on, and he did not want Simon Kramer's construction methods to degrade it. The next day, after gaining his employer's approval, he accepted.

Hot weather arrived unusually early that spring, when concrete was being poured for the three arches suspending the plaza at its periphery. This was a tricky job because steel rods known as rebars had first to be carefully placed. They would form the core to reinforce the concrete, which was then expertly mixed for maximum strength and poured into wooden forms encompassing the rebars. Larry Carlacci had been observing the process to make certain it was performed correctly. Problems developed on Friday, when the first of the three massive legs that formed the base of the tri-partite arch was being poured. Erection of the plywood forms was going slowly, to some degree because Carlacci was insisting on absolute conformity to the curvature and dimensions set forth in the plans. He insisted the carpenters remove and then refit large sections of curved plywood that they had put into place. As the delay lengthened, the construction supervisor phoned Simon Kramer, his employer, who had just returned from a leisurely lunch.

Simon rushed downtown with resurgent anger. Not only had he been held up months in getting started, even now his crew had been forced to leave a small section of the basement slab unpoured because the goddamn archaeologists were still pulling up seventeenth-century garbage, like old bottles. He needed the prestige of this project to elevate his image from that of a construction guy barely out of overalls and throwing up quick cookie-cutter office buildings to a real-estate developer of distinction. But as construction costs had mounted and cut into his projected profit, so had his fury at Ralph for unreasonably, he thought, refusing to approve the methods and materials that would lower costs considerably. Now, because of that bastard engineer Behr had put on as his rep, concrete trucks were beginning to stack up one behind the other waiting for the forms to be erected. In this heat the concrete would harden in no time. He had the best clout you could have at the concrete end, but he would still have to scrap all this concrete and wait until Monday for a new batch. This whole afternoon would go down the drain. So would his personal plans. Every Friday afternoon he and Lorna rendezvoused at her house. Unless he could straighten this mess out fast, he would have to call that off too.

Hurrying to the area where the carpenters were doing their best to put up the forms, Simon engaged in a shouting match with Carlacci, who was watching every nail that went in. But Simon saw that the carpenters would soon be done and followed Charlie Bates, his construction supervisor, to the sidewalk, where ten concrete trucks were parked. The first few had been in the sun for well over an hour.

"That first batch must be over seventy degrees. See for yourself what the stuff's like." Bates pointed out the concrete inspector behind the lead truck. The man worked for the company hired to test the concrete. "He's about to do a slump test."

The inspector filled a foot-high metal cone with wet concrete from the huge barrel rotating atop the bed of the first truck. He flipped the cone over and withdrew it. Instead of slumping the required six inches for a mix formulated to withstand seven thousand pounds of pressure per square inch, the concrete had hardened to the point where it was able to slump only four inches.

Simon instantly grabbed Bates's arm and whispered into his ear. "You keep your eye on Behr's guy. I'm going to make a deal with this son of a bitch."

Simon motioned for the inspector, a gray-haired man with a perpetual frown, to join him behind the truck.

"Don't I recognize you from somewhere?" he began.

345

Surprised to be remembered by someone of Simon's stature, the man's eyes brightened. "I worked on Three Forty-Five East and Ariel Tower for you, Mr. Kramer. My name's Stanley Shutz."

"I thought so. How you been?"

Before the man could reply, Simon began his pitch. A short while later, the man was five hundred dollars richer and walking away down the street.

Simon grabbed the hose, opened the nearby tap, and began to add water to the mix rotating in the truck's immense drum. After several minutes, the driver who had brought the concrete tried to stop him.

"That much water could weaken the mix."

"I've been doing this since before you were born. Do you know how much extra strength is designed into this mix? It could support a fucking mountain. Don't tell me about concrete, Sonny."

He handed the driver a hundred-dollar bill, told him to buy himself a hot dog on the corner, and continued to shoot water into the drum.

When the inspector ran the slump test a few minutes later, the concrete slumped six inches. He signed off, and the crane bucket was immediately lowered to be filled. Simon moved on to the trucks behind. The same procedure was followed.

Finding that the concrete in the fourth truck had not yet hardened, Simon gathered all the small metal cylinders which should have been filled with concrete from each truck in turn. After drying for a specified number of days, concrete in the cylinders would be tested by the inspection company to determine the strength of the concrete actually poured into the structure from the same truck. He filled all the cylinders with concrete from the fourth truck.

He wore a look of satisfaction at having solved the problem so quickly and cheaply as he wiped his hands on the rag proffered by Bates, who had just returned.

"That, Charlie, is why I'm successful."

Simon glanced at his Rolex watch and flicked a drop of concrete off the crystal. He could be at Lorna's in twenty minutes and still get in a decent afternoon. He clapped Bates affably on the back and jumped into his waiting limousine.

As spring crept forward, the complications in Ralph's life gradually, if imperceptibly, enlarged. The plentiful supply of office space and residential property made rents in New York City continue to stagnate and vacancies continue to increase. Although the one-hundred-fifty-story office tower at Behr Center would not be finished for many months, a luxury apartment building Ralph had recently completed on Second Avenue—in direct competition with Simon's Ariel Tower, now being publicized by Lorna—was falling behind its rent-up schedule, putting pressure on him to meet debt-service payments that somewhat exceeded net income. Hidden structural problems were forcing him to pour additional money into the Wall Street–area building he was rehabbing. And his racing stable was doing so poorly that he had not been to the track to watch one of his horses run since Patagonia's death. The Secretariat filly had been named My Enchantress, one of Ralph's private names for Amanda, but she was months away from the races.

"Losers eat just as much as winners," he groused to Ben Rogovin. "Instead of my giving you a bonus this year, maybe one of your kids would like a horse."

Ralph's private life had been filled with similarly expanding complications. Living with Gail and going out with her to public events had become different from the early days of their marriage. Their relationship had come to embody both an indulgent conviviality and, contradictorily, an edginess; they shared the intimacy of knowing each other well, which was manifested in the ease with which they could fall into conversation, and yet there was an estrangement about which they never spoke. Despite the care each took to gauge the other's mood now, they seemed to take offense more quickly than at any time since before Milo's disappearance. They forced themselves to make up quickly as well, valuing their eccentric union too much to chance any antagonism's becoming permanent. Once, Gail even ventured to admit that he was her best friend. He realized that she had become his as well.

Amanda's name came up between them only when Ralph was informing Gail of his upcoming schedule or when she happened to mention that the other woman had phoned her. Amanda had befriended her, Gail suspected, because she could not discuss Ralph with her own friends, and perhaps to smoke out as much information as she could about Gail's own intentions toward him. Gail found her stomach in knots after the phone calls and, after a while, tried to avoid them.

A related anxiety would sometimes attack her. She would wake up shaking and sweating in the middle of the night. She was all alone in life. She had never had her father, and now Ralph had demonstrated to her that she never would. For all she knew she would live the rest of her life alone and then face dying alone.

For a long while, the time spent with Amanda had seemed blissful; her bewitching charm, her cordiality, her staggering beauty could lift his spirits, while she demanded in return only his affection. But complications soon entered that aspect of his private life as well.

One morning on the veranda of his country home, while they were leisurely eating breakfast, Amanda told Ralph that she wanted to marry him. Not in some distant, cloudy future years off, but soon. She wanted him to set a date by which he would divorce Gail and marry her.

Ralph faked a cough to cover the shock. Despite a year of marriage to Gail and all the strain it had put him under and despite nearly as long seeing Amanda, he had never envisioned himself married, had never faced head-on the prospect of entering that state on a permanent and emotionally bound basis. He had always anticipated that once the divorce decree was granted, his life would become as unencumbered as before. But now Amanda was forcing him to contemplate marrying her, and he quickly analyzed what that entailed for him. He had ascertained, after close to a year of living as a pseudomarried man, that he could occupy the same house with a woman and that he had nothing against marriage to the right person. Amanda was certainly a marvelous woman, beautiful to look at, possessing everything a man could wish for in a wife. But in that instant between her question and the answer he was expected to make, he was unable to fit all those factors into a coherent whole.

"I've told you it's essential for me to stay with Gail for another year. Any talk before then is premature."

Amanda shook her head, dismissing his pronouncement as unrealistic thinking.

"We have to make plans. My parents and grandparents want me to think seriously about marriage to Cob."

"Cob?"

"Do you want that for me?"

"Of course not." He took her hand.

"And you weren't lying when you told me in Saratoga that you wouldn't walk away from your responsibility to me?"

"Of course not," he swiftly replied, aghast that she might think that of him. He had certainly meant what he had said that night in Saratoga—and still did—except that he had no idea precisely what the words had meant. To Amanda, he did not doubt, they decidedly had meant marriage.

Amanda cocked her head, worry pinching her brow. "You do love me, don't you, Ralph?"

"You know I do."

"Well then." She smiled beguilingly.

Ralph suddenly realized that in this particular field, he was dealing with a master negotiator. The skill seemed to have been bred into her many generations of select genes.

Before he could speak, she added, "I'll try my best to be a good wife to you, to make you happy you married me."

Amanda was nearly twenty-six. She had lived a carefree, if unproductive, life in the six years since ending her college career, and it was beginning to wear her down. Her sole rationale, although she hardly needed one, had always been that her social activities permitted her to engage in the search that would justify that course—the search for the right man to marry. She had always known that by reason of her family background, her looks, and her wealth, she could aim very high. Ralph had filled nearly every qualification. He was exciting, handsome, so wealthy on his own that he could not be accused of marrying her for money. Of course, he was not from an old family, but his incredible business success compensated for that—and she had enough social cachet for the both of them. He was, even for her, a spectacular catch.

In truth her family had imposed no pressure on her to marry; she had refused many excellent suitors, awaiting the perfect one, and they had never interfered. Cob was nice enough, but not special. However, his was a useful name to drop as a way of increasing the pressure she herself had decided it was necessary to put on Ralph in order to extract his commitment to marry her. She had begun to sense a new, albeit carefully cloaked, tone in Gail's voice when discussing Ralph: warmer, no longer so neutral, a definite fondness there. Amanda determined to move before that inclination grew into competition and Gail, capitalizing on her own advantages of proximity and possibly of refusing to divorce, perhaps decided to take the field against her.

Amanda's more aggressive tactics were due as well to the perception that Ralph seemed far too contented with the status quo. She had even wondered whether Ralph was claiming the necessity of that extra year of marriage in order to ensure another year in the same pleasantly uncommitted state. If he intended to marry her, Amanda had concluded, he could make that pledge now, although her engagement might necessarily have to be a covert one, known only to her family. If he did not intend to marry her, better to know that now and not lose another one of her good years when she should be seeking out the best possible match. But that latter contingency occupied little space in her thinking: in her entire life she had never failed to get what she wanted, and she had decided that to secure Ralph Behr, she had to maneuver him into making an irrevocable commitment.

"Could I drive us to the train station?" she asked a few minutes later. "I'd love to try driving your Mercedes." She usually telephoned her parents' country house from the nearby station, as if she had just arrived on the train and needed a car sent to pick her up.

Ralph called the wrong turn to her attention as she was approaching the village. Dark glasses shielded her eyes from the sun as she drove the open convertible, so he could not see them when she glanced over with a pleasant smile, but without a reply. Still traveling at a good clip, she turned through the gates of the Brookhouse estate, waving to the guards. Concerned about how to explain their arriving together, he asked her to turn the car around and drive out again. She paid him no mind and took the road that led to her own parents' house on the estate. Both her mother and father were gardening in front of the large Georgian mansion. Two gardeners stood behind them to hand them tools and early plants from the nursery; tulips, hyacinths, irises, crocuses. Amanda raised her sunglasses, lowered her window, and waved.

"Mom! Dad!" she called out.

She turned back to Ralph. "They're both avid gardeners."

"Look, Amanda—" Ralph started to say, but got no further. Charles and Patty Brookhouse, both wearing work shirts and large gloves, were approaching the convertible. Both naturally appeared surprised to see him.

"Did Ralph drive you up this morning?" Patty asked.

"No, last night. We slept together at his country house. We plan to get married as soon as he's divorced. We wanted you to know."

The shock Ralph felt at the disclosure was exceeded only by the shock on the faces of the elder Brookhouses.

"When was this decided?" Charles asked, ignoring for a moment the revelation that his daughter was engaged in an adulterous relationship.

"Well, from the first moment we met, I think," Amanda declared happily, "but we decided to let you know only this morning."

Charles cast a stern glance at Ralph. "I take it you concur in the accuracy of what my daughter has told us."

"Yes."

What could he say, Ralph realized—that she had been lying or that he had slept with her for the best part of a year without wanting to marry her? The truth was, he told himself, that he had wanted to marry her from that magical moment when they first saw each other. He had just put off admitting it because of his complicated married state. He grinned broadly at the Brookhouses.

"I don't understand," Charles replied. "You and Gail seemed to be such a wonderful young couple. We're all very fond of her. Such energy and humor."

"Well, the way it appears isn't the way it really is."

"You didn't look unhappy," Patty added, although her own restrained demeanor had always carefully concealed how she felt about her own marriage.

Ralph glanced at Amanda for an instant before he answered her parents. "I had hoped that before I got into all of this with you, my divorce to Gail would be settled."

"Then you two are separated?" Charles inquired.

Ralph took a deep breath. "Not exactly." He eyed the gardeners standing patiently by the flower beds about forty feet away. "Look, could we go somewhere to discuss this? An open convertible isn't very private."

Charles called to his gardeners to finish the planting and led the others to the garden behind the house. As they walked to a grouping of white iron chairs beneath a shade tree, Amanda pointed out to Ralph the white church steeple in the distance, visible above a grove of trees. She whispered that they would be married there, as her mother and grandmother had been, and she would wear the same dress that they had.

When they all had taken seats, Charles recapitulated. "You said, 'Not exactly.' What does 'not exactly separated' mean?"

"You must understand that what I tell you can't be repeated to anyone and that I can speak only in general terms," Ralph began. He continued only after they had nodded. "The reason Gail and I married was purely business . . . to dispose of an old family debt that couldn't be disposed of in any other way. Gail and I were just about meeting for the first time at our wedding, with no intention to remain married or to engage in any intimacy. We have separate bedrooms. Although we appear to everyone to be married, we agreed before the marriage that we would obtain a divorce two years after the wedding. That would be next year. Gail herself confirmed to Amanda what I've just told you."

The Brookhouses deliberated on what had been said, asking a couple of questions for clarification, and then Patty pragmatically summed up where matters stood between Ralph and her daughter. "As I understand it, you two would be engaged, but no one could know about it except for us."

"And Granny," Amanda added. "I have to tell Granny."

"My father would eventually have to know," Charles said to his wife with obvious trepidation.

She nodded, then spoke again to Ralph. "But no one else."

"I could be damaged if the news got out prematurely."

"We, as well," Patty observed. "If it were revealed that Amanda was having an affair with a married man, particularly one so well known, the publicity would be distasteful. And that sort of thing never goes away."

All four nodded in agreement. Charles and Patty had been so wrapped up in trying to comprehend Ralph's explanation that they realized only now that they still must discuss whether Ralph was an acceptable husband for their daughter.

"What do you think?" Charles asked his wife.

Patty had already mentally zipped through a list of qualifications, and Ralph met all but a couple. He was not from their crowd, and his public flamboyance and the consequent media prominence would focus far too much attention on the family. But Amanda's evident affection for him balanced matters out. Patty nodded at her husband, who then turned to Ralph.

"I have your word that you are sincere in all you've told us. You will divorce Gail and marry Amanda."

Ralph nodded, filled with exaltation by the simple, timeless solemnity of the moment. Charles extended his hand, and they shook. Patty kissed her daughter, who then kissed her father. Finally, Amanda threw her arms about Ralph's neck and gave him a deep, long kiss. Her parents stood awkwardly until the couple parted, and Ralph once more addressed them.

"And I have *your* word that nothing about our marriage plans will be spoken about, except among yourselves. Not even to Gail. News like that has a tendency to get around fast. She and I would both be at great risk if it did." A whiff of equivocation had wafted across his consciousness, dispersed by the sight of his beautiful, his perfect wife-to-be.

"Whatever you say, my darling," Amanda declared enthusiastically.

She kissed Ralph heartily again, taking delight in how embarrassed her parents became and in how decisively she had secured her future.

That night Amanda told her grandmother. Although aware that her granddaughter was seeing Ralph and wanted to marry him, Nina was still dismayed by the news. Her mood became gloomily anxious when Amanda suggested her as the logical person to inform her husband. She tried to dissuade Amanda or, at least, to convince her to put off thoughts of marriage until Ralph was free. Amanda remained adamant, insisting that her happiness in life rested on marrying the man she loved; even if her parents and grandparents were opposed. Nina's expression implied that she had not taken a position on the matter, but inwardly she was terrified that the marriage would lead to the disclosure that Ralph was her child.

Nina went, not to her husband, but on Monday to New York City. She shopped distractedly all afternoon until at four she was driven to a small, out-of-the-way restaurant for tea. She entered diffidently, not certain what her reception would be, but he had been awaiting her and stood up immediately, appearing hardly to have changed in the quarter century since she had last seen him. A little grayer and stouter perhaps, but still very much as she remembered him. She walked over and sat down across the table from Henry Behr.

Worried about being diverted from her mission, she immediately announced, "It is essential for both of us that you stop your son from marrying my granddaughter."

Henry was still too dazed by her phone call that requested this meeting, too dazzled by seeing her, by how desirable she still looked, her skin still clear and smooth, her eyes still wide and blue, to focus directly on what she was saying. Several seconds passed before Henry realized that Nina was stating that his son Ralph and her granddaughter Amanda had been seeing each other for nearly a year and intended to marry once Ralph divorced his wife. She wanted to break up their relationship.

Henry had been nettled when he first learned that Ralph had approached Metrobank for financing, but now he saw a grand strategy that delighted him. Moreover, he considered the romantic nature of his son's liaison very much in the Behr tradition and saw no reason to discourage such an advantageous match. "You want me to tell Ralph not to marry your granddaughter when all my life all I've wanted is to marry you? There's no real blood relationship between them, right?" When she nodded, he shook his head. "You came to the wrong teller's window for that, Nina. Let me ask you a question—for them and for us: Have you led a happier life because you married Otis and not me?"

"You could never have given me the life, the standing, that Otis has."

"Not easier, Nina—happier."

She stared into his eyes for a very long time. Then, abruptly, she pulled back her chair and walked out of the restaurant.

She cried all the way back in the car, the smoked window between front and back raised so the driver could not see her. Assaulted by the same alarm that had overwhelmed her maternal longings the instant that Ralph, as a child, guessed she was his mother, Nina could not assess objectively whether she liked Ralph as a person or as a prospective husband for her granddaughter or took a mother's pride in how he had turned out. She had, in fact, convinced herself that her hostility to the marriage was for Amanda's benefit, that her granddaughter's happiness would be secured only if she married someone from the same background as her own, possessed of the same values and assumptions. What she feared, in fact, was her husband's outrage if he learned she had produced a son who was now trying to usurp the future of his line; Otis would banish and pauper her for mocking his manhood and tainting his descent.

Composed by the time the car began the winding approach through the property to her home, she had come to the conclusion that only a massive threat to Ralph's financial welfare would force him to withdraw his marriage proposal and end the risk of exposure to herself posed by his presence within the family circle, by an inadvertent slip of his tongue or that of Henry, who would have to be invited to family gatherings occasionally. Only Otis had the power to make that threat. Although he would be angry at her—he had sometimes been viciously so during the half-century course of their marriage—because her adultery had occurred so long ago, she reasoned that his anger at that would eventually pass. What Otis would never then accept would be Ralph Behr marrying his granddaughter. He would do everything in his power to bar from his family the son of the man who had cuckolded him.

With a courage and cunning born of fear, she went to the library, where Otis was reading. She told him she had just learned that Amanda was having an affair with a married man, someone who had mocked the hospitality of Otis's house and trampled on the trust invested by his bank. To fuel her husband's anger at Ralph, but gripped by dread, she revealed one part of the secret she had protected so long: that many years before she had had an affair with Henry Behr, Ralph's father.

Otis did not say a word while she was speaking, the wrath simmering behind his gaze, but as she had expected, his mind was quickly occupied with stopping his granddaughter's marriage. Nina kept to herself the greater secret: that Ralph was her son, counting on Ralph's own self-interest to keep concealed the truth about his parentage; his revealing it would undoubtedly incite the entire Brookhouse family, perhaps even Amanda herself, to oppose the marriage.

Deferential nods and surreptitious glances and whispers followed J. Otis Brookhouse's passage through the entrance hall of the club. Ralph had been invited here several times before for business luncheons. It had seemed to him then as now to be a huge vault, the stone-block walls of which guarded the mysteries of an envied fraternity born to power and membership, the white Protestant moneyed elite who had dominated American business and society for more than a century. For Ralph and even for the members who observed his firm step and dark eyes glowing like hot coals, J. Otis Brookhouse fused all of that history, as well as present financial might, into one living symbol.

"Mr. Behr," Otis said without extending his hand to Ralph, who was awaiting him for the late afternoon meeting. The elderly banker had arranged it through their secretaries without indicating its purpose. Ralph remembered that the old man had simply called him Behr when he and Gail visited his estate. His now more formal tone did not seem to signal a warming phase.

Taking care to close behind them the doors to the paneled meeting room, Otis motioned to a wing chair and moved to one opposite. For nearly a minute before he began to speak, he scrutinized the younger man with an expression of loathing.

"My wife informs me that you are seeing my granddaughter and that you have expressed an intention to marry her. Is that information correct?"

"Yes. But appearances don't—"

"Are you or are you not married?"

"I am."

Otis's eyes glared into Ralph's. "I consider your behavior despicable, an indication of an immoral character. You are to cease seeing her immediately."

"Despite appearances, Mr. Brookhouse, I assure you that my marriage is not what it seems to be. From the start it was purely a business arrangement and will end within a year. I love your granddaughter and intend to marry her."

Otis's mouth tightened. "No, Mr. Behr, you will not be allowed to do so. My granddaughter will not waste herself on an opportunistic upstart."

"Be very careful what you say," Ralph warned.

"Oh, I will, Mr. Behar. It was Behar, wasn't it? I knew your grandfather quite well before his untimely death. He tried to wheedle his way into our circle, to charm or beg or buy his way into this very club if memory serves. He was not our kind. We all knew he was Jewish; no amount of name-changing or church-going could eliminate that. Now I see before me his grandson who, through seduction and marriage this time, is still trying to climb his way upward."

Otis's hand slammed the black leather chair-arm. *But you will not!* I control Metrobank. Not the directors. Not my son. I do. And unless you cease to see my granddaughter as of this very moment, don't think that I will not act. I will destroy you."

Teeth gritted in rage, Ralph sprang to the edge of his chair. "I give you the same warning, old man. Those bank-loan papers I signed with your bank were very carefully drawn. Step one inch outside them, and I will attack with lawsuits that will be disastrous both for you and for your bank, punitive damages as a result of your personal malice that will be so huge you both will be crawling on your knees."

The two men stared at each other for a very long time. At last Ralph offered, not a concession, but an olive branch. "Mr. Brookhouse, I don't like you or your bigoted kind. You certainly don't like me. But I'll marry Amanda if that's what she and I want. And I hope, for Amanda's sake, that by the time we do, it will be with your blessing. For my own sake, I'd be equally satisfied if it was with your hatred."

The old man had a deep affection for his headstrong granddaughter and knew she would follow her own inclination in this matter despite his own aversion to the man of her choice. He had little hold over her: she had her own money and the certainty of more in the future as additional trust funds matured.

But he would never reconcile himself to the entrance of this philandering married man, this slick Jew, this son of his wife's lover into the Brookhouse family.

Otis stood up swiftly, the weight of his years in part overcome by the vigor of his hatred. "Mr. Behr, I will never allow it!"

Ralph brooded over what had just occurred as he walked the few blocks from the club to his home. He stopped at a corner pay phone to tell Ben Rogovin that he, Jeff, and the lawyers should immediately begin to double-check the loan agreement and the Behr group's own performance under its terms, so as to be sure that Metrobank was not inadvertently permitted a means to back out. Given the merest cause, Otis Brookhouse would withdraw financing to force an end to his relationship with Amanda. He and Ben ought to start trying to line up alternative sources of financing, just in case. It would be tough to do so: he was already too heavily borrowed, and the other sources would want to know why he was backstopping his highly publicized deal with Metrobank.

Ralph continued in deep thought after hanging up, not about business matters any longer, but about the feelings that had exploded within him with Otis Brookhouse.

Ralph did not say much to Gail during dinner. Usually, if she prompted him, he would talk at least about his day at work. But he was laconic in the extreme, and Gail waited until they were in the upstairs hallway to ask him if anything was troubling him. After a moment's hesitation, he led her into the breakfast room and closed the door. He needed to confide his anguish to someone, and Gail had become the only one to whom he could.

"A long time ago my father had an affair with Nina Brookhouse. Her husband never found out, but she's always been terrified he'd learn about it."

"When was that?"

"When I was nine or ten was the last time I saw them together."

"Is she your mother, Ralph?"

The unexpected question startled Ralph. Gail already knew so much about his past, why not this? But he had spent a lifetime polishing the flawless conqueror's image he displayed to the world, believing in it. He could not bring himself to admit to the defect of illegitimacy.

"Hey, watch it," he admonished her.

"Sorry. But when you mentioned it, it occurred to me there seemed to be a resemblance between you."

Ralph shook his head. "My father and mother were married in London, during the war, years before they had me."

"You knew about the affair he had with Nina though?"

"Yes, but I don't think my mom did."

"Interesting that you and your father would both get involved with women from the same family."

"I didn't know who Amanda was when I met her."

"Maybe you didn't purposely choose her granddaughter, but you chose a woman from the same background your father did."

"What man wouldn't go for Amanda?"

Gail nodded glumly. Amanda truly had been gifted with a lavishness few women could match—certainly not she. Sometimes life was very unfair. "Your father probably felt the same way about Nina. But why is it bothering you now?"

"She told Otis I was seeing Amanda. I've just come from talking to him. Threatening each other would be more like it."

Gail felt the heat rising to her cheeks. She felt like a spy eavesdropping on controversies deep within the enemy's headquarters. "Was he angry because he somehow found out about his wife's affair with your father?"

"I don't know. It turned out he hasn't been thrilled with my family for a long time." Ralph tried to distill the essence of the dispute for her. "My being married bothered him a lot, but the major strike against me seems to be that my grandfather was a Jew."

Ralph fell silent and quickly left the room before Gail could delve further. But she comprehended why he had chosen to make these abrupt revelations to her: their family histories were linked somehow; she and her family were as much *his* key to the meaning of his past as he and his family were to the meaning to her of her own.

Ralph had rushed from the room to be by himself because he had been struck by a strange, disconcerting awareness which he had to examine before he would be willing to admit to it: that his anger toward Otis Brookhouse had not been the self-righteousness of someone whose religious affiliation was misidentified, but had been the deeply personal fury of someone whose very being was under attack by an absurd and cruel bigotry. He had reacted passionately, instinctively, it began to dawn on him, because he had *felt* like a Jew. No sudden compulsion was seizing him to adopt the religion as his own. Rather, he sensed that among the several things he was, he was a Jew, that he'd always been one but never known it until that moment.

Chapter 20

"You said this place has great cold sesame noodles," the mayor reminded Simon Kramer, as they and the others in the mayor's campaign-advisory group at Lorna's apartment dipped into the first of the cardboard containers that had just been delivered. "These are very definitely *not* great cold sesame noodles. They taste like they have peanut butter on them."

"It must be a different chef at night," Simon answered him. "To tell you the truth, I've only ordered there during the day."

The group that had taken seats around her dining table for a late supper also included Lorna, the deputy mayor, a political pollster with a supposed genius for managing election campaigns, an ex–city corporation counsel, and the mayor's closest confidante, an older man in charge of patronage, among other things, who operated out of a basement city-hall office. As finance chairman, Simon had been raising campaign funds for months, while Lorna had been advising on public and media relations, which all had agreed needed shrewd handling after the succession of municipal corruption scandals which had continued unabated through several administrations. They were tired from hours of pontificating, prognosticating, and bickering about the best strategy for the mayor's upcoming election campaign.

The mayor's confidante, a reserved, scholarly man of about seventy, had been silent throughout the long evening. He deemed the time now propitious to synthesize the group's thinking into what he and the deputy mayor had privately agreed several days earlier was the best campaign strategy. Both advisers had figured the mayor would be more amenable to accepting the advice if the older man presented it.

"We are all in agreement, I think, that the mayor gains nothing by allowing his opponents in the upcoming Democratic primary to force him to defend his record. Crack, the homeless, racial problems, those are all negative issues that benefit his detractors. Focusing on the past only serves to put him on the defensive and might confuse the public into associating the mayor with the corrupt men he appointed who betrayed the public trust."

Several people nodded, Lorna most strongly. She had been asserting since the inception of the meeting that the mayor must avoid running a campaign based on defending his record, which, irritated by criticism of his administration, he had been advocating.

"We have to sell voters on the future," the older man continued, gently directing his words to the mayor. "That's the purpose of an election campaign: to sell the voters on what a candidate is promising. The other candidates will just be able to offer speculation. But you can tie future promises to projects and programs you've already started."

"We go with a campaign slogan like 'Building a new New York,'" the young pollster–campaign manager jumped in to assert. His own ideas had been shot down, and he saw an opportunity to recoup some lost prestige.

"We thought Behr Center should be the symbolic centerpiece of your campaign," the deputy mayor explained, simultaneously establishing his co-authorship of a strategy that seemed to be going over well. "This city gets a giant project every year, but Behr Center is truly monumental. The locals may have fought against it, but believe me, everyone else you talk to is dazzled by it and really proud. They want New York to have the tallest skyscrapers in the world again and not be second best. How many foreign dignitaries have asked if you could arrange for them to see the model of the project? Between those towers and that atrium in the air, it's like fucking Disneyland." The mayor nodded. "Make it your project in the public's mind, and every time someone writes about it or mentions it on TV, you'll come to mind as well."

With a worried, apologetic nod toward Simon, the pollster felt himself duty-bound to report, "Our sampling reveals people consider the mayor too closely tied to big real-estate developers who make large campaign contributions."

"Our point here is to make the voters see that you haven't been advancing the interests of the developers themselves," the deputy mayor interjected, "but all along you've been acting for the *city's* welfare—new construction, new housing, new jobs for the people. You've got the city on the move again."

The mayor had swiftly forgiven his deputy for exploring a possible mayoralty run after his aide claimed to have done so only in the hope that their policies might live on if the mayor should make a run for even higher office. The mayor knew that the taint of the recent scandals was the real issue, and forgave the deputy because the viability of his candidacy was a valid cause for concern.

The campaign-polling specialist was nodding enthusiastically. "I want everyone here to know I got exactly these same goose bumps when I first heard the phrase, 'missile gap.'"

The mayor's elderly confidante concluded. "Your instincts were right on target when you got behind Behr Center. It conjures up a vision of a glowing future for the city, positive changes for the better, economic growth, the greatest city in the world. The opposition to it has died down now that the artists seem satisfied with the new arrangements. The architectural press loves the design. The TV news shows can't get enough of it. It's keeping companies in the city and creating a lot of new jobs. And if it's the centerpiece of your campaign, you can honestly take credit for making it happen."

Lorna pointed out the idea's marketing impact. "The people have had it up to here with the scandals and the crime and the drugs. They want something to be proud of again. Behr Center is perfect. We can open your campaign with some kind of ribbon-cutting there."

Simon punched the air enthusiastically. "It's a natural. We're still erecting the plaza and need a few weeks before it's ready, but I think the timing is right for a ribbon-cutting when it's finished." Although the arches were up, the elevated concrete slab they supported was only now about to be poured. The escalators would not be in place and all the scaffolding cleared away for several weeks.

Lorna's marketing adrenaline was flowing. She promised to produce the sort of event that would "knock their underwear off—maybe marching bands, doves of peace, skydivers, high-wire walkers, the Vienna Boys Choir, the works."

After the others left, the deputy mayor stayed behind. However, realizing that Simon Kramer was acting very much at home and that he himself was odd man out, he remained only long enough to inform Simon that he himself deserved the credit for putting Behr Center in the limelight.

Larry Carlacci sported a thick mustache; strutted like a bantam rooster in a Mets cap, jeans, and T-shirts emblazoned with the likes of Bullwinkle and the words Wossa Matter U; and had married a woman half a foot taller than his five feet four inches.

He was all toughness and bristle, taking no guff from any man. And he designed structures that had the same aggressive strength of character.

Nothing had come easy for him. Growing up in a poor, working-class home, he had learned very early that if he was going to get anywhere in life, he would have to fight harder and longer than the next guy. Realizing on the first day of school that he was the shortest by a wide margin, he picked a fight with the largest boy in class and had to be pulled, swinging, from on top of him. The others never forgot. He survived an operation in infancy to correct a congenital heart defect, meningitis at eight, and the need all of his life to take medication to cause his heart to beat regularly. At fourteen he wangled a summer job as a carpenter's helper on a construction crew rehabbing old houses. By sixteen he was still short and resigned to spending his life at that height, but he was a full carpenter working summers and weekends, which he continued to do until he had put himself through engineering school. Doubtless influenced by his carpentry experience, he had fallen in love with structural engineering, the science of overcoming gravity in construction. With graduation approaching, he made interview appointments with the best structural-engineering firms in New York City. The very first one hired him after he hauled into the interview his plans and six-foot-high models for a daring high-rise tower and an innovative bridge he had designed.

Now, at twenty-eight years old, he had what he considered the greatest job in the world. Not only had he played a significant part in designing the structures that composed Behr Center, but he was now responsible for seeing that every column, every pane of glass, every doorknob was exactly correct as the complex rose up before him.

On a Friday morning, while going through the papers on his desk, Larry began to peruse the strength tests done of cylinders of drying concrete which had been poured at the same time as the base of the first arch. Something appeared odd. Concrete cylinders from each of the first four trucks all displayed exactly the same number of pounds-per-square-inch resistance to collapse—not approximately, but exactly the same. That seemed so strange that he called the testing company and was told that the figures he had been given were indeed correct.

Larry stroked his mustache while he thought for several minutes. Then he left the construction trailer to inspect the arch visually.

362

The wooden forms that had molded the tripartite arch assembly had been removed. Like three immense longbows propped against each other, their tips met high above the center of the elevated plaza now being constructed twenty feet above grade. The plaza would be made of reinforced concrete held aloft by connection to the three equidistant arches at its periphery and, eventually, between them, the three towers—a dazzling engineering feat. As of yet, though, it was simply a vast circle of flat plywood sheets given solidity by thick and remarkably long concrete transverse beams, set like spokes of a wagon wheel beneath the slab to prevent sagging. Long temporary wooden legs kept both the drying beams and the plywood in the air.

Atop the western side of this plywood plateau, steelworkers were fashioning ridged steel rebars into a horizontal grid that would instill strength into the concrete slab to be poured around it. The pouring process had already started on the eastern side. There, a mobile crane with a lufting boom swung and raised large buckets of concrete from street level to the plaza, where workmen directed the flow of wet concrete onto the steel grid. A few were pulling long-handled bull floats to smooth and level the wet concrete. Others were vibrating it to eliminate voids and ensure adherence to the rebars. And still others, on concrete that had set a bit, were operating power floaters to smooth it. In a few days most of the plywood that formed the slab's bottom would be removed, but some of the wooden shoring poles would be left in its place. As the drying concrete cured, its strength would increase until, in about eight weeks, it would approach its designed strength.

Larry intended to spend a good part of his day inspecting the slab's construction, but now he was interested in the most easterly arch. He had named it the Number Three Arch when making the drawings, and it stood directly across the plaza from the rising office building. As best Larry could figure it, the questionable concrete composed much of the arch's base from about ten feet above grade to a few feet above the point where the elevated-plaza slab connected to it. A deep, wide notch had been correctly placed there. Like the handiwork of a mad orthodontist, metalwork emerged from the notch to interlock with the plaza grid. Atop the grid, a few feet away, a workman was spreading wet concrete toward the notch, as if to take an impression of the huge-jawed patient's bite.

Larry placed a tall ladder against the arch and scampered up to make an inspection. Not finding anything suspicious, he moved

363

the ladder around the arch and inspected the adjacent area. Nothing again. He shifted the ladder once more, climbed up nearly to the plaza level, and suddenly spotted what he feared: a crack a couple of feet wide.

"Shit!" he breathed.

He inserted his penknife into the crack. It entered all the way to the hilt with no opposition.

"Stop!" he yelled up to the workman spreading concrete.

The man had already filled in the notch, and the next crane bucket of concrete was being lowered nearby.

"Don't do any more until I speak to Bates!"

The man leaned back on the handle of the bull float, glad to take a break.

Larry scooted down the ladder and ran beneath the scaffolding temporarily supporting the plaza to the Kramer Construction trailer. Bates was on the phone. Larry pulled the receiver from his hand, barked into it, "He'll call you back!" and slammed it onto the cradle.

"Charlie, there's something wrong with the concrete in the Number Three Arch. There's a crack in it that's at least three inches deep. Probably deeper. They're already spreading concrete into the notch. You've got to stop it until we know what the problem is."

"Show me where it is." But the construction supervisor already had a pretty good idea.

Ten minutes later, Bates was back in the trailer with the door closed and speaking on the phone to Simon Kramer. Larry waited impatiently outside.

When Bates finally opened the door, his face was red and his jaw set. "Mr. Kramer doesn't think it's serious enough to stop for."

Larry was incredulous. "You told him how deep and how wide it was?"

Bates nodded.

"That whole arch could be weak," Larry said with an urgency that conveyed his concern. "I've got strength tests that look phony as a three-dollar bill. Let's get the concrete sub down here and make him explain what the hell is going on. But meanwhile, it's crazy to keep pouring concrete we may have to rip up."

"Mr. Kramer says he'll speak to the concrete sub."

"Shit!" Larry roared. He would get no further with this yes-man. Breaking off, he ran the short distance to his own trailer and telephoned Ralph's office. Myra informed him that Ralph had gone away for the weekend. She didn't know where to reach him, but he'd be calling in later in the day. Larry said it was critical that they speak.

Reluctantly, Larry asked to be transferred to Jeff, who was overseeing the Behr Center project for his brother. A couple of disagreements had occurred when Jeff pulled rank on matters Larry considered him unqualified to judge. Jeff would be back in half an hour. Larry jumped into a cab and headed uptown to be there when he arrived.

Jeff heard Larry out, pleased that today, at least, the guy couldn't run behind his back to Ralph. Jeff viewed the additional responsibility with which he had been saddled as just another ploy by Ralph to divert him from what had long been coming to him, his own operation with no interference from a dominating elder brother. His impression of Larry's complaint was that the man was letting one little crack run away with his imagination. He could imagine Ralph's rebuke if he ordered construction stopped over some niggling little scratch in a ten-foot-thick piece of concrete.

Larry appeared to be so perturbed, however, and remained so insistent that Jeff agreed to take him along to the meeting on retail space he was scheduled to attend in a few minutes at Simon Kramer's office. Before he and Simon began, Carlacci could voice his complaint.

Little was said during the short walk over. Jeff, tall and wearing a dark suit, was mentally reviewing his agenda for configuring and marketing the retail space. Larry, short and in a baseball cap and jeans, was planning how most effectively to make his plea that construction be halted for further testing.

Simon Kramer sat impassively through Larry's impassioned presentation, not registering a reaction of any kind, even when Larry concluded by saying, "That arch is one of the key supports of the plaza. If, as I suspect is the case, the concrete mix is of insufficient strength, the plaza could collapse."

Simon smiled. "I want you to know I appreciate your bringing this to our attention, I truly do. We intend to look into it, but my man Bates tells me the crack is superficial, a natural part of the drying process."

"That wasn't his opinion when he looked at it with me. Mr. Kramer, we're talking about a very significant part of the plaza structure. If that arch can't bear the load, it goes down and takes the plaza and the other arches with it. Look, I don't know

365

exactly what the condition of that concrete is, but continuing with the construction can only increase the cost if it all has to be ripped out and rebuilt."

Suddenly, Simon's anger showed. "Do you know what it costs to *stop construction*? As it is, I've already had to approve work crews over the weekend to try to regain some of the time we've lost."

"Mr. Kramer, we could have a dangerous condition here."

"Are you prepared to tell me that if we go in, we'll definitely find defective concrete in that arch?"

"We can't know until we test."

"Then let me tell you: There's no way that I'm going to stop that job on your *hunch* that something *might* be wrong." Simon's voice dripped sarcasm.

"I told him that too," Jeff added, but he was beginning to grow anxious in the face of Larry's steadfastness. "What if he's right, Simon? What if something *is* wrong? Maybe we could stop this thing, and over the weekend tests could be run, so we'd be sure."

Simon turned ferociously on Jeff. "No one is stopping that job! I gave the mayor my word, based on your brother's agreement, that twenty-nine days from now he would stand on top of that plaza—flags flying and bands playing and cameras rolling. He's been issuing statements to the press about how great the project is—worth millions of dollars in advertising to us. He held a press conference to congratulate the head of the insurance company that's taking space in your office building there. The construction schedule is so tight now that my men will be working overtime every weekend to be ready on time. But let me tell you, come hell or high water, twenty-nine very short days from now, the mayor is going to stand on that plaza and he will cut a fucking ribbon and he will give his opening campaign speech!" Simon shoved his forefinger at Jeff. "*Nothing*—understand me?—*nothing* is going to stop that!"

Rather than cowing Jeff, Simon's excessive attack had served to trigger doubts. "We'd only be suspending construction for a weekend, Simon."

"Two days I can't afford to lose."

"Is there something more here than we know about?"

Simon's eyes blazed now, and his mouth was drawn tight with rage. "You!" He pointed at Larry. "Get out of here until I send for you! This is between him and me."

Larry stalked from the room. Simon waited for the door latch

366

to click before speaking again. "I sure do know something more than I've been telling. Something about a certain East Side brownstone that seems to get a lot of traffic at night. Very odd time for a 'design firm' to do business."

Jeff's insides clenched as if his inquisitor was twisting them to the screaming point.

Simon bent forward, elbows on his desk. "Some friends found that revenue at their better establishments was beginning to decline because of unexpected competition. So they decided to meet the little lady who seemed to be in charge at the brownstone. I'm afraid they frightened her quite a bit, but what do you think they learned? The man who financed her and owns a big chunk of the place is none other than Jeff Behr. And the Behrs own the property. What a surprise!"

Simon leaned back and, heels on the desk, crossed his feet. "Now, my friends could have put the place and the lady herself out of commission for a couple of months. But they remembered that I was partners with the Behrs, and they're very good friends. So they called me up. I suggested they let the little lady alone and forget the whole thing—for a while. Now, wasn't that nice of me?"

Jeff nodded nervously. He was very frightened.

Simon was smiling again, certain of his dominance. "The time has come for me to decide whether or not to *keep* forgetting the whole thing. One option is to tell Ralph Behr what his kid brother's been doing behind his back. Imagine if he learned about this!"

"This woman, whoever she is—"

Simon went on blithely, ignoring Jeff's attempt at denial. "Maybe I should do my duty as an upright citizen and tell my friend the mayor and my friend the police chief and my friends at the newspapers all about the evil things going on at that brownstone."

Jeff's fists pressed desperately against his aching abdomen. "Stop the cat-and-mouse stuff, Simon. What are you looking for?"

Simon swung his feet down and leaned forward again. "First thing is I want that little construction-rep prick out there fired. The son of a bitch is trying to prove how important he is by making a mountain out of a molehill—a little surface scratch. He's a pain in the ass, and he's out."

"Simon, I wish I could do it—I don't like him much either—

but I can't. Ralph hired him and likes him. Besides, the guy's supervising the structural engineering."

Simon raised his voice ominously. "You didn't seem to understand me. I want him fired. How you do it is your business."

"What if I could get him to agree to hold off on testing the crack until after the ribbon cutting?"

"Fine." Simon turned accommodating. "I'm not trying to do shoddy work. You don't get as big as I've gotten, Jeff, by doing shoddy work. What I want is a little breathing space, and then I'll take care of whatever has to be taken care of. Full tests. Whatever it takes."

"Do you want anything else from me?" Jeff was sweating profusely, but the cramps were subsiding somewhat.

Simon circled the desk. He wore a relaxed grin and leaned back against the edge of the desk in front of Jeff.

"I like you, Jeff. I wouldn't want to harm you. Why do you think I told my friends to back off? Because I was looking to blackmail you?" He lifted his shoulders and flipped his palms open ingenuously. "I just wanted to do a favor for a friend, to protect you. I have trouble with your brother who fights me on every point, but you're a guy I can do business with."

Jeff rose stiffly and went to the door to recall Larry. The engineer entered, but did not take a seat. He stood with legs spread and arms locked across his chest as he listened to Jeff.

"Here's what we decided, Larry, and I'm sure you'll go along with it. If we stop construction now, there's no way we can have that ceremony on the plaza, and it's important to all of us. But just as soon as it's over, less than a month from now, we'll put that arch through every test in the book. If something's wrong, Simon will do whatever has to be done to make it right. Now, that sounds fair to me."

"No."

"Don't be hard-assed about this. There are a lot of factors to be considered."

"No."

"Jesus." Jeff was sweating. "Be a little reasonable."

"Are you going to stand there and hold it together for the next month just in case it's crumbling?"

"It can't be that bad." The cramps had begun again. Jeff fought not to let the pain show.

"I don't know if it's bad at all," Carlacci said, his face still stubbornly set. "But I'm not going to take the chance."

Jeff's mind felt stuck, unable to think of an approach that

would silence the engineer's concerns. He glanced helplessly at Simon, his tormentor, who with a phone call could shred his life into ruins. Simon stepped forward.

"Larry—it's Larry, right? Are you married, Larry? Kids? Me too. I'm concerned about safety. If it's as worrisome as you say, I wouldn't want to take a chance and keep going. Tell you what . . . my limousine is downstairs. You and I will drive right over to the site, and you can show me that arch yourself. If there's any question at all about it, I'll stop construction until we're a hundred percent sure."

"Jesus," Jeff quickly interposed, "what could be fairer than that?"

"Okay," Larry replied. "Let's go."

Simon smiled. "I just a need a minute or two to make some calls, and I'll be right with you." He eyed Jeff, smiling benignly. "Let's see how this works out."

When the door was closed behind them, Jeff felt the spasms being inflicted on his bowels suddenly end. All his life his intestines had betrayed him when he felt trapped. He considered today's repulse an admirable achievement.

He took Larry aside. His voice conveyed his authority. "The guy is trying his best. Meet him halfway. More than halfway. I don't want construction stopped unless that fucking arch is leaning like the tower of Pisa."

Uncertain whether he had left Carlacci daunted by the repercussions that would follow a failure to cooperate with Simon Kramer, Jeff's thoughts were a jumble with fear over what Simon might do about the brownstone. He waited across the street to observe if Carlacci did, in fact, accompany Simon Kramer downtown, as he had promised. Later, overcome by a sudden panic about being in his office if Ralph telephoned, he raced out of the building and picked up his car, not quite certain where he was headed.

Early that afternoon, Ralph telephoned when his plane landed on Providenciales, part of the Turks and Caicos chain in the Caribbean. The government had invited him to view the island and discuss building a major resort to attract more tourism. He had used the opportunity to spend a long weekend with Amanda at Turquoise, the Club Med complex on the island. He had been able to arrange for adjoining rooms.

After speaking to Myra, Ralph asked to be transferred to Jeff, in part to discuss some ongoing matters and in part to learn why Larry Carlacci had wanted so urgently to speak to him. Informed that Jeff was not in, he phoned his construction office on the site. Larry had not yet arrived.

"She makes great pot roast, doesn't she, Jeff?" Henry sat back in his armchair at the head of the dining table and cast a complacent glance at his wife.

"It was really great, Mom."

Distraught about Simon Kramer's threat, Jeff finally turned up late in the afternoon at the Jersey Shore house where his parents had already begun to spend their weekends. He decided he would unburden himself to Henry. His father would know what to do.

After dinner, while Rosalie cleaned up, Henry and Jeff took a stroll to the ocean. Despite his compliment to his wife, their squabbles had been increasing of late. She often stayed late at school or was too busy with her studies to cook and left it to the cleaning woman to throw on a steak or boil spaghetti for Henry. He had little to occupy his time and, with her away so much, was frequently lonely. Seeing Nina had increased his edginess and revived his dissatisfaction with Rosalie. Moreover, despite the sacrifice he considered he had made before Ralph's birth in agreeing to live with her, she too was now deserting him.

How different life with Nina would have been, he often imagined lately. Yet, as Nina had pointed out and he was gratingly aware, even his own considerable success in business could not have permitted him to offer Nina the opulent life she had chosen with Otis Brookhouse. Although he and Ralph had almost reached a point of such success that she would have been forced to regret rejecting him, the retirement he silently, frequently cursed ended any chance of that. Much of the free time that weighed so heavily on his hands was spent concocting fantasy schemes to increase his assets to a scale vast enough to be able to provoke heartache in her at not having chosen him.

And then he would come back down to earth: he knew he was kidding himself. He was a has-been. Out of the mainstream. To build up his wealth to that magnitude, he would have to get back into business full time on a major scale. He was too realistic ever to think he could win her back after so many years, but that desire had welded itself onto the yearning that had long formed the purpose of his life, reinforcing its intensity, to make her desperate with regret for having spurned him half a century before.

"How's the business going?" Henry asked.

"All right, but I've got a personal problem. You know how much I've wanted to get out of there and get going on my own?"

Henry nodded!

"Well, a few months back I needed to make more money."

"I thought you were raised to four hundred thousand a year."

"Before then. I was making good money then too I guess, for someone who's working for someone else, but I was always promised the funding to start my own company. And I was getting so itchy to make the kind of money it takes to get started that I guess I did something I shouldn't have. Remember Grandpa's brownstone?"

"Ralph was assembling a parcel there."

"I started a whorehouse in it."

Instead of berating him, as Jeff had feared, Henry began to laugh uproariously. He threw an arm around his son and led him to a bench on the boardwalk. Jeff explained about the brownstone and then tried to repeat word for word exactly what Simon had said to him that morning. He noted that his father's eyes narrowed, as they always did when his mind was racing with ideas.

However, instead of suggesting a way for Jeff to extricate himself from Simon's blackmail threat, for which Jeff had been direfully hoping, Henry said, "Tell me about Ralph's projects, about his finances, everything."

Jeff explained how slow leasing had been, how tight money had become this spring, and how careful everyone was acting around the office to conform diligently to the littlest detail in loan agreements. He went down the list of projects and prospective projects. Suddenly, Henry stopped him.

"Repeat that again, Jeff. Explain exactly how it's set up."

And as Jeff did as he was told, Henry saw a way, not only to liberate his son from the spectre of blackmail, but to change his own life completely.

For years, Ralph had taken his rare vacations at exclusive resorts. Amanda had always spent her summers in the New England sea-coast towns where her crowd cultivated the sort of reserved, isolated, and artificial simplicity that depended on great wealth and the inconspicuousness of a house filled with servants. Because Ralph had a business reason for being in Providenciales, they exposed themselves to the casual democracy of the major resort there, a Club Med, where everyone ate together at large tables and fell into conversations without having been introduced and where the bikini-clad G.O.'s, the young employees who ran all the activities, seemed almost like guests. Ralph and Amanda found themselves having a wonderful, unhampered time.

She easily won the sailing race and competed for one of the teams on Olympic day. He had not touched a basketball since twisting his ankle, but he played for a couple of hours on the open concrete court near the Florinda residences and felt so good that he wondered if maybe that painful morning last fall had been a fluke, an off-day anyone could occasionally have. He was still a young guy, as good as he ever was.

He and Amanda played tennis together and sunbathed alone on a secluded beach for hours and were driven around the island by a representative of the government. But in public at the club, they always seemed, just by purest chance, to be part of the same random group: to have happened to choose nearby chaises; to have dropped into the same rollicking water-vollyball game; to have wandered into dinner with the same large group; and to have been among the people with whom the other danced at the disco. When Ralph was recognized, he told people he was on the island for business and had decided to stay on for a couple of days of relaxation. Several women, in fact, kept hoping that his amicability might lead to more intimate intercourse, but all were soon convinced that he was, as he said, simply there for the sun and activities. No one suspected that he and the delicately beautiful blonde around whom so many male G.O.'s gravitated were lovers.

While lolling on the deserted beach with her, Ralph pondered how he felt about Amanda. And the most profound evaluation he could come up with was simply that he felt very comfortable around her. Maybe that was the best reason of all to choose her for a wife, he reasoned. Annoyingly, when he tried to imagine what she would be like to live with, he found himself comparing her to Gail. He told himself that was because he had lived with Gail for a year now—in a manner of speaking—and had come to know her so well.

Unlike Gail, Amanda wasn't one to talk much, except when she had something on her mind or sensed he might be bored and needed amusing. When Gail wanted something, she charged head first and would trample you to get it. Amanda had her beat hands down there: she was tactful and cajoling and could get him feeling so good he would be delighted to give in. She was fun to be with, he remembered, although she lacked Gail's sharp humor. That was probably better, he decided—more gracious, more lasting. Gail was so touchy, you had to be careful not to say something that would set her off, and you could never be quite sure what that was, especially lately. Amanda, on the other hand, was great about going along with things; she was thoughtful and considerate. Even if, as he sometimes suspected, she might not be in the mood, she would make love because it was something he wanted. She wasn't a wildly passionate or aggressive lover, but he figured that too was probably more enduring in a long-term relationship. And when he compared their looks, Gail dropped out of the competition entirely. Gail was nice enough looking, but so were a lot of women. Amanda was exquisite, unforgettable. Men turned and stared until she was out of sight. His own eyes drank her in as if overcome by thirst for the sight of her.

Ralph grew angry at himself. Why the hell was he thinking of it as a contest? He was engaged to Amanda. He loved her. She had everything he wanted. He opened his eyes to scrutinize her as she lay beside him on her back, eyes closed. She had removed her bikini top for an even tan. Her breasts lifted like young mountains as she breathed. He leaned forward and kissed the pinnacle of the nearest. She shivered at his unexpected touch and then realizing it was he, ran her hand affectionately through his hair.

He pulled the string on her bikini bottom, and it fell away from her hip and onto the blanket. He reached for the other bow.

"Can't we continue this later?" she asked. "Back at the room?"

"No one is watching. You always liked doing it outdoors." His hand slid down between her legs.

"I'm just not in the mood now. I was then."

"I'll bet I can get you in the mood."

"People out there on the boats have telescopes."

"They're fishing. Or doing it themselves. Nobody is paying attention to us."

"If it's important to you, I'll do it."

He rolled onto his back. "Forget it."

"Now, you're angry."

"No, now *I'm* not in the mood anymore."

"I promise we'll make love as soon as we're back in the room."

His analysis of Amanda had been far too simplistic, he decided sullenly. Even *she* was a mystery. What the hell was the difference between grass and beach? He wondered whether Gail would have acted so inconsistently. Perhaps because she had been denied love during her traumatic childhood, Gail harbored an unexpected wild streak that broke through as righteous anger when she was passionate for a cause and as almost unbridled wanton sexuality when the passion was libidinous. But then she too could suddenly become baffling, he decided, recalling how icy she had become as soon as they left Sun Valley. What about Lorna, he grimaced? If Amanda could turn moody and Gail icy, with a similarly frustrating unpredictability, Lorna could be as treacherous as a female praying mantis.

Ralph played volleyball until nearly dinner time, as if to prove he could not be yanked around by the genitals. He and Amanda finally made love in the early morning hours, after returning from the disco. He was gratified to find her amorous, anxious now to make the experience memorable for him.

Flying back to New York aboard his plane, Ralph commented on how much freer he had felt this weekend than at the toney resorts and elite social events they both ordinarily attended. "Do you notice how many of the people we know look for their pictures in the paper or magazines after those things, to make themselves believe they had fun and that the rest of the world should be jealous? This weekend *was* fun."

Amanda reminded him that the weekend had been a lark, a game. But it was not the real world.

The plane landed at nightfall at the Westchester airport where Ralph had left the Mercedes. He drove Amanda back to the Brookhouse estate and dropped her off at the main house, where her grandparents lived. They kissed good-bye, and she went inside. She was the only one in the family to whom her grandfather had been half-civil since she'd announced her engagement to the immediate family. This weekend away with Ralph had proven once again to her how right she was to love him and to marry him. She still sometimes found his manners a little, not gauche—he was never that—but a little noticeable, a little unconventional. She could curb that in time. What was most important was that she admired him. She would hate to be married to a man she didn't respect, whom she could manipulate. With Ralph she felt cared for, protected. He had told her about his meeting with Grandpa. Who else but Ralph could have stood up to him that way? But Amanda knew that her grandfather's authority in the family made his enmity toward Ralph a barrier to her marrying him. To transform the engagement into reality, she could no longer rely on the others to win her grandfather over to Ralph and their union. She would have to do it herself.

She found her grandparents in the study—Nina reading, and Otis on the first step of the ladder that followed tracks around three walls lined with bookshelves. He was just descending with a volume of Gibbon, having just finished rereading the preceding one.

Amanda joked a bit and, when he asked about her tan, explained that she had been away. She tried to describe the puzzling procedures at the resort she had just visited, where one carried one's own luggage and ate with the help. He thought it chaotic and intrusive, perhaps endurable by young people wishing to rough it, but not something to which an older adult would willingly be subjected. He was glad, however, that she had enjoyed herself.

She sat down beside him on the sofa and, taking his hands in hers, confessed that she was desperately unhappy because two men whom she loved very dearly had been fighting. He was one of them. The other was Ralph Behr. She said that Ralph's marriage was one of convenience and that she hoped to marry him as soon as the divorce could be arranged.

"Grandpa, I hope you'll somehow see your way clear to end your disapproval of him, if only for my sake."

She stared imploringly into his unreadable eyes. When he did not reply, she rose and left the room.

"Close the doors when you leave," he ordered.

From the outside Amanda pushed the heavy doors together until they closed.

Otis did not speak for several minutes. Nina could not see his expression from where she sat. Finally, he rose and turned to her. His skin appeared to be aflame. His eyes seared her with their fury.

"This is intolerable! A Jew! A flashy, devious, grasping Jew!"

"Oh, Otis, I don't think he's quite that—"

"Why?" he screamed. "Because he's your lover's son, your Jewish lover's son." His rage seemed uncontrollable. His suspicions were hitting terrifyingly close to the truth. "She confides in you. You were the one who turned her head to him. Why? What is Ralph Behr to you?"

Nina was cowering in the chair, too frightened to answer. He was determined to force an answer from her, to vent his fury somehow. He raised his hand to strike her.

"I want the truth!"

Nina buried her face in her arm. But when time passed and no blow came, she peeked up. As if something had caught him by surprise, Otis's eyes stared straight ahead at the wall behind her, and his mouth was open in an odd way. Slowly, almost imperceptibly at first, he began to fall backward, like a tree struck by lightning.

For a long fearful time, she watched him as he lay unmoving on the floor. His eyes and mouth remained open. He was breathing, but unevenly, as if his body had little experience in performing the function. Then it occurred to her—the rage and activity had brought on a stroke.

She leaned forward and looked into his eyes. They seemed to be beseeching her for help. She smiled at him. Then she stood up and walked out of the room, careful to close the heavy doors behind her. She went to tell the servants that Mr. Brookhouse did not wish to be disturbed.

Ralph had stayed the night at his country house and driven to the office early the next morning. The short vacation had been a welcome break from the increasing pressure at the office. But now he was eager to get back to work.

The first to arrive at his office, he picked up the newspapers left outside the door and let himself in. At the top of the list of messages on his desk was the urgent one from Larry Carlacci. Ralph had gotten the engineer's message and had tried to reach the engineer, but had been unable to. Now, as he dialed the construction trailer, and the phone there began to ring, his eye wandered to the front page of the *Daily News*.

Very slowly, he lowered the receiver to its cradle and stared at the headline, which read, BEHR'S MAN DEAD IN RIVER. Beneath was a photo of a body lying on a dock. Several policemen seemed to be examining it. The caption stated that early Sunday evening several men just heading back from a day of sport fishing had spotted the body of a man later identified as Larry Carlacci floating in the Hudson. They had returned to port with it and notified the police.

Ralph read the article in shock and sat back to think. Larry's wallet was on him, so robbery was not considered a motive. Could he have been contemplating suicide? Is that why Larry wanted so urgently to speak to him? Ralph could not be sure, but he prided himself on having a pretty good feel for people, and everything he knew about Larry Carlacci told him that the engineer would not have killed himself.

Phone calls from the press began lighting up the telephone console a few minutes later. Ralph stopped answering the phone until Myra arrived to tell them that Mr. Behr was too upset by Mr. Carlacci's death to make a personal statement.

Simon too was distressed at the news. He heard it on the small TV set in his limousine while traveling to his office that morning. He worriedly telephoned the deputy mayor as soon as he arrived there. He himself, he admitted, had met with the dead man only three days earlier about some minor matters and afterward had even offered to drive him down to the construction site, but the man had changed his mind just as they were about to enter the limousine. A flood of campaign publicity had already linked the mayor firmly to Behr Center. Simon expressed his thoughts on how best to position the mayor to keep him above any consequences that might ensue from Carlacci's death while, at the same time, gaining the mayor's help in dealing with them.

Then he phoned Jeff Behr at his apartment.

Gail had been the first telephone caller to whom Ralph had agreed to speak. She had met the dead man while touring Behr Center with Ralph and had felt a kinship with his quick, peppery manner. She too found it doubtful that a man like that would kill himself.

"He mentioned a wife," she remembered. "I think she might appreciate a visit tonight."

They agreed Gail would meet Ralph at his office at five.

Immediately after he hung up, Myra announced that a police detective was outside to see him.

The man who entered was about thirty years old, but premature baldness caused him to look older. His build was broad and muscular, with the beginning of a paunch leaning over his belt. His brown suit was open in front and shiny in spots from overuse. He carried a notepad.

"Don Connolly," he introduced himself. "Police." He flashed his badge and, flipping the wallet closed, dropped it back into his pocket. "Great view," he observed, glancing at the city spread out beyond the glass curtain wall. "Do you mind if I ask a few questions about Larry Carlacci?"

"No." Ralph motioned for him to take a seat on the other side of the desk.

Ralph confirmed that Larry worked for him and what his

function was and what he thought of him. The last time he saw him was last Tuesday at the weekly project meeting for Behr Center. They had spoken by phone Wednesday or Thursday. Nothing unusual. The man had not seemed depressed. What was unusual, however, was that Larry had tried hard to reach him Friday by phone, but they had never made contact. He had no idea what might have been on Larry's mind.

"Why weren't you able to speak to him on Friday?"

"I was away and couldn't reach him when I got his message."

"Where were you?"

Ralph told him. Noticing a slight reticence about providing the information, Connolly asked if anyone could confirm his whereabouts. Reluctant to reveal that he had been away with Amanda, Ralph withheld the names of the pilots who had flown him to Providenciales, but gave the name of the government official who had invited him. Connolly already knew about Carlacci's phone call.

"Your secretary says she transferred the call from your line to your brother's. Did he tell you what Carlacci wanted to speak to you about?"

"Jeff was out when I called in that day, and we haven't had a chance to speak since. This morning his secretary told me he would be coming in late. Let's see if he's here yet."

Unlike the others, Jeff had felt a mixture of relief and opportunity when Simon Kramer's early-morning phone call informed him at home about Larry Carlacci's death. Admitting fear of uncertain repercussions to both of them, Simon intimated that he would keep to himself Jeff's involvement in the whorehouse in return for Jeff keeping to *himself* the dispute they had had with Carlacci. Jeff gladly agreed, asserting what he believed—that the engineer must have been insane to have been so insistent about holding up construction without any hard evidence to substantiate his panic.

"You know," Simon asserted, "I never did drive him downtown that day."

Jeff merely said good-bye. Inwardly, he felt increasingly confident that everything would work out as his father had planned; and soon neither Simon nor Ralph would have the weapon of that damned whorehouse brownstone with which to intimidate him.

Even so, he experienced a terrible shock when the door to his office opened and Ralph announced that a police detective

378

wanted to speak to him about Larry Carlacci's death. He hid his nervousness beneath a portrayal of candor.

"Larry went over with me to Simon Kramer's office, in case any construction matters came up at the meeting, but he didn't mention anything unusual. He was kind of quiet, as a matter of fact, and we separated right after the meeting. We didn't even take the same elevator."

Connolly was persistent. "You're sure he said nothing suspicious or unusual. Nothing that might indicate he was considering suicide or that he feared something or someone."

Jeff shook his head after taking a moment to appear to be mulling over the question. "Nothing. I wish I could help. I really liked the guy. But I can't think of anything."

Connolly continued to ask questions, but drew nothing more from Jeff. After the police detective left, Jeff placed in his briefcase several files full of agreements he would need. He locked the briefcase and placed it just inside his office doorway before he went into his brother's office. Ralph was engaged in a phone conversation with a broker. Jeff waited, but did not take a seat.

"What a horrible thing about Larry!" Ralph remarked as soon as he ended the call. "How'd it go with the policeman?"

"I told him what I knew, which wasn't much." Jeff still did not take a seat.

"Larry never mentioned to you what the urgent matter was he wanted to talk to me about?"

Jeff shook his head.

"Did he seem depressed to you or frightened about something?"

"No. I couldn't believe it when I read this morning that they found him floating in the river."

Ralph shook his head. "What would have driven him to do something like that?" He reflected for a moment, then spoke again. "I hate to bring it up so soon after Larry's death, but this means you're going to have to take over his responsibilities until we can find another construction rep."

"Ralph, this is probably as good a time as any to tell you I'm leaving you."

"What is it now? You want more money again. Did I insult you or something? Otherwise, this is a lousy time to joke around."

"I'm serious. I'm leaving. And I'm taking the East Side assemblage with me."

"You're what?" Ralph was more incredulous than shocked.

"I'm taking the assemblage. It's in my name. I control all the stock."

"You were buying up the parcels for me."

"That isn't how it looks on paper. I'm the sole stockholder of the corporation at the end of the chain of dummy companies and nominees."

That Jeff really did intend to keep the properties was finally beginning to sink into Ralph's consciousness. Worried that he might become overextended, Metrobank had insisted on a clause in the Behr Center loan agreement that restricted Ralph from buying additional properties without the bank's approval until Behr Center projected a profit on the basis of firm leases. For that reason Ralph had kept the accumulating assemblage in Jeff's name. He leaned forward, his face apparently calm, but his eyes explosive with anger.

"You and I both know you were buying for me. With my money. You were supposed to sign the properties back over to me when the restriction was lifted."

"Legally, I own that property."

"I've got ten million dollars of my own money invested, and I personally guaranteed a twenty-million-dollar bank loan on them."

"I figure you owe me at least ten million dollars for the years of keeping me from going into business for myself. As soon as I get a new money partner, you'll be off the hook on the guarantee. Look at it this way: you're finally being forced to finance me, like you were always obligated to do after Dad financed you."

"I could go to court and prove you were acting on my behalf."

"But you won't. You're too good a brother." Smiling, Jeff reached for the doorknob. "And you can't afford to give Metrobank an out on the financing for Behr Center. I want you to know I appreciate it, Ralph."

Jeff hurried from his brother's office, his legs so weak they could barely support him. He scooped up his briefcase without stopping and was out the front door and in an elevator only seconds later.

Seething, Ralph stared at the door for a long while. He had always thought of Jeff as a kid, but his brother had just double-crossed him with the finesse of the shrewdest of adults. He had trusted Jeff utterly. His brother's casual disloyalty distressed him far more deeply than the monetary loss.

He dialed his father's Jersey Shore house. The phone rang several times before Henry picked up.

"Dad! Were you working out in the backyard?"

"I'm too busy to sit around a yard. It's early for you to be calling. What's up?"

Ralph related what had just occurred. He heard a quiet chuckle when he finished and then his father's voice again.

"The boy seems to have touched all the bases."

"He just stole ten million dollars and a loan for twenty more."

"Well, you promised me you'd finance him."

"In his *own* project. Up to a reasonable amount, like you did me. When he was ready."

Henry chuckled again. "Sounds plenty ready to me."

"I'm beginning to get the feeling you approve of what he did."

"It seems to me it was his to take. You put the property in his name. You owed him a start in life. You—"

Ralph heard something more than admiration for Jeff in his father's voice and asked sharply, "Are you involved with him in this?"

"Just keeping my hand in—for a rooting interest."

Ralph slowly lowered the receiver to the cradle. Even when he discovered his father's duplicity regarding Hampshire Gardens, Ralph had not broken with him, telling himself that his father was a jungle fighter who had naturally put his own and his family's welfare first. He had continued to love his father despite his new knowledge of how badly his father behaved toward others. Now, by conspiring with Jeff to bilk him, his father had betrayed him as well. That act, Ralph realized, was the culmination of the competitive resentment his father had always harbored and of the manipulation with which his father had used him all of Ralph's life: Henry Behr was incapable of unselfish love.

Ralph had always felt a deep obligation to his father for undertaking the risk of financing him in business, but Gail had been right: Ralph had been backed, not out of fatherly devotion, but as if he had been a fast racehorse too headstrong to be held back. Only once before had Henry needed to lie and scheme to obtain something from Ralph—when he sought the latter's cooperation for the marriage and divorce arrangement that would keep him out of prison. Then he had swindled Ralph out of a hundred million dollars. This time, with Jeff's help, he had swindled thirty million. No wonder he had expressed admiration for Jeff. His younger son, who had never challenged his ego, was created more in his father's image than Ralph had ever been.

Despite the anger derived from betrayal and monetary loss,

Ralph knew he would not fight to regain what they had stolen from him. Perhaps he did owe something, as they said. But if he did, he had just paid it many times over. His ties to both men were now irrevocably severed.

Neither Henry nor Jeff possessed sufficient capital to pay the high cost of carrying their new property until construction began— the interest and taxes on the land, the architectural and legal fees required to take them through the statutory approval process. Moreover, the ten million dollars invested in the land would probably be considered insufficient equity by any bank willing to finance construction. But Henry had glimpsed an opportunity to turn the tables when he heard how Jeff had been blackmailed by Simon Kramer, recognizing that Simon himself was now vulnerable to their own threats.

The following day, when Simon, Jeff, and he met, Henry hardly had to touch on that point after outlining the favorable deal he had structured. With Simon taking on the role of money and construction partner, a three-way arrangement was quickly agreed upon.

A few days later, after performing the autopsy, the city's acting chief medical examiner issued a report that confirmed what seemed apparent: that Larry Carlacci's death resulted from drowning and appeared to be self-inflicted.

Ralph and Gail had visited the widow and her young son soon after hearing about her husband's death. Expressing their sympathy, Ralph had committed himself to continuing to pay her husband's salary. But, disturbed by the medical examiner's finding, Ralph went with Gail to the funeral home in Queens to talk to Maria Carlacci again the night the body was released. She was tall, unlike her husband, but she possessed some of his toughness. She too did not believe that her husband would have killed himself. She was grateful and relieved when Ralph offered to have independent pathologists perform an autopsy on her husband's body.

"Somebody killed him," she averred. "Larry wasn't the kind who could rest easy if someone got away with it."

They conversed for several minutes, and when she left their company to comfort Larry's mother, Gail asked Ralph why he was doing this.

"He worked for me. Somebody should."

Gail would have said something, but a large, balding man stepped up to them. Ralph introduced Don Connolly.

"How's the investigation going?" Ralph asked.

The detective looked away. "The investigation ended when the medical report came out. Suicide. End of investigation."

"Why are you here?" Gail asked.

"Last-ditch hope, I guess, that I'll spot someone."

"Then you don't believe it either," Ralph observed.

Connolly's manner grew more combative. "The guy just wasn't the suicide type. He was outgoing, successful in his career, happy home life. He was meticulous about details, but he didn't leave a note. He didn't even have a will. Nothing points to suicide but the drowning."

"Join the group."

"The captain wouldn't listen to me, so I called a friend who's pretty high up at headquarters. He told me point blank to drop it."

"What if you kept going on your own? I'd pay for your time."

"It's not the money."

"Orders?"

Connolly shook his head. "A police department that covered up something like this wouldn't be worth working for. No, I just don't have a lead."

Ralph revealed that he was arranging for another autopsy. Connolly's expression grew more optimistic.

"You get me something firm that differs from the acting medical examiner's report, and I'll be back on the street on this thing, regardless of what the brass say."

Ralph did not notice Max Borah watching him from across the room as he and Gail took their leave of the bereaved. Max was far more interested in observing the Behrs than in being observed himself. His curiosity about Ralph had collapsed after the debacle in Sun Valley, although he occasionally mused on the odd fact that Ralph Behr, who seemed so keen on establishing himself in the upper-class equine set, had suddenly married a woman whose father had just finished serving a twenty-year prison sentence. But the front-page news about the structural engineer disappearing from Behr Center in the middle of a workday and turning up dead in the river two days later had rekindled his mistrust of Ralph Behr. Something incriminating was out there, Max was now convinced, something Ralph Behr was trying to hide. Every journalistic instinct shouted to him that he was onto a big story.

Chapter 21

"Where are you off to?" Ralph asked Gail as she ducked into the breakfast room for a cup of coffee. He was dawdling over the newspapers, trying to figure out what to do with his Saturday.

"A couple of errands, for a start. There's a street fair. You?"

He shrugged.

"Amanda leave early?" she asked. He had spent the last three weekends with her in Connecticut.

"A friend's party this weekend in San Francisco. In a few days she'll fly directly to Europe. Want some company?"

"If you don't think she'd object."

"What's that supposed to mean?"

"Don't you think she gets a little jealous when you have to spend time with me?"

Why do I deliberately provoke him? she castigated herself. No wonder he's in love with Amanda. She's never bitchy and always says exactly the right thing. Gail recalled promising herself after Milo left that she would never again suppress her true feelings simply to ingratiate herself with a man. She was certainly making good on that vow with a vengeance. Well, if Ralph didn't like her as she was, that was his loss.

"You're being unfair," he maintained. "She just thought people wouldn't get suspicious—they'd think it was natural—if we spent less time together the closer you and I got to announcing a divorce."

"I can understand her being jealous," Gail found herself continuing blithely. "What bothers me is that you've let it interfere with our friendship."

"Tell you what—we can spend the whole day together." He motioned toward the newspapers. "We can go to that street fair. Tonight a show, maybe. Anything you want."

"I'm supposed to meet my father later. And I wanted to take a look at how the rehab's going on the new shelter."

He stood up. "Great. We'll do it together."

384

In one continuous motion, she took a last, fast sip of coffee, put down the cup, and slipped her arm through Ralph's. "We haven't had a day together in months."

Amsterdam Avenue was a long strait, with tides of pedestrians flowing up and back within banks formed by collectors hawking old bric-a-brac; racks of discount and antique dresses and bins of socks and cosmetics for sale; portable stoves turning out varieties of fast food either cooked by adjacent restaurants or native to the homelands of families busily scooping it onto paper plates; old record and photo collections; block-association bake sales; hot-dog, beer, and soda stands; deep fryers browning dripped dough for funnel cake; and rock bands and comedy groups on a mobile stage.

To a large degree the floppy hats and sunglasses with which Ralph and Gail topped their jeans and sport shirts hid their skin from the hot sun and their identities from others. Although the populist nature of the fair and the liberal West Side locale served to retard inquiries, Gail would occasionally be annoyed by some-one staring at them, as she always was, but she broke into laughter when she found herself pointing out a well-known actor who was strolling by.

Gail bought a plate of vegetable sushi, Ralph a hamburger. As they moved on, her eye was caught by antique silver combs and by a pocket watch she thought her father would like. She asked their price, but found them too expensive.

"Trust me," he assured her, "you can afford them."

She hesitated. "The watch, maybe."

"My treat." He took out his wallet, but she put her hand over it and turned back to the woman at the center of the rectangle of display cases.

"How much will you take for the watch alone?" she asked.

"Three hundred and fifty. And believe me, lady, it's a bargain."

"I'll give you a hundred and twenty-five if I get a guarantee with it."

The woman appeared stunned. "A hundred and a quarter? Forget it. Buy yourself a Timex."

"Okay then, what'll you take?"

"I don't bargain. That's the price."

"For tourists," Gail scoffed. "How much for someone who doesn't have hay in her hair?"

"All right, I shouldn't really do this. Three hundred. That's my best price."

"Two hundred."

The woman checked the code on the tag. "Two fifty."

"Two and a quarter with the guarantee."

The woman nodded. "I'll gift wrap it."

As she did, Gail proudly remarked to Ralph that she might just be learning how to deal with the thousands and millions with which he daily bargained, but she was pretty good with money in the normal ranges. "You ought to see me save money at the supermarket." Her brow tightened. "I can't remember the last time I was in a supermarket."

Continuing to weave around others as they ambled down Amsterdam, Gail was lost in thought, "I think I just don't want to acknowledge," she finally said unhappily, "that I really *have* been separated from my old friends. But I'm not in the least bit comfortable with rich people either."

"People are all the same underneath."

"They're not. They care about different things. They have to."

"And you're just not materialistic like the rich."

Her face took on a troubled look. "What I've learned is that the poor and middle class are the materialistic ones. They want the material things they don't have. The rich, who have it all and could do anything with their lives, just spend their lives protecting themselves."

"So, the angry little girl from Brooklyn no longer knows who she's supposed to be angry at?"

Gail nodded. "Except you."

"Why me?"

Embers of indignation began to glimmer behind her eyes. "Because I'm tired of being angry at myself for not fitting in anywhere anymore. Because your money and our marriage caused it." She turned to face him, her ire growing. "Because you keep running after Amanda and her family like they were the Good Housekeeping seal of approval on your life. Because, for all your brains, you can't see what's in front of your face. And because you'll still be my friend after I'm over my anger. Or am I assuming too much?"

He put his hands on her shoulders. "This thing still really bothers you."

Gail threw up her hands in exasperation and strode away. A few steps later she turned and waited for him to catch up.

"You left your hamburger back there," she noted and held out her plate. "Want to try my sushi?"

Ralph grimaced. He gestured at a jungle of green plants at the end of the block. "I'll buy you a tree for your new office."

A tall, smiling man and a short, affable woman sold Ralph a yucca plant. They tagged it with Gail's name, and from the corner, Ralph phoned his chauffeur with directions where to pick it up.

As he hung up the phone, a gaunt woman in her late thirties beckoned to him from behind the bridge table at which she sat with a stack of petitions she intended to present to the mayor and city council. The smallness of her breasts was emphasized by a very tight white T-shirt that read Low-Rise Is Beautiful.

"We want the city to declare the West Side a historic zone and put an end to development."

"I'm all for that!" Ralph proclaimed enthusiastically. "Where do I sign? Damned developers mucking up our slums!"

"Ralph!" Gail hissed at him in embarrassment.

His mouth curled in derision at Gail. "Running dog of the American imperialists!"

He picked up the pen. Carefully, at the top of the petition, he signed, "Simon Kramer."

They walked the few blocks to the building where her father lived. Gail offered a few ideas on how the three of them could spend the rest of the day, but Ralph knew exactly what he wanted to do: to have Abe Weintraub give them a tour of the Lower East Side he knew as a boy.

They started on Delancey Street, where the shirt store used to be, and strolled without plan through the area. Abe remembered it had been dirty and crowded—his parents were proud when they were able to move their residence to the then-burgeoning Bronx. But he also remembered the Lower East Side as being exciting: streets lined with pushcarts full of goods, kids playing games on the sidewalks, prostitutes on the steps of the buildings they worked out of.

Abe chuckled. "My mother used to tell me the women were just very friendly, but the other kids told me what they did. She had no respect for those women. Your grandmother was a different story."

"What do you mean?" Ralph asked, his tone bristling.

"My mother admired her for not selling herself cheap. A Jewish girl didn't have many options in those days. Look, maybe you'd rather not hear about this."

"Go on."

"She said your grandmother had been one of the grandest of

the kept women in New York. A real beauty. Very elegant. Your grandfather was insane about her. He was in synagogue one holiday with my father when he saw her and asked who she was. My father's friend told him how she made a living."

Ralph's teeth were set on edge, his gaze furious. "You're mistaken. My grandmother came from an old Boston family."

Abe retreated under the barrage of Ralph's tone. "This is all ancient history."

"My father always told me his mother was from a wealthy old-line Yankee family," Ralph repeated.

"Maybe he didn't know," Abe said quietly.

"How can you be so sure about her?" Ralph queried belligerently. He had constructed much of his sense of self and of his destiny from the Behr family history as recounted by his father.

"Because women from old-line Yankee families don't speak perfect Yiddish."

"You heard her?"

"To my mother at my bar mitzvah. She thought no one could overhear them."

Ralph's gaze tilted upward. He stared at the sky without seeing it, what remained of his belief about who he was and where he came from, his heritage as the foundation and guarantor of his irresistible future, struck down like paper stage-sets.

"How do I know you're not lying about all this?" Ralph muttered.

"*You* were the one who wanted to come down here and ask me about the old days."

If his father's duplicity had not so recently been manifested to him, he might have doubted Abe Weintraub more strongly. Ralph slowly lowered his gaze to Abe's. "She was Jewish?"

Abe nodded. "From Russia. She came here when she was young. The people down here knew all that about her. I imagine the rich Christians she ran with didn't. Eventually, both she and your grandfather became Christians. But, funny—" He paused, musing. "I was at your grandfather's funeral. He left a note asking that the funeral service be the same kind of Jewish service he remembered when he was a boy. My mother had a friend who was from Salonika, where your grandfather came from—"

"He was from France," Ralph corrected him firmly.

"If France is in Greece," Abe rejoined gently, "then he was from France. She found a Sephardic synagogue started by Jews from Salonika and Turkey. It was in an upstairs room somewhere in the Bronx, near an el, with Turkish carpets on the floors and people wailing like Arabs when they prayed."

"Damn!" Ralph said. "I didn't know . . . well, I didn't know very much of this. Only that he was originally Jewish, but not much more. Look, even if he was Jewish and born where you say, he had converted to Christianity. Why would . . ." Ralph's voice trailed off as he ruminated.

"If you want to know why your grandfather would want a Jewish funeral . . ." Abe offered.

Ralph's head snapped up. "Yes."

"Ecclesiastes says, 'Unto the place from whence the rivers come, hither they return again.' My thought is: with death facing him, he realized who he was and that all his pretentions to being anything else had just been vanity."

Ralph looked down the narrow street that intersected at the corner. He could almost see in his mind's eye the bustling crowds of immigrant Jews long-gone who had once filled the buildings and the streets and the shops: men in yarmulkes and derbies, women in high-necked, long-skirted dresses, children in knickers and pigtails bursting out of the dark tenements into the sunlight, entranced with the freedom of this new land. Today, Saturday, was the Sabbath down here. Tomorrow their grandchildren and newer immigrants would staff the stores, and the streets once more would be packed with crowds, this time seeking bargains on lingerie, designer clothing, luggage, and linens. But now the streets were silent, expectant, recollective. Ralph could sense the ghosts.

As it once had to Raphael, it came also now to Ralph that he somehow shared with the Jews who had struggled to reach and then to transcend this neighborhood a common culture and values passed down by generations of Jews, by Raphael and Sally, that had endowed them with the strength to brave the journey here. They knew no one. Few could even speak the language. And yet they strove and succeeded. One of their beliefs, Ralph mused, was that life rewarded virtues like honoring one's father. In that regard he had fulfilled the mandate of his Jewish heritage. In contrast, his father had treated that blind loyalty as gullibility, exploitable when expedient. Who had set his father *that* example—those same names from the past—Raphael and Sally—who had abandoned their Jewish identities?

After dropping her father off in a cab which then headed east to transport them home to change for dinner and the theater, Gail asked Ralph whether he felt saddened or disillusioned by what he had learned about his grandmother's true background and his grandfather's original homeland.

"At first, I felt like a kid who's had his candy stolen. But then I realized that if they *had* been accepted where they came from, they never would have put themselves through hell to travel here. They came because of the opportunities, believing that they could do anything here if they tried hard enough, even make themselves into brand-new people. That's probably where a lot of my determination to succeed comes from. It makes me feel kind of proud. My grandparents did whatever they had to do to make their way up and out of there."

"They couldn't change the important things about themselves. That's what my father seemed to think."

Ralph nodded. "And maybe it took them a long while to understand what was important and what wasn't." He reflected for a long while before continuing. "I don't feel more Jewish or less Christian now than before. What I really feel is richer, in a way I hadn't expected."

Within minutes after they arrived home, Amanda telephoned from La Guardia Airport. When she had spoken to him early that morning from San Francisco, he had had no plans for the weekend and joked that he wanted her to jump on the next returning plane so they could spend a few days together before she was scheduled to join her parents in Europe. She became so lonely for him after she hung up that she apologized to her hostess and hurried back to New York, desperate to see him. She called to let him know she was on her way, but he had already left the apartment.

"I sort of promised Gail she and I'd go to dinner and a show," Ralph tried to explain.

Amanda made no reply.

"I told her I would do something with her because I was free."

"And now you're not," Amanda reminded him firmly. "I just changed my plans and traveled all the way back across the country because you said you wanted to be with me."

Ralph was silent.

"I'm sure you feel obligated to her—you're very good about that," Amanda pressed him, "but you and I love each other, and I'm going to Europe in a few days. Seeing you tonight is not an unreasonable request for a fiancée to make."

Ralph put his hand over the mouthpiece and explained his predicament to Gail. "I hope you understand," he told her.

"Sure," Gail responded cheerfully. "Don't give it a second thought."

Ralph smiled. "Thanks."

He turned back to the receiver and made arrangements to pick up Amanda at the airport. Gail strode down the hall to her bedroom. She shut the door, removed her shoes, and threw them, one after the other, as hard as she could at her bed.

Ralph and Amanda stopped for dinner on their way up to the country. While they were awaiting their entrees, she mentioned that they could go right to his place afterward because she certainly had enough clothing with her. Before he had even thought out what he was saying, Ralph replied that they couldn't. A water pipe in the house had burst and, besides, his back problem had returned. Neither was true, and he was almost aghast at his own mendacity but, on consideration, he recognized his ambivalence about his relationship with Amanda. He loved her, to be sure, but the day had prompted awareness that he certainly felt something for Gail as well. Until he worked out his feelings fully, he did not want to engage in the kind of intimacy that Amanda had a right to believe confirmed his commitment to her.

Discerning his detachment, Amanda increased her effort to engage him in conversation throughout dinner and the drive to her family's Connecticut estate. He soon found himself amused and interested in her recounting of her San Francisco visit and the gossip about people they both knew socially. She asked Ralph to stop at the main house and come in with her. Although her parents were away, she wanted to let her grandmother know she was back.

Nina was alone in the study, seated at the desk, reviewing papers. In the days since her husband's illness, effective control of the bank had finally passed to Charles, who now had the power to back up the authority he had always appeared to exercise there. Leadership of the family and control of much of its resources had passed to Nina.

She rose immediately upon seeing her granddaughter and Ralph. A wide, spontaneous smile spread across her face.

"How's grandfather?" Amanda asked dutifully.

"Doing very well."

"I've felt so guilty since he got sick," Amanda admitted. "I keep thinking that what I said to him might have had something to do with his condition."

Nina touched her granddaughter's arm comfortingly. "You had nothing to do with it. The doctor said it was like a fuse. Eventually, the fuse ran out and the little blood vessel in his brain exploded. None of us has anything to reproach ourselves about."

"I wanted so for him to approve of my marriage to Ralph."

"I'm sure he does," Nina assured her.

"You really think so?"

"I'm sure of it. Why don't we go and ask him ourselves?"

Amanda was surprised. "Is he well enough?"

"Of course."

"Let's not bother him," Ralph objected, not sure in his own mind about the marriage that seemed now to have taken on a momentum of its own. "We have plenty of time to discuss it with him."

"No time like the present," Nina chirped. Ralph was surprised by the unlikely hospitality in her manner.

She led the way upstairs. Otis's bedroom was at the end of the hall. As soon as she opened the door, medical equipment and a nurse were visible within. Otis lay on a hospital bed, a respirator straddling his chest.

"Otis, you have company," Nina announced brightly. "It's Amanda, and she's brought Ralph. They're getting married. You remember—Amanda told you all about their marriage plans, and you and Ralph had that talk together at the club. Since his stroke," she confided to the others, "I'm really the only one who can understand what he's trying to say." She leaned over Otis's bed. "You don't object to their marrying, do you?"

She sensed Otis could hear and comprehend everything, but he could not move a single muscle in his body, not even his eyelids, preventing all communication. The hatred she thought she descried at the bottom of his eyes was matched only by her own, no longer fearing retaliation. She straightened up, grinning. "He tells me he's delighted, just delighted for you two. You have his blessing."

Amanda broke into a smile. "I was so worried."

Nina embraced her granddaughter. "Just when you think they can't possibly, things suddenly change in the least expected ways."

As she was bidding them goodnight, Nina asked offhandedly after Ralph's family and then added with a subtly arch finality. "I recall once having known your father. That was a long time ago."

As they parted from her and descended the stairs, Amanda told Ralph that she had always felt great sympathy for her grandmother because she hadn't had an easy life with Grandpa.

Ralph was struck by the strangeness of listening to his fiancée unknowingly comment on the sadness of the life chosen by the mother who had rejected him. What had been amiss, he decided, was not the life or the man Nina had chosen, but her values that had dictated those choices.

Amanda too was occupied by her thoughts. She pulled him into a drawing room to declare her unhappiness at having to wait some eighteen months to two years to marry him, until after the conclusion of all the legalities and court approvals of the divorce he and Gail would not announce for another year.

"Simply separate now," she asserted with what seemed to her to be perfect logic, "and we can get married next year."

"I've told you I have to wait another year."

"Why? You've never told me that."

"So there can be no doubt the marriage was legal."

Amanda shook her head definitively. "No judge would question anyone after a full year's worth of unhappiness." Her voice conveyed certainty that such a period would be ajudicated endless agony.

They debated for nearly half an hour with no resolution, Amanda trying to persuade him to announce his divorce immediately, so they could marry sooner. Unsure of his feelings, Ralph continued to maintain that he could not.

Ralph was gloomy as he drove back to New York City. He came upon Gail reading in the breakfast room.

"How was the show?" he asked. He had left the theater tickets for her when he withdrew to join Amanda for the evening.

"I didn't go."

"Those tickets cost a hundred and fifty apiece to buy at the last minute. Did you at least give them away?"

"A couple of bag ladies needed a place to stay for the night."

"Come on."

"They're on your bureau." She paused. "How was your evening with the aging debutante?"

Ralph's mouth tightened. "Amanda and I had a nice evening."

"Oh, good. What did you talk about?" Gail fixed on him attentively, as if the topic were supremely fascinating.

"What we've been doing. You know, the usual stuff. Some funny stories about her friends."

"Good old Muffy and Buffy and the gang? Sounds absorbing. I'm surprised you came home."

"I left Amanda at her family's Connecticut place. Something's bothering you."

"I thought Otis didn't want you hanging around."

"As a matter of fact," Ralph responded defensively, "he's now very pleased that I'm dating his granddaughter."

"Probably can't wait to sit down and break matzoh with you."

Ralph threw up his hands. "All right, let's have it out here and now. You and I had a wonderful afternoon together. You were terrific, easy to get along with, just the way it was before we came back from Sun Valley. Now, suddenly, with no warning, you're being sarcastic again, and I haven't done a thing to stir you up. Are you on the rag or something?"

Gail exploded. "Is that ever typical! The rag! As if a woman's normal biology was somehow dirty and had to be wiped up. Any show of honest anger or emotion by a woman upsets you. Your very 'manly' thought is that it was provoked by my hormones and not by your incredibly thoughtless behavior."

"What the hell have I done except shell out to you half of every last dollar I own—one hundred million of them—and try my best to be civil?"

Gail's hands were on her hips. "Aha!" she exclaimed, flinging her head up. "Back to money again! Oh, is Amanda Brookhouse ever just perfect for you! No doubt about what *she's* worth on the open market. U.S.-government-inspected, blue-blood rich. So cool she probably uses ice cubes under her arms instead of deodorant. Doesn't make scenes. Will look great in society magazine photos. Good bones, so the looks will be there a long time. And she has you around her little finger. Give me one good reason—one emotional, human reason—why you should keep running after her."

Ralph was steaming. "I don't know how this conversation got around to Amanda and how my relationship with her suddenly became your concern, but she happens to be a compassionate and loving human being."

"Who told you that—her accountant? You're so smart in business and so ignorant when it comes to people. Once you think someone loves you, you ascribe all sorts of undeserved qualities to them."

"Like my father, you mean?"

"I mean Amanda. Everything that attracts you about her is on

394

the outside, like you ran up a balance sheet of her assets. You're blind!"

Ralph was nearly out of control. "Look who's giving me advice on understanding people and love—the woman who married one of the world's great skunks and is still worried that he might not be a happy camper out in L.A."

"I have no illusions about Milo. But I ought to buy you a white cane. You can't see what's really good for you."

"That's very funny coming from the woman I was forced to marry."

Brought up short, Gail's voice was softer. "You're too dazzled by the Brookhouse name and her baby blue eyes to know it, but marrying me was the luckiest thing that ever happened to you."

Ralph's exasperation had reached its farthest limit. "Just tell me one single reason that marrying you was lucky."

"Just for starters, if you didn't have to stay married to me for another year, Amanda would already be dragging you to the altar by that ring she's got through your nose."

"Nobody tells me what to do. I *want* to marry Amanda. As a matter of fact I want to marry Amanda as soon as I can. If I could get married to her this minute, nothing would please me more."

"Did she give you permission to say that?"

"That's it! I've taken everything from you I'm going to, and that's it! I want that divorce now!"

"What?" Gail was stunned.

"I want the divorce now. I love Amanda, and I don't want to wait another year to finish off this joke of a marriage!"

"But we always said two years. We agreed to that."

Ralph too was shocked by what he had just blurted out. He had not intended to ask for a divorce. Invariably poised under trying conditions, he had nonetheless lost control as a result of Gail's provocation. Groping to comprehend the import of what he had said, he was uncharacteristically subdued when he spoke next. "When a marriage partner wants a divorce, the marriage ends. That's what divorce is."

"If it's what you want."

His tone turned belligerent again. "I wouldn't have said it if I didn't want it. Regardless of what you think, nobody tells me what to do."

For a moment Gail could not respond. Then she shouted out, "No! No way I'm going to let you jeopardize me with a divorce before the two years are up! Over my dead body!"

She spun around and ran toward her room.

"We'll see about that!" Ralph yelled after her. "You were sleeping with Milo when you were married to me, and I can prove it in court. Don't try to deny it!"

She stopped at her door. "What about you? What about you and Little Miss Muffet? The nights you came home at three in the morning. The weekends you stayed away. No judge is going to sympathize with a husband who treats his wife so shamefully."

"This is going to get very messy."

"That's not *my* problem. I don't have the majestic Brookhouse name to protect. My father was a convict, remember? I'm just an ordinary American woman you happened to marry on the spur of the moment and then discarded when someone better came along." Gail bit her lip. "How could you treat me like this after all that this marriage has put me through? I've been trying so hard to be a good wife to you."

Ralph was indignant. "*You? You?* Nobody could have worked harder to make this marriage a good one than I did. But things change. People's needs change."

"And now you can't bear to be separated from Amanda for a moment longer," she finished for him.

"She's been asking me to join her and her folks in France. I just may do that."

"I can see it now. A great cultural excursion—touring the great dresses and handbags of Europe."

Ralph felt his good nature provoked past the limit of tolerance. "And I want to be seen there in public with her . . . and have the news out by then about my divorce."

Gail slammed the door behind her.

Later, she knocked on the door between their bedrooms and called out, "You can have your divorce if you really want it."

"I said I did," he called back.

"I'll talk to our lawyer about it." She added sadly, "I really thought it was working out well between us."

"For you, maybe. For me it's been unbearable."

She kicked the door. "You son of a bitch!"

Fuck you! she thought. She would not stay together with that bastard one moment longer than was legally necessary to protect her rights.

Early Monday morning, Max Borah entered the Brooklyn court building and began to search the records. Hours passed as he culled one book after another. The room was musty with the

396

smell of old paper, but it was an odor that spurred him on. He took pride in undertaking these enervating treks ordinary reporters avoided. Diligence, persistence, that was how you found the buried treasure, the skulduggery—by digging and digging, even if it took months, until you finally uncovered one odd little anomaly you followed to the next and then the next until you had dug up an entire criminal scheme. Marilyn had provided him with the first clue, and he had just discovered the next.

He lifted the pages to better catch the window light as he read. Henry Behr and Abe Weintraub were partners in business when Weintraub pleaded guilty to fraud and grand larceny. Behr had not been charged.

Max lay the text down to consider the facts he now knew. A year ago, just after Weintraub finished serving his twenty-year sentence, his daughter divorced her husband and married the son of the business partner who had never been charged. And there was no evidence that Ralph and Gail had ever even dated before that.

He sat for a long time and then, after making photocopies of relevant pages, set off for the defrauded bank to try to find old employees who might still remember what had occurred twenty years before.

"No doubt about it," the elder pathologist declared. "He didn't drown. His lungs were clear of water."

"I agree completely," the other confirmed.

The pathologists hired by Ralph to perform an autopsy on Larry Carlacci's body had worked over the weekend to complete it and summoned him first thing Monday morning. They, Ralph, and Don Connolly stood in the hallway outside of the medical-school morgue. The doctors were still in their operating gowns.

"What *did* he die of?" Ralph asked.

"Fibrillation," said the elder physician.

Observing the puzzlement on the laymen's faces, the younger doctor explained, "Sections of the heart beat independently and without the normal rhythm."

Ralph sought further clarification. "Just a lot of wild beating without pushing the blood through, I think you're saying."

The younger pathologist nodded. "He had a history of heart problems. He was operated on as a child to correct a congenital heart defect and had to take quinidine twice a day to control arrythmia—irregular beating. From what we could tell, he hadn't received the second dose that day. Without it his heart went into fibrillation, and he died."

The other doctor spoke up. "What we can't understand is how anyone, particularly someone as experienced as the city's chief medical examiner, could mistake fibrillation for drowning."

"You're sure it was that and not drowning." Ralph needed certainty.

"Would you care to see the tissue sections?"

"No thanks." The thought sent Ralph's stomach wallowing. "But I think they should be kept in a safe."

The doctors nodded. They understood the seriousness of their assessment.

"You'll put all that into a written report?" Connolly asked. He too wanted to be sure.

"It's being typed up now."

Ralph turned to the detective. "I guess you have your case."

Connolly and Ralph left with copies of the autopsy report. Arrangements had been made for the body to be returned to the funeral home for burial. The coffin was to be sealed and buried in a waterproof vault in the ground to keep the body from deteriorating as much as possible, in case another autopsy was called for.

"I'm going right to headquarters and the chief with this," Connolly informed Ralph as soon as they were in the elevator.

"I'll take you down there."

Out on the sidewalk, Ralph headed toward his limousine.

Connolly halted. "Can we leave the trumpets here? This report is hot. I don't want to take the chance of reporters seeing you."

Ralph waved for a cab, and they stepped inside. Staring out of a window, Connolly ruminated for several minutes on what they had learned. Finally, he voiced his thoughts. "A guy who's acting chief medical examiner doesn't do something like this without a damned good reason—not if he wants to be appointed permanently. And soon afterward he was."

"How do we find out the reason?"

"Carlacci's death could be totally unrelated to that project you're building. But with no better connection to go on, I went down there yesterday. You know, they're working around the clock, but a construction site's always looser on weekends. And I learned something. Last Friday morning, before he went up to your office, Larry Carlacci was spotted examining one of the concrete arches with the construction supervisor."

"Charlie Bates?"

"That's the guy. I tried to question this Bates, but he looked frightened out of his wits and clammed up tight."

"Do you know which arch it was?"

Connolly nodded. "Number Three."

"We'll stop there first and take a look."

But when they did, going up as high as they could with a ladder, no blemishes were visible.

Chapter 22

The argument with Ralph impelled Gail into yet another round of deliberation about her future. She felt that she had grown a good deal in the last months, that the shock of Milo's perfidy had forced her to confront the seeds of her drives and defenses. Out of that self-analysis, she believed, had developed a mature understanding of the needs that motivated her and a self-knowledge that would guide her in the future. The dispute with Ralph had been the final impetus toward separation from the vestige of her emotional dependency on a man. She knew now what she was entitled to receive in her relationships with men and the limits of what she should be prepared to give.

This last argument convinced her that the conflict between her and Ralph's characters was irreconcilable, that she and he were a poorer match than even their initial incompatibility could have predicted. She saw now that at the root of their differences—liberal versus conservative, idealist versus materialist, even vegetarian versus carnivore—was the difference in their ethical commitments. She had always been someone with a penetrating ethical sense; she burned with it; it provided her purpose in life. He was a man whose ethics were nearly prehistoric—us against them. He prided himself on tenacious honesty, but it was simplistic, obscuring the fact that his ethics were short-sighted, self-centered, and avaricious when matters of value to him were at stake. She could remember him tiptoeing just this side of arcane legalistic boundaries to outwit the zoning code or the tax code or the rights of his tenants. The means he utilized continuously shifted to meet his ends. "They can't hit a moving target," he had once explained to her. She realized that, grateful for his solicitude after losing Milo, she had fooled herself into believing that Ralph possessed a far deeper empathy and integrity than he really did. Whenever she speculated that he was groping toward embracing more enduring values, he invariably slid back into a puddle of eager superficiality. She foresaw that he was doomed to lead a life that would grow tedious with ceremony and ornaments, an unfulfilled, dissatisfied life among ever-replaceable furnishings. He was settling for the predictable indicia of status because he could not grasp that the immortality he craved and would never achieve was within him.

She had also been forced to think about the money that would be hers as soon as the divorce was declared final. Resorting to a pocket calculator, she broke the figure she would receive into how many loaves of bread it could buy, how much milk for the shelters, how many pairs of stockings and of shoes at a discount store she frequented, how many women's vocational training courses, even how many publicity campaigns for worthy artists. Viewed from every perspective, it was a staggering amount. And she realized that her embarrassment over it, her denial of possessing it, had resulted from ingrained prejudice, not logic. That money provided the power to do almost anything she wanted: put up more women's shelters, print pamphlets and hire lobbyists if she wanted legislation, donate to those desperately needy.

Apart from these inclinations, she recognized as well both the weariness that had finally overtaken her after a lifetime of working for others and appreciation of the miracle of being heiress to her own storehouse of security. Even in her youth, the cash she had received every month from Henry had been modest, something like a government disability payment, and her mother had had to budget it carefully. The small salary she drew from the Coalition's budget had been equally modest, and she had always had to scrimp and barely make do. Those days seemed like a bad dream. She had come to acknowledge that even her original laudable impulse to give away immediately the great bulk of her windfall that she would never need for herself was misguided: money for good worked best over time, persistently. And she had learned from Ralph that one had to act wisely to make it grow, so that it would still be there for one's uses tomorrow.

Her soul-searching having brought an uneasy acceptance of a

future that entailed living alone and for herself and being rich, Gail began to plan that future and the changes in her life.

"I'm really sorry it turned so unpleasant for you." Jeff assumed a sympathetic expression.

What Jeff missed keenly as a result of his break with Ralph were the dinners with Gail he had frequently shared at their apartment. He had telephoned her early Monday morning and invited her to have lunch with him that day near the Coalition's office. Gail had been delighted because she liked Jeff and because the lunch, forcing a break in her usual daily routine, seemed like a good omen coming so soon after she had determined that she would change her life.

Jeff had begun the conversation by communicating his version of the split with Ralph and why he was justified in his actions. He kept to himself the new arrangement with Simon Kramer—no sense revealing that yet, even though it was signed, sealed, and delivered. His discussion of Ralph had inevitably led Gail to reveal her own premature separation from him.

The crush Jeff had developed on Gail during her first spirited clashes with his brother had gradually become reciprocated to some degree by her affectionate, if platonic, regard for him. But sensing her growing attraction to Ralph, he had not revealed the extent of his interest. Now, her imminent divorce and the loneliness she could not quite hide had revived his hope. He asked what she intended for her future.

"I'll start my life fresh. Whatever our differences, Ralph has been good for me in a lot of ways. He made me realize that I was hanging onto Milo those last months, maybe years, more out of fear of being alone than because Milo was returning the love I was giving. I always figured that the more selfless I was the more people would admire me and love me. Milo took advantage of that. There was no equality in my marriage. It was all give and no take. Ralph helped me see that." She paused. "And yet he can't see that his own relationship with Amanda is just as misguided . . . not that I care one way or another for myself whether he marries her."

"Amanda isn't just an empty-headed socialite, you know. She's very smart."

"I know," Gail admitted. "But she isn't right for him either. He could be so much more than he'll ever be with her. The sad thing is that he won't. But that's not my worry."

"Are you sure there isn't just a little bit of attraction to Ralph in this concern for him?"

Gail reflected for a moment on her own attitude. "No," she could honestly assure Jeff. "That's something else I'm over too. Once in a while I get fooled into thinking there's more to him than meets the eye, and then he does something that wakes me up to the truth: he's all surface, all action without purpose. No thanks, I'll take the money and be very glad to run."

Jeff's pulse was racing. "You know, I never could say this before—the circumstances were, well, too tangled—but now that you and Ralph are getting a divorce, I think I can. Would you have any objection to seeing me—going out, I mean?" He added hurriedly, "Look, I mean, I can understand, you've probably had enough of our family to last a dozen lifetimes."

"I'd like to spend more time with you," Gail answered genially. "But I've never dated very much—it seems I've been married all my adult life. Now's my chance to go out and meet new people and do new things. I want to take it very slowly, and wait at least until the divorce comes through."

Jeff responded with a broad smile. "Sure, that makes sense. I'm not trying to rush you or anything."

After dropping Gail off at her office in his new limousine, Jeff sat back to be driven uptown. He felt exhilarated by how well lunch had gone: she had confided in him and reacted warmly to him. She had seemed pleased by his overture although, to be honest, she had made it clear she was seeking to date others as well. But he thought, countering his own pessimism, that she knew no one else, and with the field all to himself, anything could happen between them.

He was tired of all the pointless screwing around he had done in the last year. Gail had character. She was the kind of woman you married, the kind of woman you raised a family with. And he finally had a chance with her. He had straightened his life out. Maggie had been paid off and the whorehouse closed down—Simon could hold nothing over him now. He and Simon and his father were equal partners in a major Manhattan development that would make him a multimillionaire. Like Gail he too was starting out on a great new life.

In a couple of days, he would phone her again, demonstrate his interest in how she was doing, and then ask her out for lunch again. By the time she was ready to begin dating, who knew how close their relationship could become?

* * *

Lunch with Jeff had been nice, liberating in a way. She had always taken on too many commitments to allow time for herself, fearing others would condemn her selfishness, Gail realized as she returned to her desk. But there was so much more to life than work and whether one had a man. Ignoring the messages and pleas beckoning her, Gail picked up the telephone to reduce further the isolation into which she had unwittingly wandered. She was determined to reclaim relationships that she had let lapse since her marriage to Ralph, having allowed her embarrassment over her sudden marriage and wealth to separate her from her friends. Her own discomfort, as much as theirs, had been to blame for her withdrawal, for her becoming dependent on Ralph's company and, thus, blinder to his faults. She dialed Carla's number.

"Hi, how about dinner tonight?" she asked as soon as she recognized the other woman's hello, before Carla could overcome her surprise and say no. Gail named a simple neighborhood restaurant at which they had often met.

A bit nervous, Gail arrived that night well ahead of time. The two women had seen little of each other since Gail had turned the reins of the neighborhood organization over to her. She knew Carla believed the old causes didn't interest Gail the way they once had. Talk was awkward at first, but Gail persevered, and their conversation became increasingly open and intimate. By the end of the evening, Gail was able to divulge that she and Ralph were separating. As she unburdened herself of all his shortcomings, all their differences, Carla came around the table to sit beside her in the booth. Putting her arm around Gail, she conveyed genuine sympathy.

"You sound like your heart is breaking. Deep down I always thought you married him because of the money, but I guess you really did it for love."

Gail was about to protest the other woman's misconception, but she kept silent, thankful for the concern, even if misplaced. She was willing to admit one thing, though. "It was over before it ever really had a chance to be anything."

Ralph professed to be as content as Gail with his decision to seek an immediate divorce and marry Amanda. He and Amanda had spent Sunday in the country together and drove down to the city together on Monday. While Gail and Jeff were having lunch together, Ralph and Amanda were at the Harry Winston firm, putting in an order for them to locate a superb sapphire to match the color of her eyes. She, in turn, surprised him with a gift of diamond cuff links. She was leaving by Concorde the next morning to join her parents in Paris, and she and Ralph spent that night, for the first time, at her small Manhattan apartment, no longer caring about possible gossip spread by the doormen. They made love with a zest they both attributed to regret at their imminent parting. He did not need convincing, Ralph told himself, but if he had, this day and night with Amanda had proven how much more stable and tranquil life with her would be.

As soon as they separated on Tuesday morning, Ralph once more found himself preoccupied with questions that began with Larry Carlacci's death and proceeded logically to his own real-estate development. Larry had not died of a bullet wound or strangulation, but of a natural cause. Why then was his body found in the river? Had the acting medical examiner's diagnosis of drowning been merely a mistake or was it part of a crooked scheme? But why would it be? What could have been so important about a junior-level engineer that an accredited public pathologist would risk his reputation and advancement by mis-attributing the cause of death? The primary matter with which Larry was involved was Behr Center, its structural design and the quality of its construction. When Ralph and Don Connolly had scanned the arch Larry had inspected with Charlie Bates the morning he died, nothing appeared amiss. Yet twice Bates had acted very nervous as he denied any knowledge of a problem.

Ralph had yielded on allowing the mayor's people to under-take the plaza's opening as the formal commencement of the mayor's reelection bid only after Simon had argued that it was the price one had to pay to continue obtaining cooperation from the city. Moreover, Simon pointed out, the event was being held only to signal the completion of the atrium, not the office building—not the tallest building ever erected. That would be the truly important occasion and would be Ralph's alone. Although accession of control over the kickoff event to the mayor not only meant sharing with him credit for Ralph's own conception, it would also involve allowing the mayor's people to engage Lorna's services to plan it. Yet even Ralph had to agree she was excellent at staging such ceremonies and procuring maximum exposure for a project. At last he entered into a signed contract with the mayor's campaign committee.

Ralph and Simon usually met once a week and often spoke on the phone several times each day regarding Behr Center, sometimes heatedly. When Simon phoned that day, Ralph was prepared to air his apprehensions. He did not intend to disclose his knowledge that the cause of death was different from the official one, only that Larry Carlacci had been inspecting the arch with Simon's construction supervisor on the day he died. Ralph wanted to ask what they were looking for.

The opening ceremony was to take place in two days. Having just spoken to the mayor's campaign manager, Simon opened the conversation by mentioning how preparations were going for the event. The latest news was that two award-winning high-school marching bands, with their corps of baton and flag twirlers, were set to perform, as well as a top trapeze act from the circus—the rigging would start going up tomorrow—and Lorna had coaxed the navy into sending a precision flying team overhead. With the escalators now installed and the electricians rushing to make them operational and with scaffolding and the concrete supports being taken down to clear the plaza and the colorful bunting about to be put up and with finishing touches and clean-up being expedited, Simon admitted he was breathing easier about the site's being ready in time.

He added, "I had my doubts that we'd make the date after all the delays we've had."

"By the way," Ralph mentioned casually, "did Larry Carlacci say anything to you about a problem with a concrete arch when he was up at your office the day he disappeared?"

For an instant Simon weighed disclosing that testing was required on the arch. Ralph was a man who understood political necessity and, he was sure, would appreciate the need not to halt construction these last few days, so that the plaza would be ready to kick off the campaign. Stopping now would shatter the mayor's election strategy, embarrassing and alienating a powerful politician who would instantly become a bitter enemy. However, fearing that suspicion regarding Larry Carlacci's death would consequently be drawn to him by the information, Simon rejected disclosure. He need only wait out the next two days, until the campaign ceremony. Once that was over he could test and, if necessary, repair the arch. He could even use the excuse that Ralph's query had gotten him to thinking he ought to check it out.

"Not a word," Kramer replied. "What prompted the question?"

"I heard Larry and your supervisor, Bates, were inspecting one of the arches that morning."

"Just a normal inspection, I suppose," Simon replied.

"Charlie Bates seemed pretty nervous when I asked him about it."

"He's a nervous guy."

Both men dropped the matter, but each was left disquieted by the exchange and more suspicious than usual about the other man.

That afternoon a phone call further disquieted Ralph. Don Connolly was at a pay phone at Kennedy Airport. The connection was poor, and Ralph asked for the number so as to call him right back, but Connolly had no time: his plane for Dallas was about to board. He explained that he had been tagged to be the liaison with the Texas police in the hunt for a Brooklyn cop-killer suspected of having fled to Texas. Even obscured by the static, Connolly's speech still sounded stilted, forced.

"This assignment sounds kind of sudden," Ralph observed.

"It was."

"What did your friend at police headquarters say when you handed him the new autopsy report?"

Connolly paused to listen to the public address system in the background. "They're calling my row. I've got to get going."

"But you did hand him the report."

A long silence ensued. "Yes," Connolly finally answered, and then Ralph heard a click on the line as the detective hung up.

There was no doubt in Ralph's mind that someone high up in the police department had put immense pressure on Connolly and then, to take no chances, was sending him out of town. If the city's law-enforcement authorities could not be trusted, Ralph needed the help of the federal authorities. He had no alternative.

Early the next morning, Ralph traveled to lower Manhattan to convey a confidential copy of the new autopsy report personally to the U.S. attorney, whom he had met once or twice, a man known for his honesty.

The weather for Larry Carlacci's funeral turned out be far nicer than the forecasts had predicted. Morning clouds gave way to sun and a southerly breeze that seemed warmer than the rest of the air as it gamboled across the rectangular field edged by paved paths. The rows of identical white gravestones that proceeded toward the small group of mourners gathered at the open grave imparted to Gail the impression that death was a giant Pac-Man inexorably munching his way to the end of the world. In earlier days she would have derived some pleasure out of

406

communicating that observation to Ralph, but they barely spoke to each other anymore. When they did, the tone was curt and the content limited to essentials.

The priest was an athletic-looking young man who had succeeded in convincing the bishop that death by drowning did not necessarily signify suicide. A mass had been permitted before the cortege had wound its mournful way to the Long Island cemetery and a grave in sanctified ground.

Gail had chosen to attend the funeral because of the sadness she felt for Maria Carlacci, whom she had come to know a bit in recent days, and for their young son. Mother and son stood among relatives, but apart somehow, she detected, separated by their loss from everyone else there, even from the dead man's sobbing mother. She glanced at Ralph, who stood beside and yet separated from Gail herself—not by grief, she realized, but by mutual disinterest. Soon, neither would be forced any longer to participate in the travesty of companionship.

When the service was over, she and Ralph were joined by Larry's employer, Eli Steinman. The three ambled more slowly than the others back to the automobiles. Steinman was in his fifties, of average height, and dressed in a green-checked shirt and blue-striped tie. His pants and jacket matched neither of them nor each other and appeared never to have been pressed. His hair was gray, but he seemed to be a man who probably never noticed that either. The only other person in his firm fully familiar with Behr Center's construction, because he had designed the structure, Steinman was telling Ralph that he had increased his personal surveillance of the structural work's installation since Larry's death.

"But have you looked at the work that was done while Larry was alive?" Ralph wanted to know.

Steinman glanced at him with surprise. "No, Larry was a top man."

"The day he died, he left an urgent message for me. I don't know what was bothering him. He was seen looking at one of the arches with Kramer's construction supervisor just before he went uptown to my office."

"Might be a coincidence, but Larry wasn't the type to cry wolf. You and I have a construction meeting at the office building site at eight tomorrow morning. Afterward, we can take a look at the arch and the rest of the plaza."

"Eight o'clock," Ralph confirmed.

During the drive back to the city, hearing Ralph telephone

Myra to cancel his early appointments and request that Ben Rogovin also attend the morning meeting at the site, Gail grew concerned about the implications.

"You don't think there was something criminal about his death, do you?"

"No," Ralph replied with annoyance. He did not want to expose himself to the argumentativeness into which conversations with her had recently been falling. "And probably nothing's really wrong with the arch. But a lot of little things don't make sense, and a few people seem very eager to hush up something. A problem with that arch could ruin the construction schedule."

"Sorry," she muttered sarcastically.

"Oh, Jesus!" A single word from her was enough now to incense him. "Let's hear it."

"For a moment I really thought you were doing all this out of concern for Maria or maybe to see justice done for Larry. I apologize for ascribing unselfish motives to you. Wouldn't want to give the Behrs a good name."

Staring straight ahead, Ralph extended and crossed his feet, folded his arms and growled, in a stage whisper he wanted to be sure she heard, "The sooner the better."

The early morning sun tinted to gold the pale green glass that already enclosed the first forty floors of the office building at Behr Center. The next thirty floors were exposed steel, which displayed the arrangement of diagonal supports that would buttress the tower's vertical strength. Slanting glass triangles on the narrowing upper part would eventually cover those diagonal members and setbacks, giving the finished building its look of a crystal splinter. Atop the half-finished structure, silhouetted against blue sky like ants and twigs, workmen and a crane that climbed higher after completing every five floors were installing new girders.

"If anyone else had built this building, this complex," admitted Ralph softly to Eli Steinman and Ben Rogovin as they all stared upward, "I'd never forgive myself."

The engineer nodded. "I know what you mean. If I never design anything else in my life . . ." He left the sentence unfinished, but Ralph understood that urge to leave a cry of identity to echo down through the ages.

The three men spent nearly an hour inspecting the office building and conferring with Bill O'Rourke, the head of the company managing the construction, and with executives of the major subcontractors. One of the issues under discussion was some of the design changes requested by the major tenant, the insurance company, in its space. Another was the steelwork subcontractor's contention that it could fasten the diagonal beams more strongly and reliably by adding another rivet. Productive, cooperative, the meeting smoothly advanced toward the end of the agenda. Ralph wished for the hundredth time that events had gone differently and prevented Simon Kramer from levering his way into directing the construction work on the rest of the project, the first part of which, the plaza, was now being readied for tomorrow's ribbon-cutting.

The elevated plaza had been stripped of all the wooden supports that had propped up the poured concrete during curing. Folding seats were being stacked, to be set up as soon as the sweepers had finished clearing dirt and debris from the space. Red, white, and blue bunting was being hung from the railing that now encircled the vast white disk. Wide, similarly colored strips were also being attached to the railing and their other ends to a metal ring in the atrium's center, which would be hoisted by a wire to the junction of the three arches. Trapeze rigging was being erected on one side of the plaza and a giant TV projection screen to enlarge the speakers' faces for the audience on the other. Workmen engaged in other tasks were everywhere else—painting, scraping, assembling, testing, hammering, cleaning.

Several times Ralph halted his progress across the plaza to direct workers on how to handle particular matters. By the time he and Ben Rogovin had reached the edge affixed to the questionable arch, Eli Steinman had already climbed a long ladder from ground level and was inspecting the arch's surface about a foot below the plaza level.

"Look at this," Steinman called out. The other men leaned over the railing, careful not to brush against the wet paint. He gestured with the blade of his pocketknife. "No wonder you didn't notice anything wrong. You can barely see the demarcation line, but a thin layer of concrete has been spread over the surface to patch and hide something."

He began scratching at the new concrete with his pocketknife.

"Hey, you there!" a voice behind Ralph and Rogovin yelled. "You on the ladder! Cut it out!"

A heavyset man with hands curled into fists, a flattened nose, and heavy brow ridges that often must have felt the force of other people's fists was hurrying across the plaza toward Ralph. Alerted by his voice, other men were converging as well.

"I'm Ralph Behr. I own Behr Center," Ralph tried to establish. "That's Eli Steinman, the structural engineer who designed this whole project."

The heavyset man barely glanced at Ralph as he yelled again at Steinman. "Down from there! Now!"

Ralph and Rogovin tried to argue that they were within their rights, but the man refused even to engage in discussion. Half a dozen other men now at his back, he whipped a walkie-talkie from the holster on his belt and reported a "security violation." Angry now, Ralph tried to intimidate him into backing off. Ignoring all communication, the man crowded Ralph and Rogovin toward the stairway. Steinman slowly began the climb back down the ladder. Two workmen now waited at its base.

Recovering his composure as he descended with Ralph to ground level, Rogovin quipped, "I don't know what made you more unhappy: that the guy stopped us or that he wasn't impressed when you told him who you were."

"He's a thug," Ralph grumbled.

"What was all that about?" Steinman asked when he joined them at the bottom of the stairway.

Ralph headed toward the corner. "Let's see Bates."

The license plate on the black limousine parked beside Bates's trailer read SIMON SEZ, revealing greater wit and insightful objectivity than Ralph had given the developer credit for possessing. Ralph squared his shoulders, entered the trailer, and moved toward the rear where Simon sat before architectural plans with Charlie Bates.

"We had a little run-in," Ralph began, "with someone who looks like he lost a lot of fights before he came to work for you."

Simon replied jovially. "He won his share too. Fought twice for the middleweight title. His name's Tony Di Lucca. Remember him? A little rough around the edges, but he gives us the security we're looking for."

"I think Tony ought to be trained to tell the difference between the good guys and the bad guys. He just threw us off the site."

Simon's smile grew a touch more strained. "Tony says you were scraping away at one of the arches."

"That's right," Steinman interjected. "I wanted to check something."

"That's why we give you all those reports."

Ralph stepped past Bates's chair to confront Simon. "We

410

wanted to look at the concrete. You remember I mentioned on the phone I was concerned about it."

All pretense of a smile was erased from Simon's features. "And I told you I'd check into it when we had a chance."

"That isn't what you told me. Why is there a problem with us checking into it now?"

Simon appeared astounded by the question. "Did you see the activity out there? You and I—we—the owners of this project—are trying to get the plaza ready for a major press event scheduled for tomorrow morning." Simon's tone was that of a man trying mightily to be patient as he explains the self-explanatory to a half-wit. "In case you've forgotten, I'll remind you. Those banners and streamers are going up for a reason. Not only is tomorrow the ribbon-cutting to officially open the plaza, but we have a contract with the mayor's reelection committee to kick off his campaign at the end of that very same event. Every reporter in the city will be there to finally get a look at the most highly touted real-estate project ever built. All the TV news shows are sending crews. I hear dozens of foreign TV networks have arranged to buy tapes or send crews. We've got street performers, marching bands, two ballet stars with ABT, navy jets, hot-air ballons, a dozen acts from the circus, three thousand guests, and I don't know what the fuck else. That, Ralph, is why we are not going to check anything now."

"A lot of people will be on the plaza and a lot of weight," Ralph agreed, unfazed. "What if something's wrong with one of the arches supporting them?"

"Come on, Ralph," Simon barked in frazzled annoyance, "we are talking about a wait of one day."

"But if there is an accident, what will the delay be then?"

Simon sat back and appraised Ralph. "You know what I think? I think what you really want is to make me look bad. You started right out at the beginning with those fucking delays last year and now you see an opening to take a shot at me here. You know I put my reputation on the line by promising the mayor I could get the site ready by tomorrow, and you'd love to make me and the mayor look incompetent by forcing the whole shooting match to come to a dead stop."

"Simon," Ralph started to remonstrate, "my only concern is what's happening behind the patch on that arch. And I have a hunch that Larry Carlacci was also—"

Simon jumped to his feet. "That's it! You're trying to smear me with that one too. From now on, Behr, until that ceremony is over tomorrow, you and all your people—those two," he snapped at Steinman and Rogovin, "the architects, everybody working for you—are barred from the site."

"That's ridiculous," Rogovin rejoined. "We have contracts that give us every right to be there. Ralph's company owns majority control of the project."

Simon punched a finger at the group. "The next time I want to see your faces on that plaza is at the ribbon-cutting tomorrow morning. With smiles from ear to ear because you're all so happy with the project. That's it."

Simon nodded at several men in hard hats at the other end of the trailer. One opened the door. Another, a tall, brawny man who had been leaning against a filing cabinet, reached menacingly for a wrench.

"Out!" Simon ordered. His people controlled the site.

Ralph's group departed. They did not speak again until they had retreated to the corner of the property.

"I wish there was a way to look at that concrete without having to go on the site," Ralph said, his gaze fixed on the arch in the distance.

Steinman thought a moment. "Kramer himself mentioned a way. The concrete that went into it was tested. A copy of the reports should be in your trailer."

Ralph's new construction rep on the job, a man named Dodd, drew the reports from the filing drawer. He had been pulled off the building Ralph was rehabbing in the financial area.

Steinman found the reports related to the concrete used in the arch. After a few minutes he looked up.

"Something strange." He pointed to the figures. "Identical strengths for concrete from three different trucks," Ralph realized.

"And Larry found it too. Look at the note penciled into the margin. It's got his initials and says he checked with the testing company and those are the right figures."

"How can that be?" Rogovin asked.

"It's an old-timer's trick," Steinman explained. "The metal cylinders for testing are filled with concrete from an undoctored batch of concrete, although the concrete that actually went into a beam or column might have been watered down to keep it from drying."

"Simon knew before we did that there was a problem with that arch and had a coat of concrete spread over it," Ralph reasoned. "Underneath is what Larry was pointing out to Bates."

"And then Larry disappeared," Steinman reminded him.

"I want your professional opinion, Eli. Is there a real possibility of danger if there's bad concrete in that arch?"

"We can't know one way or another what the structural strength is without testing, but a possibility? Sure. That plaza is one of the widest concrete spans in the world. The stresses are perfectly balanced. If the support on one side gives, then it collapses."

"I wasn't just talking through my hat to Kramer back there, was I? That *is* a lot of weight crowded onto the plaza tomorrow morning."

"Right in the center, where the major stress is. With thousands of people on the plaza, any failure at an outer support could be disastrous."

Ralph paused, absorbing the significance of the engineer's evaluation. He frowned ruefully. "On top of everything else, you and I would be blamed, and we could be back to square one with the construction."

"*If* the concrete is too weak," Rogovin pointed out. "But for all we know, it might be plenty strong enough. Kramer might have patched over just so we wouldn't get on his back about holding up the schedule for testing until tomorrow's event is over."

Ralph engaged the engineer's gaze before he spoke again. "Eli, are you willing to let that event go on without knowing the strength of that arch?"

"Not a chance."

"Then that's our answer."

At the department of buildings, Steinman led the way first to the supervisor of the unit responsible for structural safety to see them. Ralph strode past the receptionist and into the supervisor's office. He found the man alone and dread creeping across his jowly face. He looked like a mole with no rearward escape watching a ferret enter his tunnel. Ralph waved the curiously identical test reports at the tiny eyes and described the potential danger. The supervisor declared how proud he was to meet Ralph and how much he admired him and then he shuffled plans and papers and explained about understaffing and procedural necessities.

Ralph stomped out and, followed by Steinman and Rogovin, proceeded to the commissioner's office. He kept them waiting but, with a politician's timing, emerged with a smile and an outstretched hand just an instant before Ralph would have kicked down the man's door. He was a tall man who had parlayed affability and handsome tailoring into a career. The walls of his office were covered with photos of him with the rich and the powerful at ground-breakings and bill-signings. The largest photos were of him with the mayor, to whom hc owed his allegiance, and with the political leader who had engineered his rise to prominence.

Ralph was uninterested in his reminiscences about their previous meetings or their mutual acquaintances or chatting about the upcoming municipal elections or the local baseball teams. He refused coffee, tea, mineral water, and soda. He was intent on only one thing—getting someone to the site right away to inspect that arch and then closing down the job if that proved necessary.

The commissioner was effusive in expressing his admiration for Ralph's civic-mindedness and promised to dispatch a man, "no, a *team* of inspectors to investigate the slightest construction danger to the citizenry of this great city." He proceeded to recite examples of his regime's safety triumphs, but when Ralph cut him off to insist, first, that an inspector be designated then and there and, second, that he himself accompany that person to the site immediately, the commissioner smiled at Ralph's naivete about the procedures that had to be followed in these matters.

Ralph could take no more. "How much of a bribe does a guy have to offer around here to get you to do your job honestly?"

"That's unfair," the commissioner responded in a hurt tone. "These people might get the wrong idea."

Without raising his voice, Ralph warned that if an accident occurred because the commissioner's department failed to halt construction, Ralph would hold him personally responsible. The man blanched, fluttered his hands, protested his inability to move any faster, and hoped that Ralph could understand how committed he was to sound construction.

On the pavement Rogovin voiced the question that had occurred to all of them. "Is it red tape or is the fix in?"

Ralph shook his head. "Let's go to the top. For all my tussles with the mayor, I think he's an honest guy. It's *his* event tomorrow. He's the one on the line. We'll call his office from the car to tell them we're coming and it's urgent."

"What I want to emphasize," Ralph concluded, "is that there's a real risk of something going wrong if that arch is weak.

414

Nothing might happen tomorrow or something disastrous, as Eli here put it. We just don't know."

Throughout the recital, the mayor's arms had been rigidly locked, his expression autocratic. He glanced for an instant at his deputy. Unable to discern any contradiction to his own skepticism, he stood up.

"I'll take what you said into consideration. But listening to you would be stupid. You haven't given me a shred of hard evidence that would convince me to throw a major monkey wrench into my campaign plans by calling off that speech tomorrow."

"Don't call it off. Move it somewhere else. Look, would I hurt myself by asking you to do that if I weren't truly concerned about the plaza's safety?"

Head imperiously back, the mayor pursed his lips and eyed Ralph along his nose. "I don't know what your motives are."

He walked to the door and opened it. "I've interrupted my schedule to hear you out, and I don't believe you."

Ralph stared at the city's chief official, not hiding his frustration. "I hope we both don't regret it."

When the others left his office, the mayor's expression turned reflective. Perhaps he should have given more credence to what he had just heard. He directed his secretary to telephone Simon Kramer.

Simon swiftly disposed of the mayor's uncertainties about the plaza's safety and commended his sagacity for discerning that the Behrs were, once again, attempting to cripple his chances for reelection. "You have my word that the construction is solid as a rock."

The reporter from the *Times* noticed Ralph descending the circular stairway to the city-hall lobby with two other men and asked Ralph what was up, not expecting anything newsworthy, but knowing that, in Ralph's case, the possibility was great enough to warrant the question.

Deciding he needed to augment the pressure to cancel tomorrow's event, Ralph halted. "I'm worried about the safety of an arch that supports the plaza at Behr Center. I'm trying to get the general contractor, Kramer Construction, to test it. Until that's done, I can't vouch for its safety. You know, the mayor is scheduled to speak there tomorrow morning."

Surprised that Ralph would denigrate the safety of his own project, the reporter asked him to elaborate, but was advised to check with Lorna Garrison, whose firm was handling media relations for tomorrow's event.

From his limousine Ralph phoned the U.S. attorney, who said he was interested in viewing Ralph's evidence, but did not think a court would consider it substantial enough to halt the ribbon-cutting ceremony.

Ralph was exasperated. "What the hell do I need to bring in, an X-ray showing Jimmy Hoffa's body inside the concrete?"

The U.S. attorney, an intense, humorless man, replied, "That case is still open, you know."

About the same time, the reporter was telephoning Lorna, who said she would get back to him and then immediately telephoned Simon Kramer.

"That prick said *what* to the reporter?" Simon groaned incredulously. "Behr'll ruin himself *and* me."

"And *me*. You have a very convenient habit of forgetting I'm an owner too," she snapped. She resented Simon's continued disregard of her participation. "I still haven't received my partnership papers."

"Would I hurt you? Sweetheart, you know what you mean to me. But at the moment I've got more important problems than pressing the lawyers to draw up your partnership papers." His mind was evaluating the most recent problem. "The mayor's going to tell them everything's fine. On your end, stonewall it. Don't dignify the reporters' questions with an answer."

"If we refuse to comment, Ralph's accusation will become a headline in the morning paper. The reporters will ignore the mayor's speech tomorrow and all the great publicity we've set up. They might even believe Ralph's bull and be afraid to show up tomorrow."

"Then tell them we've had the concrete tested, and it's safe."

"Have you?" When Simon was slow to reply, Lorna suggested, "How about, 'There are no indications of any problems, but we will not stage the event unless testing confirms the arch is totally safe'? Tonight or first thing in the morning you release the test results and undercut Ralph."

"You want me to chop out a hunk of that concrete for testing right now and leave a hole in the arch during the event?" he queried angrily. "Then we really do have a problem. All the testing we've done on the concrete to date confirms the concrete is up to design specs. There's no problem with that arch. You're a partner in this project and know a hell of a lot more about

416

what's been going on than is good for you. Unless you want your hot little ass in a very big sling, you say exactly what I told you."

Lorna telephoned the *Times* reporter to inform him that tests had confirmed the arch's safety. Mr. Behr must have been pulling his leg. That afternoon, as the rumor of a problem spread, she continued to deny that one existed.

Gail attended a cocktail party that night at the art gallery. The gallery was important to her, and she would insist it be included in her divorce settlement. Moreover, she would soon be single and was determined to commence the sorts of activities that would invigorate her future social life. She certainly had the wardrobe for it now. She put on a black, very chic cocktail dress, small diamond earrings, and black patent-leather shoes and evening bag.

In recent weeks Gail had once again experienced the desire to paint. Ideas and images fought to be recognized in her brain. Bright leaps of color had been streaking in her dreams. Studying the works in the new exhibit at the gallery, she found herself impatient to pick up a brush and lose herself in the intensity of creation. Eagerness filled her so full she felt she could fly and leave rainbows in her trail if she wanted. She had stopped painting rather than wander into a professional territory appropriated by Milo. For all his bluster, his self-image had been more fragile than even she had realized. Now, when she was about to come into a sum of money so vast it might paralyze her if she did not assert the uniqueness of her identity, she was overjoyed at her own eagerness to fulfill the creative urge she had so long denied.

Gail had continued to pay the rent on the apartment in which she had lived with Milo. Tomorrow, not needed at the Coalition until late in the afternoon, she would go early to the apartment and summon a trucking company to pack and ship Milo all of his belongings immediately; she wanted them out of her apartment and the last vestige of regret for losing him out of her mind. She would spend the late morning and afternoon painting. The facility and confidence that made everything go well in one's work would take a while to develop again. But she was prepared for that and was not expecting too much—just grateful for the stability of the nest that had always nurtured her as she poised on its lip to soar upward in flight to reclaim her individuality. Maybe she would even move back into the apartment when the separation became official. She had been happy there, she remembered—living in a fool's paradise, perhaps, but happy nonetheless. She wanted to be happy again.

Gail had a wonderful evening and stayed out very late, eating and drinking and talking with old friends. Instead of traveling back uptown, she left a message with Deighton and stayed the night at her old apartment nearby.

Ralph was standing in the doorway of the breakfast room, trying to keep an eye on the corridor while wolfing down a doughnut for breakfast and seeking some mention in the newspaper of the story he had tried to plant. He was expected at Phil Rountree's office by seven thirty to read the injunction papers to be submitted as soon as court opened.

"Where the hell have you been?" he barked at Gail as she appeared at the top of the stairs. "You look like you slept in that dress."

"Here we go again."

He appeared shocked and hurt as she approached. "Couldn't you have had a little discretion and not flaunted yor adultery before we were divorced."

Gail was stunned. "My adultery?"

"What else would you call it? How do you think it looks for me—my wife shamelessly dragging herself home at dawn looking like she's peddled herself all over town."

"You hypocritical ape!" Gail fulminated. "It's perfectly fine for you to stay out nights and weekends to do whatever you want with Amanda. But if I have even a little bit of innocent fun, you get ridiculously moralistic."

Ralph's mouth was pursed with righteousness. "Well, have you or have you not spent the night with a man?"

Gail slapped him as hard and as fast as she could and sped past him to her room. "How I wish now that I had."

He never had a chance to duck.

Chapter 23

On the ride downtown from the law office to the courts, Ralph directed his new driver to take a route past Behr Center. When he arrived, crowds were already gathering on the periphery of the site to glimpse the celebrities, hoping to be allowed up to the plaza itself. He could glimpse workmen on the plaza's edge setting up equipment and circus roustabouts and TV crew members moving equipment from trucks. A neatly dressed young woman from Lorna's office, carrying a clipboard to check the names of invitees, recognized Ralph and leaned into the rear of the limousine. She had a trusting, confident face and appeared to be less than a year out of college.

"Lovely day for a party, Mr. Behr. People started arriving early even though we won't begin till eleven."

Phil Rountree spoke up. "I'm going to try my best to have them leave early too."

"It's true then," she remarked, looking back at Ralph. "Someone told me they heard on the news this morning that you're trying to stop the event. Is it really dangerous?"

Ralph shrugged. "Just in case, try to stay down here while it's going on."

"I was looking forward to seeing it."

"I don't know what to tell you," Ralph replied honestly.

She withdrew, and the limousine commenced its progress toward the court building.

Several news crews were waiting on the sidewalk at the bottom of the wide expanse of stairs that led up to the entrance of the white neoclassical edifice.

As the car slid to a stop, Rountree turned to his client. "Ralph, don't say anything defamatory about Kramer to the reporters," Rountree felt bound to advise him. "Let's confine our remarks to the courtroom, so he can't sue you for libel or slander."

"You saw the plaza. It's going to be packed. If we can't stop the damned thing, at least those people should be warned to stay away."

"Leave that to the judge."

The new chauffeur, a young black man, opened the rear door. Ralph was the first to emerge. A reporter was waiting. Ralph started to wave him off, but changed his mind when he heard the question.

"Mr. Behr, will you be claiming that Behr Center is a death trap and should be condemned?"

Rountree tried to nudge Ralph forward, but Ralph was intent on replying.

"We're here because we have questions about some of the concrete. We think it would be wiser for the mayor not to stage this event until after we can be sure. Unfortunately, Simon Kramer, the general contractor, has possession of the site now, and the mayor's campaign committee has a contract to stage the event. I saw the mayor yesterday and tried to convince him to call it off, but he refused."

"He says you're doing all this to make him look bad, that you've contributed to his opponents in the past."

"True, but the rumor now is that Simon Kramer has given him a blank check."

A woman reporter Ralph recognized from one of the local TV news shows stepped in front of him as he was about to start up the stairs.

"There are also rumors that you and your wife will soon be seeking a divorce. Would you care to comment?"

Red with anger, Rountree shoved his arm across the reporter to afford Ralph room to step by her. "Mr. Behr is here on serious business and will not respond to that kind of dirt."

As they trotted up the courthouse steps, Rountree was seething. "Can you imagine? I just hope Gail doesn't take it badly if that clip shows up on the news tonight."

"We *are* getting a divorce, Phil."

"Hire a lawyer yet?" Rountree asked without missing a beat.

"Sorry, Phil, it's been taken care of."

"We do matrimonial work, you know."

"Worry about the concrete, Phil."

Because of the urgency, Ralph's request for a temporary restraining order to halt the event was the first item on the calendar. Eli Steinman and several potential witnesses were awaiting Ralph and Rountree's arrival.

When the people in the courtroom rose and Judge Brandon entered, Ralph exhaled angrily.

"I recognize that face. I've met him at fund-raisers for the mayor."

"Oh, shit!"

No opposing counsel could have been as difficult for the Behr forces to refute as was Judge Brandon. While hammering away at their lack of firm proof, he refused to allow the testing company to supply evidence about the identical concrete-strength figures. When Rountree vehemently contended that his case depended on that testimony and refused to yield the point, the judge threatened him with contempt of court.

When Judge Brandon finally ruled against granting the temporary restraining order, Ralph slammed his fist into his palm, his frustration brought to the boiling point by his powerlessness to affect the outcome.

Rountree was philosophical. "No matter who was on the bench, it still would have been a long shot."

"What now?"

"The Appellate Division. To see if the sitting judge will grant our order—we couldn't even get a lot of our testimony heard here."

"Let's go."

In the hallway outside the courtroom, reporters sought a reaction to the decision from Ralph, but fearing what that might be, Rountree announced that his client's rush to get to the Appellate Division precluded a statement. Ralph planted himself in front of the reporters. Camera lights went on.

"I want to make clear how really worried we are about the safety of one of the arches. We tried to convince Simon Kramer, the general contractor, to postpone the mayor's ceremony until after we could test the concrete. Then we asked the mayor and now, Judge Brandon. They all refused. If anything terrible happens, it will be on their consciences."

Rountree jumped forward. "What he means is—"

"Let *me* say what I mean, Phil. We're appealing this decision immediately, but in case we don't win that one either, I would just urge people not to take the chance of attending the ceremony. We can't be sure yet if the structure is sound."

"Mr. Behr," a reporter informed him, "this won't go on the air till five. They probably won't interrupt the regular shows."

As he strode away Ralph shook his head in sadness at the continuing perversity of the circumstances he faced.

"Do you know the risk of a libel suit you're facing?" Rountree admonished worriedly.

"If I could have talked half the people into staying away, that would be a quarter of a million pounds less on that slab—and half as many people in danger." Ralph reflected. "If the mayor disliked me before, he's going to hate me now."

An hour later the appellate judge refused to grant the order.

"Somebody's got to listen to us!" Ralph railed when he and his colleagues were in the hallway outside the courtroom.

Steinman shook his head. "It's starting already." He held up his watch.

The time was three minutes after eleven.

"Maybe if I get over there—" Ralph bolted toward the limousine. Rountree grabbed his arm at the car door.

"You can't claim the plaza may be unsafe and then show up. You'll look like you made up the whole thing to get publicity for yourself and to screw the mayor."

Ralph pulled his arm away, dove into the limousine, and ordered the driver to get to Behr Center as quickly as possible. He flipped on the passenger television set as the limousine moved into heavy traffic. The mayor's campaign committee had purchased time to broadcast it live. Highlights would appear on tonight's news shows. The colors deepened into a man speaking from a podium.

". . . it ought to be called *Where* Center because everyone here this morning is asking where Ralph Behr is."

The face on screen belonged to a beloved comedian in his eighties on whom the mayor could call for a favor. He got a big laugh. Decades of familiarity with him had made laughter at his delivery almost a reflex habit.

"How about that Ralph Behr? They say he plays Monopoly with real buildings. The skyscrapers in this place will be so tall they'll have to hire astronauts to run the elevators. But seriously, he's got a problem: the Screen Actor's Guild has forbidden him from making the buildings any taller because King Kong would get a nosebleed."

The comedian concluded with a few words about his delight to be at the official opening of the project and his support of his old friend the mayor. A local talk-show host replaced him at the podium—the beloved comedian had another appointment—and introduced the program's next entertainers by reading the line, "The greatest project on earth surely deserves to be graced by stars of the greatest show on earth."

A long camera-shot revealed the three thousand guests seated in two large rectangular sections. The large open area between them contained the escalators. Behind the invited guests stood several hundred onlookers who had managed to gain access to the plaza. A tentlike framework composed of wide red, white, and blue fabric strips was strung from the apex of the arches down to the outer railings. Government officials and other dignitaries faced the guests from seats on the reviewing stand. To their left trapeze artists began to climb rope ladders to their perches. Beyond the trapeze apparatus, several bareback horses with a performer standing on the back of each were trotting up a temporary ramp to the plaza. They formed a circle in front of the reviewing stand.

As Ralph's limousine fought its way through the heavily crowded side streets cut like narrow gorges between cliffs of buildings, the television picture flickered and disappeared for short stretches. Ralph fidgeted through the blackouts and through the circus acts when they were visible.

He heard the navy jets screaming overhead before the television camera picked up their formation trailing red, white, and blue decorative smoke over the site. A bird cage filled the screen. Several doves broke upward through the suddenly opened cage door. The camera zoomed back to reveal thousands of white flapping wings moving upward on the air like a snow flurry. A few seconds later Ralph could see the doves through the limousine's side window wheeling together above rooftops.

The screen steadied. A Catholic bishop was intoning the words, ". . . and peace on earth. And dear Lord, we ask your gracious blessing on this magnificent structure. Amen."

"Amen!" Ralph repeated fervently. Despite his anxiety and although he had approved the program, he smiled at the unmistakable signs of Lorna's orchestration.

The mayor and Simon Kramer shook the bishop's hand and descended three steps to a red ribbon pulled between two groups of teenage girls, each girl wearing a different native costume. Ralph could make out one in a plaid kilt and cap, another in a Greek costume, and a third, he thought, in a dress that looked Mexican.

The mayor's election speech, to sound the themes that would shape his campaign, would come at the end of the extravaganza. Now, he stepped forward to cut the ribbon for photos that would appear on the front page of every newspaper in the city and many elsewhere. One hand on each handle, the mayor squeezed oversized scissors and sliced through the ribbon. A roar erupted from the guests.

"I congratulate my friend Simon Kramer and all those who are working on this magnificent project."

"Thanks," Ralph muttered to himself. At that moment he desperately regretted his absence. Behr Center was his vision made real, and he was not there to take the credit. Instead, he was running around the city like a lunatic prophesying a catastrophe that anyone could plainly see was not happening. A lot of very sane people were enjoying themselves and were not in the slightest danger.

And then the picture changed to a shot of both escalators, each lifting a different high-school marching band onto the plaza level in double lines, one band in green-and-white uniforms, the other in black-and-white gaucho garb. They were playing a rousing Sousa march.

"Oh, no!" Ralph cried out. "God, no!"

"You all right, Mr. Behr?" the chauffeur called back in concern.

"They're going to march. Oh, God, no, they're going to march!"

The next minutes went by for Ralph in slow motion: the young people stepping off the escalators in ordered formations and onto the large open area in the center of the plaza, the limousine creeping forward, blocked by traffic, Ralph exhorting the driver to go faster when that was clearly impossible. As sure as he knew that night followed day or that the seasons would succeed each other in turn, Ralph knew that before the last note was sounded and the last step strutted, the vibrations generated by those synchronous marching feet would set up sound waves within the concrete that would bring the plaza crashing to the ground.

The young people were high-stepping now, stamping down together with each stride, proudly displaying their skill for the benefit of the enthusiastic audience about them and the video recorders at home, which they would view that night with proud families while hoping to glimpse themselves and their friends.

Suddenly, the camera tilted back crazily—for an instant Ralph thought he spied the arches cracking near their apex—and then forward. The concrete slab began to roll in large, even waves, like an ocean about to break on a shore. Marchers and musical instruments were launched in haphazard directions. In the center of the screen, a woman in a red dress was tossed up and down by the oscillating slab like a rag doll on a blanket. Great chunks of concrete fell or tumbled by. A boy's face topped by a black sombrero suddenly filled the screen and then swept onward. No body was attached to it. Then the screen went black. At that instant Ralph heard the deep rumbling from the site, as if nearby the earth were yawning and stretching.

The TV picture cleared, showing a long shot from a new angle, possibly from the window of a building across the street from the site. The concrete surface had stopped rolling and, cracking in innumerable places, was thrusting into ridges and valleys, as if formed by continents colliding. The thousands of people trapped on the plaza were being hurled about or were trying to run from the chasms cracking open beneath their feet. Chairs and circus rigging blocked or pinned down many. The last pieces fell from above, crushing some people instantly, others after aimless bounces. The red, white, and blue bunting covered some of the victims like a mass shroud and laced through much of the rest of the wreckage in freakish irony.

Two of the arch arms seemed to be whole nearly to their tops, but the third was missing completely. The plaza began to dip to the side of the missing arch like a great white pancake about to be flipped. For an instant the stump of the third arch could be seen. People began helplessly cascading or cartwheeling down the long decline along with an avalanche of concrete. The falling edge of the plaza slab hit the ground and broke into huge chunks. People fell among them like meat into a grinder. Carnage was everywhere.

Later, Ralph would not remember doing so, but now he was screaming into the car telephone for the police dispatcher at 911 to send emergency medical teams, ambulances, police cars, and fire trucks to aid victims of the disaster. A moment later he had contacted Myra and was ordering her to hire every private ambulance service in the city to send its people and vehicles to the site.

The limousine was barely moving. Ralph reached for the door and yelled at the driver, "Get there as fast as you can to take people to the nearest hospital!"

He rushed from the car in the direction of the site, hearing the screams before he turned the corner and saw, several blocks away, the dust rising and the high mound of rubble. Behind and above it, tipped toward him like a dreadful full moon on the horizon, loomed the sheared-off disk of the plaza. He could see masses of people on the incline, many heaped into writhing formations between long concrete ridges, many trapped by them.

Rising above the sky beyond was a sight that struck him as bizarre even amid so much mind-numbing horror: three colorful hot-air balloons in playful flight.

Ralph was one of the first to arrive at the mound and began frantically to pull people out from under the debris, which rolled down at every movement. He could hear moans and cries from within the hillock and clawed at the rubble to reach them. Helping now were people who had survived the collapse unhurt and rescuers who had rushed to the site. Ralph spotted construction workers among them.

"The equipment!" he yelled. "The bulldozers! Can anyone operate them?"

A few understood and sprinted toward the machinery parked along the fringe of the site. Ralph saw two shovels near a wheelbarrow and ran to gather them. He gave one to another man and began digging furiously. Noticing that a woman's hand, all that was visible of her, waving weakly about ten feet up the incline, Ralph and another man scrambled up to her and began to dig frantically to free her. They opened a hole around her head. She began gasping for air. Another man had joined them, and Ralph moved off to aid others.

A backhoe with a clam-digger attachment had trundled up. Ralph handed his shovel to a brawny teenage boy wearing an orange-and-white high-school football-team jacket and began to direct the backhoe operator to dig away at the base of the debris, so as to undermine the high mound and perhaps free more people when the dust and fragments above rolled down and off them. Victims pulled from the rubble were being laid on the ground. Some were dead. Others had gaping wounds. Ralph caught sight of an advancing bulldozer and heard sirens in the distance. An ambulance careered around a corner. The paramedics were racing toward the accident spot an instant later.

Most of the victims were still trapped on the plaza. The cranes! Ralph remembered. The plaza's workmen had doubtless gathered on that level to watch the ceremony and been trapped themselves. No one who knew how to operate the cranes parked beside the site would have been able to get down to them to start lifting concrete off the victims, but a crane operator would be on the tower crane atop the office building.

Ralph ran around the site. The workers who had been at street level during the ceremony had already dispersed to help victims. He spied one in a red hard-hat with a walkie-talkie in his belt whom he recognized as a supervisor on the office building. The man was in the open area beneath the plaza level and crouching with his shoulder up against a heavy cube of concrete that had fallen the twenty feet to the ground. He was trying futilely to lift it off the leg of a man moaning beneath it who might have fallen through from above with the concrete. Ralph rushed to join the effort. They heaved together. Ralph shoved rocks beneath the concrete and pulled the victim out from under its weight.

"Jesus!" the workman exclaimed in horror.

Blood was spurting from the mangled limb. Ralph slipped his belt around the man's thigh, trying to stop the flow.

"Can you reach the crane operator on top of the office building?" Ralph asked as he tightened the belt.

The workman was frozen in place. Ralph shouted at him. "Get on that walkie-talkie to the tower crane! Tell the operator what's happened down here—tell all of them! Get them down here with whatever equipment and first-aid kits they have!"

"Right!"

The workman began running toward the office building, shouting into the walkie-talkie as he did. Ralph heaved the injured man across his shoulders and began trudging back toward medical help. As he emerged from beneath the plaza, he stopped some police officers who were running toward the mound and told them he knew where to find ladders that would allow them to climb up to the plaza through gaps in the slab. One took the injured man from him, and Ralph led the others to the ladders.

He himself ran to the twisted stairway and fought his way up the steps past people pushing and stumbling down to safety. At the top he held onto the railing as he stepped onto the pitched surface and raised his eyes to look about him. What he had seen below had been awful. What he saw and heard all around him now was a foretaste of the apocalypse: People everywhere screaming and clawing at folding chairs and each other to pull themselves out from between long hunks of concrete squeezed upward together like praying hands. Looking like a horrific, great-bodied spider was a huge cylindrical section of an arch beneath which protruded the legs of two men and one woman. A severed head and several limbs had landed atop chunks of concrete as if they were sculpture on display. A cable from the trapeze rigging had freakishly picked out one man to sentence to death, whipping about his neck and then forming his gallows rope when the plaza fell away beneath him.

And yet parts of the plaza and the people on it appeared to have been untouched by the calamity. The reviewing stand was

427

tilted, but many of the dignitaries still sat on it, as if afraid that movement would send it sliding down the slope. He recognized only a few of them: a city commissioner, several politicians, and a couple of prominent businessmen. A ballerina and her partner in powder blue clutched each other on a concrete knife-point too high to descend from safely. He could do no more for any of them than they could do for themselves.

Angling his feet for balance, he began moving toward the opposite side of the plaza, where a crane's boom pointed at the sky. Someone grabbed his ankle, almost tripping him. He couldn't stop, he wanted to say. Rescuers would arrive soon. He could help many more people by getting to the edge to organize the crane's lifting of concrete blocks and the evacuation of injured victims to the ambulances. But he thought he recognized the woman kneeling below him, her face gruesome with anguish.

"Simon's not moving!" she cried out.

"What?" Ralph asked, not understanding.

And then he remembered her: Simon Kramer's wife. Next to her was a man's body, face down, the dark blue suit-jacket twisted awkwardly up under his arms. Ralph skidded down the incline and turned him over. Skin the palest white, a deep gash across his throat, blood above it on his beard, and a long bib of blood down his shirt, Simon Kramer stared lifelessly past Ralph's head.

"I'm sorry, Mrs. Kramer. He's dead."

The woman's eyes widened in terror and then, sobbing, she grabbed for him and tried to shake him awake.

The hours that followed were a blur of activity and torment. Hundreds had died in the disaster and dozens more died before the day was out. Rescue workers labored to free trapped victims and rush them to hospital emergency rooms. Doctors who had raced to the site with as many medical supplies as they could carry were often forced to operate where the victims lay to save their lives. A surgeon who had served in Vietnam was later quoted as comparing the slaughter to that on a battlefield; he said he thought Beirut must be like this.

Mobilizing construction equipment to free people, bringing order to the aid efforts, Ralph played a large part in directing rescue efforts on the plaza. To lower the injured and dead to the street, he had workmen hurriedly rebuild a fallen ramp and reinforce the damaged ramp on the opposite side of the plaza that had provided access for the circus horses. Two TV crews followed him with their cameras for several minutes. A couple of times during the day reporters were able to get to him with microphones to ask if he thought the disaster had been caused by the suspect arch.

"All I know is it isn't there anymore," he said to one.

When the reporter pressed him further, he indicated that there would be time enough to assess blame later on and returned to the rescue work.

The mayor had been able to make his way to the ground from a ladder thrown up near the reviewing stand and had then quickly taken command of the police and fire-fighting teams. He was a continual presence on the air, shown and heard giving orders to subordinates or issuing a succession of bulletins throughout the day and night to the media. When reporters asked why he had not heeded Ralph Behr's warnings, he asserted that Behr had never produced hard evidence of a problem and then added, "Maybe Ralph Behr was the only one who knew the construction was faulty because he caused it."

Nightfall brought searchlights to the site, and the work continued.

Gail had ignored the first sirens moving that morning past the windows of the apartment she had once shared with Milo, but when other sirens followed and she could hear still more in the distance, she put down her brush and palette and turned on a radio, spinning the dial back and forth until she came upon the news bulletin broadcasting the first early reports of the accident. She dashed from the apartment instantly.

She ran the block and a half to the storefront where her old neighborhood center was located and stuck her head in. People there had already heard the news. Carla and several other women were gathered about the radio.

"We've got to get people over there right away!" Gail shouted at them. "Get on the phones with the alert list!"

Ducking back out, she raced in the direction of the site. If she could not stop a taxi, she would run the ten blocks there. It sounded to her like the worst disaster she could imagine.

After several hours of rescue work on the plaza, she found herself near Ralph and had instinctively joined him. At one point, the crane lifted a block of concrete, uncovering Dan Ahern beneath it, who had attended the event for the *Times*. He had a head wound and his chest was crushed, but he was still breathing and conscious. Ralph shoved an oxygen mask on him and began screaming for a doctor. One ran up and began to work on Ahern, remarking as he did that he suspected major internal injuries. His head shake conveyed that the injured man did not have much of a chance even if they *could* get him to an operating room right away.

Someone was dragging several folding stretchers back up the ramp. Gail ran for one. They slid Ahern on and lifted it. Another man grabbed a handle, and they moved quickly down the ramp. At the curb were a line of injured on stretchers awaiting ambulances. Doctors and nurses were working on the most badly injured.

"We've got to get this man to a hospital!" Ralph yelled at a policeman who had taken on the job of directing the flow of rescue vehicles.

The officer shrugged. "We've got half a dozen like that. We'll do our best."

"I'll stay with him until we can get him out of here," the doctor volunteered.

Ralph nodded numbly, and he and Gail returned to the plaza.

Some time in the early morning hours, when all the victims had been evacuated and he and Gail were about to descend, Ralph stopped for a moment to survey the wreckage, illuminated like a gruesome tourist attraction.

"Somebody should build it," he murmured resignedly.

"You're not going to go on?"

"Everyone will run like frightened chickens—the bank, the city, potential tenants. Would you buy an apartment here or rent a room at the hotel or even take the escalator up to one of the department stores? This place is now America's Chernobyl."

He dropped his head and moved toward the ramp.

The chauffeur had spent the day ferrying victims to hospitals. They found him cleaning the interior of the limousine of blood and dirt. He had bought the latest newspapers for his employer.

"What's your name?" Ralph asked him.

"Brian."

"Brian. I'll try to remember that. Take us first to Saint Vincent's and then to Bellevue."

In the back of the limousine, at rest for the first time in eighteen hours, Ralph tried to recall the victims he knew. But he had known so many—a lot of eminent citizens had attended. His tone was impassive, like someone reading statistics; the enormity of the catastrophe almost precluded sorrow for an individual.

"Simon Kramer was killed. Barney Kornbluth and his brother both—the concrete opened and then closed again as they were falling through it. Must have been a horrible way to go. Judge Hernandez. Remember—you met him and his wife at the Hilton a few months back."

She nodded. "Harold Gaber. He was planning to run for city council."

"The name's familiar."

"Head of the local community board. You sued him for a hundred million dollars after he tried to stop Behr Center."

"I guess he was right."

Ralph opened the *New York Post* to an early, partial list of casualties. He closed his eyes and dropped the paper for an instant at the sight of the column's length. He forced himself to read aloud. The first paragraph, in italics, stated that the city had opened up the gymnasium of an old school as a morgue for the hundreds of bodies. Ralph began to recite to Gail the names of the deceased he recognized.

"Estelle Atwater. Nice woman. She invited me to her parties when I first moved to New York. James W. Carroll. Harold Denizoff. That guy would turn up at a ceremony to clean a toilet. Neil Farrell's wife."

"I liked her," Gail added.

Both felt that the horror of the deaths would be somehow magnified by letting the victims go without a comment, as if they had merely been words once spoken into the wind. Ralph began to read again, this time every name: business people who had attended as a favor to the mayor or Kramer or Lorna, politicians, government officials, people from the media, three construction workers given the hour off to watch, two circus people, local activists on boards in the area with whom the mayor curried favor, the party faithful. The names seemed never to end. There would be more by morning. Gail knew many of the local people, and she had met several of the more prominent guests through Ralph.

"Dan Ahern wasn't on the list of the deceased," she noted when Ralph had concluded.

"Separate column here for the injured. He's listed in critical condition."

Dan Ahern was at Bellevue, it turned out. Doctors had operated on him for three hours. He was still in the recovery room and would then be sent to intensive care. If he survived, he would probably not be able to receive visitors for several days. Ralph kept asking if he couldn't just peek in, just say hello.

Finally, he pushed past the obstinate nurse into the recovery room. His face was grim when he emerged a short time later.

"Touch and go, they said."

At each hospital, Ralph and Gail visited every disaster victim able to receive visitors, extending whatever comfort they could. His distress at their suffering was immense. Gail, who was as distraught as he but more capable now of handling her emotions, had to put her arms around him several times until he could recover. He felt worst about the construction workers; their working for him, even if indirectly, somehow made them family in his mind, his responsibility, and he knew the medical costs and the loss of income during recovery would tax their resources even with their union-mandated insurance plans. He spent a lot of time with them and their relatives, inquiring about their means and offering money to tide them over the next few weeks.

At the last hospital Ralph was particularly shaken to encounter the young woman from Lorna's office he had met early that morning. He had counseled her to stay off the plaza. She had remained at ground level to admit latecomers and had been felled by falling concrete. Outside her room a doctor confided that one of her legs might have to be amputated. Refusing to accept that evaluation, Ralph phoned a doctor with Bellevue Hospital's microsurgery unit whom he had met at a dinner party. He arranged for the young woman to be transferred there immediately.

A television crew covering the disaster story at that last hospital took shots of Gail and Ralph with the injured and set up an interview. Ralph announced he was starting a fund to cover medical costs for those unable to pay.

Waking Brian, who had been dozing in the car, they slumped into the rear seat.

"Starting that fund—" Gail commented wearily, "that was very generous."

Ralph was staring out the window, clenching and unclenching his hands as he spoke. "I should have been able to stop that event somehow." He turned to her, his expression tense with anger at himself. "The collapse. What if something I did—or didn't do—caused it? Like hiring the wrong engineer or insisting on that fucking radical design? This happens to other people! Not to me!"

A while later, gazing unfocused out the window, he said, "Why the hell was it so important to me to build it?" Then, to himself, in a very soft voice, he added, "I didn't think I could fail."

Ralph was already gone when Gail woke amid the sweating fear of earlier months. She had dreamed she was dying alone beneath the huge concrete boulders, screaming for help that never came. She was filled with guilt upon learning Ralph had left the apartment several hours earlier.

She felt wrung out, still grieving for all the people killed and all the others injured. Her mind had not yet adjusted to the fact that the rescue work into which she had flung herself was over. There must be more to do, she told herself conscientiously. She should visit the hospitals again for one thing. There would be funerals too, starting tomorrow probably.

A call to her office disclosed that Jeff had phoned her. He had seen her with Ralph on the news and wanted to know if she was all right. She returned his call, and they spoke for a few minutes. His concern touched her. They made a tentative dinner date the following night, depending on whether Ralph needed her presence. Then she dressed and went down to one of her women's shelters, first stopping off to visit the family of a friend who lived near it, a community-board member killed in the disaster.

As soon as he had awakened, Ralph had phoned Myra to summon people to a meeting in the conference room later in the day: Ben Rogovin; the lawyers Phil Rountree and Gary Frost: his insurance broker, Harry Salzman; his financial vice president, Al Cole; and Bill O'Rourke, the head of the company managing construction for him on the office tower. Ralph wanted to hear what they had to say, but he had little impetus of his own; the alacrity of the action he was taking belied his discouraged spirit. He felt beaten down by the calamity. So many dead. So much destruction. The project seemed cursed. He had moved heaven and earth, he felt, to get it finally to the point of commencing construction. The financing had depended on an intricate arrangement of dates and guarantees now impossible to meet. He faced, at best, months of inaction while fencing with investigatory commissions and insurance companies. Simon Kramer's estate now possessed all sorts of rights that tied Ralph up and obligations it could most probably never meet, among them payments to him over the next two years totaling forty-five million dollars and probable court judgments in the hundreds of millions if Simon's negligence could be proved. Ralph could not bring himself to contemplate putting all the intricate parts together again, even if he could somehow revive his reputation for trustworthiness within the business community.

Just before the meeting, Charles Brookhouse telephoned from Paris. He offered his sympathies and then informed Ralph that he had been on the phone with James Fowler and others in the bank's real-estate department. They had spent the day assessing the damage and running up figures.

"Before I called you, though, I phoned George Hanssen of Watchman Fidelity. He has decided to cancel his lease commitment for space in the new office-building and will look elsewhere. On the grounds that you can't possibly meet the schedule to which you agreed."

"That's true."

"He thinks it would be harmful to his company's image to move into a complex which will undoubtedly prove to be one of this nation's greatest insurance disasters. If you recall, Ralph, Metrobank's financing is contingent on his lease and on similar undertakings from you."

"True again."

"Apart from the financial damage, I think Hanssen has correctly assessed how appalling the public relations implications will be. Everyone associated with this project will become a target for recriminations, regardless of actual liability. I hope you understand, Ralph, that my first responsibility is to my bank." Brookhouse paused, awaiting concurrence, but Ralph refused to make it easier for him and held his silence. Brookhouse took an audible breath and went on. "Metrobank has decided its most judicious course is to disengage ourselves instantly and completely from the project. The insurance proceeds will go a long way toward making us whole. The guarantee you signed will cover any shortfall."

Ralph's grunt indicated that he understood.

"This isn't personal, Ralph. Please understand that this is simply good business." Again Brookhouse paused. When he spoke again his voice conveyed his concern. "Ralph, if I may, I'd like to give you some private advice here. Drop this project. Pull out now. No one will blame you. The insurance should go a long way toward making you whole. Cut your losses. Protect your net worth. Preserve your capital. The bank is prepared to go further toward that end with you. Your next project—whatever it might reasonably be—Metrobank will finance it, no questions asked."

"Very kind. Truly." Ralph understood the bank's rationale for such largesse: it did not want him to publicize or prolong its connection to Behr Center by taking legal action.

"My people tell me that some public statements you made prior to the accident laid the groundwork for directing the blame at the feet of the contractor and the mayor. That was very astute. Keep a low profile in the coming weeks. Don't become so hypnotized by this one project that you lose sight of your priorities and let it pull you under. That has happened, you know."

Ralph could not tell whether Brookhouse was making a veiled reference to his grandfather Raphael's ruination during the depression. But he could discern no maliciousness in the other man's voice and acknowledged, "That's prudent advice, Charles."

"I . . . look at you like a potential son now, Ralph. I trust you take into account that I must consider Amanda's welfare in judging any course you pursue."

"Yes."

"I know you'll make the wise decision." His voice brightened. "I have a young lady here who says she will go mad if I don't hand over the telephone this very instant. Would you like to speak to her?"

"Very much."

Amanda's voice twittered like a night bird's. "Oh, Ralph, I've been so worried for you ever since we heard. Are you all right?"

"I'm fine, but it's been dreadful, Amanda." She would get the details of the accident from the newspapers, but he wanted to talk to her about how he felt, about the nearly physical pain of observing so much slaughter, about the grief that corroded his nerves and veins like acid. He spoke for several minutes, and she listened.

"It must have been terrible for you," she said in commiseration when he halted.

"Those poor people. Wives losing husbands. Sons losing mothers. It got so you began to think the lucky ones were only losing arms and legs."

"I wish I could have been there for you."

"Better that you weren't. I wouldn't have wanted you to see all that death and suffering. You can't imagine it. I saw dead people I knew and didn't even have the time to mourn for them."

"I miss you so much right now. I'd like to hold you and make all the bad thoughts go away. You'll be here next week, right? You're not going to disappoint me."

Amanda's words dazed Ralph like a punch in his solar plexus.

He felt disoriented by their apparent self-centeredness, their failure to recognize the dire crisis that had affected so many and continued to confront him.

"I want to make you forget this terrible accident," she was saying. "By then you'll have announced your divorce and—"

Slowly, he found his voice and interrupted her. "Amanda, you can't have any idea how horrible the accident was. Hundreds of people died."

"I was grief-stricken when I heard. I was so afraid you might have been one of them."

"I can't just walk away from it. This is *my* project."

Amanda's tone was concerned but firm. "Ralph, Dad gave you excellent advice. Our future is what you should keep in mind, not this one project. There'll be lots of others. Surviving whole is the important thing. Stay in the background. Let your people handle the problems. Dad always has people who handle the unpleasant matters."

A long while passed before Ralph could answer. He wanted to believe she could not have recognized the gravity of what had occurred. "From where you are, I guess it sounds very easy."

"It's only hard if you let yourself get too attached to things."

"What things?"

"Oh, you know the way you get, to a particular building or a racehorse or some dream or other."

Ralph's intercom buzzed.

"I have to get off," he told her and bid her good-bye.

"I love you, Ralph. I can't wait to see you. Till next week."

The intercom buzzed again as Ralph stared at the receiver. Finally he pressed the button and heard Myra's voice.

"Mr. Behr, there are two police detectives out here who insist on seeing you."

"Send them in."

The door opened, and two men entered. One appeared larger than his suit. The other man was trim and smaller. Both held their credentials up for view. Both appeared intimidated by having to confront Ralph.

"How can I help you?" Ralph asked, to put them at ease.

The men glanced at each other for a moment. The larger one took a deep breath, reached to the rear of his belt, and produced a set of handcuffs.

"We're here to arrest you for criminal negligence in the death of three hundred and . . . some-odd people." His eyes dropped.

"Three hundred and twenty-seven," his partner corrected.

Stunned, Ralph finally replied, "You're not kidding, are you?" realizing as he spoke how absurd was the possibility that these strangers would be playing a joke on him.

"We've got a summons here for your arrest," the smaller man informed him.

"Signed by a police chief," added the other, as if to assure him that no mistake could have been made by such an august official.

"Myra!" Ralph shouted. "Get Frost and Rountree in here right away! And get Mickey Kohler on the phone!"

The three men stared awkwardly at each other for the few seconds it required the lawyers to arrive from the conference room. As Ralph began to relate the events, Myra informed him that she had reached Mickey Kohler, considered by many the best criminal lawyer in the city. Ralph explained to the three lawyers what had occurred. On the other extension Frost answered a question asked by the criminal lawyer, and then Kohler wanted to speak to one of the detectives.

"All right, what now?" Ralph asked Kohler, when he had retrieved the receiver from the smaller detective.

"Go downtown with them. I'll meet you there and ask for bail to be set."

"Someone's trying to frame me, Mickey."

"You have any evidence to refute the charges?"

"The concrete . . . maybe."

"Put guards on it. We'll talk this over after I get you out."

They hung up. Word had spread through the office, and several others who had gathered in the conference room were now standing in the open doorway. Spotting Bill O'Rourke, whose company managed construction on the office tower, Ralph scribbled a note to him, which read, "(1) Stop office construction now—bank is nervous. (2) Put armed guards on site so debris won't get taken, especially at collapsed arch."

He stood up and waited a moment for O'Rourke to nod. Then he motioned for the note to be read by Ben Rogovin, who would make sure O'Rourke did as he had been asked.

The larger detective spoke up, exhibiting embarrassment. "Could you hold out your hands, Mr. Behr?"

Ralph tried to object.

"Orders," the detective replied with embarrassment. The handcuffs were snapped into place around his wrists. One officer in front of him and one in back, Ralph marched through the office to the front door and the elevator amid total silence. All eyes

437

followed Ralph out of the building to the waiting police car. Television lights suddenly illuminated the twilight. Reporters and cameramen rushed to block Ralph's passage.

"Do you have any comment?" one reporter shouted and aimed his microphone at Ralph. "Was it shoddy materials?"

"Are you guilty, Ralph?" shouted another.

Ralph started to answer back that he had been framed, but he felt helpless, as if every defense would be utterly futile. Deranged forces of death were now plundering this city he had once thought the most wonderful on earth, leaving behind only lies for historians and judges to dispute.

"No," was all he replied, with no conviction that he would ever be able to prove it.

Chapter 24

Ralph angrily balked at the fingerprinting part of the booking procedure until Mickey Kohler arrived and convinced him to go along with it. Humiliated and despondent, he kept silent while each of his fingers was inked and rolled across the appropriate box on the card which now bore his name. When it became evident that technicalities would hold up the arraignment until morning, Kohler and the young male assistant district attorney then on duty apologetically accompanied him to a cell.

Another prisoner, asleep on the far cot, lifted an eyelid suspiciously as Ralph entered. Then, recognizing his new cell-mate, he remarked bitterly, "Had a falling out with the ruling junta?"

Ralph took a moment to examine the other man. Well-dressed in a dark blue double-breasted suit, he appeared to be about fifty to fifty-five years of age, although perhaps the stray strands of dark hair combed across his scalp added a few years. His brown eyes were large and confident. Were it not for the man's caustic greeting, Ralph might have taken him for a businessman of some sort.

"What are you in for?" Ralph asked.

"Political crimes."

The assistant D.A. spoke up. "Fraud. He's a master. With an alias and a phony résumé he whipped up, he talked his way into being made CEO of a good-sized financial company. Then he induced a couple of prominent investment banks to raise five hundred million dollars so he could take over a firm that does consumer financing."

The man winked. "I ask you, aren't those the acts of someone out to undermine the capitalist system?"

"Building himself a regular empire, he was," the assistant D.A. continued. "The scam was brilliant."

"Brilliance is beside the point," the man said scornfully. "Business is the easiest scam. You don't need to be dishonest. Papers and numbers, numbers and paper. You juggle one with the other. The financiers begged me to take their money."

"Listen to him for five minutes, and you won't know top from bottom. He can convince you of anything."

The man stood up and, with a disarming smile, extended his hand. "M. Jeremy Rice."

"That's only his latest alias," the young assistant D.A. remarked. "He used Harold Larson when he was a surgeon."

"A surgeon?" Ralph stared at the man incredulously.

"Best mortality record in the hospital," the man interjected with considerable pride.

"What's your real name?"

The man laughed. "They'd like to know that too. What difference does it make? A name's only worth what you can sell with it." He was growing bored with the conversation. "My lawyer arrive yet?"

The assistant D.A. indicated that he had not. The man shrugged and lay down again, almost immediately returning to sleep.

"Will you be okay?" Kohler asked Ralph.

Ralph nodded and waved good-bye to the others for the night. He found himself staring at the sleeping figure, who seemed to embody a riddle, the solution to which was just out of reach. Soon, however, personal problems began to overgrow Ralph's thoughts, and he lay down on his cot to confront them.

Negative notions had rarely before penetrated Ralph's self-confidence, but that night all the invective written about his excessive vanity in pushing through so gargantuan a project appeared to rocket through his mind in an extended machine-gun burst. He cursed the egotism that had driven him to insist on having to build the biggest, the most spectacular, and never to recognize that he was human and could fail. Dan Ahern's

Times article had compared him to a superb wire-walker, but now Ralph was haunted by the memory of a terrible fall.

Charles Brookhouse had given him excellent advice, he told himself again: take the insurance, liquidate, and get out with whatever he could. It wouldn't be much. For one thing the insurance companies would stall for years making payments to him. For another, the bulk of what was left would go to Gail under the divorce settlement—to the extent he was able, he had kept her share safe when negotiating his personal guarantee with Metrobank. At least he hadn't pulled Gail down with him; that was something to be proud of in all this mess.

That was his last thought before he fell asleep. When he awoke early the next morning, all trace of his cell-mate was gone, as if he had never been there, and the previous night's depression had been replaced by a demoralized alarm. Ralph lay the untouched breakfast aside and began to stride back and forth across the small cell.

The mayor, maybe others, had sprung a perilous trap on him. He had been thinking last night about how to address his financial problems, but he could not dare waste time on extricating himself from those entanglements until he had first refuted the false accusations that threatened to imprison him permanently. He had to find out exactly what happened to that plaza and who caused it to happen. And he had better find out fast. As he had always done, he would defend himself with fierce determination—his freedom now depended on it—yet Ralph could not shake his feeling of powerlessness against the array of official weapons that were moving into position against him.

Despite the protestors outside carrying signs that deplored freeing "mass murderer Ralph Behr," the arraignment was brief and the hundred-thousand-dollar bail quickly met. Afterward, in the hall, Mickey Kohler mentioned that the U.S. attorney had phoned him about questioning Ralph this morning. "He didn't sound very friendly," Kohler added. "You and I ought to talk before we go over there."

"I'll go alone, Mickey. I've got nothing to hide."

After trying to dissuade him, the lawyer left.

Ben Rogovin handed Ralph a list of disaster victims' funerals scheduled for that day. Two were for friends. Others were for a prominent judge, a workman on the project, and a policeman. Ralph had already missed a friend's. For public-relations reasons, he could not afford to miss the policeman's. The mayor would be there for the benefit of the TV cameras.

"Gail says she'll be at these two." Rogovin pointed to the names on the list. "And any others you want her at."

Ralph nodded and pointed out others. Then he asked Ben Rogovin to meet with executives at the concrete-testing company. "How could three trucks sent from the concrete factory at different times," he wanted to know, "produce identical test figures?"

"Where are you going now?"

"To track down Charlie Bates to ask the same question. Anything else?"

"Remember Heshy Rubin?

Ralph nodded. "That fat little broker who arranged our lease with Watchman Fidelity? When he heard they'd canceled it and he'd lost his commission, he cut his wrists. Close call, but they got him to a hospital in time."

"He did it just because of the money."

"I guess so."

"Oh, Jesus."

Ralph had not seen the project site since the early morning hour when the last of the casualties was evacuated. Uniformed guards had been posted about the site, but their occasional movement was the only visible activity. To one side was the office tower, now some seventy-odd stories high, the upper section a naked Tinkertoy. Ralph trudged grimly through the debris that was recently the plaza. Now in daylight, the drama past, the several city blocks of tilted slab littered with mounds of sheared-off concrete seemed to him a vain, destructive place, unredeemed by the pity one felt when viewing newsreel films of bombing or earthquake or tornado victims picking through the rubble that used to be their homes.

Charlie Bates was alone in the trailer, a caretaker now, sitting idly. His work shoes were off. He dropped his feet from the desk to the floor as Ralph entered. His features tightened with apprehension.

Ralph spoke without bothering to greet him or take a seat. "It's got to be terrible waiting to be convicted of causing this disaster, Charlie."

"What do you mean?"

"Right now there's a lot of confusion about what happened. But as soon as that concrete is analyzed, the authorities are going to start looking for the man in charge of construction. That's you, Charlie."

441

Bates's eyes widened, but he did not reply.

"And the authorities aren't the only ones you've got to worry about," Ralph continued. "You've also got to worry about me."

"In what way?"

"Well, I'm going to sue you, Charlie, for a lot of money. I figure this project coming to an end lost me in the neighborhood of about a billion dollars. Knowing the mean streak in my lawyer, he'll probably tack on another billion in punitive damages."

"You know I haven't got much money."

"Oh, I'll sue Simon's estate too, of course, and the insurance companies if I have to, but I'll be very happy to take whatever you have, Charlie—house, car, furniture, clothing, TV. A lot of the families of the dead people will probably go after you too. And the odds are pretty good that you'll go to jail for a lot of years besides."

"I didn't do anything," the construction supervisor responded shrilly.

"Then who did?"

"Oh, no!" The whites of Bates's eyes showed all around his pupils. "I don't intend to get myself killed."

"Why would you get killed for telling me what happened?"

Bates sat silently now, refusing to reply or even to engage Ralph's eyes, although Ralph continued to threaten him for several minutes. He was far less frightened of Ralph than of something or someone he refused to disclose. Who could that be, Ralph wondered? Simon Kramer was dead. Someone in Kramer's firm maybe? The concrete subcontractor? Whoever it was, Charlie Bates was terrified of him.

"What do you expect me to believe?" The U.S. attorney, a sharp-faced man of about forty, in shirtsleeves, tie open, put his elbows on his desk and leaned forward to emphasize what he was about to say to Ralph. "First you came in here with your own private autopsy report. Then you frantically phoned to tell me something was wrong with one of the arches, but that you didn't know what. Boom! There's an accident, and who's there with an alibi, just in time to play hero, but too late to get injured?"

"I guess I'm a little slow, but I'm beginning to get the idea you think I caused the accident."

"I want you to look at something." He lifted one of several videocassettes from his desk and walked to a player and a television set that had been rolled into his office. "The TV station voluntarily gave us these. They had one or two of the cameras connected up to videotape machines in the truck. So we also got some stuff that didn't happen to get on the air. These cassettes have all the best shots of the accident happening."

As if trapped in a recurring nightmare, Ralph saw once more on the TV screen the bands marching in the large open space bordered by the reviewing stand at the far end and the two sections of guests seated to either side of the escalators. Ralph was again filled with dread, but now it was infinitely more ghastly because of the certainty of imminent calamity. Suddenly, the marchers froze in midstep, and the music ceased. The patriotic colors strung up to form the outlines of a tent stopped moving in a breeze which now held its breath. A sea gull hung in space like a tiny origami Christmas ornament.

"Keep your eye on that arch a couple of feet up from the plaza," the prosecutor declared, gesturing toward it with the remote-control unit that had halted the tape. His thumb pressed a button.

In slow motion now, band members simultaneously dropped lethargic feet toward the hard floor. The breeze seemed to spring from one fold of material to the next. The sea gull inched out of view. Ralph fixed his concentration on the arch, glad to be diverted from the death and mangling about to follow. A crack spread through it like a sly smile, and then above that, a second, like a worry line across its high forehead. The cracks were top and bottom of a large block of concrete that began slowly to topple forward onto the plaza. Above it, a very long, tapering cylinder floated downward.

"Watch the floor now!" the other man warned him.

The huge disc, like the diaphragm of a massive audio speaker, was commencing ponderous oscillations that possessed the power to fling the little figures balanced atop it into high, lazy arcs.

"The marchers," Ralph mumbled hoarsely. "All in step like that, those pounding feet had to be sending sound waves through the concrete—powerful vibrations. The arch was weak at that point and gave."

The U.S. attorney spun around, the remote-control unit pointed at Ralph like a weapon.

"But how did you know all that beforehand?"

"I've already told you, and I told you before the accident. The strength tests for the concrete poured into that arch were all identical. And a police detective named Connolly found one of the workmen who remembered that Larry Carlacci and the supervisor were looking at that arch the day Carlacci disappeared. Don't blame me because you guys refused to investigate before the accident."

"As a matter of fact we did get hold of Connolly in Texas right after you spoke to us. He said he knows nothing about Carlacci talking to this guy Bates. He says he dropped the investigation just as soon as his superiors told him to."

"Shit!" The lassitude that had gripped Ralph since his arrest fled in the face of his anger. "Look, something very crooked is happening. I don't know who's doing it or why, but I'm not going to be anybody's punching bag. You have a report from two top pathologists that the city's acting chief medical examiner gave the wrong cause of death. Somebody high up in the police department sent Connolly off to Texas when he started asking uncomfortable questions. Now I'm arrested for criminal negligence by that same police department and arraigned by a judge who wiped a county leader's ass until the mayor arranged his judgeship."

"It was *your* project that collapsed."

"I had no control over construction. That was Simon Kramer's obligation."

"We call that the Adolf Eichmann defense. It didn't work for him either."

"Kramer and I had a written contract. The mayor insisted on Kramer building the plaza as part of the settlement that let me start construction. If anybody knew who caused the weak arch, Kramer was the one."

"You're great at coming up with these defenses that can't be substantiated: first a conspiracy you can't prove and now dead witnesses—Larry Carlacci and Simon Kramer. What have you got in the way of live ones?"

"I brought you whatever evidence I had," Ralph retorted, "because I thought you were honest and cared about the truth. Now you're trying to pin the blame on me for coming to you."

The expression on the prosecutor's face did not change as he broke off eye contact and returned to his desk chair. "Simon Kramer was no angel. We've been looking into rumors that he had ties to organized crime through the concrete industry."

"What do you mean 'ties'?"

"You know about the convictions we've been getting related to the concrete industry." He paused a moment for Ralph to nod. "The Mafia allocated the big jobs among various major concrete companies at hiked-up prices and took a commission. Those not

444

chosen for a particular job wouldn't bid on it or else would bid too high to get it."

"But how does that involve Kramer?"

"We suspect he was a silent partner in one of the big concrete companies, Maxwell-Atlantic Concrete, the supplier for the plaza."

"Maxwell-Atlantic usually supplied the concrete for Kramer's jobs. No surprise in that. But he had given me a firm price for the construction that was in line with our own estimates, so I didn't care who he used, as long as they were competent."

"Or maybe you didn't care because you were involved in the scheme."

Ralph jumped to his feet, incensed and worried, taking one of the videocassettes to study further as he was about to leave—he had no intention of remaining to be harassed.

"You know," he remarked, "I used to think you were a pretty nice guy. You're really a son of a bitch."

The U.S. attorney's expression hardened with pride. "The *people's* son of a bitch!"

Ralph left the Frank E. Campbell chapel on Madison Avenue after the judge's funeral service, knowing the politic course would be to race to Queens for the policeman's funeral, but he kept thinking of the people still trying to stay alive. The newspapers had reported that the young woman at Bellevue Hospital fighting to keep her leg would be undergoing a second microsurgery operation early that morning. Although she would doubtless be under anesthetic until that afternoon, he went because most of the casualties were being cared for there.

He found several of the accident victims sitting up now. A couple of others were on crutches. He conversed with them and their families. He rarely needed to take notes to remember business matters, but now he kept drawing the pen and notepad from his inner jacket to write them. He recorded the name and phone number of a high-school clarinetist's father who lost his salesclerk job when a shoe-store branch closed at a shopping mall, the name of a local politician who might be paralyzed for life and who would require extensive rehabilitation, the name of a laborer whose father used to work for Ralph's and who needed a loan to pay the rent until disability payments started. Underneath that last note he added a reminder for himself to have Ben Rogovin direct the lawyers to rush through whatever legal requirements were necessary to initiate the indigent victims' fund.

445

Ralph was gladdened to learn that a few patients he had asked to see had been discharged, and that lifted his spirits.

He saved visiting Dan Ahern for last, dreading that the news might be bad. But Ahern had regained consciousness overnight and recognized Ralph's face peering into the room. His head was bandaged and his eyes very swollen. A light cast had been placed only on the upper half of his chest, so as to allow him to breathe, but he was inhaling with great pain and, most troubling, appeared as willing to cease as to continue.

"God, I'm sorry," Ralph exclaimed. "Believe me, if I could take back building that monstrosity now I would."

"I thought . . . it was . . . kind of majestic," Ahern whispered in spasms, his voice at the end fading like a man's departing over a hill, "for as long . . . as it lasted!"

During their minutes together Ralph tried passionately to revive the reporter's will to live. He was terrified that this good, crusty man, whose probing had forced his own principles to clarify, might die, that he might not even consider living worth the effort it took. Ralph murkily perceived beneath the worry he felt that the survival and significance of his own integrity was symbolized by Ahern's survival.

When he sensed that his visit was tiring the injured man, he promised, "I'll be back tomorrow. Is it a date?"

"I'm not going anywhere," Ahern replied.

"Tomorrow and every day till you're out of here," Ralph vowed. "It's a date, right?"

The injured man nodded. A subconscious part of Ralph believed that as long as he came back every day, his own willpower could keep Dan Ahern alive.

As he reentered the limousine and Brian asked where he wished to be driven, Ralph did not reply for a moment. He did not know. Eyeing the progress at his other buildings seemed too inconsequential at that moment to be given consideration.

"My office," he answered for lack of an alternative. He knew he should be doing something now to help his case, but was not quite sure what. He phoned Myra and directed her to reconvene the meeting adjourned summarily by his arrest the previous afternoon. She should add Mickey Kohler to the group and subtract his financial vice president Al Cole, his insurance man Harry Salzman, and the general contractor Bill O'Rourke.

Noticing the videocassette he had borrowed from the U.S. attorney, he placed it in the limousine's VCR. The pictures began to appear on the television screen, and he felt eerily like a man doomed to reexperience to the end of his days the tragedy that had destroyed him. He decided to skip the early part of the ceremony and speeded up the tape, watching the speakers and performers toddle quickly as if in a ghoulish silent film. When the trapeze artists were whipping back and forth, some workmen were shown applauding. Ralph froze the scene and leaned close to peruse it. One man he recognized was Tony di Lucca, the thuggish security guard who had driven him from the plaza.

When he reached his office, he phoned a well-known boxing promoter he knew and an acquaintance at Madison Square Garden. He asked them to make inquiries about di Lucca, emphasizing that the information was important, although he had no idea whether that would prove to be so. He had little else to pursue.

Ralph then told Myra to hold all his calls and not disturb him until everyone had arrived for the meeting. He began to ponder how to stop the attacks mounted against him. The feeling of being trapped sprang back up to loom ominously over him. The U.S. attorney had proven to be another attacker. How was Ralph to fight back against so many? He needed to put some weapons quickly into impartial hands. Not only would his freedom be in jeopardy until he was fully exonerated, but his hands were tied with respect to actions he could take to protect his financial position in Behr Center. By the time the desultory court process wound to a conclusion, he could be bankrupt. He had to force the issue quickly.

He strode into the conference room with a question for Gary Frost and Phil Rountree. Mickey Kohler would be late. "Is there some way the governor can launch an investigation fast into what caused the collapse? Everything connected with it too—who knew about it, who hid what, what happened?"

"A Moreland Act commission," Frost replied.

"What's that?"

"In the early years of this century the state legislature passed the Moreland Act, which allows the governor to create a commission to investigate a state agency or act or commission. Remember the one a while back looking into the nursing-home industry."

"Can this commission subpoena people?"

"Sure. But the investigation has to be about some aspect of state government."

"Behr Center is still technically a UDC project, isn't it?"

The others turned to Rountree. His firm had overseen the matter.

"It sure is," Rountree confirmed.

"Then we've got our state-government connection," Ralph pointed out. "How do we convince the governor to form this commission and start hearings right away?"

Rountree informed him, "You're not exactly *personna grata* with the governor right now."

"Have you spoken to him?"

"To his people. He knows we want help on your behalf, and he hasn't returned my call."

This was a blow. Rountree and the governor had once been law partners. Ralph had been a beneficiary of that relationship in the past.

Frost spoke up. "Ralph, you're a hot potato right now. For all he knows you could be the biggest murderer in New York State history. There's not much Phil can do at this point."

"If the governor thinks by ducking me I'm going to disappear, he's fooling himself. We have to convince him that his best route with the public is to look like he's acting decisively. Naming a commission to investigate is perfect. They always do that, like rounding up the usual suspects. Right now, the mayor is making all the moves, and the governor looks like a man who doesn't know what to do. But he could steal the mayor's thunder by quickly naming a commission that really tries to find out what caused the arch to fall and who covered it up."

Rogovin broke in with his customary skeptical pragmatism. "That's what *we* want the governor to do. Now, how do we get the governor to want to listen?"

"There's got to be *someone* he'll listen to. Let's put a list of people together who are close to him and would be willing to put themselves on the line for me. Damn it, I'm only asking for a fair shot at getting justice."

For several minutes names were thrown out. Suddenly, one was suggested that instantly went to the head of the list: a man who had recently resigned as the governor's chief of staff to join a prominent law firm. Rountree looked glum, knowing his own influence was eclipsed by the other man's. If successful in inducing the governor to create a commission, the new lawyer would be repaid with a nice piece of Ralph's future legal work; the lion's share of the billings had been going to Rountree's law firm, but Ralph would shift much of it to reward the governor's old employee.

*   *   *

By the end of the day, a convinced governor, who had consulted other aides as well on the matter, called a press conference. Decisive in tone and manner, he announced that he was establishing a Moreland Act commission to investigate the recent disaster at Behr Center. With him was the chairman he had settled on, a tough former federal judge, Jonas H. Rayburn. In order to get to the bottom of the disaster as quickly as possible, the other commission members would be named and subpoenas sent to key witnesses the next day. Hearings would start the day after.

After a long discussion with Mickey Kohler to prepare his testimony for the hearings, Ralph had put in an appearance at an important cocktail party; it was essential to be seen and to appear to be his old self. When he arrived home, he felt fatigued and hungry and his thoughts were as restive and out-of-sorts as his stomach. Deighton informed him that Mrs. Behr had left early and had not returned or telephoned. He ordered that dinner be sent to his bedroom, and he stomped upstairs.

He spent the evening on the telephone. He canvassed political allies for the name of someone impartial or better, someone favorably disposed, who could be suggested to the commission's chairman as the staff attorney.

His initial call, though, was to Amanda. He had been so busy following the tragedy that he had not had the time or inclination to think much about their last conversation, but now he had an impulse to speak to her, to set things right, to persuade himself that the disquieting impression of insensitivity he'd been left with then had been ill-founded, that Amanda was really the woman he knew her to be.

She was still out for the evening, but her parents had just returned. Charles took Ralph's call. He emphasized his concern with the way events had been tending in New York. "Arrest is quite a serious matter. I fear I must ask for your resignation from the Calvin Coolidge committee."

"I saw our lawyer yesterday," Gail said as she took the chair across from Ralph in the breakfast room and poured her morning coffee. "He says the divorce papers are ready. He can file whenever we tell him to. One thing—if you have no objection, I'd like to take the gallery. Of course I'd pay you for your share."

"Whatever you want. I can't think about it right now."

"Sorry. My timing was lousy. I wouldn't have brought it up right now if you hadn't told me you were in such a hurry to announce it."

Ralph nodded. "I guess we ought to wait until I'm in the clear. That okay with you?"

"I'd certainly look better not deserting you when you're in trouble." Gail paused. "Will this commission help?"

"I'm counting on it, but you never know. At least it levels the playing field."

"Please don't talk like that . . . as if the most serious matters are part of some kind of sport. I'm worried for you."

Ralph took a bite of his cinnamon bun as he glanced skeptically at her. "You couldn't have been too concerned. It's been two days since my arrest. You didn't call."

"I left a series of messages with Myra. Late yesterday I heard you'd been arrested and tried to reach you at the jail, but they said you were asleep. I phoned Ben. I've been to a lot of funerals and wakes since then."

"That's right, he told me," Ralph remembered, his tone apologetic. "Sorry. I've had a lot on my mind."

"Phoning back the woman you're divorcing isn't a top priority."

"I'm glad one of us was at that Queens funeral. I appreciate your stepping in like this."

"A lot of people came up to me to say they were behind you."

Ralph stared at Gail uncomprehendingly.

"They all think you're being railroaded," she explained. "Everyone kept saying how hard you tried to warn people and you were out there afterward trying to save them—even one or two people who argued against you when Behr Center was before the community board. They just don't believe you would have caused it."

Ralph shook his head slowly, reflecting on the implausible conditions under which he had met with community approval rather than opposition. His features hardened. "Unfortunately, it's not decided by a popularity vote."

"You're really worried about this."

"Yes," he admitted reluctantly, unable to offer his usual encouragement. "And nobody knows yet what caused that arch to give way. Maybe I pushed for too ambitious a design, maybe—"

Gail shook her head. "You wouldn't do something that would endanger people."

"Thanks," he said, touched by the avidity of her response. "I

450

guess we've come a long way in a year. What are your plans today?"

Gail finished her coffee in a final swallow. "I'm going with you now to Simon Kramer's funeral and then wherever else you need me."

"Look, if I'm taking you away from something . . ."

"I've got a dinner date with Jeff, but I can break it."

A look flashed across Ralph's face too quickly for her to be sure what it meant.

As the limousine moved along Park Avenue, Ralph grumbled about the injustice of his arrest and having to face criminal charges. "What kind of government is it that can act so high-handedly?"

"A lot of people fighting you over Behr Center asked the same question when you made that private deal with the mayor and Simon Kramer. The difference now is you're the one *without* the clout."

Ralph shook his head. "It isn't right. It's just not right."

"Welcome to the club, Ralph. You've become one of the common people."

The limousine let them off before the large sand-colored church where Simon Kramer's funeral was about to be held. A large crowd was milling around near the entrance. Ralph stopped to speak to the majority leader of the state senate, who was attending the funeral before going to a meeting with the governor. The men discussed the names of potential commission members and a staff attorney.

The conversation was brief, the majority leader agreeing to push for impartial, bipartisan appointments. Ralph cast a knowing grin at Gail as they started to move inside.

"I still have a *little* clout."

As usual a lot of eyes were on Ralph, but now they were trying to judge his guilt or innocence from a momentary frown or the relative openness of his glance. She perceived how aware he was of the increased attention by the effort he made to greet people with an informal friendliness and to move unself-consciously.

She put a hand on his arm. He jumped.

"Simon was in good health," Ralph remembered. "He went to a gym. Took care of himself. He used to brag he'd live to be a hundred. None of that mattered a bit."

Gail asked whether he expected the mayor to attend. Ralph was not sure. The mayor was caught in a dilemma: on the one hand, he should distance himself from Simon, who might be implicated in the investigation, but on the other, ignoring the funeral might reflect badly on him because Simon had been his finance chairman, a friend, and publicly supported by the mayor in seeking a role in Behr Center.

"Tough to have it both ways," Ralph commented to Gail upon noticing the mayor slip into the nave through a side access only a moment before the service began.

Ralph observed few "mourners" who were moist-eyed. Simon Kramer was not a man who elicited devotion. His wife was in tears, but she seemed more lost than lamenting. Lorna was on a side aisle beside David Hodge. She appeared genuinely bereft by Simon's death. Ralph had known other women like her, very successful in their own right, yet still turned on by power and the wealth that could be converted into power. She too would be adrift until her next association.

Ralph offered his condolences to both women after the service—to Mrs. Kramer perfunctorily and to Lorna with some solicitude. Grief had eroded Lorna's features behind the black veil that descended from her small black hat.

"I'm going to miss him, Ralph. Being with him was like a good dirty fight. Know what I mean? You always had to watch your back, but that's what made it fun." She sobbed softly into her handkerchief for a moment and then looked up again. "The bastard never put my share of Behr Center in writing for me, did you know that? I checked with his lawyers. He never even told them about it. I'm out of luck all around." A thought struck her. "Any chance that you would make good on it?"

Ralph eyed her with astonishment. "Among a lot of other good reasons not to is the fact that he died owing me forty-five million."

A soft smile lit her eyes. "He made sure we wouldn't forget him."

In the procession toward the exit, Ralph recognized a tall man about fifty years old in a black suit and tried to place him. He had seen him where? he asked himself. Simon's office? The construction site? That seemed to ring a bell. The car, he suddenly recalled—inside the car that was parked near Kramer's construction trailer. The man was Simon's chauffeur. Ralph observed him as the crowd moved slowly up the aisle. He seemed a diffident man, giving way at the slightest movement beside him, but he did not appear outwardly affected by the funeral. It occurred to Ralph that the man was probably out of a job now. Otherwise, he would be waiting in the limousine to drive Simon's family to the cemetery.

"I'll meet you at our car," he told Gail and slipped between people to make his way more quickly up the aisle.

"That's Ralph Behr, isn't it?" a small elderly lady asked Gail, who nodded. "I hope they put that killer away for a thousand years."

Gail tried to step on the woman's foot, but could not locate it as the woman drifted away from her in the herd of people moving forward.

Ralph tapped the shoulder of the man in the black suit. "You were Simon's chauffeur, weren't you?"

"Oh, Mr. Behr. Yes, I was. Matthew Miller. I thought it only right to be at his funeral. Mrs. Kramer was very generous about severance."

"You drove Simon everywhere."

"Yes."

Ralph gambled. "Then I suppose you drove him and Larry Carlacci down to the construction site the day Carlacci disappeared."

The chauffeur did not understand what Ralph was talking about, and Ralph was about to drop the inquiry. He had been pursuing a hunch that maybe Simon had lied to the police about driving alone to the site after meeting in his office with Carlacci and Jeff.

"Do you mean that man who drowned?" Miller asked. "A small man in a T-shirt and cap?"

"Yes, that's him."

"I didn't understand for a minute. It wasn't the construction site that I drove him and Mr. Kramer to, it was a warehouse near the river."

They were outside now. Ralph grasped the chauffeur's arm and drew him toward his silver-gray limousine which was parked among many others.

"Would you show me where? I'd be glad to pay you for your time."

"No trouble at all, Mr. Behr. You wouldn't be looking for a chauffeur would you?"

Ralph shook his head. "I'd be glad to keep you in mind."

As soon as Gail joined them, Miller took a seat in front, saying he would feel more comfortable there, and directed Brian to a large, single-story, red-brick warehouse near the Hudson

River close to the meat-wholesaling district on Manhattan's Lower West Side. Gail was right behind Ralph as he got out of the car.

"Maybe you ought to wait here," he told her.

"You shouldn't go alone."

She skipped up the loading-dock stairs ahead of him before he could stop her and pressed the bell beside the wide steel doors. They waited several minutes. When no one came to the door, Ralph tried to peer in through a dirt-blackened window. He rubbed away some of the dirt, but could see nothing. He tried to lift the window, but it did not give. The next, however, was more vulnerable: the screws in the latch lock yielded as Ralph applied all his force. The window slid open.

"Tell me if anyone comes," he told her and climbed into the warehouse.

The interior was gloomy and unlit. Cartons with recognizable brand names were stacked in rows up to the high ceiling that extended to the dim rear. An empty room and an office were located to one side.

Ralph turned on the single bulb in the office. A desk sat in the middle of the room and a filing cabinet behind it. Growing excited, Ralph quickly went through their drawers. Bills of lading. Vouchers. Correspondence. Minutes ticked away. Nothing was out of the ordinary. The building was evidently the warehouse it appeared to be.

He had been in the building long enough. No sense taking more chances than necessary. He extinguished the light and climbed back out the window, shutting it behind him. Gail nearly collapsed in relief. Every car that had turned into the street had made her fearful it would stop.

Ralph and Gail had reentered the limousine and were just starting to pull away when another car came around the corner and slid to the sidewalk beside the warehouse. Ralph recognized the man who stepped from the driver's side: Tony Di Lucca. Lowering his voice, Ralph informed Gail that the man had chased him off the construction site on Simon Kramer's orders. As the limousine passed Tony di Lucca, his eyes bored holes through Ralph.

Seemingly relaxed, Ralph chatted with Miller as the car drove back uptown. Innocuously, he asked, "Where did you drive Simon and the man in the T-shirt and cap after that?"

"Only Mr. Kramer. He had dropped off the other man at the warehouse. After we left here I drove Mr. Kramer to city hall."

Chapter 25

Ralph tried to meet with the deputy mayor in order to ask whether he knew about a meeting Simon Kramer may have had with the mayor the day Larry Carlacci disappeared. The deputy's secretary emerged from his office to relay the message that a meeting would be improper with Ralph presently under indictment. Perhaps, Ralph thought as he left city hall and returned to the waiting limousine. Or perhaps the deputy mayor knew something he did not want to be pressured to reveal.

Ben Rogovin was waiting on the sidewalk when Ralph and Gail arrived at the Riverside Memorial Chapel for the funeral of Martin Salazar, a prominent real-estate owner whom the mayor's committee had invited to their event at the plaza. Rogovin and Ralph chatted quietly in the third-floor hall before joining the line to offer the family their condolences, a prospect that filled Ralph with apprehension that he would be blamed for Marty's death.

Rogovin had spent a good part of the last two days at the offices of the company that tested the concrete at Behr Center. He had viewed their written records and looked into their strength testing procedures. They and now he were sure that the figures were accurate. When he asked to see their field inspector who had been on the site that day, he was told to return this morning. This morning he was not permitted to speak to the man, but was referred to the company's lawyer, who refused to comment.

Ralph directed Rogovin to bring all that evidence to Kohler; he wanted it placed in the hands of the Rayburn Commission as soon as possible.

The three entered the room where the family was receiving condolences a few minutes before the service was to start in the large sanctuary across the hall. Ralph tried to convey to each family member—the widow, two daughters, and a son-in-law—how saddened he was at the death of a man he liked and respected so much, but each eyed him with enmity and barely mumbled a response.

Gail pointed out to Ralph that the rabbi, like the Salazar family, was from the Sephardic tradition, his own grandfather's tradition. But Ralph found little difference from other Jewish funerals he had attended and sensed no conduit to his own heritage. What soothed him, however, were the ancient texts the rabbi recited: the Twenty-third Psalm, the words of prophets. Ralph found himself listening very hard, instead of using the time, as he usually did, to plan for matters he was working on. The words seemed to speak to yearnings that were unformulated questions within him.

Brian had been dispatched to a florist during the service. The car was filled with bouquets and plants, like a Rose Bowl float turned outside in, as it carried Ralph and Gail to visit hospital patients. A bouquet was superfluous in the room of the young woman whose blood vessels had been reattached to avoid an amputation. The *Post* had adopted her to epitomize the recovering injured (PLUCKY PR GAL BEATS KNIFE), and her room overflowed with flowers sent by people who had read about her. Ralph guessed her position with Lorna's firm may have facilitated the newspaper's choice. As they chatted she happily displayed her toes to Ralph and Gail. Their normal pink color indicated they were receiving an adequate blood supply.

The tour ended in Dan Ahern's room. He appeared as wan and enervated as before. To buck up the injured man's outlook and wanting so to believe it himself, Ralph told Ahern he looked better and that his breathing seemed to be a touch easier than the day before. Considering the newsman's listless questions about the Rayburn Commission a hopeful sign, Ralph explained that he intended to bring out all aspects of the matter, not just engineering evaluations regarding the cause of the collapse.

"The nurses say," Ahern whispered, "you guaranteed everyone's bills . . . who couldn't pay."

"The hospitals would treat them anyway," Ralph mumbled.

"Why the concern?" Ahern asked. "You have . . . your own problems."

Ralph shrugged. "They have a right to it. My name is on the project."

Uncomfortable, he returned the conversation to Ahern's convalescence, imploring him to do everything in his power to get well.

A flicker of animation showed in the injured man's eyes as he mentioned that Marilyn Watkins had phoned from Cincinnati to say she would visit him in a few days. Ralph knew she had found a newspaper job there after quitting the one in New York. Ralph went to the corridor pay telephone and called her to explain that Dan Ahern was in far worse condition than he may have let on. She promised to fly in that day. Ralph said his limousine would pick her up at La Guardia and be at her disposal.

On the way out, Ralph and Gail circled past the room in which a laborer named Juan Luis Ramirez was recuperating. Employed by the company renting chairs to the mayor's campaign committee, he had been badly injured when the concrete had tilted and buried him under stacks of extra metal chairs. The doctor had been examining him when the visitors had stopped by earlier. Now Ramirez, a man in his mid-twenties, lay on his bed in the far corner of the room, staring into space. Elastic bandages encircled his chest like barrel staves. His wife sat in the chair beside him, sobbing into a tissue.

"All right if we come in?" Ralph asked hesitantly.

Ramirez nodded.

"Bad news?"

"My doctor he look at the X-rays with other doctors. They talk it over. He say my back never be good."

Gail asked, "Will you be able to walk?"

"Only if I do no hard work. All my life." He glared at Ralph and then at Gail. "How I make a living for my wife and children? I never went to school. Why my family starve because I am hurt doing my job?"

"You'll get some workmen's-compensation benefits," Ralph said. "Disability too I think. I don't know if it's very much. I'll look into it."

"Somebody did this!" Ramirez cried out in anger. "He should pay for my body that cannot work no more."

Ralph's eyes burned like green suns as he leaned forward and placed his hand on the injured man's. "Somebody *will*! I give you my word to find whoever caused it or concealed it and make them pay you and everyone else hurt in the collapse."

In the corridor Gail put her arm through Ralph's. "It's not going to be easy."

"If I don't, who will?"

Ralph, Mickey Kohler, Ben Rogovin, and the governor's ex–chief of staff spent the next hours with Eli Steinman and several other structural engineers preparing evidence to be presented to the Rayburn Commission. Taking advantage of the chaos produced by the commission's hasty formation, they spent much of the rest of the day briefing commission members and staff, often only minutes after the latter had agreed to serve.

Rosalie had phoned Ralph worriedly the day after the collapse and again when word broke that he had been arrested. He had assured her that things were well with him. This time, however, she insisted on visiting him that night, he assumed for the purpose of seeing with her own eyes that he was well. When he invited her for dinner, Rosalie expressed the hope that Gail would be there too.

Ralph telephoned Gail and conveyed his mother's wish to her. She volunteered to reschedule her dinner date with Jeff.

"Look, if I'm breaking up something—" Ralph began testily.

"Ralph, you're prying."

"Well, how does it look that my brother is going out with my wife?"

"To whom? You?"

"The hearings are coming up for one thing."

"You sound jealous. It's absurd when you're getting a divorce so you can marry the professional princess, the lovely Amanda. That *is* still on, isn't it?"

"Amanda's the most wonderful, supportive woman in the whole world," he replied heatedly.

"I'll see you at home," Gail said.

The main course had been removed, the dessert and coffee served, and the servants had withdrawn when Rosalie announced that she had something to tell them. She prefaced it by explaining that she would appreciate it if they did not discuss with Jeff what she was about to say because he had become too close to Henry these last few weeks, and she did not trust her youngest son to keep her confidence until she herself could break the news to her husband.

Ralph directed a meaningful glance at Gail: she should know the sort of undependable person his brother was at heart. But he had reservations about allowing his mother, who could be embarrassingly candid in her disclosures, to say what was on her mind in front of Gail. "I have the feeling this may be the kind of family thing Gail doesn't need to hear."

"I want her here," Rosalie declared in a voice Ralph had not heard from her since he was a child being reprimanded. Rosalie had always been a factual, direct woman, her emotions hidden far below her surface like veins of minerals. Ralph had learned from his father how to handle people and situations, but from his mother he had learned to value honesty.

"Mom, this doesn't concern her. You must have guessed the truth about our marriage by now."

"*She is your wife!*" Rosalie's expression and tone then lightened. "She is also my friend. She will not be ignored like I was." She smiled at Gail. "Besides, she already knows about him."

"About who?"

"My lover."

Ralph stared at his mother without the news penetrating into his understanding: she might as well have just told him she was taking up parachute-less skydiving or inventing her own nuclear weapon.

"That's terrible!" he was finally able to say.

Reflecting for a moment, Rosalie answered with her usual intense seriousness, "No, it has been wonderful."

"Why are you telling me this?" was all Ralph could ask. "Couldn't you keep it to yourself?"

"I want you to know why I'm leaving your father. Unfortunately, it has come to the point that I care more what you think than what he thinks."

Rosalie revealed that she had been having a romance with a professor in the German department at NYU, where she was studying. A practical woman, she had decided that she was happier with him and would leave Henry. She did not want to spend the years left to her with a selfish man now that she had experienced the attentions of someone who cared for her.

Ralph was shaken by the news: his parents' marriage had always provided him with a platform of stability. With that too now in ruins, nothing seemed permanent or solid anymore.

"How can you be so sure you'll be happier?" he demanded. "A man his age—you'll probably end up nursing him in no time."

Rosalie and Gail exchanged a look of amusement. Gail spoke up. "John is only sixty."

"He is younger than I," Rosalie said and then added, "he is a very gentle and tender man."

"I don't want to hear this. Dad loves you." Ralph said the last automatically, without considering its validity.

Rosalie had, however. "That is not true. It was never true. He agreed to live with me as his wife only because he wanted me to care for you when you were born." Rosalie halted to restrain her

459

candor. Her face expressed the concern she felt. "You have known for a long time about someone named Nina, I think."

Ralph nodded. "I want to know more."

"You are sure?"

Ralph thought a long while and only when he had nodded did Rosalie explain.

"Your father and I were married during the war, but never lived together. Later, this Nina—I do not know the rest of her name—was having a child by him: you. He came to me and he asked me if I would care for the child after it was born." For the first time she dropped her eyes. "I wanted Henry. And I wanted children—" She raised her eyes again. "His children. But only if I could give them a good home for growing up. I agreed to raise you as my own child if Henry and I could live together as a true man and wife."

Ralph's voice was small and tentative. "Why did Nina agree to give me up?"

Rosalie searched her son's face. Deciding that he wanted the truth, she went on. "Henry said she was married. My impression from him was always that she was very pleased with her life and wanted an abortion, but Henry threatened to tell her husband about the affair if she did not have the baby. I think now he wanted to keep a tie to her that could someday perhaps bring her back."

"Not because he wanted me."

"I know how proud he was of you later on," Rosalie replied. Out of kindness, Ralph thought.

She explained that Henry then went off to ponder her demand and returned the next day. He said that at forty-two he was tired of a bachelor's rootlessness, and now that it was over with this Nina, was ready to settle down. He promised to be a good husband. Indeed he did settle down and even, she liked to think, enjoyed their life together. But he never gave of himself. She did not want to spend the rest of her life unloved and unappreciated, getting little and giving everything.

"You and dad . . . you were . . ." Ralph faltered.

"What you wanted us to be. Dependable. I had forgotten there could be more until I met John." She glanced gratefully at Gail. "I never even had a friend before I could speak to about such things."

"Are you sorry that you wasted all those years with us?"

"When you and Jeff were growing up was the happiest time of my life." She spoke with deep concern for his pain. "Odd to say, but you always had more of my character than Jeff. I love you . . . and I want you to understand my decision."

Ralph swung back to her. He wanted her to be happy, but his emotions were badly confused right now.

"I wish you luck, Mom."

"Thank you. That was what I wanted to hear." She rose. "Now I go to tell your father."

She kissed Ralph and Gail, and they saw her out.

Ralph turned furiously on Gail as soon as he had shut the front door. "Why didn't you ever tell me she confided in you about this . . . this German professor? What didn't you try to break it up? You encouraged her!"

Gail erupted. "You're a total hypocrite!"

She climbed briskly up the stairs, continuing to excoriate Ralph, who followed irately just behind her. "I had no obligation to break up a relationship that was making your mother happy. Quite the contrary. I was thrilled for her. John seems like a fine man. Your father, on the other hand, isn't worthy of shaking her hand. I will also point out that you haven't learned a thing from his mistakes. I gather that *his* Nina is Amanda's grandmother."

She glanced back at Ralph long enough to see his nod before resuming her climb. She shook her head in disbelief at his obtuseness. "You're set on marrying a woman just like the one who didn't marry dear old Dad, the mother you never had—her step-granddaughter, in fact. Well, I'm not a Rosalie who'll comfort you with apples when the woman you really want isn't around! And fortunately, I'm about to commence a single life without you."

Ralph halted her at the top of the stairs. "I'm sorry. I really don't want to argue. I was just very upset by what she said. It's not every day you find out your mother is divorcing your father and that you came close to being aborted."

"Accepted. I'm sorry I flew off like that. You've got to be very upset on a lot of counts. Ralph, do you want to talk about it?" She paused, not sure whether their contentiousness had alienated him.

A smile zigzagged across his face. "I'm going to miss your not being around."

They went into the breakfast room and took chairs across the table from each other. Ralph's thoughts were bitterly fixed on his father. "Every Christmastime my father used to take me to

Rumpelmayer's, and Nina would be there to see us. He probably waited all year for that day."

Ralph fell silent, meditating. When his eyes shifted back to Gail, they were angrier than she had ever seen them. His teeth were clenched.

"You really were right about my father. Do you know what I despise most in him? He takes no responsibility for anything." Ralph clenched his fists around the chair arms. "And takes advantage of people who do!"

Gail was about to respond, but Deighton arrived at the room's entrance at the same moment to announce that downstairs in the lobby were three gentlemen who wished to discuss a matter with Mr. Behr. The one who gave his name was a Mr. Di Lucca who said Mr. Behr would know who he was.

Gail spun around in her chair toward Ralph. "The guy who drove up to the warehouse as we were leaving! You're not going to let him up here?"

Ralph was intrigued. "He wouldn't come here and give his name like that if he intended to try anything. Maybe he does have something to discuss. What else do I have? Deighton, tell the doorman to let them up.

When the butler was out of earshot, Ralph instructed Gail to call the police if their business wasn't concluded in ten minutes or if she heard anything suspicious.

Ralph followed Deighton downstairs, sent the butler back to his room and waited at the front door. Two men swiftly emerged from the elevator. Di Lucca was first, appearing oversized in the small enclosure, followed by a dapper young man in his twenties. Only when they were sure the hallway was safe did they nod at someone in the elevator.

An old man appeared between them. He was small and stooped, with the large ears and elongated nose of many elderly men. He wore no tie over his shirt buttoned to the throat. His dark suit was expensive, but out-of-date, and the brown fedora with its brim turned up seemed a vestige of the thirties. But his blue-black eyes, behind lids hooded like silencers, seemed to discharge a menace as strong as the scent of gunpowder.

The trio walked forward, and Ralph blocked the front door. Di Lucca looked to the old man for instructions. The latter was staring at Ralph, gauging him.

"My name is Luigi Buvarrio," he finally said. His voice, deliberate and ancient, wrapped in a thin remnant of Sicilian accent, sounded baleful. "I think we should talk."

"About what?"

"About Simon Kramer and about concrete."

"Come in."

No sooner had the young man in the trio entered the living room than he withdrew a screwdriver from his inside pocket and went to the telephone. A moment later he had removed the plastic casing from the body and both ends of the receiver.

"What's going on?" Ralph demanded to know.

Staring at Ralph, Buvarrio put his index finger in front of his closed lips to indicate that Ralph should be silent and lowered himself with painful slowness into what appeared to be the more comfortable of the late-eighteenth-century armchairs that now graced the room.

The young man was now tracing wires and removing electrical switch plates. Then, ear phones in place and a black box faced with meters under one arm, he was sweeping a rod before him with the other arm.

"The place is clean," he finally reported.

"Good," the old man said to Ralph. "We can talk. That's my nephew Louis. Named after me." Even as he talked about his nephew, the dark-hooded eyes were fixed on Ralph. "He's a genius with that electronic stuff. Keeps me out of trouble." Buvarrio paused. "Everybody says you're a stand-up guy. Straight. They say if you give your word, you keep it." Ralph did not reply.

"You've been digging around for some information on Simon Kramer to get you off the hook. That's why I come here. I want to make a trade."

Ralph was beginning to feel more comfortable. He understood negotiation. "What do I have that you want?"

Abruptly, Buvarrio began scanning the gilt trim on the walls and the expensive antique furnishings. "Nice place. I got a place you wouldn't believe. From the outside it looks like nothing. Inside, a mansion. A lot like this." His eyes returned to Ralph's, judging them for a long time. Finally, he made up his mind about Ralph and spoke. "I'm tired. I'm an old man, and I'm tired. I've been in business a long time, a business the feds would like to close down. I'd like to spend a little time enjoying my place, my grandchildren."

"Why don't you retire?" Ralph asked, gathering that some response was expected.

He snorted. "The U.S. attorney would like to retire me, in the pen. All my life they got nothing on me—one or two of my guys

463

for a short stretch from time to time, but nothing on me. Now, with this investigation they've got going into concrete and Simon Kramer, they're breathing down my neck. I can't even phone my daughter to talk to my grandchildren without wondering about a tap. Twice I been up to the grand jury. Understand?"

"Not much."

The old man's eyes closed down to forbidding slashes. "You been asking questions around town about Tony here. There's something you want to know. I also hear you saw the U.S. attorney today." He chuckled. "I got good information, eh? I got something to sell that he and you would be very interested in. About Simon Kramer. I want you to make the deal for me with him."

"Does this have to do with the warehouse and Larry Carlacci?"

Buvarrio raised his voice only a fraction, but the insinuated threat was ominous. "First, I want your word that you'll only use the stuff that doesn't involve me and you'll forget whatever I tell you here unless he agrees to the deal I'm offering."

"I don't know what you're about to tell me, but there might be other ways to protect you if he won't agree."

The old man shook his head. "This deal is the only way you'll ever get what you want to know! Money's not going to buy it. You wouldn't believe what I've got put away. Like I said, this information is to trade with him."

Ralph had no choice. "You have my word, as long as I'm not getting into anything."

Buvarrio chuckled humorlessly. "Some other guys might be getting into something. You might be getting out."

He shifted in his seat, using the time to choose his words carefully. A tincture of wrath penetrated them. "Suppose, you know, for argument, that like the feds think, I was Simon Kramer's silent partner in the concrete company. Then suppose maybe he talked me into backing him in construction and then, a few years later, into developing new buildings. All the years I know him, I figure I can trust the guy." His hand lifted to emphasize his disbelief. "But who's to figure that all of a sudden he's going to think he's high society and his shit don't stink no more? I mean he goes crazy with ambition. He starts to think he can put up every building in the city. Then I hear the son of a bitch, who's borrowed up to his ass, is buying paintings for thousands to give away to some goddamn museum. Not even for his walls, just to give away."

The old man threw a disgusted glance at his nephew, who

nodded back. "Between what I loaned him and he owed the banks and the losses he was running up, he was becoming a real problem. With the feds digging into the concrete industry, the risk wasn't worth it. I pulled him in and warned him to start paying me back fast and making those investments bring in some money or he's gone."

"We're still supposing?"

"Right," Buvarrio continued, his voice heavy with discontent at the course events had taken. "Then suppose that just a couple of days after I lay down the law to him, first he gets into that trouble at the warehouse and then boom! the plaza collapses, and he's dead."

"Ralph," Gail's voice called from the stairway, "are you all right?"

The dapper young man sprang into the hallway, his hand inside his jacket.

"I'm fine," Ralph quickly called back in reply. "You can go back upstairs." He then leaned toward Buvarrio. "You said something about trouble with the warehouse."

"That's the trade. I got something very important for the feds. But first, they got to drop the investigation to get me—guaranteed. All this I been telling you till now, that's just for you, so you understand. And I got your word." His stare was like knives thrown to either side of Ralph's head.

Only after Ralph nodded did the old man go on. "My men and me had nothing to do with what happened in the warehouse. That asshole Kramer just showed up. Tony was there that day and saw something important he's willing to testify about, aren't you, Tony? But I want the feds' word they leave me alone and he don't face a rap. This thing don't go no farther. Especially they leave me alone. It's up them. Do they want a shot at getting me or a shot at getting somebody high up in the city— maybe even the mayor?"

"You've got evidence to prosecute the mayor?"

"I didn't say that. I said 'a shot at getting one of the big guys in the city—maybe even the mayor.' "

Buvarrio then related what happened that fateful Friday. Kramer suddenly showed up at the warehouse near the piers that Buvarrio had owned for over fifty years. As with everything else he owned, Buvarrio had placed ownership in another's name. In the case of the warehouse, for the last ten years or so, Kramer had been the owner of record. Tony, who managed the facility, and two other men were there at that time. Kramer told Carlacci to wait in an empty room for a minute while he spoke to Tony. Before anyone knew what was happening, Kramer had locked Carlacci in. As he ran out of the warehouse, he told Tony and the others he had to see the mayor and some other people, but they were not to free Carlacci until he returned in a couple of hours. They were to ignore the yelling and the pounding on the door. After a while the yelling and pounding stopped.

Kramer returned that evening. He unlocked the door. Carlacci was dead. That was when Tony phoned Buvarrio, who ordered that Kramer remove the body immediately, without help from anybody.

"With Kramer dead so he can't be tried, I don't think there's enough here to convince the federal prosecutor to grant you immunity for testifying," Ralph declared.

"I'm coming to that. Kramer made sure no one was on the street and then he dragged the dead guy's body out of there and put it in the trunk of the car he came in." The old man paused to make sure he had his listener's full attention. "It was a cop car."

"You're sure?"

"And a cop was driving. The cop helped Kramer put the body in the trunk and drove away with him."

"Did Tony recognize him?"

"Yeah, that's why I think the feds will grant him that immunity and drop everything against me. He recognized the cop, all right. The guy's on the news all the time. He's a division chief, and he's very close to the mayor."

Ralph spun around to the heavyset man behind him. "Will you name the guy for the prosecutor and then in court or at a hearing?"

Tony grunted affirmatively.

Ralph turned back to the old man. "Okay. I'll call the prosecutor."

As his subordinates carefully lifted the old man from the chair so that he could listen in on the phone extension, Ralph saw for himself what Buvarrio had admitted being, a tired old man wanting only to be left alone.

Ralph dialed the prosecutor's office. An aide promised to contact him and relay the message that Ralph and Luigi Buvarrio were waiting by Ralph's phone to speak to him.

As they waited Buvarrio remembered something. "I knew your papa when he was younger than you. He ever tell you? He tried to buy my building on time from a guy he worked for, except that guy didn't really own it. This Johnny Manzanatto got into trouble making like he owned other things belonging to me. Your father's a smart guy. If I knew then how smart, I would have backed him in business."

Ralph was struck by a possibility. "Do you know a guy named Charlie Bates?"

Buvarrio shook his head.

"He was Kramer's construction supervisor. He seems to be terrified someone will kill him if he tells what he knows about construction problems that might have led to the collapse."

Buvarrio grew exasperated. "Kramer was always doing that— threatening people to keep quiet or 'he'd have the mob rub them out.' If I get my deal, I'll have someone drop the word that this Bates can tell whatever he knows."

The phone rang. After stating that Buvarrio was on the extension, Ralph spent several precarious minutes trying to win over the U.S. attorney. Buvarrio had brought Ralph the first hard evidence, usable in court, that might begin to unravel the case building up against him. Ralph bargained as he never had before. Here was the prosecutor's opportunity to expose the direst sort of criminality at the top of the police department and maybe even in city hall. Ralph vowed he could produce two witnesses: the first was Kramer's chauffeur, who would testify that he drove Carlacci and Kramer to the warehouse and then Kramer alone right afterward to city hall; the second was Tony Di Lucca, who would swear that Kramer had locked Carlacci in a room—where he died, as the private autopsy reported, for lack of medication to control his cardiac problem—and then Kramer returned in a police car driven by a division chief, who helped him dispose of the body.

"Look at what you're getting here," Ralph urged the prosecutor. "One top cop and maybe more, the chief medical examiner deliberately lying about the cause of death to make it look like suicide, and maybe the mayor ordering them all to do it. You're giving up very little by not prosecuting Buvarrio: with appeals and delays an old man like him might be dead by the time you finally can put him in prison."

Buvarrio glared at Ralph. A long silence emptied the phone line to the U.S. attorney, who was weighing the offer.

"Buvarrio," the latter finally said, "are you still on?"

"Yeah."

"You have a deal."

467

Chapter 26

With its members and staff amicably agreed upon by leaders of both political parties, true to the governor's and its chairman's word, the hastily convened Rayburn Commission staged its first public hearing the next morning to take sworn testimony from its initial witnesses. Ralph was accompanied by Gail and Mickey Kohler as he approached the entrance of the lower Manhattan building in which the hearing was to be held. He was greeted by demonstrators protesting his release on bail. They carried signs condemning Ralph for murder. Several police officers lounged against a blue sawhorse well away from the pickets.

"I thought Rayburn told you these hearings were going to be low-key and judicial," Ralph remarked testily.

"The city administration must have stirred this one up," Kohler surmised.

"They've even let them block the entrance into the building."

"Do you want to try to find a side entrance?"

Ralph gestured toward the TV news crew. "Too late."

He put an arm around Gail and stepped forward.

"Good morning," he said into the din as he tried to push a path through to the entrance.

A middle-aged woman in mourning black suddenly threw herself at him and clawed at his clothing. "Murderer!" she screamed. "You killed my son! You killed him!"

Ralph recoiled. Kohler stepped between him and the old woman to restrain her and give Ralph time to rush into the building. Instead, Ralph spoke to her.

"I'm truly sorry about your loss, ma'am," he said quietly. "How old was he?"

The crowd quieted to hear what was being said. Ralph repeated his question. The woman halted and stared at Ralph. Her eyes filled with tears. A younger woman put an arm about her shoulder.

"Twenty-six. Billy was my brother. He was working on the mayor's campaign."

"I wish I could comfort you both in some way," Ralph said quietly, a terrible sadness harrowing his face. "I can only tell you that I'm as eager as you to see that whoever caused this tragedy is punished."

The older woman buried her head in her daughter's chest. One of the protestors tried to start up the chant again, but the others simply watched as Ralph, eyes sadly downcast in thought, moved on toward the building's entrance.

The temporary embarrassment it may have caused Ralph's public image to the contrary, the decision to stage the demonstration actually symptomized a larger misjudgment by the mayor and his advisers. Nonplussed by the swift creation of the commission, they initially ignored the substance of its assignment and reacted to its formation instead as a public-relations or election-campaign tactic, to be met by similar efforts on their own behalf. When TV news cameras were admitted into the hearing room, they attempted to blunt the inevitable flow of news film with a barrage of their own events for the TV news shows to cover. The mayor's press office flooded the media with announcements of the mayor's activities: naming a well-known lawyer and the buildings commissioner to head his own expert panel to investigate the collapse; ordering that city agencies review structural requirements in the city code; making campaign appearances at which he would outline new measures to ensure construction safety.

Ralph, on the other hand, had effectively framed the Rayburn Commission's agenda when, the day before, he provided documentation and briefings during the hectic early hours of the commission's organization and arranged to be called as the initial witness. His intent was to lift the commission's sights from determining only the proximate cause of the collapse to probing the subsequent cover-up as well, including the scheme to convict him for the crime.

The text of Ralph's opening statement had been carefully prepared. He spoke slowly, his voice soft as usual, yet searing the air with the force of his righteous integrity. While television cameras rolled, he laid out the facts in the most logical, damning way. The commissioners had intended, of course, to hear testimony regarding the questionable arch, but now they would be forced to call other people Ralph was naming in his statement— the public would now demand it. They would have to call

469

Charlie Bates, who had inspected the arch with the late Larry Carlacci and who had harbored critical information about the cause of the collapse; the field inspector who had signed the report falsely attesting to the acceptable quality of the concrete trucked to the site; the chauffeur, Matthew Miller, who had driven Carlacci and Simon Kramer to a warehouse from which only Kramer emerged before being taken to city hall; Tony Di Lucca and the police chief he would accuse of helping to dispose of Carlacci's body; the buildings department people who refused to heed Ralph's warning; and the private pathologists whose autopsy report refuted the findings of the city's chief medical examiner.

Except for an occasional gasp, the onlookers sat in shocked silence while Ralph spoke. At the conclusion, the hearing room broke into an uproar. After gaveling the room silent and warning that he would eject those disrupting the proceedings, Judge Rayburn called a short recess. Reporters and TV camera crews fought to get close enough to shout questions at Ralph.

The dean of local TV reporters thrust his microphone at him. "Are you charging that officials of the city government engaged in a conspiracy to cover up the engineer's death and make it look like suicide?"

"Yes."

"How high does it go?"

"That's what we're here to find out. One good question the commission might ask is who ordered me arrested."

Ralph stood up, politely declining to take any more questions so as not to diffuse the impact of his statement. He did not experience the elation he had anticipated when the threat of guilt was lifted from his shoulders. Rather, he could hear more clearly now the cries of the dying, for whom justice had to be done, and see more vividly the anguish of the maimed and their families, facing lives with no certainty of permanent medical and financial relief. They all seemed to be watching him, and waiting.

Ralph excused himself and moved toward his contingent seated in the first row, Gail closest. As he leaned over to elicit their opinion as to how the speech had gone, he noticed Max Borah among the journalists, staring at Gail and him with a cynical smirk.

Discreetly, Amanda always phoned Ralph at home. However, alerted to the hearing's favorable turn of events by a transatlantic call to her father from his assistant, she could not wait to offer her congratulations; she was so pleased and so proud of him. With the cloud over his innocence all but dissipated and the announcement of his divorce imminent, he need no longer be wary about hiding their relationship. She reached him at his office.

Ralph had been too concerned with lifting the onus of guilt placed on him to devote much time or worry to pondering the disharmony he thought he had perceived at the end of their last phone conversation. But, like water dripping through a night's wretched sleep onto the edge of awareness, it had wearied him subconsciously and added to his distress.

Amanda made him recount his testimony at the hearing and praised his cleverness. She told him that she adored him and wished she were with him now so he could see in her eyes the love she felt for him. Knowing how critical the hearings were for him, she understood that he couldn't be with her for a while, but she was trying very hard to be patient. He detected in her the same endearing qualities he had loved from the first. Speaking to her had made him very happy.

"I love you," he told her.

"Oh, Ralph, I miss you so much," Amanda admitted, "and don't care what my parents say about how it will look. I'm coming home to you. I can't bear to be away from you a minute more than I have to."

"That's great!" Ralph told her happily.

"It's just that I can't get away for a couple of days," she added dolefully. "There are just a few more engagements I've promised to attend— I'm guest of honor at one. But it really won't be long now."

Although he would not tell Amanda, in one sense he was pleased by the delay; her greatest charm, her ability to divert him, would only complicate further his already drastically complicated life. To be sure, his legal defense and the financial crisis confronting him required his attention, but he also needed time to think through strange, unexamined feelings he had been forced by greater priorities to put aside. One such feeling, like a subterranean river, seemed to pull him along blindly toward some unknown place: his entire soul seemed concentrated on a mission he did not understand, a purpose awaiting him in his life different from any he had ever imagined. He was such a concrete, practical man that the confusion in his goals and the turmoil in his convictions were deeply disturbing. However, because he was also a confident man who had always followed instincts that had never failed him, he felt vaguely like an explorer, not knowing what to expect or why he had even undertaken the quest, but believing that at the end he would discover it.

During the next two days, a procession of witnesses filed through the hearing room either willingly or under legal duress to offer sworn testimony that filled in details of the sketch Ralph had drawn in his opening statement.

Renowned structural engineers analyzed the collapse. They played the videotape in slow motion for the commission and pointed out where the initial break had originated that led to the plaza's collapse. They had tested concrete from the midsection of the suspect arch and averred that it had been dangerously weak, far below the strength called for in Eli Steinman's excellent structural-design specifications. The fault, they declared, was not in the design, but in the actual construction material employed. The concrete mix had been faulty. With so wide a span to support, weak concrete at any point was potentially disastrous.

Noted real-estate lawyers and construction executives testified that under the terms of the contract between Ralph and Kramer Construction, and as was customary in the industry, Kramer Construction bore full responsibility for erecting the plaza in accordance with the design Ralph provided. Documents signed by the inspector at the concrete plant and testimony offered by the concrete supplier showed that the mix was correct when it left the plant in trucks. The blame increasingly narrowed to what happened to the concrete after it arrived at the site.

At that point Charlie Bates was called to testify. He appeared fearful, although he had already spent hours revealing what he knew to both the federal prosecutor and the Manhattan district attorney. They had promised him immunity for anything he might reveal at the hearing. Upon hearing the first question after taking the oath, Bates glanced worriedly at his elderly lawyer seated beside him. When the latter nodded, Bates turned back reluctantly to face the interrogators arrayed before him.

The opening questions elicited the information that on the day the arch was poured, carpentry work on the wooden forms had taken longer than anticipated, and Bates had accompanied Simon Kramer to view the problem. Kramer had argued with the Behr representative, Larry Carlacci, over the latter's finickiness. Then Bates had taken Kramer to view the line of concrete-

472

mixing trucks stacked up by the delay. The day was hot, and the concrete in several had begun to harden.

"I explained that to Mr. Kramer. We even watched the inspector run a slump test that showed the stuff had gotten too hard."

After Bates was called upon to explain the purpose of the slump test, the attorney for the commission asked the critical question, "What did Mr. Kramer then do?"

Bates hesitated for nearly half a minute before he began to answer. "Mr. Kramer told me to go back and keep Carlacci busy . . . so he wouldn't show up all of a sudden at the concrete trucks. He went to talk to the concrete inspector."

"That's Mr. Kramer who spoke to the inspector?"

"Yes."

"Is that all you saw happening at the trucks?"

Bates shook his head. "No, before I was out of sight of the trucks, I looked back and saw Mr. Kramer pick up the hose and start shooting water into the concrete in the first truck."

"What is the purpose of adding water to concrete?"

"It softens it, lowers the temperature."

"Did you notice anything out of the ordinary happening when you returned to the trucks?"

"Yes. When I came back, Mr. Kramer was filling all the test cylinders with concrete from the fourth truck in line. You see, you're supposed to fill cylinders with concrete from each truck, so it can be tested at each stage of drying. That way you can tell how strong the batch of concrete was that actually was poured into the forms."

"But it seems that Mr. Kramer was filling all the cylinders with concrete, not from the first three trucks, but only from a truck in which he had not doctored the concrete. Anyone testing the concrete would erroneously think the concrete in them came from the first three trucks and could not know the concrete was faulty. Is that correct?"

Bates mumbled an answer.

Judge Rayburn interjected. "Louder, please. The commission can't hear you."

Bates raised his head. "Yes, that's correct."

"Why didn't you tell anyone?"

Bates's eyes stared down at his hands while he wrestled with the need to answer.

"I repeat," the commission's attorney declared, "why didn't you tell anyone?"

"Mr. Kramer said he would have me killed."

A roar exploded in the hearing room.

"And you believed that he would have carried out that threat?" the interrogator shouted over the subsiding noise.

"I wasn't about to take any chances."

"Did you have any evidence that Mr. Kramer had the capacity to carry out his threat?"

"You didn't take chances with a man like him. Larry Carlacci turned up in the river a few days after he began asking questions about that arch, didn't he?"

"Do you know anything about Mr. Carlacci's death?"

"Only that he was asking questions Mr. Kramer didn't like, and nobody ever saw him alive again."

"Thank you. I have no further questions."

A few queries were raised by commission members to fill in gaps in their comprehension, and then the next witness was called: Stanley Shutz, the field inspector who signed off on the watered concrete.

Shutz looked to be near retirement age and had gray hair and eyes and a sagging mouth. He almost disappeared into the space he occupied. His hands were shaking, and he kept his gaze down from the moment his name was called and he shuffled forward to the witness chair. He too was accompanied by a lawyer. They conferred in whispers after every question was asked, sometimes for several minutes, but each time he claimed his Fifth Amendment right to refuse to answer on the grounds that it might tend to incriminate him. Both state and federal prosecutors had issued subpoenas for him to testify before grand juries, and he was still bargaining for immunity. Unlike Bates, however, he would not receive it. He had certified the faulty concrete as acceptable and had allowed unrelated concrete to be placed in the testing cylinders, acts that led directly both to the plaza's collapse and to concealing the faulty construction. Not only had Bates's sworn testimony incriminated Shutz, which would doubtless be confirmed in court by the truck drivers, but also the testimony of engineers and of an expert witness had already established that the three identical reports could only have been produced by concrete that came from the same truck.

Several commission members castigated Shutz for refusing to testify, but he kept his silence and departed under the potential threat of contempt proceedings. The day's hearings were adjourned.

Ralph had sat in the center aisle of the front row through every moment of the hearings. Although alone most of the

474

second day, he had been joined by Mickey Kohler in the afternoon. As soon as the gavel struck, Kohler announced to Ralph that he was returning to his office to draft a motion to dismiss the indictment and was sure a transcript of the hearings would provide sufficient evidence for dismissal.

Ralph felt little elation at having been cleared. Three hundred and, now, twenty-nine lives would have been saved if only those charged with doing so had simply done their duty. Many of them would testify tomorrow—the chief medical examiner who rubber-stamped the ostensible drowning, the police chief who must have closed the case because he had helped to dispose of the body, and the buildings department people who might have been under orders to drag their feet about looking into the problem.

Max Borah sidled up and fell in step beside Ralph as he was walking down the corridor to the elevators. The reporter glanced up at him from the corner of his eye as they walked.

"It's a shame that no one has asked why you married Gail Benedict just as her father was getting out of jail. You hardly knew her, from what I've learned. But your father and hers knew each other very well. People who were around when her father went to jail say your father should have been the one to go."

The elevator doors opened.

"Any reaction to that?" Borah concluded.

Ralph stepped into the elevator, letting the doors close between them. Only then did the scowl grip his face.

The street demonstrators had disappeared after that first morning. Ralph was walking to his car when a thin, sandy-haired man who seemed to have been waiting for him stepped forward.

"Mr. Behr, may I speak to you for a moment? My name is Walters, Dr. John Walters. I'm with the medical examiner's office."

"Sure."

"Could we just walk a bit away? I hope you can understand my reluctance to be seen."

They walked to the end of the block and stood by the traffic light as if waiting for it to change.

"I'm not eager to volunteer this information," he began, "but if I were called by the commission, I'd have to, wouldn't I?"

"I imagine this relates to the autopsy."

"Yes. I was assisting when the chief or, rather, I should say, he was then the *acting* chief, received a telephone call. I couldn't be sure who it was from, but from the way he behaved, someone very important was on the line. He was nervous when he hung up and told me he intended to finish the autopsy alone. Up until that time we had uncovered nothing that would have indicated drowning."

Shortly after issuing his report of probable suicide by drowning, the acting chief was named to the post permanently by the mayor. Ralph glanced reproachfully at the pathologist. "Am I right in assuming that if the chief is indicted and loses his job, you're the next one in line for it?"

"I did this only because I thought it was my duty."

"Your sense of duty didn't seem to spur you to action when the false autopsy report was issued?"

"To have come out with all this on my own would have ruined my career. I wouldn't have looked like much of a team player, would I? It's different for you. You're a rich man. They can't touch you."

Ralph took a deep breath. "I'll see that what you've told me is passed on to the commission."

Dr. Walters nodded and crossed the intersection. Ralph returned to his car.

Brian had the radio tuned to one of the all-news stations. Periodic reports were being broadcast from the hearing room.

"They make you sound pretty good, Mr. Behr. A couple of times they had you speaking to the reporter, asking about why the mayor hasn't taken back any of the things he said about you now that you're in the clear. Probably makes you feel pretty good to give a little of his own back to him."

"Brian, I'm finding out that life doesn't give a man much of a chance to gloat." His mind was still preoccupied with Max Borah.

Brian handed him the messages Myra had called into the car. She was holding a list, she reported, of several dozen people who had phoned their congratulations on how well the hearings were going for him. He remembered there had been only a few calling to register their support the day he was indicted. And one of those had been his mother. The last message jumped out at him: his father and brother had made an appointment to see him at his office at five.

Among the hopes and plans that were buried in the rubble of the plaza were those engendered in Henry and Jeff by their partnership with Simon Kramer. Simon turned out to have died deeply in debt, with extremely thin equity margins supporting excessively high mortgages on buildings he owned. Worse was on the horizon, with the drift of testimony in the Rayburn hearings now indicating that his estate would be forced to defend enormous liability lawsuits from victims, their families, and insurance companies hoping for reimbursement. It had neither the intention nor the capability of providing the millions of dollars in funding Simon had contracted to provide for Jeff and Henry in the upcoming months. Without that money they could not pay their property taxes or installments on some of the purchased property.

When the two men entered Ralph's office, they did so diffidently, not knowing the sort of reception they would receive. Ralph did not stand up to greet them or offer a salutation. They had something to say, and he would listen—no more, no less.

"Did you hear what your mother did to me?" Henry began, his tone a combination of indignation and confusion.

Ralph nodded, remaining silent. He did not know whether his father was truly troubled or simply seeking sympathy from a son he wished to soften up. As much one as the other, Ralph decided as his father continued.

"Just like that, she told me about some other man and moved out. Just like that." Henry thought about it for a moment. "I couldn't find a thing this morning. Then the maid gets angry because I didn't have her salary ready. How am I supposed to know the maid gets paid today?" He shook his head. "What is it, thirty-five years more or less? And she walks out on me, just like that."

Jeff offered his brother a show of enthusiasm. "We're really glad to hear how well the hearings are going for you."

"Things seem to be going well for you too," Ralph replied with a steady gaze. "You've got my East Side property. And you're seeing my wife before she and I even have time to announce a divorce. Anything else I can help you with?"

Henry stepped in to cover his younger son's embarrassment. He manufactured a wide smile. "As a matter of fact, we've got a great deal for you, Ralph. And it's regarding that East Side property you love so much. You're going to be thrilled when you hear. Simon Kramer's death is a great opportunity."

Henry explained their problems. "There's a payment of eight and a half million dollars due on one of the parcels in less than a month, taxes have to be paid too, and the lawyer for Simon's estate won't make a deal with us because he says they consider

477

their rights in this property one of their best assets. They can tie us up for years. We'll be bankrupt long before then."

Henry searched Ralph's face for the empathy he had always been able to evoke, but saw only the effects of the anger stoppered within him.

"Ralph, we think you hold the key to this whole business," Henry went on, trying to retain his smile as he did. "Don't tell me you haven't thought about it—you're the craftiest real-estate man I know. Kramer owed you a lot of money at Behr Center. Under the completion bond he obtained for you from his insurance company, you can force them to finish constructing Kramer's part of the project—everything but the office building. But they're scared out of their minds—I've talked to them."

Jeff broke in. "They know they'll lose a fortune if they have to build Behr Center."

"They *have* to buy you out," Henry continued with a nod, "so that you can't force them to build. Even if they built and didn't want to buy you out, they'd *still* have to do it—they'd be so deep in the hole that the one-third ownership they take over from Kramer is too small for them to come out whole. So, either way you've got the controlling hand and can force them to buy you out. But we all know they don't want to build, and neither do you anymore. The smart thing is for you to sell out now and not risk sitting with empty buildings. That place is going to be a ghost town. You'll still own the office building that's under construction without Kramer, but you can top out at whatever height it's at right now, finish it, and maybe sell it off. You might be able to get the state to buy it from you as a favor. Or you can just let the construction lender take it over in foreclosure. But the important thing would be that nobody would have to build any more space there. Kramer's insurance company will still take a licking, but not as bad as if you forced them to build. And, compared to where you are now, you're sitting pretty."

Henry's mouth had gone dry as sand. He poured himself a glass of water from the pitcher on Ralph's desk.

Jeff moved in to fill the silence. "So you can see, Ralph, the insurance company's on a no-win hook, but it's a lot worse for them if they can't get you to sell out. That's why we're here. Dad figures you can make the insurance company force Kramer's estate to turn over to you its interest in our East Side property as part of the price the insurance company pays you for Behr Center. They don't know how valuable our property is. You can practically steal it."

478

Henry reclaimed the spokesman's role. "That's exactly the point, son. You can get out of Behr Center now with a good bit left in your pocket, including a share of the East Side property you can co-venture with us. You just have to make good on Kramer's cash obligations as they come due. We'll all be back on top together in no time. Believe me, we're ready to give you a good deal to come in with us." He widened the smile. "It's not the same without you as a partner. We're family."

He waited for Ralph's reply, but when none came, a quizzical look appeared on Henry's face. "Don't tell me you're thinking of trying to rebuild. You'd have to be crazy, even with the insurance company's completion bond. You'll have empty buildings that will bleed you dry and shove you under sure as we're sitting here." His look became bitter. "Ralph, don't make the same mistake my father made—falling in love with the crackpot notion that you have to build the biggest buildings ever. We're all in this for the bucks. Sell out of Behr Center, take Kramer's share of our property as part of the price, and you're off and running again with a great project. That way, we're all safe."

Ralph did not respond. The distance between himself and his father and brother seemed to lengthen.

Henry leaned forward, a salesman desperately trying to close a sale. "You can't let us go under, son. Do you know what people will say? They won't want anything to do with you. We're family, your flesh and blood. Banks will shun a client who doesn't live up to his moral obligations. Nobody's closer to you than we are."

Ralph finally spoke, with a quiet finality that chilled the room. "I owe nothing to either of you. You robbed me, and now you want me to finance your getaway. I don't know yet what I'm going to do about Behr Center—or about anything else—but one thing I promise you: I'll go under myself before I raise a finger to help either of you."

Henry jumped to his feet. "What an ungrateful son you are! After all I did for you!"

"Whatever you did, you did for yourself. The time for exploiting me is over."

"You think you've got me in a box and can get that East Side property for a song, but I've got one last card that will get me all the money I'll ever need and cut you down to size. I heard today that Otis Brookhouse had a stroke. He's a vegetable now, and Nina controls a lot of his wealth. She'll jump at the chance to get me back. I'm the only man in the world she ever wanted."

Ralph exploded into laughter, the first time he had laughed with his entire being in weeks. Convulsed, he rocked back and forth in his chair, his knees curled up to his chest. His laughter pounded against the walls and slammed against Henry and Jeff like punches. He lifted the phone receiver and offered it to Henry, appearing almost maniacal to them, like the messenger of some vengeful god, eyes utterly devoid of compassion, mouth twisted with the condemnation he was about to pronounce.

"Money is the only thing she's ever wanted, money and position. Not love! You're a dead man, Father. You just don't know it yet."

Ralph shifted his gaze to his brother. "The East Side assemblage is probably still in your name. There are ways you can save it. But you have to cut yourself off from him and take your life into your own hands. You have to become a man."

Jeff was bewildered. "If you could just—"

Ralph had already turned away. He had put the receiver to his ear and was telling Myra the next person he wished her to call for him. For a short time, Jeff and Henry regarded his back, and then they left.

Toward the end of the day Gail phoned Ralph with a problem. Two new battered women and their children had shown up today, but no space was available in the already overcrowded apartment-shelters. The only solution was to put them into the new building that was still being completed. She could do that only if the contractor could obtain, as she put it, "something he calls the temporary C of O. It sounds like a fly-by-night railroad."

"A temporary certificate of occupancy allows people to occupy a building that already has all the essential safety features, but isn't absolutely finished, which is when the city would issue the *permanent* C of O. The temporary's what you need, all right."

"Ralph," she asked apologetically. "I know you probably have plans for this evening, but could I ask you to stop by here for a few minutes and help us with this?"

"Where should I meet you?"

She gave him the address of the apartment where he had once met her. Ralph had let Brian have the evening off, and he telephoned for a taxi.

"Overcrowded" had been an understatement, Ralph discovered when he was admitted into the three-bedroom apartment that now housed five mothers and seven children, as well as the Coalition's makeshift offices. After admitting Ralph, a young woman he took to be a staff worker flipped the dead bolt above the knob and the lower lock, reattached the end of the chain, and set the long steel bar that traversed the width of the front door. Several women and children stared tensely at him; his masculine presence had violated the fragile security of this sanctuary from the violence of men. Unreasonably, Ralph felt brutish and guilty for his manhood.

Gail stood behind a dented metal desk at the far end of the living room. With one hand she held a baby she had rocked asleep on her shoulder. The other held a telephone receiver to her ear.

"My husband, Ralph," she announced softly to those in the room. Much of the apprehension left the taut faces.

A light-skinned black woman with livid bruises beneath her eyes sat on a wooden bench along the wall nursing her baby. The staff worker who had admitted Ralph was now dressing in pajamas her other child, a boy of about two. The woman had appeared frightened of Ralph, but now assayed a tentative smile and then immediately glanced obsequiously at Gail, seeking her approval. If the boss lady was not pleased and threw her out, she had nowhere to go.

Gail motioned for Ralph to join her. He stepped carefully over toys and children: interlocking plastic balls; a wooden train on its side, the painted smiles on the barrel-bodied occupants spilled around it belying the severity of the wreck; twin girls he judged to be about four being covered with a blanket as a bedtime story was about to be read to them.

"One second," Gail said into the receiver and then muffled the mouthpiece against her body. She smiled broadly at Ralph. "Marrying you has its advantages. The inspector at the buildings department is standing by to issue the temporary C of O."

Ralph glanced at his watch incredulously. "It's six thirty."

"It seems they're terrified of you down at the buildings department these days."

"Do you have all the inspections signed on the back of the application—plumbing, so forth?"

She nodded.

"Smoke detectors in the apartments," he continued, "two means of egress, exit signs up, stairways and roof finished, kitchen sink attached, three-fixture bathroom installed, mailboxes, intercom."

To all of these she nodded affirmatively. "The contractor is waiting there now," she explained. "We just need one floor ready."

"Tell the buildings department guy to meet us there if he wants to see for himself."

A few minutes later, Ralph and Gail walked the few blocks to the new building and went upstairs with the inspector when he arrived. He immediately found several items not yet installed and two rooms in one of the apartments on the floor not yet painted. The contractor was already inserting the peepholes in the doors and connecting wiring in the door buzzers and the exit signs. But the meticulous official was reluctant to grant the TCO because of the two unpainted rooms.

"You can see for yourself the painters will finish first thing in the morning," Ralph argued. "The paint is here."

The official refused to budge, appearing to fear that the dreadful Ralph Behr might utilize his slightest deviation from prescribed duties as the basis for criminal charges; he was going by the book. Finally, Ralph offered to paint the rooms with Gail that night.

"You really would?" she asked Ralph.

"Got any better ideas?"

The official acquiesced. On that basis they could have the temporary certificate of occupancy.

Ralph and Gail went into the living room of the last apartment on the floor, which contained the two unpainted bedrooms. Ralph was wearing a dark gray suit. He began to strip down to his underwear.

"What are you doing?" Gail asked in astonishment as he removed his trousers.

"Paint drips, remember?" He began to remove his shirt.

Gail stared at him awkwardly for a moment and then unbuttoned and slipped off her dress. Soon, except for panties and bra, her clothing too was off and folded in a pile on the newspapers laid out on the floor of the living room.

Neither he nor she had glanced over at the other until Ralph watched her walk to the front door to lock it. Noticing the look on his face when she turned back, she halted self-consciously in mid-step.

"I forgot how lovely you are," he said softly.

"God, that was a crazy week, wasn't it? What could have come over us?"

Ralph thought a moment. "It was a wonderful week."

482

Gail blushed and hurried past him into the first bedroom to be painted.

As they worked, they joked about the compromising nature of their nudity and then remembered that they were still legally man and wife.

"You're my woman," Ralph teased. He dipped his finger in the white paint and drew a heart on her chest and an R within it.

Gail threw her arms around him to press the wet paint against *his* chest. Standing side by side, they regarded themselves in the full-length mirror on a hallway door. Each was painted with a heart containing matching, if reverse, Rs.

"We look kind of like the front of a Rolls-Royce on Valentine's Day," Gail observed.

"Better."

"Isn't it funny that normal couples go from attraction, to passion, to getting to know each other, to marriage, and then to fighting and a divorce settlement? With us it all worked out backwards."

Ralph did not reply, but continued to stare at her in the mirror until she broke away and went back to painting.

Several hours later they had showered and dressed and helped two women and their children move into one of the empty apartments. A staff worker would stay with them.

Ralph and Gail walked out of the building and down the street.

"Those women felt safe," Ralph observed to her. "You must get a lot of satisfaction from that."

"I'm burned out, Ralph. Not just tonight, I mean, but generally. I don't have anything left in me to give. That may be why taking up art again seems so appealing. It's a way to remember who I am."

"The money will make it easier. You can hire more people."

"Thank God for the money. My problem is finding someone to hire who'll do what I do." She shook her head. "It never ends."

She confided how fatigued she had felt the last few months, after the shock of Milo's leaving. The trauma had helped her to realize, though, that her compulsive selflessness had emptied her life. Subjugating her own needs and burying other parts of her character had finally taken their toll.

"You were never a doormat with me like you say you were with Milo," Ralph pointed out. "You were a tiger, fighting over every little slight."

"I was a fighter for the Coalition too, and for women's rights and for every damned cause between here and Washington. I guess it was a way I could get out all that suppressed anger I didn't know was bottled up inside me. I was giving everything to everyone else, and there was nothing left for me."

They turned a corner. Down the street, extending into the blackness, was the skeleton of the Behr Center office building. Gail took Ralph's hand and quickened her step.

He resisted. "Not now. I don't want to think about the project yet. Whenever I do, I remember all the people who died there."

Gail continued to pull him forward. "Then it's time you looked at the tower again. I never told you this, but I've really come to like that building." She smiled. "It's got your unassuming arrogance."

They halted on the pavement across the street from the office building and stared up at it.

"It would have been twice as tall," Ralph murmured regretfully.

A family stood nearby, gazing at the building as well: a broad-shouldered man, a small woman, and a young boy. The man noticed Ralph, said something to his wife and then, urged on by her, walked over to Ralph.

"You don't know me, Mr. Behr, but I'm a steelworker on this job. Joe Olezewski."

Ralph extended a hand, and they shook, the man self-consciously. Ralph introduced Gail. The man introduced his wife and son, who had followed him over. He shuffled his feet for a moment, and then he spoke again.

"Mr. Behr, there's some talk you might not finish the building. I just want you to know I hope you go on with it. Not for the work. I can always get hired on other jobs."

"Then why?" Ralph inquired.

"My uncle worked on the Empire State Building. When I was a kid, he used to show me the photo of him on a beam on a high floor of that building. He was prouder of having worked on that building than anything else in his life. I felt the same way about this job, you know what I mean? This was the biggest, the greatest thing ever put up, and I was building it."

The woman spoke up. "He talked about nothing else when he came home at night, Mr. Behr. I know it has your name on it and you own it, but in his mind—in all the guys' minds—this is theirs."

Fearing she might have insulted Ralph, the man tried to correct her. "Hey, it's Mr. Behr's building. I just work on it."

"No, it was yours too," Ralph agreed in a voice subdued by the emotions the man had aroused. "It had your sweat and skill in it."

"Thanks, Mr. Behr, for saying that. That's the way it feels to me. I just hope, you know . . ."

Ralph nodded. They all said goodnight and separated. Ralph and Gail remained where they were, staring at the tower for several more minutes. Then he hailed a cab, and they went to dinner.

With the burden of legal prosecution virtually lifted from Ralph's shoulders, the conversation that night was easy and warm; neither could remember ever laughing so much. With the hearing scheduled to begin early the next morning, the evening ended more quickly than Gail felt both of them wanted.

As they were walking down the corridor to their bedrooms, Ralph asked if they could have dinner again tomorrow night. This time they would start out in the late afternoon, take a drive, and maybe find some quiet restaurant in the country. She could come to his office in the late afternoon.

Staring at him, Gail experienced a sense of wonder at the transformation he had undergone in her eyes since she had known him. Originally, he had appeared to her to be brash, limited, self-glorifying. But she had eventually been allowed to glimpse a far more complex whole. In an age of self-interest, he was humanely responsible, growing a little more so each day, refining a little more a boy's uncomplicated sense of fairness in playing the game, always groping forward somehow, even when he was on his knees. Perhaps because his ego was so secure, he had never tried to dominate her and had always met her halfway. She no longer saw his father in him, single-mindedly ruthless toward anyone blocking his acquisitiveness, but the integrity her own father had admired in his grandfather Raphael, and the concern and respect for others she admired in Rosalie. Over the course of the year, tendencies she had found objectionable had gradually fallen off him like scurf from a healing physique. He had developed into a being possessed of a worth even he did not yet comprehend or appreciate.

Impulsively, Gail leaned forward and kissed him—brushed against his cheek, really. But he was still smiling when they separated.

Chapter 27

The next day's hearings were bedlam. Lines began forming the night before to obtain the few precious seats set aside for the public. The ranks of reporters had been swelled by the addition of many members of the national press. The atmosphere was tense, explosive, as the gavel rang out the opening of the day's testimony.

One after another, witnesses confirmed precisely what Ralph had claimed they would. The day's first witness, Matthew Miller, professed to have driven Simon Kramer to a warehouse with Larry Carlacci and then alone to city hall.

Next, Tony Di Lucca recounted how Simon Kramer had locked Larry Carlacci in a room, said he was going off to see the mayor and other people, and came back later to find Carlacci dead. Kramer, he related, then dragged the body out to a police car and put it into the trunk with the aid of a police chief, whom he named. The latter was then called up, but refused to testify, claiming the protection of the Fifth Amendment.

Two private pathologists swore that the true cause of Carlacci's death was cardiac fibrillation, probably induced by failure to take medication to control chronic arrythmia; he was dead before his body entered the water. The finding was corroborated, in part, by the second in command to the chief medical examiner, who had been subpoenaed to testify. Dr. Walters recalled that he had been performing the autopsy with the chief and that he too had detected no signs of drowning, but that his involvement in the autopsy had been unexpectedly cut short by a phone call the chief received. After that call, the latter ordered him from the room and completed the autopsy himself.

When the chief medical examiner was summoned to testify, however, he insisted that he had indeed found evidence of drowning and that he had ordered his assistant from the room because this autopsy did not require two senior people.

All the while Ralph remained in the front-row seat on the

center aisle. As soon as the hearing was adjourned for lunch, reporters rushed to Ralph for his comments. He pointed out that only a city official with a good deal of authority over the then acting chief medical examiner could have ordered him to dismiss the other pathologist and falsify the cause of death.

"This afternoon, the buildings commissioner will take the stand to answer questions about why he refused to send investigators to inspect the arch after I begged him to do so. Did he make *that* decision on his own or was he also under orders from a top city official?"

Having returned to his office, Ralph was listening to a radio news report of the events at the hearing when another listener, a very anxious one, telephoned him: the deputy mayor.

"I want you to know, Ralph, I had nothing to do with it."

"With what?"

"This isn't something we can talk about over the phone. Can I come up to your office now? I'm downstairs in a phone booth."

"I remember something about your not wanting to see me because I was under indictment."

"I needed time to think."

"And to see which way the wind was blowing. All right, come up."

When the deputy mayor entered Ralph's office, he was sweating and apprehensive. He rushed to take a seat.

"I've done nothing wrong, but everyone who was at that city-hall meeting will be suspect."

"The one right after Larry Carlacci was locked in the warehouse?"

The deputy mayor nodded and brushed a hand across his mouth. Averting his eyes from Ralph's, he began to confirm what so much testimony had implied—that a tightly closed, hurriedly called meeting had been held in the mayor's office the day Carlacci had disappeared. Present with the mayor and the deputy were Simon Kramer, the buildings commissioner, and the police chief named at the hearing. Kramer informed the others that he had locked up a supervisor on the construction job because the man had gone crazy and was trying to extort money by threatening to claim construction on the plaza had been faulty. Even a totally false claim could ruin the plans to open the mayor's reelection campaign there. Kramer wanted the police to come up with some charge or other to hold the man for psychiatric observation for a few days or, preferably, weeks—until, as he put it, the fellow came to his senses. Kramer had maintained that even though the man was crazy, he held a responsible position and could provoke a good deal of negative publicity. For the fellow's own good as well, he should be committed for observation. Everyone agreed that the police chief should accompany Kramer back down to his warehouse where the man was being held and take him into custody.

Ralph interrupted. "It's just your word against the mayor's and the others' who were there."

"Not where the next meeting is concerned."

The deputy mayor took a deep breath and reached into his pocket. When his hand emerged, it held an audiotape cassette.

The deputy mayor explained. "After the guy's body turned up in the river, Kramer contacted me to arrange another meeting with the mayor. There was no way I was going to let myself get trapped into becoming an accessory by sitting in on that one. By the same token, I didn't want those two guys hatching a plot to pin something on me when they were alone."

"So you left a tape recorder running in the mayor's office."

He nodded. "In my briefcase. I left it slightly open on a chair when I went out of the room."

Ralph reached for the cassette.

The deputy mayor pulled it back a bit and said, "You're in contact with everyone—all the prosecutors, this Rayburn commission, reporters. I want you to make it clear to them all I did this as a concerned citizen."

"There seems to be an epidemic of that going around right now. All right."

"You know, Ralph, I've been thinking. I've got as good a chance as anyone to win the mayoral nomination. I could use your support."

Ralph eyed him with distaste. With one blow the deputy mayor was eliminating his mentor from a job he wanted and saving his own neck. "It seems to me that this city is entitled to a little competence and foresight this time around. Just be glad not to spend the next four years making license plates."

Ralph reached out his hand, palm up. The deputy mayor glanced at the cassette for a moment, as if reviewing his reasoning for the last time. Then he took a deep breath and placed the cassette in Ralph's hand. At that instant, at last, Ralph felt his luck returning.

* * *

The mayor called a news conference early that afternoon. In the midst of a campaign for renomination by his party, unrefuted charges could be devastating. He had to get his own version of events into the news programs to counter the impression left by the hearing.

Reporters crammed into the room, their banks of cameras and microphones aimed forward like artillery. The mayor entered with a confident air. He drew a piece of paper from his vest pocket as he stepped to the podium.

"At the Rayburn Commission hearings today," he read, "statements were made insinuating that the late Simon Kramer and others plotted with me in my office to take one Lawrence Carlacci illegally into custody and then, later, to cover up his death. Those charges are baseless lies. No such discussion ever took place. Simon Kramer was the finance chairman of my campaign. That was his role, and everything discussed that day in my office related to campaign financing. I'll take questions now."

So intent had the listeners been on the mayor's statement that no one had noticed the tall, well-dressed man slip in.

"I have a question, Mr. Mayor."

Ralph Behr strode quickly to the podium and placed a small tape recorder atop it. "Is this your voice?"

The mayor was too surprised by his appearance to stop Ralph from pressing the play button. The mayor's unmistakable voice immediately issued from the machine.

"You son of a bitch, Kramer! First you tell me you're holding a nut case who ought to be locked up and you get me to agree to have him held for psychiatric examination. The next thing I know, I'm out on a limb for helping you cover up a murder."

Cameras recorded the mayor's face blanched with fear. Simon Kramer's New York accent stabbed into the silence.

"I swear to you he was dead when I got back there. The shock almost killed *me*."

"You never told me the guy was Behr's construction representative and you also swore to me that no one would ever find the body. Of all the dumb ways to get rid of a body—"

"The point was to make it look like suicide. If the medical examiner says it's a drowning, then this whole thing ends and nothing smears you." After some mumbling Kramer's urgent tones were heard again. "All you have to do is name the guy to the job permanently."

Reporters began to yell questions, others to hush them. Then the mayor's voice could be discerned. "Simon, if this thing hadn't gone so far, I swear I'd have you arrested and wash my hands of you."

Ralph blocked the mayor from grabbing the recorder. "I know too much for you to try that," Kramer's voice went on. "Besides, who'll finance you until you win the primary and prove to the big contributors that the voters don't blame you for all the scandals? I've kept my part of that deal, haven't I?"

"You could finance a dozen campaigns for what you'll make on Behr Center. How could you let yourself get into this mess?"

"You can wash it clean as a whistle for all of us with one phone call to the medical examiner."

A few seconds later the sound of a telephone receiver being lifted came from the recorder. "This is the mayor. I'd like to speak to the chief medical examiner, please."

TV cameras swung to follow the mayor as he rushed from the news conference. All the while his taped voice was heard offering to make the medical examiner's appointment as chief permanent in return for a small favor—confirmation that Larry Carlacci had died in a drowning suicide.

As soon as Ralph turned off the tape recorder, reporters began shouting questions at him about the significance of what they had just heard.

"Plainly and simply put," Ralph responded, "the mayor acted to cover up a death. That led to a failure to investigate the arch that the dead man had insisted should be tested for a possible defect. Testimony at the hearing this afternoon should reveal that the mayor used the buildings department to continue the cover-up. As things got more and more out of hand, he probably ordered officials over there not to investigate claims that there was a defect in the concrete. Look, I'm not a lawyer, but it stands to reason that if all these city officials conspired to cover up a crime and then a potential safety hazard, then nobody can deny the disaster victims their right to receive cash damages from the city."

"Where did you get the tape?" a reporter cried out.

"From the deputy mayor. He wants everyone to know that he made it because he was concerned that just such a cover-up was being planned."

Another reporter got Ralph's attention. "What I don't understand from listening to the tape is why the mayor even entered into this alleged conspiracy to cover up the engineer's death. Why didn't he just have Kramer arrested?"

Ralph reflected for a moment. "I've been thinking about that since I first heard the tape. Maybe, as Kramer says on it, he could divulge things that would create problems for the mayor. But I really believe the mayor is an honest man. There's nothing to suggest he personally profited when Kramer bought into Behr Center. My best guess is that, like Nixon and Watergate, the mayor got trapped because he refused to bite the bullet at the very start. He let himself get talked into sending the police chief down to take Larry into custody. Turning against Kramer then could have cost him the nomination. Bad publicity for one thing. For another, Simon Kramer was an old friend and his key financial source, who had pledged immense financial backing at a time when the mayor was having trouble raising campaign money. Also, you have to remember that the mayor had tied his campaign strategy to that opening ceremony at Behr Center. He wanted to believe what Kramer was telling him. He never considered what was moral, what was legal—only what was useful. He misplaced his loyalty. It should have been given to the people of the city. But to him, in the end, everything boiled down to politics."

Dan Ahern recognized his visitor's step well before Ralph turned into his hospital room.

"I'm not disturbing you, am I?" Ralph asked softly, so as not to wake the patient sleeping in the other bed.

"I was expecting you. You haven't been by today, and I'm finding out that you're not the kind of man who breaks his word."

"Your breathing sounds better. How are you feeling?"

Ahern did not respond for several seconds, and when he did, it was not to reply to the question. His head gestured toward the TV set suspended beside his bed.

"I saw you on the news a while ago." Ahern glanced down the bed; he had more he wanted to convey, but he felt uncomfortable doing so and swallowed once or twice. Finally, settling for much less than he had intended, he lifted his gaze to Ralph's. "If it means anything to you, I'm proud to know you."

For the merest instant the embarrassment lowered between them, and then Ahern turned his gaze away. "Feeling better, thanks."

Both men were quiet for a while, letting the silence cradle them. After a while Ahern asked, "What are you going to do about Behr Center?"

"What *should* I do, Dan?"

"Build, damn it!"

Ahern's voice was so forceful that both men were surprised. Ralph waited to hear the other man's reason.

"It's just . . ." Ahern paused for thought. ". . . I don't know, you've come so far. You've fought and won so much in the last few days. To let it just die . . ."

He slumped back into the pillow. "You were always fun to watch because you took big chances and made good copy. Building those big skyscrapers was just your ego trip when this started out. But it's become more now. What you've come through means something to people. The nurses and the aides and doctors around here don't get impressed easily, but they think I must be pretty important because you visit me. You've become a kind of a giant to the average guy, a man who can accomplish just about anything."

Ralph raised his hand to cut Ahern off. "What's been happening has cut me down to size."

"I'm not talking about how you think of yourself, but what you mean to the rest of us. You sustain our faith in the aspirations we'll never achieve, the myth that we could be giants too." He glanced at Ralph again. "That's why it's so important that you don't fail, that you build those suckers."

After a long while with nothing more said, Ralph bade Ahern good-bye and, deep in thought, walked slowly from the room.

Ralph got into the front seat of the limousine beside Brian. They drove to Behr Center and slowly circled the site. Ralph motioned the car to a halt in front of the office tower and stepped out to look at it again. Last night it had been a delicate brush painting extending forever into the darkness. Today it appeared puny beneath the limitless blue sky. Still, he stared upward for a long time until he finally returned to the car.

Even as all his doubts about the viability of the project muttered their apprehensions into his ear, he could still hear the voice of the steelworker's wife telling Gail and him that the men building it considered it theirs. Suddenly Ralph knew how to build Behr Center without reducing its size a single inch. In seconds he had worked through the numbers roughly in his head, but he had to be sure.

Ben Rogovin followed Ralph past Myra's desk and into his office, eager to congratulate him on how well events had gone.

"You were great. You knocked the mayor out of the ring."

"Now what, Ben? What do I do about Behr Center? You've gone over the figures."

"Pretty carefully. Basically, we're in big trouble now that our major tenant has pulled out—even if we force the insurance company providing the completion guarantee to rebuild the plaza and, when the office building is rented up, the other two towers as well. You'll have a tough enough time renting up an eighty-story building. Complete it the full way up, and it will drain you dry, especially with no retail or anything else around it to attract tenants. Nobody wants to rent down there now. The president of one of the department stores we were hoping to sign told me it was a cemetery. Besides that, rents in general are weaker than they were. So, we'd have an empty plaza with no retail on it next to the tallest, emptiest office building in the world, and you'd have to find the financing for both now that Metrobank has pulled out."

Ralph reflected, "When you look at it that way, it doesn't make much sense to keep going, does it?"

"This one's a no-brainer. You have a shot to pull it out and make a fortune, sure, but first you have to convince an awful lot of tenants that the area will be great despite what happened and that the rest of the project will go up too. You'll have to raise a hell of a lot of money again, and this time no one will be knocking down your door to give it to you." The pessimism in Rogovin's voice increased. "The project is just too costly to build. If there was some way to cut down on the cost, then maybe you'd have an even-money shot. But let's not kid ourselves—this is New York."

Rogovin's troubling judgment was the same as that of all the other astute minds that had counseled him to walk away from the project, to take the safe course that would leave him secure. The two men reviewed the figures. The project appeared to be a financial death-trap.

"Ben, I've been thinking. What if we could lower the labor costs?"

"By how much?"

"Say twenty-five percent. That way we could lower rents."

"Just like that. What do we give the workers in exchange?"

"A share of the profits."

"You're kidding."

Ralph shook his head.

They quickly recalculated the same figures that had seemed

impenetrable only moments before. Finally, Ralph sat back. Building Behr Center successfully with this new strategy would still be difficult, but it could be done. Seeing possibilities where others had not gave him confidence. That had always been his edge.

He asked Myra to get hold of a man whose support would be essential, but with whom he had always been reluctant to do business—the head of the city's council of construction trade unions. Ralph had invariably hired other companies to act as general contractor, rather than doing that himself, because of his dislike of the back-room deals he suspected had to be made to bring projects in on time and on budget.

The labor leader took the call. He was earthy and straightforward. "Ralph, I'm about to go into a meeting, and I've got to pee. Can this wait till tomorrow?"

"The john and the meeting can wait, Mac. This is important. I'm about to make an extraordinary offer to you and your men who work on Behr Center."

"What's the offer?"

"A piece of the profits, an incentive, twenty percent. It would be the workers' project as well as mine. What I want from them in return is a big reduction in wages. A third. That could hold rents down. If the project is a success they'll make more than they ever dreamed possible, and for the rest of their lives."

"And if it isn't?" the union leader growled.

"This is *my* project, Ralph Behr's. And I haven't blown one yet."

"They'd skin me alive if I asked them for something like this."

"Try them. I'm willing to bet that if you can get the men themselves together and let me talk to them, they'll be willing to do it."

"You sound like a socialist."

"No, what I'm trying to be is a new kind of capitalist, with everybody making an investment and taking part of my risk and everybody owning a piece of the pie in exchange."

"What's wrong with paying a man a decent day's wages for a decent day's work?"

"Because times have become too tough to do business the way we've always done it. Sure as hell, we'll fall on our faces or lose out to some smart competitor who's seen the future while we were watching the past. Everyone wants to be an owner, to have an interest in what he's building or producing, a little property that won't disappear when the monthly bills are paid. Mac, this project has become too expensive the old way. Either we build it for less or it doesn't get built, and Manhattan ends up with a hole the size of Hiroshima right in the middle of its lower end. Do you want the unions to be responsible for that?"

"Don't try to lay the blame on me for that, Ralph. My men just work there."

"That's the problem. If that's all they do, those buildings and that plaza will cost too much to ever get built. But if everyone makes a sacrifice in return for some equity, it can be a big winner."

"And you think the guys working your job will go along with you on this?"

"Not only will they go along with me, I think they'll build it faster and better because they have a stake in it."

The man's voice had become strained. "Jesus, Ralph, I'll have to continue this conversation some other time: I've got to pee bad."

Ralph refused to permit his hang up. "Will you let me present it to the men and see if they'll hear me out?"

"They can't survive on two-thirds pay."

"All right, let's say their pay cut is one quarter for twenty percent of the profits." Ralph winked at Rogovin.

"You're really confident about this crazy plan?"

"Yes."

"The heads of the locals are the ones you have to meet with first. You'll have to convince them that the deal makes sense if you want to speak directly to their men." He hesitated and then, pressed to a quick decision by the urgency of his urinary condition, he blurted out. "All right, I'm set to meet with them at the end of the day. I'll give you the last half hour."

"That's all I'm asking, Mac, that's all I'm asking."

Gail arrived at Ralph's office at four thirty, having spent the day at a conference on the problems of battered women. She and Ralph had planned to drive up along the Hudson for dinner. He explained that he had to stop first at the construction trades council.

"What are you going to propose?"

Ralph chuckled. "What makes you think I'm going to propose something?"

"I know you too well. Some kind of deal on wages at Behr Center?"

Ralph tipped his head. "Pretty good."

495

"I told you, I know you, Ralph Behr. And you've taught me a lot. What did you ask them for?"

As Ralph began to outline his proposal, he handed her the projections of costs and income he and Ben had worked up for the meeting. While he spoke, Gail deciphered the meaning of the numbers. She began to ask questions—good ones, Ralph thought.

"You really have learned a lot," he observed.

"Thanks, but you haven't answered my question about how you estimated the rent-up rate for the commercial space."

Ben Rogovin and, in the last hours, Ralph as well had been talking to financial institutions. The disaster and the economic reversal he had suffered as a result of it, coupled with the spreading knowledge that Metrobank had pulled out, had made bankers gloomy about the project's prospects. To increase their enthusiasm after some time had passed, Ralph had decided to undertake an intensive schedule of gala events intended to attract large crowds to the site—street fairs, holiday parades, concerts, and the like. His aims were to erase the memory of the disaster, to acquaint people with the site's location, and to demonstrate its attractiveness and financial viability to prospective tenants and to those who could finance him. "Think my rent-up rate is too optimistic?"

"No, too pessimistic. The bankers, with their heads in ledger books—they don't understand what's happened. I don't think you yourself really understand. Everywhere I go, people congratulate me on your being proved innocent and thank me for what you did—you know, about the mayor, the accident victims. Huge crowds will show up for events at Behr Center just because they want to help you in some way. If New Yorkers are jaded and cynical, it's only because they've been burned so many times they're afraid to expect any better. But they want to."

Ralph's grimace conveyed his skepticism of the flattery. "And tomorrow it will be somebody else. Come on, banks need hard figures. Why do you think space will rent faster than I've estimated?"

"You underestimate the market. I lived and I work pretty close to the site. Adjacent areas are exploding with development. The office market is expanding around there too. Behr Center might be huge and at the high end of the scale, but it's situated in a pretty undeveloped spot that's ready to attract high-income residents and stores. And there are almost no low-income tenants."

Ralph was grinning at her. "You sound a lot different than you did when I was fighting for approval to build it."

"People have gotten used to the idea of Behr Center. They no longer see it as a threat, but as an enhancement." She ceased speaking while she stared at the figures at the bottom of the second page. She looked up in dismay. "Ralph, you end up with only twenty percent of the ownership."

"A piece goes to that labor profit-participation pool, a big piece goes to the financial institutions—they're insisting on it. They see the project as a big risk, so they want me to give up a big share of the ownership."

"But you'll have your own money in it."

"Whatever I've got. They'd like a lot more."

Gail stared at him. "How much do you have, Ralph?"

He wanted to avoid the question. "Not as much as before the accident."

"Or before you married me."

Ralph shook his head. "One thing I'm glad about is that most of your assets are safe."

"From your personal guarantee to Metrobank, you mean. Will you lose a lot to them?"

He nodded.

"But Charles Brookhouse should be willing to be lenient for his daughter's sake."

"He said he will be—on my *next* project. Metrobank has pulled out of this one, and Charles thinks I should too. There's a bright spot. He kicked me off the Calvin Coolidge committee."

Gail was too intent on the paper before her to laugh. "You're getting forced into a corner just because you want so much to build those towers."

"You think I should get out?"

Still deep in thought, she slowly began to shake her head. Her eyes lifted to his. "No. With all my heart and soul, I think you should build. What you're trying to do is important."

"Brookhouse, my father, Ben Rogovin, Morris Weitzman, probably all the other developers with any sense in this city think I'm nuts to risk everything and not just to walk away."

"They're wrong because they aren't you. They couldn't have stood up to the mayor like you did. And they could never have built Behr Center. But you *can!*" She grasped his hand. "Giving the workers a stake in the profits for part of their wages is a momentous idea. You don't know how proud of you I am."

Ralph tipped his head with little zest. "We'll see what their leaders say first. They're giving me half an hour to try to sell them on the idea, and then we can go to dinner. But I wonder if I'm not conning myself onto an express to bankruptcy. The history of this city is littered with conceited developers who choked on a project that was too big for them. My grandfather."

"Ralph, you're an idealist. For a long time I didn't understand that. Once in a while someone is born into this world who has the talent and vision to create a poem or a piece of art or an invention that no one ever imagined before . . . or, against all odds, to build something higher than anyone else would dare to. After what's happened, what you've been through and done, a lot of people are pulling for you to build those towers and make them successful." She held up the financial projections he had given her. "That's why they'll buy apartments and rent space—they all want to touch a little piece of you. The banks don't understand that, and so they want too much for their risk."

"They're being realistic, and you're not."

"Ralph, how much am I worth after the divorce?"

"I'd guess somewhere over seventy million."

Gail glanced down once more at the paper. She did not speak for several minutes. When she looked up again, she said, "I'll be your investor."

"No! That money's yours. It's your security. Your father gave away twenty years of his life for it."

"If it's mine, I can invest it wherever I want. I want to invest it in Behr Center."

"The answer is no. I won't take charity."

"It's not charity. It's an investment. Don't you think you're good enough to make this project pay off?"

Stung, he retorted, "Those estimates are conservative. I can be in profits a year earlier than that and bringing in a lot more revenue."

"Then I have nothing to worry about." She checked the paper. "You and I can share the eighty percent that doesn't go to the labor profit-participation pool."

"The banks may still want part of the profits."

"If they ask too much, you can sell shares on Wall Street, like manufacturing companies do. Ordinary people will be happy with half what the banks would ask."

Ralph laughed at the fervency of her belief in him. Despite her shrewdness about the figures, she remained so naive about the way the financial industry worked. His tone softened with gratitude. "I appreciate your faith, but I won't take your money."

"The project and the man in charge are both good investments. Besides, Ralph, you need me."

He instantly became irritated. "If this is an act of gallant self-sacrifice on your part because you feel sorry for me . . ."

Gail was incredulous. "Not for this kind of money. You just hate to admit that you can't do it all yourself."

"I'm not saying yes, but I'm not saying no. We'll talk about it at dinner."

The phone intercom buzzed. Ralph took the call and listened for a short time. His expression was pensive when he turned back to Gail.

"That was someone from Metrobank. Amanda is arriving at JFK from Paris at seven tonight. On the bank's plane. She's expecting me to pick her up at the airport. I'm going to have to cancel our dinner."

Slowly, Gail got to her feet. "This is where I came in."

By the time Gail's elevator descended to the lobby, she had made up her mind. Traveling to the Coalition's offices, she worked out all the details.

Brenda Clay had been a volunteer with the Coalition since her freshman year in college. Gail had seen her grow from a tentative do-gooder into a poised young woman. She had undertaken every job in the understaffed organization, from keeping the books to rescuing battered women under the hail of a husband's blows. Now Gail offered her the salaried director's position—running all of the shelters and programs. Gail explained that she had decided to take a vacation for a while. When she returned, she would stick to the chairperson's role and concentrate on establishing priorities, developing new programs, and raising money.

Brenda was both stunned by the offer and intimidated by the responsibility.

"I'll be available for advice," Gail assured her, "but you've had long enough to learn the ropes and take over on your own."

"I can't replace you."

Gail could still hear idol worship in the young woman's voice. "You'll have to. I'm probably going to go to Vermont for a little while—a friend has a house there I'm sure she'll loan me." Gail smiled and hugged the young woman. "You'll be fine. So will I."

For the next few hours, Gail filled Brenda in on matters coming up she might not know about and drafted and signed letters that would grant her full authority to act for the Coalition. Then Gail left.

It was a warm night. The clouds had broken late in the day and stars punctuated swatches of darkening sky. Normally she took a subway uptown after work, but she wanted to exercise her new independence, her sense of possessing lavish financial means. She took a taxi back to the Fifth Avenue apartment she had shared with Ralph for a year.

Upon entering, Gail told Deighton not to bother with dinner for her. She stopped on her way upstairs to pick up her mail neatly stacked on the side table, the third table to occupy that spot during a year of periodic redecoration. Leafing through her pile as she climbed the stairs, she came upon a thick, hand-delivered manila envelope. She reached for the banister to steady herself. Reading the lawyer's name in the upper left-hand corner, she knew exactly what the envelope contained: the divorce papers.

She entered her bedroom and placed the mail on her desk. She stared at the manila envelope and then into Ralph's empty bedroom through the open connecting doorway. He and she had begun their union as resentful enemies and had ended it as trusted companions. This had been such an eventful year for her. She had grown so much. So had he. That was a lot to expect out of any relationship.

She slipped a letter opener into the corner of the envelope and extracted the divorce papers. Shock gripped her as she saw that Ralph had already signed them, probably the day before yesterday. He had not said a word to her about it. Gail felt a deep hurt, and her hurt was turning to fury. She threw the letter opener at his room.

Why was she so unaccountably angry? After all Amanda's return was no surprise: the divorce he had requested to marry her had been postponed only because of his legal problems, and those were now resolved. Her own alternative was tears. Something long past changing wasn't worth crying over, she told herself.

"You really are a major fool," she declared scornfully at the empty room. "I'm well out of it." This was the best thing that could have happened to me, she decided. That really puts an end to any lingering illusions.

She grabbed a pen and slashed her signature across marked places in the divorce documents and then stuffed the papers into the enclosed envelope. She noticed the diamond wedding band on her left hand and ripped it from her finger, slamming it down beside the envelope. How bare her hand appeared! She had been married in one form or another for so many years. Now she had turned a corner and would not look back.

Determinedly, she stood up and walked to her closet to take down her suitcases. She placed them on her bed and began to scoop clothes by the armful from her bureau drawers and throw them into the open suitcases. She was eager, she told herself, to begin the rest of her life.

Her shoes should go in first, she remembered. Her thoughts were a jumble with her emotions.

As she came out of the closet carrying several pairs, Ralph was standing in the open doorway between their bedrooms.

"What are you doing?" he asked.

Gail dropped the shoes into a suitcase and stomped over to the envelope on her desk. She flung it at him. "Amanda will be delighted."

"Amanda is on the last plane back to Paris," he replied.

"Oh, she just hopped over for a fast embrace. Not only romantic, but she gets all those frequent-flyer points."

Gail entered the closet for more shoes. Ralph was blocking her way just outside it when she emerged.

"I told her I didn't love her and wouldn't marry her."

Gail shrugged and stepped around him. Blouses, she remembered; she had just been about to pack her blouses.

"I'm not going to marry her," Ralph repeated as she arranged the first few blouses in a suitcase.

"I guess that leaves at least one cover of *Modern Bride* up for grabs."

"I had hoped you might be a little more enthusiastic."

"My pom-poms are out being cleaned."

She was reaching into her drawer for more clothes when Ralph's hand stopped hers. "I want to tell you what happened," he said.

"Look, Ralph," she replied with exasperation, "you're a big boy. Whether or not you want to marry her is no longer any of my business. When you signed those papers, I stepped out of your life."

"The closer I got to the airport, the more miserable I became. I kept remembering that the only thing on her mind when I told her on the phone about the plaza disaster was that she didn't want it to interfere with my visiting her in Europe. Later, I figured we were all under a lot of strain and said strange things that day. But that uncomfortable feeling I couldn't put my finger on just got stronger and stronger the closer I was to the airport. When I saw her coming out of customs, I felt I was suffocating."

"Ralph, see an allergist, or an analyst, but let me get out of here."

She reached down for sweaters. She was packing all wrong, she realized, but she just wanted to get away. He followed her back to the suitcases.

"She was busy talking with a friend she had run into in customs," he continued. "It never occurred to her that she was blocking the doorway to the concourse where everyone was waiting to meet arriving passengers. I wasn't more than fifteen or twenty feet from her, but she never bothered to look around for me. Not a big thing, but something in me snapped off, like a switch. I had thought I was the most important thing in her life, as she was for me. But she had traveled three thousand miles, and I wasn't even on her mind. That did it. When she finally ended her conversation and found me, I told her it was over."

Gail placed her sweaters in the suitcase and walked back to the bureau.

"Damn it," he exploded, "can't you say something?"

"Ralph, I'm worn out," she said wearily. "I'm going away. You'll have two things you always wanted from me: my silence and my absence."

For a moment Ralph just looked at her. And then he said, "You don't have to leave anymore. We don't have to rush into a divorce now."

Gail stood thinking about what he had said for several seconds. Then she shook her head and scooped up another armload of clothing.

"It's Jeff!" he exclaimed. "You're leaving me for Jeff."

Gail's eyes rolled up. "I'm leaving because I don't want to be an afterthought who's glad to hang around just because you got tired of someone else. One thing I've learned during this year: I don't have to beg any man to love me."

"Gail, I want you to stay. All the time I was watching Amanda I kept thinking of you and how wonderful last night was."

She flung the clothing into a suitcase and rushed back for more. "It won't work, Ralph. I'm not what you really want. I'm not your shadow or your fantasy. I don't bring you an esteemed social position, and no one is going to die with envy when they see me on your arm. But let me tell you, buster, you would have been the luckiest man alive to have me for a wife."

Ralph was about to speak, but she would not let him. "I make you happy! I make you laugh and I make you think. Oh, maybe we'd fight once in a while, but only because I refuse to let you be less than you could be."

Ralph removed the previous batch of clothing from the suitcase and, right behind her, returned it to the drawer. "Anything more?"

She had already grabbed another pile of clothing to replace it in the suitcase. "A lot more! Look at what you've grown into, what you've become. That never would have happened without me. I stretch you and complete you. I'm the Jewish part of you you're just discovering. The part of you that cares about people. I'm your other half."

He retrieved that pile too and followed her back to the double chest of drawers. "And I'm yours. That's what I'm trying to tell you."

"Sure, when you're feeling sorry for yourself, when you haven't got Amanda anymore and you need an investor."

"Forget about the damned money. That goes into your name. Forget about Amanda. I just want *you*."

She was too angry and intent on her thoughts to listen. "Where were you all these weeks and months? You had social-register stars in your eyes." The relay race had stopped. "I can't fit into her mold, Ralph. But let me tell you this: the kick of knowing others are envious of you wears off. What remains is who you have to live with—who you *want* to live with—day in, day out for the rest of your life. The person who's there to console you when you're down and who you want to be proud of you when you're up. That was me, Ralph. Forget about how we met or why we married. You just never opened your eyes, Ralph. That was me."

"I love you, Gail," he finally said with a tenderness she had never heard from him before.

Neither of them moved or emitted a sound for a long time, until she replied, "That's not enough."

She started to reach into the bureau for more clothing. He stopped her.

"What would be?"

She held her breath, fearful he would not understand or remember.

Ralph smiled. "Gail Weintraub, I'm the luckiest man alive to have you for a wife."

She grabbed his face between her hands and kissed him deeply. "Your real wife from now on?"

"The realest."

They kissed again for a very long time. Finally, they came up for air and began to argue about who had loved the other first.

About the Author

Joseph Amiel was educated at Amherst College and Yale Law School. The author of the novel HAWKS, as well as several screenplays, he lives with his wife and two children in New York City.